READER'S DIGEST
CONDENSED BOOKS

THE READER'S DIGEST ASSOCIATION LIMITED
25 Berkeley Square, London W1X 6AB

THE READER'S DIGEST ASSOCIATION
SOUTH AFRICA (PTY) LTD
Reader's Digest House, 130 Strand Street, Cape Town

Printed by Petty & Sons Ltd, Leeds
Bound by Hazell, Watson & Viney Ltd, Aylesbury

Original cover design by Jeffery Matthews FSIAD

READER'S DIGEST
CONDENSED BOOKS

A MATTER OF HONOUR
by Jeffrey Archer

When Adam Scott's father dies, he leaves his son a letter: the first clue as to why, many years earlier at the end of the Second World War, his distinguished army career was cut short without explanation—and without honour. This extraordinary letter leads Adam to Geneva and a priceless Russian icon—precious not only for itself but for a secret which could change the course of history. Very soon Adam finds himself in a labyrinth of treachery, murder and intrigue.

A Matter of Honour shows world best-selling author, Jeffrey Archer, writing at the height of his compelling powers. It is a magnificent novel of pursuit and suspense which no reader will want to put down before the end.

ICE TREK
by Ewan Clarkson

Steve Larsen can't wait to get home. Reconnoitering for his travel company has brought him to northwest Alaska, where he finds the landscape bleak and the natives unfriendly. It's time to get back to civilization. But fate has a gruelling ordeal ahead for Larsen when a plane crash leaves him stranded in the wilderness; his fellow survivor and only companion is Umiak, a quiet, inscrutable Eskimo. These two men, with nothing in common except their awful plight, must now begin a hazardous trek across the mountains. Facing the bitter elements, dreadful hunger and the lurking menace of a huge grizzly bear, the white man and the Eskimo are put to the greatest test of their lives.

THE LONG KILL
by Patrick Ruell

For the last twenty years—nearly half
his life—Jaysmith has been a hired
killer, paid by a master he knows only
as "Jacob". It is Jacob who chooses the
targets, Jacob who calls the tune. But
when a job goes wrong, in the Lake
District, Jaysmith thinks that perhaps
it is time to retire: time to look around
him, to take stock of life. And for the
first time in years he finds himself
falling in love . . . But, all too soon,
Jaysmith is to discover that he cannot
put his past behind him without a fight
to the death.

This tense, urgent novel tells an
agonizing tale of a man's battle to
redeem himself. Part thriller, part
romance, it will enthral the reader on
every level.

THIS SHINING LAND
by Rosalind Laker

Norway never expected to be a target
of the Nazis—a neutral nation, she had
for long years been free and at peace.
Yet early in 1940 German troops
stormed into Oslo, horrifying the
citizens with their tactics of terror.
Resistance seemed utterly useless. But
not everyone was willing to submit to
the Nazi jackboot . . .

This powerful novel tells the story of
two brave Norwegians, Steffen Larsen
and Johanna Ryen, who joined the
growing underground movement to
defend their native land and, in so
doing, risked everything. It is an
inspiring tale of a little-known battle for
freedom, fought by a valiant people,
and movingly shows what courage can
do in the face of great adversity.

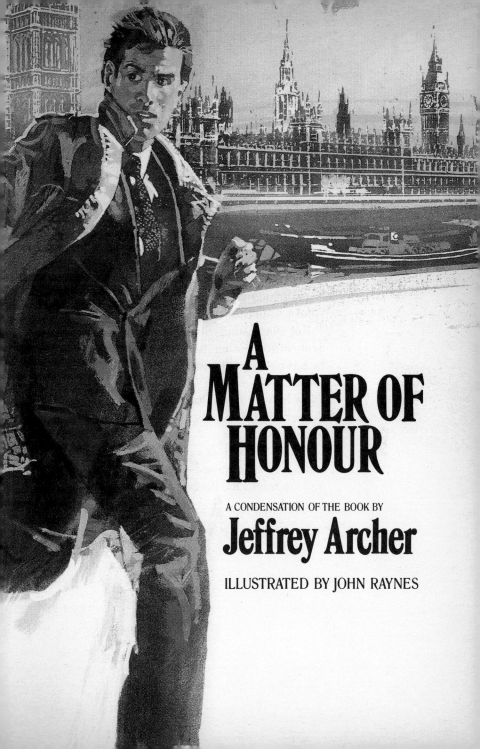

A MATTER OF HONOUR

A CONDENSATION OF THE BOOK BY

Jeffrey Archer

ILLUSTRATED BY JOHN RAYNES

With its dazzling shades of gold and red and
blue the delicately painted Russian icon of St.
George and the Dragon is a small masterpiece.

But when Adam Scott, a young former
army officer, inherits the icon in his father's will
he has no way of knowing its strange history or
the incredible secret that it holds. Nor does he
know how swiftly he will be caught up in a
desperate race among the world's super-powers
to possess it.

What's more, it is a race in which Adam
himself is the pursued—hunted by a ruthless
and ingenious KGB agent who stalks him across
Europe . . .

Chapter One
THE KREMLIN, MOSCOW

"It's a fake," said the Russian leader, staring down at the small, exquisite painting he held in his hands.

"That isn't possible," replied his Politburo colleague. "The Tsar's Icon of St. George and the Dragon has been in the Winter Palace at Leningrad under heavy guard for over fifty years."

"True, Comrade Zaborski," said the old man, "but for fifty years we've been guarding a fake. The tsar must have removed the original some time before the Red Army entered St. Petersburg and overran the Winter Palace."

The head of State Security moved restlessly in his chair as the cat-and-mouse game continued. Zaborski knew, after years of running the KGB, who had been cast as the mouse, the moment his phone had rung at four that morning to say that the General Secretary required him to report to the Kremlin—immediately.

"How can you be so sure it's a fake, Leonid Ilyich?" the diminutive figure inquired.

"Because, my dear Zaborski, during the past eighteen months the age of all the treasures in the Winter Palace has been tested by carbon dating, and what we have always thought to be one of the nation's masterpieces turns out to have been painted five hundred years after Rublev's original. It has always worried the curator at the Winter Palace that the tsar's traditional silver crown was not attached to the back of the frame, as it was to all his other masterpieces."

"But I always thought that the silver crown had been removed by a souvenir hunter before we even entered St. Petersburg."

"No," said Brezhnev drily, his bushy eyebrows rising every time he completed a statement, "the painting itself had been removed."

"Then what can the tsar have done with the original?" said Zaborski.

"That is exactly what I want to know, comrade," said Brezhnev, splaying his hands and dwarfing the little painting that remained in front of him. "And you are the one who has been chosen to come up with the answer. There is very little to go on," he added.

He flicked open a file on the desk in front of him and read aloud: " 'At the time of the Revolution, Tsar Nicholas II obviously saw Rublev's masterpiece as his passport to freedom in the West. He must have had a copy made which he then left hanging on his study wall, where the original had previously hung.' "

The head of the KGB looked perplexed. Why should Brezhnev want State Security involved in the theft of a minor masterpiece? "And how important is it that we find the original?" he asked.

Leonid Brezhnev stared at his Kremlin colleague.

"Nothing could be more important, comrade," came back the unexpected reply. "And I shall grant you any resources you may consider necessary to discover the whereabouts of the Tsar's Icon."

"But I could end up spending far more than the painting is worth," said the head of the KGB, trying to disguise his disbelief.

"That would not be possible," said Brezhnev, pausing for effect, "because it's not the icon itself that I'm after." He turned and stared out of the window. "The money the tsar might have raised from selling such a masterpiece would only have kept him in his accustomed lifestyle for a year at the most. No, it's what we feel certain the tsar had secreted inside the icon that would have guaranteed security for himself and his family for the rest of their days."

"What could possibly be that valuable?" asked Zaborski.

"Do you remember, comrade, what the tsar promised Lenin in exchange for his life?"

"Yes, but it turned out to be a bluff because no such document was hidden . . ." He stopped.

Brezhnev smiled triumphantly. "You have caught up with me at last, comrade. You see, the document was hidden in the icon all the time. We just had the wrong icon."

The Russian leader passed a single sheet of paper to his colleague. "This is the tsar's testimony, indicating what we would find in the icon. When nothing was discovered, Lenin was convinced that it had been a bluff by the tsar to save his family from execution."

Zaborski slowly read the handwritten testimony, then looked at the tiny painting, no larger than a book, that remained in the centre of Brezhnev's desk.

"Not since the death of Lenin," continued the General Secretary, "has anyone believed the tsar's claim. But now, there can be little doubt that if we are able to locate the genuine masterpiece we will also be in possession of the promised document. I also feel confident that we would receive the backing of the United Nations and the World Court if the Americans tried to deny us our legal claim. But I fear time is now against us."

"Why?" asked the chairman of State Security.

"Look at the date in the testimony and you will see how much time we have left to honour our part of the agreement."

Zaborski stared at the date scrawled in the hand of the tsar—20 June 1966—and considered the gigantic scale of his task.

Brezhnev continued his monologue. "So, we have only one month left before the deadline. But if you can discover the whereabouts of the original icon, President Johnson's defence strategy would be rendered virtually useless, and the United States would become a pawn on the Russian chessboard."

Chapter Two
APPLESHAW, HAMPSHIRE   JUNE 1966

"And to my dearly beloved and only son, Captain Adam Scott, MC, I bequeath the sum of five hundred pounds."

The old lawyer raised his head and glanced over his half-moon spectacles at the handsome young man before him. Adam put a hand nervously through his thick black hair, suddenly conscious of the lawyer's stare. Then Mr. Holbrooke's eyes returned to the papers in front of him.

"And to my dearly beloved daughter, Margaret Scott, I bequeath the sum of four hundred pounds." Adam was unable to suppress a small grin. Even in his last will and testament, his father had remained a chauvinist.

"To the Hampshire County Cricket Club," droned on Mr. Holbrooke, "twenty-five pounds, life membership." Finally paid up, thought Adam. "To the Appleshaw Parish Church, ten pounds. To Wilf Proudfoot, our loyal gardener, ten pounds, and to Mrs. Mavis Cox, our daily help, five pounds. And finally, to my dearly beloved wife, Susan, our marital home and the remainder of my estate."

Mr. Holbrooke looked up once more, then stared down at the last paragraph of his late client's testament. What could he have to add? thought Adam.

Whatever it was, the solicitor had obviously pondered the final bequest several times, because he delivered the words like a well-versed actor, his eyes returning to the script only once.

"And I also leave to my son the enclosed envelope." Mr. Holbrooke paused, holding it up. "Which I can only hope will bring him greater happiness than it did me. Should he decide to open it, it must be on the condition that he will never divulge its contents to any other living person." Adam glanced towards his mother, who looked shocked. Was it fear or was it distress? Mr. Holbrooke passed the yellowed envelope over to the colonel's only son.

Everyone in the room remained seated as Mr. Holbrooke closed the thin file marked Colonel Gerald Scott, DSO, OBE, MC, pushed back his chair and walked slowly over to Mrs. Scott. They shook hands and she said, "Thank you." Adam rose and went quickly to his mother's side.

Once they had left the office and Adam had ensured that his mother and sister were seated comfortably in the back of the family Morris Minor, he took his place behind the steering wheel. Even before he had switched on the ignition his mother offered matter-of-factly, "We'll have to get rid of this, you know. I can't afford to run it now, not with petrol at six shillings a gallon."

"Don't let's worry about that today," said Margaret consolingly, but in a voice that accepted that her mother was right. "I wonder what can be in that envelope, though," she added, wanting to change the subject.

The earlier look of fear returned to her mother's face. "I begged your father to destroy that envelope," she said, in a voice that was barely a whisper.

Adam realized this must be the envelope that had caused the only row between his parents that he had ever witnessed. It had been just a few days after his father had returned from Germany.

"I have to open it, don't you understand?" Pa had insisted angrily.

"Never," his mother had replied. "After all the sacrifices I have made, you at least owe me that."

Over twenty years had passed since that confrontation and Adam had never heard the subject referred to again.

A mile or so down a winding country lane Adam brought the old Morris Minor to a halt outside a trellis-work gate. A path led through a neat lawn to a little thatched cottage.

"I'm sure you have to get back to London," were his mother's first words as she entered the drawing room.

"I'm in no hurry, Mother."

"Just as you wish, my dear, but you don't have to worry yourself over me," his mother continued. She stared up at the tall young man who reminded her so much of Gerald. The same dark hair and deep brown eyes, the same open, honest face, even the same gentle approach to everyone he came across. But most of all the same high standards of morality that had brought them to their present sad state. "And in any case I've always got Margaret to take care of me," she added. Adam looked across at his sister. She had recently become engaged to a City stockbroker, and although the marriage had been postponed, she would soon be wanting to start a life of her own. Thank God her fiancé had already put a down payment on a little house only fourteen miles away.

After tea, Margaret cleared away and left Adam alone with his mother.

"Now that you're no longer in the army, my dear, I do hope you'll be able to find a worthwhile job," she said uneasily, as she recalled how difficult that had proved to be for his father.

"I'm sure everything will be just fine, Mother," he replied. "The Foreign Office have asked to see me again."

She looked at the clock on the mantelpiece and said, "You'd better be getting along, my dear. I don't like the thought of you on that motorbike after dark."

Adam bent down to kiss her on the cheek. "I'll give you a call tomorrow." He stuck his head round the kitchen door and shouted to his sister, "I'm off. I'll be sending you a cheque for fifty pounds."

"Why?" asked Margaret, looking up from the sink.

"Let's just say it's my blow for women's rights." He shut the kitchen door smartly to avoid the dishcloth that was hurled in his direction. Adam revved up his motorbike and drove down the A303 towards London.

He had decided to wait until he had reached the privacy of his own room in Chelsea before he opened the envelope. After all, he had waited most of his life to discover what was in it.

Adam had been told the story of the family tragedy a thousand times— "It's all a matter of honour, old chap," his father would say, squaring his shoulders. Colonel Scott had spent a lifetime overhearing the snide comments of lesser men, but Adam knew his father too well to believe, even for a moment, that he could have been involved in treachery such as was whispered.

Adam tried to piece together the few facts he had been told over the years. In 1946, within a year of his fiftieth birthday, his father, whom *The Times* had described as a brilliant tactical officer with a courageous war record, had resigned his commission from the army. His resignation had astonished his family and shocked his regiment, as it had been assumed by all that it was only a matter of months before crossed swords and a baton would have been sewn onto his epaulets.

Because of the colonel's sudden and unexplained departure from the regiment, fact was augmented by fiction. When asked, all the colonel would offer was that he had had enough of war, and felt the time had come to make a little money on which Susan and he could retire. Few people found his story credible, and that credibility was not helped when the only job the colonel managed to secure for himself was as secretary of the local golf club.

It was only through the generosity of his late grandfather that Adam had been able to remain at Wellington College, and continue the family military tradition. After leaving school he was offered a place at the Royal Military Academy, Sandhurst where he studied diligently and took part in most sports, but his greatest success came at weekends, on cross-country courses. For two years, panting cadets from Cranwell and Dartmouth saw only Adam's mud-spattered back as he went on to become the Inter-Services Champion.

When he passed out of Sandhurst in August 1956, no one was surprised that he was awarded the Sword of Honour. Adam never doubted therefore that he would follow his father and command the regiment.

The Royal Wessex Regiment accepted the colonel's son soon after he had been awarded his regular commission. Adam quickly gained the respect of his fellow soldiers. As a tactical officer in the field he had no equal, and when it came to combat duty it was clear he had inherited his father's courage. Yet, six years later, when the War Office published the names of those subalterns who had been promoted to captain, his name was not to be found on the list. It was becoming clear that Adam was not to be allowed to atone for whatever it was his father was thought to have done.

Eventually he was made up to captain, but not before he had distinguished himself fighting in the Malayan jungle against the Chinese. Captured and held prisoner by the Communists, he endured solitude and torture. He escaped after eight months only to discover on returning to the front line that he had been awarded a posthumous Military Cross. When, at the age of twenty-nine, Captain Scott passed his staff exam but still failed to be offered a place at the staff college, he finally accepted that he could never hope to command the regiment. He resigned his commission a few weeks later.

While serving his last few months, Adam learned from his mother that Pa only had weeks to live. He therefore decided not to inform his father of his resignation. He knew Pa would only blame himself and was at least thankful that he had died without realizing that his stigma had become part of his son's life too.

Adam's mind returned to the pressing problem of finding himself employment. It was true that he had another meeting lined up with the

Foreign Office, but he had been impressed by the high standard of the other candidates he had encountered.

As he swung the motorbike into the King's Road, Adam fingered the envelope in his inside jacket pocket hoping, uncharitably, that Lawrence would not yet have returned from the bank. Not that he could complain; his old school friend had been extremely generous in offering him such a pleasant room in his spacious flat for only four pounds a week.

He parked his motorbike and then took the stairs up to the flat by threes. On the fifth floor, as he pushed his Yale key into the lock, a voice from inside shouted, "It's on the latch."

"Damn," Adam muttered under his breath. He would have to wait now before he could open the envelope.

"How did it go?" were Lawrence's first words as Adam entered the drawing room.

"Very well, considering," Adam replied.

Lawrence had already changed from his City clothes into a blazer and grey flannels. He was slightly shorter and stockier than Adam, with a head of wiry fair hair and grey inquiring eyes.

"I admired your father so much," he continued. "He always assumed one had the same standards as he did." Adam could still remember introducing Lawrence to his father one speech day. They had become friends immediately.

"Able to retire on the family fortune, are we?" asked Lawrence in a lighter vein.

"Only if that dubious bank you work for has found a way of converting five hundred pounds into five thousand in a matter of days."

"Can't manage it at the present time, old chum—not now Harold Wilson has announced a standstill in wages and prices."

Adam smiled as he looked across at his friend. He could still remember those days when Lawrence had been school captain. "Late again, Scott," he would say as Adam scampered past him in the corridor. Adam had looked forward to the day when he could do everything in the same relaxed, superior style. Lawrence's suits always seemed to be well pressed, his shoes always shone and he never had a hair out of place.

Adam heard the bathroom door open. He glanced interrogatively towards Lawrence.

"It's Carolyn," whispered Lawrence.

When Carolyn entered the room Adam smiled at the tall, beautiful woman. Her long, blonde hair bounced on her shoulders as she walked towards them, but it was the faultless figure that most men couldn't take their eyes off.

"Care to join us for a meal?" Lawrence asked Adam, putting his arm round Carolyn's shoulders. "I've discovered this Italian restaurant that's just opened in the Fulham Road."

"I might join you later," said Adam, "but I have one or two papers that I ought to check through."

"Forget the finer details of your inheritance, my boy. Why not join us and spend the entire windfall on one wild spaghetti fling?"

"Oh, have you been left lots of lovely lolly?" asked Carolyn.

"Not," said Adam, "when considered against my present overdraft."

Lawrence laughed. "Well, come along later if you feel you can afford it." He winked at Adam—his customary sign for "Be sure you're out of the flat by the time we get back. Or at least stay in your own room and pretend to be asleep."

"Yes, do come," cooed Carolyn, sounding as if she meant it.

Adam didn't move until he was sure he could no longer hear her penetrating voice. Satisfied, he retreated to his bedroom and locked himself in. He sat down and pulled his father's envelope out of his inside pocket.

He opened it carefully and extracted a letter in his father's unmistakable hand and a smaller envelope which had faded with time. Written on the old envelope in an unfamiliar hand were the words "Colonel Gerald Scott". Adam placed the faded envelope on the little table by his side and, unfolding his father's letter, began to read.

My dear Adam,

Over the years, you will have heard many explanations for my sudden departure from the Regiment. I always considered it better for all concerned to keep my own council. I feel, however, that I owe you a fuller explanation.

As you know, my last posting before I resigned my commission was at Nuremburg, from November 1945 to October 1946. I was given the task of commanding the British section responsible for those senior ranking Nazis awaiting trial for war crimes. I came to know those officers quite well and I had even grown to tolerate some of them. Such views were considered unacceptable at the time.

Among the senior Nazis with whom I came into daily contact was Reichsmarschall Hermann Goering. The night before Goering was due to be executed, he requested a private interview with me. It was a Monday, and I can still remember every detail of that encounter. I received the request when I took over the watch from the Russian, Major Vladimir Kosky. As soon as I had inspected the guard and dealt with the usual paperwork, I went along with the duty corporal to see the

Reichsmarschall in his cell. Goering stood to attention by his small low bed and saluted as I entered the room.

"You asked to see me?" I said.

"Yes," he replied. "It was kind of you to come in person, Colonel. I simply wish to make the last request of a man condemned to death. Would it be possible for the corporal to leave us?"

Imagining it was something highly personal I asked the corporal to wait outside. I confess I had no idea what could be so private when the man only had hours to live, but as the door closed Goering passed over the envelope you now have in your possession. All he said was, "Would you be good enough not to open this until after my execution tomorrow? I can only hope it will compensate for any blame that may later be placed on your shoulders." I did not understand what he was alluding to at the time.

Goering's final words to me as I left his cell were simply: "Be assured. It is a masterpiece, do not underestimate its value." Then he lit up a cigar as if he was relaxing after a rather good dinner. We all had different theories as to who smuggled the cigars in for him, and wondered what might also have been smuggled out from time to time.

I placed the envelope in my jacket pocket and left him. The corporal and I then inspected the other cells to see that all the prisoners were locked up for the night. I later returned to my office to make out my report and left the envelope in the jacket pocket of my uniform with every intention of opening it immediately after Goering's execution had been carried out the following morning. I was checking over the orders of the day when the corporal rushed into my office without knocking. "It's Goering, sir, it's Goering," he said. We both ran all the way back to the Reichsmarschall's cell.

I found Goering lying face downwards on his bunk. He was already dead. In the commotion that followed I quite forgot his letter. An autopsy a few days later showed that he had died from poisoning, and the court came to the conclusion that the cyanide capsule that had been found in his body must have been implanted in one of his cigars.

As I had been the last to see him alone, my name was linked with his death. There was, of course, no truth in the accusations, but so stung was I by them that I felt the only honourable thing to do in the circumstances was to resign my commission immediately.

When I returned to England and finally decided to throw out my old uniform, I came across the envelope again. I explained to your mother the details of the incident and she begged me to destroy the envelope as she considered the matter had brought enough dishonour to our family already. Although I never opened the envelope I could never bring myself to destroy it, remembering the last sentence Goering had uttered. And so, finally, I hid it among my personal papers.

However, since the imagined sins of the father are inevitably visited upon the next generation, I feel no such qualms should influence you. If there is, therefore, anything to be gained from the contents of this envelope I make only one request, namely that your mother should be the first to benefit from it.

But if you open the envelope only to discover its purpose is to involve you in some dishonourable enterprise, be rid of it without a second thought. I feel confident that I can leave you to make the correct decision.

Your loving father,
Gerald Scott

ADAM READ THE LETTER once again, realizing how much trust his father had placed in him. His heart thumped with indignation as he considered how Pa's life had been wasted by the murmurings of lesser men—the same men who had also succeeded in bringing his own career to a premature halt. When he had finished reading the missive for a third time he folded it up neatly and slipped it back into the envelope.

He then picked up the second envelope and slowly slit it open. He hesitated for a moment before extracting two pieces of paper, both yellowed with age. One appeared to be a letter, while the other was a document of some sort. The crest of the Third Reich was embossed on the letter, above the printed name of Reichsmarschall Hermann Goering. Adam's hands began to tremble as he read the first line.

It began, *Sehr geehrter Herr Oberst Scott.*

Chapter Three

As the black Chaika limousine drove out into Red Square, two Kremlin guards sprang to attention and presented arms.

Yuri Efimovich Zaborski touched the corner of his black felt hat in automatic acknowledgment of the salute, although his thoughts were elsewhere. As the car rumbled over the cobbles, he didn't even glance at the long snake of tourists that stretched from Lenin's Tomb to the edge of Red Square. The first decision he had to make was which of his senior operatives should be charged with the task of heading the team to find the Tsar's Icon.

Within moments of leaving his leader, the chairman of the KGB had formed in his own mind a short list of two. Which of those two, Valchek or Romanov, should be given the nod still taxed him, though the deadline of 20 June left him with little time to make the choice. The driver cruised past the Ministry of Culture and into Cherkasskiy Bolshoy Pereulok, lined with its imposing grey buildings. The car remained in the special inside lane that could be used only by senior party officials.

When the car came to a halt outside KGB headquarters, the driver ran round and opened the back door to allow his master to step out, but Zaborski didn't move. The man who rarely changed his mind had already done so twice on the route back to Dzerzhinsky Square.

His professional intuition told him to select Yuri Valchek, who had proved over the years to be a trusty and reliable servant of the state. Slow and methodical, he had completed ten years as an agent in the field before confining himself to a desk job.

In contrast, Alex Romanov, who had only recently become head of his own section, had shown flashes of brilliance in the field, but they had often been outweighed by a lack of personal judgment. At twenty-nine, he was the youngest and, without question, the most ambitious of the chairman's select team.

Zaborski stepped out onto the pavement and walked towards another door held open for him. By the time he had reached his office on the top floor he had made up his mind. It would be Valchek.

A secretary helped him off with his long black coat and took his hat. He walked quickly to his desk where the two files he had asked for were awaiting him. He sat down and began to pore over Valchek's file. When he had completed it, he barked out an order to his hovering secretary: "Find Romanov."

COMRADE ROMANOV LAY FLAT on his back, his left arm behind his head and his opponent's right arm over his throat.

An attendant came rushing up to them and bent down to whisper in the coach's ear. The coach reluctantly released his pupil who rose slowly as if in a daze, bowed and then in one movement of right arm and left leg took his coach's legs from under him and left him flat on the gymnasium floor.

Romanov didn't notice the girl who handed him the phone. "I'll be with him as soon as I have had a shower," was all she heard him say. The girl who had taken the call had often wondered what Romanov looked like in the shower. Six foot tall with blond hair—he resembled a Western film star. And those piercing blue eyes . . .

THE CHAIRMAN MEANWHILE was perusing the details of Romanov's personal file.

Alexander Petrovich Romanov, born Leningrad, 12 March 1937. Elected full party member 1958.

Father: Peter Nicholevich Romanov, served on the eastern front in 1942. On returning to Russia in 1945 refused to join Communist Party. After several reports of anti-State activities supplied by his son he was sentenced to ten years in prison. Died in jail 20 October 1948.

Grandfather: Nicholai Alexandrovich Romanov, merchant, one of the wealthiest landowners in Petrograd. Shot and killed on 11 May 1918 while attempting to escape from the forces of the Red Army.

Alex, as he preferred to be known, had enrolled in the party's Pioneer organization at the age of nine. He excelled in the classroom, and at fourteen he was selected as one of the party's elite.

By the age of sixteen, Romanov had won the Lenin language medal and the junior gymnastics prize and was allowed to take up a place at university. As an undergraduate he continued to excel in languages, specializing in English, French and German.

Zaborski picked up the phone at his side. "I asked to see Romanov," he said curtly.

"He was completing his morning workout at the gymnasium, Chairman," replied his secretary. "But he left to change the moment he heard you wanted to see him."

The chairman replaced the phone and his eyes returned to the file in front of him. That Romanov could be found in the gymnasium at all hours came as no surprise: the man's athletic prowess had been acknowledged far beyond the service.

During his first year as a student, Romanov had continued diligently with his gymnastics until the university coach had written across one of his reports, "This student is too tall to be considered for Olympic competition." So Romanov took up karate. Within two years he had been selected for the 1958 Eastern Bloc games in Budapest, and within a further two years he found other competitors preferred not to be drawn against him. After his victory at the Soviet games in Moscow, the Western press crudely described him as "The Axe".

Once Romanov had completed his fifth year at the university and obtained his diploma (with distinction), he joined the diplomatic service. That was when Zaborski had first come across the self-confident young man. Each year the KGB were able to second from the diplomatic service any person they considered to be of exceptional talent. Romanov was an obvious candidate and he had always wanted to be an officer of the KGB.

As an operative, Romanov had reached the rank of major, having served successfully in the field before being appointed head of a department. His most significant achievement, however, had been the recruitment of an agent from the British Foreign Office whose rise through the ranks had assisted Romanov's own career. Romanov's appointment as head of a department had surprised no one.

The chairman turned to the last page of the report, which was a character assessment: sophisticated, ambitious, ruthless, arrogant, but not always reliable.

There was an assertive rap on the door. Zaborski closed the file and pressed a button under his desk. The doors clicked open to allow Alexander Petrovich Romanov to enter the room.

"Good morning, Comrade Chairman," said the elegant young man who now stood to attention in front of him. Romanov's suit looked as if it had been tailored in Savile Row—and probably had. Zaborski chose to ignore such irregularities, though he was tempted to ask the young man where he had his shirts made.

"You called for me?" said Romanov.

The chairman nodded. "The General Secretary has entrusted us with a particularly sensitive project of great importance to the state." Zaborski paused. "So sensitive, in fact, that you will report only to me. You can hand-select your own team and no resources will be denied you."

"I am honoured," said Romanov, sounding unusually sincere.

"You will be," replied the chairman, "if you succeed in discovering the whereabouts of the Tsar's Icon."

"But I thought . . ." began Romanov.

Chapter Four

Adam removed from his bookshelf the Bible his mother had given him, and as he opened it a layer of dust rose from the top of the gilt-edged pages. He placed the envelope between the pages and returned the Bible to the shelf.

He went through to the kitchen, fried himself an egg and warmed up some baked beans. He placed the unwholesome meal on the kitchen table, unable to put out of his mind the slap-up dinner Lawrence and Carolyn must now be enjoying. After he had finished, he returned to his room and lay on the bed thinking. Would the contents of the faded envelope prove his father's innocence? A plan began to form in his mind.

He counted ten chimes on the grandfather clock in the hall, lifted his long legs over the end of the bed and pulled the Bible back out of the bookshelf. With some apprehension he removed the envelope, unfolded the two pieces of paper and placed them in front of him on his small writing desk.

One appeared to be a personal letter from Goering to Adam's father, while the other had the look of an older, more official document. Adam placed this second document to one side and began to go over the letter line by line. It didn't help him to understand it.

He tore a blank piece of paper from a notepad, and started to copy down carefully the text of Goering's letter before replacing the original in its faded envelope. He had just begun the same process with the official document, using a separate sheet of paper, when he heard a key turning and the voices of Lawrence and Carolyn at the front door.

Adam sighed and switched off the light by the side of the desk so that they shouldn't know he was still awake. One of them must have headed towards the kitchen, because he heard the fridge door squelch closed and, a few seconds later, the sound of a cork being extracted.

Reluctantly he rose from his chair and felt his way back to the bed. He quietly lowered himself onto it and waited impatiently for Lawrence's bedroom door to close.

He must have fallen asleep because when he checked the luminous dial on his alarm clock it was ten past three. He eased himself off the bed gingerly, feeling crumpled and weary. Slowly he groped his way back towards the desk, fumbled for the light switch. The faded envelope and the official document were still laid out on the desk, alongside the first few lines of his handwritten duplicate.

Adam yawned as he began to study the document once more. It was not as simple to copy as the letter had been, because the hand was spidery and cramped. He copied out each word painstakingly, in block capitals, and when he wasn't certain of the spelling he put down the possible alternative letters below; he wanted to be sure of any translation the first time.

THE FIRST ACTION Romanov took on leaving the chairman's office that morning was to handpick a team of twelve researchers. From the moment they had been briefed they studied in pairs on four-hour shifts, so that the work could continue night and day.

The researchers had quickly been able to establish that the Tsar's Icon had remained in his private quarters at the Winter Palace until as late as December 1914. Romanov studied a photo of the small, exquisite painting: St. George in a tiny mosaic pattern of blue and gold, while the dragon was in fiery red and yellow. Although he had never shown any interest in art, Romanov could well understand why people might be moved by the little masterpiece. He continued to read details of the icon's history, but still couldn't work out why it was so important to the state.

A royal servant who had testified before the People's Court after the Revolution claimed that the Tsar's Icon had disappeared for a few days in 1915, after the visit of Ernst Ludwig, Grand Duke of Hesse. At the time, the People's Court had taken scant interest in the misplaced icon because it was on the wall of the tsar's study when they stormed the Winter Palace. What concerned them more was why, in the middle of a fierce war with the kaiser's Germany, the grand duke should want to visit the tsar at all.

The professor of history at the University of Moscow had immediately been asked for his opinion. The great academic briefed Romanov on everything that was known of the incident. Romanov pored over his report again. The grand duke, it was thought, had been on a secret visit to his sister Alexandra, the tsarina. Historians now believed that it had been his intention to secure a cease-fire between Germany and Russia, in the hope that Germany could then concentrate her war effort on the British and the French.

There was no proof that the tsar made any promises on behalf of his people but the grand duke, it seemed, did not return to Germany empty-handed. Reports showed that another palace servant had been instructed to wrap up the Tsar's Icon and pack it with the grand duke's belongings. However, the palace staff could never properly explain to the People's Court how a few days later the icon reappeared in its rightful place on the wall of the tsar's private study.

Romanov's chief researcher had underlined his conclusion in red ink. "The tsar must have replaced the original painting with a copy, having handed over the real icon for safekeeping to his brother-in-law, the grand duke."

But why, Romanov wondered, when the tsar had a palace full of Goyas, El Grecos, Titians and Rubenses, did he bother to smuggle out one icon, and why did Brezhnev so badly want it back?

He instructed his researchers to turn their talents to the royal house of Hesse in the hope of tracing what had then happened to the icon. Within ten days they possessed, between them, a lifetime's information about the grand duke and his family. As each file appeared on his desk Romanov checked it: he came to a dead end when, after the grand duke's death, the painting had been left to his son, who was tragically killed in a plane crash. Nothing had been seen or heard of the icon after that day.

By the beginning of the third week, Romanov had reached the reluctant conclusion that there was nothing new to be discovered. He was preparing his final report for Zaborski when one researcher, Comrade Petrova, stumbled across a report in the London *Times* of Wednesday, 17 November 1937. It read:

> Grand Duke George of Hesse and four members of his family were tragically killed yesterday when a Sabena aircraft carrying them from Frankfurt to London crashed in thick fog over Belgium.
>
> The Grand Duke was on his way to England to attend the wedding of his younger brother, Prince Louis. The Prince immediately cancelled his wedding plans and announced that they would be rescheduled, with a small private service.

It was the next paragraph that the researcher had circled boldly.

> Some of the late Grand Duke's personal belongings, including several wedding presents for Prince Louis and his bride, were scattered for miles in the vicinity of the crashed aircraft.

The German government announced this morning that a senior German general has been appointed to lead a team of salvage experts to ensure the recovery of any family possessions, which will belong to the Grand Duke's successor.

Romanov immediately called for the young researcher. "I want you to scour *The Times* for every day from 17 November 1937, and also check the German and Belgian press during the same period, in case you come across anything that would show what the salvage experts discovered." He dismissed her with a smile.

Comrade Anna Petrova gave no impression of being overawed by her head of department. Within twenty-four hours she barged back into Romanov's office without even bothering to knock and handed him an article she had discovered in the Berlin *Zeitung* of Saturday, 19 January, 1938.

The investigation into the crash last November of the Sabena aircraft that was carrying the royal family of Hesse to London has now been concluded. All personal possessions that were discovered in the vicinity of the wreckage have been returned to Prince Louis, who, it is understood, was saddened by the loss of a family heirloom that was to have been a wedding gift from his brother. The gift, a painting known as "The Tsar's Icon", had once belonged to his uncle, Tsar Nicholas II. The icon of St. George and the Dragon, although it was only a copy of Rublev's masterpiece, was considered to be a very fine example of early twentieth-century Russian craftsmanship.

Romanov looked up at the researcher. "Twentieth-century copy be damned," he said. "It was the fifteenth-century original. No doubt the tsar had other plans for the icon, had he managed to escape."

Romanov dreaded having to tell Zaborski that the original Tsar's Icon had been destroyed in a plane crash, because, clearly, there was something far more important than the icon at stake.

He stared down at the photograph above the newspaper report. Prince Louis was shaking hands with the general in charge of the salvage team which had been successful in returning so many of the prince's family possessions. "But did he return them all?" Romanov said out loud.

"What do you mean?" asked the young researcher. Romanov continued to stare at the faded photograph. Although the general was unnamed, every schoolboy in Germany would have recognized the large, impassive, heavy-jowled face with the chilling eyes.

Romanov looked up at the researcher. "You can forget the grand duke from now on, Comrade Petrova. Concentrate on Reichsmarschall Hermann Goering."

ADAM WOKE AT TEN TO SEVEN the next morning. Although he felt as fit as he had been the day he left the army some seven weeks before, he still completed a punishing routine of exercise every morning. He intended to be at his peak when the Foreign Office put him through a physical. In moments he was kitted out in a singlet, running shorts and gym shoes.

Adam tiptoed out of the flat, and for the next half hour he pounded the pavements down to the Embankment, across Albert Bridge, through Battersea Park, to return by way of Chelsea Bridge. Only one thought was going through his mind: after twenty years of innuendo, was this going to be his chance to clear his father's name? Adam checked his pulse the moment he arrived back: 150 beats a minute. Sixty seconds later it was down to 100, in another minute 70, and before the fourth minute was up it was back to a steady 58. It's the recovery that proves fitness, not your speed, his physical training instructor at Aldershot had drummed into him.

Back in the flat, Lawrence, smart in a grey pinstripe suit, was preparing breakfast in the kitchen while glancing at the sports pages of the *Daily Telegraph*.

"The West Indies made 526," he informed Adam forlornly.

"Have we begun our innings?" shouted Adam from the bathroom.

"No, bad light stopped play."

Adam stripped for his cold shower. Minutes later, once he had towelled himself down and thrown on his dressing gown, he joined his friend in the kitchen for breakfast. Lawrence was now concentrating on a bowl of cornflakes, while running a finger down the foreign exchange rates in the *Financial Times*.

Adam checked his watch: already ten past eight. "Won't you be late for the office?" he asked.

"Dear boy," said Lawrence, "I am not a lackey who works at the kind of bank where the customers keep shop hours."

Adam laughed.

"But I will, however, have to be shackled to my desk in the City by nine thirty," Lawrence admitted. "They don't send a driver for me nowadays," he joked. "As I told them, it's so much quicker by tube."

Adam started to make himself breakfast. "I could always give you a lift on my motorbike."

"Can you imagine a man in my position arriving at the headquarters of Barclays Bank on a motorbike? The chairman would have a fit."

Adam cracked a second egg into the frying pan.

"See you tonight then, glorious, unwashed and unemployed," jeered Lawrence as he collected his rolled umbrella.

Adam cleared away and washed up, happy to act as housewife while he was still unemployed. All he had planned before his interview with the Foreign Office that afternoon was a long bath and a slow shave. Then he remembered that Reichsmarschall Goering was still resting on the table in his bedroom.

"HAVE YOU COME UP with anything that would indicate Goering might have kept the icon for himself?" asked Romanov, turning hopefully to the researcher.

"Only the obvious," Anna Petrova replied. "It's common knowledge that Hitler put Goering in charge of all the art treasures seized on behalf of the Third Reich. But as the Führer had such fixed personal opinions as to what constituted quality, many of the world's masterpieces were judged as 'depraved' and therefore unworthy to be put on public view."

"So what happened to them?"

"Hitler ordered them to be burned."

"You are not suggesting Goering could have stolen the Tsar's Icon," Romanov asked, "only to burn it?"

"No, no. Goering was not that stupid. As we now know, he didn't always obey the Führer's every word. When it came to it, Goering did not destroy any of the denounced masterpieces. He held some public burnings of lesser-known German artists, but the real works of genius were moved discreetly over the border and deposited in the vaults of Swiss banks. Since the end of the war many of the paintings have been found and restored to their rightful owners. Others, however, have appeared on walls as far-flung as the Metropolitan Museum in New York and the Gotoh in Tokyo, sometimes without a fully satisfactory explanation."

"Have all the missing pictures now been found?" asked Romanov.

"Over seventy per cent, but there are still many more to be accounted for. Some may have been lost, but I am sure that there are still a large number lodged in Swiss banks."

"How can you be so certain?" demanded Romanov, fearful that his last avenue might be closing.

"Because the Swiss banks only return valuables when they can be certain of a nation's or an individual's right of possession. In the case of the Grand Duke of Hesse and the Tsar's Icon there was no proof of ownership, as the last official owner was Tsar Nicholas II and he, as every good Russian knows, had no successors."

"Then I must retrace Goering's steps by going direct to the banks. What has been their disclosure policy to date?" asked Romanov.

"That differs from establishment to establishment. Some banks wait for twenty years or more and then try either by extensive research or advertising to contact the owner or his next of kin. In the case of the Jews who lost their lives under the Nazi regime, it has often proved impossible to trace a legitimate owner. Although I can't prove it, I suspect they kept the rewards and split the proceeds among themselves," said Petrova. "Typical capitalists."

"That is neither fair nor accurate, comrade," said Romanov, glad to be able to show that he also had been doing some research. "In fact, when the banks have been unable to discover the rightful owner of any treasure left with them they have handed it over to the Swiss Red Cross for auction."

"But if the Tsar's Icon had ever been auctioned we would have heard about it through one of our agents?"

"Precisely," said Romanov. "Our operatives have combed Europe. They have spoken to nearly every major curator, keeper, dealer and crook in the art world and they still haven't come up with a single lead."

"Then that can only mean some unscrupulous bankers have disposed of the icon privately once they felt sure no one was going to make a claim."

"Another false conclusion, I suspect, Comrade Petrova."

"How do you know?" the young researcher asked.

"For one simple reason, comrade. The Swiss banking families all know each other intimately and have never in the past shown any propensity for breaking the law. Swiss justice is as tough on corrupt bankers as it is on murderers. Swiss bankers make so much money dealing with honest people that it has never been in their best interests to become involved with crooks. No, I'm convinced," Romanov concluded, "that while the rest of the world is under the illusion that the original icon still hangs in the Winter Palace, it has, since 1937, been lodged in a Swiss bank waiting for someone to claim it."

"A long shot," said the researcher.

"I am quite aware of that," said Romanov sharply, "but don't forget that many Swiss banks have a twenty-five-year rule before disclosure, some even thirty. One or two even have no deadline at all as long as enough money has been deposited to cover the housing of the treasure. It is those that we must check."

"Heaven knows how many banks there will be which fall into that category," sighed Petrova.

"Heaven knows," agreed Romanov, "and so will you by nine o'clock tomorrow morning. And then I will have to pay a visit to the one man in this country who knows everything about banking."

"Am I expected to start straight away, Comrade Major?" the researcher asked coyly.

Romanov smiled and looked down into the girl's green eyes. Dressed in the dull grey uniform of her trade she wasn't worth a second look. But in the nude she was quite magnificent. He leaned over until their lips nearly met.

"Just turn out the light, Anna."

Chapter Five

It took Adam only a few more minutes to check both documents again. He put the originals back into the Bible on his bookshelf. Finally he folded his copy of Goering's letter into three horizontal pieces and cut it carefully along the folds into strips which he placed in a clean envelope and left on his bedside table. His next problem was how to obtain a translation of the documents and Goering's letter without arousing unnecessary curiosity. He quickly dismissed the German embassy, the German tourist board and the German press agency, as all three were likely to ask unwanted questions. Once he was dressed, he went to the hall and began to flick through the pages in the London E—K directory until his finger reached the column he had been searching for.

> *German Broadcasting*
> *German Cultural Institute*
> *German Hospital*

His eye passed over *German Technical Translations* and stopped at a more promising entry. The address was Bayswater House, 35 Craven Terrace, W2.

Adam left the flat a few minutes before ten, the three pieces of the letter now safely lodged in the inside pocket of his blazer. He strolled down Edith Grove and into the King's Road, enjoying the morning sun. The street had been transformed from the one he had known as a young subaltern, he reflected ruefully. A record shop had replaced the local cobbler, and booksellers had given way to fashion boutiques. Take a fortnight's holiday and you couldn't be sure that anything would still be there when you returned.

At Sloane Square underground station he paid a shilling for a ticket to Paddington and, installed in a half empty carriage, once more went over his plan. When he emerged into the open air at Paddington he walked along Craven Road until he came to the first newsagent. He asked directions for Craven Terrace.

"Fourth road on the right, mate," said the shopkeeper, not bothering to look up from a pile of *Radio Times* on which he was pencilling names. Adam thanked him and a few minutes later found himself standing at the end of a short drive, looking up at a bold green and yellow sign: The German Young Men's Christian Association.

He opened the gate, walked up the drive and strode confidently through the front door. He was stopped by a porter standing in the hallway.

"Can I help you, guv'nor?"

Adam put on an exaggerated military accent and explained that he was looking for a young man called Hans Kramer.

"Never 'eard of 'im, sir," said the porter, almost standing to attention when he recognized the regimental tie. He turned to a book that lay open on the desk. " 'E isn't registered," he added, a Woodbine-stained thumb running down the list of names in front of him. "Why don't you try the lounge or the games room?" he suggested, gesturing to a door on the right.

"Thank you," said Adam, not dropping the plummy tones. He walked smartly across the hall and through the swing doors. Several students were lounging around the room, reading papers and magazines. He spotted a studious-looking girl on her own in a corner, poring over a copy of *Time* magazine. Adam strolled across and took the empty seat beside her. She glanced sideways at him and couldn't hide her surprise at his formal dress. He waited for her to put the paper down before asking, "I wonder if you could assist me?"

"How?" inquired the girl, sounding a little apprehensive.

"I just need something translated."

She looked relieved. "I will see if I can help."

Adam took the envelope from his inside pocket, extracted the first paragraph of Goering's letter, and handed it over to the girl. He put the envelope back in his pocket, took out a little notebook and waited expectantly.

She read the paragraph over two or three times, then hesitated.

"Is anything wrong?"

"Not exactly," she replied, still concentrating on the words in front of her. "It's just that it's a little bit old-fashioned, so I might not be able to give you the exact sense."

She repeated each sentence slowly, first in German and then in English, as if wanting to feel the meaning as well as just translating the words. " 'Over the last . . . past year we have come to know . . . each other somewhat' . . . no, no," she said, " 'quite well.' " Adam wrote each word down as the girl translated it.

" 'You have never hidden your distaste for the National Socialist Party.' "

She raised her head and stared at Adam. "It's only out of a book," he assured her. She didn't look convinced but nevertheless continued.

" 'But you have at every time' . . . no, 'at all times, behaved with the courtesy of an officer and a gentleman.' "

The girl looked up, even more puzzled, as she had now reached the last word. "Is that all?" she asked. "It doesn't make sense."

"No, that's it," said Adam, quickly taking back the piece of paper. "Thank you," he added. "It was most kind of you to help."

He was relieved to see the girl shrug resignedly and return to her copy of *Time*. Adam went in search of the games room.

When he swung the door open he found a young man in a World Cup T-shirt and brown suede shorts. He was tapping a table-tennis ball up and down listlessly.

"Care for a game?" said the boy, not looking at all hopeful.

"Sure," said Adam, removing his jacket and picking up a bat. For twenty minutes Adam had to play flat out to make sure he lost. As he replaced his jacket and congratulated his opponent he felt sure he had gained the young man's confidence.

"You put up good fight," said the German. "Give me good game."

Adam joined him at his end of the table. "I wonder if you could help me with something?" he said.

"Your backhand?" asked the young man.

"No, thank you," said Adam, "I just need a paragraph of German translated." He handed over the middle paragraph of the letter. Once again, the would-be translator looked puzzled.

"It's from a book, so it may seem a little out of context," Adam said, unconvincingly.

"OK, I try." As the boy began to study the paragraph, the girl who had already translated the first section came into the games room. She made her way towards them.

"This hard to make out, I am not good translation for," the young man said. "My girlfriend better, I think. I ask her. *Liebling, kanst Du dies für den Herrn ins Englische übersetzen?*" Without looking at Adam he passed the second paragraph over to the girl who immediately said, "I knew there was more."

"No, no, don't bother," said Adam, and grabbed the piece of paper away from the girl. He turned back to the boy and said, "Thank you for the game. Sorry to have bothered you," and walked hurriedly out into the corridor.

As he left the building he saw that the boy and his girlfriend were following him.

Adam ran down the drive and hailed a passing taxi.

"Where to?" said the cabbie.

"The Royal Cleveland Hotel."

"But that's only just round the corner."

"I know," said Adam, "but I'm already late."

"Suit yourself, guv," said the cabbie, "it's your money."

As the cab moved off Adam peered out of the back window, to see his table-tennis opponent in conversation with the porter, who was pointing to the taxi.

He relaxed when the cab turned the corner and they were out of sight. In less than a minute the taxi had drawn up outside the Royal Cleveland. Adam pushed through the revolving doors of the hotel and hung around in the foyer for a few moments before returning to the pavement again. It was twelve thirty. He had time for lunch before going on to his interview with the Foreign Office. He headed across Bayswater Road into the park at a brisk pace, knowing he couldn't hope to find a pub until he reached Knightsbridge.

Adam recalled the table-tennis match. Damn, he thought. I should simply have thrashed him. It would have given him something else to think about.

ROMANOV'S EYE RAN DOWN the list of fourteen banks, but the names meant nothing to him. He knew he would have to seek advice from an expert.

He unlocked the top drawer of his desk and flicked through the red book held only by the most senior ranking officers in the KGB. He dialled a number on his private line and asked to be put through to Aleksei Andreovich Poskonov, chairman of Gosbank, the National Bank. It was some time before another voice came on the line.

"Comrade Romanov, what can I do for you?"

"I need to see you urgently," said Romanov.

"Really." The gravelly tones that came from the other end of the line sounded distinctly unimpressed. Romanov could hear pages being flicked over. "I could manage Tuesday, say eleven thirty?"

"I said it was urgent," repeated Romanov. "It concerns a state matter that can't wait."

"We do have one or two problems of our own, you may be surprised to hear," came back the unrepentant voice. Romanov waited. "Well, I suppose I could fit you in at three forty-five today, for fifteen minutes," said the banker.

"Three forty-five it is, then," said Romanov.

"In my office," said Poskonov. The phone went dead.

Romanov began to write down the questions he needed answered. He couldn't afford to waste a single second of his allocated fifteen minutes. An hour later he asked to see the chairman of the KGB. This time he was not kept waiting.

"Trying to play the capitalists at their own game, are we?" said

Zaborski, once Romanov had outlined his intentions. "Be careful. They've been at it a lot longer than we have."

"I realize that," said Romanov, "but if the icon is in the West I'm left with little choice but to use their methods to get my hands on it."

"Perhaps," said the chairman.

Romanov knew better than to interrupt the brief silence that ensued.

"Don't worry, I'll give you all the backing you need—although I've never had a request quite like this one before."

"Am I allowed to know why the icon is so important?" Romanov inquired.

Zaborski frowned. "I do not have the authority to answer that question, but as Comrade Brezhnev's lack of enthusiasm for the arts is well known, you must have been able to work out that it is not the painting itself that we are after." He rose from his desk, walked over to the wall and tore another page from the calendar. "And we've only twelve days left to find the damn thing."

AT THREE FORTY-FIVE PRECISELY Romanov was ushered into Poskonov's office.

The young major was momentarily taken aback by the sheer opulence of the room: the long red velvet curtains, the marble floor, the delicate French furniture. He was reminded, not for the first time, that money still remained the most important commodity in the world—even in the Communist world. He stared at the old stooped man with the thinning grey hair and bushy walrus moustache who controlled the nation's money.

"What can I do for you, Comrade Romanov?" inquired the banker with a sigh, as if addressing a tiresome customer.

"I require one hundred million American dollars' worth of gold bullion, immediately," Romanov announced evenly.

The chairman's bored expression suddenly changed. He took several short, sharp breaths before extracting a large white pill from a box and swallowing it. It took fully a minute before he seemed calm again.

"Have you gone out of your mind, comrade?" the old man inquired. "You ask for an appointment without giving a reason, you then charge into my office and demand that I hand over one hundred million American dollars in gold without any explanation. For what purpose do you make such a preposterous suggestion?"

"That is the business of the state," said Romanov. "But, since you have inquired, I intend to deposit equal amounts in a series of numbered accounts across Switzerland."

"And on whose authority do you make such a request?" the banker asked in a level tone.

33

"The General Secretary of the Party."

"Strange," said Poskonov. "Leonid Ilyich has not mentioned this to me."

Romanov stepped forward, picked up the phone by Poskonov's side and held it out to him. "Why don't you ask Leonid Ilyich yourself, and save us all a lot of time?" He pushed the phone defiantly towards the banker, who picked it up and placed it to his ear.

A voice came on the line. "You called, Comrade Chairman?"

"Yes," replied the old man. "Cancel my four o'clock appointment, and see that I am not disturbed until Major Romanov leaves."

"Yes, Comrade Chairman."

Poskonov replaced the phone and, without another word, rose from behind his desk and walked round to Romanov's side. He ushered the young man into a comfortable chair under a bay window and took the seat opposite him.

"I knew your grandfather," he said in a calm, matter-of-fact tone. "I was a junior clerk when I first met him. He was very kind to me but he was just as impatient as you are."

Romanov laughed.

"You'll forgive my curiosity, Major, but if I am to hand over one hundred million dollars in gold I should like to know what it will be spent on. I thought only the CIA put in chits for that sort of expenses without explanation."

Romanov laughed again and explained to the chairman how they had discovered that the Tsar's Icon was a fake and how he had been set the task of recovering the original. When he had completed his story he handed over the names of the fourteen banks. The banker studied the list while Romanov outlined the course of action he proposed to take.

There was an exasperated grunt from the other chair when Romanov had finished. "May I be permitted to suggest an alternative to your plan?"

"Please do," said Romanov, relieved to be gaining the old man's cooperation.

The old man paused to light a cigarette. "Correct me if I have misunderstood any of your requirements. You suspect that lodged in one of these fourteen Swiss banks is the original Tsar's Icon. You therefore want me to deposit large amounts of gold with each bank in the hope that that will give you immediate access to its chairman. You will then offer the chairman the chance to control the entire hundred million if he promises to cooperate with you?"

"Yes," said Romanov. "Bribery is surely something the West has always understood?"

"I would have said you were being naive if I hadn't known your grandfather; though to be fair it was he who ended up making millions of roubles, not me. Nevertheless, how much do you imagine is a lot of money to a major Swiss bank?"

"Ten million, twenty million?"

"To the Moscow Narodny Bank, perhaps," said Poskonov. "But every one of the banks you hope to deal with will have several customers with deposits of over a hundred million each."

Romanov was unable to hide his astonishment. "Then I will need a thousand million?" he asked.

"No, no, no. We must approach the problem differently. You do not catch a poacher by offering him a rabbit stew."

"But if the Swiss are not moved by the offer of vast amounts of money, what *will* move them?"

"The simple suggestion that their bank has been used for criminal activity," said the chairman.

"But . . ." began Romanov.

"Let me explain what I mean. Why not tell each of the fourteen banks that, after extensive research, we have reason to believe that one of the nation's most valuable treasures is thought to have been deposited in their vaults? And rather than cause a diplomatic incident—the one thing every Swiss banker wishes to avoid at any cost—perhaps they would consider checking all items that have not been claimed for over twenty years?"

Romanov looked straight at the old man, realizing now why he had survived several purges. "I owe you an apology, Comrade Poskonov."

"No, no, we each have our own little skills. Now, if you will allow me to contact each of the chairmen on this list and tell them no more than the truth—namely, that I suspect the Tsar's Icon is in their bank—most of them will be disinclined to hold on to the masterpiece."

"I cannot overstress the urgency," said Romanov.

"Just like your grandfather," Poskonov said. "So be it. I shall speak to every one of them today. At least that's one of the advantages of the rest of the world waking up after us. Be assured, I shall be in touch with you the moment I have any news."

"Thank you," said Romanov, rising to leave. "You have been most helpful."

The chairman of Gosbank closed the door behind him and walked back to the bay window. He watched Romanov run down the steps of the bank to a waiting car.

I couldn't have supplied you with the one hundred million in gold bullion at this particular time, even if the General Secretary had ordered me to, he thought to himself. I doubt if I have ten million dollars' worth of gold left in the vaults. The General Secretary has already ordered me to fly every available ounce to the Bank of New York—and so cleverly was his ploy disguised that the CIA had been informed about the deposit within an hour of its arrival. It's hard to hide over 700 million dollars in gold, even in America. I tried to tell him . . .

Poskonov returned to his desk and began to phone the fourteen banks.

ADAM STEPPED OUT of Tattersalls Tavern, on the corner of Knightsbridge Green, and headed towards the Royal Thames Yacht Club. It seemed a strange place for the Foreign Office to hold an interview, but so far everything connected with his application had been somewhat mysterious.

He arrived a few minutes early and asked the ex-Royal Marines sergeant on the door where the interviews were taking place.

"Sixth floor, sir. Take the lift in the corner."

As Adam stepped into the lift, a rather overweight, bespectacled man of roughly his own age followed him. Adam touched the sixth button, but neither man spoke on the journey up. The large man stepped out of the lift in front of Adam.

"Wainwright's the name," he informed the girl at the reception desk.

"Yes, sir," said the girl, "you're a little early, but do have a seat over there." She gestured towards a chair in the corner, then her eyes moved on to Adam and she smiled.

"Scott," he informed her.

"Yes, sir," she repeated. "Could you join the other gentleman? They will be seeing you next." Adam went over and picked up a copy of *Punch* before settling down next to Wainwright.

Adam took a more careful look at the other interviewee. "Do you by any chance speak German?" he asked him suddenly.

"German, French, Italian and Spanish," Wainwright replied, looking up. "I'd assumed that was how I managed to get this far," he added somewhat smugly.

"Then perhaps you could translate a paragraph from a German letter for me?"

"Delighted, old fellow," said Adam's companion, who removed the glasses from his nose and waited for Adam to extract the middle paragraph of the letter from his envelope.

"Now, let me see," Wainwright said, taking the little slip of paper. "Quite a challenge. I say, old fellow, you're not part of the interviewing team by any chance?"

"No, no," said Adam, smiling. "I'm in exactly the same position as you—except I don't speak German, French, Italian or Spanish."

Wainwright seemed to relax. "Now let me see," he repeated, as Adam took out the small notebook from his inside pocket. " 'During the past year you cannot have failed to . . . notice that I have been receiving from

one of the guards a regular . . . regular supply of Havana cigars. One of
the few pleasures I have been allocated'—no, 'permitted—despite my
. . . incarceration.' That's the nearest I can get. 'The cigars themselves
have also served another purpose,' " Wainwright continued, obviously
enjoying himself, " 'as they contained tiny capsules . . .' "

"Mr. Scott, the Board will see you now," said the receptionist.

"Do you want me to finish it off while they're finishing you off, old
chap?" said Wainwright.

"Thank you," Adam replied, "if it's not too much trouble."

WHILE ALEX ROMANOV waited impatiently for the results of the
inquiries by the chairman of Gosbank he reread the research papers and
checked all new intelligence sent in by his agents.

Then the chairman of the bank called him over.

This time Romanov was ushered up to the finely furnished room
without a moment's delay.

"You must have wondered if I had forgotten you," were Poskonov's
opening words. "But I wanted to have some positive news."

The chairman's secretary entered the room and placed two empty
glasses, a frosted flask and a plate of caviar in front of them.

Romanov waited in silence.

"I have, over the past few days, managed to talk to the chairmen of all
the banks on your list," Poskonov began, as he poured two vodkas. "It
will please you to know," he continued, "that twelve of them have
already agreed to cooperate with us. Five have in fact already phoned
back, four to say they have run a thorough check but have come up with
nothing that remotely resembles an icon."

"And the fifth?" inquired Romanov.

"Now that, I suspect, may be our first breakthrough," continued
Poskonov, referring to the file in front of him. "Herr Dieter Bischoff of
Bischoff et Cie, an honourable man with whom I have dealt many times
in the past, has come up with something that was left with the bank in
1938. It is unquestionably an icon, but he has no way of knowing if it is
the one we are looking for."

Romanov leaped up from his seat in excitement. "Then I had better go
and see for myself," he said. "I could fly out today."

The chairman waved him back into his chair. "The plane you require
does not leave Sheremtyevo Airport until four thirty-five. In any case, I
have already booked two seats on it for you. You will obviously need an
expert to accompany you, unless you know considerably more about
icons than you do about banking. I also took the liberty of booking you
on the Swissair flight. One should never fly Aeroflot. It has managed only
one aviation record, namely that of losing the most passengers per mile

flown. I have also fixed an appointment for you to see Herr Bischoff at ten o'clock tomorrow morning.

"I note from your file that you have never served in Switzerland, so may I also recommend," went on the old man, showing off, "that you stay at the St. Gotthard while you are in Zürich. The manager, Jacques Pontin, will take excellent care of you. And that brings my little investigation up to date. All I can do now is wish you luck in Zürich."

"Thank you," said Romanov. "May I be permitted to add how much I appreciate your kindness."

"My pleasure, comrade. Let's say I owe your grandfather a favour, and perhaps one day you will find you owe me one, and leave it at that."

Romanov tried in vain to fathom the meaning of the old man's words as he descended the wide marble staircase.

BY THE TIME ROMANOV had returned to Dzerzhinsky Square, his secretary informed him that Herr Bischoff's assistant had telephoned from Zürich to confirm his appointment at ten o'clock the following morning. Romanov asked her to call the manager at the St. Gotthard Hotel and book two rooms. "Oh, and confirm my flight with Swissair," he added, before going to see the chairman and brief him on his meeting with the head of the National Bank.

"Thank God for that," were Zaborski's first words. "With only nine days left at least you've given me something to discuss with Brezhnev, who has taken to phoning me at one o'clock every morning."

Romanov smiled.

"Good luck, comrade. Our embassy will be alerted to your every need. Let us hope fervently that you will be able to return the masterpiece to the walls of the Winter Palace."

"If it is in that bank, it will be in your hands by tomorrow night," said Romanov.

When he walked into his own office he found Petrova waiting for him.

"You called for me, comrade?"

"Yes, we're going to Zürich in three hours' time. The flight and the rooms are already booked."

"In the names of Herr and Frau Schmidt, no doubt," said his lover.

Chapter Six

When Adam emerged from the interview he felt quietly confident. The interviewer's final words had been to ask him if he would be available for a medical in a week's time. Adam had told them he could think of nothing that would stop him attending.

Back in the waiting room Wainwright looked up and handed him his piece of paper.

"Thank you very much," said Adam, trying, by slipping it into his inside pocket without looking at the results, to look casual.

"What was it like, old chap?" his companion asked cautiously.

"No trouble for a man who has French, Spanish, German and Italian as part of his armoury," Adam assured him. "Best of luck, anyway."

He took the lift to the ground floor and decided to walk home, stopping on the corner of Wilton Place to buy a bag of apples from a barrow boy who seemed to spend most of his time on the lookout for the police. Further on he came to a sudden halt. What had attracted his attention was a sign reading "The German Food Centre". An attractive girl with a cheerful smile was sitting at the cash register near the doorway. Adam strode into the shop and went straight over to her without attempting to purchase a single item.

"You have not bought anything?" she inquired, with a slight accent.

"No, I'm just about to," Adam assured her, "but I wondered, do you speak German?"

"Most girls from Mainz do," she replied, grinning.

"Yes, I suppose they would," said Adam, looking at the girl more carefully. She must have been in her early twenties, and he was immediately attracted by her friendly manner. Her shiny, dark hair was done up in a ponytail with a big red bow. Her white sweater and neat pleated skirt would have made any man take a second look. "I wonder if you would be kind enough to translate a short paragraph for me?"

"I will try," she said, still smiling.

Adam took the envelope containing the final section of the letter out of his pocket and handed it over to her.

"The style is a bit old-fashioned," she said, looking serious. "It may take a little time."

"I'll go and do some shopping," he told her, and started walking slowly round the long, stacked shelves. He selected salami, frankfurters, bacon and some German mustard, looking up now and then to see how the girl was progressing. She was continually interrupted by customers and nearly twenty minutes passed before he saw her put the piece of paper on one side. Adam immediately went over to her and placed his purchases on the counter.

"One pound two shillings and sixpence," she said. Adam handed over two pounds and she returned his change and the little piece of paper. "This I consider a rough translation, but I think the meaning is clear."

"I don't know how to thank you," said Adam.

"You could perhaps invite me to share with you your frankfurters," she laughed.

"What a nice idea," said Adam. "Why don't you join me for dinner tonight?"

"I was not serious," she said.

"I was," smiled Adam. The queue behind him began to look restive, so he grabbed a leaflet from the counter, retreated towards the back of the store, and scribbled down his name, address and phone number. He waited for two customers in front of him to pay, then handed over the leaflet to the girl.

"I've put my name and address on the centre page," Adam said. "I will expect you for dinner at about eight this evening. At least you know what's on the menu."

She looked uncertain. "I really was only joking."

"I won't eat you," said Adam. "Only the sausages."

She looked at the leaflet in her hand and laughed. "I'll think about it."

Adam strolled out into the street, whistling. Back at the flat he put the food in the fridge and went into his bedroom to assemble the full text of the Goering letter. He took out his notepad and began to copy out the translations: first, the paragraph supplied by the girl from the YMCA, then Wainwright's, and finally the section of the letter translated by the lovely girl from Mainz. He read the completed draft through slowly.

> Dear Colonel,
>
> Over the past year, we have come to know each other quite well. You have never disguised your distaste for the National Socialist party, but you have at all times behaved with the courtesy of an officer and a gentleman.
>
> During the year you cannot have failed to notice that I have been receiving from one of the guards a regular supply of Havana cigars—one of the few pleasures I have been permitted despite my incarceration. The cigars themselves have also served another purpose, as each one contained a capsule with a small amount of poison. Enough to allow me to survive my trial, while ensuring that I shall cheat the executioner.
>
> My only regret is that you, as the officer in charge of the watch during the period that I am most likely to die, may be held responsible for something to which you were never a party. To make amends for this I enclose a document in the name of one Emmanuel Rosenbaum which should help with any financial difficulties you face in the near future.
>
> All that will be required of you—

"Anyone at home?" Lawrence shouted. Adam collected up the pieces of paper and quickly inserted them alongside the other documents in the Bible, seconds before Lawrence put his head round the door.

"Bloody traffic," said Lawrence cheerfully. "I can't wait to be appointed chairman of the bank and be given the luxury flat on the top floor, not to mention the chauffeur and the company car."

Adam laughed. "Had another hard day at the office, darling?" he mocked, before going into the kitchen and starting to remove food from the fridge.

"Guess who's coming to dinner," said Lawrence.

"A rather attractive German girl, I hope," said Adam. "It could hardly have been described as a formal invitation so I'm not even certain she'll turn up."

"If that's the situation I may as well hang around in case she gives you the elbow and you need someone to help you eat that lot."

"Thanks for the vote of confidence, but I think you'll find it's your turn to be missing, presumed dead. Anyway, what about Carolyn?" said Adam.

"Carolyn was yesterday's girl, to quote the esteemed Harold Wilson. How did you come across your fraulein?"

"She was serving at a food store in Knightsbridge. I have no idea what her name is, come to think of it," said Adam. "But I am hoping to find out tonight. As I said, your turn to disappear."

"*Natürlich.* As you see, you can rely on me to provide a helping hand if you need anything translated."

"Just put the wine in the fridge and lay the table."

When eight o'clock chimed the table was set and Adam had everything ready. By eight thirty both of them stopped pretending and Adam served up two plates of frankfurters, salami and lettuce with baked potatoes and sauerkraut. He then hung up his apron and sat down opposite Lawrence, who had begun pouring the wine.

"Oh, *mein liebes Mädchen*, you look ravishing in that tweed jacket," said Lawrence, raising his glass.

Adam was just about to retaliate with the vegetable spoon when there was a loud knock on the front door. Adam leaped to open it. Standing in the doorway was a man of well over six foot with shoulders like a professional bouncer. By his side, dwarfed by him, was the girl that Adam had invited to dinner.

"This is my brother, Jochen," she explained. Adam was immediately struck by how beautiful she looked in a dark blue patterned blouse and pleated blue skirt. Her long dark hair, now hanging loose, shone.

"Welcome," said Adam, more than a little taken aback.

"Jochen is just dropping me off."

"Yes, of course," said Adam. "Do come in and have a drink, Jochen."

"No, I thank you. I have a date as well, but I will pick up Heidi at eleven o'clock, if all right by you?"

"Fine by me," said Adam, at last learning her name.

The giant bent down and kissed his sister on both cheeks. He then shook hands with Adam before leaving.

"I am sorry to be late," said Heidi. "My brother did not get back from work until after seven."

"It was no problem," said Adam, leading her into the flat. "If you had come any earlier I wouldn't have been ready for you. By the way, this is my flatmate, Lawrence Pemberton."

"In England the men also need a chaperon?" said Heidi.

Both men laughed. "No, no," said Lawrence, "I was just on my way out. As you can see, the table is only laid for two. I'll be back around eleven, Adam, just to make sure you're safe." He smiled at Heidi, put on his coat and closed the door behind him.

"I hope I don't drive him away," said Heidi.

"No, no," said Adam, as she took Lawrence's place at the table. "He's already late for his girlfriend." He quickly topped up her wine, pretending it hadn't already been poured.

"So I am going to eat my own sausages, after all," she said, laughing. The laughter didn't stop for the rest of the evening, as Adam learned about Heidi's life in Germany, her family and the holiday job she had taken while on vacation from Mainz University.

"My parents only allow me to come to England because my brother is already in London. It is to help my language course."

"So how long will you be here?" Adam found himself asking.

"Another two months," she said, "if I can stand the job."

"I hope you stay the full two months," said Adam.

"So do I," she replied, smiling.

When Jochen arrived back punctually at eleven o'clock, he found Adam and Heidi washing the dishes.

"Thanks for a most interesting evening," she said, wiping her hands.

"Not a good word," reprimanded Jochen. "Lovely, happy, delightful, enjoyable perhaps, but not *interesting*."

"It was all those things," said Adam, "but it was also interesting. May I come and buy some more sausages tomorrow?"

"I would like that," said Heidi, smiling, "but don't hold up any customers this time, with translation demands. By the way, you never tell me why you needed the strange paragraph translated."

"Next time perhaps," said Adam, looking a little embarrassed.

"And next time you can bring my sister home yourself," said Jochen, as he shook Adam's hand firmly.

After Heidi had left, Adam sat down and finished off the last glass of wine, aware that he hadn't spent such a lovely, happy, delightful, enjoyable and interesting evening for a long time.

MAJOR ROMANOV AND ANNA PETROVA emerged from the customs hall at Zürich Airport and took their places in the back of a black limousine with dark windows.

When it drew up outside the St. Gotthard Hotel, Jacques Pontin, the manager, was stationed at the door, waiting to greet the new arrivals. He introduced himself immediately, and as soon as he had checked them both in he summoned a porter. A moment later a handsome young man dressed in green livery appeared.

"Suite seventy-three," Pontin instructed, before turning back to Romanov. "Please do not hesitate to call upon me if there is anything you need, Herr Romanov."

"Thank you," said Romanov. The porter took Anna and Romanov in the lift to the seventh floor and led them to a corner suite. The suite was in a different league from any Romanov had ever experienced in either Moscow or Leningrad. When he saw the array of gadgets in the marble bathroom he reflected that in Russia even prosperous travellers took their own bath plugs with them.

"Your room is through there, madame," the porter informed the researcher, and unlocked an adjoining door. Although smaller, the room maintained the same unassuming elegance. The porter handed Romanov his key and was passed a five-franc note. The porter bowed, and closing the door behind him left Romanov to unpack while Anna Petrova went to her own room.

Romanov started to undress and then studied himself in the bathroom mirror. He was vain about his looks and even more vain about the state of his physique. He was six foot tall, and at twenty-nine his muscles remained hard and taut.

By the time Romanov had returned to the bedroom, he could hear the shower beating down in the adjoining bathroom. He crept over to the door and edged it open. He could see quite clearly the outline of Anna standing in the steaming shower. He smiled, noiselessly moved across the thick carpet, and slipped into the researcher's bed. He waited for her to turn off the shower.

ADAM JOINED LAWRENCE in the kitchen for breakfast and peered over his flatmate's shoulder, trying to take in the latest Test score.

"Why can't we produce any really fast fast bowlers?" he asked rhetorically.

"Can't stay and chatter with the unemployed," said Lawrence, picking up his briefcase. "The Shah of Iran wants to discuss his financial problems with me."

Left on his own, Adam boiled himself an egg and burned some toast before he turned to the newspaper to learn of the latest casualties in

Vietnam and President Johnson's proposed tour of the Far East. After he had cleared up, he settled down at his desk to consider how to get the official document translated without arousing further suspicion.

Almost absent-mindedly he extracted from the Bible the letter he had read the night before. The final paragraph still puzzled him. He read Heidi's translation once again:

> All that will be required of you is that you present yourself at the address printed on the top right-hand corner of the enclosed document, with some proof that you are Colonel Gerald Scott. A passport should prove sufficient. You will then be given a bequest that I have left to you in the name of Emmanuel Rosenbaum.
>
> I hope it will bring you good fortune.

Adam turned his attention to the document. He was still quite unable to discern what the bequest could possibly be, let alone whether it was of any value. He mused over the fact that such an evil man could involve himself in such an act of kindness hours before he knew he was going to die—an act that now left Adam himself with no choice about his own involvement.

"Breakfast in bed?" Anna murmured hopefully.

"Dressed in ten minutes, or no breakfast at all," came back the reply. Anna lowered her feet onto the thick carpet and headed off towards the shower.

During breakfast in the dining room Romanov mulled over the approach he intended to take with the bank if Petrova were able to confirm that the icon was in fact Rublev's original masterpiece. Then suddenly, without warning, he said, "Let's go."

Petrova caught up with her superior only moments before the lift gate closed. "Why?" she asked, but Romanov did not speak until they were both back in his suite. He then threw open the large window that overlooked the railway station.

"Ah, it's outside your room," he said, looking to his right, and quickly walked through to the adjoining bedroom. He marched past the dishevelled double bed, jerked open the nearest window, and climbed outside. Petrova had no choice but to follow. Once Romanov had reached the bottom rung of the fire escape, he ran to a passing tram. Petrova would never have made it if she hadn't been lifted bodily onto the tram by Romanov's sheer strength.

"What's going on?" she asked, still puzzled.

"I can't be sure," said Romanov, looking out of the back of the tram. "All I do know for certain is what the local CIA agent looks like."

The researcher looked back in the direction of the hotel, but all she could see was a mass of anonymous people walking up and down the pavement.

Romanov stayed on the tram for about a mile before he jumped off and hailed a passing taxi going in the opposite direction.

"Bischoff et Cie," he said, as he waited for his puffing assistant to join him.

The cab headed back in the direction of the hotel, winding in and out of the morning traffic, until it came to a halt in front of a large brown granite building. By the side of the imposing doors, carved into the stone and inlaid with gilt, were the words "Bischoff et Cie". There was no clue as to what kind of establishment lay within.

Romanov turned a heavy wrought-iron knob and the two Russians stepped into a spacious hall. To their left a smartly dressed young man was seated behind a solitary desk.

"Good morning," said Romanov. "We have an appointment with Herr Dieter Bischoff."

"Yes, Herr Romanov," said the receptionist, checking the list of names in front of him. "Will you please take the lift to the fifth floor." There they were greeted by a lady in a neat plain suit who escorted them to a comfortable room which more resembled a reception room in a country house than a bank.

"Herr Bischoff will be with you in a moment," the lady said, withdrawing. Romanov remained standing while he took in the room. Three framed black-and-white photographs of sombre old men in grey suits took up most of the far wall, while on the other walls were town and country scenes of nineteenth-century Switzerland. A magnificent oval Louis XIV table with eight carved mahogany chairs dominated the centre of the room. Romanov felt a twinge of envy as he thought that he could never hope to live in such style.

The door opened and a man in his mid-sixties, followed by three other men in dark grey suits, entered the room.

"What an honour for our little bank, Herr Romanov," were Herr Bischoff's first words as he bowed and shook the Russian by the hand. Romanov nodded and introduced his assistant, who received the same courteous bow and handshake. "May I in turn present my son and two of my partners, Herr Muller and Herr Weizkopf." The three men bowed in unison, but remained standing while Bischoff took his seat at the head of the table. At his gesture Romanov and Anna sat down beside him.

"I wonder if I might be permitted to check your passport?" asked Bischoff. Romanov took out the little blue passport from his inside pocket and handed it over. Bischoff studied it closely, then returned it, saying, "Thank you."

He then raised his hand and one of the partners immediately left them. "It will only take a moment for my son to fetch the icon," he said.

Romanov didn't speak again until Herr Bischoff's son reappeared with a small box and handed it over to his father.

"You understand," the old man confided, "the icon may not turn out to be the one for which your government is searching."

"I understand," said Romanov.

"This magnificent example of Russian art has been in our possession since 1938, and was deposited with the bank on behalf of a Mr. Emmanuel Rosenbaum."

Both visitors looked puzzled.

"*Nevozmozhno*," said Anna, turning to her master. "He would never . . ."

"I suspect that's exactly why the name was chosen in the first place," Romanov said curtly to Anna, annoyed at her indiscretion.

"May I see the icon now?" he asked, turning back to the bank's chairman.

Herr Bischoff placed the box in the centre of the table. The three men in grey suits took a pace forward. "Under Swiss law we must have three witnesses when opening a box in someone else's name," explained the old man.

Romanov nodded curtly.

Herr Bischoff unlocked the metal box with a key he produced from his pocket, while his son undid a second lock with a different key. The little ceremony completed, Herr Bischoff pushed up the lid of the box and turned it round to face his guests. Romanov put his hands into the box like an expectant child with a Christmas stocking, and drew out the icon. The painting he held in his hand was quite magnificent, a small wooden rectangle covered in tiny pieces of red, gold and blue making up a mosaic of a man with all the worries of the world on his shoulders. The face, although sad, evoked a feeling of serenity.

It was Anna who finally spoke.

"A masterpiece it is," she said, "and undoubtedly fifteenth century, but it's not St. George and the Dragon. It is the icon of St. Peter, you see, he holds the keys . . . painted by Dionisiy in 1471, and although it is undoubtedly one of the finest examples of his work, it is not the Tsar's Icon."

"But does it belong to the Russian people?" asked Romanov, still hopeful of some reward for all his trouble.

"No, Comrade Major," said the researcher emphatically. "It belongs to the Munich Gallery, from where it has been missing since the day Hitler was appointed Reichschancellor."

Herr Bischoff scribbled a note on a piece of paper in front of him. At least one bank in Munich was going to be happy to do business with him in the future.

Romanov reluctantly handed back the icon to Herr Bischoff, only just managing to say, "Thank you."

"Not at all," said Herr Bischoff, replacing the icon in the box. Romanov began to rise, as he considered nothing more could be gained from the meeting. At least he had discovered Goering's alias.

"I wonder if I might be permitted to have a word with you in private, Herr Romanov?" asked the elderly banker.

"Of course."

"It is rather a delicate matter," said Herr Bischoff, "so I thought you might prefer your associate to leave us."

"That won't be necessary," said Romanov, unable to think of anything Bischoff might have to say that he wouldn't later need to discuss with Petrova.

"As you wish," said Bischoff. "I am curious to discover if there was any other reason behind your request to see me. I think I know why you selected this bank in particular to start your inquiry."

"I didn't select you," said Romanov. "You were only one of—" he stopped himself.

"I see," said Bischoff, looking confused. "Then may I be permitted to ask you a few questions?"

"Yes, if you must," said Romanov, impatient.

"You are Alexander Petrovich Romanov, the only son of Peter Nicholevich Romanov?"

"Yes."

"And grandson of Count Nicholai Alexandrovich Romanov?"

"Is this to be a history lesson on my family tree?" asked Romanov, irritated.

"No, I just wanted to be sure of my facts, and I am even more certain now that it would be wise if your associate were to leave us for a moment," suggested the old man diffidently.

"Certainly not," said Romanov. "In the Soviet Union we are all equal," he added pompously.

"Yes, of course," said Bischoff, glancing quickly at Anna before continuing. "You are your father's only surviving child?"

"I am," confirmed Romanov proudly.

"In that case this bank is in possession . . ." Bischoff hesitated as a file was put in front of him by one of the men in grey.

"Don't say anything more," said Romanov quietly.

Bischoff looked up. Petrova was now sitting on the edge of her seat, enjoying every moment of the unfolding drama, and was disappointed when Romanov turned to her and said, "You will wait outside."

When he was certain the door was closed behind her, Bischoff slid the file across the table. Romanov opened it gingerly. On the top of the first page was his grandfather's name. Below were printed row upon row of incomprehensible figures.

"I think you will find that we have carried out your grandfather's instructions in maintaining a conservative portfolio of investments with his funds."

"What does this figure at the foot of the page represent?" asked Romanov.

"The total value of your stocks, bonds and cash at nine o'clock this morning. It has been updated every Monday since your grandfather opened an account with this bank in 1916."

"*Bozhe Moi*," said Romanov, as he took in the final figure. "But what currency is it in?"

"Your grandfather had faith only in the English pound," said Herr Bischoff.

Romanov was speechless.

"It may also interest you to know that we are in possession of several boxes which your father deposited with us soon after the war. He assured me he would return, but we never heard from him again. We were saddened to hear of his death. You might prefer, in the circumstances, to return and investigate the boxes at another time."

"Yes," said Romanov quietly. "Perhaps I could come back this afternoon?"

"The bank will always be at your service, Your Excellency," replied Herr Bischoff.

No one had addressed a Romanov by his title since the Revolution. The Russian sat in silence for some time.

Eventually he rose and shook hands with Herr Bischoff. "I will return this afternoon," he repeated, before joining his companion in the corridor.

Neither uttered a word until they were outside the bank. Romanov was still so overcome by what he had learned that he failed to notice that the man he had so deftly avoided at the hotel was now standing in a tram queue on the far side of the road.

Chapter Seven

The two men sat in a stark room dominated by a wooden table and several wooden chairs. A small black crucifix was the only ornament on the whitewashed walls. The pastor, elbows on the table and head in hands, stared down at the copy of the document. When he heard Adam's request he had invited the young man into the privacy of his little office at the back of the German Lutheran church.

After some considerable time, the pastor offered, "This is a receipt, if I am not mistaken. Roget et Cie, who must be Swiss bankers based in Geneva, have in their possession an object described as 'The Tsar's Icon'. If I remember correctly, the original can be viewed in Moscow. It appears," he continued, "that if the holder of this receipt presents himself in Geneva he will be able to claim the aforementioned icon, deposited there by a Mr. Emmanuel Rosenbaum. I confess," said the pastor, looking up for the first time, "that I've never seen anything like it before." He handed the document back to Adam.

"Thank you," said Adam. "You have been most helpful. Do you happen to know if icons are at all valuable?"

"I must confess that I am not the man from whom to seek such an opinion. But no doubt the art auctioneers Sotheby's, or Christie's, could help you."

"I'll pay them a visit next," said Adam. He added, "You have been most kind."

"Not at all," said the pastor. "I was only too pleased to assist you."

ADAM WALKED BRISKLY down Piccadilly towards the Ritz then turned left into Bond Street to look for Sotheby's. He passed Cartier's and Asprey's and finally spotted the gold lettering above a little newspaper kiosk on the far side of the road.

He crossed the street and entered the front door by the side of the kiosk. He felt unsure of his surroundings and not certain to whom he should turn for advice. Then he heard a voice say, "Up the stairs and straight through, madam. The sale is due to start in a few minutes."

Adam turned and saw a man in a long, green coat. The name "Sotheby" was embroidered over his left-hand pocket.

"Where do I go if I want something valued?" Adam asked.

"Straight along the passage, sir, and you'll see a girl in reception."

Adam thanked him and walked along to the reception area.

"May I help you, sir?" asked a girl behind the counter.

"I'm not sure," began Adam. "I need some advice concerning an icon."

"Have you brought the piece with you, sir?"

"No, it's still abroad at the moment."

"Do you have any details? Artist's name, date, size? Or better still, do you have a photograph of the piece?"

"No," said Adam sheepishly. "I only know its title. But I do have some documentation," he added, handing over the receipt he had shown the pastor.

"Not a lot to go on," said the girl, studying the German transcript. "But

I'll ask Mr. Sedgwick, the head of our Russian and Greek icon department, if he can help you." She spoke briefly into the phone then said, "Mr. Sedgwick will be down in a few moments."

Adam studied the pictures on the wall as he waited.

"Wonderful example of the artist's brushwork," said a voice behind him. Adam turned to face a tall, cadaverous figure with a ginger moustache and thinning red hair. His suit hung on him as if from a coathanger. "My name is Sedgwick," he announced.

"Scott," said Adam, offering his hand.

"Well, Mr. Scott, why don't we sit over here and then you can let me know how I can help you."

"I'm not sure you can," admitted Adam, taking the seat opposite him. "It's just that I have been left an icon in a will and I was hoping it might turn out to be valuable."

"A good start," said Sedgwick. "Now, am I to understand you do not have a photograph of this particular icon?"

"That's right," said Adam. "The icon is still abroad. I've never laid eyes on it. All I know is that it is known as 'The Tsar's Icon' and that the subject is St. George and the Dragon."

"How strange," said Sedgwick. "Someone else was inquiring after that particular painting only last week, but he wouldn't leave his name."

"Someone else?" asked Adam.

"Yes, a Russian gentleman, if I wasn't mistaken. He wondered if it had ever passed through our hands. I was able to explain to him that the great work by Rublev remains in the Winter Palace for all to see. One can always be certain that it's an original from the Winter Palace because the tsar's silver crown will be embedded in the back of the frame. Since the fourteenth century many copies of Rublev's masterpiece have been made and they vary greatly in quality and value. Do you have any document-ation on your icon?" Sedgwick inquired.

"I have a copy of the receipt that was left to me in the will," said Adam, and handed it over.

Mr. Sedgwick studied the paper for several moments. "Excellent, quite excellent," he said eventually. "It seems to me that a copy of the Tsar's Icon, painted by the court painter of the time, belongs to you. But you will have to go and pick it up yourself, that is certain."

"But is it worth all that trouble?" asked Adam. "Can you give me any idea of its value?"

"Hard to be precise without actually seeing it," Sedgwick said, returning the document.

"So what is the lowest figure I might expect to get for it?"

The older man frowned. "Ten," he said, after considerable thought. "Perhaps fifteen, but with an absolute top of twenty."

"Twenty pounds," said Adam, unable to hide his disappointment. "I'm sorry to have wasted your time."

"No, no, no, Mr. Scott, you quite misunderstand me. I mean twenty *thousand* pounds."

Chapter Eight

"A little more caviar, comrade?" inquired Petrova across the lunch table.

Romanov frowned. His excuse about "strictly confidential information only to be passed on at the highest level" had merely elicited a knowing smile from his companion, who did not believe that her boss's pressing appointment was at the consulate that afternoon.

Anna held out a spoon brimming with caviar and pushed it towards Romanov as if to feed a reluctant baby.

"Thank you—no," said Romanov firmly.

"Suit yourself," said the young woman, before it disappeared down her own throat.

Romanov called for the bill and paid it. "I'll see you back in the hotel later," he said curtly.

"Of course," said Petrova, still lingering over her coffee. "What time shall I expect you?"

Romanov frowned again. "Not before seven," he replied, and left the table without a further word. Once in the street, he set off in the opposite direction from the bank, but he doubted if he had fooled Anna, who was eyeing him suspiciously through the restaurant window; or the CIA agent, who had waited patiently on the far side of the road for nearly two hours.

By three o'clock Romanov was once again seated in the private room on the fifth floor, looked down on by the photographs of three Herr Bischoffs, with the fourth Herr Bischoff sitting opposite him and the fifth standing behind him.

"We are in possession of five boxes which have remained unopened since your father visited us in 1945," began Herr Bischoff. "Should it be your desire to inspect the contents . . ."

"Why else would I have returned?" asked Romanov, already made impatient by the measured voice and studied ritual.

"Indeed," said Herr Bischoff smoothly. "Then all we now require is that you sign a disclaimer in order to legalize the situation under Swiss law." Romanov looked apprehensive.

"It is only a formality." Herr Bischoff slid a sheet of paper across the table. There were over twenty clauses of German, all in small print. Romanov scrawled his signature between the two Xs. He made no attempt to discover what he was signing. If they hadn't stolen his grandfather's heritage already, why should they be bothering to try now, he considered.

"Perhaps you will be kind enough to accompany me," said Herr Bischoff, quickly passing the sheet of paper to his son who left immediately. He rose and led Romanov silently to the chairman's private lift in which they travelled all the way to the basement.

When the doors opened Romanov might have thought they had entered a jail had the bars not been made of highly polished steel. A man who was seated behind a desk on the far side of the bars jumped up the moment he saw the chairman and turned the lock on the steel door with a long-shafted key. Romanov followed Herr Bischoff through the open door then waited until they were both locked inside. The guard preceded them down a corridor, at the end of which Herr Bischoff's son was waiting in front of a vast circular steel door. The old man nodded and the younger Herr Bischoff placed a key in a lock and turned it. Then the chairman stepped forward and undid a second lock. Father and son pushed open the nine-inch-thick door but neither made any attempt to enter.

"You are in possession of five boxes. Numbers 1721, 1722, 1723, 1724 and 1725," said Herr Bischoff as he removed a small package from his pocket, and he added, "The key inside this envelope will open all five boxes." Romanov took the envelope and turned towards the open cavern.

"Once we have left," said the old man, "we shall pull the door closed. When you require it to be opened you have only to press the red button on the side wall to alert us. But I must warn you that at six o'clock the vault locks itself automatically and it cannot be reopened until nine the following morning. A warning alarm will sound at five forty-five." Romanov checked the clock on the wall: three seventeen. He couldn't believe he would need over two hours to find out what was in the five boxes. The two Herr Bischoffs bowed and left.

Romanov waited impatiently for the vast door to close behind them. He looked round the room and estimated that there were two or three thousand safes lining the walls, and more private wealth in that one vault than most countries on earth could call on. He checked the numbers of his own boxes, three small ones above two large ones, making a perfect cube.

He decided to start with one of the small boxes. He turned the key and opened the box slowly before pulling out the stiff drawer to discover that it was full of papers. He flicked through them, to find they were title deeds to tracts of land in Bohemia and Bulgaria—once worth millions, now controlled by the Socialist state. Not worth the paper they are written on, thought Romanov, as he moved to the second box, which he discovered contained the bond certificates of companies once managed by his grandfather. The last time they had declared a profit was in 1914. The third box contained just one document, his grandfather's will. It took only moments to discover that he was the lawful owner of everything—and nothing.

Dismayed, Romanov knelt down to study the two larger boxes, both of which looked big enough to hold a cello. He hesitated before placing the key in the lock of the first, turning it and pulling out the vast container.

It was empty. In desperation he quickly unlocked the fifth box.

The box was split into twelve compartments. He raised the lid of the first and stared down in disbelief. Before him lay precious stones of such size, variety and colour that they would have made anyone gasp. Gingerly he lifted the lid off the second compartment, to find it contained pearls of extraordinary quality.

It took Romanov a further hour to go through the contents of the remaining ten compartments. When he reached the last one he felt thoroughly exhausted. He checked the clock on the wall: five thirty. He began to replace the lids on each of the compartments, but during the treasure hunt he had come across one object of such magnificence that he could not resist removing it. He paused as he held up the heavy, solid gold chain, weighted by a medallion that hung from it. On one side was an engraved picture of his grandfather—Count Nicholai Alexandrovich Romanov—while on the other was a profile of his grandmother, so beautiful that she surely could have worn any of the jewellery in that treasure trove with distinction.

Romanov slipped the chain over his head and tucked the medallion under his shirt. When he had replaced the lid on the last compartment he slid the box back into place and locked it.

His mind turned to Poskonov. Had the old banker known all along, or was it just a coincidence that he had been sent to this bank first?

Then he considered how he could possibly enjoy such riches.

One false move and the state would not hesitate to send him to the same grave as his father and grandfather. He would have to be at his most skilful when he next came into contact with the old banker, otherwise he might not live to choose between power in his homeland and wealth in the West.

"After I have found the Tsar's Icon, I will return," he said, quite audibly. Suddenly the alarm bell rang out. He pressed the red button and the great doors swung open to reveal two anxious-looking Herr Bischoffs.

"We were beginning to get quite worried about the time," said the old man. "I do hope you found everything to your satisfaction."

"Entirely," said Romanov. "But what happens if I am unable to return for some considerable time?"

"It's of no importance," Herr Bischoff replied. "The boxes will not be touched again until you come back."

"What temperature are they kept at?"

"Ten degrees Celsius," said Herr Bischoff, somewhat puzzled.

"Are they airtight?"

"Certainly," replied the banker. "And watertight. And anything left in them is totally safe from any investigation."

"Excellent," said Romanov. "Because there is just a possibility that I shall want to return tomorrow morning with a package of my own to deposit with you."

"CAN YOU PUT ME THROUGH to Mr. Pemberton, please?" asked Adam.

There was a long pause. "We don't have a Mr. Pemberton working here, sir."

"That is Barclays International in the City, isn't it?"

"Yes, sir."

"Mr. Lawrence Pemberton. I feel certain I've got the right branch."

The silence was even longer this time. "Ah, yes," came back the eventual reply. "Now I see which department he works in." Adam heard a phone ringing in the background.

"He doesn't seem to be at his desk at the moment, sir, would you like to leave a message?"

"No, thank you," said Adam, and replaced the receiver. He sat thinking, not bothering to switch on the light as it grew darker. If he was to carry through his idea he needed some information which Lawrence, as a banker, should find it easy to supply.

A key turned in the door and Lawrence entered the flat and switched the light on. He looked startled when he saw Adam.

"How does one open a Swiss bank account?" were Adam's first words.

"I can't imagine one would find it that easy if all one had were next week's unemployment cheque," said Lawrence.

"It may surprise you to learn that it was a serious question."

"Well," said Lawrence, taking the question seriously, "anyone can open a Swiss bank account as long as they have a worthwhile sum to deposit, say, at least ten thousand pounds."

"What would someone need to do if they had inherited money in a Swiss account?"

"They would have to prove that they were the person entitled to inherit the deposit. That's not a problem if you're in possession of the correct documentation, such as a will and proof of identity. We deal with such matters every day."

"So, if I were entitled to a million pounds worth of gold in a Swiss bank, left to me by an Argentinian uncle, and I was in possession of the right legal documents to prove I was the beneficiary, all I would have to do is go and claim it?"

"Nothing to stop you," said Lawrence. "Although under the law as it currently stands, you would have to bring it back to this country, sell the gold to the Bank of England and then pay death duty on that sum." Adam remained silent. "Your best bet would really be to leave the gold where it is. Under this government, if you fulfilled the letter of the law, you would end up with about seven and a half per cent of its true value."

"Pity I haven't got an Argentinian uncle," said Adam.

"He doesn't have to be Argentinian," said Lawrence, watching his friend's every reaction closely.

"Thanks for the information," said Adam, and disappeared into the bedroom.

The last pieces of the jigsaw were beginning to fit into place. All he needed now was a copy of the will to show that the receipt from Roget et Cie had been left to him. He could then prove that he was the owner of a worthless—or priceless—copy of the Tsar's Icon. He lay awake that night recalling the words in his father's letter. "If there is anything to be gained from the contents of this envelope I make only one request of you, namely that your mother should be the first to benefit from it."

WHEN ROMANOV RETURNED to the hotel, he found Petrova in her room reading, her legs dangling over the side of the chair.

"I hope you had a fruitful afternoon?" she inquired politely.

"I did, my little one. Why don't we have a quiet supper in my room so I can tell you all about it while we celebrate in style?"

"What a magnificent idea," said the researcher. "And may I be responsible for ordering dinner?"

"Certainly," said Romanov.

Petrova dropped her book on the floor and began to concentrate on the extensive *à la carte* menu.

Romanov was impressed when their banquet finally appeared. Anna had chosen gravad lax with dill sauce to start with, accompanied by a half bottle of Premier Cru Chablis 1958. Between mouthfuls Romanov told her of his family inheritance, and as he described each new treasure the researcher's eyes grew larger and larger.

Romanov's monologue was only once interrupted, by a waiter who wheeled in a trolley on which was a rack of lamb surrounded by courgettes and tiny new potatoes. To accompany this particular dish, there was a Gevrey-Chambertin.

The final course, a raspberry soufflé, required, in the researcher's view, the finest Château d'Yquem. As she drained her glass unsteadily, Romanov suggested it might be time for them to go to bed, as they had to catch the first flight back to Moscow the following morning. He wheeled the trolley out into the corridor and placed a "Do not disturb" sign over the doorknob.

"A memorable evening," smiled the researcher, as she kicked off her shoes. Then, as Romanov unbuttoned his shirt, she let out a gasp of surprise.

"It's magnificent," she said in awe.

Romanov held up the gold medallion. "A bauble, compared with the treasures I left behind," he assured her.

"Comrade lover," Anna said in a childlike voice, pulling him towards the bed, "you realize how much I adore you?"

"Mmm," said Romanov.

"Well, if that gold chain is nothing more than a mere bauble, perhaps you might allow me to wear it occasionally?"

"Occasionally?" said Romanov, staring into Anna's eyes. "Why not permanently, my darling?" and without another word he removed the gold chain from around his neck and placed it over the girl's head. Anna sighed as she fingered the thick gold links of the chain, which Romanov still held.

"You're hurting me, Alex," she said with a little laugh. "Please let go." But Romanov only pulled the chain a little tighter.

"I can't breathe properly," gasped the researcher. "Please stop teasing." But Romanov only continued to tighten the chain around her throat.

"You wouldn't tell anyone about my windfall, would you, my little one?"

"No, never, Alex. No one. You can rely on me, but please stop now," she choked, her delicate hands now clutching desperately at his blond hair. But Romanov only continued to pull the chain tighter and tighter. "I'm sure you understand that I must feel absolutely certain that you would not share our secret—with anyone," he explained to her. But she did not hear because her neck had already snapped.

ON HIS MORNING RUN along the Embankment, Adam mulled over the tasks that needed to be carried out next.

If he took the morning flight out of Heathrow on Wednesday, he could be back in London by the same evening, or Thursday at the latest. But there were still several things that had to be organized before he could leave for Geneva.

"Three letters for you," said Lawrence, as Adam entered the flat. "Mind you," he added, "two of them are in buff envelopes." Adam picked up the letters and left them on the end of his bed en route to the shower.

Once he was dressed he opened the letters. He began with the white one, which turned out to be a note from Heidi thanking him for dinner and hoping she would be seeing him again some time. He smiled and tore open the first of the buff envelopes, which was a missive from the Foreign Office requesting him to attend a medical, to be conducted by a Dr. John Vance at 122 Harley Street at three o'clock on the following Monday.

Finally he opened the other brown envelope and pulled out a letter from his bank in Pall Mall, informing him that they were in receipt of a cheque for five hundred pounds from Holbrooke, Holbrooke and Gascoigne, and that his current account was in credit to the sum of £272.18.4d. The account showed that Adam, for the first time in his life, had run up an overdraft—a situation that he knew would have been frowned upon had he still been in the army.

What would his brother officers have said if they had known that he was now about to remove two hundred pounds from the account with no real guarantee of a return?

Adam rejoined Lawrence in the kitchen. "How was the Shah of Iran?" he asked.

"Oh, very reasonable really," said Lawrence, turning a page of the *Daily Telegraph*. "Promised he would do what he could about his current financial embarrassment."

"Where did you eventually take him to lunch?" asked Adam, enjoying the game.

"I offered him a shepherd's pie at the Green Man, but the fellow became quite snotty. It seems he and the empress had to pop along to Harrods to be measured up for a new throne. Would have gone along with him, of course, but my boss wanted his wastepaper basket emptied."

Lawrence had changed considerably over the years since he had left school. He had seemed so serious in those days, and certainly destined for great things. No one would have thought it possible that he would end up as an investment analyst at Barclays. At Oxford, contemporaries had half joked about his becoming a cabinet minister.

After Lawrence had left, Adam fried himself an egg and a couple of rashers of bacon, then sat down to scribble a note to his sister, enclosing a cheque for fifty pounds.

At nine thirty he made a phone call to Mr. Holbrooke, who agreed to put a copy of his father's will in the post that afternoon.

Adam's other requirements could not be carried out over the phone, so he locked up the flat. His first stop was at his bank, where he joined a queue at the foreign exchange counter and finally ordered fifty pounds in

Swiss francs, fifty pounds in cash and a hundred pounds in traveller's cheques.

Adam signed the traveller's cheques in the cashier's presence and she handed over five hundred and ninety-four Swiss francs and fifty pounds in cash.

A bus journey took Adam to the British European Airways terminal in Cromwell Road, where he asked the girl to book him a return economy ticket to Geneva.

"That will be thirty-one pounds please, sir."

Adam paid in cash and placed the ticket in his inside pocket, before returning to the flat for a light lunch. Later he phoned Heidi, who agreed to join him for dinner.

ROMANOV WAS WOKEN BY the ringing of the phone.

"Yes?" he said.

"Good morning, Comrade Romanov, it's Melinac, the second secretary at the embassy, in Berne. Have you seen Comrade Petrova since you reported her missing?"

"No," replied Romanov. "And she didn't sleep in her bed last night."

"I see," said the second secretary. "Then your suspicion that she may have defected is beginning to look a serious possibility."

"I fear so," said Romanov, "and I shall make a full report to my superiors the moment I get back to Moscow. I shall point out that you have done everything possible to assist me with this problem, Comrade Second Secretary."

"Thank you, Comrade Major."

Romanov replaced the phone and walked across to the girl's bathroom. He stared down at the body hunched up in the bath. After throwing a towel over it and locking the door, he went into his own bathroom for an unusually long shower.

After he had finished breakfast he returned to the phone to call Jacques Pontin, the hotel manager.

"Good morning, Herr Romanov."

"I have a delicate problem that I was hoping you might be able to help me with. I am in possession of a rather valuable object that I wish to deposit with my bank and I wouldn't want . . ."

"I understand your dilemma entirely," said the manager. "And how can I be of assistance?"

"I require a large container in which to place the object."

"Would a laundry basket be large enough?"

"Ideal, but does it have a secure lid?"

"Oh, yes," replied Pontin, "very secure. We often have to drop them down lift shafts."

"Perfect," said Romanov.

"Then it will be with you in a matter of moments," said Pontin. "May I suggest that it is taken down in the goods lift at the rear of the hotel, thus ensuring that no one will see you leaving?"

"Very considerate," said Romanov.

"Then I shall also arrange for a taxi to be waiting for you. When will you require it?"

"In no more than half an hour."

"You will find it parked outside the goods entrance in twenty minutes' time. Will there be anything else?"

"Perhaps you would be good enough to have my account prepared so that there will be no delay."

"Certainly, Herr Romanov."

Romanov put the phone down and made two local calls. As he replaced the phone there was a gentle tap on the door. Romanov went to answer it. A young porter stood in the corridor, a large laundry basket by his side. "Please return as soon as the taxi has arrived," said Romanov and pulled in the basket. He locked the door, wheeled the laundry basket into the main bedroom, undid the leather straps and threw open the lid. Then he unlocked the bathroom door and lifted Petrova's stiff, naked body in his arms before trying to cram it into the basket. Rigor mortis had already gripped it and it didn't quite fit in. Romanov held his fingers out straight and brought them down suddenly on the right leg with such force that it broke like a branch in a storm. He repeated the action on her left leg. He then tucked the legs under her body.

Romanov wheeled the basket into the researcher's bedroom and tipped all her possessions into the basket on top of her. Once he had removed the gold medallion from her neck he covered up the body with a hotel bathtowel, and sprayed it with a liberal amount of the Chanel No. 5 that had been left by courtesy of the hotel. Finally he strapped the lid down securely and wheeled the creaking basket back towards the outer door of his suite.

There was a knock at the door before Romanov had finished packing his own suitcase. He opened the door and the porter entered. He tugged at the laundry basket, but it took a firm shove from Romanov's foot to get it moving. The porter sweated his way down the corridor as Romanov walked by the side of the basket, carrying his suitcase. When they reached the rear of the hotel the basket was wheeled safely into the goods lift and Romanov stepped after it.

When the ground floor doors opened Romanov was relieved to be greeted by the manager, who stood by a large Mercedes with its boot already open. The taxi driver and the porter lifted the laundry basket and wedged it into the boot.

"Shall we forward your bill to the consulate, Herr Romanov?" asked Jacques Pontin.

"Yes, that would be helpful . . ."

"I do hope everything has worked out to your satisfaction?" said the manager as he held open the back door of the Mercedes for his departing guest.

"Entirely," said Romanov.

"Good, good. And will your young colleague be joining you?" asked the manager.

"No, she won't. She has already gone on to the airport."

"I am sorry to have missed her. Do please pass on my best wishes."

"I certainly will," said Romanov. With that he slipped into the back seat and the car moved off.

Romanov checked in his suitcase at the Swissair office, and then asked to be driven to Bischoff et Cie. Herr Bischoff's son, accompanied by another man, was waiting by the front door to greet him.

The taxi driver waited by the open boot while Herr Bischoff's companion, a heavily built man of at least six foot four, lifted out the laundry basket as if it were a sponge cake. Romanov paid the fare and followed Herr Bischoff into the lift.

"We have fully prepared for your deposit, following your phone call," said Herr Bischoff. "My father was only sorry not to be present personally."

The lift travelled to the basement where the guard unlocked the great steel cage. Romanov and young Herr Bischoff proceeded at a leisurely pace down the corridor, while the giant wheeled the basket in their wake.

Standing with folded arms by the vault door was another of Bischoff et Cie's partners. The partner placed his key in the top lock of the vault door without a word. Herr Bischoff then turned the second lock and together they pushed open the great steel door. The giant left the laundry basket near Romanov's five boxes.

"Will you require any assistance?" asked Herr Bischoff as he handed the Russian his personal sealed envelope.

"No, thank you," Romanov assured him, but did not relax until he had seen the vast door close behind him.

He stared down at the one large empty box: it was smaller than he had recalled. Beads of sweat appeared on his forehead as he unlocked it, pulled it out and raised the lid. It was going to be a tight fit. Romanov unstrapped the laundry basket and removed everything except the body. He stared down at the contorted face, then lifted the researcher and dropped her into the box. He had to adjust her limbs in order that the box could be shut: had Anna been even an inch taller the exercise would have proved impossible. He stuffed the girl's belongings down the sides of her body, leaving only the Chanel-scented towel behind in the laundry basket.

He replaced the lid on the airtight box before pushing it securely back in place and locking it. He hesitated for a moment, glancing at the second large box, but accepted that this was not the time to indulge himself: that would have to wait for another occasion. Satisfied that everything was back in place he strapped down the lid of the laundry basket and wheeled it back to the entrance of the vault. He pressed the little red button.

"I do hope you found everything in order," said the young Herr Bischoff.

"Yes, thank you," said Romanov. "Would it be possible for someone to return the laundry basket to the St. Gotthard Hotel?"

"Of course," said the banker, who nodded towards the large man.

"And I can be assured that the boxes will not be touched in my absence?" he asked, as they walked down the corridor.

"Naturally, Your Excellency," said Herr Bischoff, looking somewhat aggrieved at such a suggestion. "When you return," he continued, "you will find everything exactly as you left it."

"Well, not exactly," Romanov thought to himself.

When they reached the entrance to the bank, the young Herr Bischoff bowed. "We shall look forward to seeing you again when you are next in Zürich, Your Excellency," he said.

"Thank you," said Romanov, and walked out onto the pavement to find the taxi waiting to take him to the airport.

He cursed: this time he spotted the agent he had seen earlier outside the hotel.

Chapter Nine

The chairman of the KGB studied the report on the desk in front of him: something didn't ring true. He looked up at Romanov. "Your reason for visiting Bischoff et Cie was that they were in possession of a fifteenth-century icon that might have been the one we are searching for?"

"That is correct, Comrade Chairman."

"But the icon turned out to be of St. Peter."

"Confirmed by Comrade Petrova in her report."

"Ah, yes, Comrade Petrova," said Zaborski, his eyes returning to the report in front of him. "And later that evening Comrade Petrova mysteriously failed to keep an appointment with you?"

"Inexplicably," said Romanov. "Then she failed to turn up for breakfast as arranged, and when I went to her room all her personal belongings had gone."

"Which convinced you she had defected?"

"Yes, sir," said Romanov.

"But the Swiss police," said Zaborski, "can find no trace of her. So I keep asking myself, why would she want to defect? All her immediate family live in Moscow, and this was not her first visit to the West. Perhaps she disappeared because she might have been able to tell us something you didn't want us to hear."

Romanov felt a shiver of fear as he wondered how much Zaborski really knew.

"Perhaps she could tell us why you felt it necessary to return to Bischoff et Cie a second time." Zaborski paused. "I think I may have to open an inquiry into the disappearance of Comrade Petrova. Because, Comrade Romanov, by the time you returned to the bank a *third* time, every second-rate spy from here to Istanbul knew that we were looking for something."

Romanov remained silent. He began to feel confident that Zaborski was guessing. If he had suspected the truth the interview would have taken place in the basement, where a less intellectual approach was employed.

Zaborski fiddled with the paperweight of Luna 9 on his desk before continuing. "The General Secretary informed me, at one o'clock this morning, that he is distinctly unimpressed by your latest efforts. He *is* interested in finding the Tsar's Icon, however, and so, for the time being, comrade, he has decided there will be no investigation. But if you ever act in such an irresponsible way again you will be facing a tribunal, and we all know what happened to the last Romanov who faced a tribunal. Do I make myself clear, comrade?" he barked.

"Very clear, Comrade Chairman," said Romanov, and turning smartly on his heel he quickly left the room.

The chairman of the KGB waited for the door to close before his eyes settled back on the file. What was Romanov up to? He flicked down a switch on the little console by his side. "Find Major Valchek for me," he ordered.

"I'VE NEVER ACTUALLY had champagne and caviar," admitted Adam, as he looked up at the beautiful girl who sat opposite him.

"Well, don't get frightened, because I can't imagine caviar on this particular menu," teased Heidi. "But perhaps soon, when you are the proud owner of the Tsar's Icon, that is if Mr. Rosenbau . . ."

Adam put a finger to his lips. "No one else knows about that, not even Lawrence."

"That may be wise," Heidi whispered. "He will only expect you to invest all your money in his bank."

Adam ordered coffee and turned his gaze back to Heidi. "Funnily enough," he continued, "the only time I have ever rung Lawrence at the bank it was as if the telephonist had never heard of him."

"A bank that size must have over a thousand employees. You could go years without knowing everyone who worked there."

"I suppose you're right," Adam said, as two coffees were placed in front of them.

"When do you plan on going to Geneva?" Heidi asked.

"Early tomorrow morning. I hope to be back the same evening."

"You choose my one day off to fly away," she said.

"Then why not come with me?" he asked, stretching across the table to take her hand. "Better than sharing my sausages, and you could be most useful. I don't speak German or French and I've never been to Switzerland except on a school skiing trip—and then I kept falling over."

Heidi sipped her coffee. "Well?" said Adam, still holding her hand.

"The Swiss speak perfect English," she said eventually, "and should you have any problem with the bank, you can always get in touch with Lawrence."

"It would only be for the day," said Adam. "Do say you'll come."

"On one condition," said Heidi thoughtfully.

"Separate planes?" said Adam, grinning.

"No, but if the icon turns out to be worthless you will let me pay for my ticket."

"I agree to your terms," said Adam. He leaned over and kissed Heidi on the lips. "Perhaps it will take more than one day," he said. "Then what would you say?"

"I would demand separate hotels," replied Heidi. "If it wasn't for the high cost of the Swiss franc," she added.

"HOW WAS ZÜRICH?" Poskonov asked as he lit a cigarette.

"Like a Polish tractor: the bits that worked were fine," replied Romanov.

"From that I assume that the bits that didn't work failed to produce the Tsar's Icon," the chairman said.

"Correct. But Bischoff turned out to be most helpful. My every need was catered for."

"Good man, Bischoff," said the banker. "That's why I sent you to him first."

Romanov studied the old man carefully, looking for some sign that he knew exactly what had been awaiting him at the bank. "Was there any other reason you sent me to him first?" he asked.

"Lots of other reasons," said Poskonov, "but we'll not bother with them until you have found your icon."

· "Perhaps I'd like to bother now," said Romanov firmly.

"I've outlived two generations of Romanovs," said the old man, raising his eyes. "I wouldn't want to outlive a third. Let's leave it at that for now. I'm sure we can come to an understanding later."

Romanov nodded.

"Well, you will be pleased to learn that I have not been idle in your absence. But I fear my results also resemble a Polish tractor."

The banker waved Romanov to a seat before he reopened his file, which had grown in size. "Originally," the chairman began, "you presented me with a list of fourteen banks, eleven of which have now confirmed that they are not in possession of the Tsar's Icon."

"So that still leaves us with three," said Romanov.

"Correct, comrade. The first is Bischoff et Cie, whom you have already visited. But the other two have refused to cooperate."

"Why is it your influence does not extend to them?"

"Because other interests exert a stronger influence," replied Poskonov. "If, for example, your major source of income emanates from the Americans, no amount of pressure will ever allow you to deal with the Soviet Union. That being the case, there still has to be an outside chance that one of these two banks is in possession of the Tsar's Icon. As they are never going to admit as much to Mother Russia I am not sure what I can recommend you to do next." The banker sat back and waited for Romanov to take in his news. "You are unusually silent," he ventured.

"You have given me an idea," said Romanov. "I think the Americans would describe it as a 'long shot'. But if I'm right, it will be the Russians who will get the home run."

"Baseball is a game that I've never understood, but I suspect you will still need this, whatever your long shot." Poskonov removed a piece of paper from his file and handed it to Romanov. On it were the words: Daumier et Cie, Zürich (refused); Roget et Cie, Geneva (refused).

"No doubt you will be returning to Switzerland very soon."

Romanov stared at the banker.

The old man returned his stare. "I wouldn't recommend you to visit Bischoff et Cie on this trip, Alex. And remember, you won't find me as easy to get rid of as your Anna Petrova."

Chapter Ten

The elderly-looking man took his place at the back of the taxi queue at Zürich Airport. It was hard to estimate his height because he looked so bent and frail. His large overcoat reached almost to the ground and the fingers that could only just be seen peeping from the sleeves were covered by grey woollen mittens. His face was dominated by a nose that would have flattered Cyrano de Bergerac. One hand clung on to a worn little leather suitcase bearing the initials E.R.

The old man shuffled forward slowly until it was his turn to climb into a taxi. The operation was a slow one, and the driver was already drumming his fingers on the wheel when his passenger told him in guttural tones that he wanted to be taken to the bankers, Daumier et Cie.

When the old man arrived at his destination he took some time sorting out which coins to pay with, then pushed himself slowly out onto the pavement and stood gazing at the marble building. A man in a smart blue uniform opened the door for the old man and he shuffled over to the girl behind the reception desk and said in stilted German, "I have come to see Herr Daumier. My name is Emmanuel Rosenbaum."

"Do you have an appointment?" she asked.

"I fear not."

"Herr Daumier is in conference at the moment," said the girl, "but I will find out if there is another partner available to see you." After a phone conversation she took him to a small room with two chairs.

The old man was unable to hide his surprise at the age of the boy who eventually appeared. "I am Wilfried Praeger," said the young man, "a partner of the bank."

"Sit down, sit down," said Mr. Rosenbaum. "I cannot stare up at you. My name is Emmanuel Rosenbaum. I left a package with you in 1938, and I have returned to collect it."

"Do you have any proof of your identity, or any documentation from the bank?"

"Oh, yes," the old man replied, and handed over an Israeli passport and a receipt that had been folded and unfolded so many times that it was now almost in pieces.

The young man studied both documents carefully. Everything seemed to be in order.

"May I leave you for a moment, sir?"

"Of course," said the old man, "after twenty-eight years, I can wait for a few more minutes."

Shortly after the young man had left, the woman returned and invited Mr. Rosenbaum to move into a more comfortable room. Within minutes the junior partner returned with Herr Daumier.

"I don't think we have ever met, Herr Rosenbaum," said the chairman courteously. "You must have dealt with my father."

"No, no," said Mr. Rosenbaum. "I dealt with your grandfather, Helmut. I saw your father on only one occasion, and was sad to learn of his premature death," he added.

"I wonder if you have any further proof of identity, other than your passport?" Herr Daumier asked politely.

Emmanuel Rosenbaum, giving the banker a tired look, turned his wrist face upwards. The number 712910 was tattooed along the inside. "I apologize," said Daumier, visibly embarrassed. "It will take me only a few minutes to bring your box up, if you will be kind enough to wait."

Mr. Rosenbaum's eyes blinked as if he were too tired even to nod his agreement. The two men returned a few minutes later with a flat box, about two feet square, and placed it on a table. Herr Daumier unlocked the top lock while the other partner acted as a witness. He then handed over a key to Rosenbaum saying, "We will now leave you, sir. Just press the button underneath the table when you wish us to return."

"Thank you," said Rosenbaum, and waited for the door to close behind them. He turned the key in the lock and pushed up the lid. Inside was a package about eighteen by twelve inches covered in muslin and tied securely. Rosenbaum placed it carefully in his old suitcase. He then locked the box and pressed the button under the table.

"I do hope everything was as you left it, Herr Rosenbaum," said Herr Daumier when he returned. "It has been some considerable time."

"Yes, thank you." This time the old gentleman did manage a nod.

"May I mention a matter of no great consequence?" asked Herr Daumier.

"Pray do so," said the old man.

"Is it your intention to continue with the use of the box? Because the funds you left to cover the cost have recently run out."

"No, I have no need for it any longer."

"There was a small charge outstanding. But in the circumstances, Herr Rosenbaum, we are happy to waive it."

"You are most kind."

Herr Daumier bowed and the junior partner accompanied their client to the front door, helped him into a taxi and instructed the driver to take Mr. Rosenbaum to Zürich Airport.

At the airport, the old man took his time reaching the check-in desk. He produced his ticket, then shuffled into the departure lounge, which he was pleased to find was almost empty. He collapsed onto a comfortable sofa in the corner and made sure he was out of sight of the other passengers in the lounge.

Rosenbaum flicked back the little knobs on the old suitcase and pulled out the parcel. His fingers wrestled with the knots for some time before they came loose. He then removed the muslin to check his prize. He stared down at a masterpiece—"The Cornfields" by Van Gogh—which he had no way of knowing had been missing from the Vienna National Gallery since 1938.

Emmanuel Rosenbaum swore, which was out of character. He packed the picture up safely and returned it to his case. He then shuffled over to the girl at the Swissair sales desk and asked her to book him on the first available flight to Geneva. With luck he could still reach Roget et Cie before they closed.

THE BEA VISCOUNT landed at Geneva Airport at eleven twenty-five local time.

"Perfect," said Adam. "We shall be in Geneva well in time for lunch, a visit to the bank and then back to the airport for the five past five flight home."

A light drizzle was falling as they left the aircraft. Adam unbuttoned his raincoat and attempted to shelter Heidi beneath it as they ran across the tarmac to the immigration hall.

"Good thing I remembered this," he said.

"Not so much a raincoat, more a tent," said Heidi.

"It's my old army trenchcoat," he assured her, opening it up again. "It can hold maps, compasses, even an overnight kit."

"Adam, we're just going to be strolling round Geneva in the middle of summer, not lost in the Black Forest in the middle of winter."

He laughed. "I'll remember that whenever it pours." He turned, touched her hair gently and kissed her on the lips.

The airport bus took only twenty minutes to reach Geneva, nestling in the mountains beside its magnificent lake. The bus came to a halt in the centre, opposite the massive single-spouting fountain that shot over four hundred feet into the air.

They stepped out of the bus, pleased to find the light rain had stopped.

"First we must find out where our bank is so that we can have lunch nearby before going to pick up the booty. We'll drop in at the first bank we see and ask them to direct us to Roget et Cie."

Heidi pointed to the Banque Populaire on the far side of the avenue. "Let's put your plan into action."

When they had crossed the road Heidi inquired of the doorman the way to Roget et Cie. They followed his directions until Heidi spotted the discreet sign chiselled in stone by the side of a high wrought-iron and plate-glass door.

"Looks impressive," said Adam, "even when it's closed for lunch."

"What were you expecting—a small branch in the country? I know you British don't like to admit it, but this is the centre of the banking world."

"Let's find that restaurant before our *entente cordiale* breaks down," said Adam, grinning. As the sun was trying to find gaps between the clouds they chose a pavement cafe overlooking the lake. Both selected a cheese salad and they shared a half bottle of white wine. Adam was enjoying Heidi's company so much that he began to tell her stories of his army days. She had to stop him and point out that it was nearly two. He reluctantly called for the bill.

When they had returned to the bank Adam pushed open the heavy door and walked over to a woman seated behind a desk.

"Good morning. My name is Adam Scott. I have come to collect something that has been left to me in a will."

The woman smiled. "Have you made an appointment?"

"No," said Adam. "I didn't realize that I had to."

"I'm sure it will be all right," said the lady. She picked up a phone, and held a short conversation in French. Replacing the phone she asked them both to go to the fourth floor.

As Adam walked out of the lift, he was surprised to be met by someone of his own age.

"Good afternoon. My name is Pierre Neffe and I am a partner of the bank," said the young man in perfect English, leading them to a small, exquisitely furnished room. "Now, how can I help you?"

"My father," began Adam, "died last month, and left me in his will a receipt for something I think you have had in your safekeeping since 1938. It was a gift given to him by one of your customers." Adam hesitated. "A Mr. Emmanuel Rosenbaum."

"Do you have any documentation relating to this gift?" inquired Monsieur Neffe.

"Oh, yes," said Adam, digging into the map pocket of his trenchcoat. He passed over the Roget et Cie receipt to Monsieur Neffe, who studied it and nodded. "I wonder if I might be permitted to see your passport, Mr. Scott?"

"Certainly," said Adam, handing it to him.

"If you will excuse me for one moment." Monsieur Neffe left them.

"What do you imagine they are doing?" said Heidi.

"Checking if my receipt is authentic. 1938 was rather a long time ago."

As the minutes ticked by, Adam began to believe it was all going to be a complete waste of time.

"You could always take one of the pictures off the wall and put it in your trenchcoat," teased Heidi. "I'm sure it would fetch a good price in London. Perhaps even more than your icon."

"Too late," said Adam as Monsieur Neffe reappeared with another banker whom he introduced as Monsieur Roget.

"Good morning," said Monsieur Roget. He shook hands with both Adam and Heidi. "We have on file a letter from Mr. Rosenbaum giving clear instructions to the bank that the box is not to be opened by anyone other than"—he looked at the piece of paper he had brought with him—"Colonel Gerald Scott, DSO, OBE, MC."

"My father," said Adam. "But as I explained to Monsieur Neffe, he died last month and left me the gift in his will."

"I would be happy to accept what you say," said Monsieur Roget, "if I might be allowed a sight of a copy of the death certificate and of the will itself."

Adam smiled at his own foresight and once more delved into his trenchcoat to remove a large brown envelope. He took out copies of his father's death certificate, the will, and a letter from Mr. Holbrooke marked "To Whom it may Concern", and passed them to Monsieur Roget, who read all three documents slowly. Monsieur Roget then turned and spoke to Monsieur Neffe, who swiftly left the room, only to return a minute later with a copy of the English Law Society Register for 1966.

Adam was impressed by the bank's thoroughness as Monsieur Roget checked that the number and address on the Holbrooke letterhead corresponded with the number and address in the yearbook. "We have one small problem, Mr. Scott."

"And what is that?" asked Adam, nervously.

"I'm afraid Mr. Rosenbaum's account is somewhat overdrawn, and the bank's rule is that an overdraft must always be cleared before any box can be opened."

Adam's pulse raced. He hadn't brought enough money to cover this eventuality.

"The account is only one hundred and twenty francs in debit," continued Monsieur Roget, "which is the charge for housing the box over the past two years, since Mr. Rosenbaum's deposit ran out."

Adam breathed a sigh of relief. He took out his wallet, signed a traveller's cheque and handed it over.

"And finally," said Monsieur Roget, "we will need you to sign a form of indemnity for the bank."

Monsieur Roget passed over a long form containing clause after clause in tightly printed French at which Adam only glanced before passing it over to Heidi. She studied each clause carefully as Monsieur Roget explained to Adam that it was a standard disclaimer clearing the bank of any liability over what might be in the box, and Adam's legal claim to it. Heidi looked up and nodded her agreement.

Adam signed on the dotted line with a flourish.

"Excellent," said the banker. "All we have to do now is go and retrieve your box."

"I suppose it could be empty," said Adam once the two of them were left alone again.

"And it-could be packed with gold," said Heidi.

When both men returned a few minutes later, Monsieur Neffe was carrying a flat metal box, about twelve inches by nine and some three inches deep.

Adam was disappointed by its modest size, but didn't show his feelings. Monsieur Roget proceeded to undo the top lock with the bank's key and then handed Adam a small faded envelope with signatures scrawled across the waxed seal.

"Whatever is in the box belongs to you, Mr. Scott. When you have finished, perhaps you would be kind enough to let us know. Until then we shall remain outside in the corridor." Both men left the room.

"Come on," said Heidi, "I can't wait."

Adam opened the envelope and a key fell out. He fumbled with the lock and then at last pushed up the lid. Inside was a small flat package wrapped in muslin and tied with string. The knots took some untying but finally an impatient Adam tore off the string before slowly removing the muslin. They stared at the masterpiece in disbelief.

The simple beauty of the golds, reds and blues left them both speechless. Neither of them had expected the icon to be so breathtaking. St. George towered over the dragon, a massive sword in his hand, about to plunge it into the heart of the beast. Fire belched from the dragon's jaws, and the saint's cloak was a rich scarlet.

"It's magnificent," said Heidi, eventually finding her voice.

"I wish my father had seen it, perhaps it would have changed his life."

"Don't forget he wanted it to change yours," said Heidi.

Adam finally turned the icon over to find on the back a small silver crown inlaid in the wood. He stared at it, trying to recall what Mr. Sedgwick of Sotheby's had said that proved.

There was nothing else in the box, which Adam locked again. He tucked the muslin round the masterpiece, tied it up firmly and slipped the little painting into the map pocket of his trenchcoat.

Heidi smiled. "I knew you'd prove you needed the coat, even if it didn't rain."

Adam walked over to the door and opened it to the two bankers. "I hope that you found what you had been promised," said Monsieur Roget, benevolently.

"Yes, indeed," said Adam. "But I shall have no further need of the box," he added, returning the key.

"As you wish," said Monsieur Roget, bowing. "And here is the change from your traveller's cheque, sir," he said, passing over some Swiss notes to Adam. "If you will excuse me I will now take my leave of you. Monsieur Neffe will show you out." He shook hands with Adam and bowed slightly to Heidi before he left.

"I hope that you will enjoy a pleasant stay in our city," said Monsieur Neffe, as the lift took its leisurely pace down.

"It will have to be very quick," said Adam. "We must be back at the airport in just over an hour."

The lift stopped at the ground floor and Monsieur Neffe accompanied Adam and Heidi to the door, where they both stood aside to allow an old man to shuffle in. Although most people would have stared at his nose Adam was more struck by his penetrating eyes.

When the old man eventually reached the woman sitting at the reception desk, he announced firmly, "I have come to see Monsieur Roget."

"What name shall I tell him, sir?"

"Emmanuel Rosenbaum." The woman picked up the phone. When she had replaced it she asked, "Would you go to the fourth floor, Monsieur Rosenbaum?"

When he got there another middle-aged woman accompanied him to the waiting room and told him Monsieur Roget would be with him shortly.

He did not have to wait long before a smiling Monsieur Roget appeared.

"How nice to make your acquaintance, Monsieur Rosenbaum, but I'm afraid you have just missed Mr. Scott."

"Mr. Scott?" the old man uttered in surprise.

"Yes. He left only a few minutes ago, but we carried out the instructions in your letter."

"My letter?" said Mr. Rosenbaum.

"Yes," said the banker, opening for the second time that morning a file which had remained untouched for over twenty years.

He handed a letter to the old man.

Emmanuel Rosenbaum removed a pair of glasses from his inside pocket, unfolded them slowly and proceeded to read:

12 September 1946

Dear Monsieur Roget,
    I have left in your safekeeping a small icon of St. George and the Dragon. I am transferring the ownership of that painting to a British army officer, Colonel Gerald Scott, DSO, OBE, MC. If Colonel Scott should come to claim the icon at any time please ensure that he receives my key without delay.
    My thanks to you for your help in this matter.

Yours sincerely,
Emmanuel Rosenbaum

"And you say that Colonel Scott came to collect the contents of the box earlier today?"

"No, no, Monsieur Rosenbaum. The colonel died quite recently and left the contents of the box to his son, Adam Scott. Monsieur Neffe and I checked all the documents, including the death certificate and the will, and we were left in no doubt that they were all authentic. He was also in possession of your receipt." The banker hesitated. "I do hope we did the right thing, Monsieur Rosenbaum?"

"You certainly did," said the old man. "I came only to check that my wishes had been carried out."

Monsieur Roget smiled in relief. "I feel I ought also to mention that your account had run into a small deficit."

"How much do I owe you?" asked the old man, fumbling in his breast pocket.

"Nothing," said Monsieur Roget. "Mr. Scott dealt with it."

"I am in debt to Mr. Scott. Are you able to tell me the amount?"

"One hundred and twenty francs," said Monsieur Roget.

"Then I must repay the sum immediately," said the old man. "Do you by any chance have an address for him?"

"No, I'm sorry, I am unable to help you there," said Monsieur Roget. A hand touched his elbow and Monsieur Neffe whispered in his ear. "It appears," he continued, "that Mr. Scott was returning to England immediately. When he left here he was on his way to Geneva Airport."

The old man lifted himself up. "You have been most helpful, gentlemen, and I will not take up any more of your time."

"IT'S FLIGHT BE 171 and your seats are 14A and B," the man behind the check-in counter told them. "You will be boarding at gate number nine in about twenty minutes. Have a good flight, sir."

"I have seven hundred and seventy Swiss francs left," said Adam, thumbing through some notes, "and while we're here I must get my mother a box of decent liqueur chocolates."

Heidi pointed to a counter where Adam selected a large box of Lindt chocolates which the girl behind the counter giftwrapped and placed in a carrier bag. "Not much time for anything else except perhaps to pick up some wine in the duty-free."

"I'd like to find a copy of *Der Spiegel* before we go through customs."

"Fine," said Adam. "Why don't we try the paper shop over in the corner?"

"A call for Mr. Adam Scott. Will Adam Scott please return to the BEA desk on the ground floor," came booming out over the public address system.

Adam and Heidi stared at each other, then returned downstairs and walked over to the man who had checked them in. "I think you put a call out for me," said Adam. "My name is Scott."

"Oh, yes," replied the man. "There's an urgent message for you," he said, reading from a pad in front of him. "Please call Monsieur Roget at Roget et Cie, on Geneva 271279." He ripped off the piece of paper and handed it over. "The phones are over in the far corner, and you'll need twenty centimes."

"Thank you," said Adam. The message gave no clue as to why Monsieur Roget should need to speak to him.

"I wonder what he can want," said Heidi. "It's a bit late to ask for the icon back."

"Well, there's only one way I'm going to find out," said Adam, passing over the bag to her. "Hang on to that and I'll be back in a moment."

"I'll try and pick up my magazine at the same time, if I can find a newspaper shop on this floor," said Heidi as she took the brightly coloured bag which contained the chocolates.

"Right," said Adam, "meet you in a couple of minutes."

"ROGET ET CIE. Est-ce-que je peux vous aider?"

"I am returning Monsieur Roget's call," said Adam, making no attempt to answer in French.

"Yes, sir. Whom shall I say is calling?" asked the telephonist, immediately switching to English.

"Adam Scott."

"I'll find out if he's available, sir."

Adam swung round to see if Heidi had returned to the BEA counter, but as there was no sign of her he assumed she must still be looking for a newspaper shop. Then he noticed an old man shuffling across the hall. He could have sworn he had seen him somewhere before.

"Mr. Scott?"

"Yes, Monsieur Roget, I am returning your call."

"Returning my call?" said the banker, sounding puzzled.

"There was a message left at the BEA counter asking me to phone you, urgently."

"There must be some mistake, I didn't leave any message. But now that you have rung, it might interest you to know that just as you were leaving Monsieur Emmanuel Rosenbaum visited us."

"Emmanuel Rosenbaum?" said Adam, "but I assumed he was . . ."

"COULD YOU ASSIST ME, please, young lady?" Heidi looked up at the old man who had addressed her in English, but with such a strong mid-European accent. She wondered momentarily why he had assumed she spoke English.

"I am trying to find a taxi and I am already late. I fear my eyesight is not what it used to be."

Heidi replaced the copy of *Der Spiegel* on the shelf and said, "They're just through the double doors in the centre. Let me show you."

"How kind," he said. "I do hope I am not putting you to too much trouble."

"Not at all," said Heidi, taking the old man by the arm and guiding him towards the door marked "Taxi et Autobus"

"ARE YOU SURE it was Rosenbaum?" said Adam anxiously.

"I'm certain," replied the banker.

"And he seemed happy about me keeping the icon?"

"Oh, yes. His only concern was to return your one hundred and twenty francs. I think he may try and get in touch with you."

"BEA announce the departure of their flight BE 171 to London Heathrow from gate number nine."

"I must leave," said Adam. "My plane takes off in a few minutes."

"Have a good flight," said the banker.

"Thank you, Monsieur Roget," said Adam, and replaced the receiver. He turned towards the BEA counter and was surprised to find that Heidi had not yet returned. His eyes began to search the ground floor for a paper shop. Then he spotted her walking out through the double doors, helping the old man he had noticed earlier.

Adam called out and quickened his pace. Something didn't feel right. When he reached the automatic door he had to check his stride. He could now see Heidi standing on the pavement, opening a taxi door for the old man.

"Heidi," he shouted. The old gentleman suddenly turned and Adam found himself staring at the man he had seen at the bank. "Mr. Rosenbaum?" he questioned. Then, with a movement of his arm that was so fast and powerful it took Adam by surprise, the old man threw Heidi into the back of the taxi, jumped in beside her, and pulling the taxi door closed, shouted at the top of his voice, "*Allez vite!*"

For a moment Adam was stunned, then he dashed to the side of the taxi but only just managed to touch the handle as it accelerated away from the kerb. The car's sudden momentum knocked Adam backwards on the pavement, but not before he saw the petrified look on Heidi's face. He stared at the numberplate of the departing car: B-7-1-2 was all he could catch, but at least he recognized that it was a blue Mercedes. Desperately he looked round for another taxi.

A Volkswagen Beetle drew up on the far side of the concourse. A woman stepped out of the driver's seat and walked to the front to open the boot. A man joined her from the passenger's side and lifted out a suitcase before she slammed the boot lid back into place.

On the kerb, the two of them embraced. As they did so, Adam

sprinted across the road and opening the passenger door leaped inside and slid into the driver's seat. The key was still in the ignition. He turned it on, threw the car into gear, slammed his foot on the accelerator and shot forward as the embracing couple stared at him in disbelief. Adam set off at speed, following the signs to the centre of Geneva.

He had to concentrate hard on remaining on the right-hand side of the road. "B712 . . . B712," he repeated to himself again and again. He checked the numberplate and the passengers of every taxi he passed, but there was no sign of Heidi.

Then he saw a Mercedes in the outside lane some considerable distance ahead of him. He pressed the accelerator harder—90, 100, 110, 120 kilometres an hour. Metre by metre he began to narrow the gap as he tried to fathom out why the old man would want to kidnap Heidi in the first place. Could it be Rosenbaum? But he had wanted him to keep the icon, or so the banker had assured him. None of it made sense, and he drove on, wondering if at any moment he was going to wake up.

At the next roundabout only three cars divided Adam from the taxi. "A red light, I need a red light," he shouted, but the first three traffic lights on the approach road into the city remained stubbornly green. And when one finally turned red, a van suddenly pulled in front of him. Adam cursed, leaped out of the car and started running towards the taxi, but the light changed back to green just before he could reach it and the Mercedes sped away. Adam sprinted back to the Volkswagen and only just managed to drive the car across the junction as the light turned red again. His decision to get out of the car had lost him several crucial seconds and when he looked ahead he could only just spot the taxi in the distance.

When they reached the Avenue de France, running parallel with the west side of the lake, both cars weaved in and out of the traffic, until the Mercedes suddenly turned left and climbed up a slight hill. Adam threw his steering wheel over to follow it, and watched carefully as the taxi turned left again. In order to follow, Adam veered in front of a bus so sharply that it was forced to slam on its brakes.

The taxi was now only a couple of hundred yards ahead, when suddenly it swerved into the kerbside and screeched to a halt. Adam skidded to a halt directly behind it. He leaped out of the car and ran towards the parked vehicle. The old man jumped out of the taxi and sprinted up a side street carrying Heidi's airport shopping bag and a small suitcase.

Adam pulled the back door open and stared at Heidi. "Are you all right?" he shouted. Heidi did not move a muscle. Adam put his hand on her shoulder and looked into her eyes but they showed no response. He began to stroke her hair and then, without warning, her head fell limply onto his shoulder, like a rag doll. A small trickle of blood ran from the corner of her mouth. Adam felt cold and sick and began to tremble. He looked at the taxi driver. His body was slumped over the wheel.

Adam refused to accept that they were dead. He kept holding on to Heidi as he stared beyond her: the old man had reached the top of the hill.

Why did he still think of him as an old man? He was obviously not old at all, but young and very fit. Suddenly Adam's fear turned to anger. In a split-second decision he let go of Heidi and darted up the hill after her killer. He moved as fast as he could but his trenchcoat slowed him down, and by the time he too had reached the top of the hill the killer was a clear fifty yards ahead of him, weaving his way through the cars on the main thoroughfare. Adam watched the man leap onto a passing tram, but he was too far behind and could only watch the tram moving inexorably into the distance.

The man stood on the tram steps and stared back at Adam. He held up the shopping bag defiantly with one hand. The back was no longer hunched, the figure no longer frail. Adam stood for several seconds in the middle of the road, helplessly watching the tram disappear out of sight.

He tried to gather his thoughts. Behind him he could hear the sirens of ambulances. Adam tried to start sorting out in his mind the madness of the last half hour. None of it made sense. He would surely find it was all a dream . . . then he touched the side of his coat, touched the package that held the Tsar's Icon. The killer hadn't gone to all that trouble for £20,000—murdering two innocent people—why, why, why, was the icon so important? What had the Sotheby's expert said? "A Russian gentleman had inquired after the piece." Adam's mind began to whirl.

When he heard the whistle behind him he felt relieved that help was at hand, but as he turned he saw two officers with guns pointed at him. He started to run, and despite the trenchcoat, doubted if there was a member of the Swiss force who could hope to keep up the pace he set. He turned into the first alley he came to. It was narrow—not wide enough even for two bicycles to pass abreast. Once beyond it, he selected a one-way street. It was crammed with cars, and he was able to move swiftly in and out of the slow-moving traffic.

In a matter of minutes he had lost the police, but he still ran on, continually switching direction until he felt he had covered at least two miles. He turned into a quiet street and halfway down saw a fluorescent sign advertising the Hotel Monarche. It didn't look much more than a guesthouse. He stopped in the shadows and waited, taking in great gulps of air. After about three minutes his breathing was back to normal and he marched straight into the hotel.

Chapter Eleven

He stood naked, staring at the image of Emmanuel Rosenbaum in the hotel mirror. He didn't like what he saw. First, he removed the teeth. He had been warned that his gums would ache for days. Then, painstakingly, he shed each layer of his bulbous nose, admiring the skill and artistry that had gone into creating such a monstrosity. It will be too conspicuous, he had told them. They will remember nothing else, had come back the experts' reply.

Next he began on the lined forehead; as the wrinkles disappeared, so the years receded. After that, the flaccid red cheeks, and finally the two chins. Sharp rubbing with a pumice stone removed the number from the inside of his arm. Once more he studied himself in the mirror. The hair, cut short and greying, would take longer to restore.

Moments later he stood under a warm shower, his fingers massaging deep into the roots of his hair. It took half a bottle of shampoo before it had returned to its normal colour, but he realized that it would take considerably longer before he stopped looking like a staff sergeant in the United States Marines.

In a corner of the room lay the long baggy coat, the shiny, shapeless suit, the old shirt and tie, the woollen mittens and the Israeli passport. Hours of preparation discarded in a matter of minutes.

His back still ached from all the stooping. He stood up, then touched his toes and threw his arms high above his head fifty times. He rested for one minute before completing fifty press-ups.

He was beginning to feel like a human being again. He put on a freshly ironed cream silk shirt and a new suit.

Before making one phone call to London and two more to Moscow he ordered dinner in his room, so that no one would see him—he had no desire to explain how the man who had checked in had been thirty years older than the man who was eating alone in his room. When his meal arrived he tore at the steak and gulped the wine like a hungry animal.

He stared at the colourful airport carrier bag but felt no desire to finish off the meal with one of Scott's liqueur chocolates. He was angry at the thought of the Englishman getting the better of him.

His eyes then rested on the little leather suitcase that lay by the side of his bed. He opened it and took out the icon from the Winter Palace that Zaborski had suggested he should always have with him so that there could be no doubt when he came across the original of St. George and the Dragon.

A little after eleven he switched on the late-night news. They had no photograph of the suspect, only one of that stupid taxi driver who had

driven so slowly it had cost the fool his life, and then they showed the pretty German girl who had tried to fight back. It had been pathetic, one firm clean strike and her neck was broken. The television announcer said the police were searching for an unnamed Englishman. Although the Swiss police had no photograph of Scott, Romanov didn't need one. It was a face he would never forget. In any case, his contact in England, a man code-named "Mentor", had already told him a lot more about Captain Scott in one phone call than the Swiss police could hope to discover for another week.

LYING MOTIONLESS ON HIS HOTEL BED, Adam tried to make sense of all that had happened. If Goering had left the icon to his father, and Goering's alias had been Emmanuel Rosenbaum, then a real-life Emmanuel Rosenbaum didn't exist. But he did exist: he had even killed twice in his attempt to get his hands on the Tsar's Icon.

Adam switched on the bedside light, then pulled the small package out of the pocket of his trenchcoat. He unwrapped it carefully. St. George stared back at him—no longer looking magnificent, more accusing. Adam would have handed the icon over to Rosenbaum without a second thought if it could have saved Heidi.

By midnight Adam had decided what had to be done, but he didn't stir from his tiny room until a few minutes after three. He quietly opened the door, checked the corridor, and then crept down the stairs, past the sleeping night porter and out of the front door. Once outside Adam checked the street, but there was no sign of movement. He walked in the shadows by the side of the road and when he reached the corner he saw the phone box he was searching for. In the box he pressed in a twenty-centime coin and waited. A voice said, "*Est-ce-que je peux vous aider?*"

"I want to make a reverse charge call to London," said Adam firmly.

"Yes," said the voice. "And what is your name?"

"George Cromer," replied Adam.

"And the number you're speaking from?"

"Geneva 271982." He reversed the last three digits: he felt the police could well be listening in on all calls to England that night. He then told the girl the number in London that he required.

"Can you wait a moment, please?"

"Yes," said Adam as his eyes checked up and down the street, looking for any unfamiliar movement. Only the occasional early morning car sped past.

He could hear the connection being put through. "Please wake up," his lips mouthed. At last the ringing stopped and Adam recognized the familiar voice which answered.

"Who is this?" Lawrence asked, sounding irritated but wide awake.

"Will you accept a reverse-charge call from a Mr. George Cromer in Geneva?"

"George Cromer, Lord Cromer? The Governor of the Bank of Eng . . . Yes, I will," he said.

"It's me, Lawrence," said Adam.

"Thank God! Where are you?"

"I'm still in Geneva, but I'm not sure you're going to believe what I'm about to tell you. While we were waiting to board our plane home a man pulled Heidi into a taxi and later murdered her before I could catch up with them. She's dead, Lawrence! And I'm afraid the Swiss police think I'm the killer!"

"Now just relax, Adam. I know that much. It's been on the evening news and the police have already been round to interview me. It seems Heidi's brother identified you."

"What do you mean, identified me? I didn't do it! You know I couldn't do it! It was a man called Rosenbaum, not me."

"Rosenbaum? Who is Rosenbaum?"

Adam tried to sound calm. "Heidi and I came to Geneva this morning to pick up from a Swiss bank a gift that Pa had left me in his will. It turned out to be a painting. When we returned to the airport, this Rosenbaum grabbed Heidi thinking she had got the painting, which doesn't make sense because the damned icon's only worth twenty thousand pounds."

"Icon?" said Lawrence.

"Yes, an icon of St. George and the Dragon," said Adam. "That's not important. What's important is that . . ."

"Now listen carefully," interrupted Lawrence, "because I'm not going to repeat myself. Keep out of sight until the morning and then give yourself up at our consulate. I'll make sure that the consul will be expecting you. Don't arrive until eleven because London is an hour behind Geneva and I'll need every minute to see that everything is properly organized."

Adam found himself smiling for the first time in twelve hours.

"Did the killer get what he was after?" Lawrence asked.

"No, he didn't get the icon," said Adam. "He only got my mother's chocolates . . ."

"Thank God for that. Be sure to keep out of sight of the Swiss police because they are convinced you killed Heidi."

"But . . ." began Adam.

"No explanations. Just be at the consulate at eleven. Now you'd better get off the line," said Lawrence.

"Right," said Adam, "and . . ." but the phone was only giving out a long burr. Thank God for Lawrence, he thought. He hadn't sounded like

Lawrence though, and it was strange that he didn't seem to need to ask any questions. It was as if he already knew the answers . . .

Adam checked the street once again before stealing back to the hotel. The porter was still asleep. Adam was back in his bed by five minutes past four. He didn't sleep. Rosenbaum, Heidi, the Russian gentleman at Sotheby's . . . so many pieces of a jigsaw, none of them fitting into place.

But the thing that worried him most was the conversation with Lawrence.

THE TWO POLICEMEN ARRIVED at the Hotel Monarche at twenty past seven that Thursday morning. They were tired, discontented and hungry. Since midnight they had visited forty-three hotels without success. They had checked over a thousand registration cards and woken seven innocent Englishmen. They still had three more hotels to check before they went off duty.

When the landlady saw them coming into the hall she waddled towards them. She loathed the police. Twice in the last year she had been fined for her failure to register every guest. If they caught her once more she knew they would take her licence away. Her slow mind tried to recall who had booked in the previous evening. Eight people had registered, but only two had paid cash—the Englishman, Mr. Pemberton was the name he had given, and Maurice who always turned up with a different girl whenever he was in Geneva. She had destroyed both their cards and pocketed the money. Maurice and the girl had left by seven, but the Englishman was still asleep in his room.

"We need to check your registration cards for last night, madame."

"Certainly, monsieur," she replied with a warm smile, and handed over the six remaining cards.

"Did an Englishman stay here last night?"

"No," said the landlady firmly. "I haven't had an Englishman for at least a month. Would you like to see the cards for last week?"

"No, that won't be necessary," said the policeman. "But we will need to check your unoccupied rooms."

"I've already checked them once this morning," said the landlady.

"We still need to see for ourselves," the other officer insisted.

The landlady picked up her passkey and waddled towards the stairs, which she climbed as if on the final ascent of Everest. She knew she would lose her licence the moment the policemen entered room twelve. She turned the key in the lock and the two walked in ahead of her while she remained in the corridor.

"Thank you, madame," said the first, as he stepped back into the corridor. "We are sorry to have troubled you." He put a tick on his list next to the Hotel Monarche.

As the two policemen made their way downstairs the landlady walked into room number twelve, mystified. The bed was undisturbed and there was no sign of anyone having spent the night there. "I wonder where he is," she muttered.

For the past hour Adam had been crouching behind a derelict coach in a railway goods yard less than half a mile from the hotel. He had watched the early morning commuters flooding in. By twenty past eight he judged they were at their peak and slipped out to join the crowd. He stopped at a kiosk to purchase a *Herald Tribune*, a city map of Geneva and a bar of Nestlé's chocolate.

There were still over two hours to kill before he could present himself at the consulate, but he could already see the building he had picked as his next sanctuary. He steered a route towards it that allowed him to mingle with other people and avoid open spaces. His timing was perfect. He reached the main door of the cathedral as hundreds of worshippers were leaving the early morning Communion service.

Once inside St. Peter's he felt safe. He made his way slowly down a side aisle, dropped some coins in one of the collection boxes, lit a candle and placed it in a holder below a statue of the Virgin Mother. He fell on his knees, but his eyes never closed. After about twenty minutes Adam was distressed to see that there were only a handful of people left in the cathedral: some old ladies dressed in black filled a front pew, fingering their rosaries; a few tourists were craning their necks to admire the roof.

Adam rose slowly and walked over to a confessional box partly hidden behind a pillar. A small sign said that the box was not in use. Adam slipped in, sat down and pulled the curtain closed.

First he took out the *Herald Tribune* from his trenchcoat pocket, and then the bar of chocolate, which he began to munch greedily. Next he searched for the story. His eyes passed over the headlines until he saw the paragraph he was looking for: "Englishman Sought after Murder of German Girl and Swiss Taxi Driver." Adam began to tremble when he discovered they knew his name: "Captain Adam Scott, who recently resigned his commission from the Royal Wessex Regiment, is wanted . . . please turn to page fifteen." Adam began to turn the pages. ". . . for questioning by the Geneva police in connection with . . ."

"Au nom du Père, du Fils et du Saint Esprit."

Adam looked up from the paper, startled. He considered making a dash for it. But instead some long-ago training from his Catholic upbringing took hold and he found himself saying automatically, "Father, bless me, for I have sinned and wish to confess."

"Good, my son, and what form has this sin taken?" asked the priest in accented but clear English.

Adam thought quickly, I must give him no clue as to who I am. He looked out through the gap in the curtain and was alarmed to see two policemen questioning another priest by the west door. He drew the curtains tight and turned to the only accent he could ever imitate with any conviction.

"I'm over from Dublin, Father, and last night I picked up a girl and took her back to my hotel."

"Yes, my son?"

"Well, one thing led to another, Father."

"And is it your intention to marry this girl, my son?"

"Oh, no, Father, I'm already married."

"It is a night you must put behind you. Let it be a lesson to you, my son, and may the Lord find it in his mercy to forgive you this abominable sin. Now you must make your act of contrition."

When Adam had completed the act of contrition the priest pronounced absolution and told him he must, as penance, say three decades of the rosary. Adam once again checked through the curtains. The police were no longer anywhere to be seen.

"Continue to pray to our Blessed Lady to keep you from the evils of temptation."

Adam folded up his newspaper, pushed it into the trenchcoat and bolted from the little box. He took a seat at the end of the pew, lowered his head and began to whisper the Lord's Prayer as he opened the map of Geneva. He located the British consulate and estimated that it was just over a mile away from the cathedral. Seven streets and a bridge had to be negotiated before he would be safe. It was still too early to leave St. Peter's so he waited another thirty minutes.

He watched a party of tourists as they were conducted through the cathedral. As they neared the great door at the west end, Adam rose and walked quickly to the porch only a yard behind the tourists. They shielded him into the square. He ducked under an awning, then walked around three sides of the square to avoid the one policeman on duty by the north corner. He crossed the road and headed up a one-way street.

He managed the next three crossings without incident, but with only two hundred yards to go he could feel his heart thumping. There was only one policeman in sight, intent on directing traffic. Adam kept his back to the officer. He could now see across the road the garden square that had only been a tiny green blob on the map. On the far side he spotted a Union Jack hanging over a blue door.

Never run the last few yards, especially when it's open ground, his sergeant had told him many times. He crossed the road and stood on the edge of the small park, only fifty yards away from safety. A policeman was patrolling the opposite pavement, but Adam suspected that was only because there were several consulates standing adjacent to one another.

He watched the officer carefully. It took the man two minutes to reach the French consulate before he turned and continued his leisurely walk back. Adam ducked behind a tree in the corner of the park and waited for the policeman to reach the furthest point of his beat.

He checked the consulate door, relieved to see there was no guard in sight. He looked up at the bay window on the first floor and saw two men staring out as if waiting expectantly for someone to arrive. Adam set off as the cathedral clock struck eleven. The policeman was now a few paces from the French consulate. Adam crossed the road with a measured stride. When he reached the tramlines in the centre he had to stop suddenly to let a car pass by. The policeman turned to start his journey back.

For several seconds Adam remained motionless between the tramlines, then he took a confident pace towards the British consulate. A tall man of athletic build, his head covered in a stubble of short fair hair, stepped out to greet him.

Adam would not have recognized him, but for the eyes.

Chapter Twelve
THE FOREIGN OFFICE, LONDON   16 JUNE 1966

When Sir Morris Youngfield left the prime minister at number 10 Downing Street he was still unable to work out why the possession of any icon could be so important.

He marched back to the Foreign Office, where he found Tessa, his secretary, in his room sorting out papers.

"I want a D4 committee assembled immediately," he said to the woman who had served him loyally for fourteen years. "And ask Commander Busch to join the team."

Sir Morris knew he couldn't hope to get to the bottom of this one without the cooperation of the Americans.

As ROMANOV MOVED towards him, Adam took a pace back from the tramlines to allow a tramcar to pass between them. When the tram had passed Adam was no longer to be seen. Romanov snarled at such an amateur trick, sprinted the twenty yards necessary to catch up with the tram and, to the astonishment of the passengers, leaped on. He began checking over the faces row by row.

Adam waited for the tramcar to travel another twenty yards before he emerged from behind a tree. He swore under his breath. The policeman was now only a few paces from the consulate and heading towards it. Adam looked back at the tram which had just been passed by another which was heading towards him. To his dismay, he saw his adversary leap from one platform to the other with the agility of a top-class gymnast. With the policeman now right outside the consulate door, Adam was left with no choice but to turn and sprint back in the direction he had come from. After fifty yards he glanced over his shoulder. Heidi's killer, the man he knew only as Rosenbaum, had started running towards him.

Adam tried to lengthen the distance between them. At the first crossroads he saw a plump lady coming out of a phone box a few yards away. He changed direction quickly and leaped into the empty box, crouching in the far corner. The door slowly squelched shut. Rosenbaum came hurtling round the corner and was twenty yards past the box before he realized that Adam had shot out and back down the road in the opposite direction. Adam knew he had at least five seconds before Rosenbaum could hope to see which direction he had chosen. One and two and three and four and five, he counted as he ran along the road. He checked right, before mounting three steps and pushing through some swing doors. He found himself in front of a small counter, behind which sat a young woman holding a small wad of tickets.

"*Deux francs, monsieur*," said the girl. Adam quickly took out two francs and made his way down a passage and through more swing doors. He waited for his eyes to become accustomed to the dark. It was the first performance of the day and the cinema was nearly empty. Adam chose a seat on the end of a row that was an equal distance from two exits.

He stared at the screen while he formulated a plan. Whenever the screen was bright enough he checked the map, and using the top of his thumb as a one-inch ruler he estimated that the nearest border to France was only eight miles away, at Ferney-Voltaire. From there he could travel home via Dijon and Paris. Having decided on his route, the next problem was how to travel. He settled on hiring a car. He remained in his seat to double-check the routes, then folded up the map and left the cinema.

WHEN SIR MORRIS ENTERED the room, he found the D4 committee already assembled.

He glanced round the table at the handpicked men. On his left, the old warhorse Alec Snell, who had served at the Foreign Office longer than any of them, was touching his moustache nervously as he waited for Sir Morris to take his seat. Next to him sat Brian Matthews, a grammar-school boy with a double first and a chip on both shoulders. Opposite them was Commander Ralph Busch, the CIA representative co-opted onto the committee, who after five years attached to the US embassy in Grosvenor Square considered himself more British than the British. At the far end of the table sat Sir Morris's second-in-command.

Some said he was a little too young, but then everyone except Tessa had forgotten that Sir Morris had held his job at the same age.

Sir Morris settled in his seat at the head of the table.

"Gentlemen," he began—the only lady present being Tessa, whose existence he rarely acknowledged—"the prime minister has given this D4 his full blessing. And he requires detailed reports to be sent to him every twelve hours, wherever he is, and at any time of the night or day should there be some unexpected development. So, as you can see, there is no time to waste. This particular D4 has co-opted as part of its team Commander Busch from the CIA. I have worked with Commander Busch several times over the last five years and I am delighted that the American embassy has chosen him to represent them."

The man seated on Sir Morris's right bowed slightly. At five feet nine inches, with broad, muscular shoulders and a neat black beard, he looked every inch the sailor whom Player's cigarettes were always trying to please.

"From the latest reports I have received," Sir Morris continued, opening the file in front of him, "it appears that Scott never reached the consulate this morning. BEA have confirmed," said Sir Morris, consulting his notes, "that Scott received a call from Roget et Cie while he was at the airport. After considerable pressure from our ambassador and from Interpol, we have learned from Monsieur Roget that the purpose of Scott's visit to the bank was to pick up a bequest from a Mr. Emmanuel Rosenbaum. Further checking shows that a Mr. Rosenbaum arrived in Zürich yesterday morning and travelled on to Geneva in the afternoon. None of this would be of any great significance if Mr. Rosenbaum had not boarded the aeroplane to Zürich from"—Sir Morris couldn't resist a dramatic pause—"Moscow. I think it is not unreasonable therefore to assume that Mr. Rosenbaum works for the KGB. What still remains a mystery is why he should kill two innocent people for a relatively obscure icon. That brings my report up to date. But have you come up with anything?" he asked, turning to his Number Two.

Lawrence Pemberton looked up. "Since our meeting this morning, Sir Morris, I have spoken to Scott's sister, his mother, and the firm of solicitors who administered his father's will. It transpires that Scott was left with nothing of any real importance in the will apart from an envelope which his mother says contained a letter from Reichsmarschall Hermann Goering." There was an immediate buzz, until Sir Morris tapped his knuckles on the table.

"Do we have any idea of the contents of Goering's letter?" asked Sir Morris.

"No, sir. But one of our examination entrants, a Mr. Nicholas Wainwright, was asked by Scott to translate what we now believe was a paragraph from the letter. We know this because Wainwright later asked the examination board if it was part of his test."

Lawrence extracted a piece of paper from the file in front of him and read out the paragraph:

> "During the year you cannot have failed to notice that I have been receiving from one of the guards a regular supply of Havana cigars—one of the few pleasures I have been permitted despite my incarceration. The cigars themselves have also served another purpose, as each one contained a capsule with a small amount of poison. Enough to allow me to survive my trial, while ensuring that I shall cheat the executioner."

"That's all?" said Sir Morris.

"I'm afraid so," said Lawrence, "although I believe it confirms what Scott told me last night was his reason for travelling to Geneva. There is no doubt in my mind that the package he went to pick up contained the icon of St. George and the Dragon left to his father by Goering."

"St. George and the Dragon," said Matthews, interrupting. "That's the icon that half the KGB have been searching for during the past two weeks. My team have been trying to find out why."

"And what have you come up with?" asked Sir Morris.

"Very little," admitted Matthews. "But we began to assume it must be a decoy because the Tsar's Icon of St. George and the Dragon hangs in the Winter Palace in Leningrad, and has done for three hundred years."

"Anything else?" asked Sir Morris.

"Only that the section leader in search of the icon is Alex Romanov," said Matthews.

Snell gave out a low whistle. "Well, at least we know we're dealing with the First Division," he said.

There was a long silence before Sir Morris offered, "One thing is clear. We have to get to Scott first and we must assume that it's Romanov we're up against."

"What do you imagine would be the outcome if Romanov or this Rosenbaum, who must also be part of the KGB, manages to get to Scott before we do?" asked Matthews.

"A civilian up against one of the Russians' most ruthless agents—that's all we need," said Commander Busch.

Lawrence inclined his head towards the American. "I've known Adam for most of my life," he said. "Ironically, it was I, without his knowledge, who recommended that he should be interviewed for a place in one of our Special Sections. If Romanov or any of his cohorts come face to face with Scott, they'd better remember that he won a Military Cross in Malaya."

"But if the situation demanded it," asked Snell, "would Scott be able to kill Romanov?"

"I would have said no before Rosenbaum murdered his girlfriend," said Lawrence.

"I wouldn't be confident of his chances, even now," said Matthews.

"That's because you don't know Adam Scott," retorted Lawrence.

Matthews lowered his eyes in order to avoid a clash with his boss. His boss! Lawrence was ten years his junior. A shortlist of two and they had chosen another Oxbridge man to be undersecretary. Matthews knew that as far as the Foreign Office was concerned, he had gone to the wrong school and the wrong university. He should have taken his father's advice and joined the police force. There were no class barriers there.

Sir Morris ignored the signs of hostility, which had become fairly common since he promoted Pemberton in preference to the older man.

"Are we allowed to know," asked Snell, looking straight at Busch, "why a relatively obscure icon is of such importance?"

"We are as mystified as you," said the American. "All we can add to your current information is that two weeks ago the Russians deposited gold bullion in New York to the value of over seven hundred million dollars, without any explanation. We are, of course, not certain there is any connection."

"Let's get down to what we actually know, and stop guessing at what might be." Sir Morris turned back to Lawrence. "What's the position now?"

Lawrence undid a folder with a red band round it and the words "Immediate Action" printed across the top. "We have seventeen agents in Geneva, and the Americans are flying in a further twelve today. With the Russians and the Swiss also roaming the city in search of Scott, I can only believe someone will have come across him by tonight. One of our biggest problems is that the Swiss are not willing to cooperate. As far as they are concerned, Scott is a common criminal on the run. We have started checking out all the obvious places and we are in constant touch with every agent. So if Scott suddenly appears out of nowhere we should be able to go to his aid at a moment's notice."

Lawrence looked up, to observe that one of the team was carefully taking down all these details. "Added to that, the GPO are intercepting every call made to me at Barclays' DCO. But it won't be long before Adam works out that that's only a front. After our conversation last night he is bound to have become suspicious."

THE CINEMA DOOR OPENED onto the busy pavement and Adam slipped into the stream of commuters now returning home. Checking everything within 180 degrees, he covered three blocks. Then he spotted a red Avis sign swinging in the afternoon breeze on the far side of the road. He safely reconnoitred the crowded crossing, but once his foot touched the far pavement he froze. Just ahead of him in the crowd stood a man in a raincoat. He was continually looking around. Was he one of Rosenbaum's men, one of the Swiss police, or even British? There was no way of telling whose side he was on. Adam's eyes never left the man as he took out an intercom and whispered into it.

"Nothing to report, sir. Still no sign of our man, and I haven't seen any of the KGB either."

Adam, unable to hear the words, turned into a side road and almost knocked over a boy selling papers. "*Le soldat anglais toujours à Genève*" the headline blared. Quickly he crossed another road, and stared at the hotel in front of him. There would be no point in his trying to hide there.

As he started to move away, an empty touring coach drew up and parked outside. Smart blue lettering along its side proclaimed "The Royal Philharmonic Orchestra". Adam watched as some musicians walked out of the hotel and climbed onto the coach carrying their instrument cases. One was lugging a large kettledrum which he deposited in the luggage compartment. When the next group of musicians came through the double doors Adam walked quickly forward and stepped into the midst of them. He then continued on past them through the door. The first thing he spotted in a crowded lobby was a double bass leaning against the wall. He glanced at the label round the neck of the unwieldy case. "Robin Beresford".

Adam walked over to the counter and gestured to the clerk. "I need my room key quickly—I've left my bow upstairs and now I'm holding everyone up."

"Yes, sir. What room number?" asked the clerk.

"I think it's number 312, or was that yesterday?" said Adam.

"What name, sir?"

"Beresford—Robin Beresford."

The clerk handed him key 612. His only comment was, "You were three floors out."

"Thank you," said Adam. He walked rapidly over to the lift and went up to the sixth floor. He made his way quickly along the passage to room 612.

As he turned the key and opened the door he said firmly in as good French as he could manage, "*Service de chambre*," but as no one responded, he stepped in and locked the door behind him. An unopened suitcase had been left in the corner. Adam checked the label. Obviously Mr. Beresford hadn't even had time to unpack.

Adam looked round the room. There was no other sign of the hotel guests apart from a typed itinerary on a side table:

"European Tour: Geneva, Frankfurt, Berlin, Amsterdam, London.
Geneva: Bus 5.00; Concert Hall rehearsal 6.00; Concert performance
7.30; Encores 10.00.
Programme: Mozart's Third Horn Concerto; Brahms's Second Symphony; Schubert's Unfinished Symphony."

Adam looked at his watch. He felt safe to remain in the room until it
was dark.

He picked up the phone by the bed and dialled room service.
"Beresford, 612," he announced, and ordered himself some dinner
before going into the bathroom. On the side of the basin was propped a
complimentary plastic bag containing soap, a tiny toothbrush, toothpaste
and a plastic razor.

He had just finished shaving when he heard a knock on the door and
someone calling, "Room service." Adam quickly covered his face with
lather again and put on a hotel dressing gown before he opened the door.
The waiter set up a table without giving Adam a second look. "Will you
sign the bill, please, sir?" he inquired.

He handed Adam a slip of paper. Adam signed it "Robin Beresford"
and added a fifteen-per-cent tip.

"Thank you, sir," said the waiter and left. As soon as the door closed,
Adam's eyes settled on the feast of onion soup, rump steak with green
beans and potatoes, and raspberry sorbet. A bottle of wine had been
uncorked and needed only to be poured.

After he had finished the meal he wheeled the trolley out into the
corridor and placed the "Do not disturb" sign on the door. Then he lay
down on the bed and began to consider what had happened in the last
twenty-four hours.

He still couldn't accept what he had gone through. If only he hadn't
pressed Heidi into joining him on this journey. A week before she hadn't
even known him, and now he was responsible for her death. He would
have to explain to her parents what had happened to their daughter.
Before Adam could face them he had to have some explanation for the
things he hadn't yet begun to understand.

"ANTARCTIC IS IN POSSESSION of an icon of St. George and the Dragon.
But we know from our files of that period that that particular icon was
destroyed when the Grand Duke of Hesse's plane crashed over Belgium
in 1937."

"That may well be what is written in your files," said the man on the
other end of the phone. "But what if your information turns out to be
wrong and the icon was found by Goering but not returned to the grand
duke? What if the Russians have now discovered the existence of the
original icon?"

"Are you suggesting they might also get their hands on the original document?" asked Busch.

"Precisely. So you must be sure to get to Scott before the Russians do, or, for that matter, the Foreign Office."

"But I'm part of the Foreign Office team."

"And that's precisely what we hope that the Foreign Office will go on believing."

"'AND WHO'S BEEN SLEEPING in my bed?' said Mother Bear."

Adam woke with a start. Looking down at him was a girl who held a double bass firmly by the neck with one hand. She was nearly six foot and she was considerably heavier than Adam, so that she made the bow she was holding in her right hand look like a toothpick. She had long, gleaming red hair that was in such contrast to the rest of her that it was as if her Maker had started at the top and then lost interest. She wore a white blouse and a flowing black skirt that stopped an inch above the ground.

"Who are you?" asked Adam, startled.

"I'm not Goldilocks, that's for sure," parried the girl. "More to the point, who are you?"

Adam hesitated. "If I told you, you wouldn't believe me."

"I can't imagine why not," she said. "You don't look like Prince Charles or Elvis Presley, so go on, try me."

"I'm Adam Scott."

"Am I meant to swoon, or scream and run away?" she inquired.

Adam realized that the girl couldn't have watched television or read a paper for at least two days. He switched tactics. "I thought my friend Robin Beresford was meant to be booked into this room," he said confidently.

"And so did I until I saw you on my bed."

"You're Robin Beresford?"

"You're quite sharp for someone who has just woken up, but you still haven't explained what you're doing on my bed."

"Is there any hope of you listening to me for five minutes, without my being thrown out?" asked Adam.

"Yes, but don't bother with any more fairy stories," said Robin. "My father was a born liar, and by the time I was twelve I could see through him like a pane of glass."

"I should have a seat if I were you," said Adam. "What would you like first, the good news or the bad news?"

"Try me on the bad news," said Robin.

"The Swiss police want to arrest me for murder."

"What's the good news?" Robin asked.

ROMANOV STOOD IN the Russian consul-general's office in Geneva and studied the group of men who had been flown in at short notice. They all had long records of service to the state, but only one of them, Valchek, was known personally to Romanov, and he worked too closely with Zaborski to be trusted.

"Comrades," Romanov began, the moment they had all settled, "there is no need to remind you that we have been entrusted with a vital assignment for the Motherland. We must maintain a tight surveillance over Geneva in case Scott is still holed up somewhere in the city. My own guess is that, like all amateurs, he will wait until it's dark, perhaps even first light, before he makes a run for the nearest border. The French border will be his most obvious choice. The English have never bothered to master the German language, although a few of them can manage to speak passable French, so he's more likely to feel safe in that country. It also offers him the opportunity to cross only one border before reaching the coast. If he's stupid enough to try to leave by plane, he will find that we have the airport covered; if by train, we have the stations manned. But my guess is that he will try to escape by motor vehicle.

"I shall therefore take five men to the French border with me, while Major Valchek will take another five to Basle to cover the German crossing point. The rest of you will remain on surveillance in Geneva, relieving those agents who are in the field already. And don't expect Scott to be roaming around looking like a tourist on holiday. Study your picture of him carefully."

Romanov paused for effect. "The man who brings me the Tsar's Icon need have no fear for his future prosperity when we return home."

He pulled out the duplicate icon from his coat pocket and held it high above his head for all to see. "When you have the original of this your task will be done. Study it carefully, comrades. And remember," Romanov added, "the only difference between this and Scott's icon is that his has a small silver crown embedded in the back of the frame. Once you see that crown you will know that you have found the missing masterpiece."

Romanov looked down at the silent men. "I underestimated the Englishman. He's good, and if any of you are hoping to kill him before I get to him, you'll have to be *very* good."

Chapter Thirteen

"Not bad, Scott, not bad at all," said Robin when Adam had finished his story. "Either you're one hell of a liar, or I've lost my touch. Am I permitted to see this icon?"

Adam got off the bed and pulled out the package containing the Tsar's Icon from the map pocket of his trenchcoat. He passed it across to her. She opened the package and stared at the face of St. George without making any comment. "It's beautiful," she said at last. "And I can understand anyone wanting to possess it. But no painting could be worth the tragedy and trouble you've had to go through."

"I agree it's inexplicable," said Adam. "But Rosenbaum, or whatever his real name is, has killed twice to get his hands on it, and he's already convinced me that so long as I am in possession of the icon, I'll be the next in line."

Robin turned the painting over. "What does that mean?" she asked, pointing to the tiny silver crown embedded in the wood.

"That proves it was once owned by a tsar, according to the man from Sotheby's. And it greatly enhances its value, he assured me."

"Still, it couldn't be worth killing for," said Robin. She handed the icon back to Adam. "What other secret is St. George keeping to himself?"

Adam shrugged and frowned, having asked himself the same question again and again since Heidi's death. He returned the silent saint to his trenchcoat.

"What was to have been your plan if I hadn't interrupted your sleep?" asked Robin. "Other than making the bed?"

Adam smiled. "I hoped to call Lawrence and check if he had any more news for me. If he couldn't help, I was going to hire a car and try to get across the border to France and then on to England. I feel sure that Rosenbaum and the Swiss police will have all the airports and stations fully covered."

"No doubt Rosenbaum will have thought that much out as well," said Robin. "So we'd better try and get in touch with your friend Lawrence and see if he's come up with any bright ideas."

"You don't have to get involved," said Adam hesitantly.

"I am involved," said Robin, walking across to the phone. "Tell me the number and once I've got your friend on the line I'll pass him over to you and then no one will realize who's phoning."

The phone didn't complete its first two rings before Robin heard a man's voice on the line. She immediately handed over the receiver.

"Hello, who is that?" asked the voice. Adam suddenly realized that Lawrence never announced his name on the phone.

"Lawrence, it's me."

"Where are you?"

"I'm still in Geneva."

"We were waiting for you at eleven o'clock this morning."

"So was Rosenbaum."

"What does this Rosenbaum look like?"

"A six-foot, fair-haired, blue-eyed monster, who seems determined to kill me."

"And are you still in possession of our patron saint?"

"Yes, I am," said Adam. "But what can be so important about . . ."

"Put the phone down and ring me back again in three minutes."

The line went dead.

"Is everything all right?" asked Robin, breaking into Adam's thoughts.

"I think so," said Adam, a little mystified. "He wants me to ring back in three minutes. Will that be all right with you?"

"This tour's already costing eight thousand pounds of taxpayers' money, so what difference can a few international calls make?" she said.

Three minutes later, Robin picked up the receiver and repeated the number. After one ring Lawrence was back on the line.

"Only answer my questions," said Lawrence.

"No, I will not answer your questions," said Adam, becoming increasingly annoyed with Lawrence's approach. "I want one or two of my own answered before you get anything else out of me. Who is Rosenbaum?"

Lawrence didn't immediately reply.

"You'll get nothing further from me until you start telling the truth," said Adam.

"I have every reason to believe Rosenbaum is a Russian agent whose real name is Romanov," said Lawrence.

"A Russian agent? But why should a Russian agent be so keen to get his hands on my icon?"

"I don't know," said Lawrence. "We were rather hoping you might be able to tell us."

"Who's we?"

Another long silence. Then Lawrence said, "I work for the Foreign Office."

"In what capacity?"

"I am not at liberty . . ."

"Stop being so pompous, Lawrence. In what capacity?"

"I'm the Number Two in a small section that deals in . . ." Lawrence hesitated.

"Espionage I think is the current jargon," said Adam. "Well, if you want my icon that badly you had better get me out of this mess."

"Where are you?"

"The Richmond Hotel."

"In a public phone box?" asked Lawrence.

"No, in a private room."

"Registered in your name?"

"No, of course not!"

"Right. Don't leave the room until seven am, then phone this number again. That will give me enough time to get everything in place."

"Is that the best you can do?" said Adam, but the phone had already gone dead. "It looks as if I'm stuck with you for the night," he told Robin as he replaced the phone.

"On the contrary, it is I who am stuck with you," said Robin, and disappeared into the bathroom. Adam paced around the room before he tested the small sofa. By the time Robin returned, clad in a pair of sky-blue pyjamas, he had selected the floor as his resting place.

"Not very comfortable is it?" said Robin. "But then British Intelligence didn't warn me to book a double room." She climbed into the bed and turned out the light.

Adam slept intermittently, his mind switching between why the icon should be so important, how Lawrence knew so much about it, and most crucial of all, how the hell he was going to get out of the hotel alive.

ADAM WOKE WITH A START just before he was due to phone Lawrence. Only Robin's steady breathing reminded him he was not alone. Suddenly he became aware of a strange sound coming from the corridor outside— two or three steps, a pause, then whoosh, two or three steps, a pause, another whoosh. A newspaper shot under the door and the steps moved on. Adam saw that his photograph dominated the front page of the *Herald Tribune*.

Robin was still asleep. He picked up the phone and took it into the bathroom, closing the door.

When he got through to Lawrence he said, "Things have become worse now. I'm still holed up in the hotel but my picture is on the front page of every paper."

"I know," said Lawrence. "We tried to prevent it, but the Swiss wouldn't cooperate."

"Then I may as well give myself up to the Swiss," said Adam. "Damn it all, I am innocent."

"No, Adam, in Switzerland you're guilty until proven innocent and you must have worked out by now that you're involved in something far more important than a double murder."

"What could be more important than a double murder?" asked Adam angrily.

"I can understand how you feel, but your only chance now is to carry out my instructions to the letter and treat with suspicion every person with whom you come in contact."

"I'm listening," said Adam.

"Remember everything I say, because I am only going to tell you once. The Royal Philharmonic Orchestra are staying in the same hotel as you and are going to Frankfurt at ten o'clock this morning. Leave your room at five to ten, join the orchestra in the lobby and then make your way to the front where you'll find their coach parked. We will have a car waiting for you on the far side of the road. The car is a black Mercedes and you will see a man in a grey chauffeur's uniform holding the door open for you. We have already arranged that no other car will be able to park on that side of the road between 9:30 and 10:30, so you can't mistake it. There will be another man in the car and you will then be driven to the safety of our consulate. Do you need me to repeat any of that?"

"No," said Adam, "but . . ."

"Good luck," said Lawrence, and the phone went dead.

By seven thirty Adam had showered, while Robin remained in a deep sleep. He sat on the sofa and went over Lawrence's plan in his mind. Robin finally woke. She blinked at Adam and a large grin appeared on her face.

"So you didn't murder me while I slept," she said. "Aren't you meant to have phoned London by now?"

"I already have."

"And what is the master plan to be?" she asked.

"I will be leaving with you," said Adam.

"Most of my one-night stands don't bother to stay that long," she remarked on her way to the bathroom. Adam laughed and turned his attention to the paper.

"Does that mean we're sharing a room in Frankfurt as well?" Robin asked a few minutes later, when she came out of the bathroom.

"No, as soon as we're clear of the hotel I leave you at the coach and make my own way to a car on the far side of the road."

"That sounds more like the men in my life," she said. "But at least we can have a farewell breakfast," she added, picking up the phone. "I'm nuts about kippers. How about you?"

The waiter arrived with breakfast about fifteen minutes later while Adam hid in the bathroom. When he reappeared he showed no interest in the food, so Robin ate four kippers and most of the toast. Nine o'clock passed; a porter took away the breakfast trolley and Robin began to pack. The phone rang, making Adam jump. Robin picked it up.

"Yes, Stephen," she said. "No, I won't need any help with my luggage. Not this time." She put the phone down.

"I'll carry the double bass for you if you like," offered Adam.

"I'd like to see you try," said Robin. Adam walked over to the large instrument case that was propped against the wall. He tried from all angles but could only hold it off the floor for a few moments. Then with one flick Robin had the stem on her shoulder and the instrument balanced perfectly.

"It's a matter of skill, my puny friend," she said. "And to think I believed all those stories last night about you outrunning half the Swiss police force to spend the night with me."

Adam tried to laugh. He picked up his trenchcoat, checking that the icon was inside. He couldn't stop himself shaking from a combination of fear and anticipation.

Robin looked at him. "Don't worry," she said gently. "It will be over in a few minutes." Then she saw the newspaper.

"I should sue them if I were you."

"Why?" asked Adam.

"You're a lot better looking than that."

Adam smiled and gave her a hug. "Thanks for everything," he said. "But now we have to go."

"You're sounding more like one of my lovers all the time," said Robin, mournfully.

Adam picked up her suitcase while Robin once again jerked the stem of the double bass onto her shoulder. She opened the door and checked the corridor: two of her colleagues were waiting by the lift, otherwise there was no one in sight. Robin and Adam joined the two musicians and after "Good morning" no one spoke. Adam sheltered behind the double bass as the lift trundled down to the ground floor.

Robin waited for her two colleagues to leave before she shielded Adam as best she could all the way across the foyer. His eyes were now fixed on the front door. He could see the coach taking up most of the road and several members of the orchestra already clambering in.

"Oh, I forgot," said Robin. "I'm meant to put this thing in the compartment at the back of the bus."

"Do it later," said Adam sharply. "Just keep going until you reach the coach door." Then he saw the car on the far side of the road. He felt dizzy with relief. A man was seated in the back just as Lawrence had promised. Ten o'clock struck somewhere in the distance. Another man, dressed in chauffeur's uniform, hat pulled down over his forehead, stood by the open car door. Adam stared towards him as the man's eyes scanned the hotel entrance. His uniform wasn't a good fit.

"Into the bus," hissed Adam.

"With this thing? They'll kill me," said Robin.

"If you don't, he'll kill *me!*"

Robin obeyed, despite the adverse comments as she lumbered down the aisle with her double bass screening Adam from the gaze of anyone on the far side of the road. He wanted to be sick.

Adam slumped into a seat next to Robin with the double bass alongside them in the aisle.

"Which one?" she whispered.

"In the chauffeur's uniform."

Robin glanced out of the window. "He may be evil, but he's damned good looking," she said.

"Everybody's in," called a man from the front of the bus. "But I've counted and we seem to have one extra."

Oh, my God, thought Adam, he's going to throw me off the bus.

"My brother," shouted Robin from the back. "He's only travelling with us for part of the journey."

"Oh, that's OK then," said the manager.

"He's started looking at the bus," said Robin. "But I don't think he can see you. No, he's turned his gaze back to the hotel entrance."

"I didn't realize you had a brother," said the manager, who was suddenly standing beside them. The coach moved out of the square.

"Neither did I until this morning," mumbled Robin, still looking out of the window. She turned and faced her boss. "Yes, I forgot to mention to you that he might be in Switzerland now. I do hope it's not going to cause a problem. Adam, this is Stephen Grieg, the orchestra's manager."

"What time are we expecting to reach Frankfurt, Stephen?" called a voice from the front.

"Must leave you now," said the manager.

"Now," said Robin, "may I learn what's next on the agenda?"

"I think Rosenbaum'll stay in Geneva for at least an hour, two at the most, so with luck I'll get a fifty-mile start on him." He unfolded his map and ran his finger along the road the coach was travelling on.

"That means you could make Zürich Airport before he has a chance to catch up with you," said Robin.

"Perhaps," said Adam, "but that would be too much of a risk. We now know for certain that Rosenbaum has a professional organization behind him so I must expect the airports to be the first place he will have covered. And don't forget the Swiss police are still on the lookout for me as well."

"So why don't you come to Frankfurt with us?" asked Robin.

"I've thought about that already, but ruled it out as too much of a risk," said Adam. "When Rosenbaum has had time to think about it, the one thing he'll remember is this coach. Once he's found out the direction we're heading in he's sure to come after us."

Robin's eyes returned to the map. "So you'll need to decide where and when to get off."

"Exactly. I can risk about sixty to seventy miles."

Robin's finger ran along the main road. "About here," she said, her finger stopping on a little town called Solothurn.

"Looks about the right distance."

"But once you're off the bus what will you do for transport?"

"I've little choice but to walk or thumb lifts."

"With your luck, Rosenbaum will be the one person who stops to pick you up."

"Yes, I've thought about that," said Adam. "I would have to find a long stretch of road where I can see without being seen for about a hundred yards, and then thumb lifts only from cars with British numberplates."

"They taught you a trick or two in the army, didn't they?" said Robin. "But how do you intend to cross the frontier with your passport?"

"That's one of the many problems I haven't been able to come up with a solution for."

Robin was silent for a moment. "Once you're on your own, will you contact Lawrence again?"

"Yes. I've got to let him know what happened this morning, and warn him that someone must be passing information to Rosenbaum."

"Could it be Lawrence himself?"

"Never," said Adam.

Robin turned to look at him. "What you actually mean is you don't want to believe it could be Lawrence."

Adam thought about his relationship with Lawrence and wondered if you really could know someone for fifteen years and then find you did not know them at all.

"Just be wary how much you let him know," advised Robin.

Adam checked the map and went over all the different possible routes he could take once he had left the bus.

"Got it," said Robin suddenly. "A way to solve your passport problem. I'll substitute yours for the member of the orchestra who most resembles you. Whenever we cross a border they only count the number of people on the bus and the number of passports, and as long as they tally the customs officials don't bother to check everyone individually. No one will notice anything strange until we're back home in Britain on Sunday night."

"Not a bad idea, if there is anyone who remotely resembles me."

"We'll have to see what we can do," said Robin, her eyes moving slowly from face to face. "There are two of our lot who bear a passable resemblance to you. One is about fifty years older and the other is four inches shorter. Let me have your passport," she said. Adam handed it over and then watched Robin walk to the front and sit next to the manager who was chatting to the driver.

"I need to check something in my passport," Robin broke in. "Sorry to bother you."

"No bother. You'll find them all under my seat in a plastic bag," he said, and continued his conversation with the driver.

Robin bent down and started to shuffle through the passports as if searching for her own. She picked out the two possible substitutes and compared the photographs. The shorter man's photo looked nothing like Adam. The other, that of a violinist who was older than Adam, would pass, as long as the officials didn't study the date of birth too carefully. She put the passports back in the plastic bag, placing Adam's in the middle.

Robin made her way back to her seat. "Take a look at yourself," she said, slipping the passport over to Adam.

"Not bad. It's certainly my best chance in the circumstances. But what will happen when you return to London?"

"You'll be back in England long before us," said Robin. "So put this one in an envelope and send it direct to the RPO in Wigmore Street, W1. I'll see that they send yours back."

Adam vowed to himself that if he ever got back to London, he would become a life subscriber to the Friends of the Royal Philharmonic. "I only wish I could take you with me for the rest of the trip," he said.

Robin smiled. "Well, you can always find me in Frankfurt, Berlin or Amsterdam—just in case you get bored!" Then, on impulse, she scribbled some names and dates down on a piece of paper. "These are the hotels we'll be staying at," she said, handing the paper to Adam, "if you ever need another room for the night! Now, can I have a last look at the icon?"

Adam slipped the painting out of his map pocket, careful to shield it from anyone else's view. Robin stared into the eyes of St. George before she spoke again. "When I was lying awake last night waiting for you to ravish me, I passed the time by trying to fathom out what secret the icon holds."

Adam smiled. "Well, did you come to any conclusions?"

"Yes," said Robin. "My first idea was that the crown on the back"—she turned the icon over and stared at the little piece of silver embedded in the wood—"indicates, as your expert suggested, that this is the original by Rublev and not a copy as you were led to believe."

"I had already considered that," said Adam, "but although it would place a far higher value on the work, it is still not enough to explain why Rosenbaum would kill indiscriminately for it."

"Perhaps it's not the icon he's after, but something else. Something hidden in or behind the painting."

"That was the first thing I checked," said Adam smugly. "And I'm convinced that it's a solid piece of wood."

"I don't agree with you," said Robin as she began tapping the wood all over like a doctor examining someone's chest. "I've worked with instruments all my life, watched them being made, played them; and this icon is not solid right through. But if something is hidden inside it was

never intended to be discovered by laymen like ourselves." She handed
the icon back to Adam. "Do let me know if you ever discover what is
inside." Adam returned the icon to his trenchcoat pocket.

"Two kilometres to Solothurn," said Robin, pointing out of the
window at a signpost.

Adam rose from his seat. "I'll see you off," said Robin, and they both
made their way up the aisle. When Adam reached the front of the coach
he asked the driver if he could drop him off just before they reached the
next village.

"Sure thing," said the driver without looking back.

"Leaving us so soon?" said the manager.

"Afraid so," said Adam. "But thanks for the lift." The driver pulled
into a lay-by and opened the doors.

"'Bye Robin," said Adam, giving her a brotherly kiss on the cheek.

"Goodbye, baby brother," said Robin. "Give my love to Mother." She
smiled and waved to him as the door swung closed and the coach
continued its journey to Frankfurt.

Adam was on his own again.

Chapter Fourteen

Professor Brunweld was rarely treated with any respect. It seemed to him
to be the fate of academics. "The President," was all they had said, and
they had got him out of bed in the middle of the night and escorted him
to the Pentagon. They wanted his expert opinion, they had assured him.

Once they had handed him the document they left him alone. He
studied it for over an hour and then called for them. It was, he told them,
authentic, and if the Russians were still in possession of their copy, also
signed in 1867, then his adopted country was in all sorts of trouble.

He began to realize how serious it was when they told him that he
would not be allowed to leave the Pentagon until Monday. That didn't
surprise him once he'd seen the date on the bottom of the treaty. Three
days of solitude away from his demanding students and chattering wife:
he would never have a better opportunity to settle down and read the
works of Proust.

ROMANOV KNEW HE COULDN'T risk standing by the side of the car for
much longer. He was too conspicuously dressed not to be noticed by
everyone who came out of the hotel. Three minutes later he threw his
grey cap onto the back seat and instructed Valchek to get rid of the car
and return to the consulate.

Valchek nodded. He had carried out Romanov's orders to kill the two

British agents as if he had been asked to fix a burst water pipe. The only thing that hadn't run to plan was when Valchek found the dead chauffeur's uniform wouldn't button up on him. There had been the suggestion of a smirk on Valchek's face when Romanov realized he would have to be the chauffeur.

Romanov slipped into the shadows and waited for half an hour, by which time he was sure the plan must have been aborted from the London end. He hailed a taxi and asked the driver to take him to the Soviet consulate.

Something had happened outside the hotel that didn't quite fit. On the way to the consulate he kept playing the last thirty minutes over in his mind, as if rewinding the reel of an old film; but some of the frames still remained blurred.

Once Romanov was back in the consulate, Valchek followed him into his office.

"Tell me what you saw when we were at the hotel," said Romanov, changing back into his own clothes. "Do you remember anything unusual taking place while we were waiting?"

"Nothing in particular," said Valchek. "People continually entering and leaving the hotel—but I'm sure Scott wasn't among them."

"You are fortunate to be so certain. What happened next?"

"Next? You instructed me to go back to the consulate and wait for you to return."

"What time was that?"

"It must have been about seven minutes past ten. I remember I checked my watch when that coach left."

"Coach?" said Romanov.

"Yes, the one that was being loaded up with musical instruments. It left about . . ."

"Instruments, that's it!" said Romanov. "Now I remember what was worrying me. A double bass that was carried into the coach. Ring the hotel immediately and find out who was on that bus and where they are heading." Valchek scurried away.

It was ten fifty-five. They were going to have to move, and move quickly. Romanov pressed the intercom by the side of the phone. "I want a fast car, and a superb driver."

Valchek returned as Romanov replaced the receiver. "The bus was hired by the Royal Philharmonic Orchestra, who are on a European tour and heading for Frankfurt."

ADAM STROLLED AWAY from the village, having checked everything with a professional soldier's eye. The road was deserted but for a little boy who was relentlessly kicking a plastic football. The boy turned when he saw Adam and kicked the ball towards him. Adam kicked it back and the boy smiled widely. The smile disappeared as he watched Adam continue up the hill. There were only a few old houses on the main road. On one side was a dangerous ravine with tree-covered hills rising in the distance, while on the other side stretched green fields in which cows, bells round their necks, munched happily.

Adam went further up the hill until he came to a sharp bend. Standing on the corner he could see down the hill for about half a mile without being seen. He soon became expert at picking out cars with British numberplates as much as two or three hundred yards away. For twenty minutes he thumbed optimistically at seven English cars heading towards Lausanne, but they all ignored him.

By eleven twenty Adam decided he could no longer risk being seen on the road. There was no alternative left to him now but to walk. He shrugged and began to climb down one of the steep trails that led into the ravine in the hope of meeting the other road that was marked on the map. He cursed the open ground. If only he'd started an hour earlier.

"FASTER!" SAID ROMANOV, aware that it was not possible. Not once did the consul's driver miss a gap, a light, a chance to overtake. In fact once they were on the highway the speedometer rarely fell below 130 kilometres an hour. "We must beat them to the border," Romanov kept repeating. After they had covered one hundred kilometres in fifty-five minutes, the three men began watching ahead of them for the coach, but it was another thirty kilometres before Valchek was able to point and shout, "That must be them, about a kilometre up the hill."

"Force them off the road," said Romanov. The driver swung out to overtake and then cut across, forcing the coach driver to swerve in to the side.

Romanov jumped out of the car and ran towards the coach, his eyes already searching for anyone who might be attempting to escape. He banged on the door impatiently until the driver swung the doors open. Romanov leaped on. He took out his passport from an inside pocket, flashed it in the frightened driver's face and shouted, "Swiss police. Who's in charge here?"

Stephen Grieg stood up. "I am the manager of the company, and . . ."

"When you left your hotel in Geneva this morning, did you take on any extra passengers?" Romanov interrupted.

"No," said Grieg. "Unless you count Robin Beresford's brother Adam, who only travelled with us as far as Solothurn."

"Which one of you is Robin Beresford?" said Romanov, staring around at a sea of male faces.

"I am," piped up a voice from the back. Romanov marched down the bus, saw the double bass case, and everything fitted into place. Yes, that was what hadn't rung true. Why hadn't she put the double bass in the boot with all the other large instruments? He stared down at the woman who sat behind the monstrous instrument.

"Your brother is the one called Adam?"

"Yes," said Robin, trying not to sound nervous.

"Quite a coincidence. The man I am looking for just happens to be called Adam as well."

"Common enough name," said Robin. "Perhaps you've never read the first chapter of the Bible?"

"Six foot one inch, dark hair, dark eyes, slim and fit. Not a convincing brother for you," added Romanov studying her.

Robin pushed back her red hair but didn't rise to the bait. Romanov could sense from the nervous expressions on the faces around him that it was Scott who had been on the bus. "Where was your *brother*," Romanov emphasized the word, "intending to go once he had left the coach?"

"I have no idea," said Robin, still not changing her expression from one of uninterested politeness.

"I will give you one more chance to cooperate with me. Where was your brother heading?"

"And I'll tell you once more, I don't know."

"If you refuse to answer my questions," said Romanov, "I shall have to arrest you."

"On whose authority?" asked Robin calmly.

"On the authority of the Swiss police," Romanov said confidently.

"Then no doubt you'll be happy to show me proof of your identity."

"Don't be insolent," Romanov said sharply.

"It is you who are insolent," said Robin, standing up. "You drive in front of our coach like a lunatic and burst in like a Chicago mobster. I have no idea who you are, but if you touch me, there are forty men on this coach who will beat you to pulp. We are guests of the Swiss government, and in a few moments when we cross the border we will become guests of the West German government. You're about to get yourself onto every front page in the world and you will bring a totally new meaning to the words 'diplomatic incident'." She leaned forward and pointed a finger at him. "So get lost!"

Romanov stood staring at her for some moments and then backed away. The coach driver closed the door the moment Romanov got off and quickly drove back onto the highway.

The entire orchestra turned round and gave Robin an ovation. It went unappreciated. Robin had collapsed back into her seat, shaking uncontrollably, only too aware that not one of the forty men on that coach would have lifted a finger against Rosenbaum.

SIR MORRIS YOUNGFIELD glanced round the table: everyone was in place despite the few minutes' notice he had given them.

"Let's hear the latest report," he said, looking across at his Number Two.

"Not clever, sir, I'm afraid," began Lawrence. "Two of our most experienced agents were selected to pick up Scott at the Richmond Hotel, but our men never turned up at the hotel and they haven't been seen since."

"And where do we imagine Scott is now?" asked Matthews.

"We've also drawn a blank on that," said Lawrence. "We feel certain he must have got on the coach with the girl"—he looked down at the sheet of paper on the table in front of him—"Robin Beresford. But he wasn't on it when we were waiting for them at the border. The orchestra is due in Frankfurt in about one hour so we will be able to find out more then."

"Meanwhile, what else are we doing?" asked Sir Morris.

"Keeping a close eye on Romanov who, incidentally, turned up on the French border last night. One of our old hands recognized him despite the fact that he's cut his hair very short."

"So Scott could be anywhere by now?" said Matthews. "Do you think he'll contact you again?"

Lawrence hesitated. "Almost certainly, if he's still alive," he said, without expression.

Sir Morris stared at him but didn't comment.

"If Romanov is still in Switzerland, Scott must still be alive," said Busch. "Because the moment he gets his hands on the icon he will head for Moscow."

"Agreed," said Lawrence, "and we have men checking every flight to the USSR. I therefore suggest we assemble again tomorrow at seven am, unless Scott contacts me before then."

ADAM SLIPPED AND STUMBLED the last few yards down the ravine. His hands were bleeding, his trousers smeared with earth. He sat for two minutes trying to get his breath back as he looked back up towards the road. He had taken just under an hour to cover what a stone could have managed in three seconds. Still, there had been one advantage: no one could have seen him from the road. Anyone could see him now, but he had no alternative.

Judge by eye, check by map. The map wasn't much help but he estimated the distance to the far ridge to be about two miles. At least the map promised him there was a road, about twenty minutes' walk away, on the other side of the ridge. He checked that the icon was securely in place and then set off.

ROMANOV HAD HARDLY UTTERED a word since he had been unceremoniously forced to leave the coach, and Valchek and the driver certainly hadn't ventured any opinions. Romanov knew the girl had called his bluff, but he couldn't afford a diplomatic incident which would undoubtedly have been reported back to Moscow.

Solothurn was about forty kilometres back in the direction they had come from. As soon as they reached it they split up to see if they could discover any clues as to the route Scott might have taken. None of the locals whom they questioned had seen anyone resembling Scott that morning, and Romanov was beginning to wonder which border he should now head for when he saw the driver kicking a football back to a little boy. Romanov ran down the hill and was about to remonstrate with him when the boy turned and kicked the ball hard at Romanov himself. Romanov picked it up in anger and held it high above his head. The boy ran up and jumped towards the ball but couldn't reach it.

"Have you seen a stranger this morning?" Romanov asked, in slow deliberate French.

"Yes, yes," said the boy. "But he didn't score a goal."

"Where did he go?" asked Romanov.

"Up the hill," said the boy. To the child's dismay, Romanov dropped the ball and began to run. Valchek and the driver followed.

"Non, non," cried the little boy. Romanov looked back to see that the boy was pointing out over the ravine.

Romanov quickly turned to the driver. "Get the car, I need the binoculars and the map." A few minutes later the Mercedes drew up by Romanov. The driver jumped out and handed the glasses to him, while Valchek spread a map out on the car bonnet.

Romanov focused the binoculars and began to sweep the hills in the distance. It was several minutes before his gaze settled upon a climbing brown speck.

"The rifle," were his only words.

Valchek ran to the boot of the car and took out a Dragunov sniper's rifle with telescopic sights. He assembled the long, slim weapon and checked that it was loaded. He then raised it, nestled it in his shoulder and focused on Scott.

"Kill him," said Romanov.

Valchek was grateful for the clear, windless day as he kept the rifle sight in the middle of the Englishman's back, waited for three more strides, then slowly squeezed the trigger. Adam had almost reached the top of the ridge when the bullet tore through him. He fell to the ground with a thud. Romanov smiled and lowered the glasses.

Adam knew exactly what had ripped through his shoulder and where the shot must have come from. He instinctively rolled over until he reached the nearest tree. And then the pain began. Although the bullet had lost a lot of its power at such a distance, it still stung like an adder's bite, and blood was already beginning to seep through his trenchcoat from the torn muscle. He turned his head and gazed to where he knew Romanov must be standing, waiting to take a second shot.

He looked back towards the ridge. Only thirty yards to safety, but he would have to run over the top, remaining exposed for several vital seconds. Even if he made it, Romanov would still be able to reach him by car within thirty minutes.

Nevertheless, that was his one chance. Very slowly he crawled up the slope, thankful for the tree, which he could still use as protection. He knew that once he had covered ten yards he would be exposed. He moved four more lengths of his body and stopped.

You can't hold a rifle up in your shoulder for ever, Adam thought. He counted to two hundred slowly.

"He's going to make a run for it," Romanov told Valchek, "which will give you about three seconds. I'll shout the moment he moves." Romanov kept the glasses trained on the tree. Suddenly Adam jumped up and sprinted. Romanov shouted, *"Now!"* Valchek squeezed the trigger as Adam threw himself over the ridge. The second bullet whistled by the side of his head.

Romanov cursed, knowing that Valchek had missed. He turned to the open map. "He should reach that road in about ten minutes," he said, putting his finger in the middle of a small red line that ran between Neuchâtel and the French border. "Unless the first bullet hit him, in which case it could take him longer. So how long will it take you to get to that border?" Romanov asked the driver.

"About thirty minutes, Comrade Major," came the reply.

Romanov turned and looked back towards the hills. "Thirty minutes, Scott, that's how long you've got to live."

When the car sped away, the little boy ran home as fast as he could. He quickly told his mother everything he had seen. She smiled understandingly. Children had such vivid imaginations.

ADAM JOGGED TOWARDS the road at a steady pace, finding that running caused him even more pain. He was anxious to stop and check the wound but waited till he reached the road. The bullet had torn through the outer flesh of his shoulder muscle. He was relieved to see that the blood had only made a small stain on his trenchcoat. He folded a handkerchief in four and placed it between his shirt and the wound. He knew he daren't risk a hospital. As long as he could get to a pharmacy by nightfall, he felt sure he could deal with the problem himself.

Adam was now only a few kilometres from the French border.

Desperately he began to thumb at any car that passed, no longer bothering with its nationality. Unfortunately there were far fewer cars driving towards the French border than there had been on the road to Frankfurt, and they all ignored his plea. Time was running out when a yellow Citroën drew in to the side of the road.

The woman in the passenger seat wound down the window. The driver leaned across, took a lengthy look at Adam and said in a broad Yorkshire accent, "We're on our way to Dijon. Any use to you, lad?"

"Yes, please," said Adam, relieved that his scruffy appearance had not put them off.

"Then jump in the back with my daughter."

Adam obeyed. The Citroën moved off. Adam looked back, thankful to see an empty road behind him.

"Jim Hardcastle's the name," said the man, who had a large, warm smile perpetually imprinted on his chubby red face. His dark ginger hair was plastered down with Brylcreem and he wore an open-necked shirt. "This is the wife, Betty," he said, gesturing with his elbow towards the woman in the front seat. She turned towards Adam, revealing the same ruddy cheeks and warm smile. "And sitting next to you is our Linda," Jim Hardcastle added. "Just left school and going to work for the local council, aren't you, Linda?" Linda nodded sulkily. Adam stared at the young girl, who could have been attractive but whose first experiments with make-up hadn't worked very well.

"And what's your name, lad?"

"Dudley Hulme," said Adam, recalling the name on his new passport. "Are you on holiday?" he asked, trying to keep his mind off his throbbing shoulder.

"Mixing business with pleasure," said Jim. "But this part of the trip is rather special for Betty and myself. We hired the car to tour Italy, and now we're on our way to the annual conference of the IMF. You may have heard of us." Adam nodded knowingly. "International Mustard Federation. I'm export director for Colman's." Adam wanted to laugh, but because of the pain in his shoulder, managed to keep a straight face.

"This year they've elected me president, the high point of my career in mustard, you might say. Tonight I shall be making a speech of welcome to delegates from all over the world."

"How fascinating," winced Adam, as the car went over a pothole.

"It certainly is. People have no idea how many makes of mustard there are." Jim paused for a second, then said, "One hundred and forty-three. There's no doubt the Frogs make one or two good attempts and the Krauts don't do too badly, but there's still nothing to beat Colman's. British is best after all, I always say. Probably the same in your line of work," said Jim. "By the way, what is your line of work?"

110

"I'm in the army," said Adam.

"What's a soldier doing thumbing a lift on the borders of Switzerland?"

"Can I speak to you in confidence?" asked Adam.

"Mum's the word," said Jim.

"I'm a captain in the Royal Wessex, at present on a NATO exercise," began Adam. "I was dumped off the coast at Brindisi in Italy last Sunday with a false passport and ten English pounds. I have to be back in barracks at Aldershot by midnight Saturday." Mrs. Hardcastle turned to take a more careful look at him.

"So where's the problem in getting back to England?" asked Jim.

"The border officials have been briefed that eight British officers are attempting to get over into France. The Swiss would love to be the ones to pull us in. Only two officers out of twelve made it back to barracks last year," said Adam, warming to his own theme. "Both were promoted within weeks."

"The Swiss," said Jim with disdain. "They never join in a war—happy to fleece both sides at the same time. They won't pick you up, lad, believe me. I'll see to that."

"If you can get me across the border, Mr. Hardcastle, I'm confident I will be able to make it all the way back to Aldershot."

"Consider it done, lad."

THE FUEL INDICATOR was flashing red. "How many more kilometres can we do when that happens?" demanded Romanov.

"About twenty, Comrade Major," said the driver.

"Then we should still make the French border?"

"Perhaps it might be safer to stop and fill up."

"There is no time for safety," said Romanov. "Go faster."

"Yes, Comrade Major," said the driver, who decided it was not the occasion to point out that they would run out of petrol even more quickly if he was made to push the car to its limits. The Mercedes touched 160 kilometres per hour and Romanov relaxed only when he saw a sign saying, "*Rappelle! Douanes 5 km*". Moments later the engine spluttered as it tried helplessly to continue turning over. The sheer momentum of the heavy Mercedes took them another kilometre before the car slowed to a complete stop.

Romanov did not even look at the driver as he jumped out of the car and began running the last three kilometres towards the border.

"I'VE COME UP WITH AN IDEA," said Jim, as they passed a signpost warning drivers that the border was only two kilometres away.

"What's that, sir?" asked Adam, who could now feel his shoulder beating like a tune hammered by a child on a tin drum.

"When it comes to the time for us to present our passports, you put your arm round Linda and start cuddling her. Leave the rest to me."

Linda went scarlet. Adam looked across at the mini-skirted, pink-lipped girl and felt embarrassed by the predicament her father had placed her in.

"Don't argue with me, Dudley," continued Jim confidently. "I promise you what I have in mind will work."

When they reached the Swiss border a few moments later, Adam could see that there were two checkpoints about one hundred yards apart. Drivers were avoiding one line of traffic in which a row was going on between a customs official and an irate lorry driver. Jim drove straight up behind the gesticulating French driver. "Give me your passport, Dudley," he said. Adam handed over the violinist's passport.

The argument continued in front of them. Adam looked out of the back window, waiting for the moment when Romanov would appear. When he turned back, he was relieved to find that the lorry in front of them was being told to pull over to the side and wait. Jim drove quickly up to the customs post. "Get necking, you two," he said.

Adam obeyed, took Linda in his arms and kissed her perfunctorily, one eye still open, watching for Romanov.

"The wife, the daughter and the future son-in-law," said Jim, handing over the four passports.

The official started to check.

"What was all the trouble about, officer?"

"Nothing for you to worry about," said the customs officer, flicking through the passports. "I hope it hasn't inconvenienced you."

"No, no," said Jim. "They didn't even notice," he said, pointing over his shoulder and laughing.

The official handed the passports back and waved them on.

"Sharp-as-mustard-Jim, that's what they call me back in Hull." He looked over his shoulder at Adam. "You can stop that now, Dudley, thank you." Adam felt Linda release him with some reluctance.

She glanced at him shyly, then turned towards her father. "But we still have to go over the French border, don't we?"

"WE HAVE ALREADY BEEN ALERTED to look out for him and I can assure you he hasn't been through this post," said the senior customs officer. "Otherwise one of my men would have spotted him. But if you want to double-check, do so."

Romanov went quickly from officer to officer showing them the photograph of Adam, but none of them could recall anyone resembling him. Valchek joined him a few minutes later and confirmed that Scott was not in any of the cars still waiting to be allowed over the border.

The senior official emerged from his post in the centre of the road. "Any luck?" he asked.

"No," said Romanov glumly. "Could I have missed any of your staff?"

"Doubt it—unless there's a couple of them taking a break in the bar up towards the French border point."

Four customs officers and a French waitress were in the bar as the two Russians made their way to the counter. Romanov took a cup of coffee and a sandwich over to the table where two of the border guards sat. One of them was telling his colleague the trouble he had had with a French lorry driver who was trying to smuggle Swiss watches. Romanov pushed the photograph of Scott across the table.

"Have you seen this man today?"

Neither showed any sign of recognition and the elder returned to his story. Romanov sipped his coffee, and noticed that the younger man's eyes kept returning to the photo. He asked once again if he had seen Scott.

"No, no," said the young officer, a little too quickly.

"How long ago?" Romanov asked quietly.

"It wasn't him," said the officer, sweat now appearing on his forehead.

"If it wasn't him, how long ago wasn't it him?"

The officer hesitated. "Twenty minutes, maybe thirty."

"What make of vehicle?"

The young officer hesitated. "A Citroën, I think."

"Colour?"

"Yellow."

"Other passengers?"

"Three. Looked like a family. Mother, father, daughter. He was in the back with the daughter. The father said they were engaged."

Romanov had no more questions.

JIM HARDCASTLE MANAGED to keep a one-sided conversation going for over an hour. "Naturally," he said, "the IMF holds its annual conference in a different city every year. Last year it was in Denver in Colorado, and next year it'll be in Perth in Australia, so I manage to get around a bit."

"I'm sure you do," said Adam, trying to concentrate on his benefactor's words while his shoulder throbbed on.

"Where in Dijon would you like to be dropped off?" asked Jim as he drove into the outskirts of the town.

"Anywhere near the centre that's convenient for you."

"Just holler when it suits you then," said Jim. "Of course, I always maintain that a meal without mustard . . ."

"Can you drop me on the next corner?" said Adam suddenly.

Jim drew the car up alongside the kerb and Adam kissed Linda on the cheek before getting out. He then shook hands with Mr. and Mrs. Hardcastle.

"Nice to have made your acquaintance," said Jim. "If you should ever be Hull way, look us up." He took a card out of his top pocket and passed it over. "Well, good luck."

As the car moved off Adam watched them disappear. He walked quickly down a side street, relieved to find that all the shops were still open. He began to search for one with a green cross above its door. He had to walk only fifty yards before he spotted one and entered it.

"Do you speak English, by any chance?" he asked the pharmacist.

"Passable, I hope," came back the reply.

"I need some iodine, cotton wool, and a bandage. I fell and bruised my shoulder on a rock," Adam explained.

The man quickly put the order together without showing much interest. "That will be twenty-three francs," he said.

"Will Swiss currency do?"

"Certainly."

"Is there a hotel anywhere nearby?" asked Adam as he paid.

"Round the next corner, on the other side of the square."

Adam thanked him and left. The Hôtel Frantel was, as promised, only a short distance away. He walked up the steps, to find several people waiting at reception. Adam swung his trenchcoat over his bloodstained shoulder and strode past them across the entrance hall as though he were a guest of several days' standing. He followed the sign to the cloakrooms.

He opened the door marked with a wheelchair and found behind it a sizable square room with a high-seated lavatory and a washbasin. Adam locked himself in and let his trenchcoat fall to the ground. Slowly he stripped to the waist. He then ran a basinful of warm water.

He was thankful for the endless first-aid seminars every officer had had to go through. Twenty minutes later the pain had subsided and he even felt comfortable.

He picked up his coat with his right hand and tried to throw it back over his shoulder. The movement caused the icon to fall out of the map pocket and onto the tiled floor. As it hit the ground, Adam feared that it might have broken. He stared down anxiously and then fell to his knees.

The icon had split open like a book.

Chapter Fifteen

When Adam returned to the Hôtel Frantel an hour later few guests would have recognized him as the man who had crept in earlier that afternoon. He wore a new shirt, trousers and tie, and a double-breasted blazer. The trenchcoat had been ditched because the icon fitted snugly into the blazer pocket.

He booked himself into a single room in the name of Dudley Hulme and took the lift to the third floor.

Lawrence picked the phone up even before Adam heard the second ring. "Where are you?" were his first words.

"It's my turn to ask the questions," said Adam. "You must be aware by now that someone on your so-called team has a direct line to the Russians, because it was Romanov and his friends who were waiting for me outside the hotel in Geneva, not your lot."

"We realize that now," said Lawrence.

"We?" said Adam. "Who are we? Because I'm finding it rather hard to know who's on my side."

"You don't believe that . . ."

"When your girlfriend is murdered, and you get chased across Europe, shot at and . . ."

"Shot at?" said Lawrence.

"Yes, your friend Romanov took a shot at me today, hit me in the shoulder. Next time I intend it to be the other way round and it won't be the shoulder."

"There won't be a next time," said Lawrence, "because we'll get you out safely if you'll only let me know where you are."

The memory of Robin's words, "Just be wary of how much you let him know," stopped Adam from telling Lawrence his exact location. There was a long silence before he said, "I'm in Dijon."

"Give me your number and I'll phone you back within the hour."

"No," said Adam, "I'll phone *you* back in an hour."

"Adam, you've got to show some faith in me."

"Now that I know what it is you're all after, I can't afford to trust anybody." Adam replaced the phone and stared down at the icon which lay open on the bed. It wasn't the official appearance of the document that most worried him. It was the date—20 June 1966—that read like a death warrant.

"GOODNIGHT, SIR," SAID THE DOORKEEPER, adding sympathetically, "another late night for you." The senior civil servant acknowledged the doorman by raising his rolled umbrella a few inches. It had indeed been another late night, but at least they had caught up with Scott again. He was beginning to develop quite a respect for the man. Although how they failed to pick him up in Geneva still required a fuller explanation than the one Lawrence Pemberton had supplied the D4 with that afternoon.

He set off at a brisk pace and hailed a passing taxi.

"Malet Street," he told the driver, before getting in the back.

He allowed himself a wry smile as he thought how the D4 had all accepted his plan. It had the double advantage of ensuring enough time for them to get their best men into position, while keeping Scott well out of sight in a deserted hideaway. Lawrence Pemberton had agreed to remain in the office to make sure all the loose ends were tied up and that nothing could go wrong this time.

"Eight shillings, guv'nor," said the taxi driver, as he drew up in Malet Street. He paid and the moment the taxi had rounded the corner he began walking away. In moments he turned into a side road and disappeared down some stone steps to a basement flat. He inserted a key in the lock, turned it quickly, stepped inside and closed the door behind him. In the next twenty minutes he made two telephone calls—one international, one local.

He checked his watch: nearly ten past eight. Scott would be fully briefed by now, he thought. Poor bastard. If he had never opened that envelope the icon would have ended up with its rightful owner.

ON THE HOUR ADAM PHONED, and listened carefully to all Lawrence had to say.

"I'll take one more risk," said Adam. "But if Romanov turns up this time I'll hand over the icon to him personally, and with it a piece of property so valuable that no amount of money the Americans could offer would be sufficient to purchase it back."

When Adam put the phone down, Lawrence and Sir Morris played the conversation back again and again.

"I think 'property' is the key word," said Sir Morris.

"Agreed," said Lawrence, "but what piece of property could be that valuable to both the Russians and the Americans?"

Sir Morris began slowly rotating the globe that stood beside his desk.

"WHAT DOES THAT BUZZ MEAN?" asked Romanov. "We are not running out of petrol again, are we?"

"No, sir," said the chauffeur. "It's a new calling device. It means they expect you to check in."

"Turn round and go back to that petrol station we passed a couple of kilometres back," Romanov said quietly.

"Fill up while I phone Geneva," he said, the moment he saw the petrol station. He ran to the phone box while Valchek still kept a watchful eye out for a yellow Citroën.

"I am answering your signal," said Romanov when he was put through to the second secretary at the Russian embassy.

"We've had another call from Mentor," said the second secretary. "How far are you from Dijon?"

"IT'S AN EMERGENCY," the voice said. "Antarctic is in Dijon and he's found out what's in the icon. He told Pemberton he was in possession of a piece of property so valuable that no amount of money we could offer would be sufficient to purchase it back."

"Indeed," said the voice.

"The British think the important word is property," said the caller.

"They're quite wrong," said the voice on the other end of the line. "It's purchase. The Russian ambassador here in Washington has requested a meeting with the secretary of state on June 20 and he's bringing with him a gold bullion order to the value of over seven hundred million dollars."

"So where does that leave us?"

"On our way to Dijon, so that we can be sure to lay our hands on that icon before the Russians do."

"But I've already agreed to go along with the British plan."

"Try not to forget which side you're on, Commander Busch."

"Yes, sir. But what are we going to do about Antarctic if we get the icon?"

"It's only the icon we're after. Once that's in our possession, Antarctic is expendable."

ADAM HAD DECIDED not to carry out Lawrence's instructions to the letter. He intended to be waiting for them, and not the other way round. He locked the bedroom door and returned to reception, where he paid for the room and the telephone calls he had made.

"Thank you," he said to the receptionist, and turned to leave.

"Dudley!"

Adam froze on the spot.

"Dudley," the voice boomed again. "I almost didn't recognize you in those clothes." A hand thumped him on the shoulder—at least it wasn't the left shoulder, he thought as he stared at Jim Hardcastle, who had Linda at his side.

"I—er—I thought I was spotted in town, so I had to get a change of clothes and keep out of sight for a few hours."

"Why don't you come to the dinner?" said Jim. "No one will see you there."

"Wish I could," said Adam, "but I can't afford to lose any more time."

"Anything I can do to help?" said Jim conspiratorially.

"No, I've got to get to . . . I have a rendezvous just outside the town in less than an hour."

"Wish I could take you there myself," said Jim. "Do anything to help a soldier, but I'm a bit stuck, tonight of all nights."

"I could always take him, Dad," said Linda. She was wearing a tight-fitting black crepe dress that started as low and ended as high as it dared. She looked up hopefully.

"You've only just got your licence, lass. Don't be daft."

"You always treat me like a child when there's something worthwhile to do," came back her immediate response.

Jim hesitated. "How far is this rendezvous?" he asked.

"About five, maybe six miles," said Adam, "but I'll be fine. I can get a taxi easily."

"The lass is right," said Jim, and taking his car keys out of his pocket, he turned to her and said, "but if you ever let on to your mother I'll kill you." Jim took Adam by the hand and shook it furiously.

Linda led Adam away to the car park. "Which direction?" she asked.

"The Auxerre road," said Adam, looking down at the directions Lawrence had dictated to him over the phone.

Linda set off at a slow pace. "I'm very nervous," she said, and she put her hand on Adam's knee.

"Yes, I can tell you are," said Adam. "Don't miss the turning."

Linda swung off the main road onto a country lane while Adam kept his eyes peeled for the building Lawrence had described. It was another two miles before it came into sight.

"Draw in to the side," said Adam, "and turn the lights off."

"At last," said Linda, sounding more hopeful, as she stopped the car.

"Thank you very much," said Adam, as he touched the door handle.

"Is that all I get for risking life and limb?" asked Linda.

"I wouldn't want you to be late for the dinner."

"That dinner will be about as exciting as a dance at the Barnsley Young Conservatives."

"If you stay much longer your life could be in danger," Adam said.

Linda turned ashen. "You're not joking, are you?"

"I wish I was," said Adam. "Now, when I get out of this car you must turn round and go back to the hotel, and never mention this conversation to anyone. You're a fantastic girl," he added, and gave her a long, warm kiss. He then got out of the car and watched her head off back in the direction of Dijon.

He had an hour and a half still to go before they were due, and by then it would be dark. He jogged over to the airfield and studied its burnt-out buildings. It was exactly as Lawrence had described it.

Looking across the runway, he spotted an ideal place to hide while he settled down to wait.

FLIGHT LIEUTENANT ALAN BANKS was thankful that the moon was shining so brightly that night. He circled the little Beaver round the airfield once more, and studied the two runways carefully. The airport had been out of action for such a long time that none of the manuals included a ground plan of it.

"I can make a landing on the north–south runway more easily," Banks said, turning to the SAS captain who crouched in the back with his five men. "How near to that hangar do you want me to go?"

"Stay well clear, at least a couple of hundred yards," came back the reply. "We still don't know what to expect."

The pilot swung the Beaver round to the south and put the nose down. He spotted a burnt-out Spitfire that had been left derelict on the corner of the runway. He descended confidently; as the little plane touched down it bounced along the pitted surface.

The six SAS men stared cautiously out of the side windows. They had been briefed to pick up a lone Englishman called Scott and then get out fast. It sounded easy enough but it couldn't be, otherwise they wouldn't have been called in.

Flight Lieutenant Banks brought the plane to a halt and swung the fuselage round in a full circle ready for a quick getaway. He pressed the button that cut the engines and turned the lights out. The whirring slowed to an eerie whisper. They were early.

Adam watched the new arrivals suspiciously from the cockpit of the Spitfire. He wasn't going to make a run for it across that open ground while the moon shone so brightly. His eyes never left the little unmarked plane as he waited for some clue as to who the occupants might be. A few minutes passed before six men dropped out of the side of the aircraft and lay flat on the tarmac. They were dressed as Lawrence had said they would be, in SAS battle kit, but Adam remained unconvinced when he recalled Romanov's chauffeur's uniform.

The captain raised his hand and the six men began to crawl towards the hangar where Pemberton had said Scott would be waiting. They became more and more confident that Pemberton's warning of an enemy waiting for them was unjustified.

At last a mass of clouds covered the moon and a shadow was thrown across the whole airfield. The SAS captain checked his watch. Five minutes to go before the rendezvous was due. He was the first to reach the door of the hangar and he pushed it open with the palm of his hand. He wiggled in through the gap. A bullet hit him in the forehead even before he had found time to raise his gun.

"Move, laddies," shouted the second-in-command, and the other four were up in a flash, firing in front of them and running for the protection of the building.

As soon as Adam heard the Scottish accent, he jumped out of the cockpit and sprinted across the tarmac towards the little plane, whose propellers were already beginning to turn. He jumped on the wing and

119

climbed in beside the surprised pilot. "I'm Adam Scott, the man you've come to pick up," he shouted.

"I'm Flight Lieutenant Alan Banks, old chap," said the pilot, thrusting out his hand. Only a British officer would shake hands in such a situation, thought Adam, relieved if still terrified.

"We ought to get going," said the pilot. "My orders are to see you get back to England."

"But what about those men?"

"My instructions are to get you out. Their orders are to take care of themselves."

"Let's at least give them a minute," Adam said.

They waited until the propellers were rotating at full speed. Suddenly the firing stopped and Adam could hear his heart thumping.

"We ought to get moving," said the pilot.

"I know," replied Adam, "But there's something else I still need to know as well."

Years of night marches made it possible for Adam to see the dark figure running towards them long before the pilot.

"*Get going!*" he said.

The pilot moved the joystick forward and the plane started moving slowly down the crumbling runway. Suddenly the running figure was firing long bursts at them. The pilot looked back to see a tall man whose fair hair shone in the moonlight.

"Faster, man, faster," said Adam.

"The throttle's full out," said the pilot, as Romanov's bullets began ripping into the fuselage.

By then the plane was going faster than the man and Adam let out a shout of delight when it left the ground and started to climb steadily. "Where to now?" he asked, relief flooding through his body.

"I had hoped England, but I'm afraid the answer is as far as I can manage. Look at the fuel gauge," said Alan Banks, putting his forefinger on a little white indicator that pointed to "empty". "Those bullets hit my fuel tank."

Within moments the propellers on the left side of the aircraft spun to a halt. "I am going to have to put her down in a field." Then he pointed to a large expanse of land. "Hold on tight," he said, as the plane spiralled down. Adam found himself gripping the side of his seat.

"Relax, these Beavers have landed on far worse places than this," said Banks, as the wheels touched brown earth. "Damn mud! I hadn't anticipated that." He cursed as the wheels lost their grip and the plane nosedived forward. A few seconds passed before Adam realized he was still alive but upside down, swinging from his seat belt.

"What do I do next?" he asked the pilot, but there was no reply. He tried to get his bearings. Once he was able to grip the side of the fuselage he undid the belt and collapsed onto the roof of the plane.

He picked himself up, relieved to find nothing was broken, and clambered out of the plane, glad to feel the safety of the ground. He found Alan Banks some yards in front of the aircraft, flat on his back.

"Are you all right?" Adam asked.

"I'm OK. Sorry about the landing, old chap, have to admit it wasn't up to scratch. We must try again some time." He slowly sat up.

"Can you walk?" Adam asked.

"Yes, I think so," said Alan, gingerly lifting himself up. "Damn," he said, "it's only my ankle, but it's going to slow me down. You'd better get going without me. That bunch back there with the arsenal can only be about thirty minutes behind us. Which lot are chasing us, by the way?"

"The Russians," said Adam, who was beginning to wonder if perhaps there was a second enemy. He touched the icon instinctively and was relieved to find it was still in place. The pilot's words had only made him more determined to get back to England.

"Which way?" asked Adam.

The pilot looked up at the Great Bear. "I'll head east, seems appropriate, so you'd better go west, old fellow. Nice to have made your acquaintance," and with that he limped off.

"I'M NOT SURE HOW much longer I can last, Comrade Major."

"You must try to hold on, Valchek. We cannot afford to stop now," said Romanov. "I know that plane isn't far. I saw it falling out of the sky."

"At least let me die a peaceful death on the side of the road, rather than endure the agony of this car."

Romanov glanced across at his colleague, who had been shot in the abdomen. Valchek's hands were covered in blood, and his shirt and trousers were drenched as he clutched his stomach like a child about to be sick. The driver had been shot dead.

Romanov had Mentor to thank for ensuring that they had been there first. But he must now quickly warn him that someone else was briefing the Americans. Romanov felt some satisfaction in having tricked the Americans into turning their fire on the British.

Valchek groaned. "Let's turn off into the forest," he begged. "Leave me and let me die in peace."

Romanov noticed a gap in the trees ahead of him. He switched his lights onto full beam and swung off the road onto a dirt track and drove as far as he could until the thicket became too dense. He switched off the headlights and ran round the car to open the door.

Valchek could only manage two or three steps before he slumped to

121

the ground. Romanov bent down and helped him to ease himself up against the trunk of a large tree.

"Do not waste any more of your time on me, Comrade Major. You should go while you still have Scott in your sights."

Romanov frowned. "But if the Americans were to find you, they might force you to talk."

"You know better than that, comrade."

Romanov rose and, after a moment's thought, ran back to the car.

The bullet from the 9mm Makarov went straight through Valchek's temple and blew away one side of his head. He slumped to the ground. He would probably not have talked, but this was not a time for taking unnecessary risks.

Chapter Sixteen

Adam lay flat on his stomach in the bottom of the barge as it progressed at a stately pace down the river.

The bargee stood behind the wheel counting the three hundred Swiss francs for a second time. It was more than he could normally hope to earn in a month.

Suddenly, in the distance, Adam heard what sounded like a gunshot. He listened anxiously for any other unnatural sounds, but all he could hear was the gentle splash of the water against the barge's hull. Though they were not moving very fast, he was grateful to be resting. He touched the icon, something he found himself doing every few minutes since he had discovered its secret.

The bargee's eyes never left him for long. The man smiled at Adam, took both hands off the wheel and placed them by the side of his head to indicate that Adam should sleep. But Adam shook his head. Midnight had passed and he wanted to be away long before first light.

Adam's shoulder still ached relentlessly. He walked up to the wheel. The river was wider now than when he had first leaped on board.

Adam pointed in the direction they were moving. "*Quelle ville?*"

The bargee removed his pipe. "*Ville? Ce n'est pas une ville, c'est Sombernon,*" he said, and put the stem back between his teeth.

Adam returned to his place in the bow. Curling up against the side of the boat he rested his head on some old rope and allowed his eyes to close.

ANOTHER HOUR PASSED before Romanov spotted a figure limping up a hill only a few hundred yards from the main road. A broad smile came over Romanov's face when he realized he could reach him long before he could hope to reach the road. When Romanov was within a few yards of him, Flight Lieutenant Banks turned round.

Romanov left him thirty minutes later, hidden behind a tree with a broken neck. He couldn't waste any more time trying to discover which way Scott was heading.

"YOU KNOW SCOTT better than any of us," said Sir Morris, "and you still have no feel as to where he might be now, or what he might do next, do you?"

"No, sir," admitted Lawrence. "The only thing we know for certain is that he has an appointment for a medical on Monday afternoon, but somehow I don't think he'll keep it."

Sir Morris ignored the comment. "But someone was able to get to Scott, even though we didn't call a meeting of the D4," he continued. "That icon must hold a secret that we still haven't even begun to appreciate."

"And if Scott is still alive," said Lawrence, "nothing is going to convince him now that we're not to blame."

"And if we're not, who is?" asked Sir Morris. "Because someone was so desperate to discover our next move that they must have taken one hell of a risk during the last twenty-four hours. Unless, of course, it was you," said Sir Morris.

"Even if it was me," said Lawrence, his eyes resting on a picture of the young queen which stood on the corner of his master's desk, "it doesn't explain how the Americans got there as well."

"Oh, that's simple," said Sir Morris. "Busch has been briefing them direct. I never doubted he would from the moment he joined us. What I hadn't anticipated was how far the Americans would go without keeping us informed. Now, do you think Scott can still be alive?"

"Yes, I do," said Lawrence. "I have every reason to believe that the man who ran to our waiting plane was Scott. The French police have informed us that our plane crashed in a field twelve miles north of Dijon but neither Scott nor the pilot were to be found."

"And if the French reports on what took place at the airfield are accurate," said Sir Morris, "Romanov escaped. Do you think it possible that the Russians have caught up with Scott and are now in possession of the icon?"

"Yes, sir, I fear that is quite possible," Lawrence said. "But we can't be sure. However, the monitoring service at Cheltenham picked up extra signals traffic to all Soviet embassies during the night and, most revealing of all, the active measures section of the KGB, First Chief Directorate, has booked pages of advertising space in newspapers right across Europe and America."

IF IT HADN'T BEEN for the ceaseless throbbing in his shoulder, Adam might not have woken so quickly. The barge had suddenly swung through ninety degrees and started heading east. Adam indicated to the bargee that as the river was far wider now he should ease them nearer to the bank so he could jump off. The old man shrugged his shoulders, pretending not to understand, as the barge drifted on.

Adam looked over the side and despite the dim light could see that the river was quite shallow. Taking the icon out of his blazer pocket he held it high above his head and leaped into the water. It came up to his waist.

He waded to the nearest bank, the icon still held above the water, and clambered up onto the towpath. He was soon able to distinguish the Plough and plot a course due west. After an hour of soggy jogging he began to make out a light in the distance about a mile away. He started to squelch his way towards it.

As he got nearer he could see, in the first rays of the morning sun, that it was a large cottage. A little cobbled path led up to a half open wooden door. Adam tapped gently with the knocker.

The door was pulled back by a woman of perhaps thirty, with rosy cheeks and an ample waist, who couldn't mask her surprise when she saw Adam.

Adam smiled. "*Anglais*," he told her, and added, "I fell in the canal."

The woman burst out laughing and beckoned Adam into her kitchen. He walked in to find a man, evidently dressed for milking. The farmer looked up and when he saw Adam he joined in the friendly laughter.

When the woman noticed that Adam was dripping all over her spotless floor she quickly handed him a towel from the rack above the fire and said, "*Enlevez-moi ça*," pointing to Adam's trousers.

Adam turned to the farmer for guidance, but his host only nodded his agreement and mimed pulling down his own trousers.

Adam removed his trousers, shoes and socks, but the farmer's wife didn't budge until he had finally removed his underclothes and wrapped the towel round his waist. She stared at the large bandage on his shoulder but then quickly picked up everything except his blazer and took them over to the sink while he stood by the fire and dried himself.

The farmer beckoned him to join him at the table, pouring a large glass of milk for his guest and another for himself. A delicious aroma arose from the pan where the farmer's wife was frying a thick slice of bacon cut from a joint hanging in the smoky recess of the chimney.

The farmer raised his glass of milk high in the air.

"Winston Churchill," he toasted. Adam took a long gulp from his own glass and then raised it dramatically.

"Charles de Gaulle," he said, and finished off the warm milk as if it had been his first pint at the local pub.

The farmer's wife placed in front of Adam a large plate of sizzling eggs and bacon, and he began to devour the freshly cooked food which was the first meal he'd managed since the dinner he'd ordered at Robin's expense.

The farmer left for work and when Adam had finished the last scrap of food the farmer's wife poured him a large, steaming cup of coffee.

He tapped the blazer pocket almost automatically to make sure the icon was still safely in place, then he pulled it out and studied it. He turned it over, hesitated, and then pressed the silver crown hard. The icon split in half like a book revealing two tiny hinges on the inside.

He glanced up at the farmer's wife, who was setting up an ironing board by the side of the stove and showed no interest in Adam's discovery.

Once again he stared down at the inside of the icon which was now laid flat on the table in front of him. The complete surface was covered by parchment, which was glued to the wood. Adam swivelled it round so that he could study it more clearly. The scrawled signatures in black ink, and the seals, gave it the look of a legal document. Adam had been surprised originally to discover it was written in French until he came to the date on the bottom—20 June 1867—and remembered from his military history lectures at Sandhurst that long after Napoleonic times most international agreements continued to be conducted in French. Adam began to read the script again slowly.

His French was not good enough to enable him to translate more than a few words. Under *Etats Unis* William Seward's bold hand was scrawled across a crest of an eagle. Next to it was the signature of Edward de Stoeckel below a crown that mirrored the silver ornament embedded in the back of the icon. It had to be some form of agreement executed between the Russians and the Americans in 1867.

He then searched for other words that would help to explain the significance of the document. On one line he identified, *"Sept million deux cent mille dollars d'or (7.2 mille)"* and on another *"Sept cent douze million huit cent mille dollars d'or (712.8M) le 20 Juin, 1966."*

His eyes rested on a calendar hanging from a nail on the wall. It was Friday, 17 June 1966. In three more days the document would no longer have any legal validity. No wonder the two most powerful nations on earth seemed desperate to get their hands on it.

Adam wondered how the icon had ever fallen into the hands of Goering. He must have bequeathed it to his father unknowingly—for had he realized the true importance of what was hidden inside it, he would surely have been able to bargain for his freedom.

"Voilà, voilà," said the farmer's wife, waving her hands as she placed warm socks, pants and trousers in front of Adam. He quickly snapped

125

the icon closed, and then studied the masterpiece carefully. So skilfully had the wood been cut that he could no longer see the join.

Adam thought of the words in his father's letter: "But if you open it only to discover its purpose is to involve you in some dishonourable enterprise, be rid of it without a second thought." He did not need to guess how his father would have reacted in these circumstances. He replaced the icon in his pocket and began to get dressed.

He could think of no adequate way of thanking the farmer's wife for her hospitality and her lack of suspicion or inquisitiveness, so he took her gently by the shoulders and kissed her on the cheek. She blushed and handed him a small plastic bag containing three apples, some bread and a large piece of cheese. She led him to the open door.

Adam walked outside into his other world.

Chapter Seventeen
THE WHITE HOUSE, WASHINGTON DC   18 JUNE 1966

"I don't want to be the first damn president in the history of the United States to hand back an American state rather than found one."

"I appreciate that, Mr. President," said the secretary of state. "But—"

"Where do we stand on this, legally?"

"Abraham Brunweld, the leading authority on documents of this period, confirms that the terms of the lease are binding on both sides. He looked at our copy of the treaty, which is deep in the vaults of the Pentagon. Since the Yalta Conference, it has never seen the light of day. The treaty was signed on behalf of Russia by their foreign minister, Edward de Stoeckel, and for the US by the then secretary of state, William Seward."

"Can this agreement still be valid today?" asked the president, turning to his chief legal officer.

"It certainly can, sir," said the attorney general. "But only if the Russians can produce their copy of the document. For over fifty years, we've believed the Russians' copy was destroyed at the time of the Revolution. Brezhnev must have come across something within the last month that convinced him that their copy had only been mislaid. If they produce their copy, the UN and the international court at The Hague would have no choice but to support the Russian claim."

"God damn it, is there a precedent for this kind of stupidity by a head of state?"

"The British," chipped in the secretary of state, "will be facing a similar problem in 1999 when ownership of the New Territories of Hong Kong returns to the Chinese. They have already accepted the reality of the situation and have made it clear to the Chinese government that they are willing to come to an agreement."

"Do I have any alternative to accepting the situation?" asked the president.

"Short of military action to prevent the Soviets claiming what they will rightfully see as theirs, no, sir," replied the secretary of state.

"So one Johnson buys the land from the Russians in 1867 and another has to sell it back in 1966. Why did Seward and the president ever agree to such a damn cockamamey idea in the first place?"

"At the time," said the attorney general, removing his spectacles, "the purchase price of the land in question was seven point two million dollars and the Russians agreed to purchase it back at ninety-nine times its original value or, in real terms, seven hundred and twelve point eight million dollars in gold bullion. Ironically, Seward was proud of the fact that he had demanded such a high premium in the repayment clause. At the time he had every reason to believe it would be impossible to repay. But years of inflation have made the asking price cheap. The Russians have already lodged the full amount in a New York bank to prove it."

"The land is worth that amount in annual oil revenue alone," said the president, looking out of the Oval Office window towards the Washington Monument. "Not to mention the chaos it's going to create in this country if the Russians do get their hands on their copy of the treaty. Don't forget I was the president who asked Congress to spend billions of dollars putting the early-warning system in there."

Neither adviser felt able to contradict his leader.

"So what are the British doing about all this?"

"Playing it close to the chest, as usual, Mr. President. It's an English national who is thought to be in possession of the Russian copy of the treaty at the moment and they still seem confident that they will get their hands on him and the icon before the Russians do."

"Meanwhile, we just sit and wait for the Soviets to move seven hundred and twelve million dollars of gold from their New York bank to the US Treasury before midnight on Monday?"

"They must also deliver their original copy of the agreement to me at the same time," said the secretary of state. "And they have only sixty hours left to do that."

Chapter Eighteen

After leaving the cottage, Adam had walked to the nearest small town. While it was still so early he felt safe jogging towards the "*centre ville*", but as soon as the early-morning workers began to appear on the streets, he opted to look for somewhere to hide while he considered his next move. He came to a halt outside a multistorey car park and decided he was unlikely to find a better place.

He ran down the steps to the lowest level of the car park, which was badly lit and almost empty. Two cars were parked in the far corner, and the thick layer of dust suggested that they had been there for some time. He crouched down behind one of them and began to plan how he could reach the coast by nightfall.

He was deep in thought when he heard a scraping noise that made him jump. Out of the gloom a man appeared, pulling behind him a plastic dustbin full of rubbish. As he came nearer his eyes searched slowly round the area for more rubbish, but he didn't notice Adam tucked away behind the furthest car. Satisfied that his task was completed, he dragged the dustbin across the floor and pushed it outside. After about two minutes, he returned and pulled open a door that Adam hadn't previously noticed. He took off his dirty, long brown coat and replaced it with a grey one. He then disappeared through the exit.

Adam waited for some time before he stood up and crept to the little door. He pulled it open, removed the long brown coat and headed back to his place in the corner. He ducked down as the first cars of the morning arrived. A short dapper man in a smart pinstripe suit and carrying a briefcase jumped out of a car and proceeded towards the exit. Adam waited until he was gone before he stood up and tried on the brown coat over his blazer.

For the next hour he watched the cars as they continued to arrive at irregular intervals. All the owners carefully locked their car doors before disappearing.

When he heard ten o'clock strike in the distance Adam decided that there was nothing to be gained by hanging around any longer. He crept out from behind the car and began to make his way towards the exit, when a British-registered Rover swung round the corner and nearly ran him down. He jumped to one side to let the car pass but it screeched to a halt beside him and the driver wound down his window.

"All—right—park—here?" the driver asked, emphasizing each word in an English accent.

"*Oui, monsieur*," said Adam.

"Other—floors—marked—*privée*," the man continued, as if addressing a complete moron. "Anywhere?" His arm swept round the floor.

"*Oui*," repeated Adam, "bert ay merst paak you," he added, fearing he sounded too much like Peter Sellers.

"Fine," said the man. He got out of the car, and handed Adam his keys and a ten franc note.

"*Merci*," said Adam, pocketing the note and touching his forehead with his hand. "*A quelle—heure—retournez—vous?*" he asked, playing the man at his own game.

"One hour at most," said the man as he reached the exit. Adam waited by the car for a few minutes but the man did not come back. He climbed into the driver's seat, switched on the ignition and checked the fuel gauge: a little over half full. He drove the car up the ramp and out onto the road, looking for a "*Toutes Directions*" sign. Once he had found one, it was only minutes before he was out of the town and travelling up the N6 to Paris.

He opened the bag the farmer's wife had given him and took out an apple and a piece of cheese. His mind began to drift to Heidi, as it had so often in the past two days.

If only he had never opened the letter . . .

WHEN ADAM FINALLY REACHED the outskirts of Paris, he proceeded to the Boulevard de l'Hôpital. He had decided he would abandon the vehicle in a large public car park: with any luck it might be days before anyone came across it.

He drove down the Rue de Rivoli and turned into Place André Malraux. He could hardly have picked a better place, as it was packed with foreign cars.

Adam backed the Rover into the furthest corner of the square. He then wolfed down the last piece of cheese, hid the brown coat in the boot, and locked the car. He was only a few yards away from it when he saw a young policeman checking the Rover's numberplate and speaking into an intercom. Adam inched slowly away. He only needed to manage another six or seven paces before he would be lost in the crowd.

Five, four, three, two. Just one more step . . . "Alors!" screamed the lady on whose foot Adam had stepped.

"I'm so sorry," said Adam involuntarily, in English. The policeman immediately looked up and stared, then shouted something into the intercom and began running towards him.

He swung round quickly and sprinted towards the exit. The square was full of tourists and Adam found it hard to pick up any speed through the dense crowd. He could hear the policeman's whistle a few paces behind him. He ran across the Rue de Rivoli, through an archway and into another large square.

By then a second policeman was coming, from his right, leaving him with no choice but to run up the steps in front of him. When he reached the top he turned to see at least three other policemen in close pursuit. He threw himself through the swing doors and past a group of Japanese tourists who were surrounding the Rodin statue that stood in the hallway. He charged on, past a startled ticket collector and up the long marble staircase. "*Monsieur, monsieur, votre billet?*" he heard shouted in his wake.

At the top of the staircase he turned right and ran into the Impressionist Room—Monet, Manet, Courbet—desperately looking for any way out. On into the Eighteenth Century—Fragonard, Goya, Watteau—but still no sign of an exit. Through the great arch into the Seventeenth Century—Murillo, Van Dyck, Poussin—as people stopped looking at the pictures and turned their attention to what was causing such a commotion. Adam ran on into a huge square room with three exits. He slowed momentarily to decide which would be his best bet and became aware that the room was full of Russian icons. He came to a halt at an empty display case. "*Nous regrettons que ce tableau soit soumis à la restauration.*"

The first policeman entered the large room. There were now only two exits from which to choose. Adam swung right, only to see another policeman bearing straight down on him. Left: two more.

He came to a halt in the middle of the Icon Room at the Louvre, his hands raised above his head. He was surrounded by policemen, their guns drawn.

Chapter Nineteen

Sir Morris picked up the phone on his desk.

"An urgent call from Paris, sir," said his secretary.

"Thank you, Tessa." He picked up the phone and listened carefully as his brain quickly translated the exciting news.

"*Merci, merci,*" he said to his opposite number at the French Foreign Office. "We will be back in touch as soon as we have made all the necessary arrangements to collect him. But for now, please don't let him out of your sight." Sir Morris listened for a few moments before he said, "And if he has any possessions on him, please keep them safely under lock and key. Thank you once again." His secretary took down every word of the conversation in shorthand—as she had done for the past seventeen years.

ONCE THE POLICE HAD SNAPPED the handcuffs on Adam and marched him off to a waiting car, he was surprised how relaxed they became. Once in the car, he noticed that there was a police car in front and yet another behind. Two motorcycle outriders led the little motorcade away. Adam felt more like visiting royalty than a criminal who was wanted for two murders, two car thefts and travelling under false identification. Was it possible that at last someone had worked out that he was innocent?

130

When Adam arrived at the *Sûreté*, he was immediately ordered to empty all his pockets. One wristwatch, one apple, his remaining traveller's cheques, eight francs, and one British passport in the name of Dudley Hulme. The inspector asked him politely to strip to his vest and pants. Once Adam had done so, the inspector carefully checked every pocket of the blazer, even the lining. He hadn't found what he was looking for.

"Do you have anything else in your possession?" the officer asked in slow, precise English.

"No," was all Adam replied.

"You must be dressed," the inspector said abruptly.

Adam put on his shirt, jacket and trousers but the inspector kept his tie and shoelaces.

"All your things will be returned to you when you leave," the inspector explained. Adam nodded as he slipped on his shoes, which flapped uncomfortably when he walked. He was accompanied to a cell and locked in. It had a small wooden table with two wooden chairs, a single bed and one small window. He took off his jacket and lay down on the bed. At least it was an improvement on anything he had slept on for the past two nights, he reflected. Could it have been only two nights ago that he slept on the floor of Robin's hotel room in Geneva?

As the minutes ticked by, he made only one decision: that when the inspector returned, he would demand to see a lawyer.

When an officer eventually appeared half an hour later, he was carrying a tray laden with hot soup, a roll, a steak with all the trimmings and a plastic cup filled to the brim with red wine. Adam wondered if this was simply his last meal before the guillotine. He followed the officer to the door.

"I demand to speak to a lawyer," he said emphatically, but the policeman only shrugged. "*Je ne comprends pas*," he said, and slammed the door behind him.

SIR MORRIS TOLD THEM his news and then studied each of them round the table carefully. He would never have called the D4 if he hadn't felt sure that Adam was at last in safe hands. Matthews continued to show no emotion, Busch was unusually silent, while Snell looked almost relaxed for a change. Lawrence was the only one who seemed genuinely pleased.

"The French police have Scott locked up," announced Sir Morris, "and I have already contacted Colonel Pollard, our military attaché at the embassy. He will take Scott back to be debriefed at our embassy." Sir Morris turned towards his Number Two. "You will fly over to Paris tonight and conduct the debriefing yourself."

"Yes, sir," said Lawrence, looking up at his boss with a smile.

Sir Morris nodded. A cool lot, he considered, as he stared round the table wondering which one of them it was who served two masters.

"Good. I don't think I shall need any of you again today," he said as he rose from his chair.

Mentor smiled as Sir Morris left the room. His task had already been completed. So simple when you can read shorthand upside down.

A BLACK JAGUAR bearing CD plates arrived at police headquarters a few minutes earlier than expected. The inspector, who was standing on the steps as Pollard jumped out of the car, looked at the flapping Union Jack on the bonnet and considered the whole exercise was becoming rather melodramatic.

Pollard, a short, thickset man dressed in a dark suit, regimental tie and carrying a rolled umbrella, looked like so many of those Englishmen who refuse to acknowledge that they could possibly be abroad.

The inspector took Pollard directly through to the little room where Adam had been incarcerated.

"Pollard's the name, Colonel Pollard. British military attaché stationed here in Paris. Sorry you've been put through this ordeal, old fellow, but a lot of paperwork had to be completed to get you out. Bloody red tape."

"I understand," said Adam, shaking the colonel by the hand.

"Still, the problem's been sorted out now," continued the colonel. "I know you'll be relieved to hear that the French police won't be laying any charges."

The colonel didn't know just how relieved Adam did feel.

In the hall Adam had to identify and sign for his personal belongings. He put them all in his pocket except for the watch, which he slipped over his wrist, and his shoelaces, which he quickly inserted and tied. He wasn't surprised they didn't return Dudley Hulme's passport.

"Don't let's hang around too long, old fellow," said the colonel, beginning to sound a little anxious.

"I'm just as keen to get out of this place as you are," said Adam. He followed Colonel Pollard and the inspector out to the waiting Jaguar. A chauffeur held the door open for him; Adam laughed.

"Something funny, old fellow?" asked the colonel.

"No. It's just that the last chauffeur who was doing that for me didn't look quite as friendly."

Adam climbed into the back of the Jaguar and the colonel slipped in beside him.

"Back to the embassy," said Pollard, and the car moved off briskly.

Adam stared in horror at the flapping Union Jack.

132

Chapter Twenty

When Adam awoke he was naked, and his arms and legs were bound tightly to a chair with nylon cord.

When he looked up all he could see was Colonel Pollard standing over him. The moment the colonel was satisfied that Adam had regained consciousness he turned and left the room.

Adam turned his head to see all his clothes laid out neatly on a bed at the far side of the bare room. He tried to manoeuvre the chair, but he could barely manage to make it wobble from side to side, and after several minutes had advanced only a few inches towards the door. He switched his energies to trying to loosen the cords round his wrists, rubbing them up and down against the wood of the slats, but his arms were bound so tightly that he could only manage the slightest friction.

The door swung open. Adam looked up as Romanov strode through, followed by another man whom Adam didn't recognize. The second man was clutching what looked like a cigar box as he took his place somewhere behind Adam. Pollard followed him, carrying a plastic sheet.

Romanov looked at Adam and smiled, enjoying his humiliation. "My name is Alexander Petrovich Romanov," he announced with only a slight accent.

"Or Emmanuel Rosenbaum," said Adam, staring at his adversary closely.

"I am only sorry that we are unable to shake hands," Romanov added. "But I felt certain precautions were necessary. First, I should like to congratulate you on having eluded me for so long, but as you will now realize my source in London can work every bit as quickly as your friend Lawrence Pemberton."

"Your source?" said Adam.

"Don't be naive. You must be painfully aware by now that you're in no position to be asking questions." He turned to Pollard and said sharply, "Put Captain Scott back in the centre of the room. He seems to have managed to move at least a foot in his getaway attempt."

Pollard did as he was bid, first spreading the plastic sheet on the floor, then manoeuvring Adam till the chair was at its centre.

"Thank you," said Romanov. "I think you have already met our Colonel Pollard," he continued. "That's not his real name, of course, and indeed he's not a real colonel either, but that's what he always wanted to be, so when the opportunity arose, we happily obliged. In fact he did serve in the British army, but I fear that he entered the service of king and country as a private soldier and left it some eighteen years later, still as a private soldier.

"I confess," continued Romanov, "our mistake in flying the Union Jack upside down was lax, but we must be thankful that you did not spot it until the car doors were safely locked. And now I think the time has come for you to be introduced to our Dr. Stavinsky."

Stavinsky stood immediately in front of Adam, the cigar box still tucked under his arm, and seemed to be sizing him up. Adam stared at the diminutive figure in the badly creased grey suit.

"It is a pleasure to make your acquaintance, Captain Scott," he began, his thin lips parted in a grin. "You could of course make our association very short by simply letting me have one piece of information. In truth"—he let out a small sigh—"I only require to know the whereabouts of the Tsar's Icon."

Adam didn't reply.

"So, it seems I must follow the normal procedure in such circumstances. You may have wondered," added Stavinsky as if it were an afterthought, "why I am carrying a Cuban cigar box. When I was a chemistry student at the University of Moscow I specialized in one particular aspect of the science—Scientific Interrogation."

Adam feigned indifference as he tried not to recall his worst days in the hands of the Chinese.

"Once I had been introduced to the 'cigar box'," continued Stavinsky, "I became enthralled. I could not wait to experiment." He paused to see what effect he was having on Scott, and was disappointed to be met by the same impassive stare.

"Still no response, Captain Scott, but I am in no hurry. Especially as I suspect, in your case, the whole operation may take a little longer than usual, which I confess will only add to my enjoyment. So I will ask you once and once only before I open the box. Where is the Tsar's Icon?"

Adam spat at Stavinsky.

"Not only ill-mannered," remarked Stavinsky, "but also stupid. Because in a very short time you will be desperate for any liquid we might be kind enough to offer you."

Stavinsky placed the cigar box on the floor and opened it slowly.

"First, I offer," he said, like a conjurer in front of a child, "a six-volt nickel-cadmium battery. Second, a small pulse generator. Third, two lengths of wire with electrodes attached. Fourth, a tube of collodion glue. And finally, two syringes and a phial, which I shall not require unless it becomes necessary for us to progress to stage two in our little experiment, or even stage three."

Stavinsky placed everything in a straight line on the floor in front of Adam.

"Now, a few details about the nervous system. By sending a small electrical impulse to the end of a synapse, it is possible to pass on a large electrical message to thousands of other nerves within a fraction of a second. This causes an electric shock. In the Moscow school this is known as stage one and there is no necessity for you to experience this if you are now willing to tell me where I can find the Tsar's Icon."

Adam remained impassive.

"I fear we will have to move from the theoretical to the practical."

Adam began reciting to himself the thirty-seven plays of Shakespeare. How delighted his old English master would have been to learn that after all these years Adam could still recall them: "Henry VI part one, Henry VI part two, Henry VI part three, Richard II . . ."

Stavinsky picked up the collodion glue and smeared two lumps of it on Adam's chest.

". . . Comedy of Errors, Titus Andronicus, The Taming of the Shrew . . ."

The Russian attached the two electrodes to the glue, screwed the wires to the six-volt battery, and connected it to the tiny pulse generator.

". . . Two Gentlemen of Verona, Love's Labour's Lost, Romeo and Juliet . . ."

Without warning, Stavinsky pressed down the handle of the generator for two seconds, during which time Adam received a two-hundred volt shock. He screamed as the volts forced their way to every part of his body. But the sensation was over in a moment.

"Do feel free to let us know how exactly you feel. You are in a soundproof room, and therefore you won't be disturbing anyone else in the building."

Adam ignored the comment and, gripping the side of the chair, mumbled, ". . . Richard III, Midsummer Night's Dream, King John . . ."

Stavinsky pressed the plunger down for another two seconds. Adam felt the pain instantly. The moment it was over he felt violently nauseated, but he managed to remain conscious.

"Impressive. You have definitely qualified to enter stage two, from which you can be spared immediately by answering one simple question. Where is the Tsar's Icon?"

Adam's mouth had become so dry that he couldn't speak.

Stavinsky turned towards the door. "Do go and fetch the captain some water, Colonel."

"The Merchant of Venice, Henry IV part one, Henry IV part two . . ."

A moment later Pollard was back, and a bottle was thrust into Adam's mouth. He gulped half the contents down.

"Mustn't overdo it. You might need some more later. But that won't be necessary if you let me know where the icon is."

Adam spat towards his adversary.

Stavinsky slapped Adam hard across the face with the back of his hand. Adam's head slumped.

"You give me no choice but to advance to stage two," said Stavinsky. He looked towards Romanov, who nodded. Stavinsky's thin lips parted in another smile. "After a lifetime of dedicated research my professor came up with an ingenious solution known as 'M'. If you inject 'M' into the nervous system, messages can be transmitted to all your nerves many times more efficiently, thus creating a far more interesting effect."

". . . Much Ado About Nothing, Henry V, Julius Caesar . . ."

"I see you are determined that I should proceed," said Stavinsky, removing a syringe from the floor and jabbing its needle into a phial, half filling it.

He moved behind Adam. "I am now going to give you a lumbar puncture which, if you attempt to move, will paralyse you from the neck down for life. The injection will not kill you because, as you already know, that is not in our best interest."

Adam didn't move a muscle as he felt the syringe go into his back. "As You Like . . ." he began. Then excruciating pain swept his body, and suddenly, blessedly, he felt nothing.

When he came round there was no way of telling how much time had passed. His eyes slowly focused on his tormentor pacing up and down the room impatiently. Seeing Adam's eyes open, he stopped, smiled, and walked over to the chair. "As I promised, a far more interesting sensation is awaiting you."

". . . Troilus and Cressida, All's Well That Ends Well . . ."

As the handle plunged down the volts seemed to find their way to every nerve ending in his body. Adam let out such a scream that if they had not been in a soundproofed room anyone within a mile would have heard him. Stavinsky and Pollard rushed forward to the chair and quickly undid the nylon cords. Adam fell on his hands and knees, shaking and vomiting uncontrollably.

"Couldn't afford to let you choke to death, could we?" said Stavinsky. As soon as the sickness subsided, he threw Adam back onto the chair and tied him up again.

"Where is the Tsar's Icon?" shouted Stavinsky.

". . . Measure for Measure, Othello, King Lear . . ." Adam said, his voice now trembling.

"You are a brave man, Scott," said Romanov, "but this is madness. Just tell me where the icon is and I will send Stavinsky away."

". . . Macbeth, Antony and Cleopatra . . ."

Romanov let out a sigh and nodded. Stavinsky pushed the plunger down once again. Adam screamed again, as he felt the volts reach the millions of little nerve endings in his body. When once more he had been released, he lay on the floor. Stavinsky stared down at him. "Most impressive, Captain Scott, you have qualified for stage three."

WHEN LAWRENCE ARRIVED at Orly Airport that evening he was looking forward to a quiet dinner with Adam at the ambassador's residence. He was met at the barrier by the real Colonel Pollard.

"How is he?" were Lawrence's first words.

"I hoped you were going to tell us," said Pollard. Lawrence stopped in his tracks and stared at the tall, thin soldier.

"What do you mean?" said Lawrence.

"Simply that I followed your instructions to the letter and went to pick up Scott at the *Sûreté*. When I arrived I was informed that he had been taken away twenty minutes before by someone else using my name. We contacted your office immediately but as you were already en route the ambassador ordered me straight to the airport while he phoned Sir Morris."

Lawrence staggered and nearly fell. The colonel came quickly to his side. He didn't understand what Lawrence meant when he said, "He's bound to believe it's me."

WHEN ADAM REGAINED consciousness, Romanov stood alone in front of him.

"Sometimes," said the Russian, continuing as if Adam had never passed out, "a man is too proud to show lack of resolution in front of the torturer or indeed one of his own countrymen, especially a traitor. That is why I have removed Stavinsky and the colonel from our presence. Now, tell me where you have put the icon."

"Why should I?" said Adam belligerently. "It's legally mine."

"Not so, Captain Scott. What you picked up from the bank is the priceless original painted by Rublev, which belongs to the USSR. And if that icon were to appear in any auction house or gallery in the world, we would immediately claim it as a national treasure. For over fifty years the Soviet Union has had only a copy."

Adam's eyes opened wide in disbelief as Romanov removed from the inside pocket of his overcoat an icon of St. George and the Dragon. Romanov turned it over, and Adam registered the significance of the missing crown.

"Like you," continued Romanov, "I only have this one on loan—but if you tell me where the original is, I will release you and give you the copy in exchange for the original. No one will be any the wiser and you'll still be able to make yourself a worthwhile profit."

"Old lamps for new," said Adam with a sneer.

Romanov's eyes narrowed menacingly. "Surely you realize, Scott, that unless you return the icon you are going to cause considerable embarrassment for your country and you will probably end up in jail. All you have to do is to tell me where the icon is and you can go free."

Adam didn't even bother to shake his head.

"Then the time has obviously come to give you some further information," Romanov said, extracting a single sheet of paper from his inside pocket.

"This paper gives the details of the death sentence pronounced in Moscow in 1946 on a certain Major Vladimir Kosky, the Russian guard in charge of the Soviet watch the night Reichsmarschall Hermann Goering died. Major Kosky was found guilty of smuggling cyanide into the Reichsmarschall's cell." Adam's eyes widened. "Ah, I see I have dealt the ace," said Romanov. "Now I think you will finally tell me where the icon is. It's a fair exchange. Your icon for my icon, plus the legal judgment that will finally vindicate your father's honour."

Adam closed his eyes.

Romanov was unable to hide his anger. He walked to the door and flung it open. "He's yours," he said.

Dr. Stavinsky reentered the room, smiling, and continued as if nothing had interrupted him. "Stage three is staggering in its simplicity. A rapid analgesic that when injected into the nervous system causes an immediate recovery," said Stavinsky, holding up another little phial. "When injected into your bloodstream it will aid recovery so quickly that you may even wonder if you ever went through any pain in the first place."

Stavinsky stood in front of Adam and half filled a second syringe. Adam felt the needle and moments later the fluid entered his bloodstream.

He could not believe how quickly he felt himself recovering. Within minutes he no longer felt sick or disorientated. Then Stavinsky thrust his palm down on the generator handle and Adam found a new level at which to scream.

"Now, where is the icon?" Stavinsky shouted.

In the Louvre, Adam wanted to scream, but he was unable to speak, even in a whisper.

Stavinsky proceeded to fill the second syringe again and again injected Adam with the fluid. Once again it was only moments before the agony subsided and he felt completely recovered.

"Ten seconds, we go again . . ."

"Cymbeline, The Winter's Tale, The Tempest. Aahhhh . . ." Adam screamed, and immediately fainted. Then he felt the syringe jab into his flesh again.

Romanov stepped forward and looking straight at Adam said, "I feel Dr. Stavinsky and I have earned a little supper. When we return, fully refreshed, Dr. Stavinsky will repeat the entire exercise."

Romanov and Stavinsky left, and Colonel Pollard entered the room. He came over to Adam and offered him the water bottle. Adam gulped down the liquid and was genuinely surprised by how quickly he was recovering.

"I'm going to throw up," he said suddenly, and thrust his head forward. Pollard quickly undid the knots and watched Adam slump to his hands and knees. He threw up some spit and rested before the colonel helped him back into the chair. As he sat down Adam gripped both sides of the chair firmly, then with all the strength he could muster jack-knifed forward, swung the chair over his head, and brought it crashing down on top of the unsuspecting colonel. Pollard collapsed in a heap, and never heard Adam utter the words, "Henry VIII and Two Noble Kinsmen— I'll bet that's one you've never heard of, Colonel. Mind you, to be fair, not everyone thinks Shakespeare wrote it."

Adam waited for a few more seconds as he tried to measure what was left of his strength. He picked up the water bottle and drained it of its last drops. He then crawled across to the bed and pulled on his clothes. The blazer's lining had been ripped to shreds so he stumbled like an old man towards the colonel, removed his Harris tweed coat and slipped that on.

Adam made his way to the door and opened it an inch—nothing happened. He stared through the crack but all he could see was a dark corridor with a light shining through a pebbled pane in a door at the far end. He began to creep towards it. Then he saw another beam of light coming from under the door to his right. He was only a pace away from it when it opened abruptly and out stepped a man in kitchen overalls. Adam froze against the wall as the kitchen-hand removed a packet of cigarettes amd a box of matches from his pocket and headed for the glazed door, opened it and walked out. Adam watched the silhouette outlined against the pebbled window, a match being struck, a cigarette being lit.

Adam crept towards the outer door and opened it. The smoker turned round and Adam's left hand landed firmly in his stomach. As the smoker bent over Adam's right fist came up to the man's chin with all the force he could muster and the smoker sank to the ground.

Adam dragged the limp body across the grass, dumped it behind a bush and tried to work out his bearings. He could just make out a high wall ahead of him in the moonlight. Summoning up every ounce of energy, he ran to the wall and remained motionless in its shadow. Slowly and silently he moved round the wall, yard by yard, until he reached the front of what he now felt sure was the Russian embassy. The great wooden gates at the front entrance were open, and every few seconds limousines swept past him. At the top of the embassy steps he saw the ambassador shaking hands with departing guests.

There were two armed gendarmes on the gate who stood rigidly to attention and saluted as each car went by. Adam waited until a vast

BMW, the West German flag fluttering on its bonnet, slowed as it passed through the gates. Following closely behind, he walked straight between the guards towards the road.

"*Bonsoir*," he said lightly to the guards as the car moved forward: he was only a yard from the road. Walk, he told himself, don't run. They saluted deferentially. Don't look back. He kept his eyes firmly to the front.

ADAM HAD ENDED UP in a badly lit one-way street. "*Tu cherches une femme?*" a voice asked from the shadows of a recessed doorway.

"Wha—?" said Adam, stepping sharply into the road.

"From Britain, eh? Do you search for a girl?" The voice had an unmistakable French accent.

"You speak English?" said Adam, still unable to see the woman clearly.

"You have to know a lot of languages in my profession, *chéri*, or you'd starve."

Adam tried to think coherently. "How much for the night?"

"Two hundred francs," said the girl.

Although he had no money Adam hoped this girl might at least lead him to safety.

"Two hundred is fine."

"*D'accord*," said the girl, at last stepping out of the shadows. "Take my arm and if you pass a gendarme say only, 'Ma femme'."

Adam stumbled forward.

"Ah, I think you drink too much, *chéri*. Never mind, you can lean on me, yes."

"No, I'm just tired," said Adam, trying hard to keep up with her pace.

"My apartment is just round the corner," she assured him.

Adam was not confident he could get that far and took a deep breath when they arrived at a block of flats. He just managed to reach the front door.

When they got upstairs to her flat Adam staggered towards the only chair in sight and collapsed into it. In the light he was able to see the girl properly for the first time. Her blonde hair was short and curly and she wore a red blouse, skin-tight black skirt and black mesh stockings.

She knelt down in front of him. "Would you please give me the two hundred now?" she asked, without harshness. She ran her hand along his thigh.

"I don't have any money," said Adam quite simply.

"What?" she said, sounding angry for the first time. Placing her hand in his inside pocket she removed a wallet and asked, "Then what's this? I don't play games." She handed the thick wallet over to Adam, who

140

found it was jammed full of French francs. The colonel was obviously paid in cash for his services.

Adam extracted two one-hundred-franc notes and dutifully handed them over.

"That's better," she said, and disappeared into the other room.

In the wallet Adam discovered a driving licence and a couple of credit cards in the colonel's real name of Albert Tomkins. He quickly looked around: a double bed took up most of the floor space. Apart from the chair he was settled in, the only other pieces of furniture were a dressing table and a tiny stool with a red velvet cushion on it. To his left was a small fireplace with logs stacked neatly in one corner. With what strength was left in his body, Adam pushed himself up, wobbled over to the fireplace and hid the wallet between the logs. He lurched towards the chair and fell into it as the door reopened.

This time the girl wore only a pink transparent negligée. She walked slowly across the room and once more knelt down in front of him.

"How you like it, *mon chéri?*"

"I need to rest," said Adam.

"For two hundred francs you sleep in any 'otel," she said in disbelief.

"I only want to be allowed to rest a few minutes," he assured her.

"*Les Anglais!*" she said, and began to try and lift Adam out of the chair and towards the bed, where he landed half on and half off the mattress. She undressed him deftly, lifted his legs up onto the bed and covered him with the sheet and blankets. He was already asleep.

Chapter Twenty-One

When Adam eventually awoke the sun was shining into the bedroom. He blinked as he took in his surroundings and tried to recall what had happened the night before. The girl was nowhere to be seen or heard. Then he remembered the wallet.

He sat upright, gathering himself before standing up and trying to walk. Although he was still unsteady it was better than he had expected. When he reached the fireplace he fell on his knees and searched among the logs, but the colonel's wallet was no longer there. He went to the tweed jacket hanging over the back of the chair. The pockets contained a passport, a driving licence, a bunch of keys, a few assorted coins, but no wallet. With a string of oaths he collapsed onto the floor.

He heard a key in the lock and the girl sauntered into the flat carrying a shopping basket. She was now dressed in a pretty floral skirt and white shirt. The basket was crammed with food.

"Woken up, 'ave we, *chéri? Est-ce-que tu prends le petit déjeuner?*"

"Where's my wallet?" asked Adam coldly.

"On the table," said the girl, pointing. She had left the wallet in the most obvious place.

"It not necessary of you to 'ide it," she reprimanded him. "I'm not a thief." With this she strode off into the kitchen.

Adam suddenly knew how big Tom Thumb felt.

"Coffee and croissants?" she shouted.

"Fantastic," said Adam. He paused. "I'm sorry. I was stupid."

"Not to think about it," she said.

"I still don't know your name," said Adam.

"My name is Jeanne."

"Can I have a bath, Jeanne?"

"The door in the corner." Adam made his way to the bathroom and found Jeanne had provided everything a man might need. After a warm bath and a shave he felt almost normal again, if still somewhat fragile. He tucked a pink towel round his waist before joining Jeanne in the kitchen. She was removing warm croissants from the oven. Adam spread one liberally with jam and devoured every crumb on the plate.

"Tell me, Jeanne," he said finally, looking up at her, "are you still available for work?"

"One of my regulars is at two, and I must be back on the streets by five. So it would 'ave to be this morning," she said matter-of-factly.

"No, no, that's not what I meant," said Adam.

"You could quickly give a girl a complex," said Jeanne. "You're not one of those weird ones, are you?"

"No, nothing like that," said Adam, laughing. "But I would be willing to pay you another two hundred francs for your help."

"Is it legal?"

"Absolutely."

"*Alors*, that makes a change. What am I expected to do?"

"For one hour I want every man in Paris to fancy you. Only this time you won't be available—at any price."

"SCOTT CONTACTED ME a few minutes ago," said Lawrence to the assembled D4.

"What did he have to say?" asked an anxious Sir Morris.

"Only that he was returning to Geneva," said Lawrence.

"Why Geneva?" asked Matthews.

"I'm not certain," said Lawrence, "but he said it had something to do with the German girl, or the bank."

"Did you trace the call?" asked Busch.

"We only got the area," said Lawrence. "Neuchâtel, on the German–Swiss border."

"Good. We're in business again," said Sir Morris. "Have you informed Interpol?"

"Yes sir, and I've personally briefed the German, French and Swiss police," added Lawrence, which were the only true words he had spoken since the meeting began.

JEANNE TOOK FORTY MINUTES to get herself ready and when Adam saw the result he let out a long whistle.

"No one is going to give me a second look walking behind you," he told her.

"That is the idea, *n'est ce pas?*" Jeanne said, grinning.

"Now, are you sure you know exactly what you have to do?"

Jeanne checked herself once more in the long mirror. "We 'ave rehearse like military exercise four times already."

"Good," said Adam. "You sound as if you're ready to face the enemy."

Jeanne handed a plastic bag to Adam, who stuffed it into his jacket pocket. They walked down the stairs and out onto the pavement. Adam hailed a taxi and Jeanne told the driver, *"Les Jardins des Tuileries."*

Once they had arrived, Adam paid the fare and joined Jeanne on the pavement. *"Bonne chance,"* said Adam as Jeanne set off to walk twenty yards ahead of him. Her pink leather skirt and tight white sweater made almost every man she passed turn and take a second look.

Adam was still twenty yards behind her when she reached the entrance to the Louvre. By the time she had reached the swing doors, Adam was approaching the bottom step. She continued on up the marble staircase with Adam still following discreetly behind.

Jeanne proceeded into the first of the large crowded rooms and began counting to herself, noting as she passed through each gallery that there was at least one attendant on duty in each. At last she arrived in the room Adam had described to her so vividly. She strode purposefully into the centre and paused for a few seconds. Some of the men began to lose interest in the paintings. Satisfied by the impact she was making, she flounced over to the guard, who smiled at her.

"Dans quelle direction se trouve la peinture du seizième siècle?" Jeanne asked innocently. The guard turned to point in the direction of the relevant room. The moment he turned back, Jeanne slapped him hard across the face and shouted at him at the top of her voice, *"Mais voyons, pour qui me prenez vous?"*

Only one person in the Icon Room didn't stop to stare at the spectacle. *"Je vais parler à la direction,"* she screamed, and flounced off towards the main exit. The entire charade was over in less than thirty seconds. The bemused guard stared after his assailant in bewilderment.

Jeanne continued through the centuries more quickly than H. G.

Wells. Moments later, she joined Adam at the top of the marble staircase leading down to the front entrance.

As they walked back down the steps together, Adam handed her the plastic bag and was about to set off again, when two attendants threw out their arms, indicating that they should halt.

"Do you wish a run for it?" she whispered.

"Certainly not," said Adam very firmly. "Just don't say anything."

"Madame, excusez moi, mais je dois fouiller votre sac?"

"Certainly you can search her bag," said Adam. "It's an icon, quite a good one, I think. I purchased it in a shop near the Champs-Elysées only this morning."

He removed the Tsar's Icon from the bag and handed it over to the attendant, who seemed surprised by the way things were turning out. He asked in broken English if Adam would mind if one of the gallery's experts were to look at the painting.

"Only too delighted," said Adam. "It would be fascinating to have a second opinion."

The senior attendant was beginning to look unsure of himself. *"Je dois vous demander de me suivre,"* he suggested in a tone that was suddenly less hostile. He ushered them quickly through to a little room at the side of the gallery. The attendant put the Tsar's Icon in the middle of a table that dominated the room. Adam sat down and Jeanne, still bemused, took the seat beside him.

"I'll only be a moment, sir." The senior attendant almost ran out, while two other attendants remained stationed near the door.

When the door eventually opened again, an elderly man with a scholarly face preceded the senior attendant.

"Bonjour, monsieur," the man began. "I understand that you are English," and without giving either of them more than a glance, he picked up the icon.

He studied the painting with great care for some time before he spoke. Adam felt just a moment's apprehension. "Most interesting. I would suggest late nineteenth century. Fascinating. You do realize it's a copy?" he said as he handed the icon back to Adam. "The original Tsar's Icon of St. George and the Dragon hangs in the Winter Palace in Leningrad. I've seen it, you know," he added, sounding rather pleased with himself.

"You certainly have," said Adam under his breath, as he placed the icon back in its plastic bag. The old man bowed low to Jeanne before he shuffled away.

"I was only doing my duty," said the senior attendant.

"I can only admire the way you carried out the entire exercise," Adam said pompously.

144

The attendant accompanied the two of them to the entrance of the Louvre, and they walked down the steps and into the Paris sunshine.

"Well, now can I know what that's all about?" asked Jeanne.

"You were *magnifique*," said Adam, not attempting to explain.

"I know, I know," said Jeanne. "But why you need Oscar-winning show by me when the picture was always yours?"

"I had left it in their safekeeping overnight. And without your bravura performance it might have taken considerably longer to convince the authorities that it belonged to me in the first place."

Adam realized from the look on her face that Jeanne had no idea what he was talking about.

"You know, that was my first time in the Louvre?" she said, linking her arm in Adam's.

"You're priceless," said Adam, laughing.

"That I'm not," she said, turning to face him. "Two hundred francs was our bargain."

"Correct," said Adam, taking out the colonel's wallet and extracting two hundred francs, to which he added another hundred. "A well-earned bonus," said Adam, kissing her on both cheeks.

She pocketed the money gratefully. "I think I'll take an evening off," she said. "And when you're next in Paris, *chéri*, look me up. I owe you one—on the house."

"I WOULD LIKE TO RENT a car which I will be dropping off at the coast. I haven't decided which port yet," Adam told the girl behind the counter.

"*Bien sûr, monsieur,*" said the girl. "Would you be kind enough to fill in the form, and we will also need your driving licence." Adam filled in the form slowly, copying the signature from the colonel's driving licence before handing it over with the full amount required in cash.

The girl counted the notes carefully before checking the back of the licence against the signature on the form.

She removed an ignition key from a hook on the board behind her. "It's a red Citroën, parked on the first floor," she told Adam. "The registration number is stamped on the key ring."

Adam thanked her and walked quickly up to the first floor, where he handed the key over to an attendant, who drove the car out of its parking space for him.

The attendant returned the key and Adam handed him a ten-franc note. Exactly the same sum as another man had given the attendant only hours before. That man had wanted to be informed if an Englishman who fitted Adam's description tried to hire a car. What had he promised? Another hundred francs if the attendant phoned within five minutes of seeing him.

145

Chapter Twenty-Two
THE KREMLIN, MOSCOW   19 JUNE 1966

Leonid Ilyich Brezhnev entered the room, hardly allowing the other four members of the inner Defence Council enough time to stand.

The General Secretary took his place at the head of the table and nodded to his colleagues to sit. On his right sat Marshal Malinovsky, Minister of Defence, on his left Andrei Gromyko, the young Foreign Minister. Beside him sat the Chief of the General Staff, Marshal Zakharov, and, on his left, Yuri Zaborski. Even the seating plan confirmed Brezhnev's displeasure with the chairman of the KGB.

He raised his eyes and stared up at a massive oil painting of Lenin. If only he had realized the icon was a fake in the first place, Brezhnev reflected . . . But he knew that Vladimir Ilyich Lenin was beyond criticism. He would have to find a living scapegoat.

His eyes rested on Zaborski. "Your report, Comrade Chairman."

Zaborski fingered a file in front of him although he knew the contents almost off by heart. "The Englishman, Adam Scott, was caught and . . . questioned by Comrade Dr. Stavinsky in the privacy of our embassy in Paris, but he would give no clue as to where we would find the icon. After three hours, interrogation was momentarily suspended. It was during this period that the prisoner managed to escape."

"Managed!" interjected Brezhnev. "Don't you realize that we had within our grasp the opportunity to turn the very land the Americans use for their early-warning system into a base for our short-range missiles? It would have been possible to site those missiles less than one thousand eight hundred kilometres from Seattle—two thousand kilometres from Chicago."

Zaborski made no attempt to speak. When Brezhnev began again it was almost in a whisper: "And for such a prize we would not have had to sacrifice one life, one rocket, one tank or even one bullet—because all this was ours by right. If we fail to locate the Tsar's Icon in the next thirty-six hours we will have lost our one opportunity to remove a star from the American flag."

Foreign Secretary Gromyko inquired, "Comrade Chairman, may I ask why Major Romanov was allowed to remain involved in such a sensitive operation after it was suspected he had killed researcher Petrova?"

"Because," replied Zaborski, at last looking up, "in my judgment there was no one who could have taken over Romanov's place at such short notice—"

There was a timid knock on the door. All the faces round the table showed surprise.

"Come in," shouted Brezhnev.

The great door inched open and a secretary approached nervously, deposited a telex on the table, and almost ran from the room.

Brezhnev slowly unfolded his tortoiseshell glasses before picking up the missive. Once he had read it through, he looked up at the expectant faces in front of him. "It seems an Englishman put an icon in the Louvre last night and picked it up this morning."

The blood drained from Zaborski's face.

The four ministers round the table all began talking together, until Brezhnev raised his vast hand. "I intend to act on the assumption that it will still be we who get to the Englishman first." He turned to his foreign minister. "Instruct Anatoly Dobrynin in Washington to demand an official meeting with the US secretary of state for late tomorrow."

Gromyko nodded as Brezhnev turned his attention to the chief of the general staff. "See that our strategic forces in all zones are in a state of readiness to coincide with the timing of the announcement of our diplomatic initiative." The General Secretary finally turned to the chairman of the KGB. "Do we still have advertising space booked in every major newspaper in the West?"

"Yes, Comrade General Secretary," replied Zaborski. "But I cannot be sure they will be willing to print your statement."

"Then pay every one of them in advance," said Brezhnev. "Few Western editors will withdraw a full page advertisement when they already have the money in the bank."

"But if we then don't find the icon . . ." began the chairman of the KGB.

"Then your last duty as chairman of State Security will be to find a way to withdraw all the advertisements," said the General Secretary.

Chapter Twenty-Three

Adam wound down the car window and immediately the warm summer air flooded in. He had decided to avoid the main road to Calais in favour of the N1 to Boulogne. He considered it possible that Romanov would have men watching at every port on the Channel coast although he doubted if Lawrence or the Americans were aware he had escaped.

Once he had cleared Paris, he was confident that he could average seventy kilometres an hour, but what he hadn't anticipated was running into a hundred or more cyclists bobbing along ahead of him. He honked his horn loudly as he passed a group of four men quite near the front, clad in red, white and blue British T-shirts.

He switched on the car radio and tuned in to the news. The report of the second Test match at Lord's made him feel he was already back home, and then one piece of appalling news very nearly caused him to swerve off the road.

A young RAF pilot had been found dead in a field near the Auxerre–Dijon road after his plane had crashed in mysterious circumstances. Adam cursed at the thought of Alan Banks becoming another victim of Romanov.

"IT WAS FOOLISH OF YOU to contact me, Romanov. You're not exactly a hero of the Soviet Union at the present time."

"Listen, old man, I don't have to be a hero any longer, because I may never come back to the Soviet Union."

"Be warned: Mother Russia has extremely long fingernails."

"Because of my grandfather's foresight, I can afford to cut them off," the caller said, touching the gold medallion he wore beneath his shirt.

"Why should I remain silent?"

"Because if I haven't got my hands on St. George within the next twenty-four hours, I'll phone again with the details of how you can hope to collect a larger golden handshake than you'll get from your present employers."

The banker offered no comment.

The ambassador's secretary rushed into the room without knocking. "I told you, no interruptions," shouted Romanov, covering the mouthpiece with his hand.

"But we've located Scott."

Romanov slammed down the phone.

In Moscow the old Russian banker wound the tape back. Poskonov smiled and listened to Romanov's words a second time and came to the conclusion that he had left him with only one alternative. He booked a flight to Geneva.

"ROBIN?"

"Adam! Where are you phoning from?"

"I'm just outside Paris on my way back home," Adam said. "Are you sticking to the schedule you outlined on the bus?"

"Sure am, just as I told you. Why, are you still desperate to spend the night with me?"

"Sure am," said Adam, mimicking her. "When do you get home?"

"The orchestra is taking the ferry from Dunkerque at six thirty tonight. Can you join us?"

"No," said Adam. "I have to go back by another route. But, Robin, when I reach London can you put me up for the night?"

"Sounds like an offer I can't refuse," she said, and then repeated her

148

A Matter of Honour

address to be sure he had remembered it. "When shall I expect you?" she asked.

"Around midnight tonight."

"Do you always give a girl so much notice?"

ROMANOV READ THE DECODED MESSAGE a second time. "Scott returning Geneva. Check German girl and bank." He looked up at the senior KGB officer who had handed him the missive.

"Does Mentor think I'm that naive?" said Romanov to his colleague. "We already know, because Scott was stupid enough to contact his girlfriend in Amsterdam, that he's now on his way towards the French coast. We've had her phone tapped at every hotel the orchestra has stayed in."

"Then why should Mentor want to send you in the opposite direction?"

"Perhaps he's switched sides," Romanov said, coldly.

He turned to the colonel. "We know it won't be Dunkerque, so how many other possibilities are we left with?"

"Cherbourg, Le Havre, Dieppe, Boulogne or Calais," replied the colonel, looking down at the map laid out on the table in front of him. "My bet would be Calais," he added.

"Unfortunately," said Romanov, "Captain Scott is not quite that simple. As the motorway takes you direct to Calais, Scott will expect us to have that port well covered. I think our friend will try Boulogne or Dieppe first."

He checked the timetable the second secretary had supplied him with. "The first boat he could hope to catch leaves Boulogne for Dover at three, and then there's one from Dieppe to Newhaven at five. Assuming we can beat him to the coast, Colonel, I think Captain Scott is once again within our grasp."

ONCE ADAM HAD LEFT the *Relais Routier* where he had eaten a quick lunch it was only minutes before he began to catch up with the cyclists as they pedalled on towards Boulogne. He remained in the centre of the road to avoid the bobbing cyclists, but had to slam his brakes on suddenly when an Italian and a British rider collided in front of him. The two men were thrown to the ground and the British rider remained ominously still at the side of the road.

Adam felt guilty about not stopping to help his fellow countryman but feared that any holdup might prevent him catching the three o'clock boat. He spotted the British team van ahead of him and speeded up until he was alongside. Adam waved at the driver to pull over.

The man behind the steering wheel looked surprised but stopped and wound down the window. Adam pulled up in front of him, leaped out of

149

his car and ran to the van. "One of your chaps has had an accident about a mile back," shouted Adam.

"Thanks, mate," said the driver and turned round and sped back down the road.

Adam drove on until he had passed all the leaders. A signpost informed him it was thirty-two kilometres to Boulogne: he would still make the three o'clock sailing comfortably. He began to imagine what life might be like if he could survive beyond Monday. Jogs in the park, Foreign Office interviews, even acknowledgment of the part he had played in delivering the icon into safe hands. The problem was that he hadn't yet decided who had safe hands.

A helicopter looking like a squat green bullfrog swept over him; now that would be the ideal way to get back to England, Adam considered. He watched as the helicopter turned and swung back towards him. A moment later he heard the whirl of the blades as it flew across his path at a considerably lower level.

Adam gripped the wheel of the car as an impossible thought suddenly crossed his mind. As he did so the helicopter swung back again and flew straight towards him.

Leaning over the top of the steering wheel and staring upwards, Adam could see three figures in the helicopter. He banged his fist on the steering wheel in anger as he realized how easy it must have been for them to trace a car signed for in the one name they would immediately recognize. He could sense Romanov's smile of triumph as the chopper hovered above him.

Adam swung right off the main road towards a village called Fleurville and pushed the speedometer to well over ninety. The helicopter, dog-like, followed his path.

Adam took the next left and headed back onto the Boulogne road, desperately trying to think what he could do next. Every time he looked up the helicopter was there above him.

A road sign depicting a low tunnel ahead flashed past, and as Adam entered it, he actually felt safe for a brief moment. He slammed on the Citroën's brakes and skidded to a halt about thirty yards from the end of the tunnel. He switched on his side lights and they shone brightly in the darkness. For several seconds he watched as cars slowed down before safely overtaking him.

He jumped out of the car and ran to the end of the tunnel where he pinned himself against the wall. The helicopter was already turning back and heading straight towards the tunnel. Adam watched it fly over his head, and moments later heard it turn again. As he waited, two hitchhikers passed by on the opposite side of the tunnel, chatting to one another.

150

Adam looked desperately at the two young men and shouted, "Were you hoping to get a lift?"

"Yes," they called back. Adam staggered across the road to them.

"Are you all right?" one of them asked.

"No, I'm not," Adam explained simply, "I drank too much wine at lunch and because of the cycle race the road is just crawling with police. I'm sure to be picked up if I go much further. Can either of you drive?"

"I only have my Canadian licence," said the taller of the two youths. "And in any case we are heading for Paris and your car is facing in the opposite direction."

"It's a Hertz Rent-a-Car," Adam explained. "I picked it up in Paris this morning, and I have to return it by seven tonight. I don't think I can make it in my present state." He added, "I'll give you one hundred francs if you will return it safely for me. I can't afford to lose my licence, I'm a commercial traveller." Neither of them spoke. "My papers are all in order, I can assure you." Adam handed them over to the taller man who crossed back over the road and used the car lights to study the papers before talking to his friend.

Adam could hear the helicopter blades whirling above the tunnel entrance.

"I suppose that's all right," the taller one said eventually. "But don't you want to come back to Paris with us?"

Adam hesitated fractionally. "No. I have to get to Boulogne."

"We could drive you to Boulogne and still have enough time to take the car to Paris."

"No, no. That's very considerate. I can take care of myself as long as I feel confident that the car will be delivered back as soon as possible."

The taller one shrugged, while his companion opened a rear door and threw their rucksacks onto the back seat. Adam remained in the tunnel while they started up the engine. He could hear the purr of the helicopter blades change cadence: it had to be descending to land in some nearby field.

"Go, go, for God's sake go," he wanted to shout, as the car shot forward. He watched them reverse beyond the tunnel and they tooted as they passed him, disappearing in the direction of Paris. Adam was about to start walking towards Boulogne when he saw two tall, thin figures silhouetted at the far entrance of the tunnel against the clear blue sky. He didn't move a muscle, praying they hadn't spotted him.

And then suddenly one of them started walking towards him. The other remained motionless. Adam knew he could not hope to escape again. He cursed his own stupidity.

"Don't let's waste any more time, Marvin, we already know the limey's heading back to Paris."

"I just thought perhaps . . ." began the one called Marvin, in a Southern drawl.

"Leave the thinking to me. Now let's get back to the chopper before we lose him."

Marvin was only twenty yards away from Adam when he turned round and began running back to his companion.

Adam remained rooted to the spot for several minutes. A cold, clammy sweat had enveloped his body the moment he realized his latest pursuer was not Romanov. Suddenly he had become painfully aware that he had been left with no friends.

He did not move again until he heard the helicopter rise above him. Peering out, he could see the Americans heading in the direction of Paris.

He staggered outside. What next? He had less than an hour to catch the boat. He wasn't sure whether to thumb lifts or simply get as far away

from the main road as possible. How long before the Americans reached the car, and realized it was not him inside?

Cyclists began to pass him again as he jogged slowly towards Boulogne. He even found enough strength to cheer the British cyclists as they pedalled by. The British team van followed close behind and Adam gave it the thumbs-up sign. To his surprise the van came to a halt.

The driver wound down the window. "Weren't you the fellow who stopped me back there?"

"That's right," said Adam. "Has your man recovered?"

"He's resting in the back—pulled ligament. What happened to your car?"

"Broke down about a mile back," said Adam, shrugging philosophically.

"Bad luck. Can I give you a lift?" the man asked. "We're only going as far as Boulogne on this stage, but jump in if it will help."

"Thank you," said Adam, with relief.

The driver leaned across and pushed open the door for him. "My name's Bob," he said. "I'm the British team manager."

"Mine's Adam."

"Where are you heading?"

"Boulogne," said Adam, "and with luck I could still make my crossing by three."

"We should be there about two thirty," said Bob. "We have to be: the afternoon stage starts at three."

"When will your man be able to ride?" asked Adam, pointing over his shoulder.

"He won't be competing in this race again," said the team manager. "I shall have to leave him in Boulogne and do the last leg myself."

There was no sign of the helicopter as they drove into the outskirts of Boulogne. Bob took Adam all the way up to the dockside.

"Thanks again," he said as he jumped out of the van. "Good luck with the next stage."

Adam checked the time: twenty minutes before the boat was due to sail. He bought a passenger ticket and checked to see if anyone was watching him, but no one seemed to be showing the slightest interest. He had just started towards the ship when a black speck appeared in the sky. There was no mistaking it—the sound was enough.

Adam looked up at the gangway, now only yards away from him, then back to the speck as it grew larger in the sky. The ship was due to leave in twelve minutes—still time enough for his pursuers to land the helicopter and get on board. If he got on and the Americans followed, they were bound to discover him. But if the Americans got on and he stayed off, that would still give him enough time to reach Dieppe before the next sailing . . .

Adam jogged quickly back towards the large crowd that was waiting for the start of the next stage of the road race. As he did so the helicopter started hovering, like a kestrel looking for a mouse.

"I thought you were desperate to be on that ship."

Adam swung round, his fist clenched, only to face the British team manager now dressed in riding gear.

"Changed my mind," said Adam.

"Wouldn't care to drive the van on to Dunkerque for us?" asked Bob hopefully.

Adam tried to remember what time Robin had said her boat left from Dunkerque.

"Six minutes," a voice said over the loudspeaker.

"OK," said Adam.

"Good," said the team manager. "Quickly, follow me."

154

They headed towards the van, where Bob unlocked it and handed Adam the keys.

"*Deux minutes.*"

Adam jumped up into the driver's seat and looked over towards the boat. He saw Marvin and his colleague striding up the gangplank.

"*Une minute.*"

"Just get the van to Dunkerque and leave the keys at the British checkpoint. We'll see you when we get there," said Bob, and ran to the starting line to join his team mates who were anxiously holding his bike.

"*Trente secondes.*"

Adam watched the gangplank being hoisted up as the starter raised his gun.

"On your marks, set . . ."

The gun went off and Adam shot forward towards Dunkerque as the two Americans started their journey to Dover.

Chapter Twenty-Four

The coach trundled in with only ten minutes to spare and Adam greeted Robin as she stepped off.

"Just couldn't keep away from me, could you?" she said.

Adam burst out laughing and threw his arms round her. "It's good to see you," he said.

"I thought you were going back to England by some mysterious route. You know, spy rocket, or something even more exotic."

"I'll explain everything once we're on board," said Adam. Neither noticed the KGB agent who had trailed Robin from Berlin. He stood in a phone booth on the dockside and dialled an overseas number.

"I wouldn't have believed a word of your story a week ago," she said, "but for two things."

"Namely?"

"First, a senior official of the Foreign Office returned Dudley Hulme's passport to him in Amsterdam. Which reminds me to give you yours back." She rummaged in her bag before taking out a dark blue passport and handing it to him.

"And the second thing was that I had the doubtful pleasure of coming face to face with Comrade Rosenbaum."

ROMANOV AND POLLARD waited expectantly at Dover harbour. Romanov stationed himself so that he could look through the customs hall window and watch the ferry as it sailed in, and told Pollard to cover the car exit.

On the ferry from Dunkerque the captain switched on his ship-to-shore radio and spoke clearly into the small microphone. "This is the MV *Chantilly* calling the Dover harbour master. Are you receiving me?" He flicked up the switch in front of him and then heard, "Harbour master to MV *Chantilly*. Receiving you loud and clear, over."

"This is the captain speaking. We have an emergency. A male passenger has fallen out of a lifeboat onto the deck and contracted multiple injuries to his arms and legs." Adam groaned as the captain continued. "I shall need an ambulance standing by at the quayside to take him to the nearest hospital once we have docked. Over."

"Message received and understood, Captain. An ambulance will be waiting for you when the ship docks. Over and out."

"Everything will be all right, my dear," said Robin in a gentle voice that Adam had not heard before. "As soon as we arrive, they are going to take you straight to a hospital."

"I must get back to the bridge," said the captain gruffly. "I shall instruct two stewards to bring a stretcher down for your brother."

"Thank you, Captain," said Robin. "You have been most helpful."

"It's quite all right, miss. You might advise your brother in future that it's in his best interests to drink less before he comes on board."

"I've tried," said Robin, sighing. "You couldn't believe how many times I've tried, Captain." Adam held onto his leg and groaned again.

"Um," said the captain, looking down at the gash on Adam's shoulder. "Let's hope it turns out not to be serious. Good luck," he added.

"Thank you again, Captain," said Robin as she watched the cabin door close behind him.

"So far, so good," she said. "By the way, your breath smells foul."

"What do you expect after making me swirl whisky round in my mouth for twenty minutes?"

ADAM WAS LIFTED carefully onto the stretcher, then carried out onto the deck by two stewards. They waited at the head of the gangplank and placed Adam gently on the deck while a customs officer and an immigration officer ran up to join them. Robin handed over his passport. The immigration officer flicked through the pages and checked the photograph.

"Is he bringing anything in with him that needs to be declared?" asked the customs official. Adam couldn't stop himself from touching the icon.

"No, I wouldn't let him buy any more booze on this trip. I'll be responsible for checking his personal belongings through."

"Right. Thank you, miss. Better see he gets off to the hospital then."

The two stewards carried Adam down the gangplank. He waved gamely at Robin as they placed him in the ambulance.

ROMANOV SPOTTED ROBIN as she came through customs. "This time I know exactly how Captain Scott hopes to get off the ship, and we will be waiting for him when he least expects it. Go and hire a car to take us to London," he barked at the colonel.

The ambulance shot out through the customs gate with its lights full on and bells ringing. En route to the Royal Victoria Hospital the attendant watched his patient's remarkable recovery with disbelief. He was beginning to feel the scale of the emergency might perhaps have been exaggerated.

Romanov stood by the gate and smiled as he watched the coach carrying the musicians emerge from the ship. As his eyes ranged up and down the coach he quickly picked out Robin Beresford. Just as he had anticipated, the double bass was propped up by her side, making it impossible to see who was seated next to her.

"You don't pull that one on me a second time," Romanov muttered, just as the colonel appeared by his side, red in the face.

"Where's the car?" the Russian demanded, not taking his eye from the coach.

"I've booked one provisionally," said the colonel, "but they'll need your international licence. I forgot, Scott has got mine."

"Make sure Scott doesn't try to get off that coach," said Romanov. He ran to the Avis desk at the same time as Adam was being examined by a young doctor.

"Nasty laceration," the doctor said finally, cleaning Adam's shoulder wound. "Can you circle your arm?" Adam turned the arm in a full circle and straightened it again. "Good. No break, at least. You have been in the wars lately. I'm going to give you an anti-tetanus injection." Adam turned white. "Funny how many grown men don't care for the sight of a needle," said the doctor, as he placed a large bandage over Adam's shoulder. "You can go now, but please report to your GP as soon as possible after you get home."

ROMANOV FOLLOWED THE COACH out of the main gate and in the direction of London. "Are we going to intercept them on the way?" asked the colonel nervously.

"Not this time," said Romanov, without explanation. He never once allowed the coach out of his sight all the way in to the capital.

ADAM WALKED OUT of the hospital, took a taxi to Dover Priory station and purchased a single ticket to London. He walked onto the platform, keeping a wary eye out for anyone acting suspiciously. He didn't notice the dark-haired man in a blue duffel coat leaning against the W.H. Smith stall reading a newspaper.

157

The London train drew in, and Adam jumped on, selecting a carriage full of teddy boys who were apparently returning from a day at the seaside. He thought it unlikely anyone else would wish to join them.

By the time the train had pulled in to Canterbury no one had entered the carriage other than the ticket collector. Adam felt strangely safe in the corner of that compartment even when he noticed a dark-haired man in a blue duffel coat pass by the compartment door and look in carefully.

Adam was jolted out of his thoughts by a noisy claim made by what appeared to be the gang leader.

"There's a foul smell in this compartment," he declared, sniffing loudly.

"I agree, Terry," said his mate, who was sitting next to Adam. "And I think it's quite close to me." Adam glanced towards the young man, whose black leather jacket was covered in small shiny studs.

In moments all four of the boys were sniffing. "I think the smell's getting worse," their leader concluded.

"It must be me," said Adam.

The youths stared towards the corner in disbelief, momentarily silenced by Adam's offensive.

"I didn't have time to take a shower after my judo lesson," Adam added.

"What belt are you?" demanded Terry belligerently. "Go on, tell me, a black belt," he sniggered.

"I haven't been a black belt for nearly eight years," said Adam casually, "but I've recently been awarded my second Dan."

A look of apprehension came over the four faces.

"I was thinkin' about taking up judo myself," continued the leader. "How long does it take to get any good at it?"

"I've been working at it three hours a day for twelve years and I'm still not up to Olympic standard," replied Adam as he watched the man in the duffel coat pass by the compartment again. This time he stared directly at Adam.

"Of course," continued Adam, "the only quality you really need is nerve, and no one can teach you that."

"I've got nerve," said Terry belligerently. "I'm not frightened of nothing. Nor nobody."

"Good," said Adam. "Because you may be given the chance to prove your claim before this journey is over. At this moment I'm being followed by a private detective who is hoping to catch me spending the night with his client's wife."

The four of them stared at Adam with something approaching respect.

"You just point out this detective and we'll sew him up for the night," said the leader.

"That might turn out to be unnecessary," said Adam. "But if you could delay him for a little when I get off at Waterloo East, that should at least give me enough time to warn the lady."

"Say no more, squire," said the leader. "Your friend will be delivered to Charing Cross all trussed up like a British Rail parcel."

"That's him," whispered Adam as the duffel-coated man passed by for a third time. They all looked out into the corridor but only saw his retreating back.

A few minutes later Adam slipped out of the compartment, walking in the direction opposite to that of the man in the blue duffel-coat. When Adam reached the end of the carriage, he turned to find that the man was now following quickly behind him, but as he passed the open compartment, two leather-clad arms shot out and the man disappeared inside with a muffled cry.

The train drew slowly into Waterloo East station.

ROBIN REMAINED TENSE as the bus drew into Wigmore Street and came to a halt outside the RPO headquarters. A dark green Ford had been following them for at least thirty miles.

As she dragged her double bass off the bus she looked back to see that the Ford had stopped about fifty yards down the road and turned off its headlights. The man she now knew was called Romanov was standing on the pavement looking like a caged animal waiting to spring. Another man, whom Robin did not recognize, remained seated behind the wheel. She walked straight into the RPO headquarters without stopping.

When the last musician had left the bus Romanov and the colonel searched the vehicle, despite noisy protests from the driver. Robin eyed them nervously from an upstairs window as the two of them jumped back into the green Ford and drove off. She continued watching the car until the back lights had faded away in the darkness.

THE COLONEL BROUGHT THE CAR to a halt opposite Baker Street station. Romanov jumped out, walked into a telephone booth and started thumbing through the A-D directory. Only one Robin Beresford was listed and it was the same address that the young KGB agent had given him. He dialled the number and after ten unanswered rings smiled at the realization that she lived alone.

"What now?" asked the colonel, once Romanov was back in the car.

"Where's Argyle Crescent, NW3?"

"Must be out towards Hampstead. I'll check in the A to Z. What's the plan?"

"Rather than waiting for Miss Beresford to come out we will be waiting for her to come in," said Romanov.

ROBIN SLIPPED OUT of the back of the RPO headquarters about thirty minutes later. She kept telling herself that Romanov was not coming back, but found it impossible to stop herself shaking. She hailed a taxi, checked the driver and the back seat, as Adam had advised her, then climbed in.

ROMANOV ARRIVED at Robin's front door a few moments after she had hailed the taxi. The name holder on the side wall indicated that Miss Beresford resided on the fourth floor.

Romanov secured entry to the main door within moments. The colonel followed him up the dark staircase.

Romanov slipped the Yale lock faster than Robin could have opened it with her own key. He convinced himself no one else was around, and said, "Settle down, Colonel. I don't expect the lady will keep us waiting too long."

The taxi drew up outside the house that Robin pointed to. She jumped out and tipped the cabbie extra because at last she felt safe. It seemed ages since she had been home. All she was looking forward to now was a hot bath and a good night's sleep.

ADAM STEPPED OFF THE TRAIN at Waterloo East a little after midnight and was pleased to find the underground was still running. He waited around on the underground platform for some time before the train drew in slowly.

There were several stations between Waterloo and his destination, and he waited nervously at each stop, aware now that he must have caught the last train. He only hoped Robin had carried out his instructions faithfully. The train eventually pulled into his station at twelve forty.

The ticket collector was able to give him the directions he needed. It was a relief to reach his final destination so quickly because there was no one else around to ask the way at that time of night. He moved slowly towards number twenty-three. There were no lights on in the house. He walked straight up the path, fitted a key in the lock, pushed open the door quietly and then closed it noiselessly behind him.

Chapter Twenty-Five

He pushed open the gate and made his way slowly up the path in the pitch darkness. Once he reached the corner of the house he searched for the third stone on the left, where he always hid his spare key. Like a burglar he pushed it into the lock quietly.

He crept into the hall, switched on the light and climbed the stairs.

Once he had reached the landing he turned the knob of his bedroom door and pushed.

As he stepped in an arm circled his throat like a whiplash and he was thrown to the ground with tremendous force. He felt a knee pressed hard against his spine and his arm was jerked up behind his back in a half nelson. The colonel lay on the floor, flat on his face, hardly able to move. The light switch flashed on.

"Don't kill me, Captain Scott, sir, don't kill me," he implored.

"I have no intention of doing so, Mr. Tomkins," said Adam calmly. "But first, where is your employer at this moment?"

The colonel bleated out, "He went back to the embassy, once he realized the girl wasn't going to return to her flat."

"Just as I planned," said Adam, but he didn't lessen the pressure on the colonel's arm as he described in vivid detail everything that would now be expected of him.

The colonel's face showed disbelief. "But that is impossible," he said. "I mean, he's bound to noti—ahhh."

The colonel felt his arm forced higher up his back. "You could carry out the whole exercise in less than ten minutes and he need never be any the wiser," said Adam. "However, I feel that it's only fair that you should be rewarded for your effort."

"Thank you, sir," said the fawning Tomkins.

"If you succeed in delivering the one item I require, and carry out my instructions to the letter, you will be given in exchange your papers and wallet, and a guarantee of no prosecution for your past treachery. But if, on the other hand, you fail to turn up by nine thirty tomorrow morning with the object of my desire," said Adam, "all those documents will be placed thirty minutes later on the desk of a Mr. Lawrence Pemberton of the Foreign Office."

"But think what would happen to me then, Captain Scott, sir, if you carried out your threat," moaned the colonel.

"I have already considered that," said Adam, "and I have come to two conclusions."

"And what are they, Captain Scott?"

"Spies," continued Adam, not loosening his grip, "at the present time seem to be getting anything from eighteen to forty-two years at Her Majesty's pleasure, so you might, with good behaviour, be out before the turn of the century, just in time to collect your telegram from the Queen."

"And the other conclusion?" the colonel blurted out.

"Oh, simply that Romanov could arrange for you to spend the rest of your days in a very small *dacha* in a suitably undesirable suburb of Moscow. Because, you see, dear Tomkins, you are a very small spy."

"I'll bring it to you by nine thirty on the dot, sir. You can be sure of that. But for God's sake have yours ready to exchange."

"I will," said Adam, "as well as all your documents, Tomkins."

Adam lifted the colonel slowly off the ground and shoved him towards the landing and on down the stairs.

"The car keys," said Adam.

"But it's a hire car, sir," said the colonel.

"And I'm about to hire it," said Adam.

"But how will I get myself back into London in time, sir?"

"I have no idea, but you still have the rest of the night to come up with something. You could even walk it by then. The keys," Adam repeated, jerking the colonel's arm to shoulder-blade level.

"In my left-hand pocket," said the colonel, almost an octave higher.

Adam took the car keys, opened the front door, and escorted the colonel onto the pavement.

"You will go and stand on the far side of the road," said Adam, "and you will not return to the house until I have reached the end of the road. Do I make myself clear, Tomkins?"

"Abundantly clear, Captain Scott, sir."

"Good," said Adam, releasing him for the first time, "and just one more thing, Tomkins. In case you think of double-crossing me, I have instructed the Foreign Office to place Romanov under surveillance and put two extra lookouts near the Soviet embassy with instructions to report the moment anyone suspicious turns up or leaves before nine tomorrow morning." Adam hoped he sounded convincing.

He got into the hire car. "See you at nine thirty tomorrow morning. Prompt," he added.

As Adam drove away, for the first time since Heidi's death he felt it was Romanov who was on the run.

"What a great honour for our little establishment," said Herr Bischoff, delighted to see the most important banker in the East sitting in his boardroom sharing afternoon tea.

"Not at all, my dear Bischoff," said Poskonov. "After all these years the honour is entirely mine. And kind of you to be so understanding about opening the bank on a Sunday. But now to business. Did you manage to get Romanov to sign the release form?"

"Oh, yes," said Bischoff, matter-of-factly. "He did it without even reading the standard clauses, let alone the extra three we put in."

"So his inheritance automatically returns to the Russian state?"

"That is so, Mr. Poskonov. But what happens when Romanov returns to the bank and demands to know what has become of his inheritance?" asked the chairman of the bank, anxiously.

"He will not return," the Russian banker promised. "You have my word on it. Now, I would like to see what is in those boxes."

The two banking chairmen took the private lift to the basement and Herr Bischoff accompanied his guest to the underground vault.

"Do take as long as you like," he said, "but at six o'clock the great door will be automatically locked until nine o'clock tomorrow morning. At five forty-five, an alarm will go off to warn you that you only have fifteen minutes left." Herr Bischoff handed Comrade Poskonov the envelope with Romanov's key inside it.

As soon as the massive steel door had been swung closed behind him the Russian checked the clock on the wall. He had over two hours to sort out what could be transported to Brazil and what would have to be left behind.

He opened the first of the small boxes and found the deeds to lands which the state had owned for decades. He growled. The second box contained the shares of companies once brilliantly successful, now shells in every sense of the word. And to Poskonov's disappointment the third of the small boxes only contained a will proving everything belonged to Romanov's father and his immediate heirs. Had he waited all these years to discover that the gold, jewels and pearls were nothing but an old man's fantasy? Or had Romanov already removed them?

Poskonov opened the first of the large boxes and stared down at the twelve little compartments. He removed the lid of the first one tentatively, and when he saw the array of gems that shone in front of him his legs felt weak. He put both hands into the box and let the stones slip through his fingers like a child playing with pebbles on a beach.

He went through the remaining boxes and when the alarm went off he was lost in a daydream, already enjoying his new-found wealth. He glanced at the clock. He would return the following day and remove once and for all all that he had earned by fifty years of service to the state.

When the last lid had been replaced he checked the clock on the wall: six minutes to six. Just enough time to glance in the other box.

He turned the key and pulled the large box out. Just a quick look, he promised himself, as he lifted the lid. When he saw the decaying body with its grey skin and stiffened limbs he reeled backwards and, falling to the floor, clutched at his heart.

Both bodies were discovered at nine the next morning.

ADAM SAT ON HIS BED at the Royal Garden Hotel considering the implications of his plan, for nearly an hour. Then he picked up the phone beside the bed and dialled the number Robin had given him. The phone rang several times before it was answered by an elderly voice saying, "Mrs. Beresford."

"Good morning, Mrs. Beresford. My name is Adam Scott, I'm a friend of Robin's. I was just phoning to check that she reached home safely last night."

"Oh, yes, thank you," said Robin's mother. "It was a pleasant surprise to see her. I'm afraid she's still asleep. Would you like me to wake her?"

"No, no, don't disturb her," said Adam. "I only rang to fix up a lunch date. Can you tell her I'll call back later?"

"I certainly will," she replied.

Adam replaced the receiver and smiled. Each piece of the jigsaw was fitting neatly into place. He began to put Tomkins's passport, personal papers and wallet into a large envelope. Then he removed the icon from his jacket pocket, turned it over and carefully examined the little silver crest of the tsar. He flicked open the colonel's penknife and began the slow and delicate task of removing the crown.

Thirty minutes later, Adam took the lift to the ground floor and settled his bill.

At nine twenty-three he asked the doorman to bring the green Ford up from the car park. He waited by the hotel entrance.

As the minutes passed, he began to fear that Tomkins wouldn't turn up. If he failed, Adam knew that the next call would have to be to Lawrence, not Romanov.

His reverie was disturbed by a honk on a car horn; the green Ford had been parked by the entrance.

"Your car is waiting on the ramp," said the doorman, as he returned the keys to Adam.

"Thank you," said Adam and handed over the last of the colonel's pound notes. He dropped the wallet into the large envelope, which he sealed.

He stood waiting for another two minutes before he spotted the colonel puffing up the slope to the hotel entrance. He was clutching a small carrier bag.

"I've done it, Captain Scott, sir, I've done it," he said as he reached Adam's side. "But I must return immediately or he's bound to notice it's gone."

He passed the carrier bag quickly to Adam who opened it and stared down at the object inside.

"You're a man of your word," said Adam, "and as promised you'll find everything you need in there." He passed over his own package, along with the car keys, without speaking. He pointed to the hired car.

The colonel ran to it, jumped in and drove quickly away.

Adam checked his watch: nine thirty-five. He hailed a taxi. "The Woodwork Shop, King's Road."

Adam spent twenty minutes in the shop while the craftsman carried out his unusual request. Adam paid him two half crowns and walked back into King's Road, to hail another taxi.

"Where to, guv'nor?"

"The Tower of London."

EVERYONE WAS IN HIS PLACE for the D4 meeting at nine thirty, and Busch was on the attack even before Lawrence had had a chance to sit down.

"How in hell did you manage to lose him this time?"

"I must take the blame myself," said Lawrence. "We had every port from Newhaven to Harwich covered, but the moment my man saw Romanov leave the quayside at Dover and follow the coach, he assumed he must have seen Scott."

"But we were given a second chance when Scott got on the train," persisted Busch. Lawrence stared at the American, waiting to see if he would admit that his two CIA agents had lost Scott at Boulogne.

"My man on the train," said Lawrence emphatically, "had only one opportunity to make private contact with Scott, and at just that moment he was grabbed and beaten up by a bunch of louts."

"So, as far as we can tell, Scott, the Tsar's Icon and Romanov are still holed up somewhere in London?" said Snell.

"It looks that way," admitted Lawrence.

"Perhaps all is not lost then," suggested Snell. "Scott may still try and get in touch with you again."

"I think not," said Lawrence quietly. "Scott knows that one of us in this room is a traitor, and he thinks it's me."

"GOOD MORNING. Soviet embassy."

"My name is Adam Scott and I need to get in touch with Major Romanov."

"We do not have a Major Romanov working at the embassy," came back the polite reply.

"I'm sure you don't, but it wouldn't surprise me if you were to find him very quickly once he knows who is calling."

There was a long silence at the other end, then, at last, Adam heard a familiar voice ask, "Who is this?"

"You know very well who it is," said Adam curtly. "I want to make a deal."

"A deal?" Romanov repeated.

"I'll swap you my icon—which, as you so vividly pointed out, is worthless to me—in exchange for your copy, which is not. But I require the papers that prove my father's innocence."

"How do I know you're not setting me up?"

"You don't," said Adam. "But you're the one with nothing to lose."

The pips began to sound across the line, and Romanov asked for Adam's number.

"Mansion House 9121," said Adam.

"I'll phone you back," said Romanov, then turned to the local KGB operative who sat opposite him. "How quickly can we find out where Mansion House 9121 is located?"

"About ten minutes," the aide replied. "But it could be a trap."

"True, but with nineteen hours to go before the icon has to be in America I don't have a lot of choice. The next thing I need is a motorbike and a superb driver."

ADAM COULD DO NOTHING about the middle-aged lady who was occupying his phone booth. He had nervously walked out to check the bridge, and she had slipped in.

It was ten forty-five. He knew he couldn't risk waiting a minute after eleven but was confident that Romanov would have traced where he'd made the call from long before then.

The talkative woman was another twelve minutes before she eventually put the phone down.

Adam began to watch the Beefeaters as they patrolled under Traitors' Gate. Traitors' Gate—how appropriate, Adam thought. He had chosen the spot because he could see clearly up and down the path leading to the drawbridge and felt he could not be taken by surprise. And in desperation there was always the moat that surrounded them on all sides.

When the phone rang, it sounded like an alarm bell. He picked it up nervously.

"Scott?"

"Yes."

"I can see you clearly. I will be at the end of the bridge in less than one minute. Be sure you're there with the icon. If you're not, I shall burn the papers that prove your father's innocence, in front of you."

The phone went dead.

Adam stepped out of the phone booth and looked up and down the road. A BMW motorcycle drew up at the end of the bridge. A rider dressed in a leather jacket sat astride the bike but it was the man seated behind him who stared directly at Adam.

Adam began to walk slowly towards the end of the bridge. He put a hand in his pocket to be sure the icon was still in its place.

He was about thirty yards from the end of the bridge when the second figure got off the bike and started walking towards him. When their eyes met, Romanov stopped in his tracks and held up a small, square frame. Adam simply tapped the side of his pocket and continued walking. Both

166

men advanced towards each other like knights of old, until they were only a few paces apart.

"Let me see it," said Romanov.

Adam slowly removed the icon from his pocket and held it to his chest for his adversary to see.

"Turn it over," said Romanov.

Adam obeyed, and the Russian could not hide his delight when he saw the little silver crown of the Tsar embedded in the back.

"Now you," said Adam. Romanov held his icon away from his body, as if brandishing a sword. Rublev's masterpiece shone in the summer sun.

"And the documents," said Adam, forcing himself to speak calmly.

The Russian pulled some papers from his jacket and slowly unfolded them. Adam stared at the official court verdict for a second time.

"Go to the wall," said Adam, pointing to the side of the bridge, "and leave the icon and the documents on it."

Romanov obeyed as Adam proceeded to the wall on the other side of the bridge and placed his icon in the middle of it.

"Cross slowly," called Adam. The two men moved back across the bridge, passing a couple of yards from each other until they had come to a halt at each other's icon. The moment the painting was within his reach, Romanov grabbed it, ran and jumped onto the motorcycle. Within seconds the BMW had disappeared into the dense traffic.

Adam did not move. Although it had only been out of his sight for just over an hour, he was relieved to have the original icon back. He checked the documents and placed them in his inside pocket. Adam began to relax, when suddenly he felt a sharp prod in the middle of his back. He jumped round in fright.

A little girl was staring up at him.

"Will you and your friend be performing again this morning?"

WHEN THE BMW MOTORCYCLE drew up outside the Soviet embassy, Romanov leaped off, ran up the steps and straight into the ambassador's office without knocking. "It worked just as I planned," he said, as he handed over the icon to the ambassador.

The ambassador turned the painting over and saw the little silver crown of the tsar. Any doubts that he might have had were now dispelled.

"I have orders to send the icon to Washington in the diplomatic pouch immediately. There is no time to be lost."

He pressed a button on the side of his desk. Two men appeared instantly.

"There is a plane standing by at Heathrow to take you to Washington," he said to the couriers. "You should touch down at around five o'clock

Washington time, easily giving our comrades in America enough time to fulfil their part of the contract."

The two men nodded, and when the icon had been placed in the pouch, they sealed the pouch in the ambassador's presence and left to be driven to Heathrow.

"Vodka, Comrade Major?"

"Thank you," Romanov replied.

The ambassador went over to a cabinet and took out two glasses and a bottle. "It would not be exaggerating to say you have played your part in establishing the Soviet Union as the most powerful nation on earth," he said as he handed over a vodka. "Let us therefore drink to the repatriation of the people of the Aleutian Islands as full citizens of the USSR."

"How is that possible?" asked Romanov.

"I think the time has come to let you know," said the ambassador, "the significance of your achievement." He told Romanov of the briefing he had received from Moscow that morning.

Romanov was thankful he had never known how much was at stake.

"To the Aleuts," he said, raising his glass. "But what is happening in Washington at this moment?"

"Our ambassador has already requested a meeting with the American secretary of state, scheduled for eight this evening. He is also setting up a press conference at the embassy to follow that meeting. President Johnson has requested that the networks should allow him to address his fellow Americans at peak time this evening on a matter of national importance."

"And we achieved it with only hours to spare," said Romanov, shuddering at the thought of how close it had been.

"You must join me for lunch, comrade," said the ambassador. "Although your orders are to return to Moscow immediately my secretary assures me that the first plane leaving Heathrow for Moscow does not depart until eight this evening. I envy you the reception you will receive when you arrive back in the Kremlin tomorrow."

"I still need the £1000 for . . ."

"Ah, yes," said the ambassador, "I have it ready for you."

BUSCH BARGED into Lawrence's office.

"Romanov's got the icon," he shouted.

Lawrence's jaw dropped. "How can you be so sure?" he demanded.

"I've just had a message from Washington. The Russians have requested an official meeting with the secretary of state to be arranged for eight this evening. We've always known that goddamned friend of yours, like his father, was a lousy traitor."

"He could be dead," said Lawrence quietly.

The phone on his desk rang. He grabbed it as if it were a lifeline. "A Dr. John Vance wants a word with you, sir," said his secretary. "He said you had asked him to call."

"Put him on," Lawrence said. He couldn't quite place Vance.

"Good morning, Mr. Pemberton," said a voice. "You asked me to call you after I had examined Scott."

"Scott?" repeated Lawrence, not believing what he was hearing.

"Yes, Adam Scott. You wanted him to complete a medical."

Lawrence was speechless.

"I've given him a clean bill of health," continued the doctor. "Some nasty bruises and a shoulder wound, but nothing that won't heal in a few days."

"Mr. Scott isn't there with you at this moment, by any chance?"

"No," said Vance. "Left my surgery about ten minutes ago. He said something about having to see a friend off at the airport."

ROMANOV CHECKED HIS WATCH. He had left easily enough time to keep the appointment with Mentor and still catch the plane. He thanked the ambassador for lunch, and climbed into the back of the anonymous black car. The driver had already been briefed as to where the major wanted to go.

Neither of them spoke on the short journey, and when the driver drew into Charlotte Street, Romanov stepped out and walked quickly across the road. He pressed the bell.

"Are you a member?" said a voice through the intercom.

"Yes," said Romanov, who heard a metallic click as he pushed the door open and walked down the staircase. Once he had entered the club he spotted Mentor seated on his own at a little table in the far corner of the room.

Romanov nodded and the man got up and walked straight past him. Romanov followed as the member entered the only lavatory. Once inside, Romanov checked that they were alone. Satisfied, he led the man into a cubicle and slipped the lock to engaged. Romanov removed the thousand pounds from his pocket and handed it over. Mentor greedily ripped open the packet and began to count. He never even saw Romanov straighten his fingers, and when the hand came down with a crushing blow on the back of Mentor's neck he slumped forward and fell to the ground in a heap.

Romanov yanked him up; it took several seconds to gather the ten-pound notes that had fallen on the floor. Romanov then undid the member's trousers and let them fall around his ankles. He sat the man on the lavatory seat. He then slipped under the large gap at the bottom of the door leaving the cubicle locked from the inside. All that could be seen from the outside were the man's splayed legs and fallen trousers.

Sixty seconds later, Romanov was back in the car and on his way to Heathrow.

ADAM ARRIVED AT HEATHROW two hours before the Aeroflot flight was due to depart, at eight o'clock. He stationed himself with a perfect view of the forty-yard stretch Romanov would have to walk to board the Russian aircraft.

"BEA ANNOUNCE THE DEPARTURE of their flight 117 to Moscow. Would all first-class passengers now board through gate number twenty-three." Romanov left the departure lounge and walked the long corridor to the plane. He couldn't resist taking the BEA flight rather than Aeroflot even though he knew Zaborski would frown at such arrogance. Romanov walked to the waiting plane a few minutes after six fifty. On board, he was annoyed to find that he had been placed next to another passenger, but was thankful that he had been given the window seat.

"Would you care for a drink before takeoff?" the stewardess asked.

"Just black coffee for me," said his neighbour. Romanov nodded his agreement.

The stewardess arrived back a few minutes later with the two coffees and helped the two men pull out their tables.

Romanov took a sip of his coffee but it was too hot, so he placed it on the table in front of him. He watched his neighbour take out a packet of saccharine from his pocket and flick two pellets into the steaming coffee.

Romanov stared out of the window and watched the Aeroflot plane start to taxi out onto the runway. He tried his coffee a second time: just as he liked it. He took a long gulp and began to feel a little drowsy. He leaned back in his seat. He would take every honour the state could offer him. He might even position himself to take over from Zaborski. If that failed, his grandfather had left him another alternative.

He was leaving London with only one regret: he had failed to kill Scott. But then he suspected that the Americans would take care of that. For the first time in a week he didn't have to stop himself falling asleep . . .

A few moments later the passenger seated next to Romanov picked up the Russian's coffee cup and put it next to his own. He then flicked Romanov's table back and placed a woollen blanket over the Russian's legs. He slipped the BEA eyeshades over Romanov's head, covering his open eyes. He looked up to see the stewardess standing by his side.

"Can I help?" she asked, smiling.

"No, thank you. All he said was that he did not want to be disturbed during the flight as he has had a very hard week."

"Of course, sir," said the stewardess. "We'll be taking off in a few minutes," she added, as she picked up the two coffee cups and whisked them away.

Romanov's neighbour tapped his fingers impatiently on the armrest. At last the chief steward appeared at his side. "There's been a call from your office, sir. You're to return to Whitehall immediately."

"I had been half expecting it," he admitted.

ADAM STARED UP at the Russian plane as it climbed steeply and swung in a semicircle towards the East. He couldn't understand why Romanov hadn't boarded it. Surely he wouldn't have taken the BEA flight. Then he stared in disbelief. Lawrence was striding across the tarmac towards the terminal, a smile of satisfaction on his face.

Epilogue
SOTHEBY'S, NEW BOND STREET, LONDON   18 OCTOBER 1966

"We now move on to Lot number thirty-two," said the auctioneer, from the raised platform at the front of the crowded room. "An icon of St. George and the Dragon," he declared, as an attendant placed a little painting on the easel next to him. The auctioneer stared down at the faces of experts, amateurs and curious onlookers.

"I haven't felt this nervous since I came face to face with Romanov," whispered Robin.

"Don't remind me," said Adam.

"It is not, of course, the original, which hangs in the Winter Palace in Leningrad," continued the auctioneer, "but it is nevertheless a fine copy, probably executed by a court painter circa 1890," he added, giving the little painting an approving smile. "Do I have an opening bid? Shall I say eight thousand?" The next few seconds seemed interminable to Robin and Adam. "Thank you, sir," said the auctioneer, looking towards an anonymous sign that had been given somewhere at the front of the room.

"How much did the expert say it might go for?" Robin asked Adam again.

"Anywhere between ten and twenty thousand," he reminded her.

"Nine thousand," said the auctioneer, his eyes moving to a bid that appeared to come from the right-hand side of the room.

"I still think it's amazing," said Robin, "that in the end we let the Russians have the original icon back."

"Why?" asked Adam. "After all, it belonged to them in the first place and of course the treaty had been extracted." He paused. "I think the really amazing thing is that Lawrence persuaded the Russians to let us have the copy in return."

"And that you ended up with it," added Robin. "Even more amazing."

"Yes, as an example of diplomatic ingenuity, it was Lawrence at his most brilliant," said Adam, smiling.

"Ten thousand from the front of the room. Thank you, sir," said the auctioneer.

"What are you going to do with all that money?"

"Buy you a double bass, get a wedding present for my sister and hand over the rest to my mother."

"Eleven thousand, a new bid in the centre aisle," said the auctioneer. "Thank you, madam."

"No amount of money can bring back Heidi," said Robin quietly.

Adam nodded thoughtfully. "The foreign secretary saw Heidi's parents last week. At least he was able to confirm that I had only been telling them the truth."

"Twelve thousand." The auctioneer's eye returned to the front of the room.

"Did you see the foreign secretary yourself?"

"Good heavens, no, I'm far too junior for that," said Adam. "I'm lucky if I get to see Lawrence, let alone the foreign secretary."

Robin laughed. "I consider you were lucky to have been offered a place at the Foreign Office at all."

"Agreed," said Adam, chuckling to himself, "but a vacancy arose unexpectedly."

"What do you mean, 'unexpectedly'?" asked Robin.

"All that I can tell you is that one of Lawrence's old team, a rather embittered old chap called Matthews, was 'retired early'," said Adam.

"Was that true for Romanov also?" asked Robin, still desperately trying to discover all that had taken place since they last met.

"Thirteen thousand," said the auctioneer, his eyes returning to the lady in the centre aisle.

"After all, he can't have survived for long once they discovered you had done a switch that gave the Russians back the copy while Romanov ended up presenting you with the original," said Robin.

"He's never been heard of since," admitted Adam innocently.

"I suppose I will have to go to my grave wondering what treaty was inside that icon?"

Adam looked away from the girl who had saved his life.

"Destined to remain the Foreign Office's best-kept secret, I'm afraid."

"What happened when you produced those court papers proving that it was not your father who had smuggled the poison into Goering's cell?" asked Robin.

"Lawrence paid an official visit to the colonel of the regiment and furnished him with the conclusive evidence. They're going to hold a memorial service for Pa and have commissioned a portrait for the regimental mess. Mother has been invited to unveil it."

"Fourteen thousand for the first time then," said the auctioneer raising the little gavel a few inches in the air.

"She must have been over the moon," said Robin.

"Burst into tears," said Adam. "All she could say was 'I wish Pa could have lived to see it.'"

"Fourteen thousand for the second time," said the auctioneer, the gavel now hovering. His hammer came down with a thud. They both looked up.

"Sold to the gentleman at the front for fourteen thousand pounds."

"How do you fancy a celebration lunch at the Ritz?" asked Adam.

JEFFREY ARCHER

It has often been said that Jeffrey Archer's own story reads like an international best-seller. Born in Somerset in 1940, the son of an army officer, he seemed marked for success while still a student at Oxford University: here he gained an athletics blue, was president of the University Athletics Club, and represented Great Britain for sprinting. Another achievement was to raise one million pounds for Oxfam by persuading the Beatles to perform a special concert.

After leaving Oxford he was elected to the Greater London Council as its youngest-ever member, and in 1969 he became the youngest Member of Parliament. A promising political career stretched ahead for this young Tory; but in 1974 a company in which he had invested heavily failed, leaving Archer nearly half a million pounds in debt.

So, at 34, he resigned from the House of Commons and started again from scratch. He decided to write a book. His first novel, *Not a Penny More, Not a Penny Less*, was an instant, staggering international success, and since then five more best-selling novels have followed, including *Kane and Abel*, which has appeared as a television series.

His success has bought Archer a stunning London flat overlooking the Thames, and the Old Vicarage, Grantchester, a house immortalized in a famous poem by Rupert Brooke. The vicarage was lovingly restored by Jeffrey Archer's wife, Mary, who teaches chemistry at Cambridge University, and is also home to their two sons. But Jeffrey Archer is not one to sit at home resting on his laurels. Ever eager for a challenge, he has returned to political life as Deputy Chairman of the Conservative Party, a job which involves an exhausting round of speechmaking, press conferences and organization.

Jeffrey Archer states firmly that he will not be writing again until after the next election, but fortunately for his legions of fans, *A Matter of Honour* was finished before Archer took up his new appointment. "It's a modern *Thirty-Nine Steps*," he says. "Because I still fervently believe that the old-fashioned heroes are best."

ICE TREK

A CONDENSATION OF THE BOOK BY

EWAN CLARKSON

ILLUSTRATED BY NEVILLE DEAR

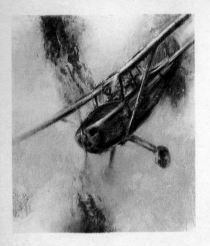

Two men stranded in the vast, frozen wilderness of northwest Alaska, two men who could not be more different: Umiak, a reserved, diffident Eskimo, and Larsen, an ambitious, self-confident American. Neither expects to share the other's company for longer than a short plane journey—but when the light aircraft crashes, killing the pilot, Umiak and Larsen are thrown together in a desperate struggle for survival.

With no chance of rescue and with winter closing in, their only hope is to begin a hazardous trek across the mountains. Threatened by hunger and cold the two men pit their wits against the hostile elements, and to Larsen's chagrin he discovers superior strengths in his reluctant companion. But all rivalries must be forgotten as they flee the greatest danger of all: a stalking grizzly bear, hungry for human flesh . . .

An empty can, caught by the wind, rattled across the icy stones. The brief summer had almost passed. The sea was restless, stained with the blood of the dying sun, and the wind from the west was cold with the breath of the ice floes. The floes were not yet visible. They lay beyond the horizon some thirty miles out to sea, but soon, Steve Larsen knew, they would be just offshore, jostling and growling amongst themselves as they groped for a blind stranglehold on the land.

East lay the wilderness, brooding and dark, a vast expanse of rolling hills and flat desolate marsh, of bog myrtle and cotton grass, and a few wind-bitten, sun-starved willows, an endless waste that was the tundra.

Between, on a strip of land that lay curved like a bear's paw out into the sea, lay the settlement, a few prefabricated houses randomly scattered on the thin turf that flanked the shore. All around lay a chaotic litter of snow machines, dog sleds, dinghies and outboard motors. Oildrums were everywhere, painted bright red for easy location in the snow. Here and there drying frames for fish or hides, built of windfretted driftwood, stood skeletal against the sky. Empty now, they served as perches for the ravens that scavenged along the shingle shore, where shreds of torn plastic snapped and crackled in the wind.

The Eskimo settlement was almost deserted. Most of the men were still away in summer employment, and the women had taken themselves, with their children and old folk, to summer camps where they spent their time berry-picking. Larsen pulled his parka hood over his cropped blond hair. He was a lanky Swedish-American from the Midwest, a man fast approaching middle age who refused to admit it. Stepping gingerly between the mounds of decaying blubber that littered the tide line, he picked his way to the shelter of an abandoned boat.

Larsen squatted down on his haunches. It was a trick he had acquired as a US marine, during interminable days and nights in damp steaming jungles on the other side of the world. Even now, years later, he could still squat for hours without discomfort.

He gazed northward, his pale blue eyes watering a little with the effort, to where a series of flat ridges climbed steadily towards hills that were shrouded in mist. Earlier, he had walked some way over those ridges, ancient raised beaches where for years archaeologists had burrowed in the permafrost, trying to piece together the lifestyle of the people who for thousands of years had made their homes there. He had picked up a flint arrowhead and rather guiltily shoved it in his pocket, knowing that this was a violation of the Antiquities Act, which forbade the collection of native artifacts.

He looked out to sea. Once there had been a land bridge out there, linking Alaska with Siberia. Over the marshy plain hunters had journeyed, following the great game herds that were their livelihood. Then the sea had risen, separating the two continents, but even the icy waters had proved no barrier. For centuries people had crossed these straits in frail skin boats, for trade, brides and barter. Now, the continents and their people were divided by a power very different from the forces of nature, an idea in the minds of men.

Larsen was accustomed to thinking of communism as a product of the East, and capitalism of the West. Now he found himself in the topsy-turvy position of looking west towards communism, while capitalism lay behind him to the east. He was on the shores of a land whose people were the last descendants of a culture older, longer-lasting, better tried and tested than either of the other two. Now these people were being tempted, coerced, into a monetarist system which might or might not sustain them, and were losing the skills which had enabled them to survive since long before the dawn of agriculture.

Larsen felt in his pocket for the arrowhead and pulled it out. It was tiny, leaf-shaped, exquisitely crafted, the point still sharp enough to pierce the skin. Was all this endeavour, this ingenuity and invention, to perish like the arrowmaker himself? Was the Eskimo culture to be replaced by the squalor he now saw surrounding him? If so, it was a pity, the more so since he himself had hoped to cash in on that lifestyle before it disappeared entirely.

Though much of his war he preferred to forget, especially the long, fever-ridden days spent in the Vietnamese jungle, yet there had been good times too, and a chance to travel, and after his discharge the hunger for new places lingered. He had reasoned that if he felt this way so must numbers of others, and that they might be prepared to pay to have their hunger satisfied. So he set up his own travel agency, specializing in tours to out-of-the-way places, and he proved himself right. The business was a success, and he could have expanded, but he preferred to stay small, to offer a personal service and to charge highly for it. So he ran the agency on his own; or almost, for he had started with one girl assistant, Sylvie, who was now a woman, and with whom he had fallen deeply in love.

Earlier that year he had learned that Congress was to create a number of new national parks and nature reserves in the remotest regions of Alaska, and that the native peoples, the Eskimos and Indians, were to be allowed to retain their traditional rights to hunt and fish, and to continue, so far as they wished, their subsistence lifestyle. It occurred to him that some wealthy white Americans might enjoy the combination of a wilderness experience and a chance to view the Eskimo way of life. So, as soon as he could spare the time, he had come north to explore the possibilities of such a tour. He had quickly been disillusioned.

The region was too inaccessible, the terrain too hazardous and the climate too harsh to tempt any but very young, strong and adventurous people—who could never afford the cost. There was also a distinct lack of amenities. He had discovered that even the most elderly tourists would endure considerable privations during the day, as long as they were promised a hot shower and a soft bed at the end of it. Here, he could make no such promise.

Then there was the reserved attitude of the people themselves. "It's like this," one of them had explained, "I can't kill a seal to order, especially with a bunch of pointy-toed tourists breathing down my neck. Would you like it if you were fixing your car in your driveway, and a crowd of us gathered round to watch, laughing and taking photographs?"

Even if the natives had been more friendly there were other problems. The summer peak of the tourist trade did not fit in with the seasonal pattern of hunting activity. The spring whaling and sealing would be over, the autumn caribou hunt had yet to begin, and in July, he had been told, the bugs were unbearable.

So Larsen had his doubts, and these he now expressed out loud in a message to his assistant, speaking softly into the personal tape recorder he always carried.

"Sylvie honey, this is just about the end of the trip, and our hopes. There are no walrus, no polar bear, no caribou and no wolves, at least not within fifty miles, and these Eskimos don't look the part somehow, not a fur-lined parka among the lot of them. Most of them seem to be dressed in an assortment of government surplus clothing. Worse, they just aren't interested in tourists, or in trading souvenirs."

He paused. There was one last chance. Away to the east lay a mighty chain of mountains, the Brooks Range, effectively isolating the Arctic from southern Alaska. Deep in the heart of this mountain barrier, situated in a broad valley which bisected the range, one of the few land routes from north to south, lay the tiny native settlement of Anaktuvuk.

There was no access by road or rail. The supply road to the oilfields at Prudhoe Bay lay even further to the east. The only way in to Anaktuvuk Pass was by air. Yet here, less than forty years ago, a group of nomadic Eskimos had settled down to hunt the caribou and the wild sheep and the bear. They also, Larsen had been told, ran a profitable sideline in native souvenirs, which they sold in cities further south. The pilot of the plane he had chartered was willing to fly him there, and if the place turned out to be as big a disappointment as this coastal settlement, then at least he would be halfway to Fairbanks and a jet service back to the States.

He pressed the record button again.

"I'm flying back to civilization shortly, but tomorrow I'll head east about three hundred miles, to a place in the mountains where I'm told the natives carve souvenir masks. I'll bring one back for you. In fact, I expect I'll be back in the office myself before you get this tape, but I'll mail it for you anyway. Take care! Steve."

He switched off the recorder and rose to his feet. With his right shoulder hunched against the wind he started briskly back along the dusty dirt trail that led towards the settlement. Already he could hear the faint drone of the aircraft coming to take him back to the nearest coastal town, and he felt thankful he would not have to linger long.

The four-seater Cessna was waiting on the airstrip. It was old and battered. Some of the dents looked as though the plane had flown through a barrage of golf balls. "Hailstones," the pilot explained cheerfully. "We run into them all the time."

Larsen shuddered. The knowledge that the pilot would have had to apply at regular intervals for a certificate of airworthiness did little to calm his mind.

Tibbett, the pilot, was a Texan, though Larsen would not have guessed it. The man was so small he might have been a professional jockey. Handy, though, for a bush pilot, thought Larsen. The less pilot the plane has to carry, the more freight it can bear.

The Texan was sitting now at the controls of the plane, chewing on the burnt-out stub of a cigar. He threw away the cigar as Larsen climbed aboard, but the rank smell lingered.

"Find the North Pole then?" he queried.

"Didn't know it was lost," grunted Larsen. "Now, if you could fly me to a Scotch?"

"Like an Apache arrow, boy," said Tibbett. "Mind, it will cost you. I

182

swear that stuff's so precious by the time it's been freighted in that it's worth more than all the gold that came out of the Klondyke!"

Larsen let him ramble on. He had a bottle of Scotch in his hotel room. He buckled on his seat belt as the engine roared reassuringly to life, and sat back in the cramped confines of the cabin, trying to relax and barely bothering to look down as the plane lurched and bounced a thousand feet above the tundra. He was tired and hungry, and the chill wind from the sea seemed to linger in his bones.

The seaport was as squalid as the settlement, but busier, noisier, and more crowded. Yet he was grateful for the warm blast of air that hit him as he entered the hotel. It was run-down and seedy, smelling of fish and fried bacon, unwashed humanity and warm wet wool, but at least his bed was comfortable and the food was good.

A modern hotel was under construction close by, built with some of the money awarded to the natives in partial settlement of their land claims. The half million square miles of wilderness that was called Alaska, the great land, was being carved up. The state was acquiring about a third. The natives had settled for less than half of that, but in addition would receive almost a hundred million dollars in compensation—money that was being managed now by regional corporations run by the natives themselves.

Up in his room, Larsen took the bottle from his holdall, poured a generous measure into his toothmug, and lay back on the bed. He was not as a rule a solitary drinker, but it was cheaper than drinking in the bar. Since practically every essential of life up here had to be flown in, the cost of living was nearly twice what it was in the rest of America, that union of states referred to almost contemptuously by Alaskans as "the lower forty-eight".

He poured himself another drink. After all, he wouldn't be needing the Scotch much longer.

Dinner was good. Larsen chose reindeer steak, mainly because it was half the price of beef. After indulging an appetite sharpened by the Arctic air, and reluctant either to step outside or suffer the solitude of his room, he made for the bar. He ordered a beer, wincing at the price, and leaning back, surveyed the scene.

The air was thick with the haze of tobacco smoke. The clients were mostly Eskimo, fishermen or construction workers in thick plaid shirts. Others, Larsen guessed, were drinking their way through their social security cheques. A group of whites, probably oilmen, played cards at a nearby table.

"Mr. Larsen?"

The voice at his side made him start. The man was older than he, with the black hair, high cheekbones and dark slit eyes of an Eskimo. He was tall, touching six foot, and very thin. "My name is Umiak. It means whaleboat." He giggled nervously, as if he were accustomed to people laughing at the joke.

Larsen waited. What did you say to a man called whaleboat?

"You will forgive me." It was an order rather than a request. "I heard you were flying to Anaktuvuk in the morning, and your pilot has agreed to take me along." He giggled again, irritatingly. "I don't weigh much, and of course I will pay my share of the charter."

Larsen shrugged. He held out his hand. "Welcome aboard, Mr. Umiak."

The man's grip was firm, his palm calloused; he had the hands of a manual worker. Yet he had the air of a leader, with an assurance flawed only by that nervous laugh. It came again, grating. "What takes you to a place like Anaktuvuk, Mr. Larsen?" he asked.

For a moment Larsen was tempted to tell the stranger it was none of his business. Then it occurred to him that the man could be a useful contact with the natives. So he explained.

Umiak was silent for a moment. "Anaktuvuk is hardly a tourist resort, Mr. Larsen. I personally hope it never becomes one. You might find some examples of native art, if the owners are willing to sell, but most of the inhabitants are too busy leading their own lives to bother to perform for wealthy sightseers."

Too busy sitting around getting legless like this lot, thought Larsen. I'll get no help from this arrogant bastard.

Before Larsen could make any retort Umiak changed the subject. "Our pilot seems to be enjoying himself."

Larsen had not noticed the little Texan until then. Tibbett sat at a table in the corner, his shirtsleeves rolled up above the elbows, challenging all comers to an arm-wrestling contest. He seemed to be leaning rather heavily on the Scotch, and Larsen said so.

Behind them the bartender gave a short rasping bark of a laugh. "Don't worry about him, gentlemen. Drunk or sober, he couldn't pilot his way out of a paper bag. He's only had a few hundred hours flying time, mostly crop-spraying in Alabama, so I'm told. He still has to get through a winter up here. If he can survive until the spring, he might make a bush pilot."

He's trying to faze me, thought Larsen. "Anyway, I hear the forecast is good for tomorrow," he said mildly.

Umiak shrugged. "The stars were dancing when I came in. That means wind. Besides, the mountains breed their own weather, especially now that it's autumn. Still, all forms of transport are hazardous in this country. It's something you learn to live with. And I'm told that the highways in the lower forty-eight can be quite dangerous."

Umiak drifted away to talk to someone further down the bar. Taking advantage of this a young Eskimo girl sidled over and whispered in Larsen's ear. He refused her and she turned away.

He looked into his empty glass. Another few beers and the girl's offer might sound too good to refuse. He went up to his room. He had finished the Scotch before he was able to sleep.

MORNING DAWNED BRIGHT and clear, but biting cold, as if the icy claws of winter were already reaching out. Over breakfast Larsen learned from the proprietor that Tibbett was already up and gone, and had left a message to join him at the plane. Of Umiak there was no sign, so Larsen set off alone, hoping the fresh air would clear the lingering whisky fumes from his head.

The pilot, visibly hungover but cheerful, was studying a map as he arrived. Larsen looked at it over his shoulder. Never before had he seen a chart so devoid of man-made features. No towns, no villages, no roads, no railways, only a scrambling of mountains interlaced with the wandering ribbons of countless rivers, and here and there a few isolated lakes. To the north lay an unmarked expanse of tundra slashed by the sweeping curve of the Colville River.

"Here's where we're heading," said Tibbett, pointing with his cigar to a dot on the map. "Anaktuvuk Pass. No great architectural splendours, I'm afraid. Just a collection of prefabricated houses and shacks, and a winter trail that leads nowhere. There's no other settlement for miles, so we can't miss it, and even if we do we're bound to hit the new service road to Prudhoe Bay." He let fall a shower of ash over the map and swept it aside. "Down here is the territory marked out for the Noatak reserve. Wild country, and further east it's even wilder: the Brooks Range, designated as the Gates of the Arctic National Park."

"We flying over that?" asked Larsen incredulously.

"Hell no," said Tibbett. "We stay up here, over the foothills of the north slope. Still, you should get a good view of the mountains to the south."

"Visual Flying Regulations?" queried Larsen.

"Pretty well. This old rust-bucket doesn't rate anything very so-phisticated in the way of electronics, and anyway half of them are no use out here. Still, I've flown the route a time or two, so I'm getting to know it now." He folded the map, and stowed it into a pocket in the door of the Cessna.

Larsen went to load his holdall in the luggage compartment behind the passenger seats, only to find the space almost filled by two large cardboard cartons. "Freight," explained the Texan. "You're lucky, it could have been a team of huskies." He glanced at his watch, then shrugged. "Chief Umiak should be here any minute. He may be on time, but then again he may not. Time means nothing to these people."

"Is he really a chief?"

"Hell, I wouldn't know. He skippers a whaleboat. Gives him some sort of social standing with his kinsfolk. Hereabouts they only hunt whales in the spring, so for the rest of the year he works for the new native cooperative, looking after their land and money."

Suddenly he laughed. "Boy, you should've seen them in the bar last night after you'd gone to bed ... Money! I tell you, we might as well have poured those millions straight down the drain, because that's where most of it is going."

"If your government paid you compensation for land they'd taken from you, I imagine you'd say it was nobody's damn business *what* you did with it."

Neither American had heard Umiak approach. For a moment Tibbett flushed with embarrassment and anger, then he relaxed. "You're right, it's none of my business."

Umiak, who was carrying a holdall in one hand and a gallon can in the other, made no further comment. He climbed aboard the Cessna, seating himself in one of the passenger seats behind the pilot. He was neatly but warmly attired as though for a day's hunting, his trousers tucked into knee-length boots, a heavy wool jacket belted over a blue wool shirt. On his head he wore a peaked cap with flaps that pulled down to serve as earmuffs.

After a moment's hesitation Larsen joined him, leaving the Texan alone up front. The Cessna quivered as the engine warmed to full power. Then they bounced and jolted along the airstrip and took off into the sun.

Gradually the drone of the engine seemed to lessen as Larsen's ears adjusted. Below them the tundra stretched in a wide circle to the horizon, a jewelled tapestry of fawns and browns, interwoven with threads of silver and crimson and gold, splashed with patches of muted green and olive. Small round ponds glistened like diamonds, and here and there the land was patterned with giant hexagons fashioned by the frost. Always in attendance, small against the earth, lay the dense black shadow of the plane, like an albatross.

Slowly the land began to rise, and in the valleys snow lay in grey-white drifts, draining away into silver tongues of streams that flashed briefly in the sunlight. Umiak seemed wholly engrossed in the scene, shifting occasionally in his seat as some detail of the terrain caught his eye. Once he tapped Larsen on the knee, pointing. "Caribou," he said excitedly. Larsen stared down, but could discern nothing.

The plane was climbing now, gaining height as the ground rose beneath them. Snowfields were more numerous and wider, so that Larsen had to shield his eyes from the reflected glare of the sun. To his right mountains were rising like a wall.

Individual peaks began to show, to the north as well as the south, black against the sky. The ride grew bumpier, and Larsen felt his ears pop as the plane climbed even higher. From time to time they crossed wide valleys, where rivers twisted among rocks and gravel bars that told of earlier floods. To the north the sky was blue, but to the east and south it was paler, whiter, and the far tops of the mountains were lost in haze. Suddenly Larsen noticed that the shadow of the plane no longer held station beside them. The sun had vanished.

Steadily the sky darkened. Then the storm hit them, wrapping them in a veil of snowflakes which spattered in starshells over the windscreen of the plane. Umiak leaned forward, shouting to the pilot to turn north and fly out of it, but the Texan only shook his head and pointed upwards. The first flash of lightning split the air, and the plane shook as the thundercrack drowned the roar of the engine.

The storm was but a local disturbance of the elements among the jagged summits of the mountains. One of many thousand such events—a sudden rise in the temperature of the air trapped in a valley, a fall in barometric pressure, a wind eddying out of an unnamed abyss, any of these factors could spawn such a storm, which might die in infancy, or grow into a monster that could rage for days.

But now hailstones added to the din and, as the Cessna began to climb, hurricane-force winds swept the little plane south. The hailstorm came thicker, together with slushy wet snow sweeping in like waves whipped from a stormy sea. Ice began to gather on the leading edges of the wings, its weight forcing the plane down, only to flake away in ragged chunks, causing the Cessna to lift once more.

Grimly the pilot wrestled with the controls, cursing as the plane bucked and lurched. Behind him Umiak sat quite still, his head bowed, his face expressionless. Only his clenched fists betrayed his anxiety. Wildly Larsen looked about him. They were deep in the mountains now, and as he watched through a rent in the clouds the gigantic black wall of a precipice reared up beside them. Instinctively he flung up an arm to protect himself, and then the plane leaped skyward and the mountain peak flashed past the window and fell away below them.

187

Suddenly he remembered reading that on average four planes crashed in Alaska every week. Strangely, he felt no fear, only a deep regret that his life was about to end uselessly, with so many ambitions unfulfilled. If I have to die, he thought bitterly, why can't it be for some purpose?

Then, as if in answer to his unspoken prayer, the storm began to abate. The snow and hail turned to rain, the clouds began to whiten, and the lightning now flickered far behind them. The rain lessened, giving way to white, cottonwool mist. All three men relaxed. Tibbett pointed away to his left. "Guess we maybe drifted a bit off course," he shouted. "I'm going to try and fly out of this. Take a look around."

There was no warning of danger in the mist ahead. Quite gently the Cessna slid onto the shoulder of a snow-covered hill, the rounded flank of an unnamed mountain on the northern slopes of the Brooks Range. It was almost a normal landing, and for a moment it seemed as though the pilot would succeed in bringing the plane to a halt. Then one wing-tip clipped the side of the hill and the plane slewed sharply round into a leaning column of granite, a ragged clenched fist of rock. There was a scream of tortured metal as the propeller bit vainly into the rock. The control panel buckled and the windscreen shattered. The pilot's last act in the face of death was to cut the engine ignition, thus reducing the risk of fire.

Larsen caught a final fleeting glimpse of the pilot's face, his eyes staring and his mouth open, as the leaning granite buttress smashed into the top of his head, crushing his skull. Then Larsen himself felt an inexorable force fling him forward, and knew no more.

The door of the plane burst open and a flurry of icy wind swept into the cabin, ice-laden, stinging with tiny particles of frozen snow. The full fury of the storm returned.

Umiak reached over and closed the door. For a long time he sat silent, his eyes bright, his whole being intent and listening, alert for fresh danger. It was, he thought, like the moment when the great whale lies still, when the danger and the risk of failure has passed and when, despite the splash of waves and the chatter of the excited crew, you sit alone in a circle of silence, before reality returns and the hard work of towing the carcass back to land begins.

Then he laughed softly to himself, a low throaty chuckle quite unlike the nervous giggle he was prone to when in the company of white men and ill at ease. The giggle was an affliction of which he was not proud, but which he had tried in vain to suppress. Now he laughed not because there was anything funny about his situation but from the sheer joy of finding himself still alive.

The pilot was dead, of that he had no doubt. Blood ran down into the collar of his coat and the metallic reek of it mingled with the fumes of petrol, oil and hot engine. Umiak looked across at Larsen, slumped forward against his seat belt. He must have hit his head at the moment of impact, but Umiak could hear him breathing noisily. He sat the man upright, frowning as he did so.

White men were useless when it came to coping with hardship and cold, even when they were well. And this one was hurt—Umiak had no way of telling how badly. He would just have to wait and see, but it would be easier if Larsen died.

A thought came to him. Scrambling forward, he began to search, first in the cockpit and then, finding nothing, about the body of the pilot. Almost immediately his fingers closed on what he was seeking, the butt of a revolver stuck in the waistband of the dead man's trousers. It was a poor weapon, a thirty-eight of inferior manufacture, but it was fully loaded, and at least the Texan had kept it cleaned and oiled. He hoped he would not need it, but its weight in his jacket pocket made him feel more secure.

He sat back in his seat to wait for the passing of the storm. The plane shook with the force of the wind. The temperature in the cabin dropped and Umiak curled himself up, to conserve heat. Beside him, Larsen breathed more easily, and by and by Umiak fell into a doze.

With a deep, shuddering sigh Larsen came swimming back to consciousness. The plane trembled around him and for a moment he thought they were still airborne. Then recollection came flooding back, and with it the knowledge that the pilot was dead. He glanced across at Umiak slumped in his seat, his face turned away. He too appeared to be dead. At once Larsen was seized with a feeling of helpless rage against this bleak and desolate land.

Then his anger passed as a throbbing pain bit deep into his skull. He lay back in his seat, gasping, and saw Umiak turn his head and look at him expressionlessly.

"We're in trouble," the Eskimo remarked. He said it almost absent-mindedly, as a man might speak who had forgotten his latchkey. "You must have taken a knock," he went on. "You've been out quite a while."

Larsen was shaking with the cold. Umiak remembered seeing a vacuum flask in the cockpit of the plane. Luckily it had survived the crash, and was full of hot coffee. He poured a cup and Larsen took it eagerly.

The coffee was harsh and black, but it stilled his shaking, and he drained the cup. "Where are we?" he asked. "There's a map, isn't there? I was looking at it before we took off."

Umiak shrugged and pointed to the empty map pocket in the door of the plane. "It was stuffed in there, but the door flew open when we crashed. The wind must have carried it away."

For a moment panic seized Larsen. "We've got to look for it."

"In this?" Umiak pointed outside. "It could be twenty miles away by now, and torn to shreds among the rocks."

Larsen sighed in despair. Then anger gripped him once more. "But don't you know where we are? Dammit, you live here."

Umiak smiled patiently. "Nobody lives here."

Helplessly Larsen looked about him. "Then we're trapped. We've got to get out, get back to civilization." A thought struck him. "They'll come looking for us, surely? As soon as we're missed they'll send a plane or a helicopter?"

Umiak sighed. It was just as he had feared. This white man was like all the rest, desperate to do anything except the one thing that made sense, to wait, to do nothing, to conserve body energy until it was needed. "Until this storm passes no one will come looking, and we cannot move. Better to rest, to sleep perhaps, until we see."

"How long, for God's sake?" demanded Larsen.

"A few hours maybe. Perhaps a day or more." Privately, Umiak thought it could be a week, but he felt it best not to say so.

Larsen subsided. It made sense to stay with the plane. It was more likely to be spotted from the air than a human figure. They could make a fire, make smoke, use the upholstery of the plane, and the wiring. Burning plastic gave off thick black smoke. Suddenly he remembered his conversation with Tibbett earlier that morning. According to him Umiak was a person of some standing in his community. "You're expected, aren't you, in Anaktuvuk? Won't you be missed?"

Umiak smiled, but his eyes were bleak. "I'm not expected. I only decided to take the trip when I heard there was room on the plane. As for being missed!" He was about to laugh, but checked himself. "There're lots of people will miss me. The Department of Fish and Game, the Bureau of Land Management, federal agencies. They'll miss me, but I imagine they'll all feel kind of relieved to know I'm no longer around to bother them any more."

"And your own people?" persisted Larsen.

"Sometimes I think they too would prefer to be left alone to go their own way, rather than have me continually nagging and goading them to stand up for their rights."

Despite his impatience, Larsen was tempted to laugh. The man was being so negative. So what was the matter with this guy? Clearly he had been well educated, was even a politician of sorts. Where were his inventiveness and resource?

As if he had asked the question out loud Umiak answered him, voicing his earlier thoughts. "Sometimes the hardest thing of all in an emergency is to do nothing."

It was then that Larsen remembered the tape, the recorded message he had mailed to his assistant before leaving that morning. When he didn't show up on time Sylvie would start telephoning around. She was like that.

190

She'd get things moving, a few days would be all it would take, and they could survive that long. Reassured by this thought, his mind turned elsewhere.

The body of the pilot still sat at the controls. "What are we going to do with him?" Larsen demanded.

"Leave him where he is. He's blocking the draught."

Larsen glanced sharply at Umiak, but the man seemed perfectly serious, and indeed Larsen could see that he spoke the clear truth. "Besides," Umiak went on, "his weight is helping to hold the plane down. If we throw him out we could quite easily turn over, in this wind."

Larsen hadn't thought of that. For all they knew, they could be lodged very precariously, perhaps close to a sheer drop. Until they could see their surroundings there was no way of telling. Relax, he told himself. Relax and wait, like the man says.

His head ached. Umiak had already closed his eyes and curled back into his favourite foetal position. Larsen tried to do the same but his mind would not let him rest. Suddenly he remembered the cartons loaded into the luggage compartment behind his seat. What was in them?

One felt light, the other heavy. He ripped open the lighter one first: it contained popcorn, bag after bag of roasted popcorn. Larsen sighed. Just the thing for a baseball game, but with nothing else to eat he had a feeling he was going to get awfully sick of popcorn. He opened the other carton, less optimistic now.

"Freezer bags," he exploded. "What in hell would an Eskimo want with a thousand assorted plastic freezer bags?"

Umiak opened one eye. His expression was pained. "We found that when we left our hamburgers lying loose in the snow the huskies ate them," he said sarcastically.

I asked for that, thought Larsen ruefully.

Umiak had closed his eyes again. Without opening them he said softly, "The word Eskimo is an insult to my people. It is a term applied by some uncouth forest Indians, meaning eaters of raw meat. It is inaccurate and offensive, as it was meant to be. We are *Inuit*, the people."

Larsen's mind harked back to Umiak's outburst earlier that day, over the waste of native funds. This guy sure is touchy, he thought. Still, I'm stuck with him, so I guess I'll have to try to get along. Aloud he said, "No offence meant. I'm people too."

"No offence taken," answered Umiak. "I just thought you'd be interested to know."

There was silence in the plane. Gradually the light faded. Outside the wind continued to blow. Larsen pulled his coat tighter round him, folded his arms and closed his eyes. For a brief moment he was conscious of the rocking of the plane, and then he fell asleep.

FIRE!

Larsen woke in panic. They badly needed fire. He was cold, colder than he could ever remember. But as a nonsmoker he carried neither lighter nor matches. He could not recall seeing Umiak using tobacco and he was filled with sudden terror that they might be stranded without the means of cooking or heating. Then he remembered that the pilot had smoked cigars. He was sure to have the means of making fire about his person.

It was still night, and Larsen could barely make out the huddled shape of Umiak beside him. It was a moment or two before he realized that the plane was no longer rocking and shaking. The wind had dropped.

Forcing his fingers to uncurl he rubbed at the frozen moisture that rimed the window, and peering out he could just discern a dim whiteness that might have been either snow or mist. By laying his cheek against the frosted pane and squinting up he could see a patch of sky, ablaze with a scattering of stars. He tried to read his watch but failed, so began to massage his arms and legs, trying to restore his circulation. Gradually he began to recover. He thought of waking Umiak, but on reflection felt that it would be unwise. So he passed the time exercising in his seat, flexing his muscles and manipulating his joints, and gradually he began to feel a little warmer. Then he recalled how, in the jungle, where the all-pervading dampness made it impossible to light a fire, they had made small stoves out of ration tins filled with petrol-soaked sand. You had to be careful lighting them or you would lose your eyebrows, but once lit they burned steadily for quite a while. Cheered at the recollection, he noticed that the cabin of the plane was slowly filling with pale grey light.

"Have you ever tasted seal oil, Mr. Larsen?"

Larsen jumped, and then grinned across at the dark eyes that solemnly regarded him. "No. What's it like?"

"You might care to try some." Umiak busied himself in the baggage compartment behind the seats. He took one of the freezer bags, emptied a packet of popcorn into it, and decanted a couple of ounces of liquid from the gallon can he had stowed there.

"This is special," he announced. "It was to have been a gift for a friend of mine in Anaktuvuk, but our need is greater than his. It is made from the oil of the *oogruk*, the bearded seal, which is best, and it's flavoured with *quogak*, a kind of sorrel." He shook the bag so that the popcorn was liberally soaked with oil. "Here, try," he said. "But be careful, it is strong."

It was. But when Larsen had finished coughing he found it was not, after all, so disagreeable. It was at once hot and sour, with overtones of fish. The oily feel in his throat afterwards was perhaps the most disagreeable aspect of the experience. In a surprisingly short time he felt full, and left Umiak to finish the remainder of the bag.

"Now we must drink," said Umiak.

The coffee was barely warm, and there was less than a cup each, but it cleaned the film of oil from Larsen's tongue. "If only we had more oil," mused Umiak, "I could make a lamp."

Larsen told him about his idea for a stove, and Umiak listened, his eyes glittering with interest. "We need a can of some sort."

Larsen pointed to the gallon can containing the seal oil. Umiak nodded. "Later I'll put the oil in a freezer bag. It will be safe there and then we can use the can." He stood up. "Meantime, I have more urgent needs." He opened the door and stepped out of the plane.

After a few moments, Larsen followed. It was full daylight now, and he saw that they were in a narrow valley. Above them the mountains towered so high that they had to crane their necks to see the peaks. The plane lay half buried in snow, in the shadow of the hill.

Across the valley the slopes were bathed in sunlight, swept almost clear of snow by the wind and shining red and gold in the morning light. A tiny stream trickled across the valley floor, glistening between sparkling white bars of sand. Umiak produced the top of the vacuum flask. "Come," he said, making his way to the stream. "We must drink."

"Why?" queried Larsen, as Umiak pressed him to a second cup of icy water.

"You must drink plenty in the cold, because you don't sweat. And if you don't sweat you overload your kidneys. A man can get in plenty of trouble that way."

"Better if this stuff was a bit warmer," grumbled Larsen, but he did as he was told. Already Umiak had deserted him and crossed the stream, clambering up the slope of the hill. Almost immediately he returned.

"Fruits of the Arctic," he announced, holding out a handful of blueberries.

Larsen regarded them sourly. His breakfast still sat queasily on his stomach, in company with the water he had drunk. "Those won't keep us going for long," he remarked.

"They will if you eat enough of them," retorted Umiak. "My people pick hundreds of pounds every year, and store them for the winter. They are rich in vitamins and minerals, and the sugar in them will give you the energy to withstand the cold."

Larsen tried to visualize a hundred pounds of berries, and failed. "I still don't think we're going to get fat on them."

"Bears do," said Umiak, and then he stood very still. Larsen saw fear flicker in his eyes. "Bears do," he repeated softly, staring up towards the head of the valley.

Then a tentacle of fear reached out and gripped Larsen too. This, he knew, was bear country, the last stronghold of the grizzly bear, perhaps

193

the most dangerous quadruped in the whole of the Americas, and they were alone and unarmed. "Do you think . . . is it likely that there are bears around here?" he asked.

Umiak hesitated and then shrugged. "Unlikely," he said. "We're probably too high up in the mountains, and anyway soon the bears will be denning up for the winter."

Thoughts of winter brought a fresh tremor of fear to Larsen. "I've been thinking," he said, anxious to change the subject. "The way the plane is, it's going to be in shadow all day. If we could manhandle it down here it would be warmer. Also it would be more noticeable from the air."

Umiak nodded. "First, though, we must deal with the pilot."

Together, one pushing, the other pulling, they manhandled the corpse out of the plane. It lay on its back in the snow, the limbs stiffened in death so that they stuck up in the air. Umiak searched the pockets. Almost at once he found the lighter and held it up in triumph. Larsen felt a wave of relief. "You've been thinking about that too?"

Umiak nodded and went on searching, but there was little more of any use to them. A wallet, some change, a cigar case and keys—Umiak bundled them in the dead man's handkerchief and set them to one side. Then he began to strip the corpse of its clothing. Without thinking, Larsen made an exclamation of protest.

"Our friend is not likely to feel the cold any more," Umiak rejoined calmly. "We will have more use for his clothes."

"They'll be too small for either of us," demurred Larsen. "He was only a little guy."

"Take off his trousers," Umiak explained patiently. "Split them down the crutch, and you've got a pair of leggings. The sleeves of his coat and shirt will make mitts, wrist warmers and so on. You were cold last night, weren't you? You're going to get colder. We're going to need all the insulation we can get."

Naked, the corpse seemed somehow less human. Dragging it by the heels they hauled it across the snow to a site where the ground was littered with loose boulders. They found a niche between three large rocks, and bundling the body in they began to pile loose stones over and around it.

They worked in haste, each man silent, preoccupied with his own thoughts. Umiak was thinking of the *Wendigo*. Far to the south, where dense forest covered the land, the natives had a belief that if a man lingered too long in the woods he would become possessed by an evil spirit which would drive him mad and make him turn cannibal. How long, Umiak wondered, would it be before the spirit of the *Wendigo* entered one or other of their two souls, if they were trapped in this valley for any length of time?

Larsen likewise was thinking of the body of the dead pilot in terms of a

194

supply of meat. It would not be the first time in the United States that survivors of a disaster had kept themselves alive by cannibalism. Larsen was no stranger to death, and in his time had been witness to far more gruesome sights. In the tropics the body would have begun to decompose by now, but up here in the cold a body would keep for weeks.

Suddenly Larsen's stomach revolted at the thought of eating human flesh and he turned aside, vomiting. Umiak worked on in silence, choosing the heaviest rocks he could find. Though not noticeable to human nostrils the smell of death, he knew, was already being signalled across the wilderness, attracting the attention of any carnivore that might be hunting nearby. Meantime, he was not too displeased at this sign of squeamishness on the part of the white man. Once a man adapted to the idea of cannibalism, it was but a short step from eating one who had already died to an appraisal of those comrades still living.

Later Larsen sat on a rock in the sun. The stream had risen slightly as the warmth of the day melted the snow on the mountain slopes, but it was still little more than a trickle among the stones. By damming the stream and scooping out the sand and gravel behind the dam, Larsen was able to create a pool deep enough to wash in.

Earlier they had manhandled the Cessna out of the shadows and down the mountain slope to a flat hummock of ground beside the stream. The starboard wing had fractured on impact with the hillside. During the night the wind and the weight of driven snow had completed the break and now it lay where it had parted from the plane, halfway down the slope. They had anchored the plane by piling boulders around the wheels and against the tailplane, and patched the hole in the windscreen with freezer bags, stuck down with the best part of a roll of the sealing tape supplied with the bags. It would not hold in a gale, but was better than nothing. By the time they were finished Larsen was sweating under the sun, though the moment he stepped back into the shadow of the hill the air struck chill as a tomb. Now, with Umiak away across the valley picking berries, he took time to bathe in the icy water, partly to refresh himself, partly to rid himself of a feeling of contamination, the taint of death. He had finished dressing, and was pulling on his shoes and socks, when Umiak returned.

The berries were fat and round, bursting with juice, but Umiak had not been over-finicky. There were bits of leaf and twig and small insects mixed among them. Umiak divided his harvest into two equal piles and began to eat, grinning as he watched Larsen pick out the debris. "Eat," he teased. "Leaves, bugs, berries, it is all food."

Larsen did as he was told, and found the rich flavour of the berries masked any other taste. "Pity the stream isn't a bit bigger," he remarked idly. "I could have had a go with my fishing rod."

Umiak stopped eating. "You have fishing tackle with you?"

Larsen nodded. "I always carry a few bits and pieces with me, on the off chance that I might get a bit of sport. It's not much. A little telescopic rod that just fits in my holdall, a few flies, lures and assorted hooks. It's not a lot of use up here though."

Umiak finished the last of his berries. "May I see it, please?"

Larsen went to the plane and came back with his rod and reel, and two tobacco boxes filled with an assortment of lures, flies, sinkers, hooks and swivels. Umiak ignored the rod, but tested the strength of the nylon line, and picked out half a dozen of the smallest hooks. "May I use these?"

"Sure," said Larsen, intrigued.

Swiftly Umiak stripped line off the reel, cutting it with his teeth into lengths about two feet long. To each length he tied a hook, and then, as an afterthought, cut several longer lengths of line. Gathering them together he set off without a word across the valley to the berry patch. Larsen followed.

The berries still clung thickly to the low bushes. Choosing his berries with care Umiak inserted a hook into the fruit, tying the other end of the nylon thread to a stout branch. When he had used up all his hooks he fashioned snares from the longer lengths of nylon, attaching one end to the twisted roots of the shrubs, and spreading the snares flat in the thin powdering of snow that covered the thick moss growing at the base of the bushes.

Larsen watched in silence. Finally, Umiak pointed to the ground, at something Larsen had not noticed before. It was a dropping, though whether from an animal or bird he could not tell. Further on he saw another one, and then, as his eyes grew accustomed to finding them, he saw the ground below the bushes was liberally sprinkled with them.

"Ptarmigan," explained Umiak. "They must come here regularly to feed on the berries. I hope we'll get one or two." He paused to make minute adjustments to a couple of the snares. "The trick is to get the snare slightly larger than their feet. Too small, and their feet won't go through. Too big, and they'll step right in and out again."

"When will they come?" queried Larsen.

"Tonight, tomorrow, who knows?" said Umiak. "They'll come though, as long as there are berries left."

They set off back to the plane. On the way Umiak asked, "Have you any more surprises in your bag, Mr. Larsen?"

Suddenly Larsen remembered his knife. It was the sort of penknife beloved of small boys, no more than a toy, an intricate maze of folding blades and gadgets, all wholly impractical but delightfully ingenious. His mother had given it to him when he joined the marines, and though he had never done more with it than peel the occasional apple, he had kept it about him since her death as a sort of memento. Reluctantly, and with a

196

faint feeling of embarrassment, he produced it for Umiak's inspection.

He had expected ridicule. Instead Umiak stared at it intently, and then began a prolonged and meticulous examination, testing every blade and gadget, opening and closing each one several times. He reminded Larsen of a small boy presented with a gift, and then he remembered the tiny arrowhead, and it occurred to him that Umiak was descended from a race of men obsessed with miniaturization.

Wistfully Umiak handed the knife back. "Take care of that beautiful thing, Mr. Larsen. We may well have need of it."

In fact they found a use for it straight away, converting the gallon can into a petrol stove, using dry sand from beside the stream. Together they designed it, cutting a flap of metal from one side of the can, but leaving it hinged to act as a windshield or perhaps, they hoped, a hotplate. They had trouble draining petrol from the fuel tank of the plane, but at last they had about half a gallon in one of the plastic bags. The fire burned well but, to Larsen's chagrin, with a sooty black flame.

"Seal oil from the can," explained Umiak. "It always smokes. Soon it will clean. A hot drink of water would be nice," he added.

Larsen felt a wave of frustration. "There's nothing to boil it in."

Umiak sat silent for a while. Then he got up and began pottering among the stones. Larsen sat on alone, hunched over the flames of the stove, straining his ears in the hope of hearing a plane. There was nothing, no sound save that of Umiak clattering among the rocks. The valley was devoid of life, and not even a raven showed in the sky above the crags.

His reverie was interrupted by Umiak, who appeared at his side with a handful of round flat pebbles, which he proceeded to pile on the stove. Then he squatted back on his heels, watching the flames play over the stones. Nearby he had built a nest of rocks and moss, lining it with a plastic bag which he had half filled with water. When he judged the pebbles hot enough he deftly shovelled them out of the flames, using two flat slates he had chosen for the purpose. Swiftly he transferred them to the water, which hissed and bubbled as the stones sank. In a few moments the water was too hot to touch.

Umiak dipped the cup in the water and offered it to Larsen. The brew did not look inviting. The stones had blackened with carbon from the residue of the seal oil, and bits of it floated on the surface. Larsen shook his head.

"You should have some," Umiak insisted. "Better to drink hot water than cold. You drink cold water, you burn energy heating it inside you, energy you can't afford to lose."

Larsen was not tempted, however. He was tired of lessons in survival. Sensing this, Umiak drained the cup and then sat silent. This white man depressed him.

Abruptly he got up and wandered away down the valley, following the course of the stream as it wound between the stones that littered the valley floor. To his right the snow-clad mountains lay in deep shadow. To his left the sun bronzed the tawny hide of the hill, with its darker mane of berry bushes. Snow lay in broad scattered drifts, sculpted by the wind into strange shapes that etched blue-black shadows on a background of sparkling white. For the stream there had to be a way out of the valley, but there was no guarantee that a man might follow.

The scene was not alien to him, for some years ago he had hunted regularly in these mountains, though further away to the east. Alone, he knew he could survive, and this knowledge, blended with an instinctive love of the land of which he felt so much a part, left no room in his mind for fear or concern.

The presence of the white man did, though. There was a fundamental difference between the two races, in their attitude to the world about them. For ten thousand years his people had learned to live with the land, and to make the best use of all that it had to offer. At some point during that time the white men, the strangers, had chosen not to adapt their ways to natural cycles, and instead had learned to domesticate stock and to cultivate crops. From that point on they had been compelled more and more to fight against the forces of the wild, until now it was as if they had built a sort of spaceship they called civilization. Once deprived of their life support systems they could not long survive.

In the days to come Larsen would grow to need him. The man was not yet prepared to accept this, and Umiak was not sure how to convince him without antagonizing him. On the other hand, he did not need Larsen. Almost without conscious thought, his hand stole to the pistol concealed in his pocket.

It would be so easy. All he had to do was to walk up behind the man and shoot him in the back of the head. It would be kinder than simply abandoning him to his fate, kinder even than having him suffer cold and hunger and the danger of frostbite. One shot would free him for ever from this land he appeared to hate and fear so much.

Yet even as he considered the prospect he knew it would be too easy. All his life he had worked for a better understanding between his people and the white strangers. Now, here he was, seeking to justify an easy way out, not, he had to admit, for Larsen, but for himself. He was forced to smile at his own duplicity. All the same, he mused, it might be wise to keep his options open.

Though his mind wandered his eyes were busy. He crossed a faint meandering trail that was possibly the path of a ground squirrel, and noted a few bitten heather shoots where ptarmigan had grazed. A shadow flickered across the sun, and gazing skywards he spied an eagle sailing on stiff outstretched wings. It circled once and was gone. There was nothing to attract it in this barren valley.

Larsen too saw the eagle. Its presence served only to accentuate the helplessness of his plight. In a day, without effort, without suffering hunger or cold, it could cross a stretch of country that might take him a month to travel.

Umiak was now no more than a mere dot on the horizon, and as Larsen watched he disappeared into a fold of the landscape, the dead ground hiding him from view. With him gone the silence was profound. He could hear his own breathing, and the steady beat of his heart. Almost, he felt, he could hear the blood coursing through his veins. He threw a stone to break the stillness, and it clattered eerily among the rocks. The mountains threw back the sound, hollow, lifeless.

Time passed, and Umiak did not return. Where had the stupid fellow gone? Perhaps he had met with an accident, fallen over a cliff—or perhaps a bear had got him. In spite of himself Larsen looked around, his eyes probing the deep shadows of the hills.

As quickly as it had arisen, the small ripple of fear passed. Funny, he thought, how even the company of a fellow human you didn't like was more comforting than utter solitude. He was tempted to call Umiak's name, but pride prevented him. Then he heard the plane.

The drone was faint. He looked up, but the sky was empty. The plane was somewhere beyond the mountains. Unless it flew directly overhead it would miss them. Somehow he had to attract attention, and the only way was with smoke.

He ran to the Cessna, cursing himself for not preparing a fire earlier. Frantically he searched for something to burn. His hand fell on the dead pilot's jacket and he hurried away with that, anxious not to start a blaze near the aircraft. There was some petrol left in the plastic bag and he threw that over the coat before flicking the lighter.

The fumes ignited in an explosion of flame, burning fiercely but giving off little smoke. The drone of the plane grew fainter, but just as he was beginning to despair the sound of the engine grew louder again. The plane was turning.

Seal oil smoked, and Umiak had a bag full. Larsen ran again to the plane, seized the container, and sprinkled the contents over the fire. The seal oil sputtered at first, partly dousing the flames, but then beginning to burn with a yellow flame that gave off a dense sooty vapour. A column of smoke rose steadily into the sky above the valley between the twin walls of the mountains, forty, fifty, sixty feet. Then, to Larsen's dismay, it stopped rising, levelling off into a flat pall halfway up the mountainside as the warm rising air met the impenetrable dense cold air of the mountaintops.

He cursed. At his feet the fire still smouldered, and savagely he kicked at it. One of the pilot's sleeves flared briefly, wrapping itself and its coating of blazing seal oil round his leg, igniting his trousers and searing his leg.

Frantically he leaped away, but the jacket clung to his leg. His attempts to free himself fanned the blaze. He thought of running down to the stream, but it was too far off. In blind panic now he shook his leg, and mercifully the jacket fell away. Still the cloth of his trousers smouldered on, and only then did it occur to him to smother the fire with snow. Hopping around on one leg, he scooped up handfuls, soaking the material until the last spark was extinguished. Then he stood sobbing with relief, yet too fearful to inspect the full extent of his burns. Not till then did he become aware of the silence. The plane had gone.

ANCIENT SHEEP DROPPINGS lay among the short wiry stems of the grasses. Umiak had paid them scant attention. Sheep, like the stream, could go where no man might follow, and their presence here in the valley was no assurance of an easy way out. He looked away downstream. Somewhere amid the jagged peaks there had to be a pass. By now he had wandered a long way from the plane, but he decided to go further.

Then, a few hundred yards downstream, he found a wolf scat, shrivelled and wind-dried, and he knew that the way out was sure. Feeling lighter at heart, he turned back to the plane. He still nursed a faint hope that he might come across the lost map, though he knew the chances were slim. As he gazed around he heard the sound of the engine.

His first impulse was to run back towards the Cessna, but then he checked himself and listened. The sound came from the north, far beyond the mountain peaks. The noise rose and fell, in slow regular intervals. The plane was circling. It was possible that it was searching for them. It was equally possible that it had been chartered by some of his own people hunting for caribou, for now was the time when the great herds began their winter migration south. It might be a biologist doing a wolf count, or a white hunter looking for a bear. The reasons for a plane circling in the vicinity were many. Then, as he listened, the drone faded and died, and then there was no sound save the gentle murmur of the brook as it trickled by at his feet.

It was, after all, most unlikely that the plane was searching for them. Their pilot hadn't had time to send out any distress call. No one in the outside world knew where they had crashed. To find them the rescue services would have to search a corridor some thirty miles wide and three hundred miles long, over tundra and muskeg swamp, river and lake and poplar thicket, spread amid mountain peaks and unnamed hidden valleys. They would check the obvious sites where a plane in difficulties might touch down. They would search the lakes, the gravel bars, the odd airstrip constructed by prospectors. They would ask others flying over the region to keep an eye open for wreckage, but beyond that there was little they could do.

He came to a decision then. The resources of the valley in which they lay could not sustain them for long, and for Larsen and him there was only one way out: on foot, before starvation and cold destroyed them.

As he topped the ridge these thoughts were forgotten. A fire smouldered near the plane, and Larsen was hopping and leaping and slapping at his leg. He hurried down.

Half angry, half ashamed, Larsen explained what had happened. Umiak could not believe that anyone would be so stupid as to waste nearly a gallon of precious seal oil just to make smoke. The man had thrown away what was perhaps their only hope of survival in the days to come. For a moment Umiak was tempted to kill him on the spot and leave his body to the ravens and the wolves.

Then he began to laugh. After all, this was the sort of misfortune that he and his kind had laughed at since the dawn of time. If a man fell through the ice, if a sled overturned, if a man shot himself in the foot, it was an occasion not for grief, but for mirth. Now the thought of a man setting his own trousers on fire struck him as so funny that he laughed until the tears came to his eyes.

Humiliated at being made the butt of Umiak's childish humour, Larsen limped moodily down to the stream with his holdall and began to bathe his leg. The ice-cold water soothed it, and was perhaps the best treatment he could have applied under the circumstances.

One burn was severe, though not crippling. The great danger, he knew, was infection, even in this cold climate. As with all burns, the wound at the moment was sterile, but beneath the dead skin, sheltered from light and air, organisms would multiply, and without antibiotics to combat them he had only the defences of his own body. Abscesses might develop. There was even the risk of gangrene.

Larsen was bandaging his leg with strips of cloth from a spare shirt he carried in his holdall when Umiak approached, bringing a wad of soft clean moss to pad the burn. Larsen accepted the peace offering, and it gave him a measure of comfort. Each man was eager to break the silence, but reluctant to speak first. "Where do you suppose we are?" asked Larsen at last.

"I've been trying to work it out," replied Umiak. With his finger he drew a long sausage shape in a patch of melting snow and placed a dot at either side. "This," he said, pointing to the sausage, "is the Brooks Range, a chain of mountains dividing the land in two. Now we left here," he went on, pointing to the left-hand dot, "to fly to here"—indicating the other dot. "Flying time would have been over three hours in that old plane, and we'd only been up and flying for about an hour and a half."

"Which puts us smack in the middle of the mountains," groaned Larsen.

"Not quite," said Umiak. "Not yet in the middle, still on the edge. It's hard to tell down here in this valley, but I think we must be towards the northern end. If so, then there's nothing but open tundra to the north. To go south we'd have to cross the length of the mountains, and though there are settlements along the rivers there we'd have a hard time finding them."

"What about turning back?"

Umiak shook his head. "Again, there would be miles of open tundra to cross. The only settlements are on the sea coast, and we have no way of knowing where they lie. There is a compass in the plane, but even if it still works, without a map it is useless."

"So we head east," said Larsen. "But it seems to me we're not a lot better off. We still have to traverse the mountain range and there's no guarantee we'll hit civilization, even if we survive. How far is it? A hundred, two hundred miles? How long will that take us? A week? A month?"

Umiak sighed. So many questions. "If we travel far enough we're bound to reach the oil road that runs north to Prudhoe Bay. But it's not quite as simple as that. To walk in a straight line over the mountains is out of the question."

He began to draw again on his map. "The rivers on this side of the mountains generally flow north, to join one great river. But others flow east and west out of the mountains. Let's suppose we follow this stream at our feet. When we find one joining it from the east, we follow that.

"A man is never quite lost as long as he has a stream to follow. Besides, there will be berries, game of some sort, shelter and perhaps firewood along the river banks. There may be fish to catch with that rod of yours. The rivers will not freeze for a while yet."

"But it could take weeks," Larsen protested. "And the longer it takes, the worse the weather is going to get. Wouldn't we be better off waiting here a while longer?"

As gently as he could, Umiak murmured, "The wilderness has kept my people alive for ten thousand years; it is a good place to be, providing you obey the rules. Besides, a few years ago I hunted west out of Anaktuvuk Pass, with the friend I was on my way to visit yesterday. Sooner or later we may come to a region I remember. Also, there are odd cabins and old campsites used by my people on their hunting trips. Who knows—we might meet up with such a party on our way."

Larsen sat a long while in silence. He desperately wanted to escape from this barren land, to relax in a hot bath and savour the warmth and comfort of a clean bed, to sink his teeth into a good steak and hear the tinkle of ice in a glass as he poured whisky over it. He wanted to hear the roar of traffic and feel a firm pavement under his feet. But the way out of this valley, and the days of journeying ahead, filled him with dismay.

He turned on the lean, olive-skinned man sitting in silent reflection beside him. "If this goddamned wilderness is such a good place to be, why aren't your own people living here?"

At first Umiak seemed reluctant to answer, and then he began softly to speak, hesitantly, as a man might recall events long past. "This land is vast and my people were few, and for centuries they wandered the hills and river valleys. They followed the deer and fished the streams, they harvested the roots and berries and birds' eggs in their season. They knew where the bears dug their dens and the beaver built their lodges. Others lived near the sea and hunted the seal and the walrus and the whale. From time to time people would meet, and trade caribou skins for whale oil, or exchange the skins of the bearded seal, which makes the best ropes and footwear, for the soft pelts of fox or lynx, or for meat which did not taste of the sea.

"Then the white men came. Whalers and fur traders. In return for our labour and meat and furs they offered us whisky, tobacco and iron, and cloth and guns. So the people came to settle near the rivers and the coast, near to the white men and the goods the white men brought.

"Now it is true that we did not need all these things. But are we so very different from you? Before you invented the automobile and the television, you did not hanker after them, but once they existed everyone had to have one. So it was with us.

"The white men brought us other gifts, syphilis and smallpox and measles and tuberculosis. In return they robbed the land of its wealth, and when they no longer needed whalebone and furs they went away, leaving our people sick and starved. Then the Bureau of Indian Affairs took our children away from us and boarded them in schools. They cut their hair short and dressed them in Western-style clothing. They taught them many things: to read and write and to speak the white man's tongue. But they did not teach them to fish and hunt, where to look for edible roots, or how to snare birds. Because our children were not allowed to be with their parents they could not learn these things. The girls did not know how to dress fish or tan hides. The boys did not know how to run on snowshoes and hunt the deer and hare. They did not learn to know their land.

"So for a long time the people abandoned the ways that had served them so well. But we are wiser now. We appreciate much what the white man has to offer, but we have learned the value of the old ways too, and we are relearning lost skills. The people of Anaktuvuk are among those who left the mountains for the coast. Twenty-five years ago they left the coast and returned to the hills. They are there still. Others may follow..."

Abruptly Umiak stood up. "The shadows grow longer and the night will be cold. I suggest we take out the seats from the plane, and with the carpet make ourselves a bed inside. It will be warmer if we share it. That is, if you have no objection?"

They set to work with Larsen's little knife and the tool kit from the plane, ripping up the carpet and removing the seat upholstery. Glad of the activity, Larsen felt his spirits lift. "If we are going to sleep together, you'd better call me Steve," he joked.

Umiak considered this. "I don't think that would be at all appropriate," he said finally.

"Suit yourself," said Larsen. He was unable to decide whether to be insulted or amused. Either way, it was not important.

As they worked the light rapidly began to fade. Clouds were gathering among the mountaintops, and before long the crags were hidden in dense black mists, condensing into icy squalls of rain that soon turned to snow.

Larsen huddled with Umiak in the shelter of the cabin as snow began to gather on the fuselage, a wet grey slush that rapidly whitened as the blizzard grew in intensity. This was just a taste of the conditions that sooner or later they would have to face, ill-equipped and ill-clad, without shelter of even the most rudimentary kind. He shivered, more with dread than cold.

Soon the valley was blotted out by swirling flakes. Then, abruptly, the storm passed and the night cold bit into their bones as stars frosted the moonless sky.

IT WAS EXTRAORDINARY how much popcorn a man could eat without feeling satisfied. Larsen hoped it would not prove binding. He had enough problems without that. Perhaps the berries, plus the leaves and bugs he had eaten, would help to counteract the effect.

At least he was comfortable, lying there in the dark, and almost warm under the carpet they had ripped from the floor of the plane. It smelled musty and foul, but at least Umiak didn't smell, lying close at his side, his breathing soft and even. Funny how uptight he had been about the use of Christian names. He'd heard that Eskimos were inclined to be over friendly, but he hadn't found it to be so.

From where he lay he could see the slope of the hill, freshly dusted with snow and sparkling now with the reflected light of the stars. Bare outcrops of rock assumed strange shapes against the white. As he watched they seemed sometimes to move. He could have sworn just then that one passed slowly across the hill.

Gradually he fell asleep, despite the pain of the burn on his leg. Once he woke, half dreaming, imagining that he had heard the clatter of stones in the night. All was still, silent save for Umiak's breathing, and he drifted back to sleep.

The ptarmigan came to the berry patch with the dawn, before the men awoke. They had almost completed their summer moult and only a few flecks of brown showed against their white plumage. First one and then another began to struggle helplessly as the hooks caught and the nylon line held them fast. Alarmed, the rest of the flock took flight. Soon the hooked birds hung still.

Larsen woke refreshed but hungry. He looked out of the window of the plane and his shout woke Umiak. Together the two men fell out of the plane and raced across the snow. As an alternative to popcorn, the thought of stringy fowl was infinitely appealing.

"We share," said Umiak.

"Roast ptarmigan," Larsen murmured ecstatically.

"Soup," corrected Umiak.

The two stopped and glared at each other. Umiak held three birds, and he had the air of a man who would not part with his prize easily. "It's more nourishing, more economical..." he began.

"Look," said Larsen. "I'll do a deal with you. Let me roast one on the stones you will be heating for your soup, and you can have the other two."

Umiak nodded, his face expressionless. He hefted the birds in his hand, and gave the heaviest one to Larsen.

The meat was tough, and though the skin was charred the flesh near the bones was almost raw. Larsen had eaten his bird before Umiak had finished making his soup. Now he sat, sucking on the bones, still hungry, as Umiak began to fish portions of juicy meat from the freezer bag in which he had stewed them, washing them down with fragrant gravy. He seemed to take an age over the meal, and the smell of the soup tormented Larsen almost beyond measure. He made up his mind proudly that even if Umiak offered him a share he would refuse, but the man made no such gesture.

The shadows were shrinking now, the sun shedding a thin warmth as it lit the snow with rosy light. Larsen let his gaze wander over the valley, struck by the beauty of the scene. Then his jaw dropped. "Oh my God," he breathed.

Umiak stared in the direction Larsen was pointing. The cairn of stones that covered the dead body of the pilot had been broken into during the night, torn apart, the stones scattered in the snow. Some of them had been so heavy that it had taken their combined strength to manhandle them into place. From the grave a broad trail of beaten snow stretched away to disappear down the valley. Whatever had stolen the corpse had dragged it away.

Larsen jumped to his feet, only to feel Umiak's restraining hand. The man was trembling. "Don't follow," he said. "I think there may be very much danger."

"From what?" demanded Larsen.

"Bear," said Umiak. "Only a grizzly, and a big one, could have moved those stones and dragged the body away."

Larson was silent for a while. "You mean the body's been eaten?"

"Half eaten, at least. Look!"

Far away down the valley black specks floated in wide, lazy circles high in the sky. As they watched one drifted down, only to rise again and join its fellows. "Ravens," observed Umiak. "They have found what is left. The bear will have eaten its fill and tried to hide the remains. But it will stay on watch, close to the corpse, and it will attack anything that goes near."

"So what do we do?" asked Larsen.

"About the body, nothing. The bear will stay with it until there is nothing left. Two days, maybe three. It must be a hungry bear. Usually by now he would be looking for somewhere to den up for his long winter sleep. This one still prowls the hills, so I think the sooner we move out the better."

"Wouldn't we be safer in the plane?"

"You can see what the bear did to the grave. How long do you think it would take him to break into the cabin?"

Suddenly Larsen remembered the shadow on the hill, and the rattle of stones in the night. His fear of the journey diminished in the face of the greater dread of what might befall him here in this lonely valley. "Right," he said. "Let's get out of here."

"Do you think you could dismantle the control panel of the plane?" asked Umiak.

Larsen shrugged. "I guess. Why?"

"We could use the wiring behind it. I think I can make a sledge from the broken wing of the plane, so we can take with us some fuel and bedding, and anything else we think will come in useful. But we need the cables because the going will be rough, and everything we take will need to be tied to the sledge. Also, we need the cables to pull the sledge with. We ought to be ready to move off tomorrow. If deep snow comes, we may be trapped here in the valley."

Together the two set to work, Larsen stripping electric wiring and control cables from the plane, while Umiak constructed the sledge. He did most of the work with Larsen's small knife. Watching him, Larsen could not help being impressed by his dexterity and economy of movement. Larsen thought again of the arrowhead in his pocket and began to understand how these people had survived for so long.

While Larsen filled freezer bags with petrol, knotting each one tightly before slipping it inside another, Umiak cut two rectangles out of the underside of the wing, folding the aluminium under so no sharp edges remained. Though he measured each one only by eye their two holdalls fitted snugly into the recesses. The spaces inside the wing between the cross struts formed a cache for a supply of berries and popcorn.

Most of their spare clothing they wore against the cold. A leg of the dead pilot's trousers replaced the one Larsen had set on fire. Umiak studied the remains of the garment thoughtfully, and then set them to one side. They worked steadily through the day, pausing only for the inevitable meal of popcorn and berries. By now Larsen was so hungry he welcomed the leaves and other debris mixed in with the fruit.

By late afternoon the sledge was finished. Umiak had used the control cables for hauling lines, and to make all secure he threaded cable through holes punched along the sides of the wing. In the morning their bedding could be lashed on top. One holdall was packed with freezer bags containing petrol.

The last red rays of the sun had faded on the peaks, and it was time to turn in for the night. Larsen felt himself rapidly growing drowsy. The burn on his leg caused him discomfort, but the pain was not unbearable, and at least sleep was a relief from both hunger and cold. He was just drifting into slumber when he heard the howl of the wolves.

He jerked bolt upright. Beside him Umiak gave a quiet chuckle. "The old bear will not sleep tonight," he murmured. "A wolf pack has come to share in his feast."

Thereafter Larsen lay wakeful, trying not to let his mind dwell on what might be happening out there. He had never regarded himself as a timid or imaginative man, yet this desolation was getting to him, and another thought bothered him too. All the while he had the feeling that as far as Umiak was concerned he was useless freight, a burden to be shed should the occasion warrant it. He had no proof of this, only a nagging doubt.

Umiak too lay without sleeping. He was fretting about the gun, now pressing uncomfortably against his side. He wished he had told Larsen about it at the start, but distrust had prevented him from doing so. Sooner or later, though, the white man would come to know of its presence. What would he do? It lay between them, a symbol of power, and there was no way of knowing whether Larsen would respect the power, or try to wrest it from him. It occurred to Umiak simply to throw the gun away, but he dismissed the thought. He would just have to deal with the situation if and when it arose. On that philosophical note he fell asleep.

Some of the wolves slept too. The others lay in the snow waiting, the white stars glittering in their eyes. They lay in a wide semicircle, well out of reach of the bear. They had not killed for five days, and the smell of the dead man was strong in their nostrils.

Most of the viscera had been eaten, the liver, kidneys, heart and lungs. Flesh had been torn in great strips from the body, but still much meat remained, and now the bear moved the carcass, grasping it in his jaws and carrying it to the shelter of the rocks. Then he lay on guard, one massive curved paw protecting his prize, moaning deep in his throat as he nosed the remains.

With the coming of dawn the wolves made their move. Slowly the pack inched closer, and the drowsing bear woke in terrible rage as the lead wolf bitch ran a few paces towards him. Immediately she backed off and then, as the bear subsided, ran in from the side.

The bear lashed out, and had the blow connected it would have crushed her skull. But she swerved aside so that the great claws scythed empty air. At that moment her mate nipped the bear in the hind leg. The bear swung round and charged, and instantly the rest of the pack grabbed at the corpse. The bear rushed to retrieve it, seizing it by an arm and biting down so hard that his jaws severed the limb from the body. Bewildered, the bear dropped the arm to retrieve the greater part of the trunk, so leaving the limb to the wolves.

The bear backed away uphill, dragging the body with him. The wolves followed. The deadly game would continue until there were no spoils left worth fighting for.

THE MORNING DAWNED GREY, and a light snow was falling as the two men prepared to depart. Umiak muttered and glanced anxiously at the sky, but Larsen was eager to set off. Apart from a nagging hunger, he felt good. The large blister that had formed over the burn on his leg had broken. He made no attempt to cut away the dead skin, but redressed the burn, throwing away the soiled moss and rag and replacing it with a fresh pad.

The makeshift sledge ran smoothly over the frozen, wind-packed snow. Earlier, Umiak had poured water from the stream over the underside and this had frozen in the cold morning air, forming a protective skin over the aluminium. They had agreed to share the task of pulling it at all times.

Though the temperature was well below freezing the dry cold was less chilling than Larsen had feared. What slight breeze there was blew at their backs as they followed the stream along its easterly course. At first the going was easy, then the stream turned north, and as they gradually lost altitude the ground became more uneven.

Here the valley widened out between the mountain walls, and the river flowed over a flattish plain formed by the deposit of silt over untold centuries. Tussock grass grew in untidy hummocks which yielded under-foot, and between them the snow had drifted soft and deep. Each step became an unknown venture, so that both men repeatedly fell and floundered. After half an hour of this Umiak suggested they make for higher ground on the flank of the mountain to their right.

To reach it they had to cross about a hundred yards of tussock. Without staves to probe the ground ahead every single step had to be considered before they moved. Simply to flounder on was to invite exhaustion and perhaps a wrenched knee. Their progress was painfully slow. Under such conditions Larsen realized that his own unspoken target of ten miles a day was optimistic.

High on a ledge above the valley the bear watched the two men depart. The wolves had robbed him of the greater part of his prize and his mood was sullen and angry. He was an old bear, his long shaggy coat unkempt and matted, fouled with carrion and tangled with knots and burrs. His claws were blunt with years of digging for roots and ground squirrels, and his teeth were worn from biting bark and bone. But his jaws still retained their terrible crushing power and his speed when roused could still bring down a running caribou.

As soon as the men were out of sight the bear descended the slope into the valley. He first checked the grave site, but only the scent of carrion lingered to tantalize him further. He prowled around the deserted plane, but there was nothing to attract him there. Moaning softly to himself he padded down to the stream. Flakes of snow drifted down and clung to his fur, lingering without melting except around his eyes and muzzle. He found the ptarmigan bones scattered among the stones and crunched them. He found the soiled moss that Larsen had discarded from his wound and ate it. Still the snow fell, powdering his hide. Like a grey ghost the bear shook his head and set off down the valley, following the trail of the two men.

Once past the tussock grass Umiak and Larsen found the going easier. The hard-packed snow was firm underfoot, and deep enough to cover all but the larger rocks. All the same, the wind blew stronger on this exposed side of the valley, and frozen particles of moisture stung their cheeks as they trudged along. To their right the mountains rose like a wall, massive ramparts from which the wind tore plumes of driven snow. Above, the sky was ashen grey.

Somewhere ahead there had to be a break in the mountains. Meantime they travelled north, hour after hour, while in front of them the valley stretched interminably, vanishing into a misty veil of driven snow that receded steadily before them.

Then, abruptly, came a narrow defile that sloped gently upwards, seeming to offer a way through the mountains. A tiny stream filtered through thickets of low windcropped scrub, while on either side the hills rose sheer. Umiak looked at it dubiously. "Could be a blind canyon," he muttered.

"Only one way to find out," observed Larsen. "At least we'll have the wind on our backs."

The sky had grown lighter and the snow had ceased to fall, but the wind carried tiny frozen flakes, a thousand needle-pointed stings, whipped from the slopes of the hills as they headed up the gorge. The chasm formed a funnel for the wind, increasing its intensity.

Now massive outcrops obstructed their way. Several times they had to cross the stream, or skate precariously along the steep slopes of the valley, the sledge skidding along sideways as it hung below them. Twice they had no option but to pick it up and carry it over the rough terrain. At last, exhausted, they collapsed in the lee of a large rock, seeking a moment's respite from the chill of the wind.

"As a boy," said Larsen, "I often wondered why the early explorers usually travelled in great circular routes. I think I know why now. It was because nothing would persuade them to turn back and face obstacles they had already crossed."

Umiak grunted. "Unless this wind drops, we cannot turn back. It's forward or nothing for us, and soon we must find a place to spend the night. We'd better move on."

The way grew steeper. Ahead of them lay a ridge, flat against the sky, but always when they reached it another appeared on the horizon. Each step became an effort, the cable biting ever harder into Larsen's shoulder, and as the time passed hunger began to obsess him. How long now, he wondered, had it been since he had enjoyed a good meal? It seemed a lifetime.

Then the way ended abruptly. They found themselves in a small hollow, a natural amphitheatre round which the mountains rose on every side. The two men stared in dismay. "There must be a way out," exclaimed Larsen.

"There *may* be," corrected Umiak. "But this is not the time to look. We must find shelter, and quickly, for there is much to do."

To Larsen there seemed to be no place suitable to offer any protection from the cold and wind, but Umiak was already searching among the rocks, and soon Larsen heard him call. He plodded over, dragging the sledge behind him.

The site Umiak had chosen was no more than a crevice in the rocks, a lidless stone coffin just over six feet long and three feet high. There was barely enough room for the two of them to lie side by side. It offered some shelter from the wind, but little more. "The sledge," asked Umiak, "will it rest on top?"

It did, though somewhat lopsidedly, and there were gaps all round. Umiak began at once to stuff these with plugs of snow and moss. "Go and gather bushes to make a bed," he instructed Larsen. "And pick any berries you can find."

In the shelter of the rocks bushes grew in plenty, but though the stems were thin they were tough and wiry, scratching Larsen's hands and wrists. He was glad to stop from time to time to harvest berries, both blue and red.

Though he returned with a great armful of sprigs Umiak was not satisfied, and together the two returned for more. The little shelter was almost packed full before Umiak crawled inside and bounced around chuckling. "Good, good," he announced. "We shall sleep well tonight."

Larsen was about ready to fall asleep on his feet, but he found energy enough to grumble about supper. Umiak, however, was cheerful. "See, we have two sorts of berries tonight, blueberries and cranberries."

"And popcorn," groaned Larsen. "How long can a man survive on just berries?"

"A long time, providing he can find them."

"But surely they'll be all gone soon, with winter coming on?"

"Not so," said Umiak. "I told you, the wilderness is a good place. If the fall season was long and mild, the berries would become overripe and rotten, fermenting in the sun. But here the cold preserves them, and so plenty of berries last all winter."

"They don't do much to satisfy a man's hunger," complained Larsen. "We must have eaten pounds, but I still feel empty."

"They eat best mixed with meat and fat," admitted Umiak. "I'll set some snares before we turn in. Maybe we'll get lucky."

Despite his weariness, and Umiak's confident prediction, Larsen slept badly. He was cold, his leg hurt, and the warmth of their bodies awakened myriads of tiny biting flies that had lain dormant in their bush bedding. Umiak slept undisturbed, but Larsen merely dozed fitfully.

Not far away the bear too dozed the night away. He also was hungry, and from time to time he raised his muzzle, his dark nose questing the air. There was a smell of man, which he feared. Yet there was too a faint sweet whiff of putrefaction, the scent that had led him to the cairn on the hill.

Throughout his life the bear had fed mostly on vegetation, young grasses in the spring, roots of stunted poplar and bark of willows, berries when the crop was thickest. Yet almost every day he got some meat, the young of a ground-nesting bird, a squirrel, voles, lemmings, a snowshoe hare. From time to time he would come upon a dead caribou calf, or sick or injured adults. Such a prize was a feast, and the riper the carcass the better he liked it. Now his nose told him that an injured man lay not far away, but he feared to approach as yet, so he hungered and dozed.

THERE WAS A WAY OUT, or so it seemed. It was little more than a cleft in the mountain wall, a crack in the rim of the basin in which they had spent the night. It rose steeply, a tortured staircase of terraced rocks and ledges, to be lost in the cloud vapours that capped the barren peaks.

The two men looked at it dubiously. For all they knew it might end at an unscaleable wall of rock. Nor was there any way they could drag the sledge up it. It would have to be portaged. They debated whether to make a preliminary reconnaissance, but in the end set off carrying the sledge between them.

Almost at once Larsen slipped on the ice-covered rocks and fell, bruising his shoulder. Umiak dug out the remains of the dead pilot's trousers and cut strips of cloth, making bindings for their boots to give them a better grip on the steep ground. Even so, the going was rough. They could not climb together. Larsen, in the lead, would gain a foot or so, then take the weight of the sledge while Umiak followed. Then it was Umiak's turn to bear the load, perched precariously while Larsen scrabbled for a fresh foothold.

At length Umiak cried out for a rest. "Too hot," he complained.

"Makes a change," grunted Larsen, impatient for their ordeal to end.

"Not good," said Umiak. "Sweat now, we freeze later. The wind will be cold at the top." So they rested, while Larsen fumed at the delay. His leg felt easier for the night's rest. He had changed the dressing. The wound was inflamed and discharging freely, but the lymph was clear, with no sign of suppuration. He would have preferred to have left the wound open to the air to dry, but he feared the effects of the cold. Besides, the pad was a comfort.

After a short break they moved on. The way grew easier, and an hour later they emerged onto a flat plateau of bare basaltic rock. Here the wind savaged them, tearing at their clothing and threatening to throw them off their feet.

Flat on their faces they crawled the last few yards over the summit. At first they could see nothing. Icy mist swirled around them, the wind stung their eyes and snatched their breath away. Then, abruptly, the skies cleared, and they found themselves looking down on the thin black thread of a river far below. In front of them, and to their left, the mountain fell sheer, black precipitous rock dusted with wind-driven snow. To the south the shoulder of the hill sloped away in a gentle curve. It seemed the only way down.

After the arduous climb of the morning the descent was relatively easy, but now ahead to the east lay more mountains to cross, more valleys to traverse. It seemed a limitless expanse of snow and ice and barren rock. Larsen thrust all thoughts of the future from him and plodded on, walking because exertion was preferable to inaction. At least the wind had moderated and the cloud was thin and high, with now and then a glimpse of pale sun. Once Umiak shouted and pointed at something ahead of them. At first Larsen could see nothing, only the black rocks and scattered drifts of snow on the mountainside. Then a tiny speck of white detached itself from a larger drift. Others followed, and Larsen saw that they were wild sheep, grazing on the distant hillside. He shrugged and walked on.

Without a rifle to bring one down, the sheep were as inaccessible as if they were on the moon.

The sight of them, though, reminded Larsen of his hunger. There had been no ptarmigan in the snares that morning, and even the popcorn was running low. His system desperately craved meat. At the thought saliva filled his mouth and his stomach contracted in a sudden griping knot that made him catch his breath. It was the first and mildest of the hunger pains that were to seize him in the days to come.

When at last they reached the river they found it was shallow and swift flowing, but nowhere narrow enough to jump. Rather than wade through the icy water they veered upstream, hoping to find a place where they could cross dry-shod. As they rounded a bend, a rock lying on a gravel bar suddenly woke to life and flapped heavily away. Larsen watched the bald eagle climb up into the sky, while Umiak dropped the towline of the sled and went running down to the water's edge.

The remains of a salmon lay there. The eagle had eaten about a third, but several pounds of pink flesh still clung to the carcass. The two men looked at it, trembling with anticipation. Larsen ran back to the sledge and got the fuel and stove. Umiak prepared a pit in the sandbar and lined it with a plastic bag. Soon chunks of flesh were curding in the fragrant steam.

The fish had spawned and was well past its prime. Still, the meat was hot and filling and they finished the lot. Or rather, Umiak did, for after a while Larsen began to feel uncomfortably full. The sight of Umiak still eating provoked a wave of nausea, and he moved away. Presently, lulled by the sound of the stream flowing by at his feet, he fell asleep.

THE SMELL OF MAN was strong again. Cautiously the bear approached the niche in the rocks where the two men had spent the night. His fear of man still lingered, though waning with increased familiarity. A sudden noise or movement might have sent the bear bolting away up the hill, but nothing like that occurred.

With surprising ease the bear poured his huge bulk into the niche, in one fluid movement. Inside, his questing snout explored every corner in a series of loud snorts. Then, satisfied that nothing edible lay hidden away, he shook up the bedding, curled himself in a ball and fell asleep.

Hunger woke him later in the day. Again the man-scent was strong in the mountain defile, and the bear quickened his pace. He lost the trail for a while on the summit but soon found it again on the downward-sloping ridge. He tracked the men upstream, and lingered a moment over the fishhead and bones. Then he moved on to where a partial bridge of water-worn stone restricted the width of the stream and enabled him to cross the river without getting wet, as it had done earlier for Larsen and Umiak.

Thin snow had begun to fall and to cover the men's tracks. It did not matter to the bear, whose sense of smell could pick up a squirrel under three feet of snow, or the birth of a caribou calf from over a mile downwind. The dead pilot's trousers bore the faint but unmistakable taint of death, and by making boot bindings from them Umiak had laid a trail the bear could follow even if it was a week old. Now, unless distracted, the bear would follow wherever the men went, lured on by the lingering scent of decay, which more and more was becoming associated in his mind with the scent of man.

The snow fell thicker, adding to the sprinkling already frozen to the bear's long pelt. The heat of his body had melted some, turning it to moisture that had trickled down the guard hairs of his chest and flanks. Here, in contact with the icy air, it had frozen again to form long thin icicles, a curtain of ice that jingled faintly but musically with every movement he made. As the light faded he merged into the gloom, a ghost bear at one with the snow-covered landscape and the pitiless Arctic night.

A FEW MILES to the southeast Umiak and Larsen were preparing to pass what promised to be a long and uncomfortable night. The best they had been able to find in the way of shelter was an overhang of rock, halfway up the hillside in a long narrow pass through the mountains. They had gone supperless, and now, at Umiak's suggestion, they sat back to back, a pile of bedding and the carpet insulating them from the cold.

Sleep eluded them. The snowstorm passed, stars burned white in an indigo sky, then paled as, with growing intensity, flickering ribbons of green and white light flashed across the sky, illuminating the mountains beyond and bathing them in a soft ethereal glow.

"Ghost dancers," said Umiak. "Northern lights. My people once believed they were the spirits of the dead. Now we are told they are caused by an electro-magnetic storm high above the earth, but that doesn't lessen their beauty." Then he stirred uneasily. "This pass we are following is leading too far to the south. We must try to head north again, or we'll be lost in the mountains."

"How do you know?" queried Larsen.

"At this time of night the bands of light always flow at right angles to the poles of the earth."

Larsen digested this in silence. It did not seem to strike Umiak as at all incongruous that the ghosts of his ancestors should act as navigational aids to the living. Inevitably Larsen's thoughts returned to the unknown terrain that lay ahead. "If only we had a snowmobile," he muttered, more to himself than his companion.

"Those things," scoffed Umiak. "They'd be useless in these hills. OK on level ground I guess, but even then they spend more time stripped down on

the workbench than on the trail. Dog teams are better. At least if a dog is injured or killed you can always eat it or feed it to the others. You can't eat a snowmobile."

Larsen felt nettled by this summary dismissal of Western technology. "If snowmobiles are such a lousy idea, how come your people buy so many of them?"

"For going to the store, meeting the mail plane, hauling garbage to the dump, they're convenient. Besides, it takes a lot of meat to support a dog team, and it was hoped that the snowmobile would help conserve fish and caribou stocks. Maybe it did for a while, but a lot of people are going back to dogs now."

"How far would a dog team carry us in a day?" asked Larsen.

"Depends. Fifty, a hundred miles a day, according to the trail, the weather, how good a team you got, and how hard you push them."

Larsen sighed. Two days, and they could be out of this. So far, on foot, they'd travelled about twenty miles, mostly in the wrong direction. He wondered how much longer they could survive, how long they could endure the cold and the growing starvation.

As if in response to his unspoken thoughts Umiak said softly, "Only the now is real, you know. The future does not exist, any more than the past."

Umiak's words had a strangely oriental ring, and Larsen was struck by the thought that he was at the meeting place of east and west, where the spirits of the departed signposted the way on a journey that was without end.

The display of lights faded. In response the stars brightened, and the mountain peaks merged with the sky. In the silence of the night a sudden sound startled the two men into instant alertness. It came again, the faint but harsh clatter of a stone. Larsen felt Umiak stiffen, heard the pounding of his own heart as he strained his ears in the darkness.

It came again, nearer. Something was moving on the hill above them. Then, with the scrape of stone, a soft panting sound, deep and ominous. Beside him Umiak began to tremble. In spite of the cold Larsen felt his hands grow moist with perspiration.

"What is it?" he whispered.

"Bear, I think." Umiak swallowed. "Listen—when I tell you, not before, yell as loud and as long as you can."

Larsen waited. Long seconds passed, each an eternity in a silence more profound, more terrifying than any he had experienced in the prelude to a Vietcong attack. He felt his stomach contract with fear.

There was no further warning. Simultaneously both men saw the bear. It was approaching them from below, its massive bulk suddenly rearing up from the snow. "*Now!*" whispered Umiak, and the two yelled at the top of their voices.

One moment the bear was there and the next it had vanished without a sound, but there was no indication of how far it had gone, or for how long. As the minutes passed and the bear did not return, Larsen noticed that Umiak had ceased trembling. He found this reassuring, for he had been baffled by the other man's obvious terror. It seemed out of character in a man who did not appear to scare easily.

Larsen felt he had to know why. "If you don't mind me saying so," he began, "you seemed pretty scared for a while, back there."

Umiak's voice was low, but it was steady. "I have seen what a bear can do to a man. I lost my brother that way, when I was just a kid. They will play with you, feast on you while you are still alive. Sometimes if you scream they will bite you, just to make you scream louder..."

"Yes, well I think I'd rather not know," said Larsen hurriedly. "Do you think he'll return?"

Umiak considered a moment.

"Not tonight," he said finally. "He's had a bad scare. I think he was expecting to find us dead."

"Like our pilot," said Larsen. "So he's a bear with a taste for human flesh," he added, more to himself than to Umiak.

216

DESPITE THE FEAR, despite the cold and the hunger and the discomfort, Larsen slept. He woke to the rumble of thunder, and opened his eyes on a world of shifting light, as black clouds swirled around the desolate landscape.

To move on seemed folly, yet neither man felt inclined to linger in what could soon become a rocky tomb. Their preparations were brief. They ate the last of the popcorn and the few remaining berries, melted some snow for a hot drink, and after luxuriating for a moment in the last warmth of the petrol flames they set off into the gloom. The thunder still muttered, and vivid lightning flashes lit the peaks and crags that towered high above them.

They plodded on in silence. As they climbed upwards the snow grew deeper, sticky and soft, dragging at their feet and adding to the burden of pulling the sledge. Larsen felt weak and light-headed. His leg throbbed, every step sending a spasm of pain shooting up into his knee and thigh. He had not changed the dressing that morning, for there had been no moss among the litter of stones where they had passed the previous night.

Vainly they searched for a way out to the north. One route presented itself, a narrow defile which seemed to lead over a saddle between two peaks. They hesitated and then passed on, hoping to find an easier route. An hour later they reached the foot of an impassable glacier. It stretched before them for over a mile before vanishing into the clouds, an awesome tangle of rock and grey, fissured ice, ridged with pressure waves and split by crevasses. Without ice axes and ropes there was no way they could get themselves or the sledge across. There was nothing for it but to turn back and try to ascend the defile they had passed on the way up.

Twice they despaired of ever making it to the top. Time after time they had to turn the sled on its side to angle it around protruding boulders that barred their way, Umiak leading and Larsen bringing up the rear, favouring his injured leg and perspiring freely in spite of the cold. Each fresh foothold brought a moment's anxiety, lest he should slip and fall, and always in the back of his mind was the fear of the bear, growing ever bolder as hunger drove it on.

He was only dimly aware that they had reached the summit. He lay face down on the frozen ground, the cold air rasping his lungs, his breathing harsh and loud. At length he recovered sufficiently to sit up, only to find that Umiak had disappeared. Suddenly panic seized him and he was about to call, when he heard a rattle of stones and the other man reappeared. He looked thoughtful and grave.

"There's a break in the ground ahead," he announced, "a crevasse barring our way. It looks narrow enough to jump, but ..."

"But what?" queried Larsen.

"If I'm wrong, it's a long way to the bottom."

Larsen could only stand and wonder at the violent forces that had split the solid rock. The path ended in a knife-edge drop, the brink of a chasm which widened out on either side of them. The opposite lip looked almost close enough to touch, but its edge was raised perhaps a foot higher than their side. Beneath, the sheer rock face sloped away under their feet so that they were unable to see the depths to which it plunged. As Larsen studied the gap, it seemed in his imagination to grow wider.

They tried to bridge it, but the sledge was inches short, and they almost lost all their possessions in the black void below. Then, without warning, Umiak took hold of the towline and jumped.

He cleared the gap with inches to spare. Then he turned and waited. Larsen pushed the sledge out over the crevasse towards him, and as it hung on the point of balance Umiak heaved on the towline, Larsen gave a final push in unison, and their goods were safely across. Larsen poised himself to leap.

Then he checked. If he took off on his bad leg, he was not sure he could clear the gap. If he used his good leg, he would jar the injured one on landing. So he wavered, and all the time the gap seemed to grow wider. He was about to ask Umiak to throw him one end of the towline when a look of horror crossed the other man's face. "Jump man, quick," Umiak yelled. "The bear!"

Larsen jumped, clearing the gap with ease and landing neatly beside Umiak on the level surface of the rock. He turned, expecting to see the bear, but there was nothing, only the naked rock and the clouds. To his astonishment Umiak began to laugh.

He saw then that he had been tricked. Umiak thought he had lost his nerve, so he had gambled that Larsen's fear of the bear would prove greater than his fear of falling, and it had worked.

Larsen was a man slow to anger, not given to violent ways. But hatred of his own weakness, plus a bitter resentment at the way Umiak seemed to have dominated their partnership ever since the time of the plane crash, boiled up inside him in an explosion of rage. Umiak was laughing, and this was the ultimate insult. He gave a savage bellow and sprang.

The two men fell heavily, Larsen on top, his hands round Umiak's throat. Umiak brought his arms up inside Larsen's, his fists clenched, driving a double hammer-blow to Larsen's chin. As his opponent's head whiplashed back, Umiak's arms swept out and down, breaking the stranglehold and flinging him clear.

As he struggled to his feet Larsen came again, head down. Umiak brought his knee up, and heard the wind go out of Larsen as it connected with his midriff, but then they were rolling on the ground again, Larsen's arms locked around his waist, and they were perilously close to the edge of the crevasse.

Though slender, Umiak was as tough as the rawhide cords on which he had hauled all his life, and wrestling was his people's national sport. Grimly he twisted in Larsen's grip, forced himself up onto his knees, and then to his feet. With a heave he threw Larsen over one hip, and slammed him to the ground, breaking his hold.

As Larsen sat up and Umiak stepped back, the revolver slipped from his belt and clattered down on the rock between them. Larsen stared at it dully. It lay, squat and black, its muzzle pointing towards him. A moment ago, at the height of his rage, he might have grabbed it and used it, but now he made no move, merely watching as Umiak picked it up and stowed it back in his waistband.

Larsen began instead to roll up his trouser leg and unwrap the bandage that protected his wound. It was a gesture of submission, an acknowledgment of defeat. Umiak watched impassively as Larsen exposed the weeping sore and held a handful of snow to the wound, wincing at first and then relaxing as the cold anaesthetized it. Larsen closed his eyes with relief, and when he opened them again Umiak was standing beside him, holding fresh bandages, and also a plastic bag filled with moss, which he must have gathered previously and stowed away in the sledge.

It was a peace offering, and Larsen recognized it as such. He felt reassured, for the man who had had the forethought to pack the moss was hardly likely to blow his patient's brains out. But again he felt inadequate, for he should have done this for himself.

The leg was a mess. His calf was inflamed from knee to ankle, and where the blister had broken there was now a circle of weeping flesh, from the centre of which pus was oozing. Larsen could do no more than bind it up again, and hope that it would stand up to the strain of walking.

Umiak regarded him dubiously. Larsen was clearly close to breaking point, and would have to be nursed along. He sighed, staring about him. Dark clouds still wreathed the peaks. Until the skies cleared, he had no way of knowing in which direction to head. In the meantime, it would do them no harm to rest.

"You a good shot?" asked Larsen suddenly.

Umiak shrugged. "I can take the eye out of a seal at two hundred feet." It was a statement of fact rather than a boast. "But that's with a rifle. Revolvers are for close work."

"Like on the bear," suggested Larsen.

Umiak shuddered. "I hope it never comes to that. This gun couldn't stop a bear before he'd killed you. It would only serve to infuriate him more. Better to turn it on yourself."

Larsen digested this in silence. "Well," he said at length, "if you come across anything worth shooting, make sure you don't miss. Me, I was never any good with sidearms."

Umiak hoped that, if the time came, he would not fail the other man. Meantime, he felt the whole matter had been resolved quite satisfactorily. Rising to his feet, he began to unpack the bedding from the sledge. They both needed rest after their wakeful night.

"What about the bear?" asked Larsen.

Umiak glanced back the way they had come. "Don't worry. He won't cross that gap. Bears can't jump."

220

HUNGER PAINS WOKE LARSEN later in the day. The skies had cleared, but the Arctic wind still sighed among the rocks. Somewhere behind the mountains the sun still shone, and the snowfields blushed rose pink in the reflected light. Leaving Umiak to sleep Larsen crawled from under the carpet and set off uphill, following a gentle rise that led to a nearby summit from which he hoped he could get a view of the terrain that lay beyond.

He felt fresher, but he noted ruefully that he had sustained several bruises in his brawl with Umiak. The guy was incredibly tough. Still, he felt strangely purged, of both bitterness and anger, and, in all fairness, Umiak didn't appear to be the sort to bear a grudge.

He reached the peak he was aiming for, and the view burst upon him. He stood on a high crag, the rock face below him falling away sheer for a thousand feet. As far as the eye could see there were mountains fading into the misty distance. Between lay a chain of small lakes interlinked by the winding silver ribbons of streams, glittering in the cold northern light. Vast snowfields lay against the slopes of the hills, swept there by the relentless wind. Elsewhere the land was bare, brown and sere, except in the hollows around the lakes, where carpets of green and gold revealed patches of tundra.

For a brief moment the beauty and the grandeur of the scene made him forget their present plight. He could understand now why the region was known as the Gates of the Arctic. Then despair descended as he realized how far they still had to travel. Seen from this altitude, the wilderness seemed even greater, more isolated, more overwhelming than he had imagined, and for the first time he began seriously to wonder if it was worth even making the effort to cross such vast distances. It would be so much more reasonable just to lie down, make himself as comfortable as possible, and await the gentle caress of death.

At that moment he heard the thin whipcrack of a pistol shot, and turning, he began to run back the way he had come.

"AN OWL!" EXCLAIMED LARSEN. "You wasted a bullet on a lousy owl?"

"Not a lousy owl, a snowy owl," laughed Umiak. "When I woke she was sitting on the rock just there. I couldn't miss. Now we have plenty of meat, and good eating too." He held the great bird up by the talons so that the wings hung down, half spread. There was, Larsen had to admit, plenty of meat. The carcass was almost two feet in length, and must have weighed seven pounds.

Expertly Umiak began to strip the feathers. "Women's work," he remarked cheerfully, "but we must shift for ourselves."

They ate slowly, savouring every morsel. The flesh was tender and appetizing. Replete at last, Larsen sat back with a sigh. Half the owl remained uneaten, and though Umiak looked wistfully at the chunks of meat still floating in the broth he too refrained from helping himself further. The soupy stew slowly congealed in its plastic bag. Umiak picked out the stones they had used in cooking it, and after licking each one clean, threw it away. The remains of the stew they carefully sealed and stowed away in the sled.

They made little further progress that day. To lose height they had to follow the long sloping shoulder of a ridge and finally make a hair-raising descent over a patch of steeply sloping scree. By evening they had reached the first of the lakes, where they had hopes of finding fish, but to their disappointment the water seemed devoid of life. So they went supperless to bed. At least the owl had allayed their worst hunger and they had the remainder of it to look forward to.

For the next two days they journeyed on through the mountains, picking a tortuous route among a maze of narrow passes and defiles, wending their way past frozen lakes and glaciers, following the course of any stream that led roughly east. Twice they had to labour over rocky saddles, when mountains barred their path. The weather held fine, and though the sun hung low on the horizon its rays sent a thin warmth through their bones.

Night brought relief from the wearisome toil of the day, but misery of a different kind. Despite all their endeavours to keep warm, the cold seemed to permeate their very bones. Long hours were passed in wakefulness. Hunger and lack of sleep then combined to weaken them still further, their legs felt leaden and useless, and each step required a real effort of will.

Dusk of the second day found them plodding wearily up through a narrow gorge, following a stream to its source, with the certain knowledge that they would have yet another mountain to cross. The sun had sunk out of sight, the temperature was falling, and they had almost despaired of finding shelter for the night when Larsen noticed the cave.

The entrance was low and rounded, as though enlarged by some animal in the past, but the snow that had drifted into the entrance was devoid of tracks. Larsen peered cautiously into the darkness. "What do you think?" he whispered.

Umiak bit his thumb. "Could be occupied. Bear, or wildcat perhaps. Better make sure." He picked up a rock, and lobbed it as far as he could into the cave. It landed with a soft thud.

"Sand?" suggested Larsen.

"Or fur," said Umiak.

He tried another stone, with the same result. Still he hesitated, and Larsen began to lose patience. Before Umiak could stop him he had dropped on all fours and crawled through the entrance. Immediately the cave widened out, so that he could no longer touch the walls, and he pulled the cigarette lighter from his pocket, ready to use it if need be. The floor was of soft dry sand, and he moved to his right until he came in contact with the wall, intending to follow it round, or retrace his steps if the cave proved to be of any great size.

There was no taint of animal odour. Instead the air smelled musty and museum-like, a strangely familiar scent associated with childhood. He moved on. The wall curved steadily to the left. Evidently the cave was not very large.

Then he recoiled in sudden terror. His hand had touched fur. He knelt, frozen, hardly daring to breathe, waiting and listening for any sign of life. Then, very gingerly, he stretched out his hand again. It was certainly skin or hide of some sort, but cold and lifeless to the touch. Larsen flicked the lighter, and the flame sprang up, clear and bright.

The body of a man, clad in furs, lay upon a pile of caribou skins. His face was black and wrinkled like leather, his eye sockets staring sightlessly up at the ceiling. Larsen stared at the mummified corpse, wondering how many years, centuries perhaps, had passed since he had been laid to rest there. Then he snapped off the lighter and crawled back to report his find to Umiak.

Together they lifted the topmost caribou skin and the corpse off the pile and laid it gently against one wall of the cave. It was feather-light, mummified in the cold dry air of the cave. It was as they were spreading the rest of the skins to make a couch for themselves that Umiak kicked something with an unmistakable metallic clang.

It was a quart-size canteen of the sort supplied by the thousand in the era of the fur trade. Umiak bore it outside in triumph and filled it with snow while Larsen prepared the stove. In the flickering light of the petrol flames they were able to see further into the gloom. There was a stone lamp and a sealskin bag that still contained oil, now thick and tarry. There was a flint and steel and tinder and a pair of fur-lined sealskin boots, iron-hard with age. And there was a homemade knife with a handle made from caribou antler.

As they settled for the night Larsen voiced the question that had been puzzling him ever since he had found the body. How had it got there, and why?

"He was abandoned by his people," said Umiak shortly. "He must have been with a hunting party, and he was left, with food and fire and a couch to lie on."

"Do you suppose he was hurt?" asked Larsen. "Too badly injured to walk?"

"No," said Umiak slowly. "They would have carried him with them. My guess is that he had some sort of infectious disease, smallpox or measles, or diphtheria. They were afraid, so they abandoned him, to recover or die."

"Seems callous somehow," said Larsen with a shiver.

"It was their only chance of survival," answered Umiak. "Whole villages died in epidemics of that kind. My people had no resistance to white man's diseases, and even a cold could kill them."

Larsen felt his flesh crawl at the thought of microbes from the distant past, perfectly preserved in the confines of this cave, waiting to claim yet another victim. Then he relaxed. "I've had measles," he remarked, "and I've been immunized against most other infectious diseases."

"So have I," said Umiak. "Progress is a marvellous thing."

It occurred to Larsen that there was an ironic ring to Umiak's voice, but he chose not to pursue it. He fell asleep more easily than usual, but his dreams were haunted by brown-skinned men, their faces purulent with disease.

He woke to find Umiak busy. He had taken the sealskin boots and was trying to restore their suppleness by rubbing in the thick tarry residue of oil that was left in the bag. The smell was revolting, but Umiak seemed unconcerned. "There was a time," he remarked casually, "when a woman's first duty on waking was to take her husband's frozen boots and chew on them until they were warm and supple. I guess high school has changed all that. I can't see today's young brides taking on such duties. There's no need now anyway, what with kerosene stoves and central heating and boots made of rubber."

He went back to his work. Larsen watched him curiously in the dim light that now filtered through into the cave. "You married, Umiak?"

There was a pause. "Was once," said Umiak.

A long silence followed.

Then Umiak spoke again. "They all died. She and the two kids. I was away at the time. There was an outbreak of polio."

Larsen had almost forgotten the poliomyelitis outbreak of the fifties, and the frantic search for a vaccine that would check the wildfire spread of a disease that could paralyse and kill. How much more devastating its impact must have been up here, where there was little or no medical aid. He began to understand better the fear of the group who had abandoned their comrade to die in this cave. Thoughts of the man lying in the corner prompted another question. How had the corpse remained unmolested by wild beasts?

"At the height of the fur trade whole regions were hunted out," explained Umiak. "I mean right out, cleared of everything that moved. It was a bonanza, but it couldn't last. A man might maintain a trap line a hundred and fifty miles long, and he had to get round it fast, before the wolverines and ravens robbed his traps. To do that he needed a large dog team, ten or more, and each dog needed seven pounds of meat or fish a day. You work that out in terms of salmon and caribou needed to last maybe six months of the year. Then the demand for furs suddenly fell. The hunters ate their dogs, and then they starved."

"At least now you have oil to bring you an income," ventured Larsen.

"For how long? We've seen the whalers come and go. We've seen the fur traders come and go. How long before the oil runs out, and the oilmen go back where they came from? No, the only things that endure up here are the land and the sea, and the harvests they yield. If the caribou don't come there are the seals, and if the seals stay out at sea there are walrus. In the spring the whales and the wild geese come, and in the summer the salmon swim up the rivers to spawn. In the fall the berries are ripe, and there are always the snowshoe hares."

Larsen scarcely heard the end of this discourse. At the thought of caribou steaks a wave of nausea had swept over him and for a moment he thought he was going to retch. Then hunger pains seized him in such a vice-like grip that he doubled up and fell forward, groaning and gasping for breath.

Umiak regarded him impassively. "It doesn't do to talk about food in a situation like this," he remarked reprovingly, as though the fault was all Larsen's. "It doesn't pay even to think about it. I'll heat some water. It helps."

It was, Larsen had to admit, better than nothing, and he sipped the scalding water gratefully. Beside him Umiak had finished work on the boots. "How are your hands?" he asked suddenly.

Larsen studied them. The skin was chapped and raw, cracks had formed in the folds of his fingers and every knuckle was sore. In his mood of general misery he had paid them scant regard, but now he was aware that he had difficulty even straightening his fingers. "Rub some of this in," ordered Umiak, pushing over the sealskin bag.

Holding his breath against the stench, Larsen did as he was bid. The relief was almost instantaneous, but at the same time he could not escape a qualm of fear, wondering what infection he might be introducing into his wounds.

It was time to move on. They had planned to take the caribou skins with them as protection against the cold, but already the hair was falling out in handfuls, and the ancient uncured hides cracked as they tried to roll them into a bundle. In the end they left them in a pile as they had found them, laying the corpse of their guardian reverently back in place. They took the canteen though, the knife, the flint and steel, and even the remains of the rancid oil.

As they prepared to leave, Umiak took off his own boots and pulled on the sealskin *mukluks* he had been working on earlier. "They'd be too small to fit you," he observed.

Larsen nodded. He was not sure whether he had received an apology or a mere statement of fact. "Dead man's shoes," he said softly, more to himself than to the other man.

"What was that?" asked Umiak.

"Oh, nothing," said Larsen. "I was merely thinking out loud."

ONE AFTER THE OTHER they crawled from the cave. The early morning sunlight on the snow blinded them momentarily, so they stood for a while, their backs to the sun, shading their eyes with their hands. The air was clean and cold after the mustiness of the cave, there was no wind, and the dry chill was infinitely more bearable than mist and snow. Neither man looked down to where the snow outside the cave was scuffed by their footprints. So even Umiak failed to notice, just in front of the entrance, the deep and unmistakable paw-print of a bear.

They set off with the sledge up the defile, towards the saddle in the mountains. In the sunlight the peaks seemed flattened against the sky. The saddle shimmered in the distance, seeming to recede with every step they took. Larsen's bad leg burned and throbbed, yet he felt curiously alive. After a while his head began to ache, and he wondered if he could be running a temperature.

There was nothing he could do about it, except press on. The cable of the sledge bit into his shoulder, his boots grew heavier, the muscles of his legs seemed reluctant to obey his will, and his feet refused to follow a straight line. Once he fell to his knees and knelt, gasping for breath, until his strength returned and he was able to go on.

The saddle was nearer now. Larsen did not dare to think what lay beyond: another mountain, a blind defile, an impassable cliff? Instead he concentrated on each step, pausing when his strength threatened to forsake him altogether. Each time, Umiak waited at his side without speaking. The man seemed indestructible, unaffected by cold and hardship.

In fact Umiak himself was glad of the pauses to rest. Older than Larsen, he had noticed that in recent years he had begun to slow down, that old age was creeping into his bones. He knew Larsen was sick, and pondered the advisability of returning to the cave, but guessed that the other man would have none of it. He could only wait until the time came when Larsen could go no further.

A cold wind began to blow across their path, whipping up stinging flurries of frozen snow to add to their misery. Umiak bent his shoulder to the towline of the sledge and plodded on, taking as much of the strain off Larsen as he could. So at last they reached the summit of the pass.

Larsen fell face down in the snow, too exhausted to care. But when at last he regained sufficient strength to rise and look east beyond the ridge, joy swept through him, a lump rose in his throat and tears filled his eyes.

226

The mountain on which they stood sloped steeply away before them in one vast expanse of unbroken snow. At the foot lay a broad valley through which a wide river meandered north. To the east lay another pass, again wide and flat, with patches of scrub, orange and yellow and scarlet, showing above the snow. There was still a long way to go, but it seemed they were free of the mountains at last.

For a long while they rested there, their backs to a rock that shielded them from the wind, the sun shedding a faint warmth on their faces. Suddenly Umiak stiffened. Then he was on his feet, laughing with delight as he pointed far up the valley to the north. "Caribou!" he shouted, and then Larsen saw them, a ragged cluster of tiny black dots moving with what appeared to be infinite slowness down the valley towards them. He guessed, though, that they were moving quite fast, and his heart sank at the realization that long before they could make the descent of the mountain the caribou would be gone.

When he voiced his fears Umiak's exuberance subsided. Then Larsen's eye fell on the sledge, the battered fragment of wing-tip they had hauled so far. A crazy idea came to his mind. Feverishly he began to untie the bundle of tattered carpet they still carried as bedding. "We're going down the fast way," he announced. "Help me spread this on top of the sledge. We've no need to climb down the mountain. This time we ride."

For a moment Umiak stared in horror, first at Larsen, and then at the steep smooth slope that stretched below them. There could be hidden rocks, uneven patches, hummocks of snow that would send them airborne. Their chances of staying with the sledge were almost nil. Then a slow smile spread over his face. If he survived, this ride would be something to remember. Like driving a dog team flat out over rotten ice.

Larsen lay flat on the sledge, the towline wrapped round his mittened hands and wrists. Umiak lay on top, and he too took a hold of the cable. "Ready?" asked Larsen, and Umiak grunted in reply.

For the first few yards the sledge ran slowly. Umiak's weight pressed down on Larsen, restricting his breathing. Then the sledge speeded up. An icy wind froze Larsen's cheeks, a great roaring filled his ears, and his eyes filled with tears so that he was almost blinded. At first gently, and then with increasing violence, the sledge began to pound. His teeth rattled, his head banged against the sledge in spite of all he could do to control it. Above him Umiak's weight pounded him, bruising his ribs until he thought they would break. Desperately he tried to breathe. His vision of the world turned red, and then there was only a roaring blackness in which, dimly, he was conscious of falling.

He woke to find himself lying flat on his back. Umiak was rubbing snow into his face. He lay there helplessly, unable to speak, feeling the Arctic air rasping into his labouring lungs, and the hammer of his heart pounding in his ears. At last he was able to sit up. "Next time I ride on top," he croaked, and Umiak grinned apologetically.

They looked back the way they had come, scarcely able to believe they could have come unscathed down the mountainside which now towered above them, seemingly sheer as a wall. The sledge had travelled a considerable distance across the level floor of the valley and close by they could hear the confused murmur of the river as it flowed north.

Umiak was thinking hard. The caribou, he knew, were migrating south to their winter feeding grounds, but whether the group he had seen were the vanguard of a large herd, or the last straggling members, he could not be sure. Now he was down on the plain, dead ground hid the approaching deer from view, and mercifully the light wind blew from the north, so there was no fear that the caribou would scent their presence.

All the same, the valley was wide, and there was no cover from which to lay an ambush. In any case, to be sure of making a kill, he had to get close. He longed for a high-powered rifle and a dozen of his own people, but it was useless to waste time on such idle thoughts. He looked back up the valley, towards the south, vainly searching for some feature of the landscape that would serve his needs.

About half a mile upstream the river curved in a great meander. Here the valley narrowed, and he reasoned that if the deer maintained their course they would cross the river, rather than detour round it. If he could find some cover beneath its bank, he might bag one as they attempted to cross.

Leaving the sledge where it lay he set off upstream, calling to Larsen to follow. Larsen did his best, but he was painfully slow. At last they reached the first bend in the river and stood on a wide gravel bar looking across to the further bank.

It was a likely place for the deer to cross. From the bank they could jump halfway across the stream, and from there it was an easy scramble up the bar. Spring floods had gouged a hollow in the bank, forming a place where a man might lie. However, he had first to send Larsen over to the furthest point of the meander, so that if the deer threatened to circle round he could divert them back. It would require timing and judgment. Umiak could only hope that Larsen's inexperience would not cause him to let them down.

First, though, he had to cross the river, a prospect he did not relish. Although he knew that the deer might arrive at any moment, he took the time to remove his boots and socks. He had no intention of risking frostbite by lying in sodden footwear. The icy waters of the stream, though they rose no higher than his knees, swiftly robbed his feet of all feeling, and it was a relief to gain the opposite bank, scrub them dry, and plunge them back into the warmth of his boots.

Then there was nothing to do but wait, and wonder whether he had chosen the best site. He dared not raise his head above the bank, and Larsen was nowhere to be seen. His right hand gripped the revolver as he lay without moving, listening, waiting for the low rumble, the steady clicking, of caribou hooves.

When at last it came it seemed to be far away over the valley towards Larsen. Bitter disappointment seized him, and then, far away, he heard Larsen shout, a long ululating wail that echoed and reechoed from the mountains.

Then the rumble became a roar, a stampede that was on him almost before he could prepare himself for the onslaught. The caribon were upon him, coming not from the right or the left but directly over his head, in a flurry of black flying hooves that rained down snow and crumbling frozen earth into his face and eyes, temporarily blinding him and almost sending him rolling into the river.

He half rose to his knees. Three deer were already across the river. His left hand gripped his right wrist, his finger curled round the trigger of the gun. As one cow hit the water he fired at her head. He saw chips of white bone fly from her muzzle, but she only shook her head and scrambled on towards the opposite bank. He fired again, and this time she went down, kicking in the shallows.

Another deer stood poised on the bank above him and he fired at the broad bulk of her side, just behind the shoulder, but at that very moment she sprang, and the bullet must have passed beneath her. Desperately he fired again, saw the bullet strike water just below where her back showed above the surface. Then she was scrambling up the bank and galloping away, seemingly unscathed.

He had one shot left. He looked wildly round for a fresh target. Then to his horror he saw the first cow, the one he thought he had killed, get up, shake herself, and stagger towards the gravel bar. Suddenly he was ice cold, calm and sure of himself. His last shot took her in the back of the head. She lurched up the bank, pulled herself clear of the water and dropped dead. The gun was empty. Wearily he stared at it for a moment, and then dropped it in the river, just so much useless weight. There was no point in carrying it any further.

A FEW MILES UP THE VALLEY a lone caribou took her last faltering steps and stood splay-legged in the snow, head hanging, flanks heaving. The rest of the herd had left her far behind, and solitude brought uncomprehending fear. She was the cow Umiak had fired at twice and thought he had missed. In fact his second shot, after entering the water, had caught her high in the chest. She felt no pain, only a growing weariness that brought her to the verge of sleep. Daylight came and went to her failing sight, so that she did not sense the approach of the bear until a violent blow on her back sent her sprawling in the snow.

High above an eagle screamed, loud in the silence, and a raven, huddled on a distant crag, woke to instant alertness. Wings spread, it dropped from the cliff face, to be lifted by a rising current of air. Its appearance aroused another of its kin, and so the message was semaphored across the vast spaces of the tundra.

Far to the north the ravens carried the news to a wolf pack, lolling in a sheltered stand of stunted willow. With one accord they rose, and after milling round for a while in an excited disorganized fashion, set off at a steady swinging trot up-river.

Larsen lay under blankets and the carpet, on the raw caribou hide Umiak had flayed from the dead cow. Every bone in his body felt as though it was broken. He breathed shallowly, trying not to expand his rib cage. His pulse raced, his head swam, and from time to time violent rigors shook his whole frame. Idly, almost detachedly, he wondered if he was going down with pneumonia.

Beside him Umiak sat hunched over the petrol stove, bone-weary, almost too exhausted to stir the stew now simmering in the canteen. Earlier he had found Larsen sprawled face down in the snow, lying where he had fallen after his last frantic race to head the caribou in Umiak's direction. He had half carried, half dragged him to this bend in the river, where a low overhanging bluff gave some shelter from the wind, and a dry gravel bar, suitably hollowed, provided a comfortable place to lie. Then he had skinned and butchered the caribou, retrieved the sledge, and hauled the spoils to the campsite, over a hundred pounds of meat and fat, including the head, together with a quart of blood. He had already fortified himself with several strips of raw liver, and the fat from behind the eyeballs, a prized delicacy he was sure Larsen would not appreciate.

Now the stew was almost ready: the tongue, heart and some of the liver cut fine and boiled in river water. His stomach churned in an agony of anticipation. Even so his first act was to pour some of the soup into the lid of the vacuum flask and carry it across to Larsen, raising the man to a sitting position and folding his hands round the cup. Gratefully Larsen drained the cup and then sank back, his eyes closed, leaving Umiak to indulge in an orgy of eating.

Even as he ate, Umiak's mind was busy. He had seen the ravens gathering in the sky, but assumed that his kill was the focus of their attention. They were a familiar sight at every caribou hunt. He knew too that they were the constant companions and messengers of the wolves, and that sooner or later a wandering wolf pack would be drawn to the scene. Wolves posed no threat to their lives, but he feared for the safety of their meat supply.

He was close to exhaustion. He knew he could not hope to keep watch all night, especially after a large meal. Larsen, for the moment, could not help. He guessed they might have to rest up for several days. So far the weather had held good, and the snowfalls that heralded winter had been light, helping rather than hindering their progress. A heavy fall could render them prisoners, unable to move through the deep drifts.

Snowshoes would help. Bitterly he reflected that it was years since he or anyone else had troubled to make a pair. It was so much easier to buy them through a mail order catalogue. But even though he might be able to fashion rawhide webbing from the caribou skin, he lacked the birch and willow to make the frames. Maybe he would find some further up the side stream he had noticed from the mountaintop.

Then there was the question of fuel. The petrol supplies were running low. They might last another five days at most. Still, they could survive on raw meat.

He could eat no more. He roused Larsen and fed him again, noting with approval that the man fell once more into instant slumber. There was one more task to perform before he too could rest. He found Larsen's fishing line, and set the caribou head, its antlers still attached, a little apart from the meat cache. He tied one end of the line to an antler, hung the empty canteen on the line so that it was suspended just above the stones that littered the river bank, and drew the line round the cache, fastening the other end to his foot. Anything approaching the meat in the night would snag the line, tugging at his foot and sending the canteen clattering against the stones. Now at last he could sleep, and crawling in beside Larsen he sank into instant oblivion.

Larsen woke to full daylight, weak but clear-headed, and for the first time since the crash he felt warm. The dense caribou skin spread beneath him in the hollow insulated him from the cold and enfolded him in a cosy nest. He still felt abominably stiff and sore, but at least he could breathe easily and the hunger pains had gone. Instead he was conscious of a raging thirst.

It was this that forced him at last, reluctantly, to abandon his couch, find the cup, and stagger to the edge of the stream. It was only then, after he had drunk two cupfuls, that he missed Umiak. He gazed round him.

So it had come to this, then. Umiak had abandoned him, left him with food and water and a bed, to survive or die, just like the man in the cave . . . Yet it seemed he had taken nothing for himself, and not even Umiak could survive without the bare essentials. Maybe he had walked off, met with an accident, and was lying injured somewhere.

"*Umiak!*" he yelled. "*Umia-a-ak!*" The echoes came back from the mountains, mocking him, but no answering call came from Umiak. He fell to his knees, gazing into the black waters of the pool. His reflection stared

back, haggard, gaunt-cheeked, fringed with the beginnings of a straggly blond beard, the face of a stranger.

Suddenly he picked up a stone and flung it into the water, shattering the image. He turned away and hobbled back up the beach. He ought, he knew, to change the dressing on his leg, but he was too apathetic to care. So he sat hunched on the river bank, staring north down the valley at the featureless frozen landscape.

In the distance a dark shape materialized against the snow, emerging from a hidden dip in the ground. It was Umiak, plodding steadily along, bent under a huge burden of dry twigs.

Larsen limped forward to meet him and help relieve him of his burden. Umiak straightened his back with a grunt, and for the first time Larsen noticed the fatigue in the older man's face. "You've been busy," he commented. "Good job somebody's prepared to get up and work around here, instead of lying sleeping all day."

Umiak grinned. "I hoped you might sleep longer. You needed the rest."

"I slept well," said Larsen. "That caribou hide makes a fine bed."

"Why didn't you stay there?"

"I woke thirsty," replied Larsen, "and then you were missing . . ."

232

"You thought I'd deserted you maybe?" queried Umiak.

"Oh no! It wasn't that," protested Larsen, and then he hesitated. "Well, to be honest, it did cross my mind . . ." He broke off.

"I was at fault," admitted Umiak. "I should not have gone off and left you. We make a pact, eh? From now on neither of us leaves the other without saying where we are going and why. It's wisest, and I should have thought of it."

"I'll shake hands on that," said Larsen. Suddenly, he felt extraordinarily hungry.

An hour later both men sat replete. They had each eaten about a pound of fat caribou steak, grilled in the hot embers of the wood fire, and a canteen full of water stood heating in front of them. "Coffee would be nice," murmured Larsen.

"Tea I can offer you," said Umiak. "Labrador tea." He picked up a bundle of herbs he had brought back with the twigs, stripped the leaves from a sprig, and dropped them into the vacuum flask. Then he added water from the canteen. Larsen sipped the brew gingerly. It was strongly aromatic, almost antiseptic in taste, but he decided he liked it, and drained the cup.

233

"You know," he said dreamily. "I'm beginning to think that when the hunting was good, your people lived pretty high on the hog, if you understand the expression. Oh, I don't mean you had it easy, but you had the best."

Umiak sat silent for a while, reminding himself that this white man was like all the rest, unable to understand the glory that once had been. Yet he was beginning to, and it was important that he should.

"Life was easy, and life was hard," he began. "If a hunter woke in the morning and heard the wind blowing strong off the land, he knew the seals would be far out to sea, so he might be idle for a week or more. But when the weather was right, then the hunt took precedence over everything. He might wait a day for a seal to show up, but then, if he killed a big one, it might weigh five hundred pounds, and he had the job of dragging it four or five miles over the ice. That was hard work. And when the salmon were running, for a fortnight we might work eighteen hours a day.

"But the wilderness provided, and we took only the best: fat caribou calves, the prime salmon, the juiciest berries. We slept on the softest of skins, our wives wore a ransom in fine furs. Life was good, and we were happy. It will be good again for my people."

He paused and chuckled. "A wise man said, and he was a white man, that 'an Indian hunts to live, but an Eskimo lives to hunt.' That is very true, I think."

They both laughed, two middle-aged men slipping into an easy familiarity, a friendship suddenly transcending the barriers of race or creed.

"We ought to move on, if you can make it," said Umiak. "There's a good campsite about a mile up the valley, a rock overhang by a waterfall. Plenty of dry wood, and berries too. We could rest up there a couple of days, eat and get strong, and still have enough meat for the remainder of the trip."

Despite his weakness, Larsen was all for setting off at once, but Umiak was tired. Already, while Larsen slept, he had tramped a good six miles, half that distance with a load of wood on his back. "There's no hurry," he muttered. "I'm going to rest awhile. Why don't you play with that fishing rod of yours? There's sure to be a fish in that pool."

So saying he lay back on the bedding, and in a few moments he was asleep. Larsen began to assemble his tackle, then walked stiffly to the head of the pool and flicked a small gold spinner across to the deep water under the far bank. His third cast brought a sudden strike. His rod bent sharply, and seconds later a grayling of about a pound was flapping on the bank. Two casts later he caught a second one about the same weight. There came a lull, and then his rod bent to a heavier, stronger fish, which made several fast runs down the pool before turning on its side exhausted. It was a char, deep-flanked and red-bellied, at least three pounds in weight.

For a time he fished on, systematically working his way down the pool, but no more fish came. At last he picked up his catch and walked back to camp. Umiak still slept, so he hung the fish on the antlers of the caribou and then he too stretched himself on the ground to sleep.

THE SITE UMIAK HAD FOUND was luxurious in comparison to earlier camps. They spread the caribou hide over a thick bed of springy twigs and moss, beneath a sloping sandstone slab that gave them shelter from the weather. Dry brushwood, willow and alder lined the banks of the stream where it had been deposited by spring floods, and soon they had a bright fire of small sticks glowing among the stones. The polished underside of the sledge acted as a reflector to the flames, throwing the heat back into the shelter. They had meat, fish, and berries in plenty.

But Larsen was in a bad way. The effort of dragging the heavily laden sledge the few miles up the valley had taxed him severely. He had a raging thirst, and his flushed appearance indicated a rapidly rising temperature. His leg throbbed and burned, and a fresh abscess was forming below the site of the earlier wound, fiery to the touch.

Umiak put fresh water in the canteen and set it to warm in the flames. Then he got a pad of cloth, and as soon as he judged the water as hot as Larsen could bear he began applying poultices to the wound. For over an hour Larsen lay gritting his teeth. At last he reached into his pocket and pulled out his little penknife. "Cut it," he gasped. "Let the poison out."

Umiak took the knife, opened the smallest blade and tested the edge with his thumb. It was razor sharp. Without hesitating he plunged the point of the knife into the abscess and cut downwards. Larsen screamed as yellow pus streaked with blood spurted out of the wound.

"All over," said Umiak, glancing up at his patient, but Larsen had fainted dead away. Umiak took advantage of this to irrigate the abscess thoroughly. He thought of packing the cavity with a strip of cloth, but then he remembered his mother using willow bark as a dressing. Swiftly he gathered a handful of young shoots, stripped the bark from them, and shredded them into the canteen along with a cupful of water, boiling the whole concoction into a sloppy mush. By the time it had cooled, and he had decanted the liquid from the bark, Larsen had recovered. He made no protest as Umiak gently packed the wound with the willow-bark paste and bound up his leg, but he resisted when Umiak tried to get him to drink the bitter juice. Finally he threw it back at a gulp. Shortly after, his fever seemed to abate, and at last he fell into a deep sleep.

That night the wolves came. Umiak heard them quarrelling over the caribou entrails which he had left further up the valley, but he knew that those few frozen remains would not sustain them for long. So he sat wakeful, keeping the fire bright, guarding the precious cache of meat.

Beside him Larsen stirred fretfully from time to time, but did not wake.

There was no chance of moving on in the morning. They both needed rest, and Larsen's leg needed time to heal. Umiak guessed they still had far to go and he seriously doubted whether they could transport the food they needed to sustain them on the trip. Perhaps they could cut some of the meat into strips and dry it, perhaps smoke some of it over the fire. This would reduce the bulk and weight, and mixed with berries it would provide sufficient nourishment. Meantime it would pay to eat as much as they could. And he could only pray that the weather would hold.

Larsen woke weak but refreshed, and eager for his share of the fish Umiak had poached in the canteen. His wound was looking cleaner and healthier, and much of the inflammation had died down. The willow-bark treatment seemed to be working, so they repeated it, but when Larsen tried to stand he found the leg would scarcely bear his weight. So he rested, while Umiak dried meat and harvested berries from the hill.

Most of the day, though, they spent sleeping and eating, so that when night came they were both wakeful, and ready for the wolves. They heard them howling as the long Arctic twilight began to fall, and twice they glimpsed a dim grey shape moving on the far side of the stream. Umiak had collected a store of firewood, and between them they kept the flames of their fire flickering through the darkness. Umiak had impressed on Larsen the need to conserve fuel. Even so, Larsen was astounded at the way the fire devoured the thin, dry sticks, and the woodpile diminished rapidly.

From time to time they discouraged the wolves by pelting them with stones, yet it seemed, in spite of their efforts, that the pack was growing bolder. Larsen found himself wondering rather nervously how he would react if he was alone. Tentatively he asked Umiak how he would feel.

Umiak thought for a while before replying. "It is not good for a man to live alone," he said. "I have known trappers, living alone in the wilds for weeks on end, and they became strange in their ways." A sudden outburst of snarling as the wolves quarrelled amongst themselves interrupted Umiak, and he heaved another rock in their general direction. In the silence that followed he laughed softly. "Man and wolf alike are pack animals, timid when alone, braver when they are in company. Yet the wolf has always feared man, probably because man has learned to throw stones. The wolf never will. His paws are the wrong shape."

It was Larsen's turn to laugh. All the same, he could not repress a shudder at the thought of lying alone beside a dying campfire, surrounded by a pack of hungry wolves.

Again Umiak displayed that uncanny knack of seeming to read his thoughts. "It is what man imagines the wolf to be that makes him afraid, rather than what the wolf is."

The wolves showed no sign of venturing closer. The hours passed and Larsen was beginning to doze, when suddenly he jerked awake to hear Umiak yelling and throwing stones. The night seemed filled with fleeting grey shapes.

One actually brushed against him as he sat up and flung aside the carpet that covered him. He too began to yell and to heave rocks at random, but almost before he had begun the raid was over. The wolf pack vanished as swiftly as it had appeared.

Together they crossed the few yards of gravel to what remained of the meat cache. Only the hindquarters remained. "I made it too easy for them," Umiak muttered angrily. "If only I'd left the carcass intact. Instead, I butchered it into easily manageable chunks."

"Well," remarked Larsen dryly, "at least the problem of how to carry the meat has been solved for us. And we've still got the meat we dried, and the berries, and the hindquarters. We could be worse off ... Besides," he added, peering into the gloom, "by the look of things, we've got wolf meat to add to the pot."

A half grown wolf lay sprawled on the ground. One of their stones had scored a lucky hit, striking the wolf on the side of the head. Gingerly Umiak took hold of its tail and dragged it a foot or so across the ground. More than one man, he knew, had been badly bitten by an apparently dead wolf. This one, though, was quite dead, and they carried it back to the fire.

"You know," said Umiak, "I've never tasted wolf."

For breakfast they mixed some of the wolf meat with caribou stew, and they both found it to be quite palatable. Umiak was not surprised. "Lots of things are good to eat, if people would only try them. Porcupine, for instance, and lynx. Fox is good too, but few people eat that now. This meat is a bit like fox." Suddenly he chuckled quietly and looked at Larsen, a hint of mischief in his eye. "There's an old belief among my people that a man who eats wolf meat will father unruly children."

Larsen grinned ruefully. "There's nothing I'd like better than to put your theory to the test. Meantime, I'll just concentrate on staying alive. What do you think? Do we move on?"

"There's nothing to keep us here," admitted Umiak. "We ought to make the effort while the food lasts. We may get lucky further on, but we can't depend on it. How's the leg?"

"Feels good," said Larsen. "I'll change the dressing in a minute."

The wound looked clean and healthy and after it was redressed it gave him little discomfort. They set about breaking camp and loading the sledge. They had been careful to spread the caribou hide fur side down, to dry in the crisp Arctic wind, and it showed no sign of decay. Larsen looked at the wolf skin Umiak had draped over a rock. For the first time he was struck by the full rich beauty of the fur, black and pale tan and grey, with the long guard hairs frosted with silver, so that he almost regretted the death of the wolf. "I wonder which one of us threw the stone that killed it?" he asked.

Umiak looked at him sharply. "Does it matter?" he queried.

Larsen couldn't answer. It had occurred to him that the pelt would make a hat for Sylvie, and then his thoughts ran on as to whether she would give him some unruly children. The intensity of feeling this evoked almost overwhelmed him, and once again he was astonished at the ease with which sudden emotion could break down his self-control, here in the wilderness.

"Keep the pelt if you want it," said Umiak offhandedly. "It might just as easily have been your stone as mine."

Larsen muttered his thanks. Again he couldn't escape the feeling that Umiak had read his mind.

By late morning they were ready to move on. The sledge felt heavier now, but the going was good, the air was calm, and a slight haze cut the glare of the sun as it hung low on the horizon. The way ahead sloped gradually upwards, following a series of gentle hills. They moved slowly but steadily, pausing occasionally to rest before leaning their weight into the towline once more. Neither man knew it, but they were heading once more into the mountains.

UMIAK HAD BEEN WRONG about the bear.

Here and there across the icy wastes of the Arctic wilderness, scattered over barren rock screes or buried beneath a carpet of mosses and ferns, lie shattered fragments of bone. They are all that remain of men who have died in the mistaken belief that grizzly bears cannot climb trees, nor jump.

In fact the bear was not so very far behind Umiak and Larsen, nosing round the campsite they had left earlier that morning. He had crossed the chasm with ease, and found an easier way down off the mountain.

There in the valley he had found the caribou dying from the gunshot wounds earlier inflicted by Umiak, and gorged until he was full. Throughout that day he had lain resting, and driving away a pair of wolverines that came to share the feast. During the night they tried again, and despite his angry rushes succeeded in bearing away a substantial portion of the prize. By the end of the second day the grizzly was reduced to cracking bones for the marrow.

So he wandered down to the river, drank some of the icy water, and then moved slowly on downstream. His mantle of snow had grown thicker. Long icicles, yellowed by dirt from his pelt, hung down his flanks. His muzzle and chest were stained red, as were his paws. Only his massive head was free of snow, and his small eyes glittered dark in the sun.

238

He lingered long at the campsite, finding much to occupy his attention, scraps of caribou bone and sinew, fishheads, and the remains of the wolf. His nose told him more as he explored the odours lingering among the stones, evoking memories of the corpse he had dragged from its cairn of stones. The same scent led him away up the valley, following in the wake of the two men.

AS THE DAY WORE ON and they climbed steadily higher, mist began to develop. Soon the two men were blanketed in thick fog, dark and chill, enveloping them in fine beads of moisture, which froze in the icy wind. Despite their exertions the raw, damp cold seemed to penetrate through to their bones.

The snow lay deeper here, swept into drifts in which they floundered up to their knees. They plodded on, step after slow careful step, ever aware that the ground was still rising before them. The cloud obscured their vision, enveloped them in a silence. They had to strain their ears to catch the faint muffled murmur of the stream beside them. Neither man spoke, saving what little energy he could muster simply to keep moving.

Now the ground began to rise more steeply. From time to time, when the mist cleared a little, they caught glimpses of crags on their right. The way became more uneven, and Umiak knew that neither of them could carry on much further without a break. They had left the willow thickets far behind, and there was no fuel or shelter.

Then, quite suddenly, they broke through the blanket of cloud, and both men stopped in their tracks as they surveyed the scene before them. On all sides the mountains closed in like walls. Ahead, the stream divided, and without a word they made their way to the fork, which lay in deep shadow. Here a massive buttress of stone reared against the mountainside, towering thirty feet above the stream. At this point the water foamed through a narrow channel in the solid rock, but there was a ledge, slippery with ice, along which they could pass. They navigated it cautiously, knowing that one slip would be fatal.

Beyond, the valley opened into a small glen. Larsen eased from under the towline of the sledge and sank down onto a rock. "Which way now?"

"No way for now," replied Umiak. "First we rest, eat and drink."

At least they had plenty of food, and they ate well, for there was no sense in rationing themselves to the point where they were too weak to travel. They had taken the precaution of boiling thick caribou steaks before they left camp. That the meat was now cold, the gravy congealed with fat, didn't trouble Larsen. His hands were blackened with dirt and charcoal, Umiak's were as bad, but they each dipped into the plastic bag that held the stew without a qualm. By the end of the meal their fingers were cleaner than when they had started.

239

Larsen's clothes stank. His straggly beard itched and his hair was tangled and unkempt. He longed for a hot bath, the comfort of a clean bed, the softness of a pillow on which to lay his head. He sat back and rested against the unyielding surface of the rock. He felt he could sleep for a week.

His eyelids drooped and he fell into a doze, leaving Umiak alone with his own thoughts. He too felt desperately weary, yet he knew they must keep moving, for with each passing day their chances of survival grew less. As the nights grew longer, the cold deepened, and the weather grew worse. Now they were faced with yet another imponderable. He sat staring at the twin watercourses. Which one, if either, would lead them out of the mountains?

The day was nearly gone, and the more rest Larsen got now the better he

would be able to face the journey ahead. Meanwhile the valley was sheltered, and there were worse places to spend the night. He would explore one stream, leaving Larsen to unload the sledge and make preparations for the night. If that route proved impassable he would try the other in the morning.

Once the decision was made he felt better, and rousing Larsen, he told him of his plans. At first Larsen demurred, volunteering to take one route while Umiak explored the other, but as Umiak pointed out, that would mean leaving their food supply unguarded. Convinced, Larsen watched him depart, picking his way among the ice-covered boulders that lay strewn along the riverbed. Gradually his figure grew smaller, then vanished behind the shoulder of the hill.

Larsen wandered around, slapping his arms across his chest in an effort to restore his circulation, looking for a suitable spot to spend the night. There seemed none better than the flat space beneath the rock against which he had been leaning, so he unstrapped the bedding from the sledge and spread it on the ground.

That done he sat down again and tried to relax, but found he could not. About fifty yards below him, just above the point where the river narrowed into a foaming channel cut deep into the rock, it widened out into a small pool. Larsen fell to wondering if it held any fish. He had caught trout high in the mountains before, in just such streams as this. He had no fly tackle as such, only his spinning rod and a fixed-spool reel, but he had a small plastic bubble float and a selection of flies, and he had long ago mastered the technique of attaching a fly on a long trace below the bubble float and letting it drift downstream with the current. It was hardly fly-fishing but it was one way of taking fish.

Soon the tiny plastic bubble was meandering gently down the pool, drifting with the current. The first run produced nothing. Nor did the second, but on the third run Larsen varied his technique by letting the float down in a series of jerks. Stopping the float brought the fly rising to the surface, and halfway down he was rewarded by a slashing take as a trout went skidding slantwise across the pool.

Fish came steadily after that. The trout were small, no more than a few ounces in weight, but perfectly formed and fighting fit. Soon five lay in a neat row on an icy slab of rock, their colours fading as they dried in the cold air. Larsen fished on, his whole concentration fixed on the tiny plastic bubble that bobbed its way down the icy black water of the pool.

So he did not notice that far down the river the landscape moved. An ice-clad boulder, indistinguishable from a hundred others that littered the banks of the stream, gradually reared up until it was an eight-foot monolith silhouetted against the sky. Then it sank down again, and drifted slowly across the river and up the side of the hill.

FAR AWAY UP THE VALLEY, Umiak stood looking up at a tangled wall of jagged boulders, bound in a shroud of ice, from the base of which the headwaters of the stream oozed out. Almost tenderly, he laid his hand on one of the stones. It fell away at his touch, bringing several more in its wake, and Umiak stepped back hurriedly as the whole mass seemed to shift. The entire wall, towering above his head, was poised on the brink of collapse.

Softly he moved away, retracing his steps downstream. After a few yards he stopped and sat down on a flat slab of rock. The light was fading, and he knew he should not linger, yet he felt a strange reluctance to return to camp. Somehow Larsen seemed to drain him, exhaust him mentally and

242

physically. Alone he felt fitter, freer, more optimistic for the future, confident of his ability to survive. With Larsen, he felt he had another burden to drag, in addition to the weight of the sledge.

He sighed, and then jerked himself to his feet. The air was growing chill. He arrived back at the camp in time to see Larsen hook and land his last fish.

THE TROUT WERE A GREAT SUCCESS, more so than the fresh caribou stew that followed. Their petrol stocks were diminishing fast. They had at most four days' supply remaining, and the stew was only half cooked, the meat rubbery, the juices thin and unappetizing. Larsen found himself craving salt. Any seasoning would be welcome, but he missed salt most.

He longed too for something sweet, and for french fries and cereals, especially bread. Endless visions of sandwiches passed through his mind: salami on rye, tuna fish, egg, corned beef, toasted cheese. Looking back, it seemed to him he'd lived on sandwiches all his life.

He remarked on this to Umiak, still mopping up the remains of the stew. Umiak laughed, but sympathetically, not sneering. "Talk to my people and you will hear the same complaint, only the opposite way. After a spell of eating white man's food they long for what they call 'real food', and if they don't get it then they feel weak and ill. They say they 'feel pale'."

It was quite dark now, and under the clear skies the cold grew intense as the frost bit into the earth. The two men turned in, huddling together under their bedding. Larsen felt weary, but his leg was aching badly and robbed him of sleep. Instead he lay watching the slow procession of the stars, trying not to think, trying not to disturb Umiak.

Suddenly Larsen was aware that the night was growing lighter. The stars paled, snowdrifts showed on the dark shoulder of the hill, and jagged rocks leaped into sharp relief. "Can't be daylight already," he murmured to himself.

"Moonlight," said Umiak beside him. Larsen started with surprise. He had judged Umiak to be sound asleep.

"I've been expecting it," Umiak went on. "In a day or so, if the weather holds, it will be nearly as light as day. Then we can travel all night and sleep during the day, when it's warmer."

"For how long?" pondered Larsen. "And how far?"

"I wish I knew," said Umiak. "But one thing's for sure, every mile takes us a little nearer, and every day increases the chance that we will meet up with a bunch of hunters. This time of year the people of Anaktuvuk hunt sheep in these hills."

"We must be somewhere in the region that is going to be designated a national park," said Larsen. "There's no hunting allowed in national parks. How will your people get on?"

243

"Oh, they'll hunt, I guess, legally or illegally. Anyway, it's been promised that we will retain our traditional hunting rights, part of the deal we worked out when the state chose their lands. We've never seen ourselves as land owners, rather as land users. Take this region, for instance—we've used it for ten thousand years or more, and yet it's as unspoilt as it was the day we moved in. Which is more than you can say for most of the lower forty-eight."

Umiak chuckled. "That's why I, among others, persuaded our people to register title to their land, even though they couldn't see the sense of it, because they didn't regard it as theirs. I remember when the officials came to my home village to explain the policy of land registration. Everybody fell about laughing. One man said he was going to register a hilltop, because if too many people came up there they'd wear away the view. My father said he was going to grow tomatoes."

"Tomatoes!" exclaimed Larsen. "Up here?"

"On a sandbank, up the river. It was a longstanding joke in the village. I'd been down south you see, and I brought lots of stuff back, including several pounds of fresh tomatoes, which no one in the village had ever seen. My father liked them, and he ate a lot, maybe too many because he went off up the river and had to stop, urgently, on a big gravel bar in the middle of the stream.

"Later in the fall, there in the hollow where my father had squatted were tomato vines, some with little fruit on them. They teased him plenty, I can tell you, told him he was a great *shaman*, asked him to eat gold dust, and turn it into nuggets."

Larsen laughed. "What's a *shaman?*" he queried.

Umiak looked faintly embarrassed. "In the old religion, before the white missionaries came, with their story of a Christ who died to save men, the *shamans* were our priests, our medicine men, spokesmen who could intercede on our behalf with the spirit world. They could heal the sick, or foretell the coming of the whales. They knew where the caribou were to be found. It is said that some could control the weather. It is certain that many had strange and terrible powers."

"You believe in these powers?"

"The *shamans* are no more," answered Umiak shortly. "They have lost their power." Suddenly he laughed again. "I was telling you about the tomatoes. Point is, next year the sandbank had gone, washed away by the spring floods. That's how it is. A good fishing hole this year may yield nothing next. A berry patch may get eaten by bears, the caribou may winter in one spot for a while, and then move on. So we use land, rather than own it. Still, we did register some land, and we were wiser than we knew, because a lot of that land lay in the way of the oil pipeline. To settle each individual claim would have taken years in the courts, so your people had to do a deal. Plus we own the right to hunt and fish over federal lands which, to be honest, is all many of my people ask."

Larsen lay silent. He was growing drowsy. The pain in his leg had eased now he had taken the weight off it, and he burrowed deeper into the thick hairs of the caribou pelt on which he lay. He had quickly grown accustomed to its rank animal odour. Now he almost welcomed it, associating it in his mind with rest and warmth and sleep.

Yet it seemed to him that now the smell was stronger, ranker, overlaid with the odour of decay. Was the hide beginning to decompose? The stench came again, in a warm foul wave, and he opened his eyes.

Larsen had met fear in many of its forms but nothing had prepared him for the sight that now filled his gaze. The bear stood not six feet away. He smelled the foul carrion odour of its breath and saw the small black eyes glittering in the starlight, the great teeth bared, the crusting of yellow ice and snow streaming down the broad chest. The bear's bulk blotted out the sky beyond it.

For a moment Larsen's throat constricted with terror. He actually felt the bristles on his face stand up. His heart began to thud. Then his fear gave voice, in an ear-splitting yell, a great brassy trumpet blast of pent-up emotion.

The bear vanished.

Umiak shot upright, still half asleep. "What the hell! What is it?"

"The bear," gasped Larsen, shaking now. "It was right on top of us."

Umiak listened. Nothing stirred. The landscape lay deserted in the pale blue-grey light. "There's nothing there. You were dreaming."

Larsen snorted. "This was no dream. The bastard was there. I saw him, smelled him, I could have damn near kicked him. I tell you, he was about to mash us into the ground."

"Then where did he go?"

"Hell, I dunno. Guess I scared him off."

"Not surprising," said Umiak. "You sure as hell scared me."

Long minutes passed, both men listening, watching. Then: "There he is," said Larsen. "See that rock across the river? He's there, watching us."

Umiak looked, but could see nothing.

"Don't look straight at the rock," hissed Larsen. "Shift your gaze a little to one side. You'll see him out of the corner of your eye."

Umiak did as he was bid. Suddenly the bear leaped into focus, a round snow-spattered bulk almost indistinguishable from the other boulders strewn across the landscape. Yet even as he watched he was aware that it was moving, that it was slowly nodding its head.

"That's a good trick," said Umiak. "Where did you learn it?"

Good grief, thought Larsen in astonishment, anyone would think we were bird-watching.

"It was a dodge they taught us in the army. Came in handy on night patrol. What about that damned bear, though?"

"I think he was hoping to find us dead. Now he knows we're not, he'll wait. As long as we're awake, and together, we're safe. I think."

"You think," repeated Larsen. Slowly his fear was giving way to rage. "Why don't we scare him off?"

"Because then we wouldn't know where he was. Do you really want to sit here, wondering all the while if he's crept round behind us?"

The thought did not appeal. "Suppose he moves off anyway?"

"Let's worry about that if it happens," suggested Umiak.

Larsen's eyes began to smart with the effort of keeping the bear in sight. Once he glanced away, only to feel a lurch of panic when he failed to locate the bear again straight away. He realized he was being nonsensical. There was no reason for the bear to attack unless they threatened it. He had just begun to relax when Umiak gripped his arm. "He's on the move," he whispered. Larsen looked towards the base of the rock, but the shape had gone. The bear had melted into the night.

Then the nightmare began. As the moon went down and the darkness deepened, the two men sat on, awake in the silence of the night. Larsen could not rid himself of the vision of the bear as it had appeared to him on opening his eyes. In his imagination he smelled the rank putrescent odour of its breath. He felt the great jaws seize him, shake him, crush down into his skull. He felt his clothing ripped from his back by one stroke of those terrible claws, felt his ribs crack and the air whistle into the open cavity of his chest.

The long hours passed, and they waited. Shaking with cold and fatigue the two men watched the dawn break, saw blessed light steal over the valley, flooding the deserted landscape. But the bear never came.

THE MORNING RENEWED their courage. Umiak insisted on carrying on with his plan to explore the second valley, leaving Larsen in camp to pack their belongings in readiness to move off. Larsen would have preferred to accompany him, not wishing to be left alone, but pride prevented him from making more than a token protest. If Umiak was prepared to face the wilderness alone and unarmed, in the certain knowledge that a hungry bear lurked somewhere close by, then so was he.

He watched Umiak depart, and then sank back on a rock. There was no hurry. Their few belongings could be stowed and lashed on the sledge in a few minutes. Meantime it would do no harm to let the bedding air. He spread it out, turning the caribou hide hair side down, and then turned his attention to a chore he had been dreading, an inspection of the wound on his leg.

The wound itself looked clean, and so did what little discharge there was. But its size appalled him. The original incision, where Umiak had lanced the abscess, had now widened and grown so distorted that no trace of the cut remained. Instead there was an irregularly-shaped ulcerated pit, around which the skin curled back.

He felt totally at a loss as to how to treat it. At first he thought it might benefit from exposure to the air, but the cold caused him such intense pain that he was glad to cover it again. Padded and protected from the cold, it felt easier, and he resolved then not to touch it again if he could avoid it.

All the same, prudence made him wash the soiled dressing in the stream and spread it out on the rocks to dry. He had just completed this task and was striving to restore some warmth to his frozen fingers, when he glimpsed a streak of white racing across the hill. As he watched it appeared again, an arctic fox, fleeing from some unseen threat. Once it checked, to turn and stare down the valley, before vanishing once more.

Larsen wondered what could have disturbed it. Certainly not Umiak, for he had gone off in the opposite direction. With growing unease, Larsen walked to the foot of the pool. Then, seeing nothing, he climbed up on the rock that overhung the gorge.

Then he saw it, far away downstream but moving in his direction, the shaggy bulk of the bear that had haunted them since they had left the plane. Surprisingly he felt quite calm, detached, able to watch with interest as the bear picked its way slowly upstream. It seemed in no hurry, pausing occasionally to look from side to side before moving on. So Larsen wasted precious minutes, expecting the bear to turn aside, or head off back downstream.

Suddenly it dawned on him that the bear had no such intention. As the full danger of the situation came to Larsen his mind began to race. His heart hammered and his mouth went dry. He sank down on the rock, desperately trying to think clearly. Would he be safe up here? Would the bear pass by without scenting his presence? Or would he have to watch helplessly as the bear demolished what was left of their food supplies? Worse, it might move on and pull down Umiak, somewhere alone up there among the crags.

Then a cold hatred of the bear overwhelmed his fear. Above all, he longed to destroy it. To reach the camp the bear had to pass below him—if only he had a heavy enough rock to drop on it, but there was nothing to hand bigger than his closed fist. Still, he had time perhaps to scramble down off the rock, and climb back with one big enough. If not, yelling might scare it away.

But he didn't want to scare it away. He wanted to annihilate it, to be free of it for ever. If only he had some kind of weapon, a grenade, napalm, any of the tools of war with which in the past he had confronted the enemy.

It came to him then what he must do, and there was little time left if he was to put his terrible plan into action. He took one last glance down the valley. Unless the bear increased its pace, he had several more minutes.

With extreme care he climbed down off the rock. With his knife he cut about a foot of cable off the spare length they had salvaged from the plane. Then he tore a small strip of rag from the remains of the pilot's trousers. His hands, he noticed, worked without a tremor. He fastened the rag to one end of the short cable, and took one of the plastic bags, a whole day's supply of fuel, and fastened the cable's other end round its neck. Finally, he soaked the rag in petrol, not too much, for he didn't want flaming petrol dripping onto the bag while he held it in his hands, and not too little, in case the spirit evaporated before the time came to light the fuse. Then he

climbed back up onto the rock with the fire bomb and the lighter to wait.

The bear was still some distance away, so he had time to spare. Now he was shaking so violently he was afraid that when the time came he would be unable to work the lighter, and it took all his willpower to relax.

Meantime the bear came on towards the rock. Now he could see its breath steaming in the cold air; a few seconds more, and it would be directly below him. Larsen's thumb was poised over the wheel of the lighter, his plastic fire bomb firmly gripped in his left hand. As the bear passed beneath him he lit the rag fuse, saw the plastic bag curve outwards and downwards, a shining silver ball followed by a tiny tag of crimson and yellow. It burst squarely on the bear's head, dissolving into a shower of sparkling drops.

For a long moment nothing happened. The bear stopped dead in its tracks, began to rear up on its hind legs, and then, like a great flower blossoming, exploded into flame. Larsen gazed transfixed, horrified, at the spectacle below him, a dancing pillar of fire. Then a pall of steam and smoke clouded his vision, and a stench of singed hair reached his nostrils.

Dimly Larsen was aware of an agonized bellowing, of himself screaming and shouting, and then, as suddenly as it had begun, the fire went out. The bear was down, rolling and writhing in agony. Then it was still, and Larsen heaved a long shuddering sigh of relief. And as he gazed at the motionless hulk below him he felt a wave of savage joy in knowing that the bear's menace would stalk them no longer.

Wearily he climbed down off the rock and began packing their gear.

When Umiak returned he told him what had happened, starting with his sighting of the fleeing fox. Umiak listened without interruption, and then let out a long low whistle of amazement. "You're crazy, man. You know that? Crazy!"

Larsen nodded. "It seemed a good idea at the time."

Umiak shrugged. "Well, we can dine on bear steaks tonight. And by a fire too. The pass is clear, and the way ahead is downhill for miles. Come on. Let's see how far we can get."

All at once he began to laugh. "Of all the crazy stunts. Roasting a bear alive. Beats just about anything I ever heard!"

Larsen said nothing. His mood of savage elation had passed, and thinking of the bear's terrible death sickened him.

NOW THE WAY LED steadily downhill. The going was good on the firm wind-packed snow, and on either side the mountains receded away into the distance, as with every mile the valley broadened out into a wide sunlit plain. In the distance a river gleamed, its waters flowing east. Unless it took a dramatic turn to the north or south Umiak was sure that ultimately it would lead them to safety.

All the same, he was uneasy. Deeply ingrained in his psyche was his people's age-old belief that to cause unnecessary suffering to an animal was to bring bad luck. As a boy an old *shaman* had spoken to him of the Keepers of the Game, the spirits that watched over every animal in their care, that tolerated hunting because man had to kill to live, but who would be sure to avenge any abuse of an animal, living or dead. Few hunters now gave a dead seal a drink of water so that it would not be thirsty on its journey to the spirit world, but men still blamed their lack of success in hunting on some infringement of the ancient code.

Now Umiak felt guilty, remembering his own exultation at the fate of the bear. In the end he'd left it where it lay, untouched, food for the wolves and ravens which were more deserving than he. There was no way in which he could explain his fears and doubts to Larsen. In any case, the man had suffered enough. He trudged at his side, uncommunicative, uncomplaining, his eyes those of a sleepwalker. Umiak wondered if this was more than the aftermath of fear, rather a mental trauma that went deeper.

The long hours passed. Slowly the distant stream drew nearer. The sun was low on the horizon and their shadows walked beside them in the snow, seeming to outdistance them as they grew longer. Umiak's legs ached, and his feet were frozen beyond feeling, leaden lumps that grew heavier with every stride and threatened to cramp his muscles into agonizing knots. Beside him Larsen walked as if in a dream.

Willow thickets bordered the stream ahead, promising both shelter and fire. At last they reached the river, and a snow-covered gravel bar on the edge of a dense willow thicket. The leaves of the willows were gone now, but the stems grew tall and densely packed, offering shelter from the wind. Wearily Umiak cut a bundle of twigs and began to sweep a space clear of snow. He looked to Larsen for help, but the man was sitting on the sledge, staring stonily downstream, making no move to unpack the bedding. So it was Umiak who cut willow boughs to spread on the ground, and laid the caribou skin over them. He took Larsen by the arm and led him unprotesting to the bed, covered him with rugs, and turned to gather firewood.

When he returned Larsen was fast asleep. Umiak began to make a fire, but found he was physically incapable of the effort. His fingers refused to obey his brain. Waves of darkness swept across his vision, and twice he felt himself pitching forward, jerking himself upright just in time to prevent himself from sprawling headlong on the gravel. He had just strength to crawl in beside Larsen before he fell asleep. His last thought was that they ought to eat.

He woke to intense cold. Beside him Larsen jerked and moaned in his sleep. It must have been this that aroused him. For a time he lay still, trying to get back to sleep again, but hunger pains and a growing chill kept him awake.

The night was nearly over and the moon rode high in the sky, shedding its brilliant light over the snow-covered landscape, and Umiak noted with satisfaction that the makings of a fire lay neatly sorted at his feet. He had only the dimmest recollection of putting them there, but it would take no more than a few moments to start a blaze.

Carefully, so as not to disturb Larsen, he crept out from under the bedding, feeling the muscles of his legs and back protest. Then he laid the tinder at his feet and began to pile thin twigs round it. As the grass caught into flame he added larger twigs, and then the thickest branches he had been able to find.

Soon the blaze began to warm his face and hands. He set the sledge on its side to reflect more of the warmth, brought water from the stream in the canteen and set some caribou on the flames to cook. Meantime he allayed the worst of his hunger by chewing a strip of dried meat. Once Larsen cried out in his sleep, but still he did not wake. It occurred to Umiak that the man might sleep more peacefully if he had some food inside him, so as soon as the stew was ready he leaned across the fire and shook Larsen by the foot.

Larsen came awake with a jerk. He opened his eyes, and saw a world lurid with flames, from the centre of which a black bulk loomed out over him. He gave one gasp of fear and flung aside the bedding. Next moment he was running for his life up the valley, stumbling, falling, picking himself up and floundering on, desperate to escape the bear that had haunted him in his dreams, and had now returned to destroy him.

Astonished, Umiak watched him go. Then he called, "Larsen, Larsen, come back. Larsen, it is Umiak!"

At last, to his intense relief, he saw Larsen slow down, stop, and then turn and walk slowly back. Umiak did not move from his place by the fire, but his hand sought the knife that lay close by. If Larsen's mind had snapped, he could be dangerous. Carefully he hid the knife where he could reach it again.

Larsen, however, was sane again, sheepish and contrite. "I thought you were that goddamned bear, come to get me."

Umiak said nothing, simply offering Larsen a cup of steaming stew. Larson took it gratefully and sank down beside the fire, still panting from his exertion.

"All day I've been seeing nothing but the bear with its head on fire. All night I've dreamed about it, and then when you woke me, leaning over the fire . . ." He shuddered, and took a mouthful of stew.

For a while Umiak said nothing. Then, when he spoke, it was with a quiet assurance he did not entirely feel. "The bear is dead. You did what you had to, the only way you could. The way ahead now is clear, so you must eat and sleep, and save your strength. No more midnight races in the snow."

Larsen nodded his agreement. Soon, warmed and relaxed by the fire and the hot food, they both slept again, and this time Larsen's sleep was deep and dreamless.

Both men woke cheerful and refreshed, and once more ravenously hungry. But the moment Larsen put his weight on his injured leg he knew he was in trouble. The pain was so intense that he nearly cried out. His midnight flight had done it no good at all.

Umiak was some distance away, collecting willow branches for the fire. Larsen hitched up his trouser leg and took a look. The dressing was wet and oozing. Hearing Umiak return Larsen hid the dressing from sight. His shame over his behaviour in the middle of the night was hard enough to bear. He did not want Umiak to find out that he might have jeopardized their safety still further. At all costs, he must keep going.

But each step was agony, as if his leg pumped fire with every stride. Try as he might he could not help limping, and soon, despite the cold, he could feel sweat breaking out on his brow. Though Umiak must have noticed, he said nothing.

They forged their way steadily down the valley, following the stream but occasionally having to make wide detours in order to skirt dense willow thickets. On either side the hills rose silent and deserted. No tracks showed in the snow, no raven flew overhead. The two men were no more than tiny dots lost in the vast white silence of space. Ahead they could see mountains again. Umiak prayed that somehow the stream would lead through or round them.

Time passed, the valley grew narrower, the way downhill steeper. Now the stream was racing beside them, as if it too was anxious to escape the winter. Then they stopped, staring in dismay. Ahead of them the stream joined a river, but one which once more flowed to the north. Beyond it, on the far side of the valley, the mountains rose like a wall.

"I don't believe it," said Larsen. "I just don't believe it."

But Umiak wasn't listening. Instead he was staring up the valley. "Look!" He pointed.

Larsen stared intently in the direction of his outstretched arm. Dozens of tiny black dots littered the frozen plain, and as he watched one after another jerked skyward, as though pulled by strings, only to float back down to earth.

"Ravens," he said dully. "What of it?"

"So many," said Umiak softly. "Only a great killing would attract that number." Suddenly he grabbed Larsen by the arm. "Don't you see?" he asked excitedly. "There must have been a caribou hunt here just recently. That means my people cannot be far away."

He set off up the valley, scarcely waiting for Larsen to catch up. Across the river he could see the broad trail where the caribou had trekked southward through the snow, bloodstained patches where deer had died, and fragments of entrails strewn over the valley floor. As they neared the site the ravens rose in a black cloud. But Umiak paid little heed. Instead he pointed to twin tracks leading away like railway lines, upstream. "Snow-mobile tracks," he shouted. "If we can just find a way across the river, we can follow them."

Larsen felt a pang of dismay. The river looked dangerously fast and deep, its leaden waters swirling over hidden rocks and foaming down into deep forbidding pools. In spite of their predicament he could not help but wish that, given more fortunate circumstances, he could cast a line over some of the more inviting stretches. Now, however, he wondered if he'd survive to go fishing again.

"It's no good," he stammered, "I can't cross. I can't wade. Look."

Umiak sucked his teeth in dismay at the sight of Larsen's dressing, but then he shrugged, and turning away he began exploring upstream, and after a while he beckoned to Larsen. Larsen followed, dragging the sledge behind him. Umiak was pulling off his sealskin boots. "Give me my old boots out of the holdall," he ordered.

Larsen did so and Umiak put them on. "Should keep the cold out for a while," he commented. "Right then. Climb on my back."

"Hey, just a minute," protested Larsen.

"Climb on!" yelled Umiak. "Or stay there. It's your choice."

"No, listen a minute," insisted Larsen. "We still have freezer bags, half a dozen big ones, and some sealing tape. We can wade across dry-shod."

Umiak's face lit up. "Good job someone's got some brains."

He chose a wide, shallow stretch at which to cross and, bearing the sledge between them, they set off, feeling their way cautiously over the riverbed. Nowhere was the water more than knee-deep, but the current was so strong it threatened to sweep them off their feet. Twice Larsen stumbled and almost fell, but managed to right himself.

At last they reached the opposite bank, and Umiak changed back into his sealskin boots. Then he shook his head sorrowfully over the snow-mobile tracks. "Two days, maybe three days old," he estimated. "The hunters will be far away by now. Pity they only killed as many deer as they could carry. If they'd cached a few, we could simply have waited here until they returned."

The trail led uphill, but with it to follow they were confident, even though the tracks led south. By late afternoon they reached a lake.

"I KNOW WHERE I AM," said Umiak.

Larsen looked out over the frozen surface of the lake, rose pink in the light of the setting sun, then back at the remains of a fire, the trampled snow, the rectangle that marked the site of a tent. "Your friends must have camped here."

Umiak nodded. "Last night, maybe. It's a regular spot. I camped here myself, oh, many years ago."

"How far?" queried Larsen.

"To Anaktuvuk?" Umiak smiled brightly. "Oh, not far now."

"Look," said Larsen, "I'm not dumb. Your people stayed over for the night here. Now if they'd been on their doorstep, they'd have kept going, especially with a snowmobile. So how far? A hundred miles?"

Umiak looked shocked. "No, no, not as far as that. Forty, perhaps."

Larsen felt better. Forty miles, on a leg that was threatening to give up at any moment, was a long way. All the same, if the going was good, another two days should see them to safety. He'd make it, even if he had to crawl.

They made themselves as comfortable as possible. The brush was thicker here: alder and willow, mingled with poplar and scrub birch, grew in dense thickets, and on the slope of the hills berry bushes showed dark against the snow. But even though they had the comfort of a fire and enough food to satisfy their hunger, Larsen could not help contrasting their lot with that of the hunting party. He had visions of the tent, bright with light and cosy with the warmth of a paraffin stove; a down sleeping bag, coffee, sweet and hot, and thick caribou steaks fried in their own fat.

Umiak must have been sharing his thoughts. "Pity we didn't get here earlier," he remarked as they ate. "Some company would have been nice."

"Tired of mine then?" asked Larsen.

Umiak was immediately embarrassed. "Oh no, Mr. Larsen," he stammered. "I didn't mean..."

Larsen laughed. "That's OK, I know exactly what you meant." Umiak's formality suddenly struck him. "Tell me, what have your people got against the use of Christian names?" It occurred to him then that Umiak might not have been baptized. "Or should I say first names?"

It was Umiak's turn to laugh. "Oh I was christened all right, by a Presbyterian minister, and later on, at high school, I was taught that Christianity was the only true faith, and that the beliefs of my forefathers were just superstition."

"You didn't like it at high school?"

"No. I was glad to get back home. All the same, I learned a lot. I learned that there were other 'true' religions, like Buddhism and Hinduism, and I found there was truth in all of them, including the old beliefs of my own people."

"But that still doesn't explain why you don't like using first names."

Umiak hesitated. "Now that is perhaps a foolishness. A silly superstition if you like, but there is an old belief that if you tell another person your given name, you put yourself in his power."

Larsen was about to scoff. Then he remembered that he had told Umiak his own first name, and virtually all along he had been at the man's mercy. It was an uneasy feeling on which to sleep.

They broke camp soon after daylight. Umiak busied himself with lashing down the bedding on the sledge as Larsen tested his leg, gritting his teeth against the pain. Then they set off, Umiak setting the pace deliberately slow, following the snowmobile tracks beside a stream. On either side the mountains towered two thousand feet above them. The valley widened out, and they passed another, smaller, lake. Here the stream ended, but a little further on they topped a small rise, to find another flowing away downhill.

Larsen was blind to his surroundings, willing himself forward, conscious only of the need to keep walking, to choose where he set his left foot, to lean heavily on his right foot, step after step after step. So he failed to notice that the sun had vanished in the haze, that the mountain peaks, distant earlier, seemed now to loom over them. A grunt from Umiak brought him back to reality. "What's up?" he queried.

Umiak nodded towards the east. "Storm coming," he announced. "Big one. I think our luck just ran out."

Larsen stared into the distance. The horizon was obscured by a violet veil of cloud. Even as he watched, it grew. Ragged pinnacles smoked and fumed from its upper layers. Its underside bulged ominously, and a flicker of lightning played on its flank. "I guess we ought to take cover," he muttered.

"And fast," said Umiak, looking about them.

On their left the southward-facing flank of the hill was shaggy with stunted brush, offering thicker cover than the northern-facing slopes. Yet here the valley was over a mile wide, and to reach the scrub they would have to cross the stream. Rocks and boulders lay to their right, but closer, and it was towards these that the two men headed. Try as he might Larsen could not move faster than a slow walk. Umiak took the sledge from him and raced ahead. By the time Larsen reached him he had found a small niche in the rocks, unloaded the sledge, and was wedging it on its side as a windbreak, feverishly piling rocks against its base, anchoring it as best he could.

Larsen bent to help him, but Umiak waved him away. "Spread the bedding," he shouted, "and lie on it. For God's sake don't let it blow away. Any minute now we won't be able to stand."

Storm-force winds were already howling round them. Larsen staggered, and then flung himself forward onto the pile of bedding. As he dragged it into the lee of the sledge he saw Umiak fly past, thrown off his feet and sent sprawling in the snow. Umiak made no further attempt to stand up, but crawled slowly back, hugging the earth. Between them they unrolled the bedding so that their own weight held it down, and crawled into it. Umiak had already stowed the rest of their gear among the rocks. They could only hope it would stay secure.

Another violent gust swept the valley. The sledge trembled and shook against their backs, but held firm. They cowered against it as lightning split the sky and thunder echoed between the hills. Snow began to fly past, driven horizontally by the wind, eddying round them, flicking like frozen darts against their faces, so that they buried their heads against the sting. Larsen lay next to the sledge, Umiak beside him, shaking with cold and exertion, his breath coming in great rasping sobs, so that on impulse Larsen put his arms round him and drew him tight to his body, sharing what little warmth he possessed. Slowly Umiak relaxed, his breathing eased, and by and by Larsen thought he slept.

Outside the darkness deepened, until it seemed that night had come before its time. At intervals lightning lit the scene. Larsen felt the sledge hammering against his spine, waited for the thunder, and expected at any moment that the storm would rip their frail shelter away. So the long seconds ticked by, hour after hour, while the wind howled and screamed as it drove among the rocks. Gradually, his senses numbed by the din, Larsen fell into a doze.

When he woke it was with a sense of suffocation. Pushing the bedding back off his face, he discovered they were covered in soft, powdery snow. It was night, the clamour of the storm had ceased, and above him stars shone in the sky. Exhausted, he drifted back to sleep again.

Day broke, and with the light Larsen regained consciousness. A new sound disturbed the silence, a soft rasping that at first Larsen was unable to identify. Then he realized it was Umiak's breathing, shallow, fast, and unnaturally loud. The man appeared to be sleeping, but his face was flushed and small beads of perspiration had formed on his brow.

He was not asleep though. He opened his eyes as he felt Larsen staring, trying to smile when he saw the other man's concern.

"I'm in trouble this time," he whispered.

Larsen nodded. "Looks like you're starting pneumonia."

"Feels like it. Hurts when I breathe." Umiak closed his eyes again. "Serves me right. Too much exertion, getting overheated and then chilled. Ought to know better."

Larsen lay where he was, propped on one elbow, thinking. Umiak needed medical attention urgently. But even if he dared leave him it would be two days at least before he could summon any sort of help, and by then it would be too late. He considered loading Umiak on the sledge, and dragging him the last forty miles, but that, he figured, would be just another way of finishing him off.

"You'll have to leave me," Umiak urged. "Don't worry, I don't feel too bad as long as I lie still. No sense you waiting here until I die."

"You're not going to die," snapped Larsen impatiently. "Lie quiet while I think."

Umiak tried to laugh. "There was a Presbyterian minister at my school who taught us to read and write and speak English. He was full of sayings. Always repeating them. One was 'hard work never killed anybody'. Well, he was wrong. Hard work has killed me."

"You're not dead yet for God's sake," hissed Larsen. "Now shut up, do. Save your breath and let me think."

257

He looked out over the valley. The wind had blown large areas almost clear of snow. Beyond the stream the hill showed black in the early light. There was bound to be plenty of dry wood there. Should he try to move Umiak? He was not sure he could make it, especially with the stream to cross. He would just have to leave him for a while, and bring back as much firewood as he could carry. Then at least Umiak would be warm.

If only he could raise help. Suddenly he looked again at the hill across the valley and a wild idea came to him. He knew it was Bureau of Land Management policy to fight all bush fires in the wilderness. Half the natives were employed all summer on fire-fighting duties. If he could start a bush fire, it should bring someone running.

If necessary, he thought, I'll set the whole goddamned mountain ablaze. He patted Umiak on the shoulder. "I'm just going to get some firewood," he announced. "Shan't be long."

There were two bags of petrol left. He checked that he had the lighter, and a length of cable with which to bind a bundle of firewood, and set off across the valley floor. To his relief the stream scarcely covered the soles of his boots. The brush, when he reached it, was even thicker than it had appeared.

He worked methodically, building his starting fires with care, each one several yards apart. What little breeze there was blew up and aslant the hill, and he chose his sites accordingly. There was kindling in plenty and he set aside as much as he thought he could carry back across the valley. He hoped there would not be much left after his work was done.

When he was satisfied he took the bag of petrol and punctured a small hole in the plastic. Fuel spurted out in a thin stream, and he went from pile of sticks to pile of sticks, soaking each and laying a liquid fuse between them. When the bag was empty, he threw it on the nearest stack and flicked the lighter with his thumb.

The fires were slow to start, and Larsen watched in an agony of suspense as the flames spread, running through the undergrowth, flaring briefly, then dying down, sulking. Then came a faint crackle and a flicker. Flames began to leap and grow. Sparks flew up and dense black smoke began to rise. For a while the fire was contained in a line, and then rivers of flame began to leap uphill. The growing heat created its own wind, the flames flared higher, and all at once the whole hillside seemed to explode with a roar and a blast of heat that sent Larsen staggering back. Smoke billowed up out of the flames, rising higher and ever higher, until it towered far above the mountain peaks. In the clear air it would be seen for miles.

Satisfied that he had done all he could, Larsen turned his back on the blaze, picked up his bundle of sticks, and set off back across the valley. Halfway across he paused for a breather. The load was heavier than he had realized. Ahead of him was a wide expanse of unbroken snow, and now another idea came to him. Walking out into the centre of the snowfield he lay full length in the snow. Then he began to drag his body, snakelike, in a wide curve. And another. And then another.

HE HAD FAILED. Larsen sat dejectedly by the burning embers of the fire, and looked out across the valley at the hill. Brief outbreaks of flame blossomed on the mountainside, and a red glow showed where the undergrowth still smouldered, but the smoke pall had gone, faded into the pale blue sky. He had cooked the last of their food, and persuaded Umiak to drink some soup, but the hours passed and still there was no sign that their signal had been seen.

They were both done for now. Larsen's leg was so bad he had barely been able to hobble back to the sledge. He couldn't even bring himself to look at it. Behind him Umiak slept, but he was restless and disturbed, his breathing if anything faster and louder. From time to time he muttered in his sleep, but he spoke only in his native tongue, so that Larsen was unable to understand him.

A raven flew over, high in the sky. It circled the burnt hillside beyond the valley, and in a moment was joined by another. Soon several had gathered, no doubt waiting until the hillside cooled to eat the corpses of small animals and birds destroyed by the fire. Larsen shuddered, wondering what further carnage he had caused. Then it occurred to him that what was food for the ravens was food for man, that he ought to make the effort to see what he could harvest for himself. Yet what was the point? The fatalism that seemed to have affected Umiak now gripped him too, so that he felt wrapped in a cosy sort of relief that their struggles were over. At least he had no further to walk.

Then Larsen heard it, faint and far away, the sound of an aircraft high in the sky. Slowly he stood up, staring skywards, gazing all round, his heart hammering wildly and his knees shaking beneath him. The sound grew fainter, then louder, until at last the plane flew over the hill, a bright orange Piper twin. Larsen staggered out from the rocks and stood on a patch of snow, waving his arms as the plane roared over his head before turning and flying down the length of the valley. For a moment Larsen thought it was going to land, but evidently the pilot was reluctant to risk his undercarriage. The Piper vanished over the mountains, and Larsen was alone in the silence once more. But he knew now that they were saved, and he tried to tell Umiak the news. The sick man did not seem to comprehend. Since there was nothing else to do, Larsen crawled back inside the bedding to wait.

He must have dozed, for the roar of the snowmobiles was loud in his ears as he crawled out from his refuge. He watched them racing up the valley, thinking he'd never seen a sight more beautiful. The driver of the leading vehicle brought his machine to a halt. He was a big guy, wearing sunglasses and a walrus moustache. He did not seem pleased to see Larsen. "You guys have caused a heap of trouble," he announced.

Larsen considered this for a while. "I blame the weather," he replied.

HE CAME OUT OF THE ANAESTHETIC to find Sylvie sitting at his bedside. "What kept you?" he murmured.

Sylvie put her finger on his lips. "Don't talk. Rest. Your leg is going to be all right. You'll need further surgery when the infection clears, but we'll fly you south for that."

Larsen closed his eyes. "How's Umiak?" he queried.

"OK. He's very weak, but his temperature's down. I guess they found him just in time. He's pretty tough, though."

He's tough all right, thought Larsen, remembering the jolting ride back on a sledge towed behind a snowmobile. How Umiak had survived that ride he'd never know. Dimly he remembered being transferred to a plane. Where were they now? he wondered, and still wondering, fell asleep.

He woke refreshed and hungry, and lay for a while dreaming of all the foods he would like to eat. In the end he had coffee and toast, and it was enough. Afterwards he felt restless. The small sickbay was hot and stuffy after the cold Arctic air, and the sheets seemed to hold him in soft, suffocating bonds.

Sylvie arrived and fussed over him, arranging his pillows and smoothing the sheets.

"Where's my gear?" Larsen asked suddenly.

She wrinkled her nose in disgust. "Your clothes are burned. We emptied your pockets, though. The stuff's here beside you." She opened a drawer in the locker.

Larsen leaned over and found the arrowhead. "Here," he said. "I promised you a souvenir."

Sylvie held it up to the light. The stone was amber-coloured flint, translucent, glowing with warmth and colour. "It's beautiful," she murmured. "Where did you find it?"

Larsen told her. "The mark of man's hand in the wilderness. Seemed to me that if he could survive, then so could I. But I wouldn't have made it without Umiak."

"And but for you he would be dead by now. The pilot said that if you hadn't scraped the SOS in the snow he'd have kept going. The brush fire was almost out by the time he found it, and he didn't think it was worth reporting."

Larsen remembered his long slow crawl through the snow.

"You mean he wasn't looking for us?"

"Why should he? Nobody dreamed you'd head east. When they

eventually found the plane, they felt sure you'd head north, to the rig. We were looking in all the wrong directions."

"Wait a minute. You said rig. What rig?"

Sylvie stared at him. "About twenty miles north of where you crashed there's a new airstrip and a drilling rig. You'd have been safe there. Why didn't you go there? It's marked on the map."

"Our map blew away," said Larsen wearily. "And if the rig's recent Umiak wouldn't have known about it. Anyway, we didn't know where we were." Suddenly he began to laugh. "We sure took the scenic route home!"

BEFORE HE FLEW SOUTH he went to say goodbye to Umiak, now recovering well. Another visitor already sat by the bedside, a round, merry-faced man whose eyes were merely sparkling black slits squeezed in above his high cheekbones.

"This is my friend I was coming to visit," Umiak announced. "The one the seal oil was for," he added slyly.

Larsen, remembering how he had burned the seal oil, grinned ruefully. The stranger laughed and rubbed his ample paunch. "No matter about the oil. I'm too fat already."

"Nice of you to take it that way," Larsen said. "I wish I could feel as happy about the souvenirs I was hoping to find in Anaktuvuk. It seems I shall be going away empty-handed."

The stranger looked at him thoughtfully. "Maybe I can help in that direction. I know of one or two people, good carvers in soapstone or deer antler, who might be interested in supplying you." He took a piece of paper from his pocket and wrote on it with a stubby pencil before handing it to Larsen. "Here's my address. Get in touch with me next time you're up this way."

"Great," Larsen said. "I'll take you up on that. Thanks a lot."

"Well, I'd do anything for a friend of Joe here, and he tells me you saved his life."

"Joe?" Larsen looked sharply at Umiak, but the invalid had his eyes fixed firmly on the bedclothes.

"I'd been meaning to tell you," he muttered, "but with one thing and another . . ."

"Don't tell me you still believe in that old superstition about revealing your name," scoffed his friend. "You'll be telling me you believe in *shamans* next."

Umiak grinned shyly at Larsen, who winked back.

"Anyway," the other man went on, "I must be off. I'll leave you two to swap stories. Goodbye, Mr. Larsen. Safe journey home, and thanks again for all you did for my friend. I owe you."

He went out, closing the door behind him.

261

"I owe you, too ... Steve," said Umiak softly.

"And I you ... Joe."

Larsen held out his hand, and Umiak took it in both of his, staring hard into his face. Suddenly embarrassed, Larsen could not think of anything else to say. "You're looking pale," he stammered.

"White man's food," said Umiak, and they both laughed. "By the way, I've been thinking. When you come back here to fix up a deal for those souvenirs, maybe we could take a proper hunting trip together." He paused, grinning. "We'll be fully equipped next time. I know of some fishing that would make your eyes pop."

"I'd like that," replied Larsen. With a sudden sense of surprise, he realized that he meant it. He had lost his fear of the wilderness, and already he was feeling a faint itch to see more. He drew his hand away from Umiak's grasp. "Before I forget," he said, "a little memento of our trip." He put his hand in his pocket and pulled out the small penknife, dropping it into Umiak's lap. For a long time Umiak stared at it without speaking, then slowly his hand closed over it.

"Goodbye, Joe," said Larsen.

"Goodbye, Steve," said Umiak softly. At the door Larsen looked back to wave. Umiak was already gazing at the knife, turning it over and over lovingly in his firm, strong hands.

EWAN CLARKSON

It comes as no surprise to learn that the author of *Ice Trek* is well acquainted with life in the wild. Ewan Clarkson, whose delightful books about nature and animals are well known to Condensed Books readers, once spent a year in northern Minnesota researching a book about the American timber wolf. There he and his wife Jenny camped in national forest around Lake Superior, and endured the extremes of a winter in which temperatures plummeted to thirty degrees below zero. The experience, arduous but fascinating, resulted in his book, *Wolf Country, A Wilderness Pilgrimage*. It also fostered a lasting interest in the subarctic regions of North America and in the natives who make their living there.

That interest was rekindled ten years later when Ewan, a longtime resident of Devon, was invited by the University of Exeter to study for an MA on the grounds of "past merit"—his work as a writer and conservationist, among other things. He chose the American wilderness for his research. "I was reading a rather dull textbook on land management one day," he remembers, "when a paragraph heading jumped out at me: 'Procedure for the Removal of Downed Aircraft'. I discovered that light aircraft were lost in Alaska at the rate of two a week! The statistic stuck in my mind—and the idea came to me of a white man and an Eskimo, stranded in the wilderness after a plane crash and having to survive on their wits alone. How they faced their ordeal would dramatize the difference between their two cultures."

Clarkson himself obviously feels closer to Umiak than to Larsen. "I have a strong empathy with hunting people," he affirms. "We ourselves may no longer be hunters, but it is a part of our heritage that ought to be remembered, to foster respect for the land and the animals that once fed us." And in his picturesque Devon cottage Ewan is still making his living from the natural world. "It gives me everything I need," he says happily. "Fruit and vegetables from the garden, fish from the river. And, of course, my writing."

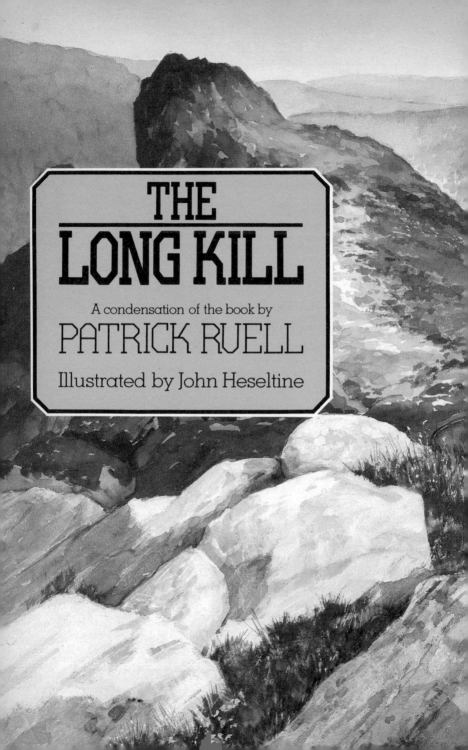

THE LONG KILL

A condensation of the book by

PATRICK RUELL

Illustrated by John Heseltine

The man known as Jaysmith is the best
in the business. The business of killing people.
And Jaysmith hasn't come to the Lake
District for pleasure.
But his latest assignment does not go according
to plan, and Jaysmith begins to think of retiring
from his terrible trade. Attracted to the magical
landscape and more particularly to an intriguing
young widow, he even dreams of putting down roots,
of leading a normal life. If only the dream
could become reality . . .
But Jaysmith's old masters will not let him go
so easily. And when danger threatens the family
he has grown to love, he must turn killer
again to protect them.

1

Jaysmith was a firm advocate of the cerebral approach.

He always shot at the head.

The head he was shooting at this bright autumn morning was a noble one even when viewed through an Adjustable Ranging Telescope at 1,250 metres. An aureole of near-white hair surrounded a tanned leathery face in which the crinkles of humour seemed at least to equal the furrows of care. It was the head of an ageing man, seventy at a guess, who must surely now be reckoning that he was going to be allowed to slip naturally from life in the fullness of his years. Another minute would teach him the error of such confidence, and also the error of whatever lust for power, pleasure or political change had put him at the end of Jaysmith's rifle.

Still, there were worse ways to die than suddenly, in your garden, looking across the peaceful fields of St. John's-in-the-Vale to the swell of the eastern fells, smoking a cigarette and feeling the warmth of a September sun on your skin.

Jaysmith began his final checks. He had worked out five possible lines of fire on the Ordnance Survey 1:25,000 sheet before leaving London. Two of them he had discarded on his first slow drive along the valley the previous Sunday. Two more had failed his strict on-the-ground examination. The last was the longest, but that didn't bother him. He preferred the long kill, the longer the better. And with his equipment, his meticulous preparation and, above all, his accuracy, distance had never posed any difficulty. That was why he was the best.

He had till Sunday morning to make the target. It was only Thursday now, but there was no reason to delay, with the weather so perfect. He stretched his muscles systematically and began to quarter the ground below him with his Zeiss binoculars.

He was squatting on a lichened rock in a steep gill cutting down through a rocky outcrop which his map told him was called Wanthwaite Crags. Eight hundred feet above him was the fell summit called Clough Head. He had checked all possible approaches before descending. The only signs of life had been the nodding head of a grazing sheep, the slow flap of a raven's wings and a tractor buzzing across a stubble field half a mile away. In any case, even in this stillness the Sionics Noise Suppressor on his M21 would scatter the sound of his shot untraceably.

He drew in a long deep breath and let it out slowly. St. John's Beck, winding through the valley below, was a ribbon of glass. The trees in the garden of the house called Naddle Foot were still as a painting. The moment was perfect.

He squeezed the trigger.

The bullet missed. It passed close enough to the old man's ear for him to flap his cigarette at a buzzing fly. Then it buried itself deep in a flowerbed on the upper level of the terraced garden.

Jaysmith sat utterly still. There were many possible explanations: a gust of wind; a slight change of atmospheric pressure; an imperfection in the bullet. But there was only one cause.

He blinked his right eye rapidly a couple of times. It focused perfectly on the M21 as he began to dismantle it. But perfect focusing was not enough. There was a weakness there. He had suspected it two targets ago, when he had shot the Austrian. And the last time out he had been almost certain. It had been a perfect shot in the eyes of the world. Only Jaysmith knew that as he squeezed the trigger, the Chinaman had raised his teacup and bowed his head into the path of the bullet.

Two weeks ago he had paid a Harley Street oculist an exorbitant fee to put a clinical label on it. It was not a condition which could be in the least detrimental to any normal activity, the man had assured him. He should have retired then. But this target had already come up, unusually soon after the Chinaman and marked urgent. Something had made him reluctant to refuse it. Loyalty to Jacob, perhaps. Or professional pride.

He packed the rifle into his specially constructed rucksack and climbed up the steep gully to the top of the crags. Here he paused and glanced back across the valley. The reprieved man in the garden was invisible. Jaysmith didn't even know his name. Jacob never provided more than was necessary for a target. In this case it had been a head-and-shoulders photograph of the man, the OS sheet NY 32 with the house called Naddle Foot ringed in red, and a deadline. Plus, of course, an order for twenty-five thousand pounds paid into his Zurich bank account.

That would have to be returned. A pity; but there was plenty left for his retirement.

Retirement! At forty-three. The thought amused him and he let out a snort of laughter as his long stride took him swiftly across the shallow saddle between Clough Head and Calfhow Pike. Then he followed the tumbling path of a long beck till he reached the old coach road where he'd parked his BMW. Even at his rapid pace, and mostly downhill, it took him over an hour, and it was with some relief that he dropped the rucksack into the hidden compartment beneath a false panel in the BMW's boot. An identical rucksack containing conventional walking gear lay in the boot. These isolated country areas were full of sharp eyes.

He had a phone call to make and he decided to make it from the nearby village instead of waiting till he got back to his hotel. Security apart, he felt eager to get it over with. It was the first admission of failure he had ever made. The best that could be said for him was that he had not altered the target.

He went into the public phone box and dialled a London number. A woman's voice answered, bright and breezy.

"Hello there! Enid here. Jacob and I are out just now but we'll be back soon. Leave your message after the tone and we'll be in touch. 'Bye!"

He waited, then said, "Jaysmith. Tell Jacob I can't make the deal. There'll be a refund, of course."

Gently he replaced the receiver and stepped out into the golden September air. He drew in a long breath, and then another. It tasted marvellous. For the first time in twenty years he felt free.

THE DANGERS OF JAYSMITH'S new sense of relaxation became apparent when he entered the hotel bar for a pre-dinner drink that evening.

"Evening, Mr. Hutton. Any luck today?" called Philip Parker, the Crag Hotel's owner-manager. It took Jaysmith a moment to react to the name.

Pseudonyms and cover stories might now be irrelevant, but they could not just be shed at will. At the Crag he was William Hutton, businessman; and in conversation with Parker he had let it slip that, as well as the fellwalking, he was on the lookout for a house or cottage to purchase. It was those sharp country eyes again; he wanted an excuse to be seen anywhere, walking or driving, during his stay.

"No," he said, slipping onto a bar stool and accepting a dry sherry. "No luck at all. But I enjoyed my walk."

"Oh good. The weather's marvellous, isn't it? Excuse me."

Parker went off to the side hatch of the bar. Parker's quietly efficient wife, Doris, looked after the kitchen and dining room, while he exuded bonhomie in the bar and at reception. He was a rotund, breezy man in his early fifties, a redundant sales executive who'd sunk his severance money into the small hotel five years earlier, and his enthusiasm for the Lake District was such that Jaysmith had soon regretted his cover story. From the start, Parker had taken an embarrassingly close interest in his alleged house-hunting and now, a dining room order dealt with, he returned to the topic.

"So, no luck then?" he said.

"No," said Jaysmith. "The market seems pretty dead. In fact, I think I've exhausted all the possibilities, so I'll check out tomorrow. I'll pay for tomorrow night, of course," he added.

He had booked in till Saturday. If he'd made his target he'd have stayed the full week in order not to excite comment, but now there was no point.

"Well, as a matter of fact," said Parker, "I heard today there's likely to be just the house you're looking for coming on the market in the next couple of days. It's called Rigg Cottage, just outside the village, up the road towards Lough Rigg. It belongs to an old lady called Miss Wilson who's finding the hill more and more difficult. She's thinking of moving down into the village. There's an old cottage become vacant, semi-detached and right next door to her best friend."

He paused for breath, grinned and glanced conspiratorially towards the dining room. Lowering his voice he said, "To tell the truth, it's Doris who told me all this. She's quite chummy with Mrs. Blacklock, the old lady in the other semi, and she passed it on, in strict confidence, of course, which is why there's nothing to be done till Miss Wilson makes up her mind. But when she does, if I know her, she'll want everything settled in five minutes, which is why it's a pity you'll not be on the spot."

"Yes, isn't it?" said Jaysmith, exuding regret as he moved fully into his William Hutton role. "A real pity."

At dinner, he ordered a full bottle of Chablis instead of his usual half and settled to a mellow contemplation of the joys of retirement. He could go anywhere, do anything. Tomorrow, back to his London flat. Next, the Continent. Italy to start with: a villa in Tuscany till autumn died. Then on to the Med, Greece, North Africa, keeping abreast of the retreating sun.

The prospect filled him with surprisingly little enthusiasm. In fact, the idea of taking time to adjust, of letting things ripen at their own speed, was not without its appeal. But where to let the ripening process take place? Not London, that was certain. Whatever pressures might remain from his old life were centred on London.

The answer was absurdly obvious. After a couple of soporific brandies in the bar, he heard himself saying to Parker, "I've been thinking. There's really no desperate need for me to be off in the morning. In fact, if that old lady's not going to make up her mind for a few days, I can easily hang on into next week. If my room's going to be vacant, that is?"

Parker smiled. "We'll be glad to have you," he said fulsomely.

2

Summer was dying like a lady this year. Leaves flushed gently from olive to ochre with no savage gale to rip them down; bracken singed at the edges and heather burned purple with no landscape-blackening downpour to dampen the glow. The locals assured Jaysmith, nostalgically, that it was not always thus.

Jaysmith took their word for it. Though he had presented William Hutton as a long-time lover of the Lake District, his only previous acquaintance had been as a small boy on a day trip to Windermere with his mother and stepfather, who had stared indifferently at the mountains and lake, explored the souvenir shops, eaten fish and chips, and left him in the coach with a packet of crisps at each of the many pub-stops on the sixty-mile journey back to Blackburn, in Lancashire.

His mother had died when he was fifteen. His stepfather had supported him for the next few years at school, till he got the exam results needed to take him to university. But first had come national service. After basic training he had been posted to Hong Kong. He went home on embark-ation leave, and the night before his departure his stepfather had told him apologetically but firmly that his stepbrother, four years his senior, was getting married and coming to live in the family home. The strain this would put on the limited accommodation meant he would have to look after himself from now on.

He had never been back to Blackburn since that day.

His first taste of the East had brought balm to the pain of rejection. From the very first moment he was fascinated. The facility with which he learned Chinese made him a valued member of his unit, but it was another talent which the army spotted that won him privileges. He turned out to be a natural marksman, capable of winning trophies at the highest level, and thus he was rapidly promoted to sergeant, well out of the way of any parades, fatigues or guard duties which might dull his eye.

For his part, he enjoyed his prowess, and even let his enjoyment spill over into civilian life, becoming a prominent member of his university shooting team. But he never dreamed that this was a talent with any commercial value. It had taken fate at its most unpredictably tragic to nudge him onto that path.

And now it had taken a fractional weakening of the right eye to nudge him off it.

For the next three days he put past and future out of his mind and set out to turn his pretended intimacy with the fells into fact. Hitherto, landscape had been considered solely in terms of best approach, best hide, best line of fire, best escape. Here in the Lake District, for the first time in two decades, he went exploring simply in search of delight. He spent the days in long, high walks, armed only with map and compass; and whether he was standing windblown on the bald head of Gable with the stark wildness of Wasdale stretching below, or descending from the gentle swell of Silver Howe in the gathering dusk towards the sun-gilt shield of Grasmere, which at the end of a long day felt very like home, he was ravished by the beauty of it all.

So, when Parker greeted him on Sunday evening with the excited news, "She's made up her mind! Miss Wilson's definitely going. I can arrange for you to see Rigg Cottage tomorrow!" Jaysmith felt surprisingly put out. He had a splendid walk mapped out for Monday, and it was irritating to have to postpone it for what was now an unnecessary piece of role-playing.

Doris Parker, who was standing alongside her husband, sensed his hesitation. She was a pleasant, down-to-earth woman, used to coping with her husband's enthusiasms. "Don't take any notice of Philip's hard sell, Mr. Hutton," she said. "There's no need to look at Rigg Cottage until you want to. I only heard at church tonight that Miss Wilson is definitely selling."

Her wide-set grey eyes fixed speculatively on Jaysmith and he smiled at her. "Of course I'd like to, if you can arrange it," he said. "I'm really very grateful."

Triumphantly, Parker went to the telephone and returned a few minutes later with the news that eleven o'clock the following morning would suit Miss Wilson very well.

Jaysmith nodded agreement. At least he would have the whole afternoon for the mountains. In any case the mountains weren't going anywhere without him!

THE NEXT MORNING he read the newspapers in detail. There was no reference to any violent death in St. John's-in-the-Vale and there had been nothing on the local news either. Presumably Jacob had not been able to make new arrangements before the deadline elapsed. That would not please him.

He put the thought out of his mind and drove up the winding road from the village to keep his appointment.

Miss Wilson was almost exactly as he had pictured her. Anything between seventy and ninety, she had snow-white hair and clear blue eyes in a cider-apple face. But any impression of gentle cosiness was soon dispelled. She carried her five feet three inches as straight as a guardsman, albeit with some help from a stick, and when she spoke it was in a clipped, no-nonsense tone.

"I'd not be moving from here if it wasn't for this leg," she informed him sternly, as if he had hinted a suspicion of some less creditable motive.

"Now the place is getting too big for me, the garden's taking over, and the hill's too steep. Not that I can't climb it, but it takes me twice as long as it once did, and me mind's back here already doing me jobs while me body's still halfway up the bank."

She proved remarkably unsentimental about Rigg Cottage, and talked about it as if it were already settled that he would buy. "The sitting room fire smokes in an east wind," she said. "I've been meaning to get it fixed these thirty years. That'll be your job now." She sounded almost gleeful.

It occurred to Jaysmith that this was a house whose faults could be freely pointed out because of its more than compensatory attractions. Built of grey-green Lakeland slate, it stood foursquare to the east, as simple and appealing as a child's drawing. The sloping garden, which overlooked the lake, was full of shrubs, mainly rhododendrons and azaleas whose blossom in June, Miss Wilson proudly and poetically assured him, burned like a bonfire. It also occurred to him that if he really were looking for a house in the Lake District, this one would be perfect.

A thought stirred in his mind. *Why not?*

He dismissed it instantly. It was one thing to decide on the spur of the moment to treat himself to an extra week in the Lake District, quite another to invest a large sum of money and, by implication, a large piece of his life here.

William Hutton, holidaymaker and property seeker, would have to speak soon. Miss Wilson had shown him the outside first. Now they moved indoors, and all was exactly as it should be, the right old furniture in rooms of the right dimensions, with just enough light coming through the leaded windows and just enough heat coming from the small fire in the huge grate.

The doorbell rang. Miss Wilson left him and returned a moment later with another woman, whom she introduced as her niece, Annie Wilson, a widow who lived out Keswick way, just back from her holidays and come for lunch.

The newcomer shook his hand. He put her age as early- to mid-thirties. She had a long, narrow, not unpleasantly vulpine face, with a sallow complexion, watchful brown eyes and thin, slightly upturned nose. She was dressed in autumn colours, dark brown slacks and a russet shirt, with her long brown hair pulled severely back and held with a casually knotted red ribbon. Her body was lean and rangy and she moved with athletic ease.

Jaysmith felt that she regarded him with considerable suspicion. Its cause soon emerged.

"You're selling Rigg Cottage?" she exclaimed to her aunt.

"That's right. I've talked about it often enough."

"I know, but it's so sudden. Didn't you discuss it with anyone? With Pappy or Granddad Wilson?"

"No, I didn't," said Miss Wilson tartly. "As you well know, else your father would have told you when you got back or James would have told you when you were staying with him. I've always made up me own mind and always will, so there's an end to it. Now tell me about you and young Jimmy. When's he coming to see me? I thought he might come with you today."

Annie Wilson laughed, and suddenly a decade was wiped off her face. "He started back at school today, Auntie. He'll be round next Sunday as usual."

"Just see he is," grumbled the old lady. "He could have been here yesterday if you'd got back earlier."

"Granddad Wilson wanted us to stay as long as possible," said the young woman. "He doesn't see much of Jimmy."

"Then he should get himself up here more often," retorted Miss Wilson. "The wedding, the christening and the funeral, that's been about the strength of it these past few years."

Annie Wilson's face lost its animation and the ten years came back with whatever was causing the pain visible in the depths of her eyes.

"Jimmy bought you a present in London," she said abruptly. She handed over a packet in gaily-coloured wrapping paper.

"I'll look at it later. I've got to show Mr. Hutton upstairs yet."

"I'll show him," offered the younger woman. "You sit down and open your present."

Jaysmith guessed that Annie Wilson wanted a chance to check him out. He played William Hutton to the best of his ability as she showed him round the bedrooms, enthusing over the views. "Have you set your heart on Grasmere, Mr. Hutton," she said, "or will anywhere in the Lakes do?"

"I love it all," he said expansively. "But Grasmere best of all."

"And you walk, of course?"

He gestured towards the eastern heights.

"It's the only way to get up there, isn't it? I wouldn't like to count the happy hours I've passed on the tops."

Which was quite true, he told himself ironically. The reward for his boast was to make her laugh and shed those years once more.

"You're as keen as that, are you?" she said, gently mocking. "You'll be telling me you're Wainwright next."

He didn't know if he succeeded in not registering his shock. Wainwright was the cover name he'd used on the Austrian job. How the hell did this woman know . . ? Then it came to him that, of course, she didn't. The name had some significance he didn't grasp, that was all.

He smiled and said lightly, "Just plain William Hutton. Is this the last bedroom?"

She nodded, her face losing its humour. He wondered if she'd noticed

274

something odd in his reaction after all. But when she opened the bedroom door and motioned him in, something about her stillness focused his attention on the room itself. It was small, with a single bed and a south-facing casement window with a copper beech almost rubbing against the glass. On the walls hung photographs of what he saw were early climbing groups, young men garlanded with ropes and wearing broad-brimmed hats and long laced-up boots, standing with the rigid insouciance required by early cameramen. The background hills were unmistakable. Scafell and the broad, nippled swell of Scafell Pike. The pictures apart, there was no sense of personality here or indeed any sign of recent occupation. But twenty years of nervous living had honed his sensitivity to atmosphere and suddenly he heard himself asking, "Did your aunt bring up your husband?"

She looked at him in amazement. "Why? What has she said?"

"Nothing," he assured her. "She said nothing. I just guessed that this had once been his room, that's all."

Now there was anger alongside the surprise, and all her initial distrust was back in her eyes. "What are you, Mr. Hutton?" she demanded. "Some kind of policeman, keeping his hand in on holiday?"

"I'm sorry," he said. "I didn't mean to be offensive. I just ..."

But she was walking away. "That's all up here, Mr. Hutton," she said coldly. "We'd better get back downstairs to my aunt. She'll be wanting to get lunch ready. I hope you're as quick with decisions as deductions."

He was very angry with himself. The remark had just slipped out and Jaysmith was not accustomed to anything but complete self-control.

Miss Wilson was holding a small pottery replica of Big Ben in her lap.

"Tell Jimmy it's very nice, dear," she said. "Now, Mr. Hutton, what do you think?"

He hesitated. When he'd arrived, he'd had it all worked out. *A delightful house, but not quite what I was looking for.* But now this formula would cut him off from Miss Wilson and her niece for ever. That was something he suddenly discovered he didn't want.

He said, "Would it be possible to come back this afternoon? It's hard to take everything in at a single viewing. You can often get mistaken impressions at a first encounter, can't you?" He glanced at Annie Wilson as he spoke.

Miss Wilson regarded him thoughtfully, then turned to her niece.

"Well, I daresay we can put up with you tramping round again, can't we, Annie? But give us time to enjoy our lunch. Three o'clock, let's say."

"Fine," said Jaysmith. "Three o'clock."

The old lady showed him out. "One thing," she said on the doorstep, "you've not asked me price, young man. It may be too high for you."

He rather liked her directness. It also occurred to him that he would

275

rather like her good opinion. He said, "If you really think of me as a *young* man, Miss Wilson, then I'll be happy to accept any estimate of the house's value based on the same principle."

A sunbeam of amusement warmed her old face. Then she closed the door. There was a little red Fiat in the drive, presumably belonging to Annie Wilson. Carefully he backed the BMW past it and drove down the hill to the Crag Hotel.

JAYSMITH ATE A SNACK LUNCH in the hotel bar and told the openly curious Parker that he had liked Rigg Cottage, but needed a second look.

"Quite right, old boy," said Parker. "Never rush into these things. On the other hand, don't hang about either. There is a tide, and all that."

"You're probably right," said Jaysmith, finishing his beer. "By the way, who is Wainwright?"

"Wainwright? You mean the walking chappie?"

"Probably."

Parker was regarding him with considerable surprise. "How odd," he said, "that someone as keen on the Lakes as you hasn't heard of Wainwright! He's the author of probably the best-known series of walkers' guides ever written. You must be pulling my leg, Mr. Hutton!"

"Of course, I know the books you mean," lied Jaysmith. "Me, I've always managed very well with the Ordnance Survey maps."

He left the hotel a few minutes later and strolled through the sun-hazed village to a bookshop he had noticed on a corner. There he found shelves packed full of the Wainwright guide books. He bought *The Central Fells*, which included much of the terrain around Grasmere. A glance through it explained its popularity: detailed routes, pleasing illustrations, lively text; something here even for the man who lived by map and compass.

It was after two thirty. Slipping the book into his pocket, he set out to walk up the hill to Rigg Cottage.

At the house he was relieved to see the little Fiat still in place, but there was no sign of Annie Wilson as Miss Wilson showed him round the ground floor once again.

"Has your niece gone?" he asked casually.

"No, she's out in the garden."

"You mentioned a boy, Jimmy. Are there any other children?"

"You've got sharp ears and a long nose, young man," said Miss Wilson reprovingly.

"If I'm going to become an inhabitant, I need to adapt to local customs," smiled Jaysmith.

His impudence paid off. "No, just the one," said the old lady abruptly. "They'd been married barely seven years when Edward died, just before Christmas last year."

Nine months and still grieving. Grief could last for ever unless life wrenched you out of its course.

"You look round upstairs by yourself," instructed Miss Wilson. "I don't bother with the stairs unless I have to."

He spotted the younger woman from the window of the room with the mountaineering pictures. She was reclining in a deckchair at the bottom of the garden with her feet up on an ornamental wall, her eyes closed against the slanting sun. Suddenly fearful that she might glance up and see him watching, he turned away and went downstairs.

"Well?" said Miss Wilson. "What do you reckon?"

"We haven't talked about a price," delayed Jaysmith.

"I thought you said you'd leave that to me," she replied, her lips crinkling. "Well, here's what the agent reckoned he'd ask for it if I put it with him, which I'm going to do if it's not sold today."

She mentioned a figure. It was hefty but, from the little bit of expertise Jaysmith had gathered to keep up his conversations with Phil Parker, it seemed reasonable.

Miss Wilson added, "But for the pleasure of not paying an agent's fee and not having hordes of strangers and more than a few nosy local devils tramping around the place, I'd knock a thousand off that, Mr. Hutton."

He scratched his chin. "That's generous of you," he said. "Very generous."

He had hoped that Annie Wilson would materialize at some point to show a protective interest in her aunt. But he saw now that the old lady would not take kindly to being protected and that the niece would remain determinedly absent till negotiations were concluded. And so if the conclusion were no sale, he would be politely shown the door and his chance would have been missed.

His chance for what? He wasn't quite sure, but Parker's words rang in his ears ... *there is a tide in the affairs of men* ...

He said, "On the other hand, I rather feel that for a cash sale, no property chain to worry about, no pressure to complete nor delay when you are ready, all this guaranteed, you might come down a little lower. Another couple of thousand, I'd have thought."

She looked outraged, but he also saw what he had already guessed—the haggler's spirit burning bright. They went at it hard for fifteen minutes.

"I'll need to go out and talk to Annie," she said at one point.

She was gone a couple of minutes only. Shortly after she returned they settled for a reduction of the agent's price by fifteen hundred pounds. She offered her hand. He took it. Her grip was firm and warm. "That's settled then. You'll have a drink. Come into the garden." He followed her out. Another deckchair had appeared alongside Annie's. "It'll be whisky to seal a bargain," said Miss Wilson, and went back inside.

Annie opened her eyes. "You've bought it then," she said neutrally. "Did you knock her down?"

"Only as far as she had decided to go," he said ruefully. "If she'd really tried her hardest, I suspect I'd have been *raising* her price. She's rather formidable, isn't she?"

He had struck the right note. She smiled at him now.

"When she came out to see you just now, what did she say?" he asked.

"Nothing," she said. "She just came out, got that deckchair you're sitting on from the shed and set it up, then went back inside. Why?"

"She told me she was coming to consult with you," he said.

She began to laugh and he laughed with her. It was a long time since there had been such a moment of shared pleasure in his life.

"You two sound very jolly, I must say," said Miss Wilson, returning with a tray on which stood a decanter and three glasses.

Jaysmith struggled to his feet to offer her the deckchair but she said, "No, I find them things too awkward for me nowadays. I'll sit on the wall here. Now, you take your jacket off and enjoy the sun."

Obediently Jaysmith removed his jacket. As he draped it over the back of the deckchair the Wainwright guide fell out of his pocket. Quickly he picked it up and replaced it, wondering if Annie Wilson's expression of amusement only existed in his mind.

He stayed for half an hour, deftly fielding questions about his background. At the end of this time the younger woman said, "I really must be off now, Aunt Muriel. I promised I'd pick Jimmy up from school."

Jaysmith rose too. He was wondering how to keep in contact with Annie Wilson when she said, "Like a lift down into the village, Mr. Hutton? I can't see your car."

"No. I walked up this afternoon."

He folded himself into the tiny car, leaving the two women to make their farewells. A moment of panic hit him as he waited. What am I doing? he asked himself. I've promised to buy a house, just so that I can talk a little longer with a woman I've only just met!

But the panic vanished like morning mist when she climbed into the driver's seat.

She dropped him at his hotel.

"Thank you," he said. "Look, I'd like to see you again."

"If you're coming to live up here, I daresay we'll bump into each other," she said with a smile.

"No. I mean sooner. What about tomorrow? Lunch, say."

She stopped smiling. "I don't often eat lunch, except when I go to Auntie's. Usually I just grab a snack."

"Me too," he said. "So why don't we eat our snacks together?"

She thought for a moment then nodded as she put the car into gear. "All right. Why not? Half past twelve suit you?"

"Fine. But where? What's the best place round here? You name it."

"Best place?" she echoed, letting in the clutch and beginning to move gently away, "Well, one of my favourites is 'The Lion and the Lamb'. Let's meet there, shall we? Twelve thirty prompt. 'Bye!" She smiled at him, her face suddenly alive with humour and mischief, and then she was gone.

That night before dinner Jaysmith studied the Cumbrian telephone directory in the bar. There were only two "Lion and Lambs" listed. One was in Gosforth, fifteen miles to the west, the other was in Wigton, thirty-odd miles north.

"Can I help?" inquired Parker, who'd been observing him from the bar.

"It's nothing really," said Jaysmith. "I just made a casual arrangement to meet a friend in a pub locally and I can't remember its name. I thought it was 'The Lion and the Lamb', but I see there's nothing near here."

"I don't know a pub of that name near here," said Parker. "No, there's only one 'Lion and Lamb' round here that I know of."

"Where's that?" Jaysmith asked.

Parker gave him the same look of surprise he'd shown at his ignorance of Wainwright.

"Up there, of course," he said. He pointed through the window, to the massive outlines of the nearer fells. One in particular seemed to loom over the hotel.

"Helm Crag," said Parker. "Home of Grasmere's tutelary deities."

"Of course. I'm sorry, my mind was too much on pubs," smiled Jaysmith, not having the faintest idea what was being said to him.

Later, in his bedroom, he made sense of it by looking up Helm Crag in his newly purchased guide book. He found it described as possibly the best-known hill in the country because of the rock formation on the summit whose silhouette was said to resemble a lion couchant and a lamb. The Lion and the Lamb!

He cursed himself mildly. Such ignorance displayed a week ago when he was still planning the kill would have been a real error of security. But now it didn't matter. He enjoyed the feeling of perfect relaxation once more.

He switched off the light and his thoughts simultaneously. Tonight sleep, when it came, was as dark and undisturbed as ever.

3

The ascent of Helm Crag was a delight: not much over a thousand feet but full of interest and beauties. He had set off in plenty of time and it was not much after noon when he reached the summit.

He laid his rucksack on the ground at the foot of the group of rocks which gave the fell its nickname, and wandered for a while, musing on that sense of peace underpinned with menace which mountains always gave him.

When he returned to his rucksack, it was gone.

"Over here," called Annie Wilson. She was sitting in a well-sheltered declivity looking westward. His rucksack lay at her feet, with hers.

"You move fast," she said approvingly. "I was barely five minutes behind you when you started climbing, but you must have gained ten on the way up."

"I never saw you," he said, frowning.

"Move like the old brown fox, that's me," she said.

He sat down beside her, recalling his first sense of a certain foxiness in her features. Dressed today in a heather-mixture shirt and dark green slacks which clung a little closer than walking trousers really ought to, she reclined among the rocks like a creature of them rather than a visitor to them. Her long dark hair hung free today and there were some small green lichens in it, picked up from the boulder behind her. The brown eyes in that narrow intelligent face had instantly registered his appraisal, so he made no real attempt to conceal it.

"Will I do?" she asked.

"You fit the occasion perfectly," he said. "And me?"

She looked him up and down, her eyes lingering on his well-worn but beautifully maintained boots. Custom-made many years ago, they were a perfect fit, light, supple and strong.

"You don't stint yourself, do you?" she said, touching the leather.

"If a thing's worth doing, it's worth doing best," he said lightly. "I've brought tongue sandwiches and a piece of salmon quiche. What about you?"

"Apples, cheese, and a bramble pie," she said.

"We complement each other perfectly. Do you mind drinking your wine out of a cardboard cup?"

"As long as it doesn't come out of a cardboard box first," she said.

They began to eat. Conversation flowed easily, but shallowly too. She refused to let him penetrate far into her personal life, and he was by need as well as by nature reticent about his own background.

"When shall you move into Rigg Cottage?" she asked.

"That depends."

"On what?"

On what happens between me and you, he thought but did not say. It was not that he was afraid to say it; simply that he was not yet ready. He was attracted to her, but he was surely too old for love at first sight?

"On business," he said vaguely.

280

"What precisely is your business, Mr. Hutton?" she asked rather sharply.

"To tell you the truth it's almost nonexistent," he said. "I ran a little management consultancy firm, but the recession's been too much. I've sold out to a competitor, so now I'm drifting into early retirement. Just a few loose ends to tie up, that's all."

"None of these loose ends could affect your purchase of Rigg Cottage?" she asked, suddenly alert.

"No, I've been making some sound investments against this day for years. The sale is secure, believe me."

"At the moment it's only as secure as your handshake, isn't it? I don't mean to be offensive."

"Don't you?" he said, slightly piqued. "It takes two to shake hands, you know. And tell me this: if someone turned up today, cash in hand, with a better offer, how would you advise your aunt to react?"

She frowned a little, then smiled. "Even your brief acquaintance with Aunt Muriel must have taught you she'd feel no need of advice from me." She smiled again and turning away said, "I spy with my little eye something beginning with H."

He let his gaze drift to the horizon. "Harrison Stickle," he said promptly.

"Good," she said. "Your turn."

"B."

"Bow Fell," she replied.

"You know you can't see Bow Fell from here," he chided. "The Langdales get in the way."

"So they do," she said innocently. "I give up then."

"Blea Rigg. There." He pointed.

"So it is," she said. "Well done."

"I pass the test, then?"

"Do you? My marking scheme is, to say the least, eccentric."

"But it was a test?"

"A tiny one," she smiled. "When I saw that brand-new Wainwright fall out of your pocket, I did wonder if you mightn't be shooting a line with all that great fellwalker stuff."

He complimented himself on having studied both his Wainwright and the OS map carefully for a good hour that morning. But perhaps it was time for a bit of truth to get himself a rest from those searching eyes.

"You're right to some extent, I'm afraid," he said. "I was trying to project a good image. To be honest, my Lakeland walking was all done when I was a mere lad. So any expertise I've got's a bit dated."

"Those boots don't look as if they've been in the coalhole for the last twenty years."

282

"No. They've been around a bit."

"Where, for instance?"

"Oh, here and there. Alps, Andes, Pyrenees, very low down in the Himalayas, rather higher in the Harz. Yes, here and there, you could say."

She looked at him darkly. "Well, that's me put in my place, isn't it?" she said. "And finally, overcome by age, you've returned to these undemanding hillocks, is that it?"

"Don't be silly," he said easily. "One thing I learned early was that any hilly terrain that takes you more than half a mile off a road in uncertain weather deserves great respect."

"What a wise man you are, Mr. Hutton. Though I'm glad to say the weather doesn't look at all uncertain at the moment."

"No, it doesn't," he agreed, looking out across the sun-gilt landscape. "What shall we do this afternoon?" he went on. "I thought we might go on to Calf Crag and then back to Grasmere down Far Easedale."

She sat upright and said, "Whoa, Mr. Hutton! Our appointment was for lunch, not a day's outing. I've got things to do this afternoon. You should have been more precise in your proposal."

"And if I had been?"

"Then I would have been tempted. It's not every day a little Lake District mouse has the chance to scurry in the wake of a Himalayan yeti!"

She started packing the lunch debris into her rucksack. He followed suit, saying, "Then let me be precise about two things. One: would you please stop calling me Mr. Hutton? Two: will you spend tomorrow walking with me?"

"What shall I call you?" she said.

"Jay," he said, after a fractional hesitation. Giving her his real name was out of the question, which left Jay, the closest familiarity he'd ever permitted. But he didn't like the cold breath of his previous life that it brought into their relationship.

"Jay? Why Jay?"

"My middle initial," he said easily. "It was used at school to differentiate me from another William Hutton and it stuck."

"All right. Jay." She tried it doubtfully.

"And I'll call you Annie if that's all right."

"No!" She was emphatic. "Anya," she said. "My name's Anya. Too outlandish for good Cumbrian folk like Aunt Muriel, but it's my name."

"All right, Anya," he said. "Yes, it suits you better. Annie is too..."

"What?" she challenged him.

"Buxom," he said.

They laughed together.

As they began the descent, Jaysmith reminded her, "You haven't answered my second very specific request."

"I was thinking about it. To tell the truth I could do with a good walk after a week in London. But I couldn't start till, say, ten o'clock, and I must be down again by half past three."

THAT NIGHT HE DREAMED, and the dream brought him awake. It was the first broken night he had had in more years than he could remember.

He dreamed of Jacob, or rather of Jacob's voice. Jacob's face he could hardly recall, except for something fairly simian about it. It was many years since he had seen it, but the voice was still fresh in his ears: dry, nasal, with its irritating habit of tagging interrogative phrases onto the end of statements, like little hooks to draw the listener in.

In his dream he picked up the phone expecting to hear Enid. Over the years one young Enid had replaced another as his route through to Jacob. What became of the old Enids he sometimes wondered. But with his employer, as with his targets, distance suited him best.

Instead of Enid, Jacob had come instantly on the line.

"You're Jaysmith," he said. "I invented you, didn't I? You're Jaysmith now and for ever, aren't you? Jaysmith, Jaysmith, Jaysmith ..."

Suddenly, with the voice still in his ear, he was back in the gill on Wanthwaite Crags. Across the valley he could see the red roof of Naddle Foot. He brought his rifle up to his eye and the terraced garden leaped into close focus. A white garden chair was there and in it a sleeping figure. He adjusted the sight till the silvery head filled the circle, quartered by the hairline cross. The sleeper woke and slowly raised his head and Jaysmith saw to his horror that it was not the old man after all, but Anya Wilson. She smiled at the gun, and his finger tightened on the trigger ...

With a huge effort of will he forced himself awake. It was four o'clock. He rose and sat by the window looking out into the night. *It is only a dream*: that was the childhood formula which used to put such things right; but now, fully awake, he knew that this dream was true. He was Jaysmith. He should have been back in London days ago, packing his belongings, easing himself into one of the alternative lives he had prepared over the years. Where could it end, this lunacy, running around after Annie or Anya or whatever she liked to call herself? She was at least fifteen years his junior, recently widowed and not yet emerged from that unthinkable pain. Suppose he did worm his way into her affections? It would be almost as bad as making her a target with his rifle.

In the morning he would rise early and pay his bill and leave, and that would be an end of Mr. William Hutton. He went back to bed, the future resolved, and slept deep. When he awoke it was a quarter to ten.

"Oh God!" he swore, touched by terror that she would not wait for him at their rendezvous point. So potent was this fear that he forwent both breakfast and shaving in his rush to get there.

She looked at him with considerable disapproval as he got into the car. "The good burghers of Grasmere will expect a much better turnout from the new inmate of Rigg Cottage," she said.

"I came out in a hurry," he said, glowering. "I had a bad night."

"Are we always so bad-tempered in the morning?" she murmured.

He got a grip on himself and smiled ruefully. "I'm sorry," he said. "As for what I'm usually like in the morning, I don't know. It's been a long time since there was anyone to tell me."

"Anyone who dared, you mean?"

"Or cared. And I did have a bad night. To tell the truth I woke in a cold sweat wondering what the devil I was doing buying your aunt's house."

He expected a hostile reaction to this: fear for her aunt's sake—anger at this hint of masculine dithering. Instead she nodded and said in a matter-of-fact voice, "Oh yes. The old four am's. They're dreadful, aren't they? You seem to see everything so clearly, and it's all black."

"You're speaking from experience?"

"Oh yes," she said. "Doesn't everyone get them?"

He shook his head. He found he didn't particularly want to press her to reveal the grounds of her own despair at this moment. "So, where are we going?" he asked brightly.

She responded to his change of mood, saying, "Well, I knew a Himalayan man wouldn't want to waste his time on pimples, so I thought we'd do Bow Fell via the Crinkles, but to fit it into our limited time allowance I've decided to cheat by driving to the top of Wrynose and starting from there."

He nodded as if this made sense to him while he worked it out on his mental imprint of the relevant OS sheets. They had climbed out of Grasmere, passing Rigg Cottage en route, and now they were dropping down again. He glimpsed the blue sheet of Elterwater before they entered its tiny village and left it on the Little Langdale road. Soon the car was climbing again and now they were on a steep, serpentine, single-track road. This was Wrynose Pass.

She parked at the head of the pass. Their path was clear, the ground firm, the gradients easy, and they walked side by side at a good pace, in a silence which was companionable rather than introspective. The Crinkle Crags, their first destination, at first merely an undulating ridge a couple of miles distant, assumed a different aspect as they got near. Instead of a gentle ridge, Jaysmith saw that they did in fact consist of a series of crags, jagged broken buttresses of rock, five in all, each a distinct and separate entity. They sat on the third Crinkle and drank coffee and looked eastwards. The sun was high in its southern swing and the contours of the fells were picked out in light and shade.

"My God, it's beautiful," said Jaysmith.

"You sound as if you'd just noticed," laughed the woman.

"Perhaps I have. I'm still not sure *why* it's beautiful, though."

"Oh, all kinds of reasons. Space, airiness, sublimity. The sense it gives of something more important than mere human guilts and sorrows." She spoke softly. Then she lay back, hands clasped behind her head, and closed her eyes. It seemed almost like an invitation and he leaned over and kissed her.

He knew at once he had been wrong. Her eyes opened wide with shock and her body stiffened.

"Sorry," he said, sitting up.

"No need," she replied, quickly regaining her composure. "It didn't bother me. Though a respectable gent like you should be careful."

"Why's that?"

"You may think you can come up here and toy with the milkmaids with impunity. But you're very exposed. There's a hundred places where someone could be lying this very moment, drawing a bead on us."

His eyes flickered round in such alarm that she laughed and said, "Hey, I'm joking. You're not going to turn out to be so important that you can't afford to be photographed making a pass on a mountain, are you?"

Jaysmith laughed back. "No," he said, "I'm not that important."

She regarded him shrewdly, as if doubting him, then said, "No matter. Aunt Muriel will know all about you when you exchange contracts, won't she? Have you contacted your solicitor yet?"

He hesitated. "Actually, I thought it would be more convenient if I got hold of a local man. There'll be searches and things, won't there? I wondered if you had any suggestions?"

"Perhaps." In a swift easy movement she rose. "Time to go. The hard bit lies ahead."

The hard bit wasn't all that hard, a fairly steep pull up the last five hundred feet of Bow Fell after they had descended from the Crinkles. There they ate their lunch and chatted until Anya, glancing at her watch, said, "Come on. We'll need our running shoes."

In fact, by dint of skirting the western face of the Crinkles as much as possible, they made good time retracing their steps to the car. Jaysmith walked a little behind for much of the way, admiring her athletic body as she set a spanking pace. .

She dropped him in Grasmere. When he tried to speak as he got out of the car she said crisply, "Sorry, I hate being late. I'll be in touch," and drove off without more ado.

A brush-off? he wondered.

He ate his dinner with little appetite and wondered where it was all going to lead. The euphoria of his decision to retire now seemed light years away: new cares seemed to be pressing in on him from all sides.

"Telephone call for you," said Doris Parker as she brought his coffee. The words filled him with alarm. He was convinced it must be Jacob, so much so that he almost said, "Jaysmith here," when he picked up the phone. Fortunately twenty years of caution made him growl, "Hutton."

"You don't sound happy," said Anya. "I hope I'm not interrupting your dinner."

"No," he said, curt with relief. "I'd finished."

"Good. I enjoyed our walk today."

"Me too. Many thanks."

"Were you serious about wanting me to recommend a solicitor?" she asked.

"Certainly."

"All right. Eleven o'clock tomorrow morning. Mr. Steven Bryant of Bryant and Grose will see you in his office in Keswick. Have you got a pen? I'll give you his address."

He noted it down, with directions.

"Afterwards, would you care to have lunch with me?" she went on. "I should warn you that I will be cooking it."

"I can't think of anything I'd rather do," he said.

"No need to be fulsome," she said. "Goodbye."

He realized after he had put the receiver down that she hadn't given him directions to her home. No matter. Presumably this Mr. Steven Bryant would be able to do that. He would certainly find her.

He took this certainty to bed with him and lay awake for a while feeling happiness lapping round his body. When at last he slipped into sleep, he took his euphoria with him. Soon it developed form and flesh and suddenly it was Anya's body, lean and brown next to his, and above them the sharp bright stars of the Lakeland sky, stars which Jaysmith saw were wheeling into another pattern, richer and softer but just as familiar.

And he knew without needing to look that the body against his was no longer the lean, brown body of Anya Wilson, but had become softer, rounder, a deep honey gold. And now he raised his head so that he could see the delicately boned face, the huge dark eyes, the uncertain smile, at once shy and inviting.

"I love you, Nguyet," he said, letting his tongue relish the strange cadence of the name which was also the Vietnamese word for moon.

"Come close, Harry," she whispered.

Gladly he obeyed her, but found there were strong hands gripping his arms, voices shouting. He could no longer see her, there was a door between them, the door of her apartment. Despite the strength of those trying to hold him back, he burst through the door and saw her again, naked, supine, but her eyes now wide with terror, blood caking her flared nostrils and more blood smudging the honey gold of her thighs.

287

The room was full of soldiers. One of them, a dog-faced man in a colonel's uniform, chattered commands. A rifle butt was driven into his kidneys while a hand dug viciously into his mop of hair and dragged him backwards screaming, "Nguyet! Nguyet! Nguyet!" as he woke up.

He fell out of the bed like a drunken man. He sat on the floor feeling the cool night air trace the runnels of sweat down his body. Last night, Jacob. Tonight, Nguyet. Why was he once again so vulnerable, after all these years? He rose and went to the window and pulled back the curtains. Above the shadowy bulk of the fells was the high northern heaven, pricked with countless stars. He watched it for a long time, defying it to re-arrange its crystal spheres into the lower, richer maze of the stars above Saigon.

Once again, it was only a dream. He closed the curtains and went back to bed.

4

He was early for his appointment next day. Keswick was a small town and Anya's directions were precise. The offices of Bryant and Grose, Solicitors were on the second floor of an old house now given over entirely to business and commerce. He went in.

"Mr. Hutton? You're expected," said the young girl in the outer office. "Just go straight in."

As he approached the door it opened and Anya appeared, smiling at his surprise.

"Hello," she said. "So you've decided to be early this morning? That's a good sign! I was just on my way to start your lunch, but I might as well introduce you now you're here. I'd like you to meet your new solicitor, Mr. Steven Bryant. Oh, by the way, he happens to be my father too!"

She started to laugh at the expression on Jaysmith's face.

"Don't look so dismayed," she said. "It may be nepotism, but he really is the best solicitor I know. Pappy, I'd like you to meet William J. Hutton. I shall expect my usual commission for the introduction. And I'll see you both in an hour. 'Bye."

She left, and Jaysmith slowly advanced to take the hand proffered by the man behind the desk.

"You'll excuse my daughter, I hope, Mr. Hutton," said Bryant. "It's good to see her enjoying a joke."

"Of course," said Jaysmith. "It's of no consequence."

But it was of consequence. For the last time he had seen the creased leathery features of the man whose hand he now held had been a week earlier, framed in the circle of his telescopic sight.

AN HOUR LATER JAYSMITH was sitting in the front garden of the red-tiled house called Naddle Foot. Alongside him, filling the bright air with the pungent smoke of a Caporal, was Steven Bryant. And by turning his head just forty-five degrees, Jaysmith could actually see the entry hole left in the flowerbed by his bullet. He shifted his chair slightly and looked instead across the valley to the fellside opposite, where he had patiently prepared to kill his host.

"Another sherry?" said Bryant in a tobacco-growl.

Jaysmith had emptied his glass unawares.

"No, thank you," he said. He studied the other man as he spoke. Distance had made him overestimate his age. The halo of silver hair was belied by his shrewd brown eyes and his ease of movement. Early sixties rather than early seventies; an estimate confirmed in the office when Bryant had said, "To be quite honest, Mr. Hutton, I've more or less given up practising law. There's a book I want to write and I've been devoting more and more time to it over the past ten years, and when I got to sixty, three years ago, I thought, to hell with the law's tedium! I still dabble a bit, but I would recommend you let me pass the actual job of conveyancing over to my partner, Donald Grose. He's very able."

Jaysmith guessed that Anya had wanted her father to look him over, and that she valued her father's judgment highly. He could not be what he seemed, a simple country solicitor: Jaysmith's expensive talents were not turned loose on such prey. But none of his own gentle probing produced the slightest clue. All Jaysmith knew was that already he sensed in Bryant a strength of will that might mean ruthlessness, and a dark watchfulness that might mean guilt. There was one other possible clue. From time to time his linguist's ear detected just the slightest nuance of foreignness in Bryant's speech.

Lunch was a simple though delicious meal of baked trout and green salad followed by a freshly baked bramble pie, washed down with a crisp Moselle. Bryant was industrious in topping up Jaysmith's glass, and when they returned to the garden to drink their coffee, the accompanying brandy balloon was full enough to swim a goldfish in.

Still icily sober, Jaysmith decided to make use of the relaxed mood Bryant obviously hoped for.

"*Anya*," he said mellowly as she handed him a cup of coffee. "That's a lovely name you chose for your daughter, Bryant."

Bryant said abruptly, "It was my mother's name. Anya Winnika."

"Polish?" said Jaysmith, trying to make his interest casual. "Were you born in Poland then?"

Anya said quickly, "Pappy was a law student in Warsaw till 1939. He got out when the Nazis invaded."

"And your parents, did they get out with you?"

289

Bryant lit another Caporal. "No," he said. "They thought they could sit it out. I found out later that when the Nazis came, they requisitioned our family house for their officers and moved my parents into the ghetto. My mother was Jewish, you see. The next time I saw Warsaw it was in ruins."

"And your parents?"

Bryant shrugged massively. "Who knows? The ghetto uprising of '43; the resistance uprising of '44; in one or the other they died, and so many with them that nowhere in the whole of that city could I find a trace of their passing. Think of that, Mr. Hutton, if you can!"

Anya put her hand on her father's arm and Jaysmith sipped his brandy. The sun still shone, but a chill seemed to have risen in the peaceful valley.

"You speak excellent English," said Jaysmith with deliberate banality.

It worked. Bryant coughed a laugh and said, "And why the hell shouldn't I? I've been speaking it longer than you, Hutton. I learned it first from my grandfather when I was a child. He was an Englishman, you see, sent to look after his firm's affairs in Gdansk—Danzig, it was then—in the 1880s. He never went back. When World War One came, he took his Polish wife's name and moved to Warsaw. And after the Second World War was over and I saw that the Russians had a stranglehold on my country, and realized that my life was to be in England, well, I reversed the process and reverted to my true patronym. I really am Steven Bryant, Hutton. Or, more properly, Stefan Bryant. Much more reassuring, isn't it, than something full of Ks and Zs?"

"Reassuring to whom?"

"To solid English burghers looking for someone to do a bit of conveyancing for them," said Bryant. "But I'm sorry to have bored you with my family history. In the interests of equity, I will now keep quiet, and you must tell us something about the Huttons and their origins." He smiled ironically as he spoke.

A trade-off! thought Jaysmith. He needed all his mental powers now to concentrate on the lies he was about to tell. Glancing at Anya, he was filled with shame, but rescue was at hand. Inside the house a voice called, "Mum? Gramp?"

Anya called, "Jimmy! We're out in the garden."

A moment later a boy of about six ran out onto the terrace. He pulled up short when he saw Jaysmith.

"Jimmy, this is Mr. Hutton. Jay, this is my son, Jimmy."

"Hello," said the boy. He was small, with his mother's brown eyes, but much fairer both of hair and complexion. His expression at the moment was rather solemn.

"Hello," said Jaysmith.

He held out his hand. Before the boy could shake it, he turned it over to reveal a fifty-pence piece in the palm. Slowly he made it move across the undulations of his knuckles and back again. Then he tossed it high in the air, caught it with his left hand and immediately offered both hands, fists clenched, to the boy, who studied them with a look of calm appraisal.

"What's the problem, Jimmy?" said Bryant after a while

"Well, I know it's in that one," said the boy pointing to the left hand. "Only, it's probably not, as it's a trick, and it'll be in that one."

"You've got to choose, Jimmy," said Anya.

"All right," said the boy with the certainty of defeat. "That one."

Slowly Jaysmith opened his left hand to show an empty palm.

"I knew it'd be the other after all," said Jimmy with resignation.

Jaysmith opened his right hand. It was empty too. Then he shot his left hand forward and apparently plucked the coin from Jimmy's ear. He handed it to the boy, who took it and glanced at his mother.

"Is it mine?" he asked hopefully.

"You'd better ask Mr. Hutton."

"It's certainly not mine," said Jaysmith. "Would *you* want a coin that's been kept in someone else's ear?"

The boy laughed joyously and thrust the coin into his pocket. "Thanks a million!" he cried. "Mum, what's for tea?"

"Nothing till you've washed your face and I've put some antiseptic on that grazed knee," said his mother, and led him into the house.

"Nice kid," said Jaysmith. "He looks fine."

"Why shouldn't he?" said Bryant.

"An only child without a father, it can be tough. How long has it been since he died?"

"Last December."

"What was it? Illness? Accident?"

"Climbing accident," said Bryant shortly. "But I think my daughter's business ought really to be discussed with my daughter, don't you? Another drop of brandy?"

"No thanks," said Jaysmith, rising. "It's time I was going. Goodbye, Mr. Bryant. Thank you for your help and your hospitality."

He found Anya in the kitchen bathing her son's knee. "I must be off," he said. "That was a marvellous lunch."

"Are you coming to Carlisle with us on Saturday?" asked the boy.

Jaysmith raised his eyebrows interrogatively.

"There's a soccer match," said Anya gloomily. "He's conned his grandfather and me into taking him, as a pre-birthday treat."

"Birthday?"

"That's the following Saturday. Fortunately Carlisle United are playing down south that day, so he'll have to make do with a party instead."

"Please come," urged the boy.

"Well, I'd love to come to the party, if I'm asked, but I can't make the match. I've got to go down to London tomorrow and I may have to stay away a couple of days."

He thought Anya looked disappointed, but it might have been wishful thinking.

"Jay, if you can hang on till I finish with this monster, I'll see you out," she said.

Jaysmith said, "I'll use the bathroom if I may."

He went upstairs and swiftly checked the landing windows. They were double-glazed and fitted with what looked like new security locks. He had already noticed an alarm box high up under the eaves. He opened a bedroom door at random. It proved to be Anya's. The straw handbag she'd been carrying in Keswick was on the bed. He opened it, and after a little rummaging he came up with a key ring which he bore off into the bathroom. He locked the door and, ignoring the car keys, carefully made prints of the three others in a large cake of soap. Carefully he wrapped the soap in his handkerchief, removed all traces from the keys, flushed the toilet and unlocked the door. Swiftly he made for Anya's bedroom but stopped dead on the threshold.

Anya was standing by the bed shaking out her handbag onto the coverlet.

"Hello," she said. "Won't be a sec. I wanted my car keys and as usual they seem to have sunk to the bottom. I keep far too much rubbish in here."

She resumed her shaking. He stepped into the room, put his hands on her shoulders, and spun her round to kiss her passionately as he dropped the keys onto the bedspread. It was more successful than his attempt on the Crinkles, in that she did not thrust him off, but she did not return the kiss and when he broke off she said calmly, "Is it the sight of a bed which brings out the brute in you?"

"I'm sorry," he said. "I think I just wanted to assure you that I'd be coming back."

"Why should I doubt it? After all, you are buying a house up here. Oh, there they are."

She had turned away from him and seen the keys.

"Am I moving too fast?" he asked gently.

"Not as long as the finance is in order, no," she said judiciously. "Aunt Muriel won't want to hang about, you know."

"You know what I mean."

"I've only just met you," she replied with sudden vehemence. "How on earth should I know if I know what you mean?"

She left the room and he followed her down the old creaking staircase. In the hall he said lightly, "You're well protected, I see."

She followed his gaze to the alarm junction box on the wall.

"Yes," she said, "we got burgled a couple of months ago. They didn't take much, but they made a lot of mess and it was rather frightening, being so isolated. So Pappy got a firm of security specialists in."

"Still here, Hutton? Goodbye once more."

Bryant was standing in the doorway of what looked like a study.

"Mum, can I have my tea now?" demanded Jimmy, appearing at the kitchen door.

Jaysmith looked at the three of them. They appeared a formidable family group, each splendidly individual but very united too. He guessed that it was going to be hard to get one without the approval of the others.

Soon he might have to decide how much he really wanted that one.

But as he followed Anya out of the hall into the autumn sunlight, and she turned and offered him her hand with a slightly crooked smile, he knew he had decided already.

5

He set out for London early on Friday morning. He had to go. Jacob was in London, and only Jacob could tell him why Bryant had been targeted and whether the instruction was still active. Further than that, he could not think.

The journey down had a dreamlike quality. Four hours later, when he parked his car and stepped out into the din of central London, it was like having left a monastery cell for an iron foundry.

Jaysmith's flat was on the west side of Soho. It was twenty years since he had come to live here, on the top floor of a building which had once had a Greek restaurant at street level. Now there was an Adult Video shop. He turned into the doorway leading onto the narrow staircase which ran up the side of the building. At the foot of the stairs squatted two youths. One had his head shaved smooth except for a spiky orange-dyed coxcomb; the other had lank black hair and a stubble of beard prickling his jowls. Neither made any attempt to move out of his way.

Holding back his irritation, Jaysmith stepped over them and made his way up the stairs. At his door he looked back in case the youths had ambitions to become muggers. All was quiet. He opened the door. It had two deadlocks on it and the windows had internal steel shutters so that the flat was in complete darkness.

He flicked on the light and glanced at the strip of light-sensitive photographic paper which he always placed on the floor near the door immediately before leaving. As he watched, it turned black.

The flat had two bedrooms, or rather a bedroom and a boxroom. This

293

last contained a small workbench with a vice and various metal-working tools. Now Jaysmith carefully unwrapped the soap taken from the bathroom at Naddle Foot and set about producing keys which matched the imprints in the cake. He worked swiftly and ninety minutes later he was satisfied.

Carefully he wrapped up the three keys with a small tungsten file for on-the-spot modifications and put the package into his inside pocket.

Now he relaxed and realized he was hungry, not having eaten anything since his breakfast at the Crag Hotel. The freezer held a selection of frozen food, and he chose a ready-made lasagna and put it in the microwave oven. After eating he felt restless and thought of ringing Anya in Cumbria. A crazy notion, instantly dismissed. He then thought of ringing his Enid number, but that would be a mistake too. He had retired. He must not show any desire to make contact. And in any case he knew that if they wished to contact him, eventually they'd get round to it.

He went through to the bedroom, lay down and waited for Jacob.

THE FIRST TIME HE EVER saw Jacob, he was lying on a bed.

He had swum out of a drug-filled sleep into a world of physical pain and emotional agony. And there was Jacob.

Just a man in a dark double-breasted suit totally unsuitable for the hot, humid climate of Southeast Asia, sitting by the bed, still as a lizard on a wall, his squashed-up face wearing its customary expression of weary puzzlement.

"You're awake, are you?" he asked. "Can you move?"

He tried. The pain in his body didn't get much worse until he tried to speak. Then he realized that the left side of his face must have been badly cut. A long strip of plaster covered perhaps a dozen stitches.

"Where's Nguyet?" he managed to whisper.

The dark-suited man shrugged.

"I should think she's dead, wouldn't you, Mr. Collins? The civil police say she was a taxi-girl, picked up under Madame Nhu's morality laws. The secret police say she was a communist sympathizer fomenting unrest at the university. The Special Force say she was a Buddhist saboteur. They can't all be right, can they? But they all agree that she died resisting arrest, and I'm afraid they can't all be wrong either.

"And you," he went on. "You'd have been dead too, wouldn't you? If those Americans hadn't happened to come along. What *did* you think you were doing?"

He closed his eyes and let the memories come rushing back. Flung out into the street in front of Nguyet's apartment, he had staggered, half demented with rage and terror, into the nearest bar. There he had emptied his wallet in front of the barman and demanded a gun. Saigon, under

President Diem's repressive regime, was a city where it was said you could get anything for money. The barman removed the cash and five minutes later a newspaper-wrapped package was put into his hands. As he left, two Americans came in. They were attached to their embassy's Cultural and Educational Mission, and Jaysmith's British Council teaching contract at the university had brought them in touch. He ignored their greeting and rushed past them. Alarmed by his appearance, the Americans followed.

As he arrived back at Nguyet's apartment block, the street door opened and the dog-faced colonel and his entourage came out.

Screaming with hate he had ripped the paper from the package and leaped forward brandishing an ancient revolver. Thrusting the weapon into the colonel's face, he squeezed the trigger. It fell off. A soldier smashed the useless weapon from his hand. Another drove him to the ground with a savage blow to the head. Then they were all at him with rifle butts and boots. Only the arrival of the Americans had saved him from being beaten to death in the street.

"I was going to kill that bastard," he said savagely. "I still am."

"Are you? This is the man, I believe, isn't it?"

A photograph was held in front of him, and he nodded.

"Colonel Tai. A very nasty piece of work. Directly answerable to Tran Van Khiem who, as you may know, is Madame Nhu's brother and head of anti-subversion forces. And you're going to kill him, are you? You'll have to be quick, Mr. Collins."

"What do you mean?"

The dark-suited man pointed to an envelope by the bed.

"You're *persona non grata*, Mr. Collins. There's a plane ticket in there, valid for this evening's flight only. If you're not on that flight, you will be arrested on a charge of attempted murder, subversion, sabotage, it hardly matters what as you're not likely to survive arrest, are you? I should catch that plane if I were you, even if it means crawling to the airport."

The superior tone got to him at last.

"Who the hell are you?" he demanded. "Are you official? From the embassy? You've got the look of one of those smooth bastards!"

The man laughed drily. "A smooth bastard, am I? Then you'd better call me Jacob, hadn't you, Mr. Collins? And am I official? No, I'm so unofficial I scarcely exist. Come here a moment, will you?"

He went to the window. Laboriously the injured man climbed off the bed and followed. His flat was in a small block on a side street off the Boulevard Charner, one of Saigon's main thoroughfares, choked now, as nearly always during the day, with cycles, motor scooters, cars and trucks. The man who called himself Jacob pointed to the intersection.

"At precisely six o'clock this afternoon, Colonel Tai will be going down the boulevard in his jeep. He will be held up there by a slight accident, right

at that corner. It's about fifty yards, wouldn't you say? An easy shot for a man who was his regimental and university rifle champion."

"How the hell do you know that? Who are you?"

"Nobody. Jacob if you like, but I prefer nobody. What do you think, Mr. Collins? Could you pull a trigger? One that wouldn't fall off, this time?"

"Oh yes," he said. "I could pull a trigger."

Jacob contemplated him for a moment. "Goodbye, Mr. Collins," he said softly. And then he was gone.

An hour later there was a gentle tap at the door.

When he opened it, there was no one there. But against the wall stood a long cardboard box with the name of a well-known brand of vacuum cleaner on it. He took it into the flat and opened it. It contained a Lee-

Enfield .303 rifle, old, but beautifully maintained. The magazine was full.

He went to the window and looked out. Fifty yards. From that distance he could not miss. He knew beyond all doubt that he was going to kill Tai, but now he let his thoughts dwell on the mysterious Jacob. Saigon in the autumn of 1963 was awash with rumour. Self-immolation by Buddhist monks; acts of sabotage by God-knows-who; arrest without trial by government forces; the sacking of the Saigon pagodas; all these had fuelled the perennial rumours of an imminent anti-Diem coup. Perhaps most significant of all was the withdrawal of American support, signalled in a variety of ways.

Tai's assassination by a Westerner would be just another such signal. That the assassin was English, not American, would mean nothing to the native populace, but it would enable the Americans to claim total innocence. Jacob was probably British Secret Service paying off some debt to the CIA.

But for the full effect of the assassination to be felt it would have to be known that the killer was a Westerner. And there was only one way of advertising that.

He stood at the window and looked out to the crossroads. Jacob needed no special plan. Tai would have his usual armed escort. It was a mere fifty yards to the apartment block's only entrance. If he survived sixty seconds after pulling the trigger, he would be a lucky man.

He didn't mind dying if that was the price to be paid for the colonel's death. But he felt a sudden reluctance to die for the man called Jacob and the mysterious security forces behind him.

There were still two hours to go.

He pulled on trousers and a shirt and went down into the street to stroll aimlessly. Only once when, among the stream of svelte and graceful Vietnamese women passing in and out of the fashionable shops, he imagined he glimpsed Nguyet, did he show any animation. But even as he pressed forward crying her name, he knew he was wrong.

And he had been wrong ever to have loved her.

He had loved his father and his father had deserted him. He had loved his mother and she had died. And his stepfather had rejected him.

In the army and at university he had been popular, active, successful, but he had not made the mistake of allowing anyone too close. When he got the chance to come to this exotic, distant place, there had been no ties at home to make him hesitate.

And here, as if the bitter rules which seemed to guide his life in England did not apply, he had relaxed once more and taken Nguyet into the deepest and most secret places of his soul.

Now she had paid the price.

He stopped suddenly. He was outside the Hôtel de la Paix, one of the city's many monuments to the French colonial dream. Without conscious decision, he went into the crowded lobby and made his way up the stairs to the top floor. Letting his instinct guide him, he turned left and walked to the end of the corridor. There was a bathroom there. He opened the door and went in.

It was a high, airy room. A posse of cockroaches scuttled beneath the high-sided cast-iron bath at his entry. Painfully, he clambered up on the side of the bath and opened the high, narrow window.

It gave him a crow's-eye view straight down the boulevard. There, about three hundred yards away, was the intersection where the colonel's jeep would be stopped in just over an hour's time.

He got down off the bath and went to the door. There was a key on the inside. He removed it, went out, and locked the door behind him.

On his way back down the boulevard, he carefully paced out the distance. Three hundred and twenty-five yards. Back in his flat, he packed his few belongings in a small grip, slipped a small pair of field glasses into his pocket and repacked the rifle in its box.

He arrived back at the hotel at a quarter to six. Approaching one of the hire-car drivers he told him he would be leaving for the airport in about fifteen minutes and gave him the grip to look after. It was Nguyet who had taught him this lesson about most of her people: trust given without hesitation was nearly always repaid in full.

No one noticed him as he once more climbed the stairs. Locking the bathroom door behind him, he took out the rifle and adjusted the sights. At five to six, he turned the bath taps on. The ancient geyser made a thoroughly satisfactory din, a series of groans, wheezes and explosions among which a gunshot would hardly be noticed. Standing on the edge of the bath, he scanned the middle distance with his glasses.

It was perfectly timed. At one minute to six he caught his first glimpse of the small convoy of two jeeps, moving very fast and scattering the other traffic with much blaring of horns. As they came nearer, he saw that one was crowded with soldiers, guns at the ready. The other had only one armed soldier sitting next to the driver, and in the back, still and solitary, was Colonel Tai.

At the intersection a bent old man pushed an overloaded handcart into the path of an ancient station wagon which slewed round, blocking the highway. The driver leaped out, shouting abuse at the old man. The jeeps skidded to a halt.

The trouble was that while there was certainly a clear shot from his apartment in the side street, from the hotel the station wagon blocked his line of fire. Any moment now, the impatient colonel might order his jeep to divert up the side street, taking him safely out of range.

But the colonel's impatience manifested itself in quite another way. Standing up in his jeep, he too began to shout at the quarrelling men. Three quarters of his head, just enough for identification, was visible above the station wagon's roof.

He squeezed the trigger.

The explosion was deafening in the confines of the small room, but he hardly noticed it as Tai fell backwards out of sight.

Stepping down, he dipped the rifle into the bathwater, rubbed the stock and butt, then slid it out of sight under the bath. Then, turning off the taps and pulling out the plug, he went to the door and unlocked it.

The corridor was empty. He walked down the stairs, across the foyer and into the street. His driver was waiting with the engine of his ancient Renault ticking over. He got in and the vehicle set off.

He arrived at the airport just in time to check in for his flight. The girl on duty said apologetically over his shoulder to someone behind him, "Sorry, sir, with this gentleman's arrival the flight is now full."

He turned, to see Jacob.

"You thought there'd be a place?" he said with mild accusation.

Jacob shrugged slightly and said, "You'd better hurry, Mr. Collins. Perhaps we'll meet again."

"No," he said, "I never want to see you again. Never."

He headed for the departure gate. He didn't look back, neither at the man called Jacob nor at the city of Saigon. He was finished with them both for ever.

HE HAD FALLEN into a light sleep when a gentle tap at the door aroused him instantly.

When he opened it he found himself looking at the two youths from the foot of the stairs. The scruffy bearded one called, "All right, sir."

A third figure appeared behind them.

"Thank you, Davey," he said to the bearded man. "Thank you, Adam. I shouldn't be long."

The youths withdrew. The newcomer nodded casually at Jaysmith.

"Hello, Jay," he said.

"Hello, Jacob," said Jaysmith.

The two men sat and viewed each other. Jacob refused wine, accepted whisky. He raised the glass and sipped it slowly.

He's aged, thought Jaysmith. For many years Jacob had been just an unchanging voice to him. Now he saw a man in his sixties, fit and active still, but shrunken somehow. But mind and method remained the same.

"You puzzled us, didn't you?" he said with a slight shake of the head. "What happened up there?"

"I missed."

Jacob showed no surprise. "After over twenty perfect hits, you deserve a miss, don't you? You're overreacting a bit, aren't you, Jay?"

"It wasn't the first time. I missed the Chinaman as well," said Jaysmith.

"Did you? That was a strange miss, wasn't it? Straight through the head."

"He moved. It was his bad luck, my good. I'd noticed some blurring before. On the Austrian job for instance. I've been to an oculist. He gave it a name, says it's unimportant, won't affect any normal use of the eyes. He doesn't know what I do for a living, of course."

"I'm pleased about that," said Jacob mildly. "But if it's so minor, can't it be corrected? Or you should change your style, Jay. Get in closer."

"Closeness kills," said Jaysmith coldly, "both ways. You want close work, you'll have to get yourself someone else. I'm finished, Jacob. That's my last word."

300

"Yes, I can see that," said Jacob. "I'm sorry, Jay. You were the best I've known. The very best. I'm sorry to lose you."

"And I'm sorry I didn't say something after the Chinaman. But this job seemed very urgent."

"Yes, it was urgent, but never mind. Win some, lose some, don't we?"

Jaysmith poured more whisky and said casually, "I wish I could have left you more time before the deadline was up. Did you manage to arrange anything else?"

The little monkey face was gloomy. "No, I'm afraid not."

"And the deadline was firm, was it? Or can it be resited?"

Jacob shrugged indifferently. "We'll have to see, shan't we?" he said.

It was not a satisfactory answer, but pushing harder could be dangerous. Jacob was no fool and very hard to read. Jaysmith wasn't deceived by the other's apparent acceptance of his reason for quitting. There were plenty of other possible reasons, principal among them that he had been bought off, and the first hint of a direct link between himself and Naddle Foot would confirm their worst suspicions.

But he had to push. "What is he anyway?" he asked idly. "Political?"

Jacob put down his glass very gently.

"How strange that you should ask," he murmured. "Your first miss in twenty years, and now your first question, Jay."

"The one triggers off the other perhaps," said Jaysmith. "I've nearly always been able to read in the papers about the targets I've hit. It's not so strange I should feel curious about the one who got away."

"No? Perhaps not. But I hope retirement isn't going to make you forget our agreement, Jay. You do remember our agreement, don't you?"

"Oh yes," said Jaysmith softly. "Like it was yesterday."

HE WASN'T LYING. What was vague in his memory was the period immediately after his return to England from Vietnam. Friendless, jobless, and in a near-catatonic state, he had lived in a bed-sit in Notting Hill. His physical injuries had quickly healed, only the long scar on his left cheek remaining as a permanent memento. But his mind bore wounds which refused to heal. Finally his doctor had called in a psychiatrist, and Harry Collins had found himself sitting in a quiet, dimly lit room, describing all that had happened.

He remembered little of this in detail, except the last few questions.

"Do you regret shooting Colonel Tai?"

"No!"

"Yet you shot him to avenge the girl's death, didn't you? Did you believe that revenge might bring you peace?"

"Yes."

"But it hasn't."

"No."

"So hitting Colonel Tai was pointless."

"*No!*"

"What, then?"

And then he had spoken with a quiet intensity. "It wasn't enough, that's all. The world is full of them, full of Colonel Tais, murdering, torturing, corrupting, betraying. There are too many, too many, too many!"

The man had given him a tablet. After he took it, he fell asleep. When he awoke he was lying on a bed and once more Jacob was at his bedside.

"What do you want?"

"I was worried about you, wasn't I?"

"Because I didn't get killed, as you expected?"

"That's right," agreed Jacob. "I did expect you to get killed. But you were cleverer than I realized. That was a fine shot, by the way. One of the finest I've known, in the circumstances. You did extremely well."

"Did I? I survived, that's true. Though I don't know why. And I've talked!" His voice rose triumphantly.

"Yes, I know. We had to keep an eye on you, of course. Guilt feelings can lead to very embarrassing behaviour, can't they? But there was nothing of guilt in your outpourings, I gather. Just a desire to carry on the good work. Would you like that?"

"What do you mean?" he demanded.

And Jacob told him. "One step at a time, at first," he concluded. "You'd never be under pressure from me. We'd supply all necessary equipment, of course. And money."

"I don't want money."

"You'd have to live," insisted Jacob. "You'd have to be comfortable, you'd have to be fit. Think about it."

He'd thought about it. The idea had occupied his mind to the exclusion of all else, including the streets of Saigon.

Jacob came back. "Well?"

"I'd need to be sure of this: I'd need to be sure that these—what do you call them?—targets, deserve to die as Colonel Tai deserved it. I'd need to know all about them ..."

"No," said Jacob simply. "You mustn't know anything more than is necessary to target them. But I'll make an agreement with you. I won't give you any sermon about patriotism or the national interest, but I'll guarantee this. I'll never give you a target who is not as guilty as Tai. And your part of the bargain is that you never ask questions. And never talk, of course. Are we agreed?"

He had nodded and Jacob had shaken his hand.

"One more thing. Harry Collins is dead. We need to start you again from scratch. Think of a name."

He had replied impatiently. "Smith. John Smith."

"It's a little nondescript. J. Smith. No, I have it. *Jaysmith*. One word. An English compromise. From now on you are Jaysmith. Jacob and Jaysmith. They march well together, don't you think?"

And so he had been rechristened. And three months after the christening, from the top of a tall building in Istanbul he had fired the shot which had been his confirmation. And now it was over.

Or would have been if he hadn't met a slim, dark woman with more sorrow in her eyes than her heart deserved to know.

"No, retirement doesn't end our agreement, Jay," repeated Jacob. "But I will tell you this, as a retirement gift. This man that you missed, I would say that he deserved to die more than any other target I've ever given you." He spoke with surprising vehemence. Rising, he held out his hand. It felt dry and cold.

"Good luck, Jay," he said. "Take care, won't you?"

One last glance round the room, and he was gone. He had shown no curiosity about Jaysmith's plans. More strangely, he had made no real attempt to probe into his reasons for retiring. At the very least, Jaysmith had expected that his visit to the oculist and the man's diagnosis would be carefully checked. Perhaps they already had been.

He went to bed that night wrestling with the problem of how to interpret what Jacob had said about Bryant. Did his vehemence about the solicitor's deserving to die spring from the frustration that the deadline was past and he would now be allowed to live? Or was it a hint that the target order would be reactivated?

He fell into an uneasy sleep, to wake at four am. He got up and began packing. There was nothing more to keep him.

He left by a rear entrance which took him over a couple of walls and down a narrow passage into Greek Street. He saw no sign of Adam with the coxcomb or Davey with the beard. When he got to the BMW, he took it on a serpentine route to the south and west out of central London.

It wasn't till he was completely satisfied there was no tail on him that he made for the M1 and headed north.

It looked lighter up there already.

6

At one o'clock on Saturday afternoon he was sitting in the bracken high above the road which ran past Naddle Foot, eating a cheese sandwich. He could see the main gate about five hundred yards away, and his binoculars hung ready round his neck.

At one thirty there was movement. A car came down the long curving drive. It was the old Rover that Bryant drove. The gate was closed, and the car stopped to let Jimmy out to open it. Jaysmith moved his binoculars to focus on the car. Bryant was at the wheel with Anya beside him. The car was now moving and he watched it out of sight, gave it another half hour to allow for an unexpected return to pick up something forgotten, then began to descend.

His first key fitted perfectly, but the second wouldn't turn. He removed it, sprinkled some French chalk on it and inserted it again. A couple of minutes' work with his file smoothed away the impediment and he was in. The third key was the crucial one. This was the one to turn off the burglar alarm during the short period of grace given to the householder after opening the front door. There would be no time for adjustment. He opened the control box, inserted the key and turned it gently. There was some resistance, then a satisfying click.

He waited another whole minute to be quite sure, then he started to search. He had no idea what he was looking for, but he had to try to find out why Bryant had been targeted.

He started with Bryant's study, which was downstairs. At the end of an hour he knew Bryant was writing a history of Poland from 1918 to the present day, and that his researches had taken him into most major British and European libraries, including those in Poland itself. But how any of this could have put him on Jacob's target list was not apparent.

Discouraged, he went on with his search. Bryant's bedroom was even less helpful than the study, its one potential source of information being a locked wall safe. Then it occurred to Jaysmith that a man like Bryant, sharp enough to retain a number in his mind, was probably also sharp enough to know that the passing years could imperceptibly blunt his memory. An aide-memoire was the answer. Where better for numbers than among numbers?

He went downstairs to the telephone in the hall. There was a book of addresses and phone numbers by it. He looked through it hopelessly. Any one of these names could be fictitious. At the back was a list of tradesmen and emergency numbers: doctor, dentist, water, gas, electricity, police, garage ...

He paused and went through into the kitchen. He had only been in here once before but his memory had served him well. What was a house without gas doing with a gas-board number?

He noted it down and went upstairs. He tried it out in various ways. Backwards proved right. The door clicked open.

His self-congratulation did not last long. The safe contained very little: a British passport and a small bundle of letters. He looked in the passport. Bryant was well travelled, presumably on his research trips. There were several entry stamps for Poland. But there was nothing at all for almost a year.

The letters were in Polish, with no address. They were signed *Ota*. The only clue to their means of arrival was a larger envelope with Bryant's name and address on it. This was postmarked Manchester.

Inside he found a sheet of paper, again without any address, and a brief scrawl which read *I'll be going again in the autumn. I'll get in touch.* It was signed *Anton*.

He took the letters downstairs to the photocopier in the study and copied them. After resetting the counter to zero, he returned to the address book by the telephone. There was only one address in Manchester, and it belonged to someone called Anton Ford. He noted it down, went back upstairs, replaced the letters and shut the safe.

Now he started on the rest of the house. He felt reluctant to go through Anya's room, but his natural thoroughness demanded it. A photograph of Jimmy in football kit stood on the dressing table, and on the bedside table was another, of the boy standing in front of his grandfather. Nowhere in sight was there a photograph of anyone who could have been her husband. Perhaps the memory of his death was still too poignant.

Jimmy's room seemed even less likely to be productive but he glanced around it just the same. It was in a small boy's most desirable state of chaos, but hanging on the wall, between full-sized posters of a footballer and a pop star, was the photograph of a man. This had to be Edward Wilson, guessed Jaysmith. He took it down and looked at it closely. It showed a burly, dark-bearded man in a heavy Norwegian sweater, whipcord trousers and climbing boots. He was regarding the camera with arrogant impatience as if he felt this was a waste of time. There was something familiar about the face: he decided it was not a face he liked very much. *I'm jealous!* he realized with astonishment. *Jealous of a dead man!*

He dropped the photograph onto the bed and quickly searched the room. There was, of course, nothing to find. What had he expected? he asked himself sourly. His irritation was chopped short by an unwelcome noise. From the landing window he saw a car coming up the drive. To his relief it wasn't Bryant's brown Rover but a bright orange VW Beetle. His relief soon evaporated as the passenger door opened and Anya got out. She reached into the back of the car and began to pull out carrier bags and parcels, helped by the woman driver with whom she was chatting and laughing. Clearly the early return had nothing sinister in it and Jaysmith concentrated now on his own predicament.

He had to get out fast, but there was the burglar alarm to consider. It was switched off, and Anya would notice this on entry. He ran swiftly downstairs and reset the alarm, then retreated into the dining room as he heard Anya opening the first of the locks. The dining room overlooked the rear garden, an area of lawn bounded by a yew hedge. This was obviously Jimmy's domain: a football lay on the grass and a game of swing-ball was set up, consisting of a tennis ball on a cord which rotated around a vertical metal pole sunk in the lawn.

The front door opened. He mentally rehearsed the turning off of the alarm, gave a few extra seconds for safety and undid the window catch. There was no blast of noise and he let out a long sigh. He slid the window up noiselessly, stepped out and let the window down. Where now? To be found skulking about outside was almost as bad as being caught within. Again, there was no time. He ran across the lawn, picked up one of the swing-ball rackets and sent the ball whizzing round the pole with a tremendous blow. Alternating backhand and forehand, he soon got a rapid rhythm going and managed about twenty consecutive hits before he sent the ball too high and the cord got tangled.

"Bravo!" called Anya's voice, accompanied by half a dozen handclaps. She was looking out of the kitchen window. "What on earth are you doing here?"

"Trespassing," he answered. "I got finished in London much quicker than I thought, so I drove up this morning. I went for a walk and thought I'd divert here to beg a cup of tea. But then I remembered you'd said you were going to some football match with Jimmy. I thought I'd stroll around the garden for a little while in case you got back. I hope you don't mind."

"Feel free," she said. "Step inside. I'll put the kettle on."

She unlocked the kitchen door and he entered. They smiled uneasily at each other for a moment. He had the feeling that she was not certain whether she was pleased to see him or not.

"Where are Jimmy and your father?" he asked.

"In Carlisle," she said. "I decided to skip the match. I met a friend, we did some shopping and she ran me home."

"My good luck," said Jaysmith.

She made the tea, her face slightly flushed. As she poured it, she said, "Mr. Hutton ..."

"Jay," he interrupted.

"Jay. I hope I get this right. Look, you're buying my aunt's house, and that's one thing. You also seem to be ... interested in me, and that's another thing altogether. I don't know you, Jay. I mean ..."

"You mean we only met last Monday. That's true. And I was looking for a house long before I met you, that's true also. You know that. My purchase of Rigg Cottage has nothing to do with you, though it's a very charming vanity."

He smiled to remove offence, but she regarded him sombrely and said, "I've thought a lot about that. I know you were looking for a house before

306

we met. But, looking back, it seems to me that you weren't looking for Rigg Cottage till after I arrived. *Is* that vanity?"

She was as sharp-scented as any fox, he realized. She had sniffed out a not-quite-rightness in him, but, thank God, it wasn't any suspicion of deception in his name and background that bothered her. It was fear of the passion which, on such short acquaintance, could cause a man to purchase a not inexpensive house in its pursuance.

He said, "I want the house."

He meant it. He was surprised to find how much he meant it. He went on, "London's a slum. I've been everywhere: up here's the only place I've ever wanted to buy a house. Rigg Cottage is the house I want to buy. End of story."

He finished his tea and stood up.

"Are you going?" she said.

"I'd better. I haven't checked in at the hotel yet."

She followed him out into the hall and began to gather together her shopping. There was one long package wrapped round with toyshop gift paper. It slipped from beneath her arm and Jaysmith caught it.

"Someone's lucky," he said.

"What? Oh, yes. It's Jimmy's birthday next Saturday."

"What have you got him?" he asked.

"It's a gun," she said.

He must have looked disapproving for she said defensively, "It fires ping-pong balls. One of Jimmy's friends got one and he was full of envy. I was a bit doubtful, but Pappy says that if you're living in the country, you've got to know about guns. You can't pretend they don't exist. It's better to learn to respect them. What do you think?"

"It seems to make sense," said Jaysmith. "You go on up. I'll bring this."

Anya hesitated at the foot of the stairs and Jaysmith said with slight exasperation, "If you prefer, I'll drop it here and you can come back for it. But believe me, my presence on your landing will hardly compromise your name at all."

She giggled unexpectedly and said, "Sorry. Come on."

In the bedroom she dropped her shopping on the bed, and hid the birthday present carefully at the back of her wardrobe.

"Where's your car?" she asked.

"Along the valley a way," he said vaguely.

He stepped out of the bedroom and headed for the stairs. Out of the corner of his eye he noticed that he'd left Jimmy's bedroom door ajar as he rushed to check on the arriving car. Had it been ajar when he went into the room? Well, it was hardly something that anyone would notice.

Then it came back to him with the force of a blow that he had left Edward Wilson's photograph lying on the bed.

"Hello," he said, "is this Jimmy's room?"

He stepped inside without waiting for an answer and by the time Anya reached the doorway, he was standing holding the photograph in both hands.

"Jimmy's father?" he said inquiringly.

"Yes, it is," said Anya. She came into the room and took the picture from him and hung it on the wall. She was very angry, he could tell.

She said in a quiet, controlled voice, "Jimmy, like most small boys, has a highly developed sense of his right to privacy. I try to respect it."

Was this the real reason for her anger? he wondered. Or was it his temerity in daring to touch the holy image?

"Oh God," he said, "I'm sorry. I shouldn't have barged in, should I? Privacy wasn't something I knew the meaning of as a child, I'm afraid."

Instantly, she recovered herself. "I've no right to lecture you. If Jimmy knew you were in here, you could probably buy his forgiveness with a bag of allsorts. He's crazy about liquorice."

"I'll remember."

As they went down the stairs he said, "Sorry if it's painful, but Jimmy's father . . . the face looked somehow familiar."

"Did it?" She was a pace behind him. "He was in the papers occasionally. He was a climber, quite well known some years ago. And when he died, it made a nice little story."

"How was that?"

"Famous mountaineer, Alpine expert, Himalayan expeditionist, falls off a hundred-foot cliff in Cumbria and breaks his back; wouldn't you say that was a nice little story?" she asked. "You probably saw the pictures."

He turned and looked up at her.

"I'm sorry," he said. "It must have been terrible."

"It was," she said. "Terrible. Could you see yourself out?" She went back up the stairs.

As he walked away from the house he was afraid she was crying.

HE AWOKE ON SUNDAY to find the weather had broken. Heavy clouds sat sullenly on the hilltops and by the time he had finished his breakfast grey vapour had slipped insidiously down the fell slopes and the valley was blind with a thin drenching rain.

It was not a day for the long kill. And a damned uncomfortable one for the short kill too, he assured himself. Bryant should be safe enough today, even if Jacob still had him down for elimination.

He was no nearer any decision on the best course of action. He had studied the letters the previous evening, but had made little progress beyond confirming that, on the surface at least, they were *billets doux*. Until he could get a Polish dictionary and translate them he only had one possible clue to the nature of Bryant's culpability, and that was the name of his courier, Anton Ford, who lived in Manchester.

He got out his road map and checked. A hundred miles, about a couple of hours' drive. He doubted if anything productive would come out of the trip, but if this weather kept up, anything was better than hanging around the hotel.

By lunchtime the weather was, if anything, getting worse. He had a sandwich and a beer in the bar, then went out into the rain. It was slow driving at first but when he hit the motorway he was able to speed up, and eventually as the mountains fell behind so the weather began to improve.

Manchester he knew vaguely. He stopped at a newsagent on his way in and bought a street map. The address he was after proved to be in the southern suburbs, an expensive-looking district consisting mainly of Edwardian villas.

He found the street he was looking for without difficulty. It was a long crescent, with several "For Sale" signs on display, including one for the house next to Anton Ford's. Jaysmith now saw a course of action. He parked the car and walked up the drive of the house with the "For Sale" sign, taking in the neighbouring house as he did so. A pale green Granada was parked in the drive, and he had a sense of being observed.

He reached the door and rang the bell. After a long while a middle-aged woman answered the summons. She looked rather bleary-eyed, and carried a tumblerful of well-iced colourless liquor.

"I'm sorry to bother you, but I've been looking at a couple of houses in the area and I saw your sign," said Jaysmith. "I know it says appointments only but the agent's office is closed, and I'm only in the district today. If it's really inconvenient ..."

She looked him up and down, and then beyond him to the BMW parked at the gate. "As long as you don't expect apple-pie order," she said, turning away.

Taking this as an invitation he followed her into the house. It occurred to him that the last time he had gone through this masquerade he had ended up buying the place. An expensive habit to get into.

The woman began to show him round. She seemed to be under some strain and the reason for this and the drink was soon made clear. Her name was Wendy Denver. She was selling the house because her husband had died of a heart attack two months before and the house was too big for her and too full of memories and she could go to live with her son in Ireland, only she hated Ireland, and she would lose contact with her friends and neighbours ...

It was becoming stream-of-consciousness stuff and, as much out of pity for the woman as self-interest, Jaysmith cut in, "Yes, neighbours are important, aren't they? I always like to know about the neighbours when I look at a house. How are your neighbours here? Easy to get on with?"

The woman considered. "Well, on this side I don't have much to do with them." Her gesture seemed to indicate the other side to Ford's house.

"And the other side?" Jaysmith asked.

But before the woman could answer the doorbell rang.

"Excuse me," she said, and left the room. Jaysmith followed her. When she opened the door a couple stood there: she a rather faded woman in a floral smock, he a brawny, suntanned man who might have been a docker or a labourer except that the silk sports shirt straining against his solid chest was by Gucci, like the slacks similarly strained by his broad thighs.

"We thought we'd drop in and see if there was a cup of tea going," said the woman.

"Come in, do. This is handy," cried Mrs. Denver. "We were just talking about you! Or rather, this gentleman here was asking questions about my neighbours and I was just about to fill him in!" She turned back to Jaysmith. "Here are two of the very best neighbours you could find anywhere. Anton and Sally Ford from next door, meet Mr. . . ?"

"Wainwright," said Jaysmith, extending his hand. There was something unpleasantly speculative about the way Ford was looking at him.

"We didn't know you had any appointments to view arranged for this afternoon," said the faded woman.

"Didn't have. Mr. Wainwright was just passing," said Mrs. Denver, and went on, "If you moved here, Mr. Wainwright, you'd be the luckiest man in the world to have neighbours like these. What I'd have done without them . . ."

Suddenly she broke off, tears streaming down her face. Sally Ford put her arm round her and led her into the lounge, closing the door behind them. Jaysmith shook his head. "I'm sorry," he said. "I didn't realize. I'm sorry I picked this house. What's she asking, by the way? We hadn't got on to prices."

His attempt at diversion seemed to work. Ford mentioned a figure, and then said, "Look, I doubt if Mrs. Denver's going to be fit to resume her sales talk for some time. I've got to pop across to my place. Why don't you come with me, and anything more I can tell you about the area, I'll be happy to. Basically the houses are the same, too. You could even look around our shack if you liked."

It was so precisely the kind of invitation Jaysmith had been seeking that he was taken aback, as if his mind had been read.

"That would be fine," he said.

FORD'S HOUSE WAS DECORATED and furnished in an expensive modern style. In the lounge Ford unlocked a cabinet and took out a flat black leather case from which he removed a small pill bottle.

"I'll just take these over to Wendy," he said. "Make yourself at home. Have a look round if you like."

He went out whistling. This was getting to be too good to be true. Jaysmith went over to the black case. It was full of pill bottles, capsules, ampoules, all neatly stored in separate compartments. He looked in the cabinet but there was nothing there. Indeed the rest of the lounge promised little, so he went into the entrance hall and after trying a couple of doors found a small room used as an office.

Quickly he went through the drawers of the stainless steel desk. The mystery of the black case was solved. The man's business notepaper revealed that he was the sales head of a large drug retailing company. His desk diary showed he was a busy man, travelling all over Europe. There had been three visits to Poland in the last twelve months. And three letters had been received by Bryant from Ota.

A filing cabinet contained nothing but business files. There was a wall safe but this was locked, and Ford's telephone book contained nothing that looked like a hidden number. He checked that Bryant's number was in it, then he heard the noise of Ford's cheerful whistling. Quickly he returned to the lounge.

Ford looked in a moment later, said, "All right? With you in a sec. Pour yourself a drink," and ran lightly up the stairs.

When he returned, Jaysmith was sipping a gin and tonic. "How is Mrs. Denver?" he asked.

"Fine. I've given her something that'll see her right."

Suddenly he smiled and the gold teeth flashed. "By the way, in case you're wondering, I am an MD. Not practising, but fully qualified. Couldn't stand the hours. Another drink? Look, try some of this stuff. Plum brandy. It's really smooth. Best thing to come out of Poland, though perhaps it's a bit disloyal of me to say so."

"How, disloyal?" asked Jaysmith, refusing the brandy.

"My parents were Polish," he explained. "My father was a doctor. He didn't like the way things were going and decided to get his family out in 1938. Three months later I entered the world, in London."

He talked easily, readily. The Ford family, consisting of the parents, an elder brother and sister, and Anton himself, had settled down in England with varying senses of permanency.

"My mother was in her forties when she had me. By the time the war ended she wanted no more change. She wanted to stay quietly in England. Father, on the other hand, always planned to go back, and in 1948 he did. My sister Urszula, who was sixteen by then and old enough to make her own choice, went with him. She thought the sun shone out of his stethoscope and had managed to grow steadily more Polish despite her ten years in England. Me, I was bilingual, but I was British. And I wasn't

311

going to leave my mother." He laughed ruefully. "My parents are both dead now, but I go to Poland on business sometimes and I visit Urszula when I can. She's got five kids and two grandchildren. And they all seem to like their rich capitalist uncle!"

They talked for another quarter of an hour and then Jaysmith rose. "You've been most kind and helpful. I hope we meet again," he said.

"Now that you've found out what kind of neighbours you'd have, I hope so too."

They shook hands and Jaysmith left.

Driving back through Manchester, he tried to analyse what he'd found out, and it came to very little. The simple explanation was that Ford, a friend of Bryant's whose business took him to Poland from time to time, acted as a courier between Bryant and his girlfriend, Ota, bringing her love letters out and presumably taking Bryant's in. There need be nothing sinister in that. But somewhere in it, he was convinced, must lie the reason for Bryant's being targeted.

The foul weather he had left with the mountains was waiting for him on his return. He did the last few miles at a careful crawl and reached the Crag Hotel just before nine. Parking as close to the door as possible, he dashed in through the rain.

Phil Parker looked out of the bar. "Mr. Hutton, glad to see you back. No weather for driving, this. There's been a lot of accidents. Young couple turned their car over on Dunmail Raise. And then old Miss Wilson's niece from Rigg Cottage ..."

Jaysmith felt his heart constrict.

"Anya Wilson, you mean?" he cried. "Has there been an accident?"

"Yes, I'm afraid so. Young Mrs. Wilson came down here to see you, in fact. Some message from her aunt about Rigg Cottage. Then the phone rang. It was old Miss Wilson. They'd just rung from Windermere Hospital. There'd been an accident ..."

"It wasn't Anya then?"

"No, I was telling you," said Parker, looking at him curiously. "It's her father, Mr. Bryant. His car evidently came off the road coming down into Ambleside from Kirkstone Pass. He's been seriously hurt, I gather. It sounds very very bad."

Parker insisted on pouring Jaysmith a large Scotch and then gave what details he had as succinctly as possible. Anya had arrived at the hotel with Jimmy at about five forty-five. On finding Jaysmith was out, she had started to write a note, and then the phone call had come.

Anya had been almost completely overthrown by the news and Doris Parker had taken control. She had organized Phil to take Jimmy up to Rigg Cottage while she herself had driven Anya to the hospital.

Doris Parker joined them at this point in the story.

"I had to leave her at the hospital," she explained. "They said Mr. Bryant was very poorly, but not in danger. I wouldn't have left her if he'd been in danger, but the girls don't come in tonight and I couldn't leave Phil to do the dinner by himself. But I'm on my way back now. Phil, keep the coffee going, will you? And if things get quiet, you might make a start setting the breakfast tables."

"Will do," said Parker. "How long do you expect to be, darling?"

Before Doris could reply, Jaysmith spoke.

"I'll go," he said. "I know Mr. Bryant. He's acting for me in my house purchase. I reckon you've done enough, Mrs. Parker. You've got your hands full here."

Doris Parker gave it a moment's thought, then nodded. She gave him brief, clear directions how to get to the hospital. Soon he was out in the night again, the BMW cutting through the tangles of rain.

He saw her as soon as he entered the hospital, standing in a telephone booth. As he approached, she replaced the receiver, turned and saw him.

"Hello," she said. She looked pale and strained, but far from being at the point of collapse.

"How is he?"

"He's all right," she said. "He's broken an arm, cracked a couple of ribs, put his knee out of joint, torn several muscles and got himself spattered with various cuts and contusions. But they haven't found all the nasty other things they've been looking for, like fractured skull and internal bleeding. They seem almost disappointed."

She tried a laugh. It didn't come out very well.

"You've seen him?"

"Briefly. There's a lot of shock, naturally, but he recognized me. He'll be in for a few days. *They* say a week, perhaps more, but they don't know Pappy."

"I'm so glad," he said. "So very, very glad."

He spoke with such intensity that her eyes blurred with tears.

"Thank you, Jay, thank you."

"Come on," he said. "I'll take you home."

"Yes, please," she said. "I've just rung Aunt Muriel. Jimmy's fast asleep, so I'll leave him there tonight."

"What was the message about Rigg Cottage?" he asked, remembering.

"Oh, nothing important—whether you'd want a survey done," Anya answered.

She lapsed into silence. But he felt a closeness, a warmth between them, which he was reluctant to break when they arrived at the gates of Naddle Foot. She awoke as he got back into the car after opening them.

"I'm sorry," she said. "I haven't been very companionable."

"If it's company I want, I'll join the YHA," he said lightly.

She opened the front door and went in, switching off the burglar alarm. He followed. The house felt big and cold and empty.

"I'll make you a drink," he said.

"Brandy," she said. "Thanks."

"What I had in mind was cocoa."

She smiled, wanly but genuinely. "You have cocoa," she said. "I'll have brandy."

He compromised and made two mugs of cocoa liberally laced with cognac. She drank greedily.

"We were both right," she said, and yawned widely.

"Bed," he said emphatically.

He led her unresisting up the stairs, opened and door and switched the light on. "I could stay," he suggested.

"Yes. If you like."

He kissed her gently on the forehead and said, "I'll use Jimmy's room, shall I? I'm sure he won't mind."

He paused in the doorway and regarded her for a moment. She stood at the foot of the bed, like a puppet resting on its strings. An easy target. All the time in the world to check the range, take aim, and fire.

"Go to bed," he said harshly. "Quickly. I'll see you in the morning. Goodnight."

7

The next morning he awoke at eight fifteen to the smell of frying bacon. Quickly he got up, washed, shaved with a borrowed razor, dressed and descended to the kitchen.

"Good morning," said Anya. "You have the gift of perfect timing."

She was no puppet this morning, but a bright-eyed, alert young fox in a heather-mix sweater and russet slacks. She placed a plateful of bacon, egg and mushrooms on the table before him.

"He's doing all right," he stated rather than asked.

"It shows, does it?" she said, smiling. "Yes, he's doing all right. I rang half an hour ago. They said he was awake, hungry, and causing trouble. Then they remembered to say that medically he was as well as could be expected."

She filled another plate and sat opposite him.

"That's great," said Jaysmith. "What time's visiting?"

"Ten thirty. So if you can drop me at the hotel car park I'll pick up my car—it's still at the hotel."

"I'll take you to the hospital," he said. "That is, if you don't mind me going along."

She considered. "No, I don't mind," she said. "We'd better get on, then. We're picking up Jimmy first. I rang Aunt Muriel too."

"Jimmy? What about school?"

"I'll let them know he's taking the morning off," she said firmly. "I want him to see for himself that his grandfather's all right. You see, he's got this idea that people go into hospitals to die. You just never see them again. Ever since his father died. Will you clear up in here while I go and ring the school?"

ON THEIR WAY TO RIGG COTTAGE, he felt able to bring up the question of the accident.

"I don't know much," Anya told him. "He'd gone over to see Donald Grose in Patterdale—some professional problem that needed sorting out. Then on the way home he went off the road coming down from Kirkstone Pass towards Ambleside. The locals call that stretch 'the Struggle'. Up there the mist and rain had cut visibility, and he must have missed a bend. He smashed through a gate into a field and turned over. He was lucky to be found."

"Who found him?"

"A local man, a farmer I think. I must look him out and thank him."

"There was no other vehicle involved?"

"Not as far as I know. I wasn't really taking things in, you understand."

The roads were still very wet and Jaysmith drove with care. At least the rain had stopped, and there was promise of sunshine above the low ceiling of mist. When they reached Rigg Cottage, Jimmy came running out to greet his mother. Leaving them together by the car, Jaysmith joined old Miss Wilson in the doorway.

"Good morning," he said.

"Morning," she replied, regarding him grimly. "No need to look so proprietorial, young man."

"Was I? I'm sorry. Though it shouldn't be long now," he said, glancing up at the old house.

"I wasn't meaning the cottage," she said. "You spent last night at Naddle Foot, I gather."

"Yes, I did," he said.

"How old are you, Mr. Hutton?"

"Forty-three," he said.

She snorted significantly.

"You feel it's a dangerous age for a man?" he asked politely.

"They're all dangerous ages," she said. "What I want to know is . . ." she paused as Jimmy came running over, followed by his mother ". . . are you sending a surveyor to look round my house or not?"

"Would you mind?" he said, very serious.

"If you mean, do I think the old place is going to fall down, the answer's no," said Miss Wilson. "But there was nothing in our agreement about 'subject to survey', that's what I told that half-witted solicitor of mine. So if you want the place surveyed, I should prefer you to do it when the house is yours, rather than waste my time when I've got better things to do!"

Jaysmith scratched his nose and looked at the ground, then went and kicked one of the posts holding up the porch and pressed his ear to the woodwork. "All right," he said. "I'm ready to complete. The money should be available today. When can you be out?"

For a moment she sucked in her cheeks and glared at him frostily, then gradually relaxed and smiled.

"You're a bit of a joker, aren't you, Mr. Hutton? I'd not have thought it when we first met. So, it'll be a fortnight today, if that suits."

"Fine," said Jaysmith, offering his hand.

They shook and the old woman said to Anya, "I'm glad that's definite. I had that brother of mine on the phone last night and I nearly told him, but I wanted to be definite."

"You think he won't be pleased?" said Anya.

"He will not, but he'll just have to lump it. Hadn't you better be off? Here, I put a jar of rum butter out for your father."

She stepped into the hallway and returned a moment later with a large jar topped with a round of greaseproof paper.

"Thank you," said Anya, kissing her cheek.

"And you'll set things in motion, young man," said Miss Wilson to Jaysmith as he got into the car.

"Yes," he said. "I'm just off to see my solicitor."

As they approached the hospital Jimmy, who had been chattering excitedly for most of the journey, fell silent. Getting out of the car, he grasped Anya's hand tightly as a nurse came down the corridor which led to the ward, accompanied by two uniformed policemen. She recognized Anya and stopped, saying to the policemen, "This is Mr. Bryant's daughter."

"Is he all right? What's happened?" asked Anya anxiously.

"He's fine," said the nurse reassuringly. "And in excellent voice. He's been insisting on seeing the police ever since he woke up this morning."

"We'd have wanted a statement in any case," said one of the men, a big raw-boned youngster. "But your dad seems to reckon he was run off the road by some idiot overtaking him down the Struggle. He seems to think we should have roadblocks out, and Scotland Yard in, looking for him."

"I daresay you'd be a little upset if you'd been put in a hospital bed by some maniac's carelessness," snapped Anya. "Come on, Jimmy." She walked away.

"Could it be true?" asked Jaysmith.

"Could be, but it'd need a real maniac to overtake on that road in those conditions. Excuse me, but who are you, sir?"

"Just a friend of the family," said Jaysmith. "Who was it who found Mr. Bryant, by the way? I know his daughter wants to thank him."

The officer checked his notebook. "It was a Mr. Blackett, of Nab Farm, Ambleside. It was lucky he came along. The car was upside down with Mr. Bryant hanging in his seat belt unconscious."

"Did Mr. Blackett say anything about another car?"

"Not that I know of. Now, if you'll excuse us, sir."

Jaysmith waited another ten minutes, then went into the ward. Bryant was sitting up in bed. With his head bandaged, his face flecked with small dressings and his arm in plaster he looked almost a caricature of a hospital patient. But his eyes were alert and he greeted the newcomer with a pleasing energy.

"Mr. Hutton, I've been hearing about your kindness. Thank you."

"It's good to see you're all right," said Jaysmith. "I gather it was a close call."

"Very close. You'd think I'd know after all my years in the legal game just how obtuse the police can be, but I can't get them to show any interest at all in the lunatic who did this!"

"Lunatic?"

"Yes. He'd been following behind me for half a mile at a steady pace, then he suddenly started crowding me. Last thing you want in those conditions is someone up your exhaust, so naturally I speeded up a bit. I'd just begun to realize how fast he'd got me going when suddenly he was overtaking and cutting back inside, on a bend. That's when I went through the gate and flipped over. Madman!"

"What was it?" asked Jaysmith. "Car? Van? Truck?"

"Car, I think," said Bryant slowly. "It's all a bit mixed up still. But I'll get it all sorted once I'm out of this place."

"You'll stay here till you're fit to move!" commanded Anya. "Jimmy!"

She rose from beside the bed and went down the ward to where Jimmy had got into conversation with another patient.

Jaysmith reached into his pocket and produced a small bottle wrapped in a paper bag. "I gather you're not damaged internally," he said. "This might help you to survive your stay."

Bryant opened the bottle, sniffed and said, "Hutton, you can visit me as often as you like."

"Don't be too grateful. It's your own Scotch. I filled it from your decanter this morning."

"Yes," said Bryant, "Anya was saying you'd stayed the night."

"It seemed best. In the circumstances."

"Yes, it probably was. In the circumstances. I suggested you might be persuaded to stay a few more nights till I came home. She did not seem enthusiastic."

Jaysmith was taken aback as much by the suggestion as by Anya's response. Was the solicitor once again probing?

The return of Anya and Jimmy ended this line of conversation, much to Jaysmith's relief, and for the rest of the visit talk centred on Bryant's and his daughter's widely differing estimates of his discharge date. An elderly doctor trailing crowds of nurses arrived with the end-of-visiting bell and smiled benevolently when invited to umpire.

"Don't want to miss the next fell race, do we?" he said. "Well, we'll see. We'll see. Let's have a look at you now."

They took their leave. Jimmy went running off, Anya in pursuit. Jaysmith glanced back at Bryant's bed. A curtain had been pulled, but not all the way round. The sheet was drawn back and Bryant's pyjama jacket was open so that the doctor could examine the considerable bruising on his chest, but it was not this that caught Jaysmith's eye. It was an extensive area of scar tissue down his left side. There was a matching area down the other side which presumably joined up with the left round his back, and in this were four little hollows, as though a child had pushed its fingers into plasticine.

At some point in his life, Bryant had been badly beaten up and shot.

The visit had clearly done both mother and boy a lot of good, but at the exit Anya stopped and said, "Damn! I wanted to find out about the man who found him. I wonder who I should ask."

"How about me?" said Jaysmith. "Mr. Blackett. Nab Farm. Ambleside."

She looked so amazed he laughed out loud. "I asked that policeman you were rude to. I thought you'd want to know."

"You don't miss much," she said thoughtfully.

"A lot," he said. "I think I've missed a lot."

In the car she said, "Would you mind if we stopped off in Ambleside? I'd like to thank Mr. Blackett personally."

He turned out to be a burly, blunt and busy farmer. His reply to Anya's thanks was, "I weren't going to leave him, were I?"

Jaysmith said, "Mr. Bryant seems to think he was forced off the road by another vehicle overtaking him. You didn't see another vehicle?"

"I could hardly see a thing," he said. "It was that bad. I got to that bend and saw the gate broke and there was some lights in the field, so I stopped to have a look."

"How long after the accident was this, do you reckon?"

He thought, then said, "Not long. Engine were still hot."

"And you didn't see another car? Or hear anything?"

There was another pause, then he said, "There might've been some-thing. Another engine somewhere, when I stopped mine and got out. But sound travels funny in them conditions. Now, I'm glad your dad's all right, missus, but I've got to get back to work." He turned and stumped away.

"One of nature's charmers," said Jaysmith as they got back into the car.

"What do I care about charm?" said Anya fiercely. "He saved Pappy's life, didn't he?"

"Yes. I think he probably did."

"You seem very interested in Pappy's story about this other car. But I don't see how it can be quite like Pappy said. Concussion can do queer things."

"What makes you think your father's got it wrong?"

"Well, if there was a road hog belting down the Struggle, how come he didn't overtake Mr. Blackett first? I mean, he was travelling so fast, while Pappy and Blackett were crawling along. It's a narrow twisting road with no turn-offs, so he can't have been between them, can he? It doesn't make sense."

She had a sharp mind, he acknowledged again. Her conclusion was that if the third car had not sped past Blackett also, it didn't exist. His conclusion was very different: if the third car had not passed Blackett, it was because it too was crawling along, a little way behind Bryant, content to keep at a safe snail's pace till the right moment came. Then the sudden acceleration, the near-contact, the violent change of direction, the crash.

But at that speed, even dropping off the road like that and turning over, Bryant was likely to survive. So the other car would stop, its driver would get out to make sure. And distantly he would see Blackett's lights approaching.

There was no guarantee that his conclusion was sounder than Anya's, but he had seen last night what the threat of her father's death had done to her. It didn't matter what Bryant was, or had been, or what he deserved. For Anya's sake, Jaysmith could not allow him to be killed.

At the hotel car park Anya refused his invitation to have a drink and got straight into her Fiat.

"This young man's got to have his lunch, then get to school," she said, ignoring Jimmy's protests. "Father wanted you to stay at the house a bit longer," she added. "I told him no."

He didn't say anything and his silence seemed to provoke her.

"Look, I stay by myself when he goes away; there's never been any of this helpless little woman stuff before."

"Does he go away often?"

"Yes, quite often," she said firmly, then corrected herself. "Not quite so often as he used to, not since I came back to live with him."

"Does he ever go back to Poland?" he asked idly.

"Why do you ask?" she said sharply.

"Just making conversation, to prolong the pleasure of your company," he said, smiling. "I remember he said he went back at the end of the war and I wondered if he'd ever made any other visits, that's all."

She frowned. "You must have misunderstood. He didn't go back at the end of the war. He was there already when the war ended."

"Good Lord. You mean he was an agent?"

"Something like that. He doesn't talk about it; if you mention it, he'll only joke that it didn't last long enough for the glue on his false moustache to dry. His version is that he got shot when they arrested him and he spent the rest of the war in hospital, recovering just in time for the peace."

"And you believe that?"

"Wherever he was, it was a million miles away from the comfort of Windermere Hospital. Look, we must dash. I'll be in touch."

"You mean it?"

"Yes."

Their gazes locked and he nodded. Last night and this morning had eased them closer together, fractionally but discernibly. The fox was at the edge of the trees, almost ready to step into the moonlit glade.

That afternoon he drove into Carlisle, forty miles away. It was the nearest town of any size, and he wanted a reference library with a Polish dictionary in it, and also the chance to use it with the minimum risk of being observed by any of the Grasmere vigilantes. The library was situated in a pleasant old sandstone building between the attractively small cathedral and the squat castle.

It didn't take him long to realize he was wasting his time. The letters to Bryant were what he had guessed, love letters. They began with the equivalent of darling, ended with expressions of love and longing, and in between lay nothing but descriptions of domestic events, gossip about mutual friends. He put the letters back in his pocket, returned the dictionary to the shelves, and went to the service desk.

Yes, they kept copies of all the Cumbrian newspapers. He was vague about dates and got a supply of weeklies covering October to December of the previous year. He found what he was looking for in the last edition before Christmas: "Tragic Death of Well-known Local Climber".

The facts were simple enough. Wilson had been climbing Pillar Rock when he fell. He had been alone and had sustained severe back and head injuries. It had been well over twenty-four hours before he was found, and he had died in the West Cumberland Hospital without regaining consciousness. Pillar Rock, Jaysmith discovered, was a crag on the eastern face of Pillar Fell, overlooking Ennerdale. Remote, steep and dangerous, it provided ascents ranging from "Difficult" to "Very Severe".

Jaysmith was slightly puzzled as to why, on what was evidently such a famous and, in climbing terms, popular crag, Wilson's fall should have gone unnoticed. It also seemed rather odd to be climbing alone.

The inquest report answered the first point. Weather conditions, it seemed, had been atrocious: sleet and snow lashed by near gale-force winds. None but the hardiest climbers had ventured out in such conditions, and then only to destinations less remote than Pillar Rock. The coroner's verdict was death by misadventure.

On the same page was an obituary appreciation, which provided the answer to Jaysmith's second mental query.

Even making allowances for local pride in a favourite son, Wilson came across as a formidable figure. Educated at Granton, a Scottish public school run on Outward Bound principles, and Trinity Hall, Cambridge, where he read law, he had eschewed the brilliant career at the Bar forecast for him, and opted for a Lakeland solicitor's life in preference to the Inns of Court. The only thing which could draw him away from his beloved Cumbrian mountains was the challenge of other, greater, mountains. He had taken part in numerous expeditions, including the joint Anglo-Australian Himalayan venture of 1974. In 1976 he had married Anya Bryant, daughter of a fellow solicitor, and there was one son, James, born the following year. While climbing in the Alps in the winter of 1977 he had been taken ill, and it was discovered that he was suffering from diabetes. Though this disease is easily controllable by diet and insulin injections, it had virtually disqualified him thereafter for any major expedition. This had been a great loss to the world of climbing and a great tragedy to Wilson, who had since become very much a loner in his Lakeland climbs.

Jaysmith drove slowly back to Grasmere, stopping en route in Keswick to call at Bryant's office to see his partner, Donald Grose. His purchase of Rigg Cottage must still go ahead despite all these alarums, and there were many details to sort out. Also, he was hopeful that Grose might be able to add some useful shading to the picture he was drawing of Steven Bryant.

Grose was professionally efficient but extremely discreet where his partner was concerned. Jaysmith left the solicitor's office with no significant new information, but a scenario was forming. Anya had married. Bryant, left alone, had launched himself into this Polish project. It was during these years that the period of his frequent visits to Poland had begun, visits during which he had either resumed or begun an affair with the woman called Ota. Then, going by the entry stamps on Bryant's passport, the visits had stopped about a year ago and they had since kept in contact by letter. This was the time in which Anya, recently widowed, had returned to Naddle Foot. So the simple explanation was that Bryant had felt reluctant to leave his grieving daughter alone for any significant length of time.

But visits even to Poland need not be long. Perhaps there was another dimension. Perhaps Bryant, finding himself responsible not only for a grieving daughter but also a much-loved grandson, did not feel he had the right to put himself in danger.

Yet something had put him in danger, despite his efforts.

It did not surprise Jaysmith. His own experience was teaching him the hard way how difficult it was to retire from danger. If you did not go looking for it, it came looking for you.

8

Two days later, against all medical advice, Bryant discharged himself from hospital. Jaysmith was involved in the homecoming. He had rung Anya each evening, ostensibly to ask how her father was, but really to check on her own wellbeing. On the Wednesday night when he rang, Anya told him that Bryant was coming out in the morning, though the hospital would have preferred him to stay till the weekend at least.

"But he's very strong-willed," she finished. "The doctor said he couldn't spare an ambulance and I said I certainly wasn't going to fetch him, and he announced that he would walk, if necessary."

"But you *are* going to fetch him?" said Jaysmith. "Want any help?"

"Well, the only compromise we got out of him was that he said he'd use a wheelchair till he's told he can start exercising his leg. Getting in and out of the Fiat's not going to be easy . . ."

"What time shall I pick you up?" he asked.

"No, it's all right, I'll meet you there and save you the double journey."

"Nonsense," he said. "That'd mean I'd have to drive him back unchaperoned. He'd probably hijack the car and make me head for the nearest pub."

She laughed and said, "All right."

Beneath her exasperation with her father, he sensed a deep relief at having him home, and this was confirmed as he drove her to the hospital the following day. She was full of life and chatter and round her throat she wore a scarlet and gold scarf, the first truly gay colours he had seen her wearing. The weather too looked as if it was doing its best for the occasion. The cloud had risen above all but the highest peaks, and in one place the sun was trying to rub its way through.

Bryant greeted him without surprise and accepted what assistance was necessary with a good grace. It wasn't till he got back to Naddle Foot and discovered that Anya had made up a bed for him in his study on the ground floor that he showed exasperation.

"I am a temporary invalid, not a permanent cripple," he said to Anya.

323

"I desire the comforts of my own house, which include my own bed."

"Well, that's fine if that's all you want," retorted Anya, "but I presume you'll also expect to enjoy the comforts of your garden and your study and your dining room. In other words you'll be wanting to be downstairs as much as upstairs and you're in no fit state to manage those stairs."

"You're right, my dear," said Bryant, suddenly and unconvincingly humble. "What we need is a man's strength around the place. Mr. Hutton, it must be costing you a fortune staying at that hotel. Why not come and spend a few days here, till Rigg Cottage is yours? No strings, but if you happen to be around when I need a shoulder to lean on, that would be a kindness to a poor, sick man."

He spoke with a heavy irony directed at his daughter. But there was more to it than that. Jaysmith felt himself once again closely observed, and Anya too, by those still-sharp eyes beneath their grizzled brows. Bryant was still probing their relationship.

Anya said, "Jay, I can't imagine why you would want to be within a hundred miles of the world's worst invalid, but if you *can* bear the prospect for a few days, then please stay. It would be a great help and might even bring a little ease to undeserved suffering and stoically borne pain. I refer of course to myself."

It was the right note. Bryant smiled almost triumphantly as if he had prepared the way for this, or had some theory confirmed by it. He said, "That's settled then. Let's have a drink to seal the contract."

THE MOVE WAS MADE that same afternoon. Parker, scenting romance, accepted his guest's sudden departure jovially, insisting that Jaysmith take a bottle of champagne to speed the invalid's recovery.

He arrived at the house just as Jimmy got back from school. The boy was delighted to see him and when he heard that Jaysmith was staying for a few days, he said with the uncomplicated approval of the young, "Smashing! You'll be here for my birthday!" and dragged him off to play table tennis in the stone-flagged basement.

Anya rescued him half an hour later so that he could go up to his room and unpack. "We eat early in the evening, six at the latest," she told him. "That way we can all sit down together at table and have a bit of evening left over before Jimmy goes off to bed. It's a child-centred house, and that includes Pappy!"

Predictably, the boy used Jaysmith's presence to delay his bedtime, and it was after nine before Jaysmith found himself sitting in front of a gently crackling log fire with Bryant and his daughter. It was an evening of quiet contentment. Seated at the table, enjoying a plain meal washed down with a jug of beer, listening to Jimmy's chatter about school life and the amiable bickering between father and daughter about whether Bryant needed help

324

to cut up his meat, Jaysmith had felt himself seduced by happiness. And now, deep in an old armchair with Anya straining her eyes to read the local newspaper by the fire's glow and Bryant half asleep, listening to a record of Ashkenazy playing Chopin waltzes, Jaysmith felt ... he did not know what. A half-remembered and never understood phrase from his sixth-form days came to him ... *the holiness of the heart's affections* ... here, for a while, for these moments at least, it made sense. Tomorrow was soon enough for death and danger.

HE AWOKE NEXT MORNING feeling more rested than he'd done in years. His bedroom was small and simple with white-painted walls and pine furniture. The morning sun was pouring through the thin cotton curtains and bursting against the white emulsion and pale wood in a haze of warm gold. He stretched and yawned, and for a moment it felt good to be alive.

Then he remembered.

He got out of bed and went to the window. It overlooked the terraced garden at the front of the house. The sun had already cleared the eastern fells and was drawing smoky curls of mist through the bracken and up the gullies. There were still plenty of clouds in the sky but now they ranged over broad acres of blue. The improvement in the weather was continuing; and with it, the improvement of conditions for a marksman.

He got out his binoculars and began to scan the distant fellside. There, not much over a fortnight ago, he had sat and plotted death for the man who now lay under his protection. He glimpsed a movement on the fell and slowly quartered the area with his glasses. There it was again. A grazing sheep.

"What is it? A hawk?"

Startled, he spun round. Anya was in the doorway with a cup and saucer in her hand. She smiled at his alarm.

"I wouldn't have thought you were the nervous type," she said.

"You move very quietly," he said. "Like a fox."

"What does that make you?" she mocked. "A chicken?"

She was in an ebullient mood this morning. She was wearing jeans and a blue-checked shirt, and she looked about eighteen.

She said, "I took Pappy his breakfast and I thought you might like a cup of tea, particularly as Jimmy is threatening to pay a call before he goes off to school."

"We're always at home to a friend," he said.

She put the cup of tea on the bedside table and he sat down to drink it. A minute or two later the door was opened cautiously and Jimmy peered round the jamb.

"Hello," he said.

"Hello. Are you going to bring the rest of you in, or did your head just come up by itself?"

Grinning broadly, the boy entered. "Mum says if I want you at my party tomorrow, I should ask you properly," he said.

"She's quite right, but I was coming whether I was asked or not. Only, if I hadn't been asked, I was going to ruin it by putting fireworks in the jelly. That way, everyone gets a bit."

Jimmy's eyes opened wide in delight. Clearly such an explosion would set the seal on his celebration. One thought led to another.

"Were you in the war, Mr. Hutton?" he asked.

"Why do you ask?" said Jaysmith.

"That mark on your face," said the boy, looking in fascination at the long scar down his left cheek. "In one of my comics there's a man with a scar like that and he got it from a bomb in the war."

"Sorry. With me it's simpler. I cut myself shaving."

The youngster's face registered keen disappointment. Anya's voice called from below, "Jimmy! Hurry up or you'll miss the bus!"

"Better go," he said. "See you later, Mr. Hutton!"

"My friends call me Jay," said Jaysmith.

"See you later, Jay!" yelled the boy as he galloped down the stairs.

Jaysmith got dressed and descended to the kitchen. Anya was drinking coffee and reading a newspaper.

"How's your father?" he asked.

"Fully recovered except for my female fussiness. At least, that's the game he's playing. He's determined he's not going to stay in bed."

"In that case," said Jaysmith, "I'd better start earning my keep."

"Stay where you are and have your breakfast," she ordered. "He knows it's only a game. He's not going to break his neck trying to get downstairs by himself, I assure you."

He finished his breakfast and went up to Bryant's bedroom, where he found his host fully dressed. He helped him downstairs and into the lounge. Anya appeared and looked critically at her father.

"You look awful," she said.

"A breath of fresh air will soon put the roses back in my cheeks," said Bryant. "I'll take coffee outside in the sunshine."

Jaysmith was alarmed, but Anya said firmly, "No, you won't. It's still damp out there and the wind's chilly. Dr. Menzies is coming to see you this afternoon and we'll let him decide on what you can or can't do."

Bryant looked disgusted but did not object. Jaysmith said, "I thought I'd go into Keswick and do a bit of shopping, if that's OK?"

"Now see what you've done," said Anya to her father. "Jay, you're a guest, not a male nurse, no matter what this poseur may have said. You must feel completely free to come and go."

"Of course," said Jaysmith. "I thought, afterwards, I might go for a bit of a walk, so don't bother about me for lunch. I'll see you later."

His shopping did not take long and soon he was driving back along the road. It was probably a useless precaution, but he wanted to leave his own car out of sight if possible. He had noticed in his earlier researches of the terrain that there were several disused quarries below the eastern line of fells. A rutted and greened-over track led obliquely off the road towards one of them. He sent the powerful BMW up the steeply curving track till he was hidden from the road by a long spoil-heap of loose shale.

It was a bleak and dismal place. Quickly he put on his boots and anorak, raising the hood less for protection against the gusting wind than as a bar to identification. He wanted to be just another fellwalker if he came within range of a pair of field glasses.

A fence ran at a crazy angle up the fellside along the edge of the quarry, presumably to inhibit sheep from grazing themselves into danger. He climbed alongside it till finally he was on the grassy slopes of the fell top. From time to time he paused and used his binoculars, trying to give the impression of a man fascinated by the flight of various birds whose identity he was totally ignorant of. As usual, Clough Head seemed untroubled by human company that day. He paid special attention to the gill which he had chosen for his own hide. The recent rains had increased the volume of water pouring down it, but there was no other visible change, no fag ends, matchsticks or boot prints; nothing to suggest any other visitor had descended there.

Satisfied at last, he settled down on a rock near the summit and suddenly, almost with a shock, he became aware of the view. On his previous visits here his sensitivity to the surrounding terrain had been purely practical. Now for the first time he saw with an unblinkered eye. There, central amid a swell of lesser peaks, was the green head of Skiddaw. Slowly he turned. And here what a turbulent sea of fells met his view. Stretching into a distance of probably fifteen miles, they crowded the skyline with a beauty at once superb and intimate. With luck he would walk on them all, yet in essence they would always remain beyond his or any man's reach.

With a sigh he dropped his gaze into the valley below and with his glasses brought Naddle Foot leaping into view. The terraced garden was empty. Either Anya's will or the uncertain weather had kept Bryant indoors. But he would not remain indoors for ever.

Jaysmith let his glasses slide up the face of the building. The windows stared blankly back. The window of his own bedroom was open as he had left it, and here he did glimpse a movement within. It was Anya, presumably making his bed. As if to confirm her presence, she now came to the window. She was holding his pyjama jacket, he saw, and neatly folding it. As he watched she raised it to her cheek as if testing its temperature and at the same moment raised her eyes so that she seemed to be looking directly at him.

He let the glasses fall and the house was instantly miniaturized. It struck him that this was not a bad place to live, this pleasant little valley with the heights in view. No, not a bad place to live, nor a bad place to die, either. The fancy occurred to him suddenly that really *he* was the target and down there in Naddle Foot, which he had once thought to threaten and claimed now to protect, they were drawing a bead on him and just waiting for a clear shot to make the kill.

Well, at least today he was sure no one was taking a shot from up here. And it would have to be from up here, unless Jacob got hold of a rank amateur. High Rigg itself was a ruined barn alongside a small stand of trees where the ground began to rise from the beck to the fell. The drawback here was a "For Sale" notice where the track joined the road. Jaysmith's house-hunting cover had served him well, permitting him to check out the barn openly, but it meant that others, either attracted by the sign or sent by the estate agent, might come bumping along the farm track at any time. He scanned the old building with his glasses. There was no sign of life except for a magpie which came floating down in a flutter of black and white to settle on the barn. He watched it for a moment. It showed no alarm. Satisfied, he swung back to the house. Anya had vanished. He searched other windows for her without success.

Friendly no longer, the lovely old house now seemed to mock him, blank as a human face behind which unreadable thoughts pulsed their dangerous secrets.

"HELLO," SAID ANYA. "Had a good day?"

She looked deliciously domestic, with an apron round her waist and a floury smear on her cheek, standing in the kitchen surrounded by the birthday baking.

"Fine. How's the patient?" he asked.

"Dr. Menzies was pleased with him, but they're old allies, those two. I'll wait to see what they say when he goes back to the hospital on Monday for his checkup. Pappy seemed a bit down at lunch, but Jimmy's with him now and that should dispel the gloom. A six-year-old on the eve of his seventh birthday's got enough joy to share with half the world."

"And enough food too by the look of it! Do you need an impartial sampler?" said Jaysmith, reaching his hand out to a trayful of lemon-curd tarts and withdrawing it rapidly as Anya whacked it with a wooden spoon.

"God!" he said, blowing on his knuckles.

"Sorry," she said, looking abashed. "Pure instinctive reaction, I'm afraid. Pappy and Jimmy have both got fighter's knuckles."

"I can believe it. If this is what joining the family means, I may not apply for admission."

She went very still, and he was angry with himself for having come so close to what in the old days would have been called a declaration.

"Jay," said Anya in a suddenly strained voice. "What is it that you want from me?"

The lounge door burst open and Jimmy erupted.

"Jay!" he yelled. "We played football today and I scored three goals. Come and play football and I'll show you. Are you any good? I bet you are. Come and play, *please!*"

Jaysmith held Anya's gaze till the strain began to dissolve.

"To be going on with," he said, "a lemon-curd tart will do nicely."

"Help yourself," she said.

"Mum, can I have one?" demanded Jimmy.

"You can have half of mine," said Jaysmith. "Your mum's conceded quite enough for one afternoon. Never push your luck. Now, I reckon I can spare ten minutes before I get cleaned up to see an action replay of your three goals. With your mother's permission, of course."

"Granted," said Anya. "But not a second more."

"Agreed," said Jaysmith. "But not a second less either. I'm a man for full measure."

Chewing his half of the tart and with Jimmy's hand firmly clamped around three fingers of his, he let himself be pulled into the garden.

AT DINNER THAT NIGHT, Jimmy's bubbling anticipation of his birthday joys set the mood. It wasn't till Anya had led him off to bed that Bryant showed any sign of the depression his daughter had mentioned.

Nursing his balloon of brandy, he said abruptly, "I rang Donald Grose this afternoon, just to check on things at the office. He said everything's going ahead full steam on your job. You'll be living at Rigg Cottage alone, I gather."

"Yes, I'll be alone," Jaysmith said. "I'll need to get someone to 'do' for me, I suppose."

"No wife and family waiting to descend on you then?"

Jaysmith smiled. Bryant certainly went for the direct approach! "Not even an aged parent," he said smoothly.

"It's a largish place for one, even if they do call it a cottage."

"Miss Wilson lived there by herself quite happily," replied Jaysmith. "Except when her nephew was with her. He did grow up there, didn't he?"

"Why do you ask?"

"I was wondering about the associations the place might have for Anya."

That was returning directness with directness!

Bryant was silent for a while. Finally he said, "Yes, Edward spent a lot of his childhood there. James, his father, is some kind of civil servant. Trade and Industry I think it is. When he was widowed it must have seemed to make sense to let the boy be brought up here rather than in some London flat."

"You don't sound as if it made sense to you."

"Don't I? Perhaps I believe a boy needs a man. Muriel Wilson's a decent enough old stick but *old* is the operative word. She's about twelve years older than her brother and knows nothing outside Grasmere. Mind you, I don't blame *her*. Soon as the boy was old enough he was off to boarding school and, when his father could manage him, he would spend at least part of the holidays in London."

"You sound as though you feel his father neglected him."

"And you sound as if you think you've got a pretty sharp ear for nuances, Hutton!" snapped Bryant. "Perhaps I do think his father neglected him. It wouldn't have been my way. But perhaps my way left something to be desired too. Anyway, I saw his father shedding tears at the funeral, and that's something I shan't forget." For a moment he was uncharacteristically agitated, but before Jaysmith could speak the door opened and Anya came in.

"What a pleasant picture!" she said. "The old men sitting round the campfire reminiscing about their wild youth. Are we back in Poland, Pappy? Or is it Jay's turn?"

Bryant smiled at his daughter and said, "No, we're not back in Poland, dear. But yes, I do think it's Jay's turn." They looked at him expectantly.

He launched on a light-hearted account of his upbringing in Blackburn. They listened attentively, but they rarely smiled and he realized after a while that his attempts at light-heartedness weren't covering up the cracks in his story and that his teenage unhappiness was seeping through.

"I never went back to the house," he concluded. "My stepfather packed up my few things and sent them on to me. I went straight up to university after national service and stayed there during the vacations. I got myself a variety of jobs to tide me over, and at the end of three years I got my degree and lived happily ever after." He smiled, stretched and yawned, to show that the narrative was finished.

"What happened next, Jay? After you got your degree?" said Anya.

"Oh, jobs," he said vaguely. "You know, the usual progression. Office boy, filing clerk, managing director."

"And now retirement at forty," said Bryant.

"Forty-three," corrected Jaysmith. "Don't forget the three. After forty, every year counts twice, so they say. And in anticipation of a long hard day tomorrow, I think I'll retire early. Unless my services as beast of burden are required?"

Anya smiled and said, "No, that's OK. I'll drag the poor old crock upstairs. Goodnight, Jay. Sleep well."

He left. It was a retreat, of course, but he did not want to be forced into the glib lies necessary to chart the period of his maturity.

9

Jimmy's birthday was a perfect autumn day. There was very little wind. The sun's heat drew the morning mists up into the sky of cornflower blue and set the colours of woodland and fellside hotly glowing.

It was excellent shooting weather.

Jaysmith washed and dressed. As he came out of his bedroom a figure with a levelled gun leaped out of ambush on the landing. Instinctively he flung himself sideways, hitting the floor with a tremendous crash and rolling away in a vain attempt at evasion. The finger was already on the trigger, and he could only lie helpless and watch as a stream of ping-pong balls hit him on the chest.

"Jimmy! I told you! You must never fire at people!" cried Anya, coming out of her room.

"I wasn't going to, honest," protested the boy. "But Jay started playing and I couldn't help it, could I, Jay?"

Jaysmith sat up and leaned back against the wall.

"No," he agreed. "You couldn't help it. But your mother's right, Jimmy. You mustn't fire at people."

"Are you all right?" inquired Anya. He reached up his hand. She took it and began to pull. He rose in an easy movement.

"You look a bit shook up to me," she said. It was true. He could feel in himself a slight nervous reaction to the incident.

"I'm not used to holding hands with pretty girls," he said.

She drew her hand away sharply and said, "You mean you're too old to be flinging yourself around like an all-in wrestler."

Jimmy, who had been recovering his ping-pong balls, said impatiently, "Come and see my presents, Jay."

"All right," said Jaysmith. "But hold on. I almost forgot."

He went back into his bedroom and returned with a gaily wrapped parcel, which Jimmy with youthful impatience ripped open immediately. It contained a box of liquorice allsorts and a pack of trick playing cards.

The new presents were added to the horde already strewn across Jimmy's bed. They included a highly colourful children's encyclopedia from Bryant and, most impressive of all, a compendium of video games from his paternal grandfather. Anya saw Jaysmith studying this and said as if in explanation, "Grandpa Wilson would have liked to be here."

Jaysmith had to show Jimmy how to use the trick cards, and it was only Anya's force of will and a solemn promise that he would join the boy in some target practice later that got him into the kitchen for breakfast.

"Jay, could you do me a favour?" asked Anya as he drank his fourth cup of coffee. "Could you pick up Aunt Muriel this afternoon and bring her to the party?"

"It'll be a pleasure," he said.

The telephone rang in the hall. Anya went out. After a few moments he heard her running upstairs, presumably to tell her father to take the call on his extension. On her return to the kitchen she poured herself a cup of coffee and offered Jaysmith a refill.

"No," he said, "I'm fully awake now, I reckon. What's the drill this afternoon?"

"It will be something between *The Lord of the Rings* and *The Lord of the Flies*," she said. "Hobbit appetites modulating to atavistic savagery. Between two and three, a dozen or more delighted mums and dads will dump their rapacious offspring here and drive rapidly away to enjoy a few hours of peace."

"Mixed offspring?"

"Oh no," she said, shocked. "When you're seven, it's very *infra dig* to let a mere girl anywhere near your party."

"Is Aunt Muriel the only adult help?"

"Yes. And I don't want to overtax her, of course. I was relying rather heavily on Pappy to help organize games and things . . ." She let her voice tail off.

He laughed out loud. "I'll be delighted."

"Thanks a million," she said, catching Jimmy's tone and inflection perfectly. He laughed again, stood up, and kissed her lightly on the cheek.

"I'll go and see if your father's ready to descend," he said.

As he made for the stairs he noticed that Anya had forgotten to replace the hall telephone on the hook. As he passed he heard a tinny voice emerging from it. He paused in mid-stride, picked up the telephone, put his hand over the mouthpiece and pressed the receiver to his ear.

Bryant's voice said, without enthusiasm, "You'll be in touch then."

And the other voice replied without warmth, "You can bank on it, can't you? Take good care of yourself, Stefan. Goodbye."

The line went dead. Gently Jaysmith replaced the instrument.

The voice on the phone had been unmistakably Jacob's.

MISS WILSON OPENED THE DOOR before he could ring when he arrived at Rigg Cottage. Despite the warmth of the autumn sun she wore a thick tweed coat and a fur hat.

"No use you coming in just to come out again," she said, stepping over the threshold and firmly closing the door behind her. A few more days and it would be his front door, thought Jaysmith, not without amazement. He helped her into the car. She made herself comfortable and looked round critically.

"Fancy motor," she commented. "Foreign, I daresay."

"I bought it abroad," he said. "Cheap."

"Cheap!" she echoed disbelievingly. Then, as he negotiated the hill down into Grasmere, she said out of the blue, "You've got your feet under the table then."

"Sorry?"

She did not deign to elaborate.

"I'm glad to be of help to Anya," he said.

"She's a good girl," said the old woman. "She married a bit too early, I sometimes think. Edward wasn't always an easy man—from a boy, he wasn't easy. I should know. I had the bringing up of him."

This was the first hint of criticism of the man whom he still, absurdly, thought of as his rival, and Jaysmith felt a rising greed to hear more.

"In what way, not easy?"

"He could be moody," she said. Then, family solidarity suddenly making itself felt, she added sharply, "But we can all be moody, can't we? And he was a grand lad in a lot of ways. Not afraid of hard work. A heart like a lion."

Like a lion. He thought of that face he had only seen in photographs, with its heavy mane of dark hair and almost sullen gaze. Yes, there had been something leonine about it.

A blare of horns brought him back to awareness of his driving. He had turned north on the main Windermere-Keswick road and was second in a line of cars, behind a slow-moving farm truck piled high with bales of hay. A metallic-gold mini had started queue-jumping, nipping in between cars and causing much irritation. It took the final stage, from two cars behind the BMW to beyond the hay truck, in a single swoop. Jaysmith saw, as it flashed by, a young man with a shock of ash-blond hair, sun-goggles, and a cigarette drooping from his lips.

"He's in a hurry," said Miss Wilson. "He'll be lucky to get there in one piece. Youngsters!"

The widening of the road as it climbed up Dunmail Raise permitted Jaysmith to overtake the hay truck without problem, and as they made their way through St. John's-in-the-Vale they overtook the golden mini, which had pulled off the road ahead. Jaysmith realized, glancing in his mirror, that it had stopped at the mouth of the track leading to the old barn.

A few minutes later they reached Naddle Foot, and Anya greeted them with relief. "There's quite a lot here already," she said. "Parents apologetic, but some urgent appointment is taking them to the far end of the country, and they know I won't mind little Fred turning up a mite early, will I?"

"And do you?" asked Jaysmith.

"Not really," she said with a wide smile. "Jimmy would have burst if we'd had to wait much longer for his party to begin. They're all out in the back now, raising hell. Aunt Muriel, come and say hello to Pappy before I toss you to the lions."

They found Bryant sitting in the lounge looking out of the French windows which opened onto the rear garden, where Jimmy and three other boys were playing a wild game of football. Bryant and Muriel Wilson greeted each other with a wary courtesy.

"I'm well enough," Bryant was saying in response to a formal inquiry after his health. "What of you? All ready for your move? What's that brother of yours think about it?"

"He can think what he likes," Miss Wilson replied with spirit. "It's me own house. There's no family entail or owt of that."

"You have *told* him you're moving haven't you, Auntie?" asked Anya anxiously.

"Last Sunday he rang. I told him then. I was able to tell him about your accident too," she said to Bryant, reducing his misfortune to a trifle compared with the sale of Rigg Cottage. "What were you thinking of, man? Speeding down the Struggle on a night like that?"

"I was not speeding," snapped Bryant. "Unfortunately some idiot in a Dinky-car was. I was forced off the road!"

"Hmm," said Miss Wilson, conveying volumes of scepticism. "Now where's that nephew of mine? Doesn't he want his present?"

"Jimmy!" called Anya. "Aunt Muriel's here."

The boy came running in, flushed from his exertions.

"Hello," he said, halting before the old woman.

"Is that all I get?" she said sternly.

"Sorry," he said, and gave her a swift kiss. She handed over a parcel wrapped in bright striped paper which looked as if it had been used before.

"Don't tear it," she instructed as Jimmy began the assault which was his normal method of unwrapping gifts. The paper came off to reveal a radio-controlled police car.

Jimmy's delight was unbounded. "That's *smashing!*" he yelled. "Thanks a million!" Giving his great-aunt a now uninhibited kiss he rushed out to show off his new treasure to his friends.

"You shouldn't have, Aunt Muriel," protested Anya. "It's far too expensive."

"Nonsense," said the old woman, gathering up the wrapping paper and smoothing it out. "He might as well have it now as when I'm gone. And there'll be a tidy bit of cash to have, especially when Mr. Hutton here gets round to paying his debts."

The imputation that he was dragging his feet in closing a deal which had been processed at something like ten times the normal speed made Jaysmith stare. Then Anya nudged him sharply in the side. He saw that she was having difficulty holding back her amusement, and suddenly he was smiling too.

"Come and enjoy the sunshine, Auntie," said Anya. "It'll get nippy later on."

Pulling her coat round her to indicate that perhaps it was nippy already, the old woman followed the younger into the garden, where Jimmy was demonstrating the manoeuvrability of his police car to his admiring friends.

"They've come a long way since Dinkies," said Bryant. "With one quarter of the technology they use for making toys now, we'd have won the war in half the time."

"Dinkies," said Jaysmith slowly. "You mentioned them earlier too. You said when you had your crash, you were overtaken by some idiot in a Dinky-car. You mean it was a small car ...?"

"It was a Mini, bright yellow I think. I've never liked them, they seem to do something to their drivers ..."

"You mean, you've remembered about the accident? You never mentioned it to me!"

"Should I have done?" said Bryant, puzzled. "You were out, I think. It was yesterday; it suddenly came back. I rang the police. They didn't seem very interested. Not half as much as you, certainly!"

He was regarding Jaysmith with open speculation. The ringing of the front door bell postponed the need for explanation, however. Gratefully he excused himself and went to answer the summons. It was another young guest, the first of a steady stream which kept him occupied for the next twenty minutes, directing them through the house to the back garden where Anya was organizing a series of energy-sapping games in the hope of rendering them all quiescent by teatime.

When the last car drew away he went to the BMW and got his field glasses. Running lightly up to Jimmy's room, he positioned himself so that he could see the winding road and followed it back. The end of the track where the gold Mini had stopped was not within sight, he discovered. He turned his attention to the ruined barn. It stood blank and still in the sunlight.

Probably there was no connection whatever between the golden Mini he had seen on the road through the valley and the yellow Mini Bryant thought he remembered on the Kirkstone Struggle. But the thought of some nervous newcomer pumping bullets into a garden which contained

Anya and Jimmy and Miss Wilson and fourteen happy young boys, as well as Bryant himself, was not one he could live with a moment longer than necessary.

He went down the stairs, fearful of being spotted and summoned, moving swiftly past the lounge door out to the BMW once more. The rifle in the concealed compartment was no use to him. Instead he sought out his only other armament, a broad-bladed, razor-edged knife in a metal sheath.

Concealing it in his waistband, he strolled back to the house, to exit via the kitchen door into the garage, which was on the north side of the house. Keeping the bulk of the building between himself and the distant barn, he strode out across the neighbouring fields till he hit the curving beck, in a direct line with the barn, and advanced through the shallow water till he was beyond the ruined building.

Now he climbed up the bank. If there was a watcher in the barn, his attention would be all on the house. He looked down the track which ran across fields to the road. There was no sign of the Mini where it had been parked earlier. He felt the beginnings of relief. But thoroughness required that he check out the barn, anyway. And after a few seconds of cautious approach, he could glimpse the metallic sheen of gold.

It took him another fifteen minutes to reach the trees. There was no sign of the driver, either here or in the barn which was some twenty yards away. He went forward to the car.

The doors were unlocked, ready for a quick getaway. He opened the driver's door very quietly and peered in. The Mini was the 1275 GT version, fitted with every refinement.

He tried the glove compartment. It fell open at his touch. He jerked back with a small gasp as tresses of ash-blond hair slithered out over his hand.

It was a wig. He draped it over his fist, trying to envisage the young profile he had glimpsed briefly as the mini overtook him. What was under the wig? A crew cut perhaps?

Then he saw it clearly. A gleaming razored skull with its arrogant, absurd coxcomb of bright orange spikes.

Adam. Adam the watcher, Adam who knew him, and who must have seen him.

It was time to get away from the mini. He gently closed the door. The click it made still seemed too loud, but it didn't matter anyway. Some instinct told him he was not alone.

"Please put your hands on top of the car, Mr. Jaysmith. And please don't make any sudden movement, I beg of you."

Slowly Jaysmith put his hands on top of the mini. And slowly he turned his head.

10

The young man was standing about twenty feet away. He wore a green and brown camouflage jacket with a matching hat. There were leaves on his shoulders and mud stains on his knees. He must have been lying there in some shallow fold of ground, completely unmoving, for God knows how long. It was a talent to be respected. As was the pistol he held in his hand.

It was a Heckler and Koch P9, which delivered 9mm Parabellum bullets at a muzzle velocity of 11,180 feet per second. Jaysmith's mind automatically recalled the technical information. It also registered that the weapon was levelled with professional steadiness at the centre of his chest.

"I saw you at the house," said Adam, touching with his free hand the field glasses which hung round his neck. "I saw you go out to the car twice. You went back inside the second time and then after a while I could see the young woman was getting worried about something. She went inside and when she came out, she shook her head at the old lady. And I began to wonder. So I came down from the barn and hid. And I was right."

"You didn't know I was at the house till you saw me, then?"

"No," said the young man, with an overtone of pain. "I didn't."

He doesn't want to believe I've turned traitor, thought Jaysmith. But he can't see any other explanation.

"What happens now?" he asked.

"I'm thinking about it," said Adam.

Jaysmith laughed. "Look, let's just sit down and talk around things. I'm not even armed!"

He stretched his arms to prove the point. Adam took a step back but still kept the HK P9 levelled. There was a noise somewhere over to their left.

"Someone's coming!" whispered Jaysmith urgently. "For God's sake, put that thing away!"

The gun vanished inside the combat jacket, but the hand went with it. Jaysmith walked round the car, looking at it admiringly.

"Nice little job," he said. "Though I bet it's heavy on petrol."

Joining in the game, Adam said, "Not really. It depends how you drive."

"I've seen how you drive," said Jaysmith. "You passed me this afternoon, didn't you know that?"

"No," admitted the young man. "I didn't notice. But I wasn't looking, was I?"

"No excuse!"

The noise came again, the crackling underfoot of twigs and dry leaves, accompanied almost simultaneously by a long *baa*.

"God! It's only a sheep!" laughed Jaysmith.

This time the young man turned his head. The sheep peered at them through the trees, a comic sight, and Adam laughed too, until he felt the knife blade at his throat.

"Pull the gun out slowly," said Jaysmith.

Nervously the young man began to withdraw his hand too quickly. The fine-edged blade nicked his skin.

"*Slowly*," said Jaysmith.

The gun crept into view.

"Drop it."

It fell to the earth.

"Now walk backwards with me. Good. Far enough. Now sit down, hands clasped beneath you. Excellent."

Adam sat in the required position and Jaysmith took four quick paces forward and scooped up the gun.

"Now let's take a walk. On your feet, but keep your hands clasped behind you. Let's get under cover, shall we?"

He urged Adam before him into the barn. Inside, it was dark and musty, a shaft of light falling through a hole in the roof. Jaysmith kept a safe distance behind the other, ordering him to sit down on his hands once more before he himself approached the seated man. With a deft flick, he cut the strap which held the field glasses and caught them as they fell.

Sheathing the knife, but keeping hold of the gun, he moved towards the loading-window which faced south towards Naddle Foot. "I have excellent peripheral vision," he said. "Don't stir."

He trained the glasses on the house.

The children were still playing in the back garden. There was no sign of Muriel Wilson or Bryant, but he could see Anya who was clearly supervising some team game. Her face, flushed with exertion and youthful with sharing her son's happiness, seemed almost incandescent in the golden heat of the autumn sun. He felt like an envious voyeur.

Adam interrupted his reverie. "Mr. Jaysmith, look, what *are* you doing in that house? Does Jacob know you're there?"

He sounded puzzled, but that could be part of an act.

"Don't muck me about, son," said Jaysmith wearily. "If Jacob knew I was there he'd have told you, wouldn't he? Let's concentrate on you. What the hell are *you* doing here?"

"I'm just observing. Jacob told me to keep an eye on the house, that's all."

"Balls," said Jaysmith. "I suppose you were just *observing* when you ran Bryant off the road last Sunday?"

"Yes, that's how it started," said Adam. "Jacob wanted Dave to come up last Saturday after he'd seen you on the Friday night, remember? But on Saturday morning Dave went down with flu and I was told to come instead, just to observe. I got up here on Saturday night and on Sunday I started watching. It was really dreadful weather, wasn't it?"

"Get on with it!" growled Jaysmith.

"Well, in the afternoon, first the woman left with the child. Then Bryant appeared. I followed him. He went along the main Penrith road and then turned off through a place called Dockray and down to Patterdale village. He went into a house and stayed there about an hour."

"And then?"

"When he came out he didn't go back the way he'd come but set out up Kirkstone Pass and down the other side into Ambleside. The visibility was absolutely dreadful. I was crawling along behind him when suddenly I got this brilliant idea. I thought here was the perfect chance to get rid of Bryant with no questions asked, and do myself a bit of good in Jacob's eyes too. So I accelerated past him and forced him through the wall. Unfortunately, before I could check he was dead I saw this other vehicle approaching, so I got out quick. I expected him to be dead. I rang Jacob and left a message telling him what had happened. When he rang back, he was furious. He'd found out Bryant was still alive and he wasn't happy!"

"What happened then?"

"I was told to get back down to London. Then on Thursday night Jacob said Bryant was out of hospital and I was to come back up here and start observing again. And almost the first thing I observed was you. Mr. Jaysmith, what *are* you up to?"

Jaysmith almost smiled at the note of pleading.

"That's for Jacob's ears alone," he said. "But if it's any comfort to you, I'm not in the employ of an enemy power or anything like that. I mean no one any harm. Now, let's go and find a telephone, shall we? I think the time has come for me and Jacob to talk."

He could see no alternative. It had to happen some time. His only real hope had been that Bryant was no longer targeted, but that was clearly a vain hope now. He had no desire to complicate matters further by using violence against any of Jacob's operatives unless absolutely forced to it. This was between Jacob and himself.

"Now that we've established that neither of us wants to harm the other, please may I have a cigarette?" said Adam.

"So you can harm yourself?" said Jaysmith. "Go ahead."

Adam smiled, and slowly produced a gold cigarette case and matching lighter. He went out first and Jaysmith followed. Outside the barn he tucked the HK P9 into his waistband under his shirt. He judged the danger of conflict was now past, but he was still careful to maintain a safe distance between them.

As Adam reached the Mini, he took a last drag at his cigarette and flicked it away. It landed in some dry bracken.

"Whoops, sorry," he said. "Mustn't set the place on fire, must I?" And he stooped to retrieve the glowing butt.

This totally natural hiatus in his progress brought Jaysmith close up behind him. Again, he had a split second's foreknowledge of what was going to happen. As Adam, half crouched, swung his elbow back into Jaysmith's crutch, the older man was already flinching away. It meant he took the blow in the groin rather than directly in the testicles. The result was agony, but not total immobilization, and through the pain he could still feel amazement at the young man's decision to attack. He fell heavily on his side and tried to roll away from the follow-up, but Adam hit him with his full body weight while his hands attempted to gouge his eyes.

He is serious, thought Jaysmith, shaking his head violently to keep the grasping fingers out of his eye sockets. He managed to roll over onto his left side and grasp the gun in his waistband. Adam rose up slightly and struck at his wrist, numbing it halfway up to the elbow. The gun was almost loose and now the young man grabbed for it and pulled it free. Jaysmith sought his intention in his face. All he could see was death. Given a few moments to reflect, to consider, the youth might see reason. But these few moments were not Jaysmith's to give.

Adam pulled himself up so that he was kneeling astride Jaysmith and could get a clear shot at his head. Rolling onto his back, Jaysmith lifted his right hand to cover his face.

"No!" he cried. It came out like a plea for mercy. An older adversary might have known that men like Jaysmith did not ask for mercy, might have recognized that it was merely a stratagem of delay. But Adam was a young man and for a moment he hesitated. Jaysmith's left hand found the haft of his knife and as Adam teetered on the edge of decision, the blade sliced up through his belly, beneath his rib cage and into his heart. For a few seconds his face twisted into a mask of almost comic betrayal, then the ruptured heart jetted blood over Jaysmith's hand and arm in its final spasm.

HE SAT ON THE GROUND for a long time, looking at the body by his side. This was the closest he had ever been to one of his killings. He knew now why he always went for the long kill.

At last he rose, and lifted the body and carried it to the car.

The boot of a Mini proved to be no place to stow a body. There was even less room than might have been expected. As in his own car there was a false panel which removed to reveal a hidden compartment. It contained a Heckler and Koch 33K rifle.

So much for Adam's claim that he was a mere observer. Jacob did not

340

issue weapons like this just in case his operatives fancied bagging a few pigeons. It made Jaysmith feel a little better, but not much.

Finally, after taking out the spare wheel, he got the body in. He removed the bloodstained sweater he was wearing, used it to clean up his hands, which were caked with blood, and tossed the garment into the boot with the body. So what if Jacob's men found it? He was a marked man anyway. His feet and the lower part of his trousers were still wet from the beck but fortunately the dark material did not show up the dampness very much. Despite the autumn sunshine, he found he was shivering.

He did a last check round, then got into the car and drove the half dozen miles to Keswick as fast as he could and put the car into the large and crowded car park behind the main street. He purchased the maximum ticket from a machine, stuck it on the windscreen, then walked swiftly away in search of a public phone box.

In the booth he hesitated. Twenty minutes ago he had been determined to contact Jacob and lay his cards on the table. But twenty minutes ago Adam had been alive. Now the case was altered. He needed more time to think.

He looked up "Taxis" in the directory and five minutes later he was on his way back to Naddle Foot. He glanced at his watch and was amazed to see that barely an hour had passed since he had left the house.

Barely an hour for him, but a lifetime for Adam.

He had hoped to enter the house unobserved but he was out of luck.

"And where have you been, young man?" demanded Miss Wilson.

She was standing in the doorway of the dining room. Behind her he could see a table loaded with delicacies. Before he could answer Anya appeared.

"Oh, you're back," she said indifferently.

"I'm sorry," said Jaysmith. "I got ... called away. What can I do to help?"

"Very little, now," she retorted frostily. "I've had to organize all the games, so Aunt Muriel's had to do all the work in here. Now it's all ready. You've timed your return perfectly."

"Don't be daft," said Miss Wilson. "Never cut off your nose to spite your face. Sit him at the table and put him in charge."

"Oh, all right," said Anya. "Think you can manage that?"

"I think so. I'll just have a quick clean-up first."

She studied him critically and said, "Yes, you look a bit dishevelled. Where's your sweater?"

"I must have left it somewhere," he said. "I got a bit warm. I won't be a minute."

He ran upstairs, away from her curiosity. When he descended a little while later, the boys were already gathering at the table.

"Here's Jay!" yelled a very excited Jimmy. "Where've you been, Jay? We've been playing with my gun and I told them you got ten out of ten and they wouldn't believe me. You did though, didn't you, Jay? You must be the best shot in the world!"

They'd had a practice session with the ping-pong gun after breakfast, when Jaysmith had discovered that up to about six yards it was fairly accurate. Jimmy had been hugely impressed.

Jaysmith took his place at the table and soon discovered that Anya's scheme to wear them out before tea had failed miserably. Team rivalries excited by their outdoor games continued, and disputes broke out which were usually settled either by missiles above, or wrestling bouts beneath, the table. His penance was extended to the post-prandial period when Anya announced that Uncle Jay had kindly agreed to entertain them with a few tricks. In revenge, after doing a couple of coin and card tricks, he contrived a Uri-Geller-type bending of a couple of teaspoons and soon had the whole group energetically assaulting the household cutlery.

"I'll make you pay for replacements," said Anya.

"No more than I deserve," he said.

"What did happen to you? Stage fright?"

"No. It was business. Someone turned up out of the blue. They must have found out at Parker's hotel that I was staying here. I didn't want to clutter up the house with my own affairs, not today, so I suggested we drive into Keswick and sort things out over a drink. Sorry, I should have told you I was going."

"No need. You're your own boss. Was it OK?"

"What?"

"The business."

She looked at him with a clear, deceit-challenging gaze.

"So-so," he said.

"Not a disaster then? He just got the sweater, not the shirt off your back? Oh *Andrew!*"

A plump red-faced boy who was a local farmer's son was proudly displaying a trifle ladle which had clearly been bent into horseshoe shape by main force.

Half an hour later the first parent arrived to collect her offspring, and another thirty minutes after that the last guest departed. Jaysmith went out into the garden to help Jimmy collect the scattered apparatus of play, then ran Aunt Muriel back to Grasmere.

THAT NIGHT, JIMMY TRIED to extend his birthday as long as possible, but sheer exhaustion defeated him in the end. "Goodnight then, Gramp. Goodnight, Jay," he said wearily, as his mother led him from the room. "Thanks a million."

The three adults ate a snack supper in the lounge and watched a film on television. Bryant was dozing off before the end. Awoken by the swell of music which signalled a happy ending, he announced that he was ready for his bed also.

"And then there were two," said Jaysmith, re-entering the lounge after helping Bryant up the stairs.

"One, soon," said Anya, yawning. "Fancy a nightcap?"

"Yes, please."

She poured him his customary whisky and water without further inquiry.

"I'm sorry if I sounded a bit testy this afternoon," she said.

"You had every right to."

"Not to treat you like the paid help, I didn't," she said.

"I hoped I was being treated like a friend who'd let you down," he answered.

She had finished her whisky and now rose and poured herself another. She seemed restless and nervy.

"Jimmy was asking me if we'd still be able to pay visits to Rigg Cottage," she said, "after you'd moved in, I mean. I said I thought you might tolerate him for a couple of minutes a month."

"I'd be delighted. And flattered."

"Don't be too flattered. There's a conker tree in the garden which he considers to be his own property."

"I see. And what about you? Would you still visit the cottage too?"

"I suppose so. I'd have to bring him, wouldn't I?"

He smiled ruefully. "I see that again I'm not to be flattered."

"No, I'm sorry, I didn't mean to sound rude ..."

She sounded flustered. He took a deep breath, rose, and went towards her. She pretended to think he wanted another drink and held the decanter before her like a buttress.

He said, "No, that's not what I want. Anya, listen, I'm sorry if this is too soon but ..."

She interrupted him, saying, "Pappy says he thinks you're getting interested in me."

He was taken aback. "You needed your father to tell you that?" he said.

"No! Of course not," she retorted with a flash of spirit.

"Well then," he said. He was standing very close.

She turned away from him, which seemed a perfect invitation to grasp her round the waist, but she twisted out of his hold. "Let's get one thing out of the way," she said in an unpromisingly harsh voice. "This 'too soon' business. Understand me, this isn't a promise, or a commitment, or even a postponement. It's merely to clear up what's becoming a tiresome assumption on your part and an oblique deception on mine. Edward died

344

almost a year ago ..." She turned now to face him. "But I am not still mourning his death," she went on. "In fact I don't think I have ever mourned it. I was *glad* my husband died; not wholly, but certainly *glad*. And while sometimes I can't deny that I've felt very guilty at feeling so glad, what I am definitely not is a grief-stricken widow!"

She banged the decanter down, finished her second drink and said, "Now I think I'll go to bed too, if you'll excuse me. You'll put the lights out and see the fire's safe, won't you?"

"Yes," he said. "I'll see the fire's safe."

As if taking her words literally, he sat for nearly two hours after she had left, watching the burning log decay until all that remained was a bed of dark-grey embers fretted with gold.

This he stirred once with the poker, then went to bed.

11

When he awoke the next morning Jaysmith lay for a while, expecting the despairing weight of his predicament to come crashing through the flimsy barrier of residual slumber. Instead, he found himself listening to the birdsong outside his window and finding pleasure in it. The *chook chook*— that was surely a blackbird; the gentle twittering song must come from the family of house martins he had noticed in the eaves; that rapid repetition of notes belonged to a song thrush; and more distantly came the unmistakable cawing of the rooks in the tall beeches near the road.

As he shaved he studied his face in the glass and with genuine bewilderment asked, "Who *are* you? *What* are you?"

Yesterday he'd killed a man and yet this morning he searched himself for remorse, for grief, for pity, and searched in vain.

Adam would be missed. Jacob would investigate, replacements would arrive, Jaysmith's involvement could not long remain hidden. After that, what? The most likely scenario would be for himself to be targeted alongside Bryant. Yet he felt no fear.

The truth was, he realized with amazement, he was hooked on happiness! Anya's words to him the previous night had given him a shot of hope. Grief, remorse, pity, fear—for the moment there was no room for these. It wasn't that they were absent, just that they were not wanted on this particular voyage.

Soon enough they would have to be unpacked. Soon enough.

After breakfast he drove in to Keswick to pick up newspapers for the household. Jimmy went with him. Jaysmith avoided the main car park but after they had got the papers and Jimmy had been provided with a huge chocolate ice-cream cone, he felt sufficiently secure among the already considerable press of tourists to stroll within sight of the car park. The yellow Mini was still there. As he returned to the BMW, he checked back a couple of times to see if there was any sign of a tail, but spotted nothing.

He felt uneasy at the thought of Anya and Jimmy being exposed to whatever threat hung over Bryant, and now himself, and though he was eager to find some time alone with Anya, he was as much relieved as disappointed when after lunch she told Jimmy to get ready for their Sunday visit to Great-Aunt Muriel in Grasmere.

"Do we have to go?" protested Jimmy. "I only saw her yesterday."

"That was special," said Anya firmly. "We always go to Grasmere on Sundays."

"And the old girl expects her pound of familial flesh," interposed Bryant sardonically.

Anya shot him a reproving glare and ushered Jimmy out of the room.

"What about you?" said Bryant. "Are you joining this dutiful expedition to Rigg Cottage?"

"Hardly," said Jaysmith. "I'm not invited, for a start."

"No. But the place is almost yours, isn't it?" said Bryant, surprisingly illogical for a lawyer. "And you seem to like the old bird."

"So I do," said Jaysmith. "You don't seem to be all that fond of her, though, or do I misinterpret?" Bryant's expression was not encouraging, but Jaysmith pressed on boldly. "Perhaps you didn't care for your son-in-law much. No one's said anything—it's just my guess that this is at the root of the antagonism between you and Miss Wilson. A clash of blood loyalties?"

"You're a sharp bastard, aren't you?" mocked Bryant, running his fingers through his halo of grey hair. "But even if you're right, it's still hardly reason enough for me to lay out my daughter's business before a stranger, is it?"

"Anya put me right on a couple of things last night. No details, but she made it plain that her memories of married life, her attitude to her husband's death were ... ambiguous. I'd like to know more, but I don't want to risk causing pain by probing. Anything you can tell me, anything which might help me to help ... You see, I love her," said Jaysmith flatly.

"*Love!* You've only known her a couple of weeks!"

"Nevertheless."

"And how does she feel about you?"

"It takes sharper eyes and a greater wit than I've got to know that," said Jaysmith. "What do you think?"

"I think nothing. But if she put you right about Edward, that must mean something," mused Bryant. Then he came to a decision. "All right, Hutton, I'll tell you what I can without breaking Anya's confidence. So, Edward Wilson. I never liked the man from the start. My daughter was eighteen, just finishing school, with a university place open for her in a good law faculty. I had high hopes for her, not just selfish hopes either. It was *her* future that seemed bright; it was *her* future that seemed in danger when she fell in love with Wilson. She was adamant that she was going to be married. Nothing I could say swayed her in the least. In the event, I walked her up the aisle and gave her away. I might as well have sold her into slavery. At least I'd have got a price!"

He spoke with such bitterness that Jaysmith was filled with alarm.

"For God's sake, what happened?" he demanded.

"I told you, I'm not breaking any confidences," said Bryant. "But what I saw with my own eyes I'll tell you. I saw a happy, laughing, open and confident child on the threshold of life turn gradually into a taciturn, reserved and introspective woman. She was a girl of such brightness, Hutton! Bright in thought, speech, movement, dress. And now there was none of this. It was early spring to late autumn with no summer between."

"But the boy—she must have had him very quickly. That must have helped?"

"In the first year," said Bryant. "And I suppose he helped from the point of view of company and occupation. But in real terms Jimmy's birth just bound her to Wilson even more, at first because she had a double loyalty now, to husband and her child's father, later because Wilson made it clear that if she went, he would do everything in his power to make certain Jimmy stayed."

"If she *went?* Then she was contemplating leaving him?"

"It came to that. That's when she spoke to me openly for the first time. I was away a lot in the early years of her marriage and perhaps didn't pay enough attention to what was going on."

"Away in Poland?"

"That's right."

And, of course, thought Jaysmith, once he became aware of Anya's problems, any thought of making a new life in Poland with Ota must have been put aside.

"You still haven't told me much about Edward Wilson," said Jaysmith.

"He is not a man I care to talk about," said Bryant. "He was a strange, solitary man, not unpersonable, not without charm. When he was a boy his life was divided between Grasmere, boarding school and visits to his doting father in London."

"You don't like the father either?"

"I met him at the wedding, at the christening and at the funeral. He struck me as a solitary, like his son, who'd put what few emotional resources he had into their relationship. No, I didn't care for the man. I think he would like to treat Jimmy in the same way if he could, but there's no chance of that. To get back to Edward, you know he was a climber?"

"I know he ended up at the foot of Pillar Rock with a broken back, and that he was a diabetic."

"That's right. For most sufferers these days it is merely a long-term inconvenience. But for Edward it struck at the most important area of his life, which was not, I assure you, his family or his profession. It meant the end of his career as an expeditionist, as it was too risky to take him on long and arduous expeditions. Edward Wilson wasn't a man to accept a secondary role. He severed all connections with official mountaineering bodies; he turned his back completely on the climbing fraternity and he became what I think he'd always been really, an utter loner. Everyone at the inquest knew that no other climber in the country would have been out alone in those conditions doing what he did."

"I see," said Jaysmith slowly. "But it's still odd he wasn't found for two days."

"Odd?" said Bryant sharply. "Not at all. No one was looking for him, so why should he be found? Anya was visiting me here. It wasn't till I took her back to the farmhouse that we realized Wilson was missing. She still feels guilty about that, of course. It's natural. But time will cure that, I know. It's been a slow change these past months, but she's coming out of it. Much more quickly in the last few weeks. That may be something to do with you, but any personable man showing an interest might have helped the process, particularly if he appeared mature, middle-aged, safe."

"That's how you see me, is it? said Jaysmith, smiling.

"No," said Bryant seriously. "I don't believe it's how *I* see you at all. But at least I can talk to you." He smiled widely. "There's a bottle of Islay malt in the sideboard. Why don't you fetch it and a couple of glasses?"

"Are we celebrating something?"

"Do we have anything to celebrate?"

"Hope," said Jaysmith.

"Yes. Perhaps you're right. *Nadzieja!*"

"What's that?"

"Hope in Polish. That's where my hope really lies, you see, Hutton. I've been thinking things out. There's a woman there ...."

"You'd go back to Poland? To live?" asked Jaysmith.

"I'd think about it, if once I was happy that Anya and Jimmy were in good hands," said Bryant.

Jaysmith raised his glass. "*Nadzieja*," he said.

The two men drank together.

THAT SUNDAY EVENING was one of the happiest Jaysmith had ever passed. Anya and Jimmy had returned from Grasmere after a pleasant visit, but not without relief at being home. They dined late, to let Aunt

Muriel's tea settle, and Jimmy inveigled Jaysmith into playing the video game his other grandfather had bought him for his birthday. It was a complex and highly expensive piece of equipment and Jimmy was delighted with it. He would have played all night, but Anya said, "We're eating soon, Jimmy, and you've still got some of your thankyou letters to write. Have you written to Grandad Wilson yet?"

"Don't need to," said Jimmy. "Can't I thank him when he comes?"

Bryant said without enthusiasm, "He's coming up, is he?"

Anya glanced at Jaysmith apologetically and said, "Aunt Muriel said he wanted to come up before the house sale went through. He doesn't really approve, I gather."

"Well, if he's got any ideas about stopping it, he's out of luck," said Bryant gleefully. "Contracts have been exchanged, finance is all tied up, not all the wheeling and dealing of Whitehall can stop Rigg Cottage becoming Jay's next week."

"Perhaps he just wants a last look at the place before it passes away from the family," said Anya.

"If it does," murmured Bryant slyly.

"Sorry, Pappy?"

But to Jaysmith's relief Bryant did not repeat his comment.

They had a casual meal, and after Anya had put her son to bed they sat at their ease before the crackling log fire and drank whisky and talked in a pleasant, desultory manner for another hour. The room was lit only by a single standard lamp and the fire's shifting glow. Bryant at last announced that he was for his bed. Jaysmith rose to help him and they slowly processed up the stairs.

When he came down again, Jaysmith found Anya kneeling before the fire with her arms outstretched as though embracing the heat.

"You'll ruin your skin," he said.

"Perhaps. But you wouldn't like a cold-hearted woman, would you?"

He knelt beside her, feeling awkward.

"Is that an invitation?" he asked, putting his arm round her waist.

"Is this an offer?" she replied.

He turned her towards him and kissed her. It was not an easy or elegant manoeuvre and after a few seconds she disengaged herself and pushed him away. For one chilling moment he thought she was going to resume her seat. Instead, she pulled a couple of cushions off the sofa, dropped them on the rug in front of the fire and lay back on them. He kissed her again and ran his hands over her small firm breasts beneath the fine woollen sweater. A convulsion ran the whole length of her body, and then her thin arms were round his neck, drawing him down with a strength which surprised him. She kissed him, wrapping her limbs around him as if intent on fusing their bodies together against all hope of separation. They struggled with each other's garments, and then the violence of their embrace was delayed no more.

Afterwards she lay quietly in his arms, and then began to cry. "I'm sorry," she said. "I'm sorry."

"Why?" he asked gently. "I mean, why do you cry?"

"Shame, I think. Something like that. Remembering. That's how it was with Edward in the beginning. And you're the only other man, ever."

They lay quietly for a while, deep in their separate yet parallel thoughts.

"You feel guilty about him, don't you?" said Jaysmith. "Tell me why."

She rose on one elbow. "It was after he found out about his diabetes that he changed," she said slowly. "After he found out that he wasn't going to be eligible for any more expeditions."

"Hardly your fault," said Jaysmith.

"I was all he had afterwards," she said fiercely. "I should have been able to offer . . . something."

"You were all he had because he chose that you should be, surely?" said Jaysmith. "Didn't he establish you in some out-of-the-way farmhouse before he found out about his illness? He obviously foresaw another twenty years of shooting off to the Himalayas or wherever, but it never crossed his mind that his wife might like to be living somewhere a little less isolated while he was away."

"I didn't mind the farmhouse. I helped choose it, after all. And to be alone with your husband never seems such a terrible prospect to a newly wedded wife, does it? But things change, in all kinds of ways. I had Jimmy, and right from the start, I found Edward's attitude . . . disturbing. He was very proud of Jimmy, I could tell that, but very resentful of anyone else having much to do with him. And almost as soon as he could walk, Edward was wanting to take him out on the fells. I put my foot down. Besides, I was already getting worried about the kind of expeditions Edward was making by himself. He used to tell me about some of them at first, but when I protested about the danger he was putting himself in, almost wilfully it seemed, he stopped telling me. Another failure, you see."

"You're a real sin-eater, aren't you?" observed Jaysmith. "And what was his reaction when you got between him and Jimmy?"

She didn't reply.

"So he hit you," said Jaysmith. "Often?"

"I didn't say anything about him hitting me!" she protested. "He wasn't really a violent man. He did strike me, occasionally, but never more than one blow."

"Moderation in all things! But you got to the point of wanting to leave him, despite his moderate behaviour?"

"Did Pappy tell you that?"

"He told me you were staying here when your husband was killed."

350

"That's true," said Anya. "In the middle of last December, Pappy announced he was giving a party the Saturday before Christmas and asked me to help with the preparations and be hostess. He invited Edward to the party, but Edward, of course, refused. Pappy came to pick us up on the Friday, just to be sure, I suppose. I took Jimmy with me. Edward didn't care for that, but I told him straight that I wasn't leaving the boy in the farmhouse."

"I suppose he suspected you might be going to bolt?" said Jaysmith.

"He asked me that. I told him I wasn't. He trusted me."

"All the same, it might have been a good opportunity. What did your father say?"

"He asked the same question, as soon as we got back here. I just told him nothing had changed, I wasn't running and I wasn't risking losing Jimmy. He didn't persist. I loved being busy preparing for the party, and it was all a tremendous success. But come Sunday, I said it was time I was getting back. Thank God I did. I couldn't have lived with myself if I'd made up my mind to leave Edward and then found out later what had happened!"

"You seem to have accepted pretty full responsibility as it is," remarked Jaysmith. "But come on, don't stop now. All or nothing."

"It was mid-afternoon when we reached the farm, but the weather was so foul it was dark already. There were no lights on, no fires. It was clear to me at a glance that the place had been empty for twenty-four hours at least. I looked for Edward's climbing gear. When I saw it was gone, we called out the mountain rescue. They set out that evening but with the weather like it was there wasn't much hope of finding him then, and it was Monday morning before they spotted him. He was deep in coma by then and he died within hours of getting to hospital. His back was broken too, so it was probably for the best. They were kind at the inquest. They called it misadventure. But I knew better."

"Why? What did you know?"

She stared at him, her brown eyes filled once more with that intense feeling he had first mistaken for grief, but now knew was guilt.

"He'd been looking for death every time he went out on those solo climbs," she stated flatly. "But so far, despite all the dangers, his skill had always won. This time he stacked the odds against himself. He didn't go into a coma because he was lying out there among the rocks without insulin. He fell among the rocks because he went into a coma. I know. I checked the ampoules later. He deliberately didn't inject himself before he went out on the Saturday."

"But you can't be certain it was deliberate," protested Jaysmith. "Perhaps he just forgot."

"That would be bad enough," she said. "But I'm sure it was deliberate."

"Why? Because that makes you feel more guilty?" said Jaysmith angrily. A hundred refuting arguments rose in his mind, but he voiced none of them. "I'm glad the bastard's dead!" he said vehemently.

"What do you mean?"

"I want you to be free of him," he stated with simple force. "I want you!"

"It was my firm impression you'd just had me," she said.

"I want more than that," he said. "I want everything about you, and I want it on a permanent basis!"

He spoke with an intensity that clearly impressed her.

"We'll see," she said, rising. "I'll make us a pot of coffee, I think."

He stared up at the long slim legs and the curve of the boyish buttocks and he reached out and grasped her wrist.

"No," he said.

"No?"

He drew her down towards him once more.

12

Next morning he was awoken by the rattle of wind in the old sash window of his bedroom. Summer had gone again. The sky was a shifting patchwork of greys, and round the beeches in the garden swirls of bright leaves were dancing a mournful morris. He stood by the window and watched them and felt his thoughts scatter around his mind as drily and as pointlessly.

Last night it had been different. They had not shared a bed. No promises were asked and none were spoken, but promises had been made in every touch and breath and silence, promises which he now knew he'd had no right to make. Last night, everything had seemed possible. He could tell her the truth. Or he could keep silent and become Jay Hutton permanently. Either way, confessing or silent, he had felt utterly confident of waking this morning and finding a solution under his pillow.

Now he stood and watched the death-dance of the leaves and knew that there was only one faint hope of a solution. He had to talk to Jacob. He must attempt to persuade Jacob to abort. Why was Bryant targeted anyway? What was the man supposed to have done? He was a simple country solicitor, half retired; what *could* he have done? There must have been a mistake ...

With a groan he acknowledged the futility of this line of thought. The best he could reasonably hope for from Jacob was a reassurance, in acknowledgment of his own long and efficient service, that Anya and the boy would in no way be endangered by the removal of Bryant.

And Adam's body lay between him and even that basic assurance.

Breakfast, despite Jaysmith's inner sombreness, was a gay meal. Anya was alight with a happiness which shone out in her speech and movements. Bryant observed, guessed the cause, and showed his own pleasure in a kind of sly avuncularity which might have amused Jaysmith in another place, another time. He felt obliged to volunteer to take Bryant for his hospital appointment, but was relieved when Anya firmly insisted that she was taking him.

"I want to hear what they've got to say for myself," she said. "Otherwise I'll just get a load of nonsense. Come on, Pappy. We'd better be on our way. We don't want to be late."

AFTER THEY'D GONE he went out to the BMW. He could have telephoned from the house now it was empty, but somehow he felt uneasy at the thought of dialling that number on Anya's phone. Besides, he had another reason for wanting to visit Keswick. He wanted to check on Adam.

By contrast with the tourist bustle of the previous morning, the streets were almost empty this morning. There were still quite a lot of cars in the main car park, but the yellow Mini was not among them.

He went into the Royal Oak Hotel on the main street and ordered a pot of coffee. While it was coming he went to the public telephone and dialled the London number.

There was no ringing tone, only a single highpitched note. He tried again, then dialled the operator and asked him to try. After a few moments the man said, "I'm afraid that number is out of service, sir. If you'll tell me who you're trying to ring, I'll check if there's another number listed for them."

"That's OK," said Jaysmith, and replaced the receiver.

As he drove back to Naddle Foot he was still assessing the implications of the cancelled number. By now, Jacob must know of his involvement. If he knew that and was not interested in making contact, then the obvious decision must have been taken—to target him also.

Why not? His protection of Bryant, his killing of Adam, could mean only one thing in Jacob's eyes—that he had gone over to the other side, to Bryant's masters, whoever they were.

He pulled into the side of the road and watched the traffic go by. There was no suspicious slowing of any vehicle as it passed. He started the car again and drove on.

As he travelled up the drive to the house, all looked still, but as he parked before the front door, he thought he saw in the rear-view mirror a shift in the light-catching planes of a huge hollybush at the edge of the garden. He got out of the car, ran lightly up the steps, opened the front door and stepped inside. Pausing only to switch off the alarm system, he went straight through the kitchen and out of the back door, his hand on the HK P9 inside the windcheater he was wearing.

As he entered the shrubbery which ran alongside the house and began to make his way towards the front garden with great stealth, he saw through the screen of leaves and branches ahead a more solid area, vague at first, emerging to form the shape of a man.

Drawing the gun, Jaysmith advanced. Alerted by the telltale rustle of leaves, the man turned, saw him, and started to run.

"Stop!" yelled Jaysmith, bringing the gun up in the two-handed aim position. The man's foot skidded on the dewglossed grass and he crashed down onto his hands and knees.

"Hold it there!" commanded Jaysmith. "Don't move!"

The man, who was wearing an expensive dark-grey Crombie and a matching Homburg which had slipped over his forehead as he fell, stood up, adjusting his hat and brushing at his knees.

"For heaven's sake, Mr. Wainwright," he said wearily, "neither of us is going to harm the other, so why not put that thing away?"

Jaysmith found himself looking into the face of Anton Ford.

WITH THE GUN FIRMLY PRESSED against Ford's spine, Jaysmith ran his free hand over, then under, the grey coat but found no weapon.

"Right, let's go inside," he said.

"I'll be glad to. This damp grass isn't doing my shoes any good."

The shoes had been designed for elegance rather than athletics and were showing the strain. Inside, Ford removed his overcoat to reveal a dark-blue mohair suit. He tossed his coat over the back of the sofa, sat down, and examined his knees.

"Grass stains," he said, with annoyance. "I hope the dry cleaner can deal with them."

Jaysmith had put the gun away, but left the safety off. He now sat down also, a safe distance away, and said, "What are you doing here, Mr. Ford?"

He kept his voice harsh and aggressive, but in truth he was bewildered. Ford's expensive clothing and lack of armament did not chime with his being here as one of Jacob's service crowd. And what was it the man had called him—Wainwright? That was the name he'd given when he first met Ford in Manchester. Why was he using it now?

"I suppose I *could* say I was house-hunting," said Ford, his weathered boxer's face creasing momentarily into a smile. "But that's never very convincing, is it?" He seemed perfectly at ease, but the fingers of his right hand were plucking nervously at the gold identity bracelet round his left wrist.

"What *are* you doing here?" repeated Jaysmith.

The mask dropped suddenly. "What the hell do you imagine I'm doing here?" Ford demanded. "I had to find out for myself, didn't I? I mean, I can't believe it, that's the top and bottom of it. I know that someone's said that about every traitor ever unmasked, but the fact remains it's true, and I can't, not till he tells me himself!"

Jaysmith kept his face blank as his mind raced to fit together the implications of this.

"I don't see why it should be such a trouble to you." he said.

"You don't see?" growled Ford, his skin flushing a pinkish red. "What kind of a man are you? It's me who's going to have to tell Ota, isn't it?"

"Ota?" said Jaysmith. "And why should that bother you?"

Ford looked both angry and amazed.

"Why should it bother me?" he demanded. "You mean it wouldn't bother you to have to tell your own sister that the man she's in love with has sold out everything she ever believed in?"

His sister! Jaysmith cast his mind back to their first encounter. His elder sister (Urszula, wasn't it?) had gone back to Poland with his father, married, had five children, was widowed. And Urszula was Ota! No wonder Ford had been ready to bear messages for her, and probably to her as well.

Yet there had to be more. He said cautiously, "Doesn't the evidence speak for itself?"

"Evidence? You mean Tusar's arrest? That was always on the cards. The man was a drunk. Every UBEK agent in Krakow must have heard him shooting his mouth off about the government at some time or other. As for Lomnicki ..."

He paused. Jaysmith prompted him, "Yes, go on. And how did they know enough to arrest Lomnicki?"

He knew instantly he'd made a mistake.

"Arrest? Why do you say *arrest* when you know they shot him down in cold blood?" Half rising, Ford demanded, "Who the hell are you, Wainwright?"

"Sit down!" commanded Jaysmith, producing the pistol again. Slowly Ford subsided, and with a sigh Jaysmith eased the gun back into his pocket.

"OK," he said, "you're right. I don't understand half of what you're telling me. But I'd be very grateful if you'd explain. What about a whisky? I'm sure Bryant wouldn't object."

The ease with which he found the bottle and the glasses relaxed Ford even more than the disappearance of the gun, but there was still suspicion in his voice as he said, "If you're not one of Jacob's men, who are you? You're not with the others, are you?"

Jaysmith handed him a glass of whisky and smiled. "Hardly," he said.

"If I were UBEK or KGB, I'd know all about Lomnicki, wouldn't I? No, I'm a friend of Bryant's. Sorry, let me correct that. I'm a friend of Anya's. A close friend."

"Of Stefan's daughter?"

"That's right. You know her?"

"I have never met her," said Ford, frowning. "I have only been here a couple of times before and then she was married and living elsewhere."

"Didn't Bryant talk about her?"

"Very little. To tell the truth, he talked very little about himself."

"Yet you feel you know him well enough to be convinced he is innocent?"

Ford's face darkened. "I know my sister."

Jaysmith said, "Mr. Ford, let me put my cards on the table. I'm in love with Anya. By chance I discovered that her father was in danger and that it seemed to have something to do with his visits to Poland. I got your name and address from the covering note with some letters you forwarded. I was, I still am, eager to protect Bryant, for his daughter's sake more than his own, I freely admit. Please will you tell me what you can to help me help him. I am no one's man, but I am not without influence."

Ford's face was still stony with suspicion. Jaysmith added urgently, "Look, Ford, I know enough already about you. I know you're a courier, I know that you work for Jacob ..."

"Jacob? Who works for Jacob? Not me. I've never met him in my life, though I've heard enough about the bastard!"

"But Bryant deals direct with Jacob. I overheard them talking together on the phone here."

"Did you? That surprises me. He must be in real trouble then. But how the hell do you know what Jacob's voice sounds like?"

"I heard Bryant use the name, that's all," lied Jaysmith. "And it was what this man Jacob was saying that made me realize Bryant was threatened."

This flimsy piece of extemporization seemed to convince Ford. The tension left his body and he held out his glass for more whisky.

Jaysmith poured and said casually, "So. You're a courier, are you?"

Ford smiled wanly and said, "So much for secret service! All right. That's what I am, from time to time, from place to place. And Stefan, he's even less. That's what makes all this business so stupid!"

The floodgates were now open and he spoke freely. He had been recruited in the early seventies via another Polish expatriate whose attention had been attracted by Ford's strong anti-communist attitudes plus the ready access his job as a drug company salesman gave him to eastern Europe.

"I carry things, that's all. What I carry, I often do not know. What's it matter? I'm told it will help in the anti-Russian struggle, and that's quite enough for me."

"How did you meet Bryant?" Jaysmith asked.

"I didn't. Urszula did."

"You mean Ota."

"That was a family nickname. Her second name's Dorota, and Ota was the best she could manage as a child. When she got older, she insisted on being called Urszula. That's when I got worried, when I went to visit her and met this stranger she allowed to call her Ota!"

"How had they met?"

"She works in the university library in Krakow. Stefan had permission to use its facilities for research into some book he's writing. It was a common interest, the identity of Poland or some such thing."

"You say you got worried. Why?"

"It's a neurotic country, Poland," said Ford gloomily. "You suspect everything. The thing was Ota—Urszula—was getting more and more involved with the protest movement. I won't deny there was a selfish side to my concern. If Urszula drew UBEK's attention to herself, they were certainly going to be interested in her young brother with a British passport, too. So when I saw how friendly she and this Stefan Bryant were becoming I passed his name on to my London control and suggested they should check."

"And the result?"

"The good news was that he was absolutely clear. The bad news was that he'd actually done some undercover work with the SOE during the war, and someone then got the bright idea of recruiting him into the courier service too. So all I'd managed to do to protect my sister was to get the man she was involved with into the same dangerous game as myself."

"And how much actual responsibility did—does—Bryant have?"

"As little as me," shrugged Ford. "Less. He works purely into Poland while I'm much more general. A mere message carrier, or at the most the occasional parcel."

"Then how does it come about that a mere messenger can be marked out as a traitor responsible for the betrayal and deaths of important people?" mused Jaysmith.

"It's just not possible!" proclaimed Ford. "I refuse to believe it!"

His vehemence surprised Jaysmith. Then it hit him.

"It's Urszula you're bothered about, isn't it?" he said. "The only real access to information that he would have must be Urszula. In fact his only known contact with Poland during the past year has been these letters you brought back for him from Urszula."

"There was nothing in them. Nothing!" protested Ford. "I read them. They are love letters, nothing more, nothing less!"

Jaysmith hastily poured some more whisky. "Who told you what was happening?" he asked.

"A friend in London. He works at the control bureau. He visited me yesterday afternoon on another matter to do with my next visit to Poland. During the conversation he suggested I would be wise not to try to see Bryant before I left ..."

"Were you planning to?" demanded Jaysmith.

"I'd already telephoned him, yesterday morning," said Ford. "To ask if he had any letters he wished me to take to Urszula. He has not seen her for nearly a year, you know."

"And did he have a letter?"

"Yes. Also he told me about this accident. I said I would come to see him next weekend, before I went, so that I could pick up the letter and be able to give Urszula a firsthand report on how he looked."

"And yesterday afternoon you were warned off," mused Jaysmith. He'd been right not to trust the telephones in Naddle Foot. They must be bugged.

"What did your friend say?" he asked.

"Very little at first. He tried to give the impression it was just a routine checkup. But I remembered the other time they'd checked on him and I got angry and told him I would go to see Stefan anyway, and then he told me how serious it was. I couldn't believe it. I *know* my sister could not be involved in such a thing; I was almost as certain of Stefan too. I had to speak to him, and I didn't dare use the phone."

"So you drove up to see him."

"What else could I do?" protested Ford. "I parked a long way down the road in case anyone was watching. And I pulled this absurd old hat down over my eyes and wrapped a scarf round my face."

"And when you heard my car approaching, you hid," mocked Jaysmith gently.

"I am not a secret agent like in the thrillers, Mr. Wainwright," said Ford, not without dignity. "The risks I take are a smuggler's risks: knowing when to smile at customs officials, when to be indignant. I carry no weapons, have no expertise in kung-fu, would probably have a heart attack if I had to run a hundred yards. Of course I bloody well hid!"

"Just now, when you said that your London friend tried to give the impression it was just a routine security check on Bryant, you remembered another check. When was that?"

"About six months ago. It happens to all of us from time to time." He laughed. "That's what I thought you were doing when we first met, Mr. Wainwright. I didn't like the sound of those questions about the neighbours you'd been asking poor Wendy Denver. Then I left you in my house alone. I have a security camera hidden in my study, you know. I

358

checked when I came back and there you were, rummaging around. I nearly challenged you there and then!"

"Tell me about this check on Bryant," said Jaysmith.

"At the time it seemed straightforward enough. Two men called on me at my office. They were quite open. They showed me their credentials, and said it was just a routine check on Bryant. They started by asking about Stefan's relationship with my sister."

"Did that surprise you?"

Ford shrugged. "It's their business to know such things, but I knew that Stefan and Urszula had kept their affair very quiet from the start. And once Stefan began to work as a courier, they had a double reason to keep a low profile. But like I say, it's hard to keep anything from the Service. What did bother me was that they knew about the letters. Technically I should have mentioned in my reports that I was carrying letters between the two of them, but it was a private matter, a family matter, so I hadn't bothered. Yet somehow, God knows how, they knew."

"And were you reprimanded?"

"Obliquely. It was suggested that I ought now to be completely open."

"They didn't seem too bothered about the letters, then?"

"No. In fact they told me specifically it was OK to carry them."

"These two men, what were they like?"

"Like? Well, youngish. One was blond, a good-looking young chap. The other wasn't quite so young, long black hair, one of those stubbly beards, nose a bit twisted, as though someone had broken it for him."

Adam and Davey! No simple security vetters these, but Jacob's men. Jaysmith glanced towards the window. Time was passing.

"What did they ask about Bryant?" he pursued.

"They just made me go back over every contact I'd had with him for almost a year," said Ford.

"Was there anything in particular that might have interested them?"

"Maybe one thing," said Ford slowly. "About six months earlier, that is a year ago from now, Stefan had got in touch. He was going to Poland in a short time. That was his last visit as it turned out. Anyway, he asked if I could do something for him in my capacity as a drug salesman. Someone over there in Krakow had asked for it specially."

"What was it?" interrupted Jaysmith.

"It was one of my firm's packs of insulin capsules," said Ford. "The men questioning me didn't seem all that interested in this, but I had to mention it, of course. For all I knew, Stefan had told them already. But, as I explained, there was no danger. Even if Polish customs spotted them, all that Stefan had to do was say he was a diabetic. *What's that?*"

Jaysmith had heard the sound a moment earlier but he had been so riveted by what Ford was telling him that he had ignored it.

"It's a car," he said. "It sounds like Anya's Fiat. You'd better be on your way."

"Why?" demanded the other in surprise.

Jaysmith frowned. He had a dozen reasons for not wanting Ford and Bryant to talk just now. "Trust me," he said. "It's better this way. For Stefan and Anya, I mean. I'll get in touch in a day or two and put you in the picture, I promise."

Ford hesitated.

"There is no way your sister can be involved in any of this, believe me," Jaysmith went on slowly. "Jacob's seen the letters. He'll have had them analysed upside down and sideways. Urszula's completely clear."

Even as he infused the lie with sincerity, he realized he was probably telling at least part of the truth. Hadn't Anya said there'd been a burglary a few months earlier as a result of which they'd got the alarm system fitted? It must have been Jacob's men, already looking for evidence of Bryant's treachery. And all they had found had been the letters, which they had photographed for closer study. For what reason had Bryant's name gone on the target list? And why not just arrest him and squeeze everything he knew out of him?

Unless of course it was all part of some great bluff and Bryant's killing was to appear someone else's responsibility.

Ford came to a decision. "All right," he said. "You be in touch."

They heard the front door open and Anya's voice calling, "Jay! We're back."

"In here," called Jaysmith.

Ford went through the French windows into the garden. Anya came into the lounge and Jaysmith went towards her to make sure she was delayed sufficiently for Ford to get clear. She came into his arms with a movement so natural that he felt a surge of shame at his own duplicity.

13

That night Anya came openly to his room, only insisting that her alarm clock be set for six o'clock so that she could be back in her own bed before Jimmy woke.

The checkup at the hospital had gone well. Bryant was mending, there were no complications, the prognosis was a full recovery in a matter of months. Bryant himself was visibly lightened by the news. As for Anya, her delight was manifest in her every word and movement during the evening, and the promise of pleasure she gave him whenever their eyes met or hands brushed was paid in triple measure from the moment the bedroom door closed and he folded her tenderly to him.

They slept. Later he awoke and lay in the darkness, recalling their mutual pleasure. If news of her father's expected progress towards recovery could bring her to such a pitch of joy, into what depths of pain and despair would his death plunge her? Ford's visit had told him as much as he was likely to find out about Bryant's "crime". He had to act on what he knew now, and the alternatives were few and unattractive.

Sleep did not return to him that night and when the alarm began to shrill at six o'clock, his hand had muffled it in a moment. But she was awake already, stretching sensuously.

"Oh God," she said, "I'm so happy."

Then she slipped out of his arms and bed, picked up her wrap and pulled it with coquettish slowness around her shoulders, laughing at his expression.

"There'll come a time when you'd prefer a cup of tea and the morning paper!" she said. "See you at breakfast."

After the door had closed behind her, he rose and went to the window. The sky was blue, but pale as a marsh forget-me-not fast fading in the summer's drought. The fell tops were clear. He raised his eyes to them and felt a surge of longing, almost sexual in its intensity, to be up there, to be walking with the wind on his face and his mind clear of all past guilt and future care.

He had fallen in love with more than a woman, he told himself, wonderingly. He had fallen in love with a landscape too. The two were linked in a way he did not attempt to analyse further than by saying that the woman he wanted was here, and the place he wanted to be with that woman was here also.

He turned from the window and sat on the bed. The courses open to him were indeed few. He could concentrate either on getting Bryant out of harm's way or on persuading Jacob to de-target him. To get Bryant out of the way would mean revealing himself to the man. It would almost certainly mean revealing himself to Anya also, for, however Bryant might feel about entrusting his own safety to the hands of a self-confessed professional assassin, he was certainly not going to trust his daughter's future to those same polluted hands.

But now things had changed. Anton Ford had done more than give the background of why Bryant should be a security target. He had unconsciously dropped into Jaysmith's lap a weapon to make the solicitor malleable and keep him silent.

Stefan Bryant, a few weeks before Edward Wilson's death, had obtained a pack of insulin ampoules from Anton Ford. Suppose he had doctored them so that their contents were diluted or completely useless. Suppose, driven by rage at Anya's unhappiness, guilt at his own imagined neglect at letting it happen, and despair at her inability to break out of it, he had substituted this dud pack for a real one when he collected Anya to host his Christmas party.

Did Bryant have it in him to be so ruthless? It was Jaysmith's reading of the man that he did. His wartime experience proved he had the nerve and the stomach for it, if the cause were right. And how much righter a cause can a man have than his child's happiness?

If Bryant had set out to kill his son-in-law, then the threat of having this revealed to Anya would be a powerful weapon. And yet it was a weapon that Jaysmith felt the strongest revulsion against using. No; it would be a last resort. His mind was made up. Somehow or other he would contact Jacob and ask for a parley.

But he would not go empty-handed to the conference table.

He had a writing case with him. He took out some sheets of paper and spent the next half hour covering them with his small, neat handwriting. By the time he'd finished, there were sounds of life in the house: taps running, Anya's voice urging Jimmy to hurry, the boy's footsteps accelerating to their normal breakneck pace.

On his way downstairs Jaysmith looked in on Bryant. "Can I use your copier? I noticed you had one in your study," he asked.

"Did you? Quite the lynx-eyed detective, aren't you?" growled Bryant. "Well, what you didn't notice was that since Friday when Anya used it to run some things off for Jimmy's party, it's not been working. You want to watch that girl, Hutton. What she touches often seems to fall apart."

"Does it? She must have had her hands on your temper this morning then," said Jaysmith with a smile. "Is there a photocopying shop in Keswick, do you know?"

"No idea," grunted Bryant and then, as if to make amends for his surliness, added, "But there's a machine in my office. Use that if you like."

"That's kind of you, I will," said Jaysmith.

He left for Keswick straight after breakfast. It had been a comfortable domestic meal with the pair of them very much at ease with one another.

"We're like an old married couple," he said as she accompanied him to the door. "Little wife seeing hardworking hubby off to the City."

He accompanied his remark with a satirical peck on the cheek but she fastened her arms round his neck and kissed him so hard that he tasted blood when they broke apart.

"You did that like it was the last time," he said. "Much harder, and it might have been."

She didn't respond to his smile but said seriously, "There's something about you, Jay, which makes every time feel like the last time. You're not going to run out on me, are you?"

"Jilt you, you mean?" he said, still aiming at lightness. "You can always do me for breach of promise!"

"Seriously, Jay," she said steadily. "This is for real, isn't it? We're going to last?"

"It's for real," he said. "Whatever happens, never doubt that, my love. I haven't loved anyone for twenty years. She was the first and she died. Now there's you. You're the last, Anya. After you, no one, nothing. This is for ever."

He kissed her again passionately. Suddenly he too felt her sense of finality, as if it had been contagious. But it was absurd. He was only going to Keswick.

"See you later," he said, smiling. And left.

JAYSMITH DID NOT DRIVE direct to the solicitor's office. There was something else he had to do first. He skirted Keswick and turned south on the road into Borrowdale. After a couple of miles he turned left and began to climb, crossing the picturesque hump of Ashness Bridge and turning off the road into the trees half a mile further along. There were no other cars yet and no sign of anyone on foot.

He opened the boot, unclipped the false bottom and took out the rucksack which contained the M21. Assembling it, he found the target he was looking for, the trunk of a fallen tree resting against a grassy bank. He began to pump shots into the decaying wood. It took just a few minutes to dig the bullets out with the short-handled spade he had brought from the car.

Ten minutes later he was crossing Ashness Bridge once more. He parked in Keswick, not far from where he had left Adam's Mini. On his way to the solicitor's office he stopped at a stationer's and bought several small padded envelopes and a couple of large ones.

Donald Grose was not in, but the pretty young secretary smiled at him and said, "There you are, Mr. Hutton. Mr. Bryant phoned to say you'd be coming in to use the copier."

And probably thus told Jacob too. Not that it mattered. By the time the message got to London and its significance was analysed, even if they guessed at the truth it would be far too late. And in any case Jacob would know soon enough.

The copying did not take long. With the girl's permission he went into Bryant's little-used office and prepared his packages, filling them and printing the address neatly in black ink. Finally he put half the small packages in one of the large padded envelopes, and the rest in the other. As he finished, the door opened and the girl appeared.

"It's Miss Wilson for you, Mr. Hutton. I'll put it through here, shall I?"

He waited till she had closed the door, and lifted the phone.

"Mr. Hutton?" said Miss Wilson's unmistakable voice. "I rang you at Naddle Foot and Annie said I'd catch you here. It's about furniture. I've worked out what I can fit into Betty Craik's old house and that leaves quite a lot of stuff I can't take with me, large items mainly. There's the kitchen dresser, for instance, and a big chest of drawers in me bedroom. I thought I'd give you first refusal before going to the trouble of shifting them to a saleroom. Are you interested?'' She was as abrupt and direct as ever.

"Yes," said Jaysmith, knowing he was really saying yes to a dream of normality, yes to the hope of a settled future.

He looked at the pair of bulky envelopes he held in his hand. Threats were useless unless their object knew he was being threatened. He picked up the phone again and tried the old London number. All that sounded was the unobtainable tone.

And then he laughed out loud and said, "Idiot!" There was an obvious and direct line to Jacob under his nose.

He dialled Naddle Foot. Anya answered. "Hi," he said. "Listen. Aunt Muriel got through to me. There's some furniture she thinks I might like to buy. I'd like to look, so I'd better excuse myself for lunch and hope to get back this afternoon."

"I'll do my best to survive," she said lightly.

"You do that. Oh, by the way, I seem to have mislaid my wallet. I think I may have left it on the dressing table in my bedroom. Could you check for me?"

"Hang on."

He waited till he heard her footsteps running lightly up the stairs, then he said harshly, "Tell Jacob I want to talk. Tell him, any action before we talk and he'll regret it. He'd better believe it! Tell him I'll be in the bar at the Crag Hotel in Grasmere between twelve thirty and one. He can ring me there. Tell him to ask for Mr. Hutton."

He heard Anya's footsteps returning.

"Jay? Sorry, it's not there," she said anxiously.

"It's OK," he laughed. "I've found it. It had slipped down the lining in my jacket somehow. There must be a tear."

"You need looking after," she answered.

"Oh yes, I do," he said, "I really do."

As he drove through Grasmere, the threat of deterioration in the weather was fast being realized. The sun still shone in the eastern sky, but the wash of cornflower blue was now smeared by high trails of clouds and over the western fells a heavy mist was advancing. The lake's surface was like grey skin, wrinkled by the chilling wind which at every gasp stripped the remaining leaves from the trees.

Jaysmith had posted his packages in Keswick before leaving. At the very least they should give him a breathing space, and in such a space, surely an accommodation could be reached? But it wouldn't be easy.

Under threat, Jacob might stay his hand, but it would take more than a mere threat to persuade him to reverse the target directive. What he couldn't believe was that Jacob would have targeted Bryant on the flimsy evidence that he himself had now had a chance to consider. Bryant hadn't been anywhere near Poland for a year; his only communication had been with Urszula, via Anton Ford. Why on earth should Urszula send information to him in this way? No, it made no sense. God knew what as-yet-unrevealed evidence of Bryant's guilt Jacob had at his disposal. And no one knew better than himself just how ruthlessly Bryant was capable of acting if he thought that those he loved were being threatened. At least Jacob could have no suspicion of that!

Jaysmith was suddenly filled with frustration. What was the point of parleying with Jacob? Providing a negative was never easy, not unless you had a positive to balance it out. And what did he have to offer? Nothing!

Or did he? He had a name, at least: Ford.

Ford! Jaysmith's mind began to race.

If Bryant was pressurable by threats to Urszula, then so was Ford. If Urszula was going to talk freely of her work with Solidarity to Bryant then why not to Ford? And who was it that had still been visiting Poland, still seeing Urszula? Ford. Ford whose concern for Bryant might seem exaggerated unless you saw it as a reaction to what must have been a devastating onslaught of guilt, as he realized that the sister he was protecting by his acts of treachery was indirectly going to have her life destroyed by them.

It made such sense that he could not see how he had missed it till now, but he was glad he had, for that made it more believable that Jacob and his men had missed it too.

Buoyant once more, he turned into the driveway of Rigg Cottage and, stepping out of his car, stretched his arms and turned his face upwards to the watery glow in the grey sky.

"It's a bit late to be looking for broken tiles," said Miss Wilson sharply from the entrance porch. "Come you in, before I catch my death."

He entered and felt at once a sense of comfortable homecoming. Despite her businesslike approach, the old lady did not ignore the social niceties and there was a pot of tea to be drunk and some freshly baked shortbread to be eaten before the inspection began.

The old lady had been meticulous in her preparations for her imminent move. Every article was labelled. Those she was taking with her all had her new address on them, plus the room into which they were to go. Of the rest, some pieces were labelled *James*, and *Annie*, and the remainder had blank labels attached. Miss Wilson also provided a check sheet on which the saleroom valuer had indicated his estimate of the likely fetching price of each item.

"It'll be low," she averred. "They'll not raise a body's expectations, and likely they'll have some of their own contacts looking to buy up cheap to sell dear. But we'll take it as read seeing as you've got your feet under the family table, so to speak."

She said this too neutrally for Jaysmith to be able to gauge an attitude.

His task was easy. He had no furniture of his own and everything in Rigg Cottage looked so much in place that he found himself agreeing to take practically all that was on offer. Miss Wilson ticked off the list and carefully wrote *To Stay* on the blank labels in a strong, round hand. In the room which had once been occupied by Edward Wilson, he noted that the mountaineering pictures had James Wilson's name on them.

As though to a spoken question, the old lady said, "I thought they'd bring a bit too much back to Annie, and James is keen to have them. He'll see they go to young Jimmy in the end."

Returning downstairs he said, "Will you get your solicitor to send me a bill?"

"Don't be daft," she said. "I'm not giving him owt else to charge me for. You add it up and give me a cheque."

Smiling, he did so, on William Hutton's account.

She folded up the cheque and said, "Will you stay and have a bite of lunch? I got an extra chop, but then James said he wouldn't be in."

"Your brother's here, is he?"

"I told him he'd best get up quick if he wanted to see the place before it was sold," said Miss Wilson. "So, you'll stay then?"

Jaysmith glanced at his watch. It was twelve twenty.

"I'm sorry," he said. "I'd love to but . . ."

"No? Well, no doubt you're a busy man." She accompanied him to the front door, then she said, "Hold on a minute. If you're not staying, I won't waste the chops. I'll come down into the village with you, bank this cheque and call in at my new house. I've got a few things to do there."

She was ready in a minute. He dropped her outside the bank.

It was just on twelve thirty when he reached the Crag. Doris Parker was busy in the dining room while Philip was in the bar.

"Mr. Hutton!" he said. "It's good to see you. What'll it be?"

"Whisky, please. How are things?"

"Still pretty busy, thank God. Not in here, but there's a party having lunch. I've got to take these drinks through. If anyone comes in, tell 'em to ring the bell."

"OK," said Jaysmith. "By the way, I'm expecting a telephone call, so if it rings, don't rush. I'll yell if it's not for me."

"Fair enough," said Parker, and left.

The bar was empty except for a young couple by the fire. After a while they got up and headed for the dining room and Jay took their place by the welcome flames. He stretched out his hands and warmed the whisky glass, then slowly drank the golden liquid as if he were drinking the flames themselves. It was a moment of pure tranquillity unsullied by plans or fears or even thought itself. Then a voice spoke behind him.

"Mr. Hutton, isn't it? I thought I recognized you. I'll join you, if I may."

He looked up, aghast. Before him stood Jacob.

14

To the casual eye, Jacob was a faintly comic figure. He wore an ancient dogtooth tweed jacket with leather-patched elbows, a pair of baggy corduroy trousers, and on his head was an inverted sauceboat, also of tweed, which might once have been a deerstalker.

Yet Jaysmith felt menaced.

"Sit down," he said. "I'll get you a drink."

"Not yet. Later, perhaps," said Jacob, sitting. "You looked a bit startled, Jay. Why was that?"

"I didn't expect to see you in person."

"No, I don't suppose you did. But you can't trust phones, can you, Jay? I was close enough to get here myself, and I wanted very much to see you face to face, Jay. What are you playing at, Jay? Tell me. I'd very much like to know." He sounded genuinely anxious.

"I've got reason to believe you've made a mistake in targeting Bryant," Jaysmith said flatly. "I think you've got the wrong man."

"The wrong man?" echoed Jacob. "It's not impossible of course. Mistakes do happen, don't they? I take it Adam was a 'mistake'."

"I'm sorry about Adam. It wasn't my idea. He seemed to push for it."

"Suicide, was it?" The irony was mild. "Yes, I'm curious, Jay, I admit it. At first I thought you must have been turned, didn't I? But by what? Money? Perhaps. Conviction? Not likely. In any case, if you'd been turned, then you'd simply have warned Bryant and he could have taken off, couldn't he? So do tell, what's it really all about?"

Jaysmith went through the motions of draining his almost empty glass before he spoke. "All right," he said. "I have become . . . involved with the Bryant family. It has become important to me that they are not harmed."

"Involved?" Jacob savoured the word. "Involved with the Bryant family? As far as I recall, there are only two others. A grandson. And a daughter."

"I met the daughter." Jaysmith stared unblinkingly at the old man, as if defying him to smile. Jacob returned the gaze seriously and said, "And did your meeting with the daughter predate your decision to abort this target?"

"No!" said Jaysmith, feeling ludicrously offended. "What I told you was the truth. I missed. It was my eyesight. You must have checked with my oculist."

"Indeed," said Jacob. "So, you decide to withdraw, to retire, and *then* you meet this woman, is that it?"

Jaysmith nodded.

"And then you discover Bryant is her father. And then, naturally, you start to feel you cannot stand by and let him be killed, do I read you correctly?"

He nodded again. "I love her," he said. Then he repeated more quietly, as if for his own benefit, "*I love her.*"

There was a silence after this, deep enough to make Jaysmith start like a nervous horse when Phil Parker's voice said, "Anything you require, gents, while I'm here?"

He had reentered the bar and was opening a bottle of wine.

Jaysmith said, "I'll have another Scotch. A large one."

He glanced inquiringly at Jacob who said, "A half of bitter would be nice, wouldn't it?"

Parker poured the drinks. Jaysmith paid and the hotel owner left the bar with the wine.

Jacob just stared thoughtfully at his beer. "You love her," he said finally. "And you'd like to marry her. She's a widow, is she not? Of how long standing?"

"Ten months."

"Not very long. And there's a child. You'd like to marry her, but what of the child? Dump him on Bryant, perhaps? Is that why you want to keep him alive?"

There was a note of scorn in his voice which stung Jaysmith.

"Don't be offensive!" he rasped. "I love the boy too, but even if I didn't, I wouldn't expect a woman like Anya to agree to being separated from him for more than the length of a honeymoon."

"*Honeymoon!*" said Jacob, his squashed-up face almost straightening out in amazement. "You're a man of unsuspected fantasy, Jay. Marriage! Honeymoon! Aren't you forgetting something, Jay? Aren't you forgetting what you are? What makes you think that after a career like yours, you're fit for any close human relationship, let alone something so impossibly intimate as marriage? Have you told this woman about yourself? *Will* you tell her about yourself? What do you imagine she will say, Jay, when you tell her about the men you've killed?"

The savagery of the attack reduced Jaysmith to silence for a moment. He felt great anger, and also the beginnings of despair as one part of his mind acknowledged the justice of what Jacob had said.

"That's between me and her," he said at last. "But one thing's certain.

Feeling for her the way I do, I can't stand by and see her father killed."

"Of course not," Jacob said softly. "And the purpose of this meeting is to persuade me and my masters to change our minds, is it?"

"To persuade *you*, Jacob," said Jaysmith wearily. "I'm sure you are quite capable of taking care of your masters. Listen to me, Jacob. I know it sounds absurd, the way you put it. But I'm not just asking a favour; and I'm not just offering a threat, though I've got a threat to offer, believe me. But what I genuinely believe is that you've got the wrong man!"

"You said that before," said Jacob. "Then you asked me to tell you why Bryant was targeted. If you don't know why, then you can't know he's the wrong man, can you?"

"I think I do know why," said Jaysmith. "But I'd like to hear it from the horse's mouth."

Jacob slowly sipped the bitter. "I've no right to tell you anything about Bryant, and you've no right to ask. Still, despite all this, I'm going to tell you as much as I can." He paused, then resumed. "Bryant is intermittently and in a small way one of our Iron Curtain couriers. He's not really very important, one of a dozen like him. Unfortunately he has got himself into a relationship with someone who *is* important, a Polish woman who's a fairly key figure in subversive circles in the Krakow district. UBEK, their secret police who are KGB-trained, have discovered the situation and used it rather nicely, I think. Because the woman loves Bryant, she talks freely to him; and because Bryant loves the woman he talks freely to UBEK. Now isn't that a nice economic bit of organization!"

"But this is crazy!" interrupted Jaysmith. "Even if it's true it doesn't justify him as a target. He can be stopped, simply by arresting him! Or used, by feeding him false information! Why kill him, for God's sake?"

"I think you underestimate the damage he has caused," said Jacob gravely. "People have died and disappeared because of Bryant. Not just Solidarity people either. What he has told UBEK, together with what they suspected already, has pointed them towards some of our own people. One was killed just recently. That's why Bryant has to go, and go with a bang, so to speak. It's an unambiguous statement that we know what's been going on, that we know that what happened to our man was not an accident, and that it had better stop there if they don't want a general escalation."

"And for this you'd kill him? As a gesture?"

Jacob said, "Don't sound so horrified, Jay. Retirement doesn't rub out the last twenty years, you know."

He didn't rise to the gibe, but said, "I still think you've got the wrong man."

"Do you now? But then who is the right one? I presume you have another candidate?"

"Anton Ford," he said.

Jacob was not impressed. "Well, it would have to be, wouldn't it? Who else do you know to put on your short list, Jay? But go on. Explain your thinking."

Jaysmith argued his case as best he could. "You've got to admit there's a reasonable doubt," he concluded.

The bar door opened and a group of people came in, but Jacob ignored them.

"What you've told me about Ford has made me think, I must admit," he said. "That's why I came up here, actually, to have a chat to him. Your own little invitation just fell quite fortunately, and I diverted here as soon as I heard about it. I'm not unsympathetic to your dilemma, believe me. If I can be even half persuaded, well, a gesture which kills the wrong man would have them laughing from here to the Urals, and I don't care to be laughed at. So why don't we go and see Ford together? Will you join me? We've got him, of course. We picked him up on his way from Naddle Foot yesterday."

It was said most naturally and Jaysmith's instinctive reaction was to rise and accompany the other without question. Instead, he shook his head.

"First, there's something you should know," he said. "Just to make sure that I don't end up staying with Ford."

"Ah yes. The threat."

From his pocket Jaysmith took one of the sheets he had photocopied that morning. He passed it over.

Jacob read it without changing expression. "Very impressive," he said. "I'd forgotten some of these. And I see we have an anniversary too. Many happy returns. With a *curriculum vitae* like this one you could easily get a job in South America, I should think."

"I'm not applying for a job, Jacob," said Jaysmith. "I've arranged for a copy of this *curriculum vitae*, confession, call it what you will, to be sent to the authorities in every country concerned, and to newspapers also. As for references, that was easy. One thing I've always left behind me is a single bullet. Accompanying each of these sheets will be a bullet fired this morning from my M21. I've used that rifle on more than half of my kills. A simple forensic check will confirm the bullets are from the same weapon. I think this should cause a lot more embarrassment than your masters would be able to tolerate, don't you?"

"Perhaps," said Jacob. "And when does this get sent out?"

"Oh, in a couple of days, unless my distributor hears from me in a very specific way."

"Very ingenious," approved Jacob, returning the sheet. "But totally unnecessary. Shall we go now?"

He led the way out of the bar.

"Is it far?" asked Jaysmith as they reached the BMW.

"Not far. Pointless taking two cars, I think. Will you drive?"

"I don't mind," said Jaysmith, unlocking the passenger door and letting Jacob in.

As he walked round to the driver's door, a voice called to him. He turned. Approaching was Miss Wilson. In her hand she clutched a piece of paper which she waved in his face.

"I've just stood an age in a queue in that bank and when I got to the counter they wouldn't accept your cheque," she said wrathfully. "Look at it! You've put the wrong date. It's not 1963, is it? You're twenty years out."

He examined the cheque. She was right.

"I'm sorry," he said. "I don't know what I was thinking of." He altered and initialled it.

But he knew very well what he had been thinking of. Twenty years before, on this day in 1963, he had shot Colonel Tai.

He returned the cheque to Miss Wilson, who had spotted Jacob in the front seat of the car and was looking at him with puzzlement. He opened the door and got out, glancing towards a black Metro parked by the car park exit. Its driver began walking rapidly towards them. He wore an anorak with the hood up and his head was bowed against the wind but there was something familiar about him. Jaysmith, however, found his attention diverted by a puzzling turn in Miss Wilson's conversation.

"So this is where you got to," she said accusingly. "What are you up to?" She was not, he realized, addressing him.

"Just a friendly chat, isn't that right, Mr. Hutton?" replied Jacob.

Full of bewildered suspicion, Jaysmith rasped, "What's going on, Jacob?"

"Jacob!" exclaimed Miss Wilson. "Well, I've not heard anyone call him that since our father died. Muriel, he'd say, you're a rough tough lass and if you'd been a lad, I should have called you Esau. But as for this other smooth young thing, I just about got him right. James, which they used to call *Jacobus*; my second-born, Jacob, the smooth man!"

The man from the Metro was close now. Under the monklike hood was the beard-shadowed face of Davey, Adam's companion. His right hand, in his anorak pocket, was bulkier than a hand ought to be.

"What the hell's going on?" Jaysmith repeated.

Jacob smiled at him and said, "You are, of course, already acquainted with my dear old sister, aren't you, Mr. Hutton?"

"Of course he is," said Miss Wilson. "He's buying my house, isn't he? And he knows just whose house he is buying, James; and he knows it's nowt to do with you." She turned to Jaysmith. "I don't know what he's been saying to you, but it's mine to sell, and the deal's settled."

371

Jaysmith was too dumbfounded to do more than nod.

"Right then," she said. "Now I'll be off and see if they'll take this cheque *this* time!" She turned on her heel and stumped away.

Davey was standing close behind Jaysmith now and he felt an unmistakable hardness against his spine.

"I hope you haven't changed your mind," said James Wilson. "But just in case you have, let Davey here persuade you to change it back."

"No need for Davey," said Jaysmith. "No need at all. You and I have a lot of talking to do, Mr. Wilson."

He got into the car. Jacob nodded at Davey who, with some reluctance, retreated towards the Metro. "Let's go," he said.

JAYSMITH DROVE SLOWLY and with great care out of Grasmere. He asked and received no directions. Jacob seemed as little inclined to speech as he was, but sat staring gloomily out of the window. Occasionally the wind would tear open a gap in the cloud and a pillar of sunlight would tremble momentarily on a peak or in a valley. One such pillar lasted longer, focusing on the dramatic bulk of the Castle Rock of Triermain, and this brought Jaysmith to his first awareness that he had driven nearly ten miles in a trancelike state and was now heading into St. John's-in-the-Vale and back to Naddle Foot.

The realization was enough to break the paralysing spell. Naddle Foot was no place he wanted to be in the company of the man by his side. And not only Jacob. A glance in the rear-view mirror confirmed that the black Metro was matching the BMW's pace a couple of hundred yards behind.

Things were falling into place in his mind which made a long, intimate conversation with Jacob very desirable. But a conversation without witnesses.

He slammed down the accelerator of the BMW. The car surged forward on the twisting road and in a few seconds was out of sight of the Metro. He kept his foot hard down till he saw ahead on the right the angled track which led up to the disused quarry he had visited four days earlier. Swinging the wheel hard over, he went racing up the steep track, rounded the bend at the top and, to ensure minimum visibility from the road, sent the car grinding up the steep bank of waste which bounded the amphitheatre of the quarry, till the engine stalled.

He pulled the handbrake on and in the ensuing silence they heard the roar of the Metro's engine as it screamed by below them, along the road.

Jacob did not speak but peered forward with mild curiosity at the ravaged face of the fell.

"Now that's what I call a view," he said finally.

It was difficult to tell if he was being ironic.

"Let's talk," said Jaysmith harshly, "about Bryant."

372

"If you like."

"Yes, I bloody well like! Bryant's no spy, no traitor, is he?"

"There is some evidence, wouldn't you say?"

"Of course there's *evidence!* When you decided you wanted him killed and that I should do your dirty work for you, of course you made sure there was evidence! Even *you* are answerable to someone!"

"Yes, I am, aren't I? And to experts too."

"Then you must have made a bloody good job of it. How far did you go, Jacob? Did you actually provide the bodies too?"

Jacob's eyes opened wide. "You mean did I betray my own people just to point a finger at Bryant? Come on, Jay, why on earth should I do a thing like that?"

"Because you're totally unbalanced," said Jaysmith contemptuously. "I'd like to believe that it was your precious son's death that tipped you over, but by all accounts he was such a nutter himself, he must have got it from somewhere!"

This made contact. Jacob turned a little pale and rubbed the back of his neck as though attacked by a sudden pain. But his voice remained as controlled as ever as he asked, "Why do you say all this, Jay? What do you think I have done?"

"I think," said Jaysmith slowly, "that when your boy, Edward, died, you were devastated. Perhaps it was the hint of suicide . . ."

"Not that," interrupted Jacob swiftly. "Not Edward. He was strong, positive; he loved the danger of climbing, he loved pushing himself to the limit; but he wouldn't slacken the odds in that way. In the end he might have fallen to his death, but not off a piffling rock face in the Lake District; not because he'd decided not to take his injection!"

"No? What did you imagine had happened then?" demanded Jaysmith.

"This is your show, isn't it?" replied the other. "You tell me."

"I'm not sure. You must have had some idea of the kind of man he was, some idea of the kind of hell Anya had had to live through. So you decided to take a closer look at her father, at Bryant. You had their home burgled, didn't you? But you found nothing except the letters from Ford's sister. Was that the first you knew of the affair? God, they must have been discreet! And Ford was acting as an intermediary, so you sent your boys to talk to him. What were they looking for? Anything? Nothing? Something damaging to Bryant, simply because you didn't much like Bryant? But they came up with gold. They came up with the business of the insulin capsules, didn't they? And suddenly Bryant wasn't just a man you didn't like, a father-substitute for your grandson Jimmy, he was a murderer! Edward's killer! You must have wanted to kill him with your own hands then. But that's not your way, is it, Jacob? You targeted him. You put him at the end of my gun."

"And that was an error, wasn't it?" murmured Jacob.

"You don't deny it then? None of it?" cried Jaysmith.

"How strange. I think you'd really prefer it if I denied it all, wouldn't you? Because it would make you less of a tool. But that's all you've ever been, Jay. A weapon, a hit-man, nothing more."

"Nothing more," echoed Jaysmith. "You may be right. But that didn't entitle you to use me as a private executioner, Jacob! That didn't entitle you to turn me into a simple murderer!"

Jacob laughed. "There's your weakness," he said. "All these years you've acted the hard emotionless executioner, but always you needed reasons, reassurances. You had to be convinced that everyone you killed deserved his death as much as poor old Tai! Not that he deserved it all that much. He was only doing his job, wasn't he?"

Jaysmith felt rage surging up from his belly to his brain. Only the sense that Jacob was deliberately provoking him enabled him to keep control.

"All right," he said quietly. "Perhaps I did need that reassurance about my targets. That makes it all the worse to have pointed me at Bryant."

"You fool!" said Jacob, contemptuously. "At least I condemned him for a crime; most of the others died for the sake of a policy!"

So, thought Jaysmith dully. Now I know. I sold my soul—sold it for twenty years of emptiness, of ignorance, of simple misuse. No profit or delight. A simple public hangman.

"Come now, Jay," said Jacob with something approaching glee, "don't take it to heart. Remember what Eichmann said in his glass box. You were only following orders!"

There was no conscious reaction, just a distant cry of rage and despair in a voice he recognized as his own. Then his hands were at Jacob's throat, and Jacob's face was flushing a streaky purple, when the door was dragged open and Davey slammed his pistol barrel hard against Jaysmith's head.

He fell back in his seat with the tacky hotness of blood oozing down his neck. The muzzle of Davey's gun was boring into his jaw line. He looked up into the man's face and to his dull surprise saw there a physical longing to squeeze the trigger.

It was Jacob who prevented this. Massaging his throat, he croaked, "You took your time, didn't you?"

"I had to turn round," growled Davey. "Shall we get on with it?"

"Soon. Get in the back, will you?"

The bearded man slipped into the back seat. Rain was streaming off his bulky anorak. Jaysmith gingerly raised his hand to his head, and behind him Davey moved menacingly.

"It's all right," said Jacob, some of his old calm returning with his old voice. "Jay, you're bleeding."

"Just a bit. There's a first-aid kit in the glove compartment."

"Be my guest," said Jacob.

Jaysmith slowly reached forward. With luck, Jacob's body would screen him just long enough to get hold of Adam's gun and blow a hole in Davey before the bearded man had time to do the same to him. Taking a deep breath, he opened the glove compartment door.

He could have saved himself the anxiety. The HK P9 was gone.

No one spoke. He took the first-aid box out, removed a lint pad and a small antiseptic spray, sprayed the pad, closed and replaced the box as he pressed the pad to the back of his head.

"That's better," he said. "Don't want to die of blood poisoning. Jacob, I'm sorry to have lost my temper like that."

"You wouldn't be trying to humour me, would you?" said Jacob, still gently massaging his neck.

"I'm trying to find the least damaging route through all this for everyone," snapped Jaysmith, desperately playing for time.

"And what do you suggest?"

"Go ahead, kill Bryant. I know you don't want to harm Anya and the boy. That's why I had the time limit, wasn't it? They were staying with you till the Sunday!"

This clearly took Jacob by surprise, as it was intended to.

"Kill Bryant? You know, Jay, you almost sound like the man I once hoped you'd be! But what about you?"

Jaysmith shrugged. "I'll do what I should have done in the first place. Slip quietly out of view. Of course, you might have some other ideas, but don't forget my little bundle of *billets doux*."

Jacob relapsed into a reverie, his fingers steepled together under his chin, his monkey face completely still. The rain had stopped as suddenly as it had started.

Jacob roused himself. "Looks a bit brighter now, Davey," he said. "I think I'll go on to the house. You'll look after Mr. Jaysmith, will you?"

"My pleasure."

"Jacob," said Jaysmith in alarm. "What are you going to do?"

"Now you mustn't worry," reassured the older man. "I'm just going to pay a call on my daughter-in-law and her father, what's wrong with that? Perfectly natural, isn't it?"

He opened the door of the car, then turned and addressed Jaysmith once more.

"You got most things right," he said approvingly. "Except about yourself. I don't like the sound of your *billets doux*, as you call them. In fact I didn't like the sound of them from the moment my listener heard Bryant ring his office to say that you were to have the freedom of the copying machine. So I had a word with Davey here. Show him, Davey."

The bearded man reached into the pocket of his waterproof and pulled out a package. It had been opened. He handed it to Jacob, who looked at the address.

"A bank manager in Brighton!" he exclaimed. "What is it, Jay? A small account for emergencies? *Please dispatch the enclosed by airmail where appropriate on the first day of October and debit my account.* Signed *Henry Collins.* Jay, we didn't know about this, honestly. How clever of you! In Brighton. And using your own name, too, how clever to hide behind your real name. Don't look so shocked. I know one likes to think the Royal Mail is sacrosanct, but nothing is out of our reach, you know that, now don't you, Jay? And don't worry, by the way; Davey got both packages, didn't you, Davey? Including the fail-safe one addressed to your bank manager in Switzerland."

"What are you going to do?" said Jaysmith dully.

"What I said. Go down to the house. Talk a little. Jimmy will still be at school, so we can have a really good adult talk. There's another thing you didn't get quite right, Jay. Yes, I was suspicious; yes, I sent a team in to go over Bryant's house. But it wasn't Bryant I wanted investigated; it was my precious daughter-in-law! Finding those letters, and what they led to, was just a stroke of luck. Bryant arranged everything, that much is clear, but she'd driven poor Edward to despair with her insensitive, carping stupidity! She's just as guilty as Bryant, more guilty in my eyes. That's why I decided he should go first, so she could feel the pain of loss she had never felt when Edward died!"

"First?" Jaysmith seized upon the word. "*First?*"

"Oh, yes. She had her chance to survive. I wouldn't willingly deprive Jimmy of a mother, you see. But after Edward's death she refused my offer of a home and protection and settled with her murdering father. Even then, even when I knew what the pair of them had done, I gave her another chance. I asked her again when she and the boy visited me a few weeks ago. She was adamant. I offered everything, comfort, money, the best of education for Jimmy. I'm entitled to a close involvement, don't you agree, Jay? After what I've lost. Don't you agree?"

"Yes, yes, I agree," cried Jaysmith, aghast. "But you won't do anything against her now, will you? Listen, once her father's dead, she'll need someone to turn to. It'll be natural for her to turn to you ..."

"That's what I thought before," said Jacob softly. "If you'd done your job properly, Jay, I'd have been with her when the news arrived. I'd have seen her pain. I might have profited from her grief. But you botched the job, didn't you? And now things have moved on. Now she's got to know everything: what her father did; who I am; and who you are too, Jay. That's part of it also. She's got to suffer! Ten months in his grave, not even a year, ten little months and what's this grieving widow doing? Fornicating with a stranger ..."

He climbed out of the car. Before Jaysmith's outstretched hands even could make contact with the tweed jacket, Davey's gun had ploughed a new furrow along his skull and he collapsed across the passenger seat, crying out in rage and pain.

"You're useless, you know that, Jay?" said Jacob with contempt. "You're going to die, of course. Davey here will take care of that. And Bryant will die, and my daughter-in-law too. In that order. Fortunately I'll be around to take care of Jimmy. He'll be all right, believe me. I'll see to that. So don't take it too badly, Jay. You'd have had to go anyway, even with none of this. A weak man in retirement gets to thinking, gets to worrying about his life. And his afterlife. We don't like deathbed confessions, Jay, so if necessary we anticipate the deathbed. And you were a likely candidate. I'll tell you why. I checked up with your oculist. And he confirmed that you'd been to see him about your sight. But what he told me was that there was no physical reason whatsoever for the trouble you were having with your right eye. No reason whatever! It's your mind that's getting things out of focus, Jay. Just your mind. I suspect you may find something comforting in that. If you do, then good luck to you. And goodbye, Jay. Goodbye."

He slammed the door and walked away, nimble for his age on the steep and shaly slope. Soon he disappeared round the turn and a moment later Jaysmith heard the Metro's engine burst into life then slowly fade away as the car reversed down to the road.

Davey's gun pressed hard against his neck.

"And now," said the bearded man, "there's only you and me."

15

Jaysmith sat up slowly and turned to face his captor. His gun was a SIG-Sauer P230 automatic, of combined Swiss-German manufacture, beautifully made, very accurate, and as little likely to jam as any weapon on the market. Jaysmith's only immediate consolation was that whatever fate was planned for him probably did not involve having him found with a bullet in his brain.

He said thickly, "What's the plan, Davey?"

The bearded man stared blankly at him. "Jacob's going to take care of them at the house. He'll use the Heckler Koch, the one you took from Adam. It's plastered with your prints, isn't it? They said you were clever, Jaysmith. That wasn't so clever. There'll be other signs too, all adding up to you fancying a slice of the lady, the lady objecting, Daddy intervening, you going berserk. You'll be missing, natch. The mysterious third person, the stranger in the house. Crazy with guilt, you'll drive like a lunatic up into the hills. Somewhere up there, in the mist, on a narrow twisting road, you'll have an accident. This thing will turn over and over, breaking your neck. Perhaps there'll be a fire too. How's that grab you, Mr. Jaysmith?"

"It's crazy!" said Jaysmith. "For God's sake, Davey, what are you getting yourself into? You heard Jacob. You know this has nothing to do with his job, with *your* job. It's unofficial! It's private! You'd be crazy to get involved!"

The words suddenly felt prophetic as he realized there was something unbalanced about the way the man was looking at him.

"You're right, Mr. Jaysmith," he said slowly. "It *is* private. You remember Adam?"

"Yes," he said sadly, "I remember Adam."

"He was my friend," said Davey. "He was a very good friend."

There were tears in the man's eyes. It might have been touching if Jaysmith had been in the mood to be touched; it should have been frightening if Jaysmith had not moved far beyond the significance of fear.

"So what happens now?" he asked.

"I'm going to lock you in the boot of this car," said Davey. "That's how Adam ended up, isn't it? Packed in the boot of his car, twisted and crushed like a sack of garbage!"

Hastily, hoping to ward off the other's hysteria, Jaysmith said, "And then, what then?"

"Don't you listen, man? Like I said, I drive you somewhere nice and high and lonely, and I put you back in the front seat, and I see you over the edge. Then I'll scramble down and make sure you're dead. So out you get now and walk slowly round to the boot."

Davey got out of the car and kept the automatic trained on Jaysmith as he followed suit.

"You'll need the keys," said Jaysmith, taking them from the ignition. "Catch."

He threw them a yard to the right of Davey. They skittered past him down the slope. The man's eyes did not even flicker towards them as he retreated, perfectly balanced despite the steep and uneven track, to a point a couple of yards behind the car.

"You pathetic old man," he said. "Come forward slowly and pick 'em up."

Jaysmith obeyed, his own footwork much more unsure as he felt the full effect of the blows.

"Now open the boot."

As Jaysmith inserted the key in the lock, he knew that his last chance was approaching fast. Davey would not want him in the boot alive and literally kicking as they drove to the chosen accident site. And to knock him unconscious he would have to come close.

378

But the bearded man was taking no chances. "Now climb in," he ordered from his safe shooting distance, "and lie down."

Jaysmith looked at the boot floor. Beneath that false panel was his rucksack, especially constructed to carry the stripped-down M21. Even if he remained conscious, was there any chance that he could get it out and assemble it and have it ready to fire when Davey reopened the lid?

He doubted it. The boot was roomy, but it would need someone as double-jointed as Houdini to unfasten and raise the panel while lying on it.

"Get in!" yelled Davey angrily. "Or I swear I'll finish this here and now!"

"I'm getting! I'm getting!"

He climbed in, moving awkwardly as an old, tired man might be expected to. It was a piece of play-acting that came easy.

"Now crouch down, on all fours. Hold it there!"

Now he guessed Davey's intention. To render him quiescent for the next half-hour or so, he was going to come just close enough to bring the boot lid crashing down on his head.

Davey was out of his line of vision. He strained his ears through the gusting wind to hear the sound of his approach. There would be a moment when he would raise both arms to bring the lid down with maximum force. Just a moment. A second too soon and the SIG-Sauer would still be aimed; a second too late and his head would be cracked open by the solid metal.

A stone rattled close behind. He counted two seconds then swung his right hand up over his left shoulder. In it he held the small antiseptic aerosol which he had palmed as he pretended to replace it in the first-aid box. Now the sleight of hand which had so delighted Jimmy was all that stood between him and the warping of the boy's life for ever. He only had a fractional moment's touch to tell him he had the nozzle pointed the right way, and there was no chance for a sighting aim.

He squeezed the nozzle and held it down for a long, long burst before twisting round to see what had happened.

He had been lucky. The squirt of antiseptic spray had taken Davey full in the left eye. The bearded man screamed in shock and pain, but he was still able to see Jaysmith scrambling towards him and to bring the gun crashing down on his head.

Now it was Jaysmith's turn to ignore pain, and attack. The steepness of the slope and the height of the boot meant that he fell upon Davey in the literal sense, in a tangle of limbs which at least inhibited use of the gun. His fingers scrabbled at the earth, but all he got was a handful of splintered shale. At the same time he felt himself thrown off his opponent's body. He fell on his back and tried to scrabble his way back up the slope to take refuge beneath the car. Not that it would have been any refuge if Davey had decided to use the gun. But now Davey was standing right over him, using the gun as a club once more, smashing down at his skull and face. He felt his nose go and suspected that the blow must also have cracked his jaw. Dully he thought that there was no way these injuries were going to look as if they'd been received in a car crash: Davey was striking for the sheer pleasure of it.

The gun barrel caught him on the right temple, splitting it open and sending a blinding gush of blood into his eye. He cried out, the cry of despair trailing off as his body went slack.

Davey hesitated, the gun poised for another blow.

"You bastard!" he cried. "Don't die yet!"

The feeble flick of Jaysmith's right wrist, the ponderous kick of his left leg, should have been as meaningless as the last spasms of any dying man. But the flick sent the handful of shale into Davey's eyes, and the kick caught him where the ulnar nerve stretched tautly over the elbow.

The gun fell, hit a stone and, instead of sliding away down the slope, bounced under the car's boot. Davey dived sideways to retrieve it.

It was at best a brief respite. Somehow Jaysmith was upright and staggering up the slope. His idea was simply to keep the car between Davey and himself. But he had only got as far as the driver's door when the bearded man got the gun, rolled a couple of feet downhill to give himself a clear shot, and fired.

Jaysmith felt the bullet hit him in the back. Oddly its immediate effect was almost anaesthetic, but he could run no more. He fell sideways through the open door of the car across the driver's seat. His outstretched right hand rested on the handbrake. With an instant reaction that had nothing to do with thought, and a strength that had nothing to do with muscles, he pressed the release button.

Instantly the twenty-five hundredweight of metal began to move backwards down the steep track, dragging him with it. He scarcely registered the long, highpitched shriek which coincided with a momentary interruption of the steady acceleration. Then almost instantly there was a grinding of metal on stone, a slight change of angle, and suddenly acceleration had stopped altogether.

Slowly he slid off the seat till he was lying on the ground. He looked around for Davey and found him, with a shock of terror, less than twelve inches away, his open eyes staring with uncomprehending dismay into Jaysmith's face.

"Oh, you bastard," Davey said. "Oh, you tricky murdering bastard."

His body from the waist down was now pinned firmly beneath the car.

The pistol had fallen from his nerveless hand and lay just out of reach. Jaysmith rose, using the car door as a support. He kicked the pistol down the track, then tried a few staggering paces, still leaning against the car, towards the boot. What he was after was the car keys, still in the boot-lock. But when he reached the back of the car, he realized that the grinding metal noise he'd heard had been the bottom of the car scraping along a broad flat stone. The nearside wheel had then left the track and settled in a marshy ditch, bringing the vehicle's whole weight to settle on the stone. With full strength and some assistance he might have contrived to get it free, but in his present state there was no hope.

He concentrated now on Naddle Foot. He had no choice. It came as little surprise to discover that already his fingers were unscrewing the nuts which held the false boot bottom. The panel slipped out easily. Lifting up the rucksack was more of a problem, but he managed it and it wasn't till he hefted it onto his shoulders and screamed aloud with pain that he remembered he'd been shot in the back.

There was an echoing scream close to. It came from Davey.

"Help me," he pleaded. "You murdering bastard, help me!"

Jaysmith looked down at the trapped man. He was pinned facing downhill and there was no way he could twist round to look up the track. Satisfied of this, Jaysmith retrieved the automatic and put it within reach of Davey's hand.

He didn't speak but stepped painfully over the body and set off uphill. After he'd covered a slow dozen yards he heard a shot but he didn't look back. He was climbing alongside the steep line of fencing which protected the grazing sheep from the quarry. Last time he had climbed up here, a million years ago it seemed, it had taken him at most five minutes. Now he felt that hours had passed and still he seemed no nearer that jut of rock which would bring Naddle Foot distantly into view, always providing of course that the rain did not return, or the mist descend, or the blindness which seemed to be affecting his right eye pass over to his left.

No physical reason for his eye trouble, wasn't that what Jacob had said? When had he said it? Years ago, surely? But no, scarcely more than twenty minutes! It seemed impossible. No physical reason. What then? Some-thing deep inside, some repressed distaste, self-disgust, something which slowly turned away from his vile trade? He did not understand these things and it was too late to start wrestling with them now. A man was what he did, not what he wished he had done.

These thoughts carried him high up the fellside and almost to the craggy vantagepoint from which he would be able to look up the valley towards Naddle Foot. He must have lost a lot of blood, his body felt drained of strength almost to the point where the pain no longer existed. Just a few yards more. Dragging in huge breaths of cold air that rasped the exposed nerves of his broken teeth, he gained the ledge.

He sat down and with nerveless fingers scrabbled at the buckles and straps of the rucksack. At last he got it open and pulled out the Adjustable

Ranging Telescope. Raising it to his right eye, he discovered he could see nothing at all. He'd forgotten about his eye. Had it been damaged in the fight? Gingerly he touched it. It was caked with a solid patch of blood. He began to pick at it and it came away easily. He recalled that it was in fact the cut on his temple which had released the flow.

Absurdly cheered by this discovery, he cleared the blood away and picked up the sight once more.

Naddle Foot leaped across the valley towards him. But from a marksman's viewpoint, the magnification only revealed difficulties. It was distant and it was a side view, obliquely angled to the front of the house and partially obscured by trees. But he could see the front porch. And before it, partially masked from his view by a rowan tree at the edge of the garden, was the black Metro.

A cry of despair rose in his blood-tainted throat. But what had he expected? Jacob was in there. Perhaps even now it was too late. So, what now? What was there to do?

There was only one thing he could do, and that was give what warning he could. He must pump bullets at random through the side windows, against the porch, taking a chance on hitting those within, and hoping that Jacob would be thrown off balance when he realized what was happening. He tried to force his mind to an estimate of the range and flexed his fingers in preparation for the assembly of the M21. But the sky seemed to be darkening, and Naddle Foot even through the scope was fading into the surrounding fields, and his pain-racked, blood-starved body was being summoned to meet some last mocking challenge in that dismal amphitheatre below.

Then, suddenly, everything snapped back into sharp-edged focus. Out of the front porch of Naddle Foot stumbled Anya. She fell on one knee at the foot of the two steps down to the drive, recovered and dashed towards the parked car.

After her came Jacob, moving fast for a man of his age. In his hand was Adam's Heckler Koch. He caught Anya by the car, seized her, spun her round to face him and pressed the pistol against her breast. They were partially obscured by the rowan, its branches heavy with the blood-pearls of its fruit. But Jaysmith knew from his glimpse of Anya's ravaged face what must have taken place, what her desperate lips were saying.

Jacob had carried out his plan. Bryant was dead. What resistance could a man in a wheelchair offer? Anya, seeing her father dead, had turned her thoughts wholly towards her living son, soon to return home on the school bus. And now Jacob had her, was doubtless telling her the rest of his plans, describing how he proposed to bring up Jimmy, moulding him in the image of his dead father and making sure that she understood that any hope she had of rescue from Jaysmith—a hired killer—was vain.

There was no time for further speculation, in any sense. He put down the telescope and sent his fingers diving into the rucksack in search of the disassembled rifle. Out it came, piece by piece. In full health he was able to assemble it in under twenty seconds. But now his fingers were clammy with fear and fatigue, and all the time he desperately wanted to stop and pick up the scope and look once more to see what was happening so far below. But to look was to waste precious seconds which might be of the essence. He forced thought out of his mind and let his instincts deal with the familiar sequence: install bolt assembly and operating rod; engage connector lock; install and engage connector assembly; install custom-made shoulder stock to main stock; install stock with butt-plate assembly; install firing mechanism; install ART; install magazine.

It was done. He hadn't bothered with the noise-suppressor. What did noise mean to him any more? He raised the M21 to his shoulder and squinted down the scope, cold with fear that Jacob would already have forced Anya back into the house.

They were still in view, but only just. They had reached the top of the steps, with Jacob thrusting Anya ahead of him through the doorway. Obviously he didn't want to shoot her outside. His plans required that she die inside, perhaps with her clothes torn to give the impression of sexual assault. And Anya was aware of this, for she was struggling still, desperate not to be pushed back into the house where she had to die.

It was tempting to take an instant snap shot at Jacob's back, but that would accomplish nothing. This had to be a sure shot, a shot to the head, a long kill. There was wind to take into account and the light was failing, and the distance was different here from his original stand, perhaps another two hundred yards of carry.

Carefully he made his checks and adjustments. Anya and Jacob might disappear at any moment, but that must not affect his judgment any more than the growing pain in his back.

And now he was ready. All those years of pseudo-life to be reclaimed by a single shot. Anya was out of sight in the porch now and all that was visible of Jacob was a fraction of his back. Another second and he would be out of sight.

But Jaysmith waited. In him was no more fear; just a calm assurance that all he must do was wait for the moment.

And now it came.

Anya must have turned in one last desperate effort and pushed Jacob away from her. He staggered back, the gun came up in his hand, he had decided the hallway would do for his killing.

Jaysmith let out a shallow breath and squeezed the trigger.

For a moment which stopped all things, like a hair-crack in time, he thought he had once more missed.

Jacob did not stagger or twist or indicate by any movement that he had been hit. On the contrary he seemed to stand quite still. Then, though it was quite impossible, it seemed to Jaysmith that he saw the back of Jacob's head collapse slowly inwards, and the man crumpled to the ground as straight as the demands of gravity could take him.

It had been the perfect head shot, the perfect long kill.

Slowly Anya advanced out of the porch till she was out of the shadow of the house and stood in the westering sun's radiance. And slowly she raised her face to the fellside on which Jaysmith was sitting.

He looked into that dear, dear face, quartered by the cross-hairs of his scope. Jacob had told her about him. She knew he was up there, looking down at her. Her face was grave and pensive.

She's wondering what I really am, he thought. She's wondering how all

this has come to pass, how it can possibly end. She's on her own with Jimmy now. What will she do? Where will she go? Will she turn in on herself once more? Will she run like a wild fox for the cover of the high hills and crouch in her earth, fearful now beyond taming of the world of men?

Be strong, he urged her. Be curious. Stay with the police as they track me back through all those wasted years, milestoned in marble slabs, till at last they reach Harry Collins, 23, who still blushed in company; rather fancied himself as a tennis player; wrote fair romantic poetry; enjoyed very hot curries, Hollywood musicals and historical fiction; wept with joy at his first inhalation of the sounds and the scents of the Orient; and loved a woman till her loss meant more to him than the sum total of everything else in his existence.

Find him, he urged. Find him and understand.

His strength was failing fast, draining out through the hole in his back, and the rifle was growing unbearably heavy in his hands. But still he held it steady, still he kept her fixed in his unwavering sight.

She was his last and best target. It was life and hope he was firing at her and he dared not doubt his aim.

So they remained, looking at each other across the peaceful valley, till the wind drove the curtain of cloud full across the sun and her face was shadowed, and darkness drifted across his face too. The rifle slipped from his hands and fell like a challenge into the dismal amphitheatre below. A sheep grazing on the safe side of the steep fence looked up in alarm, but after a moment it decided there was nothing to fear from either the metal which had caused the noise or the still figure slumped on the ledge above. It began to rain. The sheep scrambled nimbly down the fellside in search of shelter.

Soon nothing stirred except the falling rain.

PATRICK RUELL

Patrick Ruell is only one of the pen-names of Reginald Hill, a prolific novelist and award-winning crime-writer. Born in 1936, Hill was brought up in Carlisle, Cumberland, and went to school locally before going on to study English at Oxford University. Then, after national service and a brief stint with the British Council, he became a teacher, doing a variety of jobs before ending up as a lecturer at a teacher training college in Doncaster, Yorkshire, where he now lives. Since 1981 he has been a full-time writer, and to date he is the author of some thirty volumes of thrillers, short stories and plays.

Reginald Hill and his wife Patricia (whose maiden name, Ruell, was borrowed for his nom-de-plume) are both keen walkers and frequently visit their native Cumbria for fell-walking holidays. Appropriately, it was in the Lake District that Hill was inspired to begin writing *The Long Kill*. "I was strolling alone one evening, on Loughrigg Fell," he recalls. "I was admiring the sunset and looking at the scene through my binoculars when I focussed on a house in the distance and saw a man in the garden. Suddenly the thought came into my head: *if I had a rifle, I could shoot him*. Then I began to wonder, why would anyone want to do that? What sort of story would lie behind it?"

So the character of Jaysmith was born, "made up of little bits of myself and of other people I know", and set against the dramatic background of the Lake District. More inspiration came to the author in the tantalizing form of a dream. "I hadn't even started writing *The Long Kill* yet, but I dreamed it was already published and a fantastic success, the reviews were ecstatic and so on. I had the book in my hands and I was reading it, turning the pages and seeing how the plot unfolded—and then I woke up. The only thing I could remember was the first two lines of the book!"

So, apart from its dramatic opening, we will never know what that other "dream" book contained. But we hope readers will agree that it could hardly have made more compelling reading than this one.

THIS
SHINING
LAND

A CONDENSATION OF THE BOOK BY

Rosalind Laker

ILLUSTRATED BY RAY YELDHAM

Norway, 1940—and German forces strike without warning. Suddenly this peaceful, defenceless country is in the grip of a Nazi reign of terror. But, almost overnight, a resistance movement is born, led by brave men like Steffen Larsen who are dedicated to the liberation of their homeland. Also working for the resistance is Johanna Ryen, a beautiful young girl whose growing love for Steffen is continually threatened by the war that has thrown them together. And when her undercover work necessitates fraternizing with the Nazis, Johanna faces hostility from her own people, as well as constant danger.

Chapter One

On the morning of Monday, April 8, 1940, Johanna Ryen bought her daily newspaper as usual on her way to work. After an Eastertide of sharp sunshine, which had done nothing to ease the bitter temperature, there was a strong wind blowing off Oslo Fjord and a swirl of new snow in the air. Spring was exceptionally late in coming, following a winter colder than had been known for many years. At the exclusive fur shop where she worked as secretary and bookkeeper, business had been brisk during the past few days, some customers wearing their purchases out of the shop to combat the weather.

Tucking the newspaper under her arm, Johanna turned in the direction of Karl Johans Gate. At twenty-one she was a tall girl with a good figure and long, beautiful legs. Her hair, which swung glossily at shoulder length, was a dark gold, her eyes a sparkling blue. She had an expressive face, laughed readily and was completely at ease with herself. Her mouth, wide and generous, had little need of the lipstick that brightened it to a red that matched the warm woollen cap hugging her head.

Country-bred on a valley farm on the west coast, she had had a happy childhood, spoiled by her father and two older brothers, disciplined by her mother. It had not been easy to break away from home, but after college she had needed to make a career for herself and to find out about living. She had learned a great deal since coming to Oslo and was confident that there was no situation, romantic or otherwise, that she could not handle.

On her way up the wide avenue she passed the parliament buildings and the Grand Hotel. At the head of Karl Johans Gate the royal palace stood on a rise in neoclassical splendour, its windows looking out over open ground to the city hall.

Turning out of Karl Johans Gate, Johanna reached the fur shop. She entered by the side door, collected the mail and went straight to her office. After hanging up her coat and hat, she took a quick glance at the newspaper headlines. Apart from some air skirmishes, the war in Europe seemed curiously stalemated. She was thankful her country was not involved in the conflict. Norway, together with Sweden and Denmark, was resolved that Scandinavian neutrality should be maintained, as during the Great War.

Putting aside the newspaper, she settled down at her desk to work. As always after the weekend there waş a lot of mail, including some overseas orders. The export side of the business was of particular importance to her, for it enabled her to use her knowledge of English, French and German. With some papers ready for her employer's attention, Johanna left her desk and went through the salon to reach his office. Leif Moen was not seated at his desk when she entered. He stood by the window examining one of several white-fox skins from a box on a side table.

"Good morning, Johanna," he greeted her. "What have you brought me? Ah yes. That order from Tokyo."

She liked working with Leif Moen. He was a conscientious man with smooth greying hair and well-cut features, who took a personal interest in each of his employees. Many of the sewing hands in the workshop had been with him since he inherited the business from his father some years ago. His grandfather, also in the fur business, had been a trapper in northern Norway.

After some time in Leif's office Johanna returned to her own domain. On the walls were framed designs of furs from earlier decades. They all had a certain charm, particularly the evening furs worn with beaded headbands.

When Sonja Holm, the head saleswoman who was also her friend, opened the door later, Johanna was hard at work. "It's lunchtime," Sonja said. "Are you ready?" Sonja had a round and lively face, with a dimpled smile. Older than Johanna by five years, she was married to an officer in the merchant fleet who was away at sea for long periods.

Johanna sat back in her chair with a rueful sigh. "I completely forgot the time. I can't join you today. I'm going to use my lunch break to buy some groceries. My landlady and her husband are on holiday, and so I'm preparing my own meals."

"Where have the Alsteens gone?"

"To Anna's sister in Drammen. It's a complete rest for her there, which is what she needs. Her brother-in-law is a doctor. She gets very tired nursing an invalid husband night and day, although she would never admit it."

"When do you expect them home again?"

"Not for another two weeks."

Johanna did not say that she liked having the house to herself. But she did enjoy a sense of freedom in coming and going without having to account to anyone, and if good-natured Anna had any fault, it was that her kindly concern sometimes bordered on interference. The Alsteens had no financial need to let rooms in their home, for Viktor had been a prosperous goldsmith before his stroke some years ago. A quiet and dignified man, small in stature, he was patient and uncomplaining in his infirmity. Had they had children, Anna might not have had to devote all of her time to him. As it was, they both liked having a young person in the house to bring in the outside world.

Johanna's day was exceptionally busy. When it came to an end, she was glad to catch the tram home, the bag of groceries balanced on her hip as she followed other passengers on board. With a clang of its bell the tram rattled off towards the suburb of Grefsen. As large stores gave way to smaller shops, it was strange to remember that riding on an Oslo tram had once been a novelty to her. She had never been on a train until the day she left home. To those who lived on the mountainous fjord-riven west coast, ferries were what trams were to Oslo folk.

Ahead lay the suburb of Grefsen, spread out like a country area in gentle slopes and shallow dales. Trees and orchards gave privacy to the two-storeyed pastel-hued houses set amid lawns and flowerbeds where this April only the snowdrops had managed to defy the weather.

"Grefsen!" the conductor called out.

Johanna alighted and ran across the main road to the gravel lane that would take her to the Alsteens'. The house came into sight, sturdily built and painted apple green, with blossoming plants in the lace-curtained windows.

Her first thought when she opened the front door was that the Alsteens had cut short their holiday and returned home, for there was the unmistakable scent of brewed coffee lingering in the air. But the house was in darkness. Snapping on the light in the hall, she called up the stairs, thinking that "the Englishman" might be in his rented room. "Anyone at home?"

There was no reply. She went to the kitchen and switched on more lights. The coffeepot was still warm. Two cups and saucers had been washed and left on the draining board. She picked up the note propped against the saltcellar. The writing was masculine and purposeful. "Hello, Johanna Ryen. I'm here for a few days. I gather the Alsteens are away. Maybe we'll meet some time. Steffen Larsen."

With a sigh she tore up the note. After her busy day she felt particularly unsociable and not ready to share the house with the stranger known as the Englishman. She had been newly arrived in Oslo when she first heard the explanation for his nickname.

"I've called him the Englishman," Viktor had said in his thin dry voice, every word an effort, "ever since he first came here. See that photograph." He had pointed with a frail hand towards the enlarged snapshot framed on the sitting-room wall. "It was taken at Henley Regatta, when he was sculling for Oxford during his university days in England. There's nothing more English than that."

Leaving the kitchen, Johanna went into the sitting room, where she refuelled the wood-burning stove with logs from a basket. The flames flared up, flickering on the fine antiques and rare porcelain. Johanna turned her gaze to the photograph of the Englishman. He was grinning cheerfully in the long, slender skiff, strong hands on the oars, dark hair blowing about his head.

There was more foundation for Viktor's nickname, beyond sculling: Steffen Larsen had been born of an English mother, who had wanted him educated in her own country. Bilingual, favoured nephew of a rich Norwegian aunt with whom he had lived after losing his parents, he had kept one foot in England, where he had made many friends, and the other foot in Norway, where he had established his career.

As it happened, his wealthy aunt's home was at Ålesund on the west coast, a town well known to Johanna since it was within easy reach of her own home valley of Ryendal. But she had never met him either in Ålesund or at the Alsteens', where he kept a room to use when in Oslo. A consultant engineer, he travelled a great deal, for the most part in northern Norway. Somehow, whenever he had made his visits to the capital, Johanna had always been away. Sometimes she wondered if it could have been deliberate avoidance on his part. She was well aware that Anna, an inveterate matchmaker, had contrived unsuccessfully to bring her and Steffen face to face. Very likely he wanted to retain his freedom to come and go in the Alsteens' house without needing to be sociable with a girl in whom he had no interest.

His arrival, without warning, was contrary to his usual procedure. Perhaps the explanation was indicated by the two cups left in the kitchen. She knew from Anna that he had a girlfriend here in Oslo, an English-woman named Delia Richmond, who worked at the British embassy.

Johanna turned away from the photograph and went upstairs to change out of her office clothes. She liked the room that had been hers since first coming to the city. The painted wooden walls were a faded rose colour, and there were crisp lace curtains at the window and plaited rag rugs on the pine floor. The puffy quilt on the bed was encased in a white linen embroidered cover, the pillowcases trimmed with lace. An enamelled frame on the chest of drawers held a photograph of her parents standing with her two brothers outside their two-hundred-year-old farmhouse.

After supper Johanna spent the evening in the sitting room listening to the radio. At ten thirty she went up to bed. She was already asleep when Steffen drove his car into the garage.

MILES FROM OSLO, at the mouth of the fjord, a small patrol boat was battling against a fierce sea and a rain-lashed wind. Suddenly the captain stared ahead in deep alarm, scarcely able to believe the evidence of his own eyes. Looming out of the darkness and heading into the fjord at full steam, their grey bows scything through the rough waves, were warships of great size and power. Realization dawned instantly. Invasion! "Good God! It's the German fleet!" he exclaimed hoarsely.

He snapped his orders in the same breath. The radio officer instantly sent a signal through to Oslo while the patrol boat's gun fired a warning shot across the leading cruiser's bow. Moments later there was the rush of a torpedo from a German gunboat. The patrol boat was blown to pieces.

In Oslo, upon receipt of the radio signal, lights were extinguished throughout the city in an immediate blackout. Government ministers and high-ranking military personnel were summoned to the palace of King Haakon. Confusion reigned as their meeting convened. Nobody was prepared for such a contingency, but one decision went unquestioned. The country would be called to arms.

When the German ambassador presented himself at the palace at four am, his demand for capitulation was rejected. But he drove away secure in the expectation that at dawn Wehrmacht troops would land in Oslo harbour. He believed the annexation of Norway would be complete in a matter of hours.

In the narrows of the Oslo Fjord, however, the German fleet, arrogantly lit as though for a naval regatta, was running into unexpected opposition. At the ancient Oscarsborg fortress a Norwegian officer ordered the two turn-of-the-century guns, never before fired in hostile action, to aim at the leading cruiser as she sailed past.

With a great boom that shook the old stone walls, the guns let forth across the water. The target was hit foursquare and began to sink rapidly, taking hundreds of sailors and soldiers down with it. An immediate change of plan was ordered by the German command to avoid further sinkings. Instead of being transported right into Oslo harbour, the soldiers were disembarked from the troopships far south of Oslo to face a long, rain-swept march to the distant capital.

It was early light when the wail of an air-raid siren and the thud-thud of antiaircraft fire caused Johanna to awaken with a start. Turning back the bedclothes, she put her bare feet to the floor and reached for her cream silk kimono. She drew it over her shoulders, pausing as she heard a low, throbbing hum overhead.

She ran to the window and stared out in horrified disbelief at the German bombers passing inland across the sky. Shock enveloped her. The only explanation was too terrible to comtemplate.

Suddenly there was a fist hammering at her door. A man's voice shouted through to her, "Are you awake in there? You must go down to the cellar for safety! Do you hear me?"

In her stunned state she made no answer. The door burst open. Startled, she spun round to face the intruder. The morning light caught her hair and cast a bloom over the curves of her body. Steffen Larsen stared at her, drawing in his breath.

"Move!" he exploded, belligerent in his anxiety for her.

She obeyed him at once. Pulling the edges of her kimono together, she rushed from the room, Steffen following her. Down the stairs they ran and into the cellar, he switching on the light as they went. She paused to look upward in bewilderment when a curious whine came from somewhere overhead.

"What's that?"

"Down! Get down!" Steffen shouted in warning.

He threw her with him to the floor, his body a protective shield for hers as the bomb's huge explosion nearby made the whole house shake on its foundations, blasting the small cellar window into glittering shards. All around them the collected debris of years clattered down from the shelves. As the vibration subsided, the single electric light bulb continued to swing wildly on its cord.

When he felt it was safe to move, he sat her up. "Are you all right?" He peered with concern into her pale face.

She nodded. "I think so. Everything happened so fast."

"The planes are gone now, but more may follow. We had better stay where we are for a while longer." He saw that she was shivering, and he put his jacket round her shoulders. "Here, this should help. Don't stay on that cold stone floor. There's an old sofa by the wall."

She took his advice, tucking up into a corner of the sofa. He perched on the arm next to her. "My apologies for bellowing at you in your room. I'm afraid it was necessary."

"I know that now. I was in shock. I am still, for that matter." She was noting, unconsciously, that his face had matured since the days of the sculling snapshot. He had the straight nose, square chin, classic cheekbones and light blue eyes that revealed his Norse ancestry. His

396

Englishness was in the general look of him and in the dark brown of his hair. In all, she thought, he was a man of immense physical attraction. Then her mind began to concentrate on the present crisis. "It's difficult to believe that this is happening."

"I agree. I was about to get breakfast when the announcement came over the radio. A minute later I heard the bombers."

"What did the announcement say?"

"At dawn this morning, without any declaration of war, Germany launched an invasion of Norway at targets all along the coast."

"Why?" Her look was baffled, her voice sombre.

"Well, I suppose Norway would be an excellent base from which to attack Allied shipping in the Atlantic. It's within easy range, and the fjords would provide shelter to German ships."

"That mustn't happen!" She was vehement.

"I agree, but the situation is bad. Extremely bad. We don't have a single officer or man with combat experience in the whole country. It's a hundred and twenty-five years since we last went to war. Now these Nazis are aiming to take away our independence." He slammed a fist into the sofa arm, barely able to control his fury. "We'll see them in hell first!" Restlessly he thrust himself away. "I must report for military duty. There is a general call to arms. I'll go and take a quick look round here." He hurried up the cellar steps into the house. She heard the cracking of glass underfoot and he reappeared, putting his head through the cellar doorway. "Several windows have been shattered. Come up now, but take care." His glance went to Johanna's bare toes. "Where are your slippers?"

"By my bed."

He returned a couple of minutes later to toss down her slippers. Upstairs in the hallway she paused by the sitting-room door. Steffen had cleared up some of the glass from the shattered windows and was listening to the latest bulletin on the radio. It was more bad news. Denmark had been similarly invaded at dawn and German troops were overrunning that country.

"What of Sweden?" she inquired huskily from the doorway, removing his jacket from her shoulders and putting it across a chair.

He glanced in her direction. "No attack there."

"Will it come later?"

"That's highly unlikely now, I would say. After all, the element of surprise has gone." He switched off the radio. "I have some things to do here before I report to the mobilization centre."

Before going upstairs Johanna tried to telephone her parents, but the lines out of the city were jammed. She had more success in reaching a local glazier, who promised to replace the broken panes during the morning. When bathed and dressed, she came downstairs, to be met by Steffen with a mug of hot coffee for her. She drank it while clearing up the remainder of the glass. He went back to working in the cellar, making it as secure against air raids as possible; he had already boarded up the window. He cleared the shelves of anything that could inflict injury and installed a first-aid box.

When he had finished his work, Johanna called him into the kitchen, where she had prepared breakfast. "This looks good," he said appreciatively, sitting down with her to boiled eggs, cheese, cold meats, homemade preserves and hot rolls. They both ate heartily in companionable closeness, falling into a lively discussion of the invasion and how long it might take for the Allies to send military support and aircraft. They had just finished the meal when the doorbell rang with an intruding touch.

"I'll go," Johanna said.

She opened the door to a smartly clad, English-looking young woman who had anxious grey eyes. Instinctively Johanna guessed her identity. A car carrying passengers was drawn up by the gate, its engine running.

"I'm Delia Richmond." The woman's Norwegian was flawless. "I see you've suffered some bomb damage."

"Neither Steffen nor I was hurt," Johanna replied, standing aside for her to enter. A mass of chestnut hair framed Delia's triangular face with its English-rose complexion, well-shaped nose and firm, full-lipped mouth. She was, Johanna decided, extremely good-looking. "He's in the kitchen. Come through."

"No, I'll wait here." Delia's voice was choked. "I've come to say goodbye."

Johanna found that Steffen had begun washing up. "Delia's here," she announced.

His face tightened as he went out into the hall, leaving the door wide open. It was impossible for Johanna not to hear what passed between them, or to avoid seeing that Delia darted to meet him.

"We're packing up at the embassy and getting out," she said. "Those of us able to leave at once have been told to go to Sweden and make our way home from there. We're hoping for a ship."

He was holding her arms closely. "Have you heard anything at the embassy that hasn't been on the news yet?" he asked keenly.

"The king, the crown prince and the government ministers left Oslo a while ago to travel inland. The crown princess and the royal children are already on their way to Sweden."

"What of the fighting?"

"All bad news, I'm sorry to say. There have been fjord battles along the west coast, with the Norwegian navy suffering a heavy toll. Bergen,

Stavanger, Trondheim and Narvik are all in enemy hands. In many places people woke up to find the enemy in full control of their towns before anyone knew what was happening." Outside, a car horn tooted. "I have to go." Her voice dropped a note. "It isn't easy to leave like this."

"I'll come with you to the car." He slipped his arm about her shoulder and they went side by side down to the gate.

Johanna finished clearing the table. When the car was gone, Steffen returned to the house and went upstairs to change into sturdy clothes and stout ski boots. He did not know where the army would send him and wanted to be prepared. Shouldering his rucksack, he came downstairs to discover Johanna in street clothes waiting for him in the hall. "Where do you think you're going?" he asked.

"To work. I gave the fur shop a call to say I'd been delayed, and I was told it's business as usual in the city. Everything is quiet now. I've arranged for a neighbour to let the glazier into the house. I'd like a lift into town with you."

"I've decided to catch the tram. You drive, don't you?"

"Yes, I do."

"Well, I won't be needing my car in the army. If an emergency should arise, you'd be able to get away."

"We can catch the tram together into town."

He donned a ski cap as he left the house with her. They had to run for the tram and leaped aboard just in time. "This is a crazy way to go to war," he remarked with a grin. "On a tram!"

She grinned back at him. "Let's hope you come home the same way. There's something cheerful about trams."

"Think of me every day when you travel on one," he joked.

"I will." For a second behind the cheerful banter they both glimpsed something deeper and more serious; events were bearing down on them all too quickly. She looked out of the window, trying to sustain their lighter mood. "See! All the shops are open. I told you it was business as usual."

He took his cue from her. With ease he began to talk of the west coast district they both knew so well. "I wonder how many times I've passed by your home. I know the mountains of Ryendal like the back of my hand. As for the fishing in Saeter Lake, well, that's unsurpassed anywhere in Norway."

"That's my favourite place!" she exclaimed in agreement. She had spent countless hours on the mossy banks in which the lake was set like a pale aquamarine, the speckled trout darting in its transparent depths, its pebbles showing like a floor of pearls.

"After the Germans have been booted out, we'll meet there when you're at home and I'm at Ålesund, Jo."

She smiled at his calling her Jo. That was not the Norwegian custom. It came from his being "the Englishman".

"That's a date," she promised.

"Not to fish," he insisted, smiling at her. "To talk."

She laughed softly. "Whatever you say."

Almost imperceptibly his hand moved to tighten on hers. "There's something I would like to ask you," he said. "A favour. It could be quite a while before I see my Aunt Astrid in Ålesund again. I'm her only relative. I'd appreciate it if you would call on her whenever you're at home. She is my late father's sister and a very fine person. The two of you should get on well together."

"Of course I'll visit her." As Johanna opened her bag and took down the address in a diary, she understood what lay behind the favour he had asked of her. There was the possibility that he would not come back from this war, and he wanted to ensure that Astrid Larsen would never be quite alone. Johanna felt that his request had drawn them still closer together.

Later, as they stood to say goodbye in the busy market square by the statue of Christian IV with the wide hat and the Vandyke beard, the rumble of gunfire could be heard in the distance.

"This is it then, Jo," he said quietly. "I wish we had had longer to get to know each other."

"I think this extraordinary day has condensed many weeks into a few hours."

"Those are my feelings too." He enfolded her in his arms and lowered his head to kiss her. She clung to him responsively, astonished by her reaction to the sweet impact between them. As they drew apart he stroked her face lightly with his fingertips, his eyes full of promise. "I'll find you again, Jo."

Her voice was a choked whisper. "I hope it's soon. Take care."

She watched him dodge the traffic across the square. At the corner, by a shop selling crystal and other fine glass, he turned and waved before going from her sight.

When she reached the fur shop, she went straight to her office. Plenty of work awaited her and she was thankful for it. At midmorning she managed to get a call through to her family. Her mother assured her that no German forces had reached their district. "Don't try to come home," she insisted. "Your father has heard that fighting has spread inland in some places, and you might get caught up in it." Then they were cut off.

Johanna replaced the receiver, easier in her mind now that she knew that her family was not in any immediate danger. Her thoughts returned to Steffen. Never before had someone become so important to her in such a short time. No use to tell herself that many other women, including Delia, must have been similarly attracted to him. She was convinced that something special had occurred when he first threw wide her bedroom door, as if the magnetism already between them had brought them together, sparked by the violence of the crisis overtaking their country.

JOHANNA PUT AWAY her ledgers before lunchtime. Leif Moen, half expecting further air raids, felt he should close the shop for the day.

Leaving the premises, Johanna stopped to buy a newspaper and turned when she caught the jaunty strains of a band. She moved to the edge of the pavement and looked up Karl Johans Gate towards the palace. The sight that met her shocked gaze made her stand immobile with horror. Coming down the wide avenue, headed by a German military band, was a contingent of enemy soldiers in a full marching procession that proclaimed possession of the city.

"Dear God!" she breathed.

Behind the band came a long line of troops marching three abreast. Their jackbooted feet thudded in rhythm, the skirts of their greatcoats swung in unison and, in spite of the overcast sky, the light caught the barrels of their shouldered rifles and glanced across the crowns of their heavy helmets. They were alert and in good spirits, their quick glances taking in their new surroundings. The officers actually smiled for a grim-faced photographer who stepped into the avenue to record their arrival.

On the pavement people were mute. Everyone was completely stunned. A postman, coming round the corner on his bicycle, dismounted to stare in helpless incredulity. Near Johanna, a well-dressed elderly man had tears of grief running down his cheeks. He was not alone in such an open display of sorrow.

On and on the soldiers came. The Norwegian flag, with its dark blue cross of St. Olav bordered by white on a scarlet field, was lowered from a flagpole, to be replaced by the symbol of Nazi occupation. The swastika had been unfurled over Oslo.

Johanna hardly remembered getting home on the tram. Wearily she walked up the lane and entered the house, barely noticing that the glazier had kept his word and replaced the window glass.

That evening she heard on the Oslo broadcasting station, now under German control, that their neighbour Denmark had surrendered. The Danish king and government had acquiesced to the German demands.

Then came a fresh shock. It was announced that Vidkun Quisling was about to address the Norwegian radio audience. Johanna was filled with misgivings. Quisling was the leader of Norway's small and insignificant Nazi party. In the past, its abortive attempts to gain power at election time had been something of a national joke. It would seem it was a joke no longer. From the radio Quisling's voice boomed forth into the quiet sitting room:

"Men and women of Norway! The German government has come forward with its assistance to prevent the neutrality of our country being violated by England. This protection has been rejected irresponsibly by our Norwegian government, who took flight after calling upon you to take up arms."

There followed a tirade of abuse against the government, whose authority he pronounced null and void through its own actions. Then he solemnly informed the nation that he had appointed himself the new prime minister, with his own Nazi party in full power. "I order you to show no further resistance to the German forces," he concluded.

In fury Johanna snapped off the radio. "Traitor!" she exclaimed aloud. Although not mentioned in the censored evening news, it was clear from what Quisling had said that the fighting against the invader was widespread. She hoped Steffen was safe. It was a hope that she would carry like a talisman through whatever dark days might lie ahead.

Chapter Two

Dawn brought "panic day" to Oslo. In an early-morning bulletin the Nazis had given warning that a heavy bombing raid by the British was imminent, with an attempted landing to follow. Immediately, people began to evacuate the city. Johanna made ready to leave too.

Feeling responsible for the Alsteens' possessions, she carried small valuable items down to the cellar. There she packed them with newspaper wadding into boxes, which she covered over against the chance of debris falling during the bombing.

After that she went up to her bedroom, where she hastily packed her clothes into a suitcase. When she had finished, there were still some evening dresses left in her wardrobe. Taking a large cardboard box, she laid the dresses and a few other items in it, and carried the box down to the cellar and slid it underneath a heavy cupboard.

She went back up to the hall just as the doorbell rang. Sonja Holm, her friend from the fur shop, was on the doorstep.

"Come on, Johanna! I've managed to get a taxi to take us to my mother-in-law's in the country. Get your things."

"I have a car. You can come with me."

"Better still!" Sonja ran back to the gate to dismiss the taxi. Swiftly Johanna locked up, took her suitcase and went with Sonja to Steffen's car in the garage. After piling their luggage onto the back seat, she drove out and closed the door behind them.

Congestion on the road made driving difficult. Now and again a truck full of Germans went through, a motorcycle escort cleaving a path. The soldiers themselves glanced without interest at the fleeing refugees. For them it was a familiar sight, seen often enough in other lands they had occupied.

Sonja's mother-in-law lived just far enough away from Oslo to be out of range of any battle for the city. She made Johanna and Sonja welcome, hurrying them into the house out of the cold. That evening, when the three of them listened to the news, they heard that the British raid on Oslo had not taken place and there was no further reason to believe that it would. Panic day had come to an end.

"Has it been just more German propaganda, then?" Fru Holm exclaimed indignantly. "It seems to me it was a ploy to try to make us accept Nazi protection from the British. Huh! Nobody needs protection from their friends."

Johanna and Sonja decided to return to Oslo the next morning. There was plenty of traffic heading back, although nothing like the amount that had been leaving the previous day. On the boundaries of the city there was a German roadblock.

When Johanna's turn came to drive past, she was halted by the upraised hand of a corporal, rifle slung on his shoulder. He and another soldier came forward, one on either side of the car. Johanna wound down the window.

"Is this your car, fräulein?" The corporal spoke in German, roughly and rather loudly.

She replied in his language. "*Nein*. It has been lent to me by a friend."

"It makes no difference. I'm commandeering the vehicle in the name of the Third Reich. Drive it into the field on your left."

She stared at him in disbelief. "What did you say?"

His face stiffened in anticipation of trouble. "You understand me. Do as I have instructed."

"I refuse! Who's in command? I want to speak to an officer."

"I'm in command!" his voice rasped in warning. "I'm telling you for the last time: park the car and start walking!"

Sonja plucked at Johanna's coat sleeve. "Do as he says. Please! Those soldiers are coming over here."

Johanna could feel her temper reaching a white-hot pitch. "You get out, Sonja. This isn't your problem and I don't want you to be involved. Steffen has lent me this car and I'm not giving it up."

Sonja scrambled out, retrieving their suitcases from the back seat. The corporal, realizing that Johanna was not going to obey, had his arm inside the car before she could wind up the window. Wrenching the door open, he hauled her out and flung her into a muddied snowbank. Sonja ran to help her to her feet and brushed the dirty snow from her coat.

"Don't say anything more," Sonja implored in a whisper, seeing how Johanna glared after the car as a soldier drove it into the field. "Come on. It's not far to walk home."

To her relief Johanna responded to the plea and the gentle tugging on her arm. Without another word she picked up her suitcase and started walking, her gaze set straight ahead. When they had covered quite a distance and Johanna still retained her silence, Sonja ventured a question. "You're so quiet. Are you angry with me for getting out of the car?"

"Angry with you? Of course not. There was no sense in our both getting manhandled. I've just been wishing that there was some way I could help kick the Germans out. I loathe feeling helpless."

They trudged on along the road. Their suitcases were heavy, and it was a relief to reach the Alsteens' house. Indoors, Sonja called the fur shop to see if it was open that day. Leif Moen answered the phone. When Sonja replaced the receiver, she looked puzzled.

"The shop is closed, but he'd like us to go in for a couple of hours. He didn't say why. I said we'd get there soon."

They took a tram. As they drew near the centre of Oslo the swastika was everywhere, and German soldiers were patrolling the streets. When the two women reached the fur shop, the blinds were down. Leif admitted them at the side entrance and led them into the salon, where he had opened some of the glass display cases. His instructions were that he and Sonja would select the best of the furs and take them down to the storage room in the cellar. Johanna was to list the details and attach a label to each of those furs, stating that it was not for sale.

"Not for sale?" Sonja was puzzled. "Aren't the furs just going down into the basement as a protection against air raids?"

"That is one reason," Leif said. He looked intensely serious, strained. "The second is more important, in my opinion. I do not intend to sell my choicest furs to the enemy. They will stay in the storage room until the king is back in the palace and the swastika gone for ever."

Johanna understood his feelings and was encouraged by the stand he was taking. It was similar to her refusal to give up the car without a struggle. They had both asserted themselves in the face of the enemy. She had always liked Leif Moen. Now that she knew him better, she liked him even more.

For the next half hour sables and ermines and silver foxes went swirling down the iron steps to the storage room in the basement. Finally Leif padlocked the door on what were probably the most beautiful furs in the whole country. Stock left for sale was still of high quality, but the most fabulous garments would not be seen by German eyes.

Johanna and Sonja left the shop together. They parted at the corner, Sonja to go home, and Johanna to search for some blackout material for the windows of the Alsteens' house, since a complete blackout and curfew had been ordered by the Germans. That evening, after she had hung one strip of the black fabric over the kitchen window, she began making the curtains on Anna's sewing machine. Before she went to bed she tried to phone home in Ryendal, but she was not able to get through.

FOUR DAYS LATER an Allied force of British, French and Free Polish troops landed in northern Norway and at Åndalsnes in the west, on Johanna's home fjord. By that time the whole of the south had fallen to the Germans, and the Norwegian army was engaged in bitter fighting in the west and north. Johanna was deeply concerned about her family now that the war was on their doorstep. Her two brothers were particularly in her thoughts. Erik, who was an officer on a coastal steamer, had been at home on leave on the day of the invasion, and it was unlikely he would have been able to reach a naval fighting unit. She fully expected to learn that he had gone with Rolf, a teacher, into the army. Perhaps they were with the king, who was being hunted ruthlessly by the Luftwaffe; every village where he'd taken shelter had been razed to the ground.

Thoughts of Steffen were inevitably in Johanna's mind too. It was as if his kiss had awakened something within her that she had never been aware of before. She could not recognize it as love, yet the feeling was there, impossible to ignore, and it seemed to warm her whole heart.

April gave way to May and nicer weather, and Johanna's anxiety about her family was constant. Mail had been held up, and telephones were likely to remain out of action for a long time to come, as many exchanges were in the war zone or damaged by bomb blasts. The desperate fighting continued without respite.

Then, in June, France fell. It changed the whole situation. Britain now stood alone as a last bastion of freedom fighting against the Third Reich. To strengthen England, Winston Churchill ordered the withdrawal of the Allied forces from Norway.

The first Johanna knew of this disaster for her country was when a young saleswoman summoned her to Leif's office. She found all her fellow employees gathered together gravely.

"Now that we are all here," Leif said as Johanna took a place beside Sonja, "I have some bad news. After eight weeks of fierce fighting, the battle for Norway is lost. Yesterday evening the king and the crown prince and the legitimate government sailed aboard a British ship into exile in England." He looked at his staff compassionately. "Go home to your families for the rest of the day. Remember that we have been defeated in the field, but not in our hearts."

The women began to file out of the office. Leif, halfheartedly sorting some papers on his desk, was surprised when he looked up and saw Johanna still standing there. "Yes, Johanna?"

The question burst from her in anguish. "What can we do?"

He understood her meaning and came round to perch on the desk, facing her. "I don't know. I honestly have no idea. All I do know is that as long as there are men and women with the will to retain freedom, there is hope. Hold on to that hope. In time to come it could be the salvation of our country."

A TERRIBLE DESPAIR seemed to settle over the whole nation in the weeks that followed. Then there came one bright spark of encouragement. The BBC began special broadcasts in Norwegian from London, and from there King Haakon spoke out stirringly to his people, telling them to hold fast and that freedom would be regained. Within a few days thousands of clandestinely printed copies of his speech began to flood the country. Johanna found one wound into her typewriter. She did not ask how it came there. Instead, she tucked it away in her purse for safekeeping. That evening she put it into her neighbour's letterbox, doing her part in spreading the royal message.

Everybody had to register for a ration card and an identity card. There were only about eight hundred Jews in Norway; their cards were stamped with a red J, and they also had to surrender their radios. They had already suffered the desecration of the main synagogue in Trondheim.

All public gatherings were banned. There was to be no stopping to talk on the streets, listening to the BBC was strictly forbidden and the press came under the full pressure of German censorship. Travelling beyond a restricted area was not allowed without a special permit. Johanna began to wonder whether the Alsteens would ever get home again.

One section of the population had begun to accept the German presence. The collaborators and the opportunists stood out from the rest. They were not many, but they were there; and from the start they were contemptuously labelled "quislings" by everybody else. It was a new name for traitors that had taken root in the language after Quisling's infamous broadcast.

Johanna wrote to her parents as soon as the mail began to move again, and also to her landlady, Anna Alsteen. By chance both replies came by the same post. She opened the one from home first. Her mother wrote that all was as well as could be expected in the present circumstances. Her brothers had both been in the fighting. Rolf, who had suffered a minor wound, was helping on the farm until he received confirmation of a new teaching appointment, and Erik had been recalled to service in the coastal steamers by the Germans, who were using them for their own transport. Johanna, in a wave of homesickness, longed to see them all again.

Anna Alsteen's letter was a disturbing one. She was most anxious to get home, and wrote that if her dear husband were not Jewish, there would have been no problem since they would be returning to their own residence. Unfortunately, Jews were being allowed no privileges and travelling was barred to them. Her brother-in-law was hoping to get a permit for Viktor on medical grounds, but so far the German officials were not considering any special cases. It was easy to read between the lines and recognize Anna's underlying fear that Viktor might be in some particular danger from the authorities.

By the next post Johanna received a letter from Steffen in Ålesund. She was so thankful to see it that her excited fingers could hardly tear away the censor's resealing strip along the back. The letter was as guarded in its own way as Anna's had been, and it was as easy to read between the lines.

> Hello, Johanna,
>
> Greetings from the west coast. After the events of recent weeks, it's good to be getting back to normal. There's nothing like farm work for making one feel fit. It's as if I had never been away from here. I'm looking forward to the time when you can get home for a visit. Don't forget we have a date at Saeter Lake. I've missed you. It's been far too long. Write to me. My regards to Anna and Viktor.
>
> Steffen

She laughed softly. Cleverly he had chosen not to return to engineering, which would have drawn him into the German labour force to do their bidding. Instead, he had taken up farm work near his home, an occupation less likely to be interfered with by the enemy, who would want the land to be as productive as possible.

She wrote back to him at once. The reply came by hand in a most unexpected manner one warm August evening when she was sitting in the garden after work. She saw a tall man coming across the lawn, the sun behind him, and when she shaded her eyes she recognized her elder brother, Rolf. With a shout of joy she sprang up from her deckchair and ran to him. Lithe and lean, with thick fair hair that flipped across his forehead and keen greyish-blue eyes, he was at heart the more serious of her two brothers.

"I can't believe it!" she exclaimed delightedly. "However did you get here? How's everybody at home?"

He gave her immediate assurance that everyone was well. Then came a surprising bit of information. "There's a friend of yours helping out at the farm these days. You've heard from him, I believe." He patted the pocket of his jacket. "I've another letter from him for you, and others from Mother and friends in the neighbourhood. When they heard I was going to Oslo, everyone wanted to send greetings to you."

"Come into the house and I'll make you some supper. The food won't be much, I'm afraid. Rationing has begun to pinch hard."

"You don't have to tell me. There are Germans billeted in Ryendal to ensure that local produce gets channelled in the right direction, which usually means to the cookhouses of the German army." He went with her into the house, suitcase in his hand. "Mother has sent you some food. Butter and eggs and meat."

"Butter!" Johanna said appreciatively when it was unpacked. "I haven't seen butter on the shop shelves for weeks. Now I want to hear how you were able to come to see me."

He told her he had managed to get a permit to travel to Oslo to receive confirmation of his new post at the school back home in the valley. "Normally I would have gone further afield to a bigger school," he said, "but a delegation of local people asked if I would take over ours. They wanted someone they could trust to be in charge of their children. So I accepted."

"I'm glad. It means you can keep an eye on Mother and Father."

"The same thought occurred to me."

They had a happy meal, although there were very serious moments when he spoke of friends who had been killed. He told her that Steffen had been with the king throughout his campaign; the parting of ways had come when the royal party reached Molde. From there they had sailed for Narvik in the north to make their last stand. The Norwegian troops had been told to join other units where they could, since there was no place for them on the ship. In a matter of days it was all over. Steffen then went home to Ålesund to see his aunt, and afterwards presented himself at Ryen Farm for employment.

"He explained to Father that he needed time to lie low to see what should be done next. He began work in the fields the same day and has been staying at the farm ever since." Rolf smiled at her. "He's lost no time. Already he has a group of men training in the mountains at weekends. They have no arms except those that were buried after the surrender."

Her face was alight. "Do you mean that those weapons were buried in order to continue the fight?"

Rolf nodded. "Steffen's group isn't the only one. I've heard of others. The fight isn't over, Johanna. It's just beginning." He saw her eyes fill with tears. "Hey! What's the matter?"

"I'm just so thankful to hear that. Perhaps there'll be a chance for me to join the fight for freedom."

He raised an eyebrow warily. "Hold on there. You're my sister, and I don't want you involved in any trouble with the Germans."

She decided not to protest, but she was undeterred. Somehow and somewhere, her chance would come.

When she was alone in her bedroom she read her letters, saving Steffen's until last. With no danger of the censor's interference, he had written freely of being at the farm and of how much he missed her. His words, tender and fond, formed a true love letter. A yearning to be home again swept through her.

Chapter Three

Rolf only stayed overnight in Oslo. He telephoned Johanna at the fur shop before he left the city, to let her know the good news: his appointment had been given the official stamp.

After receiving his call, Johanna passed through the shop's salon, where a German officer was seated in one of the velvet upholstered chairs watching his Norwegian girlfriend try on coats. Sonja was serving them with a face of stone. Johanna quickly entered Leif's office and closed the door behind her.

Leif greeted her with his customary smile. "Before we get to work there is something I would like to discuss with you. I noticed that you kept quiet about the copy of the king's speech that you found on your desk."

She answered him frankly. "It was my guess you had put it there discreetly, for the Germans wouldn't be pleased about that kind of distribution. Isn't that so?"

"Correct. You, and Sonja also, were as discreet as I'd expected. And so I'd like to ask for further cooperation. Do you have a good radio in your house? One that will pick up the broadcasts in Norwegian from the BBC?"

"I listen to those broadcasts every evening."

"Would you like to take them down in shorthand and type them?"

"For distribution?"

"Yes. As an underground weekly newssheet to be called *London Ekko*. Some will go out from here under Sonja's supervision."

"I'll start this evening. There is a typewriter at the house."

"And use headphones as a precaution against being overheard. Everything could be lost."

"I'll do as you say." The excitement of having been given this task was heightened by knowing that here in Oslo, as in the forests and mountains, certain members of the community were stirring. That night, and for many nights afterwards, she waited for the familiar announcement: "*Dette er London!*" Then the inspiring burst of music, which faded as the news in Norwegian began.

The best news she recorded was the successful progress of the Battle of Britain. A handful of young Royal Air Force pilots were defying the might of the Luftwaffe in the skies above England. Hitler was suffering his first defeat.

Coinciding with this news was the rebirth of spirit throughout Norway. With the coming of autumn and the crisper, invigorating days that followed, people had suddenly overcome the gloom and despondency of defeat.

Thus it had been a particularly galling day for the citizens of Oslo when Quisling moved into the royal palace. Now it also housed the official headquarters of Hitler's personal representative in Norway, Reichskommissar Josef Terboven. He was an arrogant, cold-blooded Nazi, and his aim was to see that Norway gave the fullest strategic support to the German war effort, with only minimum troops kept in the country. He foresaw no problems.

But from the start the Lutheran state church, backed by the other churches, spoke out fearlessly against the Gestapo and the Nazi regime. The judges of the supreme court resigned *en bloc* to protest against Reichskommissar Terboven's interference with the justice of the land. Sportsmen and athletes made a defiant gesture by refusing to join the Nazi Sports Association. Johanna, taking down the radio reports, perceived that the Germans had failed completely to understand the character of the people they were trying to crush.

The first snows came and the holiday season drew near. That Christmas of 1940, the first under Nazi rule, promised to be bleak. Life was particularly wretched in Oslo, where the Gestapo was establishing a terrible hold from its headquarters in the Victoria Terrasse: students had been viciously beaten in their university, and arrests had been made after struggles in the streets. Two fifteen-year-old boys had been taken away for painting "Long Live Haakon VII" on the walls of a German billet. Their parents could discover nothing about their fate.

In the shops, anything remotely luxurious had long since disappeared from the shelves, and basic commodities were not always available. Long queues of people outside the food shops were an everyday sight.

One afternoon, when the snow was drifting down in huge flakes outside, the door of Johanna's office opened and to her astonishment Steffen appeared in the doorway. "Hello, Jo."

She released a soft cry, rising slowly to her feet. In the midst of her joy at the unexpected sight of him she realized that they had grown apart over the past months. Perhaps this was a cruel trick that war played.

410

"How are you?" she asked with a catch in her voice.

"I'm fighting fit. Thanks for your letters."

"And yours." It was not how she had pictured their reunion. She had always thought they would fall into each other's arms. Instead, he was as restrained as she. It was almost at though they were strangers again. "What has brought you to Oslo?"

"I came to see you. I've spoken to your boss. He says you may leave now. I've a taxi waiting."

Steffen was wearing ski clothes, and outside she saw that his skis were in the rack of the taxi, which was powered by one of the wood-burning stoves that people had begun to attach to the backs of their cars, petrol being unavailable to any vehicle not directly involved in the German war effort. They sat in the taxi holding hands while being driven through the snowy streets to Grefsen.

At the house, Steffen stuck his skis in the snow by the porch and removed his ski boots. As he closed the front door behind him Johanna took the boots from his hand to put them in the hall cupboard. The bulb in the hall lamp was a small one, and when she turned to face him, they were in little more than a pale gloom. His face was working, and her own lips were trembling.

"Jo!" he exclaimed huskily.

She threw herself into his arms and buried her face against him. They hugged each other wordlessly, his cheek against her head. It came to her that their reunions would always be fraught with difficulty for however long the war lasted, for each time they would have to find each other again. When they drew apart, both knew that they had recaptured the promise of love that had come about at the time of their first meeting.

"Hello there," he said.

"Welcome back," she replied in perfect understanding. Then he kissed her slowly and lovingly. She was deeply stirred.

He went into the kitchen with her to unload from his rucksack some food that her mother had sent, and then padded upstairs in his socks to find a pair of sandals. By the time he came down again, Johanna had begun peeling potatoes. They talked while she prepared a meal on the electric cooker.

"I went by steamer up the fjord from Ryendal's nearest jetty," he told her, setting places for two at the kitchen table. "Then, by arrangement, I made the rest of the journey in the back of a civilian truck carrying German food supplies to Oslo."

"Is the driver taking you back?"

"No. I'm leaving for Sweden in a few hours. I'm on my way to join the Free Norwegian forces in England. The underground has prepared routes to be followed on skis to the border; with luck I should be able to

411

avoid German patrols. In Stockholm, the Norwegian legation is still organizing routes to England."

"But you needn't have come south to make a getaway. People on the west coast are slipping out in boats across the North Sea. You ran the risk of being picked up for being such a long distance from your home district without a permit."

"I had to see you again. I only hope you're glad I'm here."

"You know I am."

Before they sat down to their meal she lit a candle and set it in a china candlestick on the table. Steffen turned the kitchen lights off so that they ate in the flame's glow. Their conversation was quiet; mostly he gave her news from her home district.

Towards the end of the meal she told him of the circumstances in which she had lost his car. He was dismayed at the stand she had taken, although he fully understood her attitude. "I don't care about the car. But you could have been arrested. Don't ever take a risk like that again." His face remained sombre as he reached out to hold her hand across the table. "I've something to tell you too. Not good news, I'm afraid. It's about your father."

She felt her heart contract with dread. "What's happened?"

His clasp tightened on her hand. "In August your father made a courageous gesture of resistance that had a serious aftermath. He went to Ålesund on business and it happened to be the king's birthday. So he bought a carnation to wear in his buttonhole."

It was the flower of the royal house. "Go on," she urged fearfully.

"He was set upon by German soldiers. They tore the flower out of his lapel, knocked him down and kicked him into the gutter. They went on kicking him. He suffered broken ribs and other injuries. His recovery has been slow. The worst seems to be over now, although he has to rest a good deal."

"Why wasn't I told?" she burst out.

"It was decided that you should not be worried. You wouldn't have been allowed to travel home at that time, and there was nothing you could do."

"Is my father able to work?"

"He does paperwork and some light chores, although he has aged considerably and is slow in his movements."

Johanna's expression was thoughtful. "Now I know why my mother took on extra help in the house in August. She wrote that she'd hired a girl named Karen Hallsted. What is she like?"

He grinned widely. "In one word—beautiful. Your brother Erik fell for her when he was home on leave. My guess is that he wants to marry her."

"You must be mistaken. Erik's never serious about any girl."

412

"Karen may be the exception. She's a stunner."

"I suppose she fell for him. They always do."

"On the contrary. The cold shoulder was obvious."

Johanna was amused. "Perhaps for once he's met his match." Then her voice turned serious. "How did your aunt take your leaving Ålesund to rejoin the king's forces?"

"Courageously. She's that sort of person."

They sat talking until it was time for Johanna to listen to the BBC newscast. Steffen stayed with her while she took down the reports. As soon as the broadcast was over he moved, to stand waiting for her. She caught her breath, seeing how he was looking at her, and she went to him without hesitation. With his arm round her they went up the stairs.

In the muted glow of her bedside lamp everything was perfect between them. He made tender and beautiful love to her. For her it was the first time. Never before had she cared enough to share and be shared. Now she loved, her heart full to overflowing, their joy in each other a revelation to them both.

She lay softly in his arms and they spoke quietly. "I love you, Jo, darling," he murmured.

She curled still closer to him. "I love you too."

"I have a gift for you." There was adoration in his eyes.

She smiled. "I didn't think there was anything left to buy."

"There isn't. It's something I made for you. A jeweller completed the work. It's my special love gift."

She was deeply touched by the significance of what he had said. It was a tradition in many districts that a bride received a love gift the morning after the wedding night. It was always a piece of jewellery. "Shouldn't it be given at dawn?"

There was regret in his answer. "I'll not be here at dawn." He handed her a small package and, propping himself on an elbow, watched her unfold the tissue paper.

She gazed in delight at what she saw. It was a long string of finely shaped stones, intricately capped and linked with gold, and polished almost to iridescence, the blended greys and pearly tones and tints of pink proclaiming their origin. Hours of care had gone into bringing the stones to such perfection.

"They're from Saeter Lake—the lake that links our homes. It's a wonderful gift," she said.

"It should have been diamonds."

"No!" She slipped the necklace over her head. His love had gone into every one of the exquisite stones. Suddenly her face became serious. "I'm going to England with you."

He cupped her shoulders with his hands. "I'd been thinking along the

413

same lines, but passages and transport are difficult for our diplomats in Stockholm to arrange. They'll not give a place to a woman in preference to a fighting man."

Her head sank down in disappointment. She could not dispute his argument. She would have to let him go without her.

Then it was time for him to depart. He took her into his arms for a long kiss. Talking was over. All that was left to say to each other was in his eyes and in hers.

"Farewell, my love," Steffen whispered. They kissed for the last time. Pulling on his gloves, he left the house. She remained in the unlit doorway, shivering in the icy air while he clicked on his skis. Then with a wave to her he was away, swishing across the snow, lost from sight in the early-morning darkness.

Chapter Four

Steffen had been gone two months. Winter still had a hard grip on the land. To Johanna, Oslo seemed to get bleaker every day. Most of her spare time was spent in food queues. All the store windows had a hollow look. Many that had once displayed fine wares had little more to offer than handmade wooden items. At the fur shop a printed card in the window suggested to passersby that old furs should be repaired and restyled. In the salon itself the glass-fronted cupboards were almost empty.

Johanna had no idea, when she went home one Friday after work, that she would find the Alsteens back at Grefsen. They had returned without advance notice. At the sound of her key turning in the lock, Anna came darting across the hall to embrace her. A plump and sturdy little woman when she had left, she had lost a lot of weight; moreover, constant anxiety had ravaged her gentle features and left grey streaks in her auburn hair.

"My dear child!" Anna's tears were flowing. "Whoever thought it would be so long before Viktor and I should get home again? And how well you've looked after everything. I'm most grateful."

Johanna, moved to tears herself, patted the woman's shoulder. "I did nothing. It's just wonderful that you're here at last, under your own roof again. Where's Viktor?" she asked, removing her outdoor clothes.

"In bed. The drive from Drammen tired him, even though it was in an ambulance. Go up and see him. He's not asleep."

The door to the Alsteens' bedroom was open and Viktor was propped against the pillows, his singularly sweet smile lighting his pale, almost transparent features. The thought that moved Johanna to fresh tears was that such a gentleman, in the true sense of the word, should have been a target for Nazi vindictiveness.

"It's Johanna. Prettier than ever. Come and tell me how you've been passing the time since I last saw you." His speech was, if anything, slightly more halting than before.

She sat on the bed and took his hand. It seemed to have no weight. "I'm still at the fur shop. There's not much business these days, as skins are hard to come by. The salon staff has been reduced to just Sonja."

Johanna talked a little longer; then she made a move to get up, not wanting to add to his tiredness with too much conversation. Unexpectedly, he caught at her sleeve with his stronger right hand. "Don't go yet. I have so little time to be with you. We're leaving again tomorrow. My brother-in-law, Anders, has arranged everything."

She thought the strain of the journey had confused him, and she smiled reassuringly. "You're home to stay now."

"No, my dear. Anna and I are going to Sweden. It's safe for me there. She wants to get me away while there's still time."

Johanna sat with him until he closed his eyes and drifted off to sleep. Gently she released his hand, then went downstairs to face Anna in the kitchen. She had no need to ask anything.

Anna sank into the nearest chair. "He's told you, I can see."

Johanna sat down facing her. "Has Viktor been threatened?"

"Many times. I can't even speak of the verbal abuse we received from the Germans in the streets. Fortunately, Anders seems to have contact with the new resistance movement, and somehow he managed to get a permit for us to travel."

"How are you getting into Sweden?"

"I have permission to take Viktor to a hospital near the Swedish border. An ambulance will call for us tomorrow morning." Anna became very tense. "I have papers for you too. I was hoping that you would escape with us."

Johanna stared at her. "Why do you want me to go with you?"

"Viktor will have to be pulled in a sled. I'll be on skis. We shall have a guide, but it would be a great comfort to me to have your company." Her lips trembled. "I'm so afraid, and you're so young and strong."

Leaving the chair, Johanna knelt in front of Anna and looked up into her face. "I'll do anything I can to help you. You've always been good to me. I'll come right to the Swedish border with you and see you across, but don't ask me to leave Norway. I couldn't do it. I have to stay."

Anna shook her head in agitation. "I can't let you return here to face the consequences of our departure. It won't be long before the German authorities check to see if Viktor is at the hospital. Please forget I asked you. I should never have done it."

Johanna straightened up. "Nobody need know that I've ever been away. If it should come out, I would say that I saw you to the hospital and left you there. I assume the driver of your transport will back up whatever story I give?"

"Oh, yes. Anders told me we could trust him completely."

"Then it's all settled."

THE AMBULANCE ARRIVED the next day at the appointed time. Anna travelled in the back with her husband, while Johanna sat beside the driver, a cheerful young man with a freckled face and a shock of ash-blond hair.

"Here we go, then," he announced. "I'm Kristofer Olsen."

She gave her name in turn. "Do you work for an Oslo hospital?"

"I'm a medical student. I've never driven an ambulance before. After today this one will go back to its depot, and nobody will be any the wiser." He glanced at her. "Why are you going to Sweden? Has the Gestapo got something on you?"

"No. Nothing like that. I just promised my friends I'd see them to the border. I'll be coming back with you."

"You want me to *wait*? That could be tricky."

She was worried. "It's important I return to Oslo quickly."

He whistled softly. "Well, I guess we can fix it somehow!"

They were stopped three times at roadblocks before they reached the hospital, but there was no trouble. The early darkness of the winter afternoon closed down on them. It was snowing lightly. Kristofer checked the final details with her.

"I'll go into the hospital with Viktor, you and Anna. We go to a waiting room which has two entrances. The Alsteens stay there, and you must be seen leaving with me. I'll make sure we're remembered in reception. Anna and Viktor will leave the waiting room by the other door, which will take them to the far side of the hospital. Someone will be watching for them there. You will nip after the escape party and catch up with them. OK?"

"OK," she repeated.

Anna had Viktor sitting up when the ambulance stopped. Kristofer ran round to open the door, and then the four of them hurried into the hospital. Luckily the reception desk was busy, and they went through to the waiting room without being questioned. Two other people were there and watched as Johanna bade the Alsteens farewell.

When she came out of the waiting room, Kristofer was at the reception desk joking with two nurses. He called, "Ready to leave, frøken?"

"Yes, I am," Johanna replied.

He had a final word with the nurses and then swaggered over to

417

Johanna. Outside, they both got back into the ambulance and he swung it round the hospital perimeter, showing her the direction she had to follow and where she would find him again. He slowed down just long enough for her to get out, and then he drove off into the snowy darkness.

Johanna ran past an outbuilding and found skis waiting for her. She set off at once through the descending snow. The air was cold and getting colder still. She found the Alsteens and their guide waiting under the cover of the trees. Viktor was cosily ensconced on a sledge, wrapped in blankets like a cocoon, and the guide, who did not give his name, had the straps of the sledge securely over his shoulders.

"Let's go," he said as soon as Johanna reached them. He began to ski effortlessly ahead, and the sledge skimmed easily over the snow. Johanna followed him and Anna brought up the rear.

There was no sound except the swish of skis. The guide stopped at intervals to allow a rest out of consideration for Anna, who, in her mid-fifties, could not be expected to keep up the pace that he and Johanna could share. Occasionally when he stopped, Johanna would take the lead. Once the guide produced a thermos of hot coffee, and Anna stooped down to hold a cup to Viktor's lips.

"Are you warm enough?" she asked him.

"Oh, yes," he replied, taking sips of the coffee.

"It won't be long now." She tucked the covers closer about his face. "Try to rest. We'll soon be in Sweden."

They were not far from the border when suddenly in the forest a rifle cracked and then another. More shots followed. Almost in the same instant a Norwegian skier was rushing upon them. He took in their situation at a glance. "Get out of here! The patrol is moving in," he warned. Then he was gone.

The guide looked at Johanna. "You and I must create a diversion. This woman is too exhausted to make enough speed." He turned to Anna, slipping the straps of the sledge onto her shoulders. "Listen, you have no more than a kilometre to go. You can do it easily if you take your time. Keep going east. Don't worry about the Germans. We'll draw them away from you. Good luck!"

There was no time for farewells. Johanna could only echo the guide's last words as she sped away with him. He gave her instructions over his shoulder, and they created a zigzag route, parting to cross and recross again, giving the illusion of moving in several directions. The patrol was drawn away from the escapees. Shots rang out, sometimes perilously close, but the firing was blind. Eventually the sounds of pursuit diminished, and after a while she realized the hospital could not be far away. Then, stopping, the guide indicated the direction she should take and parted from her without looking back.

Johanna left her skis by the outbuilding, guessing that someone in the escape chain would find them and take them away. At a run she went to the far side of the hospital, where Kristofer was waiting in the ambulance. As she collapsed on the seat he belted the ambulance out of the hospital gates.

THE POLICE STATION at number 19 Møllergaten had gained a notorious reputation, entirely at variance with its peacetime image. Many of those engaged in work for the underground had been arrested and taken there. And that was where Johanna was taken for questioning by the newly formed Quisling police when it became known to the authorities that the Alsteens had vanished.

Johanna was confident of the story she had prepared, and she answered questions without hesitation. Yes, she had accompanied the Alsteens to the hospital. Anna Alsteen had been worried about her husband's condition and had wanted moral support. No, she had not seen the couple since that night. She had returned with the ambulance to Grefsen. No, the driver had not given his name, as far as she could remember.

The Norwegian sergeant gathered the papers of her statement together and summoned a policeman forward. "The preliminaries are done. Take her along for further questioning." He snapped his right arm up in the Nazi salute. "Heil Hitler!"

Johanna whitened with apprehension. His order meant that she was to face German interrogation. She was taken up to the next floor and ushered into a well-equipped office. An officer began reading her statement, his black uniform that of the SS, with the death's-head insignia. Without looking at her, he indicated with a flick of his hand that she might occupy the hard wooden chair in front of the desk.

She sat down, her back very straight, her hands folded in her lap. His profile was stern as he continued reading; there was arrogance in the thin mouth and heavy chin. Still with his eyes on the statement, he addressed her in fluent but gutturally accented Norwegian. "You deny all knowledge of the Jew Alsteen's flagrant disobedience of the law, I see. Yet you must have had some inkling of what he and his wife intended."

"They kept their arrangements to themselves. Until the police took me for questioning, I had no idea my friends had disappeared that night. I left them at the hospital."

"They were not alone. There was a guide." Abruptly he swivelled round in his chair to face her. "What would you say if I told you that you were seen near the Swedish border that night?"

She kept her voice steady. "I would say it was a lie. In any case, how could I be a guide? I'm not a native of that district."

He scrutinized her, and it seemed an eternity before he gave a laboured sigh and tossed the statement down onto the desk. "I had already given that point some thought." Sitting back, he set his elbows on the polished wooden arms of his chair and placed the fingertips of both hands together in an arc. "Had it been Ryen valley instead of that area, I would not have let the allegations rest. I have decided that nothing more will be said about this case as far as you are concerned."

She was hard put to it not to close her eyes in relief. To her surprise he held out a gold cigarette case. She shook her head. "No, thank you. I don't smoke."

He put a cigarette between his lips and lit it. "Neither did you when I last saw you," he said. "But you were too young to smoke then. Only four years old, while I was a boy of twelve." Seeing her staring at him, he gave a nod. "Yes, I'm Axel Werner. Your parents took me into their home under the Fridtjof Nansen plan." He tapped the statement on the desk. "When I saw your name, I took over your interrogation. With anyone else you would not have had such an easy time."

Fridtjof Nansen, one of her country's famous polar explorers, had instigated a plan after the 1914-18 war to bring hundreds of destitute German children into Norwegian homes. There they were cared for as members of the family, restored to health and eventually repatriated. Axel had spent most of his time with her brothers, attending the local school, helping on the farm and climbing with them in the mountains.

Johanna voiced what had come into her thoughts the moment he revealed his past association with her family. "Under other circumstances you would have been welcomed back into my home and there could have been a renewal of our friendship, but never in the uniform you are wearing."

His face tightened, yet his tone remained even. "It is time you and others like you accepted our presence here in full understanding of the benefits that living under the Third Reich will bring you. Look at Denmark. King Christian accepted our presence in the spirit in which we came, and no lives were lost. Do you know what our troops call a posting there? The Whipped Cream Front!" He laughed at that, well pleased, as he pressed his cigarette out in an onyx ashtray.

Johanna swallowed. "From what I've heard, many Danes have not accepted your regime."

He jerked his chin contemptuously. "Don't be misled by idle talk. You can best serve your country by reconciling yourself and others to a thousand years of glorious rule." A glint of fanaticism showed in his eyes. "Norway is remarkably homogeneous. Pure Norse blood down through the centuries bringing forth the fair skin and hair and blue eyes that are the mark of the true Aryan. You Norwegians and we Germans are the same type of people in every way. You shall be with us in creating a perfect race to populate the world and rid it for ever of its scum."

She regarded him incredulously. Here was a man who had spent some boyhood years in her unbigoted country, and yet he had become a rabid Nazi. "May I go now?" she requested, keeping her voice under control.

"You'll remember everything I've said to you today?"

She gave a nod. He picked up her written statement again, tore it up and threw the pieces into the wastepaper basket. "There's my gesture of goodwill." His smile was benign. He rose to come round the desk and escort her to the door. "I must talk to you more about the New Order under our Führer, some time." He clicked his heels together and bowed to her. "Until our next meeting, Johanna. *Auf Wiedersehen.*"

She wanted to run from the building, to breathe in pure, uncontaminated air. Instead, she walked quickly, keeping her gaze ahead until she was well away from Møllergaten.

In MARCH JOHANNA'S DAYS at the fur shop came to an end. She had been granted a permit to travel home. A doctor's statement that her father's health had deteriorated over the past months had gained her the necessary permission.

There would be no new girl in the fur shop to replace Johanna. Leif wanted it that way. He had become deeply involved in the nationwide resistance movement that was now taking shape, with a military core known as the Milorg directing all major subversive activities. Leif asked Johanna if she would like her name volunteered for resistance work in the Ålesund area.

"Yes," she had said. "I want to do anything I can."

Then it was time to leave. She locked up the Alsteens' house and took a taxi to the railway station. When she arrived she had to take her place in a long line of waiting passengers. The military had priority in going aboard, but Johanna managed to get a seat. The journey ahead was a long one.

The train left on the stroke of seven o'clock. Due to the blackout regulations, the blinds had to be kept down over the windows, and there was reduced lighting, making it difficult to read. The night seemed endless. Johanna dozed more than slept. It was a relief when dawn came and the blinds could be raised. On either side of the track the great mountain ranges of the west rose against the cloudless morning sky, the snowcaps tinted in the sun's first rays. Fruit trees bursting into bloom seemed to cradle the scattered farmsteads in pink-and-white clouds. Johanna's heart was reopening to everything she saw in the happiness of her homecoming.

It was almost noon and gloriously warm when Johanna left the train at the busy station of Åndalsnes, at the head of Romsdal Fjord. When she got outside the station, she followed the street down through the little town to the quayside, where a steamer waited. It would take her on the last lap of her journey along many miles of fjord to her home. On board she stood at the rail to gaze at the sparkling water that was as deep as the mountain peaks were high. To her, no photograph ever seemed to capture the breathtaking splendour of the fjord country to which she was returning after being away so long.

The time of departure was imminent, and the last passengers were coming aboard. She watched a man in nondescript clothes handing his pass to the guard at the foot of the gangway, as she had done before being allowed on board. The guard gave a nod and returned the pass to him. He tucked it into an inside breast pocket as he came up the gangway. He happened to glance up towards Johanna at the rail. Without the slightest sign of recognition he turned and went to another part of the deck. Somehow, though, she knew that he had seen her.

Remaining where she was, Johanna watched the churning of the emerald water as the steamer drew out into the fjord. Excitement was racing through her. It was a strange kind of reunion that had taken place, in which neither could acknowledge the other. But Steffen was on board!

Chapter Five

It was a peaceful voyage of several hours down the fjord. The great mountains on either side were clear as cutouts, and there was barely a ripple on the glassy green water. By chance Johanna discovered that her father's cousin, Tom Ryen, was also on board. He greeted her heartily.

"What a pleasant surprise to see you!" He was a large, bulkily built man, with sandy colouring and a broad, affable face. A widower of some years, he had been a major in the regular army and had served at Narvik during the fighting. She was pleased to see him again, having always enjoyed his company, and noted that he was as well dressed as ever, his suit and well-cut overcoat obviously new, a rare sight these days.

"So what are you doing now?" Tom asked her. "Still in secretarial work? The last I heard, you were in Oslo."

"I left there yesterday evening." She told him briefly how it had come about, although she made no mention of her work for the underground press or her part in the Alsteens' escape. "How long is it since you've been to Ryen Farm?" she asked him.

"Some months now. I've been extremely busy since putting my uniform away. I've taken on some administrative work. The wheels have to be kept turning in everyday matters."

They remained together for the rest of the voyage. Once, while strolling round the deck, they passed Steffen leaning on the rail and studying the view. Johanna did not glance back or do the slightest thing that would bring any attention to him, yet it seemed to her that an electric current passed between them.

When her destination was reached, she parted from Tom Ryen. He was going on to Ålesund, also obviously Steffen's port of call, since it was the last stop and he was still on board.

"Give my good wishes to your family," her cousin said.

"Why not come ashore and have a word with Rolf? He's sure to be there to meet me."

Tom became quite reserved in his manner, more military and stiff-shouldered. "No, I'll not intrude on your reunion with your brother. You go and see if he's in sight yet. I'll visit you before long."

She thought the change in his attitude odd, but forgot all about it when she saw Rolf waving to her from the jetty as the steamer came alongside. When she stepped from the gangway, he greeted her fondly. "How's Father?" she asked at once.

Rolf was reassuring. "He'll be all the better for seeing you. Mother is well and everything is all right at the farm." He carried her suitcases across to the waiting horse-drawn wagonette. As they drove off she mentioned seeing Tom Ryen on the steamer. Rolf's brows drew together. "We've heard rumours about him. It's said that he's in charge of an office recruiting workers to build airfields and defences for the Germans."

"Surely Tom's not a collaborator!"

"I'm afraid that these days we're discovering the difference between the wheat and the chaff."

An octagonal white wooden church at the water's edge, a nearby cluster of houses and three shops made up the hamlet of Ryendal. They drove up the valley in the early evening sunlight, past farmsteads that Johanna knew as well as her own. Most of the barns had picturesque turf roofs from which spring flowers were beginning to sprout like blooms on a bonnet. Then, ahead, the schoolhouse came into sight, painted pine green. Rolf gave a nod towards it.

"Did you hear that the teaching of English has been banned? German is to become Norway's second language."

"It must be difficult to have the Germans breathing down your neck. Your classroom should be your own."

"Dictates for nazification have been laid down that are the same as those used on the young in Germany." His voice tightened. "Throughout Norway the teaching profession is consolidating into a powerful section of the Resistance."

Johanna glanced sideways at Rolf. "I'm hoping to get a chance to do my share of resistance work locally."

He shook his head firmly. "Take it easy for a while, Johanna. The Germans have been like hornets in this district recently. One of their patrol boats was sabotaged in the fjord, and they have made a number of arrests."

She refrained from saying any more. It would be her decision, when her opportunity came.

The road climbed towards the head of the valley, and their white farmhouse came into view with its roof of curved dove-grey shingles, and blue filigreed woodwork ornamenting the window frames, lintels and porch. Further ahead lay the rust-red barn, its turf roof matching those of the other outbuildings. Their arrival had been glimpsed from a sitting-room window, and Johanna's mother appeared on the porch. Gina Ryen was a small, thin woman with a knot of silky grey hair. Her face was lined beyond her age, but her cautious smile had never lost a childlike shyness.

As Rolf drew the horse to a halt Johanna sprang down from the wagonette and rushed up the porch steps to embrace her mother. "I'm so glad to be here again!"

"Welcome home, child." Gina remained stiff-backed and withdrawn in her daughter's arms. Her intense reserve kept her from any outward show of feeling. Nothing in her composed exterior, except a spot of heightened colour in her cheeks, revealed what it meant to her to have her daughter home again. When Edvard Ryen appeared in the doorway, however, the reunion between father and daughter was exuberantly affectionate.

"I've brought you home on false pretences," he joked easily. Although prepared for a change in him, Johanna had been unable to imagine how wasted and drawn he would be. Yet she answered him cheerily in the same vein.

"I can see that, but no matter. I couldn't have stayed away in any case. With summer coming, you need me on the farm."

In the kitchen the newly employed helper, Karen Hallsted, was waiting by the table she had laid for supper. She was, Johanna thought as they were introduced, as strikingly beautiful as Steffen had described her, with her lovely, symmetrical face, lustrous violet eyes and flawless complexion. Her hair was literally her crowning glory, being a platinum colour, full of shining lights and dressed from a middle parting into a braided coil at the back of her head. Her smile was natural and sunny. Karen was a farmer's daughter following an old custom by which farm girls left their home districts to work elsewhere, a tradition that had evolved to prevent intermarriage in remote valleys.

Everybody sat down to supper. There was black bread, a little homemade butter, milk and—a marvellous sight for Johanna—a dishful of cold veal and lamb. Meat had disappeared from the shops throughout the country, and it was a long time since she had eaten anything except fish as a main course.

"After the lambing," Rolf told Johanna, "we hid some of the flock up in the summer barn, and we have cattle there too. Our neighbours are doing the same. It's not much we can keep back, but at least not everything we produce is going into German stomachs. When somebody slaughters secretly, we all share."

"Suppose the Germans should hear the cattle lowing?"

"No chance. The barn is out of earshot from the valley, and in any case, the waterfall's roar masks everything. Besides, the soldiers fear going into the mountains. A local marksman could pick them off and their bodies would never be found. So the high terrain is still ours."

The next morning Johanna wrote to Steffen's aunt in Ålesund to ask when she might call to see her. After she put the letter in the roadside postbox, she went for a long walk, covering old tracks through the woods and crossing the bridge that spanned the river. Leaning her arms on the timber top rail, she looked down into the clear and rushing water, able to discern small, pale-tinted stones similar to those that Steffen had gathered to make the necklace that she treasured. A yearning for him filled her entire being.

Johanna received a prompt reply from Steffen's Aunt Astrid. Frøken Larsen sent an invitation to lunch. Gina made up a package of some homemade beef sausages for Johanna to take, a gift more welcome than gold. A neighbour gave Johanna a lift into Ålesund in his horse-drawn trap. She alighted near the towering rock in the centre of town, where hundreds of seagulls nested, their screeching and wheeling overhead a part of the everyday scene in the busy port. Ålesund was built on three islands linked by bridges, the buildings so crammed together that the pastel-coloured warehouses rose up sheer from the seawater. The masts of tied-up fishing boats were like fences through which to view the passing sea traffic.

There was a three-mile fishing limit now. This was the route that escapees took from the west coast, and the number of German soldiers at the quayside and on duty throughout the town showed how alert a vigil was kept.

Astrid Larsen's house occupied a choice site on a wooded slope that looked out across the harbour to the open sea. It was a sizable mansion, its paintwork a pale amber with filigreed white woodwork. Simplified dragon heads at the four corners of the roof gave it the graceful look of a Viking ship.

As Johanna neared the house she came to a halt, for half a dozen

German vehicles were parked outside the gate. There were at least two large staff cars of the type used by high-ranking Gestapo and Wehrmacht officers. The military drivers of these cars lounged about, chatting together and smoking cigarettes. Then she saw an elderly, distinguished-looking woman with softly waved white hair beckoning to her from the gate. Johanna went to her, ignoring the whistles and remarks of the German drivers.

"Take no notice of them," Astrid Larsen said firmly, introducing herself as she ushered Johanna through the gate. "This way. Follow me." They entered, through a side door on a long veranda, a large and airy room. "Welcome to the small section of my home in which I'm still permitted to reside."

"Thank you." Johanna could not hold back the question that was uppermost in her mind. "Do you have any news of Steffen?"

The woman put a finger to her lips and indicated that danger lurked behind some double doors, which were padlocked on her side. "Yes, he's safe and well," she whispered. Then in a normal voice she added, "Take off your jacket. I'll hang it up for you."

Johanna obeyed, handing over the package she had brought with her as well. "This is a gift from my mother. Living on a farm means there is a little to spare sometimes."

It was gratefully accepted. "I must apologize for my haste in bringing you into the house, but I wanted to get you away from those soldiers as quickly as possible."

From the direction of the padlocked double doors there came muffled sounds. Astrid sighed. "I'm afraid that part of the house has become a Nazi officers' brothel." A look of weary forbearance showed in her eyes.

That this should have happened to such a quiet, dignified woman seemed to Johanna particularly cruel. "How long has your home been commandeered?" she asked.

"Four months. It came as a great shock to me. I was given this room, and a small pantry across the hallway that I've made into a kitchenette. A stairway gives me access to two bedrooms and a bathroom above. So here I stay, an outcast on my own property."

The large and gracious room, with its cool greens and white, seemed a fitting setting for Steffen's elegant aunt. The house must have been furnished when she was still young, for everything was of the art nouveau period. The silver objects included a pair of magnificent candelabras, each one a draped female figure holding aloft the curving stems of lilies in which the candle holders were cradled. Johanna, looking at it all, was most aware that she was in Steffen's childhood home.

"Tell me about Steffen, Frøken Larsen. It must have disrupted your life to have a young boy coming to live here."

Astrid laughed merrily. "It did indeed. But he was my brother all over again—boisterous, good-humoured, sports-crazy. I had to become both mother and father to him." She went to a rosewood cabinet and took out a large photograph album. "Perhaps you'd like to look through this while I finish making lunch."

Johanna sat down and took the album onto her lap. Turning the pages, she followed Steffen from boyhood through adolescence and into young manhood. Girls figured prominently in many of the later snapshots. Astrid must have thought of this, for during lunch she emphasized that Steffen had never before been so keen that she and a girl he knew should become friends.

"You may call me Astrid," she invited. "Steffen has done so since he became grown-up. I must say it makes me feel younger." Then she glanced at the gold locket watch she wore on a chain. "It's time. He will be here now."

"Here?" Despite her astonishment Johanna kept her voice low.

Astrid rose to her feet. "There's a small, sliding-panel doorway in the cupboard under the stairs that you'll have to get through. You'll find yourself in a cellar that is completely detached from the larger one that runs under the rest of the house. It belonged to a farm building that once stood at right angles to this site, and the Germans overlooked it when they inspected the place. It's an ideal hideout."

"But here? Under the noses of the Germans!"

"All the better. It's the last place they'd search in any emergency. Now come along."

Johanna held her breath with excitement and trepidation as she went under the stairs and crept through the small doorway into the cellar. Chill air and blackness met her. Then the sudden turning up of a lampwick showed her the man she had waited so long to see again.

"You're really here," she exclaimed spontaneously.

He reached for her as she came down the steps, and she flung her arms about his neck, caught on a wave of intense feeling. Not until she drew back did she see that he looked older and sterner, as if whatever he had been through on his escape to England had left its mark. Had he become a stranger to her again? She thought his kiss had belied that, but she could not be sure. Nothing was sure any more.

"You look well, Jo," he said approvingly. "I've been anxious about you."

That warmed her. "I wanted so much to speak to you when you came aboard the steamer. How long have you been back in Norway?"

"Only a couple of weeks." He put an arm about her waist and they sat together on a bench drawn up to an old table on which the lamp stood. "In England I was lucky enough to be picked out for special training with the British Special Operations Executive, an organization set up by Winston Churchill to direct subversive activities in occupied countries."

"Then you're here to stay."

He gave a half smile. "Let's say I'll be coming and going. My immediate task is to recruit and train agents and organize resistance in this area. Normally you wouldn't be hearing anything of this from me. One of our orders is to stay away from our families and the women in our lives. A thoughtless word in a small community could destroy a whole carefully planned operation."

"Why have you made me an exception to this order?"

"Two reasons. First, I knew I couldn't use this cellar without Astrid's knowledge. Since I hope you are going to be a frequent visitor, sooner or later you might have suspected something. It was better to give you the full facts too."

She glanced about her at the rough rock walls. The lamp could not reach into the far depths. "It's an enormous cellar. I've never seen anything like it before."

"It has the advantage of two secret outlets, impossible to discover from outside, since they pass through piled boulders from an ancient avalanche, then into a forest. If ever suspicion should fall on her, Astrid must feign ignorance of her cellar's being used by the Resistance."

"She's courageous."

"The best." He grinned at Johanna. "I hear you acquitted yourself well in Oslo. Leif Moen sent a report on you to the Milorg, which directs our subversive activities. We know all about your helping the Alsteens."

"Are they all right?" she asked. "Have you heard from them?"

"No, I haven't. But no sign of them was ever found on this side of the border. All that was received was an account of your part in getting them away. That's the second reason why I'm able to confide in you. You're in the Milorg's good books."

Johanna seized the opportunity that had presented itself. "Then surely I qualify to be one of your secret agents!"

He regarded her steadily. "I'm recruiting men."

Her retort was full of anger. "Aren't women involved in this war? Aren't we also bombed, starved and imprisoned?"

"It's not that. What's required would be beyond your physical strength. These agents may have to live for months in the mountains, leading clandestine fighting groups, able to kill with their bare hands. This is Milorg work. There are plenty of other roles that a brave and intelligent woman can play. You can be invaluable to me."

"How? Tell me?" She leaned towards him in her eagerness.

"By giving Astrid all the support you can. She's elderly and this will be a great strain on her."

428

Johanna drew back and her anger flared white-hot. "How dare you delegate such a task to me! Astrid wouldn't want me fussing over her as if she were halfway to senility. Leif didn't put my name forward for you to turn me into a nursemaid!"

Her temper ignited his, and he hauled her to her feet. "Damn it! You're in danger enough just by knowing I'm here! Do you think I'm going to put you in greater risk?"

She pulled away from him. "Have you learned nothing about me? Maybe making love when we did was a mistake. Too much happened too soon, and we're still strangers to each other. You have no more understanding of me than the Sturmbannführer who interrogated me!"

He went pale with anger and seized her by the shoulders. "All right! You'll get an assignment. I promise you it will be a tough one, and you'll stand or fall by it."

It was as though they had abruptly become antagonists despite the magnetism between them. Their strained faces acknowledged that each had created pain and turmoil for the other.

"That's settled, then." His voice was hard and his attitude cold. "You'll have to be patient. It may be weeks before you hear from me again, but don't think I've forgotten my promise to you. There's still a lot of organization to be done." He glanced at his watch. "Go back to the house. I'll wait to switch off the lamp until you're safely up those steps."

She mounted the steps, emotionally torn apart. As she slid aside the panel leading into the house, she paused to look back. It was too late. The lamp had been switched off at the same moment, to leave the cellar in total darkness, and she heard the faint thud of a secret door closing after Steffen.

Chapter Six

Johanna did not intend to waste her time while waiting for her first assignment. Already fit, she kept trim with plenty of exercise, which included hard physical work on the farm, climbing mountain paths and swimming in a shallow cove when the warm weather came. Summer was still a good time of year in spite of the occupation, for this was when marvellously hot days compensated for the winter, and the sun gave twenty-four hours of daylight.

In June school broke for the summer holidays, giving Rolf the chance to work full time on the farm. As was customary, the sheep and cattle were moved to the lush and green high pastures, to graze there until autumn. The summer barn belonging to Ryen Farm came into use again for the morning and evening milking, which Rolf and Johanna did together. If her father had been making progress, Johanna would have been more at ease, but he was getting weaker and was increasingly bedridden.

Their cousin, Tom Ryen, kept his word about coming to visit. He arrived on a Sunday, when Johanna, Rolf and Karen were in the mountains, and he had left before they returned. Edvard had doubts about Tom's loyalties, and he did not thoroughly enjoy the visit. There had been nothing pro-Nazi in Tom's conversation, but he had admitted recruiting workers for various Nazi projects.

Local friends called on Edvard regularly, but the visits he appreciated most were those that his younger son made, briefly and without announcement. The days when Erik was granted regular leave from the coastal steamer service had ended when the Germans took control. Now, on the rare occasions when he could get home, he never received more than a couple of days ashore. Johanna had yet to see him.

It was early September and the last evening at the summer barn when Rolf and Johanna arrived there to find a schoolteacher named Nesheim from the next village waiting for them. Rolf went to talk to him while Johanna made ready for the milking. A moment later her brother came through the low doorway of the barn. "Johanna, it's you Nesheim wants to speak to."

Puzzled, she went outside. "You wanted to see me?"

The schoolteacher drew near. "I have special instructions for you. Come here tomorrow evening with Rolf at nine o'clock and bring a pocket torch. A parachutist will be landing not far from here with a cache of arms. I'll deal with the container of arms, and Rolf will dispose of the parachutes. Your task will be to guide the parachutist to the unused cabin by Troll Lake. There you'll receive further instructions. Is that clear?"

"Perfectly. I've been waiting for a chance like this."

"So I was told." He gave a grim nod. "Good. Until tomorrow."

THE FOLLOWING NIGHT was rainy and black as pitch. Johanna and Rolf went up to the summer barn, where Nesheim was waiting for them. Almost without a word they set off together, Rolf collecting a spade from the barn to bury the parachutes. Within half an hour they had reached an area of plateau that was the appointed place, and they spread out to wait. When the allotted time arrived, Rolf lit a bonfire as a guide to the aircraft.

Johanna suddenly grew tense. Above the patter of rain on leaf and grass there came the distant drone of a plane. She saw Rolf's light blink in a signal to be on the alert.

Desperately she strained her ears. Then she heard a swishing sound, and as if the sky had suddenly bloomed overhead, she saw the vastness of the parachute and watched it swoop down to be lost in the blackness somewhere behind her. Now it was she who flashed her light to let the others know that the parachutist had landed. She hurried towards the landing site, a dell where the plateau dipped as if under the weight of a blanket of heather. She gave the password quickly. The parachutist was trying to pull in the rigging lines of the great billowing mass. A young woman's voice spoke out from the struggle. "I'm glad I didn't land on top of a tree!"

Then Johanna saw her face and recognized her as the Englishwoman to whom Steffen had said goodbye on the day of the invasion. The parachutist was Delia Richmond.

Rolf arrived then. After a brief greeting he gathered in the parachute and brought it under control. The container had landed at almost the same time in the opposite direction. "You take over now," he said to Johanna. "I'll join you in a minute or two, as soon as I've buried this silk."

Johanna led the way with her light. It was not an easy walk to the cabin, with obstacles of rocks and hillocks and bubbling streams all the way. Delia followed quicky and calmly. With her eyes accustomed to the darkness, she saw the cabin ahead at the same time as Johanna. The man coming down the steps to meet them was familiar to both of them. Delia darted ahead of Johanna and threw herself into Steffen's arms.

Johanna came to a standstill some little distance away, able to see by the blended shadowy shapes that they embraced. As he showed Delia into the cabin Johanna thought he must have forgotten about her. She was wrong. He had not gone inside but loomed again from the shadows, keeping a lookout. When Rolf appeared, he went ahead to reach Steffen first. Then she heard her brother say impatiently, "Come on, Johanna. What's keeping you?"

They both stood on the steps to see her in. Steffen looked searchingly into her face, as aware as she that the last time they had been together they had parted in anger. "You all right, Jo?"

"Fine," she replied, going through the doorway into the cabin. Delia was standing by a wood-burning stove that made the whole place like a warm oven. She had divested herself of her parachuting outfit and cast it into the flames. She produced some English coffee out of the pocket of the blue anorak she wore, together with a thick sweater and ski slacks, beneath the outfit. In all, she was dressed like Johanna and would have passed without notice anywhere in the country.

Johanna volunteered to make the coffee, and found four enamel cups in a cupboard. Nesheim would be halfway down the mountainside by now with the container of arms. As she waited for the coffee she listened to, but did not join in, the conversation around the table where the three of them sat. Delia was giving Steffen news of mutual friends, and there were references to parties in the past that both had attended. Johanna observed the understanding between them. She poured the coffee and took the remaining chair at the table.

"Now to business," Steffen said briskly. "Where's the important package you brought with you?" He held out a hand to Delia.

She took a slim package from an inner pocket. "Here it is."

He put it on the table in front of him. Then he took an envelope from his own pocket, which he pushed towards Johanna.

"This is the assignment I promised you. Meeting our newcomer and guiding her to this cabin was just the preliminary. The package she has brought is to be delivered by you to an address in Oslo. This envelope contains a travel pass bearing the official German stamp authorizing your journey. You'll find enough money to cover your expenses. I want you to return by the overnight train." He was regarding her steadily.

Johanna picked up the envelope. "What pretext do I use for being in Oslo if I'm stopped by the Germans for questioning?"

"You'll say you're going to see your former employer at the fur shop. I have constant contact with Leif Moen in the Resistance. If you're unable to deliver the package to the address I shall give you, Leif will take it from you, but it's preferred that it should go directly to the person awaiting it. Any diversion increases the risk of discovery." His voice took on a stern note of warning. "Remember to behave as routinely as possible. Do nothing to draw attention to yourself. Leave your smart clothes at home. You know how the average Oslo woman dresses. Aim to blend into the background. Do you have any questions?"

When she shook her head, he proceeded to give her the address of a flat in a street she knew. She repeated it three times for him, memorizing it. Then he gave her the password, which would be given in reply to her question as to the whereabouts of the previous occupants of the apartment. Again she had to practise the procedure three times. Lastly, he pushed the package across to her.

"Put it somewhere next to your body. If you carry it in your bag, it could be seen when you show your papers. Whatever happens, don't allow it to fall into enemy hands. That's an order."

She fully understood. "I'll obey it."

He nodded. "There's only one possible complication. As you may have heard, the trade unions in the factories have called a strike, and there have been mass arrests by the Gestapo in Oslo. If you see any kind of demonstration, keep away from it."

"Am I to notify you when I get back?" she asked him.

"There's no need. I'll hear that the package has been delivered before

432

you are home again. Just carry on as usual afterwards at the farm." He glanced at his watch. "You had better get home now. You've a busy time ahead."

No kiss or embrace to send her on her way. Even worse was the realization that Steffen and Delia were preparing to leave together, talking as they zipped up anoraks and donned woolly caps. Johanna took the package from the table.

"Ready to go?" Rolf asked her, waiting to leave.

"Yes, I am." She started for the door. Simultaneously Steffen and Delia turned towards her. The Englishwoman jerked up a thumb cheerily, and Steffen walked over to the door. "Good luck, Jo," he said evenly. Briefly their gaze held, each able to see how greatly the gap had widened between them.

At the farmhouse, everyone was asleep. Although tired, Johanna packed an overnight case and went through her wardrobe, busying herself to keep thoughts of Steffen at bay. Eventually she chose a dark blue suit that was neat and trim, teaming it with a polka-dot scarf. In spite of hardships, Oslo women were maintaining their standards, and if stockings were almost entirely darns, gloves mended and shoes patched, it did not detract from their general appearance. There were more ways than one to defy the Germans.

In the morning Johanna took the steamer up the fjord to Åndalsnes and disembarked in good time to catch the overnight train. It was crowded with the military, and she did not get a seat. She sat on her suitcase all the way. Due to the strike crisis, armed guards came aboard at each stop. Not for the first time she thought the general harassment and constant interference in the normal run of life was as heavy a burden as any the Nazis could contrive. During the journey Johanna had to show her papers nine times.

When the train drew into the platform at Oslo, she felt alarm at the number of armed guards who stood watching the carriages slowing to a halt. She lined up to get off with a wedge of passengers before and behind her. When her turn came to go through the open door, she saw that some of the storm troopers had formed a semicircle through which she would have to pass. Her heart hurtling against her ribs, she made to alight.

In the same instant a man behind her gave her a huge shove that sent her flying forward to fall against the nearest storm trooper. Amid the uproar that followed she saw her fellow passenger making a run for it, storm troopers in pursuit. He did not get far. As he was dragged away the rest of the guards returned to their surveillance of the passengers as if nothing had happened.

Johanna checked in her suitcase at the left luggage counter and left the railway station. In spite of the bright autumn day, the city looked gloomy to her. If anything, there seemed to be more German eagles vying with the swastika for space on the buildings. There was also a new flag in abundance, with the sun cross of Quisling's Nazi party.

She took the tram to a stop near the entrance to Vigeland Park. Without hesitation she turned into the tree-lined street where the flat was located. She pushed open the entrance door and went up the stone stairs. There was no lift. On the third floor she found the door of number 7. She rang the bell. There was no response.

She was about to ring a second time when there came the sound of cars squealing to a halt outside. As the door crashed open at street level, there came the noise of booted feet ascending the stairs. Johanna darted up the next flight to the floor above. There she paused to listen, her pulse racing. She had been just in time. The door she had just left was being pounded by heavy fists and the bell pressed urgently.

"Open up!"

A sharp order brought a lunge of shoulders to burst open the door. It was a matter of seconds before it gave. Johanna peeped cautiously over the railing to see if there was any chance of slipping past unnoticed, but there were two Gestapo SS men outside the flat. As she drew back a sergeant emerged briefly to give them further instructions.

"He's got away. Check every flat and see if you can find someone who is able to give us information. Take the upper floors first."

Johanna spun round and went up another flight. As she reached the landing she saw that one of the front doors stood open and a child, aged about four, quaint and button-nosed, was waiting in outdoor clothes, holding a rubber ball.

"Are you going to play in the park?" Johanna asked her quickly.

The child nodded. "Mama is coming too."

At that moment the young mother came out of the apartment and pulled the door shut behind her. She raised her eyebrows inquiringly at Johanna. "Were you looking for someone?" Then, attracted by the commotion on the floors below, she leaned over the railing to take a look. "Do you know what's going on down there?" she asked.

"The Gestapo has broken into one of the flats."

"Oh, dear." The woman blanched, drawing back.

Johanna took a desperate chance. "Would you let me walk to the park with you and your daughter?" she requested urgently. "What's her name?"

The alarmed mother gave her child a pat. "Tell the lady your name."

The reply came shyly, with hung head. "Margit."

Johanna stooped down to her. "May I hold your hand, Margit, when we go out? That would make me feel like one of the family."

"Yes. You can hold the ball too, if you want."

Johanna took it and looked at the mother in silent appeal. For an agonizing moment the woman was poised on the point of snatching up the child and disappearing behind a closed door. It might have gone that way if little Margit, impatient to get out, had not darted to the head of the steep flight. The woman rushed to take the child by the arm. Facing Johanna, she gulped and nodded.

"Very well. Don't tell me your name or why you're here. I don't want to know. When we reach the park, please go away."

"I will."

Johanna talked with the child as they went hand in hand down the stairs, the mother following behind. The two SS men, jackbooted and black-uniformed, were turning away from a flat door being closed by an occupant.

"Wait! Which flat are you from?" they demanded.

The mother answered. "Number twelve."

"Do you know the man Hansen who lives at number seven?"

"No. The flat changed hands only a short while ago. I don't think I've ever set eyes on him."

The questioner switched to Johanna. "What about you?"

"I've never seen him either."

The man's eyes went from her to the mother and back again. Then a curt nod permitted them to pass. A glance through the doorway of number 7 as the three of them went by showed that it was being ransacked. In the entrance hall an SS man watched them come down the stairs. Johanna opened the entrance door for mother and daughter.

"Achtung!" It was the guard in the hallway, who had stepped forward to halt them on the very threshold. Johanna and the woman froze. Then they turned. The man's leather-gloved finger was pointing to a child's mitten on the marble floor. With a gulp of acknowledgment the mother went back to snatch it up. As they went outside she pushed it back onto her daughter's hand. Then the three of them walked hand in hand to the park, Margit dancing along in the middle.

Inside the park Johanna played ball with the child for a few minutes, then took her leave, grateful for a kindness shown in an hour of great need. Leisurely she wandered on, gazing at the statues created by the famous Norwegian sculptor Gustav Vigeland. By the tall white granite monolith that dominated the park, Johanna sat down on a bench and looked up at the hundreds of sculptured figures that made the monolith curiously alive. Soon a young man took a seat beside her and opened a newspaper. A page slipped and fell to the ground almost at her feet.

"Excuse me, frøken," he said, leaning down to pick it up. "Everything has become mixed up today."

Her gaze sharpened on him. "Is that so?"

He nodded, folding the newspaper together again. "Due to an unexpected change of plan, I had to leave my apartment to meet someone off the night train from Åndalsnes, but I missed her."

She was convinced that this was her contact. Casually she launched into what she would have said if he had opened the door of the apartment. "I'm looking for the Hauge family. I wonder if you could tell me where I might find them?"

He gave her word for word the reply rehearsed by Steffen. "Do you mean Federik and Solveig Hauge, by any chance?"

"No, I don't. My friends are Rolf and Jenny."

"Jenny, eh?" he said, repeating the special password. Then he added quietly, "Put the package by the sculpture of the woman with the plaited hair, near the monolith. I'll be watching to pick it up. One more thing. Avoid going to the fur shop. The Gestapo has launched an all-out campaign against our resistance network. We don't know yet whose names are on their list, except," he added on a wry note, "it is more than apparent that mine is included. I must get away as soon as I have the package. Good day to you, frøken." He got up from the bench and strolled away.

THE DAY AFTER Johanna arrived back at the farm a contact checked to be sure she was home safely. After that she heard no more.

Of concern now was a new German restriction: all civilians, except those belonging to Quisling's Nazi party, were to hand in their radios. On the appointed September day people reluctantly and angrily obeyed.

With Teutonic thoroughness, every radio was labelled with the owner's name and then stored. In the hamlet of Ryendal, as well as in many other places, the storehouse was broken into on the first night. It was not long before most homes had access to the BBC again, with radios concealed in everything from a thermos bottle to a cut-out telephone book. Rolf, who had always been an enthusiastic wireless expert, made one for the farmhouse and concealed it in a bird's nesting box on the outside wall.

The Nazi reign of terror gathered momentum. Many patriots were shot, and arrests were wholesale. It was said that great numbers were crammed into the cells of number 19 Møllergaten under interrogation and torture. In the midst of all this alarming news there was a brighter moment at Ryen Farm when Erik unexpectedly came home for two days' shore leave.

Tall and lean in his dark uniform, Erik seemed to bring a breath of the outside world with him. His narrow grey eyes were alert and observant, and his mouth was wide, with a smile full of charm. His hair, clipped short in naval style, was stubbornly curly. He looked what he was, an easygoing and virile man able to cope with any situation that came his way.

While his sister and mother welcomed him, Karen paused only briefly in breadmaking to give him a conventional word of greeting. Yet she blushed, a hint if anyone around her needed it that she was in love with him. It seemed to Johanna that Erik was the only one in the family who had not guessed the truth. Karen wanted to keep it that way, for he would be the first to take advantage of it. He was too used to his smooth ways working for him as far as women were concerned, and her wariness had made him all the more persistent.

Karen was shaping the loaves ready for the oven. She glanced up as Erik set both hands on the opposite side of the table, leaning on them and grinning at her as she dusted off her floury palms. "How have you been spending your time?" he asked.

"I made the most of the last days of summer." She listed an account on her fingers. "Johanna and I had a final swim. Then there were picnics. Three weeks ago I managed to get a pass to travel home, where I stayed for a few days."

"What about a fishing trip up to the lake with me? I need some high-mountain air. We can go tomorrow and take a picnic."

He gave her no chance to refuse, leaving the kitchen to go and sit at his father's bedside.

Johanna saw them off to the mountains the next morning. Karen carried one fishing rod and Erik another, the rucksack on his back holding their picnic. Past Ryen Farm Erik opened the last cattle gate and then they were on a winding path that began to ascend the mountainside. Above the dwindling tree line they came onto the high pastures near a cluster of *saeter* cabins at the side of the lake. In past decades the daughters of the valley farms had stayed in these ancient turf-roofed log cabins during the summer months while tending the cattle. Now they were used by those on skiing, walking or fishing trips. Leaving her rod propped outside with Erik's, Karen took the key from a ledge and led the way into the Ryen cabin. Inside, there was a doll's-house look to the room, with its small windows and primitive furniture. She opened a window, chased out a few sleepy flies that had settled in for the winter and took the frying pan from a cupboard, in readiness for the trout they would catch. When she turned to leave the cabin, Erik barred her way.

"It's time we had a talk. That's why I wanted to be alone with you."

"There'll be plenty of time to talk when we've fished for a while." She made a move to go past him.

He gripped her arm. "You're wrong. We've little time left and a whole lifetime to discuss."

She raised startled eyes and jerked away from him. As she went out of the cabin, he looked after her for a moment or two, as if he would fetch her back. Then, on a muttered expletive, he followed her, snatching his rod from its place by the door.

She had already cast out her line. He did the same a little distance from her. She was wearing her hair loose today, caught by a large tortoiseshell slide at the back of her head, and all the autumn sunshine was in the wafting strands. From the first sight of her installed at his home, Erik had found he could not stop thinking about her. Now time had dwindled to less than anyone there realized, and he was being compelled to waste precious minutes fishing. It was even more galling that she should catch three trout of a good size while he only hooked a small one that he threw back. Deciding that enough was enough, he stuck his rod in the cleft of a rock and went round to where she stood. The three trout lay on the bank, threaded onto a birch twig.

"Surely that's plenty."

She wound in her line. "Why are you so angry?"

"I'm not angry with you. It's knowing that I'm here for such a short time, instead of having days and weeks and months to tell you that I love you. Do you hear? I love you."

Colour rushed into her cheeks and she nipped her lower lip hard. He took the rod from her and gently drew her to him. Lovingly he stroked her hair, threading his fingers through its luxuriance. Gradually she raised her face to his.

"I want you to be my wife, Karen. I'm not trying to tie you to any promises yet. I'm just asking you to remember what I've said. I love you. Who knows when I'll return, but when I do, it's my hope that you'll marry me."

She felt all restraint melt from her. That afternoon was a time of sweetness and tenderness and discovery that neither would forget. When they locked up the cabin to leave, she felt she was turning the key on the most perfect moments of her life.

Johanna saw by the way they looked at each other upon their return that there was a new understanding between them, and she was glad. Karen would be ideal for her brother.

Very early the next morning, while Karen still slept, it was time for Erik to leave. He wanted no goodbyes. In his room he dressed in practical mountain wear. Taking up a rucksack, which he had packed the day before, he crept quietly down the stairs. There was a sliver of light showing under the kitchen door. When he opened it, his mother was at the stove and breakfast was laid.

"What are you doing up so early?" he asked her in surprise.

"I couldn't sleep." No mention of wanting to see him one last time before he left or of her anxieties. "Sit down. Everything is ready."

She ate with him. Her talk was mostly of the farm. When he rose from the table, it was with the customary thanks for food received. "*Takk for mat*. I must get going now."

"I've made a packet of sandwiches for you." She took it from the sideboard and handed it to him. As he put it away she went ahead to open the front door. The chill air flowed into the house, and the whole valley was still bathed in darkness. She stepped out onto the porch.

"It'll be a wonderful morning," he said, shouldering his rucksack. "Look after yourself, Mother."

Unexpectedly, she stifled a moan in her throat and clung to him in an embrace such as he had not received from her since childhood. "Don't let the Germans get you!" she cried brokenly.

Then he knew that with some deep maternal instinct she had sensed throughout his short visit that it was likely to be his last for a long time. "Don't worry," he reassured her gently. "I'll be all right."

Quickly he broke from her, hurrying away down the porch steps to the lane. Before the trees hid the farmhouse from sight he turned and looked back. She was still on the porch and returned his last wave.

ON THE WAY towards the hamlet Erik branched off to one of the farmsteads lower down the valley. A young man of his own age was waiting by the water mill. They greeted each other quietly and enthusiastically. "Hey, there! Ingvar!"

"What a day to set off for England, eh, Erik?"

Falling into step, they reached a narrow bridge and crossed the river. On the other side they were joined by twin brothers named Oivind and Olav, bakers by trade, with a good supply of bread in their rucksacks. "This is like a school reunion," Olav joked. "Ryendal is on the march."

His brother raised a fist in a gesture of triumph. "Winston Churchill, your troubles are over! Here we come!"

They laughed and continued on together. Towards dawn they came in sight of a small town on the fjord where a large number of fishing boats were moored. Their escape plan was based on taking one hazardous chance. Some of the fishing boats went out at dawn and some at night. They were going to help themselves to one already home and unloaded. Once on board they would follow in the wake of those setting out for the day, thereby getting out to sea without challenge. The danger of being sighted by the Luftwaffe later would be great, however, for they would be heading beyond the fishing limits established by the Germans.

In the dawn light, catches of fish were being loaded onto the jetty and carted away. Further on were boats tied up for the day, their owners and the night's catch already gone. Nobody took any notice of the four men as they made their way aboard a boat. Sentries had just changed and had no reason to be suspicious.

The engine started up with its tonk-tonk sound, and they left the jetty with Erik at the wheel. The others appeared to be the crew preparing their nets for the fishing ahead. Erik did not know that the owner of the boat he was steering had returned for a forgotten pipe and tobacco pouch and was standing on the shore watching his means of livelihood depart. The man guessed where his property was bound. It never entered his mind to raise an alarm that would have brought patrol boats out to intercept the errant vessel. If he had been twenty years younger, he would have escaped too. As it was, he only wished that he had been in time to get his tobacco pouch. There had been some real tobacco in it.

The morning brought low clouds, giving protection from aircraft, and thirty-six hours later, after a relatively trouble-free crossing, Erik sailed the boat into the harbour of Lerwick in the Shetland Islands. British soldiers came on board and escorted the four of them to a public building where they were interrogated by British and Norwegian officials and issued with identity cards.

The next day they were taken by ferry to the mainland and then by train to London. After more interrogation Erik's three companions were enrolled in the Free Norwegian airforce. Erik was called for an interview with one of his countrymen in naval uniform.

"I'm offering you the chance for special work," Erik was told. "We need men who know every inlet and cove on the west coast of Norway where secret agents and supplies can be landed. It means winter crossings from the Shetland Islands in small fishing boats that will blend in with local shipping upon arrival. What do you say?"

"When do I start?"

Erik left the office well pleased. The special branch he was to join had already earned a nickname for its regular and undaunted secret crossings: the Shetland Bus.

He was to leave London by train that night. On his way into King's Cross station a dramatic headline caught his eye: JAPANESE PLANES BOMB PEARL HARBOR. He bought a newspaper and scanned the details. The United States had entered the war.

Chapter Seven

Johanna went up the stairs to the cafe above a grocery shop. The windows looked out across the wintry Ålesund waters. A number of the tables were occupied by soldiers and sailors. She made her way to a wall seat at a table in the least popular section of the cafe to wait for Steffen.

The message to meet him had come the day before. She had not seen him since the night of the parachute landing.

Not long after Erik's departure their father had had a complete collapse. The old retired doctor from the village had come to see him willingly enough, had prescribed whatever was still available in the chemist's shop for his patient's heart trouble, and had left again, grumbling about his own aches and pains. It had been a bleak Christmas, with Edvard in bed and all of them anxious about Erik. They had heard King Haakon speak on the BBC. That year, as with the first Christmas of the occupation, the king had a tree from Norway, a link from his own land. The story had touched Johanna. A Norwegian Christmas tree going all the way to London in the midst of war.

Watching the door now for Steffen to arrive, Johanna felt sick with anxiety as to how it would be when she saw him again. She had tried to accept that what had begun so gloriously between them had been no more than a brief wartime affair. Yet the truth was that her love was unchanged. There seemed no cure for it.

The cafe door opened to admit another customer. A woman. It was Delia Richmond. For a few painful seconds Johanna thought that Steffen had sent Delia in his place, but she took a seat in another part of the cafe without so much as a glance around.

Almost immediately afterwards Steffen entered. Upon seeing Johanna, he went to the counter to collect two cups of coffee and brought them across to where she was seated. "Sorry I'm late."

"You chose a busy place to meet."

"I knew it would be possible to talk here without being overheard. I have to keep an eye on Delia at the same time."

"Has she been here since I last saw you?" It was a question she could not hold back.

He nodded. "Transmitter work. She's leaving tonight. There's a chance the Gestapo are following up information that might lead to her. We can't risk it. She won't be back." He made it clear that was final.

"I wish her a safe journey."

He had taken a swig of the ersatz coffee. "This stuff gets worse!" He leaned towards her. "I haven't told you yet what a good job you did in Oslo. Congratulations."

"When shall I be used again?"

"The time will come for more assignments. There is much important work ahead for you. But there's something I have to tell you now; not good news, I'm afraid. Things have gone tragically wrong for the Resistance since the trade union strike. Virtually all our networks in Oslo have been smashed by the Gestapo."

"How did it happen?"

441

"Terrible tortures were inflicted on resistance members betrayed by Quisling informers. Inevitably information was extracted, which led to more arrests and more torture. For many there was also the firing squad." He saw the anguish in her eyes. "I'm afraid there's more. Shall we get out of here first?"

"What about Delia?"

"She'll follow us after a minute or two."

Together they left the cafe. Outside, snowflakes were swirling lightly in the air. Steffen raised his arm as if to put it about her, but thought better of it. Side by side they walked along until they came to some railings looking out to sea. Johanna spoke of what she feared to be most likely.

"Has Leif Moen been arrested?" Her arms were resting on the top rail, as were his. He turned his head to look at her.

"No. It concerns your friend at the fur shop. Sonja Holm. There was a Gestapo raid on a secret printing press. She and others who were there made an attempt to get away. She was killed."

Johanna covered her face with her hands in deepest grief. He drew her to him and held her. His act of comfort was interrupted by the harsh voice of a sentry who had just stamped into view.

"*Achtung!* Get moving. You know it's not allowed for anyone to stand about in conversation. Keep walking. *Schnell! Schnell!*" He gestured fiercely with his bayoneted rifle.

This time Steffen did put an arm round her as they moved on. She was crying silently. At a distance from them Delia followed, sauntering slowly. They stopped to say goodbye within the shelter of an archway, momentarily out of the sight of any guards.

"We'll part here, Jo," he said to her. "I wish I hadn't had to be the bearer of such sad news."

Johanna's eyes flooded again and she wiped them quickly. "It helped to hear it from you. I mustn't keep you any longer. It's not safe for you or Delia. Goodbye." As she hurried away through the snowflakes she wept for Sonja. And her grief was for everything that had been lost through the enemy occupation.

IT WAS A WEEK LATER when a German army truck came up the valley, stopping outside the farmhouse. Johanna was filled with trepidation. Helmeted soldiers jumped out, some peeling off to guard the rear of the house against any escape, the rest approaching the front door. Her mother was upstairs at her father's bedside, and Karen had gone to call on a neighbour. As the hammering of a fist came on the door Johanna opened it reluctantly. A sergeant stood there, backed by three soldiers with rifles.

"I want to see Edvard Ryen," the sergeant said in Norwegian, crossing the threshold. He had a young, bold face with jutting cheekbones, his expression stern, a truculent set to his mouth.

"He's ill in bed."

His dark brown eyes narrowed cynically. "How convenient. Where? Upstairs?"

She moved quickly to block the foot of the stairs. "I'm his daughter. I tell you he's ill. Please don't go up. What is it you want?"

"He is to be arrested as a hostage."

She stared at him, appalled. "A hostage! Whatever for?"

"You have a brother named Erik Ryen. He has broken the law, leaving the country to make contact with enemies of the Third Reich. Until he can be brought to justice, your father must stand for him. Don't delay me, frøken!"

The sergeant made a movement with his hand to indicate she should step aside. Then he looked up as Gina came hurrying to the head of the stairs.

"What do you want here?" Johanna's mother exclaimed anxiously.

The sergeant began to mount the stairs, the soldiers following him. "No hysterics," he said to Gina. "I'm here to collect your husband. He will not be alone. The fathers from two other farms have already been taken as hostages for the men who accompanied your son across the North Sea."

"Take me in my husband's place," Gina demanded resolutely.

The sergeant pushed her aside. "I'm here for Edvard Ryen. Nobody else."

As he went into the bedroom she rushed after him and took a place defensively by her husband's bed. The sergeant checked his pace and came to a standstill. He had fully expected to find his quarry well able to be jerked out of bed, but the sick man opening his eyes from sleep appeared to be at death's door.

"What is the matter?" Edvard asked weakly.

Gina took his thin hand between hers. "I think this soldier wants to ask you your name, Edvard," she said falteringly.

The sergeant was at a loss. A soldier first and foremost, he accepted that examples had to be made to subdue subversive activities, but he could not bring himself to drag a desperately sick man from his bed. "I can see the circumstances here have not been exaggerated," he said. "Therefore I must get a final decision from our medical officer. I'll be back."

The three soldiers were waiting on the landing. He detailed one to remain there, while the other two went down with him to the truck. He said to the driver, "Back to Ålesund. Let's go."

An hour later the truck returned, along with a grey military car carrying a medical officer. He had a reputation among the troops for being a skilled doctor but merciless with malingerers. When his car arrived at Ryen Farm, his mood was not amicable. He did not appreciate being brought from Ålesund on a wild-goose chase. He glanced sideways as the sergeant came running to him from the truck.

"Lead the way, Sergeant Müller," he ordered.

Upstairs in the house, Gina and Johanna awaited them at Edvard's bedside. The medical officer gave them no more than a glance. Sitting down in the chair placed ready for him, he leaned forward to pull down the lower lids of Edvard's eyes and then take his pulse. His questioning took a particular line of inquiry.

"Pain in your bones? Depression? Legs heavy and seized up? Always cold? When did all this start?" He had to lower his head to catch Edvard's answers. "How long have you been bedridden? As long as that? Hmm." He rose from the chair. "You did right to call me, Sergeant," he admitted, with a change of attitude. "To have taken this man would have landed you with a corpse on your hands in no time at all."

"Then he is to be left, sir?"

The reply came with callous indifference. "Yes. He is going to die soon. It's simply a matter of a steady deterioration."

He went from the room, followed by the sergeant. Edvard gazed after them from his pillows. He felt no surprise at what he had heard, but he wished Gina could have had the news broken to her less brutally. As she bent over him he saw there were tears running down her cheeks. With an effort he lifted his hand and cupped the side of her face. She covered his hand with her own.

KAREN, COMING from the neighbour's home, was in time to see the army car and truck leaving Ryen Farm. She drew back into the edge of a snowbank and as the truck shot past her the sergeant leaned out and looked full into her face. A stare of open recognition passed between them, their astonishment mutual. Looking back, he saw her running towards the farmhouse.

She burst into the house. "What's been happening?" she cried out in agitation.

Johanna led her into the sitting room. "Come and sit down. I'll tell you all about it."

Karen heard her through before springing up from the chair with fists clenched. "Your father is not going to die. I won't let him. For Erik's sake I'll make him hold on to life."

She would have gone flying up to the sickroom if Johanna had not grabbed her by the wrist. "Wait! My mother is with him."

Karen sat down again, her fingers entwining nervously. "I used to know the sergeant who was here today. His name is Carl Müller. He came to our village under the Nansen plan and stayed longer than most of the young people. I don't think he would have left Norway if his widowed father hadn't remarried and made a home for him in Munich. He went back and joined the Hitler Youth movement when it was formed. For a while he wrote to me." She shrugged. "There was nothing romantic in his letters as I would have hoped. Instead, he gave long accounts of doing what the Führer wished, for the greatness of Germany."

"How old were you when you last saw him?"

"We were both fifteen."

"Did he recognize you today?"

"Yes. I've no doubt at all." She gripped the arms of the chair. "I hope I never see him again. I was fond of him once. Now I hate him and everything he represents."

THREE DAYS LATER Carl Müller returned. Gina went ashen when she discovered him on the threshold.

"I'm not here on duty," he said. "Is Karen at home?"

"As you are not on duty, you may not come into the house," Gina replied. "If Karen agrees to speak to you, it must be outside."

His expression hardened. "If Karen should refuse to see me, I would have to exert my authority after all."

Gina thought with despair that the enemy had power over everything, and she was fearful. "I'll tell her you're here."

He waited where he was, stamping his feet on the porch. It had been a cold motorbike ride from Ålesund. In the old days he would never have been kept waiting on any Norwegian doorstep.

He turned his head as Karen appeared from the house, warmly wrapped against the cold. A pinched look to her face suggested she was chilled inwardly for a reason that had nothing to do with the weather. Yet nothing could detract from her beauty.

"You haven't changed, Karen. I knew you at once."

Her expression remained stony. "What do you want?"

"I only want a chance to talk to you again."

"What about?"

"Old times would do for a start. We used to be good friends." He held out a hand as if to take hers. "Shall we walk? You'll get cold standing there." When she ignored his hand and went on down the porch steps, he followed and they began to walk side by side. "Are you annoyed because I stopped writing to you?"

She turned and faced him with blazing eyes. "Annoyed? Do you think I care anything about what you did or did not do all that time ago? It's what you and your kind are doing here now that makes me hate you as I do!"

"I've done you no harm, nor am I likely to," he retorted indignantly. "You should be grateful. If anyone else had come in my place the other day, the old farmer in that house would have died in the back of an army truck."

Her attitude did not change. "No one should have come for a man with such a heart condition!"

He spoke impatiently. "There's nothing wrong with his heart!"

She became very still, her head tilting to one side as she scrutinized his face. "Why do you say that?"

"I should know what's wrong with him. I had to fill it in on my report." His eyes narrowed. "You have some doubts about it?"

"I've had doubts all along about his doctor, who is old and should have given up years ago. Would you tell me what was written on the report?"

In her eagerness to discover what he knew, her face had lost its look of hostility. The temptation to bargain with her was great, but he decided he would gain more simply by telling her outright what she wanted to know. "All right. He's suffering from pernicious anaemia. Maybe that's affecting his heart."

It was not what she had expected and it was a disease she knew nothing about. "I appreciate your telling me. I'll report it to the district nurse. The old doctor is too stubborn to listen to me, but he might take notice of her."

"Where does she live?"

"Further down the valley."

"Shall we walk there now?" He said it before he realized what he was asking of her. She had led him up the valley away from any other habitations. For her to go in the other direction would mean being seen by neighbours in the company of a German soldier. Seeing she was about to refuse him, he said, "I only asked on the basis of having proved my goodwill towards you and the family with whom you are living."

He moved as if to walk away from her. As he had hoped, she called him back. "No, I'll go with you."

As they went down the valley lane together, their talk, which he kept flowing, turned inevitably to people and events they both recalled. It was impossible for her not to smile with him now and again. For him it was an entirely new beginning, with nothing to hinder his pursuit of her.

He waited for her at the roadside while she went into the house of the district nurse. When she emerged again, her face was radiant. She ran back to him down the snow-banked path.

"Pernicious anaemia can be treated. It may not be too late. The district

KAREN

nurse will go and see the doctor. If he agrees she'll be able to give Edvard injections, and he's to have a diet rich in liver, which is easy enough to obtain on a farm. Just think! He could be cured!"

"That's good news," he said, without expression.

The excitement drained from her face. "You would have your hostage then, wouldn't you?" she exclaimed bitterly.

"Not necessarily," he replied, as if weighing his words. "Come on. Let's walk back." At his side she was anxious and silent, glancing at him continually while he looked ahead, keeping her in suspense. "Nothing is going to happen overnight. Edvard Ryen may be too far gone for any kind of recovery. I'm prepared to wait and see. As I said to you before, I'm your friend, Karen. I think you should try to trust me. You always used to."

She did not quite know how to take what he had said, yet his attempt at reassurance had been clear enough. She thought she had the key to it all. He wanted a renewal of their friendship without reservations. Perhaps he even hoped for more. She almost pitied him.

"I might trust you, but I can't trust your uniform."

"We're one and the same."

With this statement Karen knew she could never relax her guard.

ALTHOUGH THE DISTRICT NURSE was permitted to carry out the new treatment on Edvard, the old local doctor let it be known that he was thoroughly offended that a German diagnosis had superseded his. But by the middle of February there were the first faint signs of improvement in Edvard's condition.

Johanna, returning home one day from the hamlet, called in at the schoolhouse. Since Edvard had taken a turn for the better, Rolf did not come daily to visit any more, for he had too much to do at the school, including secret meetings with other teachers within the Resistance.

Recently Quisling had had a law passed, making membership in his new teachers' Nazi association compulsory for all in the profession. And every pupil was compelled to join the new youth movement for full indoctrination in Nazi ideology. The teachers, backed by the church and parents, had rejected both dictates. Nobody knew what would happen.

In the hallway Joanna was greeted by the familiar aroma of chalk and ink and blackboard. The schoolroom took up the left side of the building and Rolf's living quarters were to the right, with a staircase leading to the bedroom above. Up there, Johanna knew, Rolf's radio was hidden.

As Johanna opened the door into the schoolroom, all twenty-two of the pupils stood up with a scraping of chair legs. Rolf, who was writing on the blackboard, signalled for the children to sit down again, and gave her a nod. "Wait awhile," he invited. "Class will soon be over." Johanna

448

stood at the back of the room while Rolf finished the lesson and made an announcement to the children. "Today is the last day of school for a month. As you know, four weeks' holiday has been given to ease the fuel shortage. Do the home tasks I have set you. If any of you have problems, you know where to find me. That's all, children. Dismiss."

As they filed out Johanna strolled up to the desk and leaned on it. Rolf was wiping the blackboard clean with a duster.

"What's all this about a fuel shortage?" She nodded towards the ceiling-high stove that gave an even warmth to the room.

"Most of the country schools have all the wood they need. It's a problem in the cities, I believe." He replaced the duster and brushed off his hands. "But that's not the reason for closing the schools. Quisling has a dilemma. Twelve thousand out of the fourteen thousand teachers in this country have flatly refused to join his teachers' Nazi association. This month is to give him time to think over what to do next." He grinned widely. "Inside information has it that not only is Terboven angry with his handling of the situation, but Hitler himself is fed up with him."

She laughed. "That's the best news since Father's recuperation."

"Has Karen seen any more of that German sergeant?"

"No, thank goodness, although she's as nervous as a cat every time she hears a motorbike." Johanna swung away from the desk. "I must be getting home. You'll be coming to see Father, so I won't call again until school reopens."

But Johanna was never again to see him with his class in the schoolhouse. Before the four-week holiday was up, Rolf was arrested, along with hundreds of other teachers. The night after he was taken away, when she was certain of being unobserved, Johanna rushed down the lane to the schoolhouse to carry out what she was sure Rolf would want of her. His radio was too important to be left unused.

Inside the building, the blackout blinds hid the landing light as she switched it on. She went to a framed print on the landing, where the eaves sloped, and removed it from its nail. Behind it a panel had been skilfully cut into the wall. Carefully she prised it out. There was the radio. After lifting it down onto the floor, she thought it would be wise to check that nothing else of importance was there. Hidden deeper under the eaves was an old attaché case, which she eased forward and into the light. It held a transmitter. She admired Rolf's ingenuity. In the event of an enemy search, probably only the radio would have been found and seized. Her fingers found some aerial wire, metres and metres of it neatly coiled together. And she marvelled at the risks her brother must have taken. The Germans had detectors tracking down subversive transmitting.

Downstairs a board creaked in the kitchen. Johanna froze. Someone was in the house. It could only be a German soldier. Instantly she snapped off the light. There was no time to refit the wooden panel she had removed. Swiftly she pushed the radio back into the cavity and rehung the picture. In the hallway the door from the kitchen opened with a whine of hinges.

She held her breath, her fear intense. Somewhere on the floor beside her was the wooden wall panel that must be concealed. On her knees, she felt for it and clutched it to her. The intruder had switched on a torch. Its rays danced up the stairs and threw shadows on the sloping ceiling above her head. Like a snake she went flat, and when the rays moved back to the hallway, she crawled through the half-open bedroom door and pushed it closed behind her. Leaping to her feet, she fell against the bed in the blackness. Lifting up the mattress, she thrust the wooden panel underneath it. She was just in time.

The door was kicked open with a crash. In the light that blazed into her eyes she caught the gleam of a revolver being pointed at her. She screamed as she hurled herself onto the floor.

"Good God!" exclaimed Steffen's voice harshly. "It's you! I thought it was a German!" Word of Rolf's arrest had made the speedy retrieval of the transmitter essential. Steffen's nerves were shaken by this unexpected encounter with Johanna. Believing a trap had been set, he had been primed to kill, his finger tight on the trigger.

He came across the floor and bent down beside her. He spoke her name, shifting nearer, and she could smell the outdoor chill of his clothes, his skin, his hair. With relief from fear, all her senses were sharpened to the joy of his presence. Without stirring, she felt him reaching for her and lifting her onto the bed.

Suddenly large tears escaped one by one from her eyes to trickle down onto the pillow. He cupped her face with his hands and smoothed the tears away with his thumbs.

"Don't cry, Jo. Everything is all right now. Nothing shall ever come between us again." He covered her face with kisses. "I never loved until I met you. You're my reason for living, my love, my heart, my darling."

The tenderness in his voice was a foretaste of what was to come during the hours they were to spend together until dawn.

Chapter Eight

Packed into cattle cars, Rolf and his fellow teachers dozed on the train's journey north. Thirteen hundred of them had been arrested and held in concentration camps; only a small number had succumbed, obtaining release by joining the teachers' Nazi association.

The train began to slow down. The men stirred and yawned, getting to their feet to stamp circulation into cramped limbs. With a jolt the train came to a halt at a siding in Trondheim. There was a rattle as the bolts were pulled out of the door and it went sliding back, the bright light pouring in.

"Out! Out!" the guards shouted, rifles in their hands.

Rolf leaped to the ground and took his place in the long line. Those who were slow were thumped with rifle butts. These were five hundred teachers who had been numbered off from the others in the notorious concentration camp at Grini for transport to a labour camp far north of the Arctic Circle. From the head of the line came the barked command, "Forward, march!"

Rolf moved forward with the rest. At the time of their arrest they had been issued with prison camp uniforms, drab garments of coarse cloth that hung loosely about their legs, and forage caps that unbuttoned to protect the ears in cold weather. That protection would be needed when they reached Kirkenes, which was located only a stone's throw from the Finnish border. Spring would not reach there for another four or five weeks yet, and polar conditions would prevail. Rolf's only consolation was that they were not being sent to Germany, the fate of many Norwegians arrested on other charges.

A small wooden ship awaited them at the harbour. Her normal complement was a hundred and fifty passengers. Now she had to accommodate five hundred and, in addition, fifty guards. Prisoners were crowded in together until it became impossible for those in the hold to move in any direction. Rolf was wedged into a part of the ship where the blackness was unrelieved except by a glimmer of light showing round the hatches overhead.

The wintry seas were gale-lashed from the moment the steamer nosed out of the harbour. It took thirteen days for the vessel to make a journey that normally took four, and when the hold was opened in Kirkenes harbour, the stench was like a cesspool.

The Arctic air, sharply clean and cold, met Rolf's face like a benediction as he disembarked, helping ashore an elderly fellow prisoner who was barely able to walk. The townspeople stopped to stare in shock and sympathy at the bedraggled procession of men coming ashore.

Near a corner, a woman darted forward and dropped a winter-stored apple into Rolf's pocket, before scurrying away at a soldier's angry shout and raised rifle. Somebody else received a rolled cigarette and another a piece of dried fish. The townspeople had little to spare, but they wanted to share what they had with their countrymen. To Rolf it was a forewarning. These people knew what awaited the prisoners and wanted to help while the chance was available.

His misgivings proved to be right. Rolf could hardly believe such hell could have been created in his own land. By night they were crowded together in long huts under fetid conditions. By day they were put to heavy manual labour that was often beyond the strength of the older men. The food was no more than a bowl of watery soup and a slab of stone-hard black bread. Yet bad as it was for the teachers, it was still worse for the Russian and Polish prisoners of war who worked alongside the Norwegians. While road building, one of them was shot for breaking away to catch a yellowed cabbage leaf drifting along in a ditch. The man's compatriots showed no emotion. Death had become too commonplace.

SUNDAY AFTERNOON was quiet in Ålesund. Johanna strode along as if the ground had springs beneath the surface. The Resistance had summoned her; at last she was to be given full-time work.

Outside Astrid's house were the usual parked cars and yawning German drivers. Astrid, her silver-grey hair worn as always in immaculate waves, her dress a silk print of a mode belonging to the early '30s, opened the door when Joanna knocked.

"Come in," she invited serenely. Her composure was completely genuine. The fact that she was virtually living on a time bomb did not disturb her on her own account. When she worried, it was for younger lives put in jeopardy. "Keep your jacket on until after the meeting," she advised Johanna. "It's always chilly in that cellar."

"Am I to go down straight away?"

"Yes. They're waiting for you. Hurry along now."

Under the stairs Johanna tapped the signal on the sliding panel. Contrary to her expectations it was not Steffen who drew it back to admit her. She was helped through by a man wearing glasses, with rough brown hair, thick brows and a good-natured face.

"Glad to know you," he said, greeting her with a hearty handshake. "In the Resistance I'm known as Gunnar."

She smiled back at him. "Are we to be comrades?"

"You'll probably see quite a lot of me from now on, but our friend the Englishman is in charge." He jerked a thumb over his shoulder to where Steffen sat awaiting her at the table in the lamplight. "Everybody jumps to his orders in this region."

It was the first time she had heard Steffen's alias, and she liked his choice, a nostalgic reminder of Viktor Alsteen's nickname for him. As she went across to the chair that stood ready for her, she thought it curious that a man who loved her as much as Steffen did should be able to regard her with such an uncompromising eye. She knew why. He had explained it to her on their night together at the schoolhouse. Until he became accustomed to her facing danger in the Resistance, he had to divorce himself from his feelings for her. Otherwise he would not be able to commit her to assignments.

When she was seated in front of him, Gunnar having settled on the bench, Steffen went straight to the business in hand. "I've been waiting for something special to come up for you, Jo. Now it has. There's an important post being advertised locally, and I want you to get it. You would be working for your father's cousin, Tom Ryen."

She was astonished. "He's a quisling."

"That's why I want you in his office." He picked up a newspaper and handed it to her. She read through the circled advertisement. Her qualifications covered every requirement, including a knowledge of German.

"I'll stand a good chance if I can manage to stay civil to him, knowing he's a collaborator."

"You'll stay civil," Steffen stated flatly. "Anything else?"

"Tom will hold it against me that I have one brother escaped to England and another probably in a labour camp."

Steffen waved this point aside impatiently. "There are few families these days without a member in the Germans' bad books. But I have to warn you that you couldn't be taking on the job at a more dangerous time. Last week nineteen resistance fighters were executed by the Gestapo for less than what we're expecting you to do."

Johanna was aware of Gunnar's scrutiny, watching for cracks in her resolve. She tapped the advertisement with her forefinger. "I'll send my application to Tom this evening."

Satisfaction emerged in Steffen's penetrating gaze and he exchanged a glance with Gunnar. "That's right," Steffen endorsed. "No delays. Now Gunnar will tell you what's involved."

Gunnar leaned towards her. "Basically you are to keep your eyes and ears open for anything in conversation, letters or documents that might be of use to us, however trivial it may appear."

"What should I be looking for?"

"As you know, Tom Ryen recruits workers for every type of building erected by the Germans, from power plants to gun bunkers, and he transfers this work force from place to place as needed. These movements can reveal a great deal to our intelligence people. That's what we want from you."

Steffen commanded her attention again. She could sense his intense gravity. "You see, Jo, we believe that something especially dangerous has begun to develop."

A chill ran down her spine. "What is that?"

"It's the making of a new weapon by the Germans that has yet to be tested. All that is known is that its effect will be devastating."

"Is it being made in our country?" she asked.

"No, but a substance essential to its construction, known as heavy water, is being produced at the Norsk hydroelectric plant in Telemark." His next words came harshly. "If Germany should gain the advantage of this monstrous weapon, then it could be the end of freedom for a thousand years."

She stared at him incredulously, assimilating the horrific threat looming on the horizon. "To whom shall I report?"

"To Gunnar or to me." His face remained expressionless. "In order to make communication easier, we shall want you to move in with Astrid. She has already agreed to this arrangement." He stood up. "I'm leaving now. Gunnar will see you back into the house. We'll be in touch when and if you secure that position as Ryen's secretary."

For a week after mailing her application Johanna heard nothing. Then a standard reply came, giving her the date and time of her interview.

IN HIS OFFICE, Tom Ryen took a break with a cigarette before interviewing the next applicant. It was a German cigarette. No rolling his own out of tough, homegrown leaves. Having access to German supplies was one of the perks of the job he did, and he had not gone hungry or thirsty since he had decided to make the best of the situation when the Germans took command. He prided himself on being a realist.

Born in Bergen, with the good humour natural to Bergensers but without their appetite for hard work, Tom Ryen had settled on a career in the army. He had exerted himself until he reached the rank of major, whereupon he took events as easily as possible. His wife had been a wealthy, lively, happy woman, almost as pleasure-loving as himself. She had died ten years ago. They had had no children.

In spite of how the situation now might appear to outsiders, Tom was not in favour of the Nazis. He would have preferred conditions to be as they had been before the invasion. But that was not possible, as the Third Reich had come to stay. He was not particularly proud of his opportunism, but hardship, pursuit and torture were not what he cared to invite.

Stubbing out his cigarette, he flicked a switch and asked for the next applicant to be shown in. The door from the outer office opened. "Frøken Ryen," the temporary army clerk announced, showing Johanna into the room.

Tom rose to his feet, a broad smile creasing his face, and extended his hand. "Good morning, Johanna. This is a pleasure. I haven't seen you since we met on the steamer."

She shook hands with him, and noticed at once that he had put on a considerable amount of weight, not an easy thing to do in Norway these days. She sat down in the proffered chair. "You're looking well, Tom," she said as an opening.

"Never been better." He was still beaming at her, his sandy-lashed eyes narrowed into fat folds. "I was most interested to receive your application, Johanna. Have you had enough of life on the farm? It must have been tough having to return to it again." His own home, outside of Ålesund, had once been the house to a large farm. He and his wife had let the land out for others to work. The house itself was a treasure, with large rooms for parties, its own shallow bay for swimming, access to the fjord for sailing, and some of the best ski slopes in the district. Now he gave parties for high-ranking officers of the Wehrmacht, and many privileges had come his way in return for his hospitality, including the use of a splendid car with a generous petrol ration.

Johanna answered him easily. "I went home because I was needed there. Now that a German doctor has diagnosed his complaint, Father is in better health and things have changed. That leaves me free to take up my secretarial career again."

"I would have expected you to go back to Oslo."

"I'd like to, later on. At present the city is too unsettled."

He let her remark pass without comment, aware she was referring to the wave after wave of arrests sweeping through the capital. He preferred to ignore such happenings. "Well then, what's your shorthand speed these days?"

When the routine questions had been duly asked and answered, he was impressed by her competence. She was by far the best qualified of the interviewees, quite apart from being the best looking. There only remained one matter to settle.

"Now, about your brothers," he said heavily.

She realized the moment had come when everything was hanging in the balance. "Yes?"

"They would have been an embarrassment to me if anyone here had chosen to link our common surname. As it happens, nobody did. I prefer matters to remain that way. Do you understand?"

"Perfectly."

It was good enough for him. He was aware that many whom he recruited to work for the Germans did so through the necessity of supporting their families and not through choice, but the end result was the same. "If you should be appointed, would you continue to live at the farm?"

"No. I have an elderly friend in Ålesund, Astrid Larsen, who would be willing to let me have a room."

"That would be excellent." He was satisfied. "Well, do you want to work for me?"

She nodded her head. "I think I'd go mad if I had to return to domestic chores after getting back into an office today."

"Good. Then the job is yours. Can you start on Monday?"

She felt a heady rush of relief. "Yes, Tom. I'll be here."

As JOHANNA WALKED AWAY from Tom's office, bound for Astrid's house, she did not notice a heavily bearded fisherman across the street turn aside to study some deep-sea tackle displayed in a shop window. He watched her reflection go past. Erik, who had landed a secret agent in a neighbouring cove the night before from his Shetland Bus, wondered where his sister had been and where she was going. She looked well, which was a good sign.

Although he had made many trips across the North Sea, this was his first experience of seeing a member of his own family and having to avoid recognition. The rules laid down were strict. Too many lives were involved and too much was at stake for the slightest risk to be taken. Whenever someone had broken the rules, invariably the results had been tragic. The fishing village of Telavågen near Bergen had been wiped off the map after two resistance fighters had been found sheltered there. If it had been Karen passing by instead of Johanna, Erik would still have kept his face averted.

When evening came, he would be sailing back to the Shetlands. He ended his apparent scrutiny of the window display when his sister's reflection vanished from the glass.

IN THE FAR NORTH, the snow retreated daily from the Kirkenes area to settle in the heights. The hardships of everyone in the camp had been made worse by the bitter cold, and in the Arctic spring many were suffering from the aftereffects of frostbite. Rolf, in his patched prison uniform, turned his face to the returning sun. There was news to cheer him and his colleagues. It had just been passed to him by a local tradesman delivering goods to the camp commandant. The information would be a tonic to everyone.

Rolf made the announcement in the compound. "My friends! I have great news! Although our own imprisonment is to continue, all our colleagues left behind at the other camps are to be released. The majority of teachers in this country are to be allowed to return to their schools. Do you realize what this means? Quisling has given in! The teachers' Nazi association has been virtually eliminated, and the Hitler Youth movement planned for our pupils has fallen through." His voice gained momentum. "We've won our cause!"

There was a tremendous burst of cheering. By standing together, they had stopped the Nazi advance where it mattered most. If freedom of thought had been broken down, then the whole resistance movement would have been without a future. Now nothing would be as hard as it had been before.

Chapter Nine

It took several days before Johanna became used to her new surroundings at Tom Ryen's. Her desk was in the outer office, and there was nothing difficult about her work. It was being in close proximity to so many Germans that was unnerving.

It had not been easy letting her parents know that she was going to be working for a collaborator.

"I can't stay at home indefinitely," she had replied to her father's strongly voiced objections. He had continued to be upset until her mother calmed him down. Gina seemed to sense that Johanna had her reasons. There were many parents these days who suspected their adult offspring of being involved with the Resistance.

In preparation for her employment, Johanna and Gunnar had devised a shorthand code for recording information that might be of use. There were to be various signals, from a stick left in a certain cleft tree to a coded telephone call, by which she could let it be known that she had information to pass on.

In the office, she soon saw that Tom's inclination towards an easy life would be to her advantage. Within a couple of weeks of becoming his secretary she saw how he was shuffling work over to her that should have been his responsibility. She took it willingly, hoping eventually to glean something that might prove of use to intelligence.

The first time a German officer tried to date her she was not unprepared. She had had attentions from all ranks from the day she started work.

The lieutenant who strolled into the office was a tall young man who wore his uniform well. She was typing a letter and looked up with a faint smile of greeting. *"Guten Tag,"* she said, "do you have an appointment with Major Ryen?" The Germans always addressed Tom by his former rank.

He shook his head, coming to stand in front of her desk. *"Nein, fräulein.* It's you I want to see. I'm in the office on the next floor up. I'm Kurt Scheidt. If I may be of assistance to you in any way, please don't hesitate to let me know."

"Well, thank you. I'll remember that." She indicated the letter in the typewriter. "I am rather busy at the moment."

"My apologies. Would you be free this evening? There's a dance at the officers' mess in the garrison headquarters and I would very much like to take you there."

Suddenly the connecting door into the main office was opened wider and Tom came out, large and affable. She had never thought of him as a white knight, and yet he had come to her rescue, raising his eyebrows inquiringly at the officer. "Ah. Are you waiting to see me, Oberleutnant Scheidt?"

"Er—no, Major. I was talking to Fräulein Ryen."

"Oh, yes?" Tom commented nonchalantly. He turned to Johanna. "We'd better make it a quarter to six instead of six o'clock this evening," he said, as if confirming an arrangement with her. "I've two more letters to dictate. Come into the office now."

The lieutenant left and she followed Tom inside. "I could have managed that myself," she said with amusement.

"I know that, but these small fry must be kept at bay."

"What do you mean?" She seated herself, ready to take dictation.

"It's not important now. We'll talk about it another time."

ON THE DAY THAT EDVARD came downstairs for the first time it was Karen who guided him. Gina stood waiting at the foot of the flight. The girl cajoled Edvard briskly.

"That's it. Well done! Now another step. And another."

By the end of the week Edvard had progressed to sitting on the porch in the sunshine. One afternoon Karen had just seen him into the house and had returned to collect a plaid shawl from the chair when her name was spoken. She caught her breath in dread. Sergeant Carl Müller stood on the grass by the house.

"How long have you been there?" she exclaimed anxiously.

"Long enough to see that Edvard Ryen is back on his feet." He came slowly across to the stone steps. "But don't worry. I'll not take him while he is obviously far from well."

"Why do you have to take him at all?"

"That depends on you. Let's talk about it, shall we?" He held out a hand. Frightened and distressed, she went down the steps. When he offered his hand the last time they met, she had ignored it. This time he kept his hand thrust out like a threat, and she reluctantly gave him hers. He seized it with pleasure, closing their palms together. Again he exerted his advantage over her, saying, "We'll walk to a more populated area today." He was beaming at her. "I thought we could have something to eat in the cafe by the inlet. I managed to get hold of some civilian ration coupons for you."

She jerked her hand from his. "I won't be bribed into being friendly with you! Say what you must and be done!"

"Calm down," he said affably. "Don't misconstrue everything I say. I'm here for one reason, and I'll be completely honest with you. Seeing you again a while ago meant a great deal to me. I know we've both changed since the days when we were kids and in love. Naturally, I don't expect you to feel anything for me from that time, but as the weeks have gone by you've begun to mean something new and important to me." His sincerity came through in his voice and expression. "I'll bargain my silence about Edvard Ryen's recovery against your going out with me, if I have to. With time, I hope you'll come of your own free will."

Every vestige of colour had drained from her face. She looked as if she would have run from him if there had been anywhere she might escape his ultimatum. "I'll go out with you," she said in a hollow voice.

He was triumphant. Once more he took her hand fondly. As they walked down the lane she saw people pause in their work to look towards her in disbelief. They had heard that Johanna had gone to work for a quisling cousin, and now here was a second girl from the same household parading with an enemy soldier.

To Karen, the lane had never seemed longer. In the hamlet the same astonished looks followed her. To her relief Carl did not take her into the crowded cafe. Instead, they went to a grassy slope overlooking the fjord, where they sat down side by side, he with his arms resting on updrawn knees, she with her legs tucked under her. He did all the talking, and it was not until she saw he was becoming irritated by her lack of response that she began to comment now and again. There was little chance that he would keep his side of the bargain if he failed to get pleasure from her company.

"I don't want anyone else to know about the bond we've made," he impressed upon her. "Will you promise me that?"

"I think Gina Ryen will guess."

"Then let her guess, but don't confirm it. This is only an intermediary time for us, Karen. The day will come when we'll look back on it and laugh."

Fortunately for her they stayed by the fjord too long for him to have time to walk her home again. When she returned to the farmhouse, Gina was waiting anxiously. "Did he come back for Edvard?"

Karen swallowed. "No. It's my company he wants."

Gina stared wordlessly, comprehension dawning. She stood motionless as the desolate girl went upstairs to shut herself away in her room.

SEVERAL MONTHS PASSED before Johanna went home for a weekend. It was harvest time, and as she walked up the lane everyone was busy in the fields. At the first farmstead she had waved to those she knew. When there was no answering wave, she felt the first chill of ostracism reach her. Neighbours she had visited since childhood did not appear to see her go by. Everybody knew that she was working at the German headquarters and had concluded she was a collaborator. She did not blame her neighbours for thinking that, but their hostility would be hard to bear.

Edvard, leaning heavily on his walking stick, came unaided onto the porch to meet her. She flew up the steps and they hugged each other. "You're looking so well!" she exclaimed.

"Through being lazy, I'm afraid. As yet I can only do some paperwork. Your mother runs everything like clockwork, and young Karen is her right hand." He sank down weakly on the slatted porch seat, and Johanna sat beside him. "That doesn't mean things are fine here. Far from it. I should be out in the fields, not skulking here uselessly. Your mother is out there in my place, and as if that were not enough, a German is helping to bring in the harvest. My harvest!" He thumped his chest in outrage. "I've forbidden it, but neither she nor Karen will listen to me."

Johanna raised her eyebrows. "I didn't know about that. Is it the sergeant whom Karen knew in her school days?"

"That's him. They've been together all summer. I thought she and Erik would make a match of it, but that's gone by the board." He shook his head irritably.

"I had a cold reception on my way here. Now I know why. Karen has been stamped as a collaborator too. It can't be easy for you and Mother to have two of us tainted in everyone's eyes."

"It damn well isn't," he agreed forcibly, "particularly when you could give up your job tomorrow, and Karen has the power to send that German packing!"

She could see there was going to be a strain throughout the weekend with him. She patted his shoulder reassuringly, hoping to suggest that she and Karen had good reasons.

During her visit Johanna had plenty of chances to assess the situation. Karen had changed more than anyone. She had lost weight, and there was a brittle look to her, as if she might easily snap. On Saturday evening Carl came to take her to a dance. She left the house, and from the window Johanna saw Carl put his arm round her waist possessively. Karen neither responded nor drew away. She seemed resigned.

Johanna turned away from the window. "Why do you allow that sergeant to come here?" she asked Gina, who was darning socks. Edvard had fallen asleep while reading a newspaper and was breathing heavily, his head back against a velvet cushion.

Her mother did not look up. "He doesn't come into the house."

"That's not the point. What hold has that German got over Karen?"

Gina dropped the darning into her lap and glanced in her husband's direction. "I have the feeling that in exchange for her friendship he's prepared to keep word of your father's recovery from the military authorities."

"Oh, my God!" Johanna whispered. "Father doesn't know that. Why haven't you told him?"

"He might do something foolish."

"Give himself up, you mean?"

"I prefer not to think about it." Gina squared her shoulders, as if there were an almost unbearably heavy yoke across them. "Karen's virtue is expendable. Your father's life is not."

IT WAS A RELIEF when the weekend was over. Johanna decided it would be a long time before she went home again. Weekly telephone calls would have to suffice.

"How did you enjoy your visit?" Tom asked her on Monday.

"Not much," she replied, seizing the chance he had given her. "Thanks to you I'm in everybody's bad books."

"What do you mean?"

She told him of the hostility she had encountered in the valley and of her parents' attitude towards her.

"So you won't be going home again for a while?" He was facing her across his desk as she put the morning mail in front of him.

"That's right."

"Sit down a moment." As she obeyed, he cleared his throat. "There's something I've been mulling over. I'd like you to hear me out before you give a decision either way."

"I'm listening." She was puzzled.

"I'm speaking to you now as family and as a friend. You remember my wife, don't you? She was a wonderful hostess—vivacious and fun. I still miss her, particularly when I entertain at weekends. I'm wondering whether you would be prepared to act as my hostess. You're young and beautiful, and it would make all the difference to my guests to have you there. I promise you'd not be bothered by any of them."

Deliberately she played for time, wanting to be entirely sure of the situation. "What would you want me to do? Arrange menus? Organize your household? Book a band for dancing?"

"You have the hang of it exactly. The excellent housekeeper I once had left as soon as German officers began coming to the house. Her replacement has been far from satisfactory. You could reorganize everything and appoint whom you like."

"Give me a few days to think the idea over." She needed to consult the Resistance.

"Naturally." He was satisfied, convinced that what he wanted of her was as good as agreed to. "One more thing." He gestured to her to remain seated. "I'd appreciate it very much if you would accompany me to a party in the officers' mess this evening. We need only stay for an hour or two, but it would be a beginning for occasions to come. You see, it has been noticed that you definitely discourage German company."

She was startled, realizing her blunder. That was an aspect of her position she had not considered. Her smile came as quickly as her answer. "I'm choosy, Tom. I don't go out with small fry."

He chuckled at the echo of his own words. "Wise girl. Then you'll come with me? Good." He made the arrangements about picking her up in the car.

Back at her desk, she gazed unseeingly at her typewriter and released a long breath. Things were beginning to move fast, in a direction she had not anticipated.

TOM DREW UP outside the house on time that night. He had got out of the car and had reached the gate when Johanna came down the path from the side entrance. She was wearing a simple but superbly cut crepe de chine dress borrowed from Astrid, which showed off her slender figure. Her hair, newly washed, swung like golden silk. She carried a filmy shawl that trailed from one hand. He dashed to open the door for her. As they drove, Tom anticipated the effect she would have on the gathering they were to attend. A broad grin spread across his face.

The party was being held at the garrison headquarters, a large mansion on the outskirts of the town. As they paused on the threshold of the ballroom, the buzz of cheerful sounds, the clink of glasses and the background music supplied by army musicians did nothing to quell the surge of revulsion that rose within Johanna. She thought she had become accustomed in the office to the ever-present uniforms and swastikas, but somehow in this festive setting she was seeing them with renewed fury.

A captain of the Waffen SS broke away from his fellow officers to come towards her. As he bowed, clicking his heels, she wondered why a crack regiment like the Waffen had been posted here, the coastal region of an annexed territory, when it was surely needed at the Russian front. But she managed to summon up a dazzling smile.

"*Fräulein.* Such a pleasure. Would you like to dance?"

She danced with a number of officers, sharing her smiles among them. Deliberately she displayed no interest in discussing anything remotely connected with the Wehrmacht. It was her hope that she could establish herself as part of Tom's social circle to the point where conversations would be carried on without any special thought of her presence.

When supper was announced, Tom sought out Johanna, finding her in a group of officers who were slightly drunk and highly merry. Although she was laughing at some quip, he saw an unmistakable flicker of relief in her eyes at his approach.

"I thought it must be time to leave, Tom." She had given him no chance to suggest supper. "I have my shawl. Goodnight, everybody." The young officers were reluctant to let her go, but she slid her hand firmly into the crook of Tom's arm.

"Aren't you hungry?" he asked her, thinking with regret of the supper table he had glimpsed in an adjoining room. Among other dishes there had been cold roast pork, red cabbage, salami and apple strudel.

"I had a bite with Astrid before I came." The abundance of food on the table had sickened her. The most galling sight had been a centrepiece of an enormous bowl of oranges. Most Norwegian children had forgotten the taste of an orange, and some born after the invasion had never known it. She halted abruptly as she and Tom were about to go down the steps of the building into the courtyard. "I would like one of those oranges." She had thought of a youthful recipient.

"I'll get you a couple," he said at once.

Her request saved his life and hers. As he turned back into the mansion she followed to wait in the hallway, and in the same instant an enormous explosion split the air as an ammunition dump near the garrison headquarters went sky-high. The blast swept across the court-yard, killing the sentries and hurling the parked cars like toys into a mass of wreckage. Windows disintegrated as Johanna and Tom were thrown down across the hall floor, while overhead the wooden banisters of the gallery gave way. There were shouts and running feet, and the acrid air smelled of dust and cordite.

"Johanna! Are you all right?" Tom's voice croaked.

Dazedly she lifted her head. "I think so." She saw that he had blood running down the side of his face. "You're hurt!"

"I think one of the banisters grazed me. It's nothing to worry about. Here. Let me give you a hand." He pulled her to her feet. Together they stepped over the debris and went back into the officers' mess. The place was wrecked and there were several casualties. Johanna had some knowledge of first aid and Tom was thoroughly experienced. They worked until the medical officer and stretcher-bearers appeared.

When there was nothing more they could do, Tom steered her out into the open air. A black cloud of smoke had blotted out the stars. Soldiers were running around shouting orders. Tom took one look at the mangled wreckage of his car. "It's a long walk home. We had better get started."

Soldiers were everywhere, put on alert by the act of sabotage, and identity cards were demanded at the checkpoints. Tom's Nazi party membership card and their bedraggled appearances as survivors of the blast got them through without much questioning. He saw her to the foot of the winding road leading up to Astrid's house. Just as she was about to walk away, he thrust a hand into his pocket and drew out an orange.

"The supper table was a shambles, but I managed to find this one without any glass in it."

"Oh, Tom." She took it from him, wondering how he could be such a mixture of what she liked and what she abhorred. "Thanks for remembering."

At the house she let herself in. The landing light was on, and Astrid greeted her. "You have to go straight to the cellar, Johanna," she whispered. Then she gasped when she saw the girl's appearance. "Were you near the explosion I heard?"

Johanna nodded wearily. Reaction was setting in, and suddenly she felt exhausted. "I have an orange for the neighbour's boy," she said, putting it aside, "and I'm afraid your lovely dress is ruined."

"Nothing matters as long as you're unharmed. Go to the cellar now and tell me what happened in the morning. You look about ready to drop."

Suppressing a sigh, Johanna made her way through the stairway door and tapped the signal on the panel. Until it slid back, she had never realized that suspicion had its own animal smell. It seemed to engulf her now at the bottom of the stairs as she was seized roughly on either side and thrust forward unceremoniously into a chair. Gunnar's voice burst wrathfully from the darkness behind the beam of a torch.

"Where the hell have you been? You've kept us waiting."

She answered him in the same fierce tone, blinking against the glare. "Dancing with the Wehrmacht on behalf of the Resistance, and almost getting killed in an explosion set off by my own side. Is that reason enough for being late? Especially when I didn't know you'd be waiting here."

"What double game are you playing? You were planted in Ryen's office to seek out information, not to fraternize. It was your being sighted going into the garrison headquarters tonight that set off this present investigation."

Foreboding suddenly gripped her. "Investigation?"

"We want the truth out of you, and we're going to get it!"

Too late she remembered her instructions never to make a move on her own initiative unless her life or the lives of her fellow resistance fighters were in danger. To assume a new role without notifying anybody had been sheer thoughtlessness on her part. The Resistance was in a hypersensitive state, having suffered much from informers and double agents, and its position had never been more precarious. The seriousness of her situation was acute.

"I'll tell you how it happened." She attempted to shade her eyes from

the light with her forearm only to have it jerked down to her side. "Maybe I shouldn't have attended the party at enemy headquarters without getting it OK'd. It was forced on me. It appeared that I'd refused dates with Germans too often. Tom hinted that doubts were starting as to whether I was the right person for his office."

She could hear the faint echo of her own voice bouncing back from the stone walls. Although she could not see anybody, with the beam directed into her eyes, she sensed that several men were present in the blackness. She guessed they had been involved in the night's great act of sabotage and they were taking shelter from the hunt that was on for them.

When her explanation came to an end, Gunnar's questions were hurled at her in a barrage. "Is it not true that when you were taken in for questioning in Oslo you were released almost at once? Is that when your sympathies for the enemy were first enlisted? Is it not strange that German intervention should have prevented the arrest of your father?"

Her horror of the situation grew with every passing minute and yet she kept her head, thinking carefully before she gave her answers, determined not to be unnerved or misunderstood. As her ordeal continued she became more and more exhausted. She was allowed no respite. Finally Gunnar spat out, "I accuse you of deciding with Tom Ryen just how much useless information should be filtered through to us."

Suddenly she felt renewed strength, and her eyes glittered with triumph. "I've just recalled an item of the so-called useless information that I passed on to you, Gunnar. If it hadn't been for me, you would not have known that the Germans planned to move the bulk of that ammunition you blew up tonight north to Narvik in two days' time. I gathered the information that some of the German-conscripted labour force was to be involved in the loading."

The atmosphere seemed to change. There was movement as people stirred. The interrogation was ending. Gunnar's voice spoke to her on an entirely different note. "You acquitted yourself well. Stay where you are for the moment. People unknown to you will be leaving now." As the shadowy shapes left the cellar she slumped forward where she sat, completely exhausted. Gunnar came round the table and touched her on the shoulder. She did not move.

"How are you feeling? Everyone could see when you arrived that you'd already been through one ordeal. It made your resilience under my questioning all the more commendable."

She did not seem able to move as yet. "Did you know the Waffen SS is in our district?" she asked.

"We know. They're part of new reinforcements in transit. The Third Reich is anticipating an Allied landing in northern Norway."

"Do you think it's likely?"

"It's what we're all hoping for. Now sleep well when you get to bed. You've earned a good rest."

She heard him speak to someone before he left in the wake of the others, taking the torch with him. A match scratched and the lamp on the table was lit. Wearily she straightened her back and prepared to rise. Only then did she see Steffen standing on the opposite side of the table. With a sharp intake of breath she clenched her fists and sprang hotly to her feet.

"You! Here! And you didn't speak up once for me!"

"I did speak for you, before you came. How do you think I felt when I heard you had been in the headquarters when the explosion took place? You easily could have been killed." His voice was hoarse and muffled.

She looked at him almost in bewilderment, still dazed by all that had happened to her in the past hours. He reached out and took her into his embrace. Suddenly she pressed herself to him, with a cry that was close to pain.

Chapter Ten

It was over a month before Tom received a replacement car for the one destroyed in the explosion, and that Friday he drove Johanna out to spend the weekend at his country house, to decide what should be done to get ready for entertaining.

"When do you expect Rolf home?" he asked her as they drove. The imprisoned teachers in the Arctic were finally being released. There was no point in keeping them there when the teachers' Nazi association had fizzled out.

"I've no idea." She turned her head to answer him. "From what I read it seems they are to be let out a few at a time." She was quietly enjoying the drive. The countryside was steeped in autumn hues under a cloud-streaked sky.

Tom's voice broke into her thoughts. "We're nearly there."

She had expected his home to look smaller than she remembered it, knowing that in childhood memories proportions are invariably exaggerated. As the car drew up she was surprised to discover the house was in no way diminished. It had been built in the late eighteenth century, with filigreed ornamentation over windows and doorways and the graceful sweep of a horseshoe flight of steps to the entrance. Timber-built, it was at home in its setting of forest slope and water. A wooded island lay offshore, and a sailboat was moored alongside a couple of rowboats.

"It's still like something out of a fairy tale!" she exclaimed, getting out of the car and looking up at the house.

"Come in." He took their bags from the back seat.

Indoors, much of the furniture was of the same period as the house. Chests, cupboards and chairs were decorated with the old patterns known as rose painting; the ceiling of one room was entirely covered with these designs, while the floors were of white pine, with the knots gleaming like pieces of embedded amber. Tom went ahead of Johanna, throwing open double doors.

"I use these rooms for parties," he told her.

"I can tell that. There are wine and grease stains on those lovely floors. Where's your housekeeper?"

"I told you this place needs proper supervision. She's in the kitchen, I expect. I let her know we were coming."

There was no one in the well-appointed kitchen, which was far from clean. Johanna went out to the porch. The housekeeper, a girl of about nineteen, was asleep in a deckchair, tanning herself in the late September sun. Johanna looked at Tom. "Give her a week's wages in lieu of notice. I'll go and take a look upstairs."

Soon after, from a bedroom window, she watched the girl depart, irate and red-faced, a bulging suitcase in one hand and a carrier bag in the other. As Johanna finished her inspection of the upper floor, she met Tom coming up the stairs with their luggage. "Have you chosen the bedroom you'd like for the weekend and whenever you visit?" he asked.

She gave a nod. "The one at the end." She had selected it because it had access to a balcony above the veranda and in an emergency she could climb down.

"It's not very large," he said doubtfully. "I'm hoping you will be here often, so I want you to be happy with it."

"It's fine. And I'll see that you get a good housekeeper, don't worry about that." She knew Gunnar was already looking for a woman with resistance sympathies who would be willing to wait on Germans and prepared to support Johanna in an emergency.

The next morning the renovations and redecorating Johanna deemed necessary were begun. Through his authority it was not difficult for Tom to organize personnel to do the work. One weekend Johanna herself refinished and stained some pieces of old furniture with painstaking care. She was doing it out of love for the house and its beautiful, time-aged furnishings, not for Tom. Such things were part of the heritage that was freedom to her.

JOHANNA'S WORK WAS LEFT in abeyance on the weekend she went home to see Rolf. He was among the last of the imprisoned teachers to be released, and he had lost a great deal of weight even though rations had improved during the wait for transport home.

In the midst of the exuberant family reunion Gina happened to see from the window that Carl Müller was approaching the house. She gave Karen a nod and the girl unobtrusively left the room. Edvard did not miss the closing of the door behind her.

"That Nazi is here again, isn't he? It strikes me that there's more to her keeping company with him than meets the eye. She's not in love with him. Even I can see that."

Gina moved quickly to press a hand on his shoulder. "Don't start imagining things. And remember, we can overlook a lot for the unselfish way she nursed you through your illness."

In the hallway Karen put on her coat and went outside. The valley was still green in spite of its now being December, a trick played by the Gulf Stream, defying the snow flurries that attempted to take hold. Carl was wearing his helmet, which she hated, and was fully kitted out with his rifle and his broad greatcoat. One look at him showed Karen that something was wrong. "What's happened?" she asked as she reached him.

"There's an invasion alert. I've been posted elsewhere on the coast. I go today."

She stared at him, letting the marvellous news sink in. Her nightmare was ending. "So you've come to say goodbye."

"I'm afraid so. Walk with me where we can be alone. We've a lot of talking to do in a short time. You know I'm not one for letter writing, but I would like to hear from you sometimes."

She listened and said nothing, strolling at his side. Surely he must realize there had been tyranny in his keeping her under compulsory obligation to him. He had compelled her company and she had suffered his kisses. Only with difficulty had she kept him from going further. Now all that misery was practically over. As the lane dwindled to a mere path between the trees, she heard him say, "These past months have been good ones for me. It was a lucky day when I was sent to the Ryen farm." His arm went round her as they walked on. "That brings me to what I want to talk about." Ahead was a small wooden hut.

"Yes?"

"An army clerk looked up the military hostage file for me, and according to the entry Edvard Ryen is deceased." Carl had slowed to a standstill and her face was blooming with joy.

"Do you mean there's nothing more to worry about?"

He laughed quietly at her excitement. "Nothing at all. That's the army for you. If the files say he's a goner, that's how it is."

She shook her head at her happiness. "I don't know how to thank you for telling me this. I'll always be grateful."

She saw how he was looking at her. "You've proved that your friendship towards me is true," she said nervously.

"That's right. Now it's your turn to show equal friendship towards me." Keeping his gaze steadily on her, he lifted his chinstrap and removed his helmet. Casually he turned to the open hut by which they were now standing and put his helmet inside with his rifle. The hut was a place where hay was stored. He drew her to him, using his hold over her for the last time.

"You wouldn't want me to report to my commanding officer before I leave that there's an error in the files, would you?"

Her throat became tight and dry. She could not find a voice to speak out of the abyss of despair into which she was sinking. To resist him was to lose everything for which she had worked and endured over many months. There was no escape. The whisper broke from her pale lips. "No, I wouldn't."

He guided her into the hut. When he was finished with her, he crouched down to her pale form on the hay and tenderly stroked her face. She jerked away from his touch, shuddering. Stepping out of the hut, he looked back at her lingeringly. Then he shook his head and retraced his steps to the lane.

She could not stop shivering. Neither could she seem able to think. All that did come through to her was that Edvard was safe. And somehow that meant that Erik would be safe too.

The sound of someone entering the hut made her sit upright, convulsed with fear that Carl had returned. Instead, she saw three youths from one of the neighbouring farms. Their faces were full of loathing. The first one spoke in a tone of contempt. "You dirty Nazi-loving whore!"

She saw he had a pair of sheep-shearing clippers in his hand. "No!" she whimpered, trying to edge away. "Please. No!"

All three of them seized her. She screamed out, and a large hand covered her mouth and nose, half smothering her. Her wide, dilated eyes saw long strands of hair falling from her head as the shears did their brutal work, nicking her scalp agonizingly. When her head was completely shaved they let her go, marked as a woman who associated with the enemy.

She bolted out of the hut, her coat flying behind her, sobbing as she ran. Her instinct was to lose herself in the forest, only to hear with renewed terror the youths thudding after her. Spreading out, they herded her like a panic-stricken animal towards the valley, where she would be seen in her branded state from the farmsteads. Her mind seemed to snap and she began to scream, the piercing sound ringing far as the trees were left behind. Her pursuers fell back, their purpose accomplished.

She kept up her hurtling speed in the grip of hysteria. She neither saw nor heard those who came running out of the Ryen farmhouse to halt her. At the impact of Rolf's arms she collapsed with a suddenness that almost unbalanced him. He carried her into the house.

Gina and Johanna took charge. In the warm kitchen a shawl was wrapped round her as they seated her on the bench. Comforting elderberry tea was trickled through her chattering teeth, and the cuts on her head were bathed and treated with iodine. Her silence was as intense as her screaming had been.

She did not speak until the next day. Then, with a coloured scarf bound about her head, she came downstairs at midmorning. Johanna had just come in from a walk with her brother, and Gina was writing letters. All three of them looked towards her. It was to Gina that she spoke quite calmly. "Your husband is safe. Officially his name has gone from the hostage records. There is nothing more to fear, and Carl has been posted away."

Gina's face crumpled into tears of thankfulness. "I never wanted you to be branded in this terrible way."

"I know that. My hair will grow again. In the meantime I want to go home. I'm sorry to leave, but I have to get away."

Gina rose slowly from her chair. "What of Erik?"

Johanna, looking from one to the other of them, sensed the empathy between them.

Karen gave a curiously direct answer that was accepted as if anticipated. "I hope he forgets me. That's all I can say."

If Gina had needed confirmation of what she suspected, she had it then. Sadly she went to find Edvard in the woodshed. The previous day he had sawed a good number of logs and he was looking them over, well pleased with his returning strength.

"Sit down, Edvard," Gina said. "I've something to tell you."

When he had heard all she had to say he broke down completely, a hand over his eyes. "That poor child," he kept repeating. After a while Gina returned to the house and sent Karen out to him. Later, when she went outside onto the kitchen porch, she saw them sitting quietly together, both of Karen's arms about him.

Shortly before Johanna returned to town that evening, she went into the bedroom where Karen was packing. "I've a suggestion." She was confident of Gunnar's agreement. "I'm sure I can offer you a job. Tom Ryen needs a housekeeper at his weekend place. It's not all that far from your own village. You'd be on your own in the house most of the time."

Karen looked assessingly at Johanna. "You must have as good reason as I did for being civil to the Nazis. You too must have a purpose. I'll take the job. And later, when my hair has grown again, I'll go home and see my family."

"Then that's settled. I'll fix everything tomorrow. Tom will get travel and work permits for you. I can't tell you what it will mean to me to have a friend I can trust in the house."

IN THE FIRST WEEK of the new year of 1943, a quiet Christmas at Ryen Farm behind him, Rolf escaped to England on a fishing smack. He went through the same screening procedure as his brother and thousands of other escapees before him. His selection by the Free Norwegian airforce board went through quickly. Within a short time he was at "Little Norway" in Canada, training to be a fighter pilot.

After he gained his wings, he was posted to 331 Squadron in North Weald, not far from London. He was soon a veteran of many sorties across the Channel. The day a swastika was painted as his score on the side of his Spitfire he saw it as his first real blow against the Nazis.

He tried to trace Erik, only to draw a blank each time. His hope was that one day his brother would walk into the County Hotel or the Shaftesbury, which were centres for Norwegian servicemen in London, and they would meet that way. For all he knew, Erik might be on a battleship anywhere in the world.

On the day a third swastika was painted on the side of his plane, Rolf's life changed. He fell in love with an English girl. When he saw her across a dance hall in Epping, a village near the airport, her vivacious presence and the rich sheen of her red-gold hair eclipsed all the rest. She, seeing him come purposefully across the floor towards her, had a feeling of destiny.

"May I have this dance?"

"Yes, of course." Softly she went into his arms, light as a butterfly. There was a look of discovery on his face as he drew her out onto the floor.

"I'm Rolf Ryen. What's your name?"

"Wendy Townsend."

Chapter Eleven

For Johanna the first weekend party at Tom's house was nerve-racking. On Friday evening she had come downstairs to greet the guests, and there, standing with two army officers, was Axel Werner in his black uniform, promoted to SS security commandant. He was regarding her with astonishment.

"Johanna Ryen! I haven't seen you since you came to my office in Oslo. What a pleasant surprise."

It was anything but that for her. Apart from not wanting to come into contact with his unpleasant personality again, there was his devastating knowledge that she had been under suspicion for anti-Nazi activities in Oslo. Her involvement with Tom and her whole project were in jeopardy. She returned Axel's smile with the biggest bluff she could bring to her aid. "This should be a big moment for you, Axel. You can see that your kindly advice did not go amiss."

His conceit swelled. Thoroughly egotistical, he was totally prepared to believe he had won her over to the Third Reich during what he looked back on as a heart-to-heart talk. "Well done, my dear girl. I'm proud of you."

The taller of the other two army officers raised inquiring eyebrows. "What's all this then?"

Axel chuckled. "A little secret between us, is it not, Johanna?"

"I agree." Her smile turned to the other guests. "Axel and I knew each other as children."

"How fortunate for SS Obersturmbannführer Werner."

"Some people get all the luck," the second man commented, grinning at her.

Tom beamed as he carried out the introductions. Johanna was getting off to a flying start, just as he had anticipated. Moreover, she looked stunning, wearing a simple dinner gown of creamy velvet with a string of unusual pearly stones linked by gold. "Now, gentlemen," he said, "Frøken Hallsted will show you to your rooms. Then please join us for a drink before dinner."

Karen, waiting in the background, stepped forward. Johanna had made her a stylish turban out of a piece of silk donated by Astrid. Her hair was growing again into soft curly strands, but she was too self-conscious as yet to display it.

While waiting for his guests to reappear, Tom poured Johanna a drink in the room with the rose-painted ceiling, the firelight from the open corner hearth dancing over the centuries-old designs. "What a coincidence that you should know the SS Obersturmbannführer, Johanna."

"Where is he stationed?"

"He's in a commandeered house in Ålesund. He's here to rout out the remnants of the Resistance in the area."

"Oh, is he?" Her face was straight as she looked into the fire. "That sounds as if he will be around for a long time."

It was a very civilized dinner party that evening. Axel was in high good humour, appreciating the food and the wine and liking the fact that he had known Johanna for almost as long as Tom had. The other two guests were lively company, enjoying the presence of a young and beautiful woman. When the opportunity presented itself, both made classic passes at her. They accepted her cordial turndown with singular good grace.

In the weeks that followed, Johanna kept to her policy of never asking questions about military matters. In time she learned much to pass on to Gunnar, simply by sitting quietly and listening while the company relaxed and occasionally forgot she was there. There was much talk among the officers about the disastrous end of the North African campaign, and the Allied attack on Italy. But their confidence in the German army as the best fighting force ever was undiminished.

"If it has to be a hundred-year war, we'll still come out on top," Axel said, one warm June evening when dinner was over and some of the officers had gathered on the veranda.

"It won't take a hundred years," drawled the drink-thickened voice of a brutish-looking officer on his first visit to the house.

"What makes you so sure, Oberleutnant?" inquired Axel.

"The sweet little product in Telemark that's going to help us bring the world under the Führer's heel." The speaker lifted up and crashed down his own jackbooted metal heel, making a gash in a veranda floorboard that would be there for ever.

"Shut your mouth," another officer growled at him from the next chair. Conversation continued as though uninterrupted.

Johanna knew it was the heavy-water plant to which the drunken officer had referred. A small band of Norwegian saboteurs had entered it and blown up vital sections of the plant in February. The delaying effect on the German production of the dangerous weapon they were calling the atomic bomb had been invaluable. But something was apparently still in the wind. Johanna would pass this on for what it was worth.

KAREN'S HAIR GREW LONGER, and at last she felt able to visit her home. It was near enough for her to row there from Tom Ryen's house, cutting several kilometres off the inland journey by road. Her village had a central street running up from a cove where fishing boats were moored, a few shops standing at some distance from each other, orchards and gardens, and habitations in between. Her sister and brother-in-law, Marthe and Roald, had a flat above their bakery, and Karen had lived with them there after losing her parents. On the day she returned she went almost shyly towards the bakery door. Marthe happened to be there with Roald, saw her coming and ran to meet her. "You're home!"

They laughed and cried together. She need not have worried about how even Roald, a staunch patriot, would receive her with branded head. Gina had sent them a long letter telling them the whole story. They welcomed her like a prodigal daughter, and later that day Roald offered to give her back her old job in his bakery.

"There's been talk for a long time about Tom Ryen and the Nazi company he keeps," he said, his thin, bony face extremely grave. "I don't

474

like the thought of your being at that house of his with the carryings-on that take place there." Roald felt a keen responsibility towards his young sister-in-law.

Before Karen could make any answer, he continued, "However, I must tell you what living with us would mean. I do what I can to aid those taking a more active part in the liberation of our country. Our village is often a first port of call for small boats that come in from across the North Sea. You would not be involved in any of it. On nights when I say I'll be working alone in the bakery, you'll go to bed as Marthe does and pull the quilt over your ears. Is that understood?"

"Perfectly, except that I'll remain at Tom Ryen's house and come to see you on visits, as I have done today."

Nothing they could say would make her accept their kind offer. She had grown to like her new life. The weekends were hard work, but the quietness betweentimes was full of balm. There were moments when she thought fancifully that the old house was filled with a healing power. The emotional shocks she had suffered had ended her hopes for a future with Erik. All that was left was to pray that one day she would feel clean again.

JOHANNA WENT STRAIGHT from Tom's office on a day she was to meet Gunnar in a cafe to hand over information she had copied and hidden in a folded newspaper. Instead of Gunnar, she found to her joy that Steffen was waiting for her at a sheltered corner table. It had been a long time since their last meeting, and by the brilliance of his eyes she could tell that his excitement was equal to hers.

"Nice day." He smiled. "Would you like something to eat? I have food coupons."

She was hungry. "Yes, I would." After studying the limited menu, she made her choice. "I'm going to have boiled cod."

"I'll have the same."

When Steffen gave their order, Johanna produced a raw potato from Astrid's kitchen garden to hand over to the waitress. It was only by turning in a raw potato that customers were served a cooked one in exchange. When the cooked potato came, steaming on her plate, Johanna was jubilant. "We're in luck! This potato is larger than the one I handed in."

"Hurrah," he joked, laughing with her. Meticulously she divided their prize in half and shared it with him.

While they ate, she took up the newspaper and passed it across to him. "As arranged, here's something for you to read."

"I look forward to it." He slipped it into his jacket.

"Maybe it's of interest, maybe not. I never know."

"You're not meant to. You do your job and we'll do ours. That brings me to something else. Does Tom ever go to Oslo?"

"Not often. Once in three or four months perhaps. Why?"

"We could do with a regular courier. One with legitimate business in the city. It was hoped you might be able to persuade him to take you along if he travelled there fairly often."

"No dice, I'm afraid."

"It's a link we'll need in a while, so keep your eyes and ears open. You never know. It's possible something will come up."

"I'll remember. That's a promise."

His eyes were full of love. "I want to marry you, Jo."

Startled, she drew back slowly in her chair. "Don't say that."

"I mean it. For the first time in my life I want to put a wedding ring on a woman's finger, and it can't be done. At least not here in our own country, where at present I officially don't exist. Come back to England with me the next time I go. We can be married in London."

She shook her head vigorously. "In the early days of the occupation I would have gone with you if it had been possible. Maybe I've done nothing of real importance in my underground work so far, but the chance remains that I will come across something vital. In exile I couldn't be of that much use in the cause of freedom. Marriage has to wait until life is normal again. But our commitment to each other is as firm as ever." Moving back her chair in readiness to leave, she chuckled. "Thanks for suggesting marriage. I was beginning to think that you'd never ask!"

He grinned at her. "I meant to have you since I first saw you looking out of the Alsteens' window on invasion day."

She raised an eyebrow comically. "Now you tell me!"

"I love you."

She had to tear her eyes away from the gaze in which he held her and force herself to get up from the chair to leave the cafe. It would have been all too easy to change her mind and go with him to England.

WHEN CATERING for the weekends at Tom Ryen's house, Karen always placed an order for bread with her brother-in-law, and her sister usually made the delivery with a horse and wagonette. Throughout the summer there had been none of the secret comings and goings to which Roald had referred, but with the arrival of the darker nights of autumn the stage was set once more. Marthe's agitation was noticeable when she brought the bread into the house one Friday afternoon. Twice she dropped loaves as she was helping to unload them from the basket.

"What's the matter with you?" Karen inquired considerately. "Aren't you well?"

The reply came almost irritably. "If you must know, I do get nervous when we have important company."

"Oh." Comprehending, Karen said, "I wouldn't have asked if I'd known."

"That's all right." Marthe took the last loaf from the basket. "There's no harm in your knowing. Our visitor came in the middle of the night and tomorrow night he changes places with someone arriving by boat. I'll be glad when it's all over."

After Marthe had left, Karen finished what she had to do in the kitchen and then went upstairs to make sure everything was in order for when Tom and Johanna arrived. There were to be three houseguests, including Axel Werner, while a number of other people were coming to a party on Saturday night. Lately Tom was finding food and drink no longer as easy to come by. Fortunately, most of the guests brought bottles with them, and so far Karen's culinary skills had disguised any major shortages.

On Saturday night the party was in full swing, with dancing and noisy laughter. Three of the guests, older men with no interest in dancing, wanted a game of bridge and asked Johanna if she could locate a fourth to join them.

"I think so." She knew Axel was a keen bridge player and she went in search of him. Unable to find him in any of the rooms, she asked for him and was told he had gone out. She found another player instead, and leaving the four men on their own in the rose-ceilinged room, she carried a tray of dirty glasses into the kitchen, where Karen was washing up. As Johanna took up a cloth to dry the dishes she wondered aloud where Axel might have gone.

Karen stopped her washing and gripped the edge of the enamel sink, a look of fright on her face. "Go and find out if he's upstairs or in the bathroom or anywhere," she implored.

Johanna looked at her. "What is it? What's wrong?"

"I don't know. It may be nothing, but he's commandant of security, and my brother-in-law has a resistance fighter in his house tonight, with another coming off a boat."

Johanna dashed from the room. Upstairs she failed to find Axel and hastened back to the kitchen.

"Tell me where your brother-in-law lives! I'll change my clothes and get over there and warn them!"

"No!" Karen was adamant. "I'll go. Nobody will miss me out here in the kitchen. I can reach Roald's place without being seen if I row there." She went to her room to change into outdoor clothes and sneakers. When she returned, Johanna gave her one of Tom's torches and some last-minute advice.

"Do be careful. The area could be alive with troops if things are as we fear."

Karen slipped out into the dark and rainy night. Running swiftly from the house, she went down to the bank where the rowing boats were moored. Within moments she had cast off, gripped with fear of what would happen to Marthe and Roald if they were discovered to be hiding freedom fighters in their house.

As she rowed she caught a glimpse of headlights, which enabled her to see that there was more than one truck approaching along the twisting inland road. Her guess was that soldiers were being moved in to close upon the village. Desperately she lent her strength to the oars with renewed effort. Never had it seemed to take longer to reach the moorings below her old home.

IN THE BAKERY Gunnar was waiting, glancing constantly at his watch and pacing restlessly. It was stiflingly hot, for Roald was continuing with his night's baking. In the darkness of a room upstairs Marthe was keeping watch on the road.

"My colleague is overdue," Gunnar remarked edgily.

"How much longer are you going to give him?" Roald asked.

"I must go on waiting. He'll come sooner or later." Gunnar was about to light a cigarette when a hasty knocking came on the door. Immediately Roald gave a tense nod, and Gunnar went quickly through into the inner hallway, his revolver ready. Through a crack in the door he watched Roald admit a young woman he had never seen before.

"Karen!" Roald exclaimed. "What are you doing here?"

"I've come to warn you! Is the resistance man still in the house? He should get away at once."

Gunnar emerged from the doorway. "Who are you?"

Roald spoke for her. "My wife's sister."

Karen stepped forward in her frantic anxiety. "I've seen trucks approaching the village. More than that. I work at Tom Ryen's on the other side of the inlet, and the SS security commandant in this area left a party there early for no apparent reason."

"The Ryen house? You're Karen?"

"Yes I am. Johanna knows I'm here." She broke off as there came a tapping. The men recognized a prearranged signal. Roald opened the door. It was Steffen.

Gunnar saw the ashy pallor of Steffen's face and the way he slumped back against the wall. "What's happened?" he asked. "Are you badly hurt?"

"I was nicked in the shoulder."

Gunnar pulled Steffen's jacket aside and saw a red stain seeping through the thick wool of the jersey beneath. "You must have that wound dressed. You're losing a lot of blood."

Steffen pushed him away. "That can wait. You can't. Get out of here. Now! The mountains are your only chance. You'd never reach the fishing boat. That's cut off by a nest of Germans. I went smack into them when I came across towards the village. I only hope the skipper heard the shots, but it's unlikely."

"We'll try for the mountains together." Gunnar grabbed a wad of clean linen dough coverings from a bench and bound them round Steffen's shoulder. "These will hold until we can get you medical attention."

While he was speaking, there was a scurrying of footsteps down the stairs and Marthe appeared, trembling with fright, in the doorway. "Germans! Coming down the street in both directions!"

Karen ran to Gunnar. "I'll show you where I've left a rowing boat. Take Steffen to Tom Ryen's house. Johanna will find a place for you to hide. The house is full of Wehrmacht officers. Nobody would look for you there! Come with me."

When Steffen thrust himself away from the wall, he reeled and would have fallen if he had not been given support, Gunnar pulling his uninjured arm about his shoulders. Roald switched off the light and held the door open, and the two of them went with Karen out into the darkness. They hurried down to the water's edge in the now torrential rain. Gunnar got Steffen into the boat first, but when he held out his hand to Karen she hung back.

"I'm not going. Tell me the name of the fishing boat you were supposed to take and the signal for the skipper. I might get through to warn him by following the rocks."

"*Fjellpike* is the boat and the password is 'Midgard'."

Steffen supplied the rest of what she had to know. "There's only one place on the west side of the point where fishing boats can put in. You'll find the *Fjellpike* there."

"I know the place. Good luck."

"And to you."

Karen vanished immediately in the wet blackness as Gunnar pulled strongly away from the shore. Steffen, slumped in the bow, spoke his thoughts for both of them. "I hope she makes it. It'll be disaster for the whole crew if she doesn't."

The boat bobbed through the fierce little waves, spray showering over the two men continually. They strained their eyes for the boathouses that were the landmark. They loomed up eventually, and Gunnar located a place to moor.

After helping Steffen into the boathouse, Gunnar went to reconnoitre, darting across the grounds to feel his way to the rear of the house. As he stepped onto the porch an old board creaked and immediately the kitchen door opened narrowly. There was a gasp of astonishment.

"Gunnar!" Johanna rushed out to him.

"I've the Englishman with me. He's wounded."

"How badly?" Her voice shook.

"I don't know yet. Where shall I take him?"

"There's a storeroom off the kitchen where I can hide you. Do you want any help?"

"No. Just be ready to let us in."

Johanna went back indoors. Dodging round the table, which was loaded with dirty glasses, she reached the door into the hall and peeped through. Nobody was there. She flew up the stairs to the landing, where a first-aid box and spare bandages were kept in a linen cupboard. Taking these out and with blankets under her other arm, she returned to the kitchen and deposited the items on the stone floor of the storeroom.

At the boathouse, Gunnar found Steffen unable to get to his feet unaided. Hauling him up amid stifled groans, Gunnar once more supported him and together they staggered towards the house. When they reached the kitchen, there was a brief moment during which Steffen focused on Johanna's face before pain overtook him and he blacked out.

AT THE FJORD'S EDGE, Karen scrambled along through the rocks and boulders. Her stockings were torn and her knees were scraped where she had fallen several times, and her sneakers were sopping wet from when she had plunged her feet into the rock pools hidden in the darkness.

Then ahead, black against the water, was the crag beyond which she would find the waiting fishing boat. She scrambled up the steep slope and ran through the wet grass, knowing she was on the right side of the point and away from the place where Steffen had barely escaped ambush. In the little bay below she saw the boat lying, without navigation lights. It was here she was to start giving the password, for someone from the vessel would be waiting near the track that led down to the bay.

"Midgard!" she called in a low voice. The name of a sanctuary created for mortals by the Norse gods was appropriate to the wild night. "Midgard!"

A figure in black oilskins emerged from the trees nearby, making her start. "Karen? Is it you, Karen?"

"Erik!" she hurled herself into his arms, and as they met, all the past was wiped clean for her. She forgot the misery and self-doubts, the conviction that she was lost to him beyond recall, that Carl had destroyed what might have been. Everything she had ever wanted returned to her in his kiss. When they drew back, he laughed softly in his joy at this unexpected reunion. Then she gasped out why she had come.

"You'll be caught if you stay here!" he exclaimed. "I'll take you back to the Shetlands with me."

She thought she was crying with happiness, but she could not be sure. He paused only to flash a signal to the fishing boat to be alert for departure and then began to run with her towards the track. Below them the vessel's engine spurted into life.

"*Achtung!*" Her heart seemed to stop. A single soldier had appeared, to face them with rifle pointing. Erik thrust her behind him and fired a signal gun. A red warning star arched through the blackness down to the water below. If orders had not been given for all the captives to be taken alive, Erik would have been shot. The soldier ran forward, swearing.

"Hands up! Get your hands up! Both of you!" Then more soldiers came swarming out of the trees. They went pouring down the track, firing their rifles at the fishing boat, which was drawing out into the fjord. A sergeant snapped an order and came to have a look at the prisoners, shining a torch into Erik's face and then into Karen's. He brusquely ordered that the seaman be placed under special arrest and that the girl be escorted back into the village to join those already arrested.

As Erik was shoved forward he called his last words to Karen. "We'll find each other again one day."

"I love you," she replied, helpless with tears. A rifle gave her a sharp push. Allowed to drop her arms to her sides, she stumbled along, her sneakers slopping uncomfortably on her feet. She was chilled to the bone.

When the village came into sight, she stared in disbelief at the scene of destruction. Soldiers were putting torches to each building, the wood crackling, paintwork spitting. The fishing boats moored by the jetty were also in flames. In the red-gold light she saw the women and children of the village gathered, watching their homes burn down. The menfolk were being shepherded away into trucks, to be taken to concentration camps in Germany. Only the very old men were weeded out and sent to join a little group of their own. Every person had a dazed look of disbelief.

"Why are you doing this?" Karen cried to her escort.

"By order of the commandant. A just punishment for harbouring secret agents. There's the one we caught." He pointed ahead with his rifle. "We would have taken him alive, but he killed an officer and two men before he was brought down."

The dead Norwegian lay sprawled in his own blood. It was neither of the men who had been in Roald's bakery. Two plainclothesmen, whom she guessed to be Gestapo, were going through his pockets while Axel Werner, jackbooted feet astride, stood looking on. She could only conclude that by some devious trick of fate there had been a third agent in the village that night with some purpose of his own, and this poor stranger had been accidentally caught in the Germans' net.

"Over there!" She was pushed towards the group of women and children. Marthe had seen her coming and burst into sobs in her arms. "They've taken Roald away. We don't know what's happening to the men or to us."

After a while more trucks arrived to load up the women and children to be taken to camps in Norway. As with the men, the old women were pushed aside to be left behind.

Inside a truck Karen held her sister close. Through the flap of the canvas opening Karen could see the burning village. She watched the gilded sign above the bakery door turn brown as flames licked up the building. The unremitting rain did nothing to quell the fires, and sparks hissed and spat in the puddles.

Chapter Twelve

In the storeroom, Steffen lay unconscious on a bed of blankets. Gunnar knelt on one side of him and Johanna on the other. She handed across whatever was required from the first-aid box and helped cut away the blood-soaked jersey and the shirt beneath, to reach the wound. There proved to be no major damage. When the dressing was completed, Gunnar drew up the blankets.

"He needs rest. Lots of it. That's the only treatment in these circumstances." He sat back and looked at Johanna in her silky evening dress. He thought she made an incongruously beautiful sight in their strange surroundings of flour sacks and storage pots. Her expression was loving as she gazed down at Steffen.

"Is he in a lot of pain, do you think?" she asked anxiously.

"He's not aware of it at the moment." Gunnar saw tears in her eyes, and his tone became gentle. "Hey! He's not going to die."

She forced a smile. "I know. I'm crying with relief that his wound isn't worse than it is." Hastily she dried her eyes. "I must return to the party. You'll be safe enough here. I'll bring a jug of water for Steffen and get rid of his shirt and jersey. I'll take replacements from Tom's wardrobe."

After discarding the garments and handing the jug to Gunnar, she went out of the kitchen, fully expecting to be met by Tom expressing annoyance over her prolonged absence from the gathering. To her surprise the soldier musicians of the band were already packing up their instruments.

"Are you going so soon?" she queried. "It's barely midnight."

"Nobody is dancing now," one of the bandsmen answered. "Most of the men have gone to the fire. We're taking the ladies back to town in our truck."

"Fire?" She was alarmed. "Whose home is it?"

"It looks like the whole village."

She ran through the deserted party room to the veranda. The glow lit the sky above the trees and tinted the fjord. Several officers stood exchanging comments. Johanna spotted Tom among them and darted to him. "Shouldn't we go and help?" she suggested. "People will be homeless. There'll be lots we can do."

Tom maintained an uncomfortable silence. The officer next to him half turned to address her. "It's not that kind of fire, fräulein. This is an elimination of subversion. There'll be no homeless there. The population is to be dispersed to places of correction."

Feeling nauseated, Johanna turned back into the house. Tom, seeing her go, followed her. She sat down on a chair, and he hovered uncertainly, twisting a ring on his finger.

"It could have been worse, Johanna. You heard what was said. The people are being taken away, not shot."

"Are you trying to tell me that mercy has been shown?"

"In a way, yes. Naturally the firing of the village has upset you. But for your sake and for mine, don't show them hostility. The Germans are edgy at times like these. We don't want to get involved in any trouble."

The rest of the company departed, and Johanna returned to work in the kitchen. The houseguests had retired, and the place was quiet again when Tom heard a car approaching. As he expected, Axel Werner, the SS commandant, had returned. Tom went out to greet him. Werner looked tired and less than satisfied as he mounted the steps.

"We killed one agent," he informed Tom, "and wounded another who escaped in the undergrowth."

"Is the search still on?"

"Yes." Axel went ahead into the house, removing his shiny-peaked cap and smoothing his hair. "A seaman from the fishing vessel involved in tonight's incident was also captured."

"Is he from these parts?"

"I'm told his papers gave a name and a home address near Bergen. The Gestapo are taking him to Oslo."

"What about the fishing boat?"

"Sunk. No survivors. It failed to heed a shot across the bow from a patrol boat. A hard night. Not one that I relish."

"How about a cognac before you retire?"

Axel grunted acceptance. "Perhaps Johanna or Frøken What's-her-name could make me a sandwich?"

"That shall be done. I'll pour you the drink first."

Axel followed his host into the rose-ceilinged room and flung himself down in a chair. He was churning with sullen anger that one of his quarries had slipped the noose. His only hope was that the man would be found before the night was over. He took the drink Tom handed him and said, "The garages and boathouse and the grounds around your house will be searched during the night. Don't worry. No damage will be done." He raised his glass in salute. *"Prosit."*

"Skål."

In the kitchen, Johanna had washed up everything from the party and was carrying crockery into the storeroom when suddenly she heard chair legs scrape in the hall. She had placed a chair in front of the kitchen door to give warning of anyone's approach.

"Someone's coming," she whispered to Gunnar. "Switch off the light in there."

Tom entered, grumbling about the chair left in the way, just as the storeroom door was being closed. Johanna set down the stack of plates and looked inquiringly at Tom. "Is there something you want?"

"Axel is back. He'd like a sandwich. Can Karen fix it?"

Johanna swallowed hard. "She's finished with chores here this evening. Leave it to me."

Tom noted the shadows under her eyes. She looked exhausted, almost brittle with stress. The village fire had been hard on her.

"I'll give you some help since Karen has gone to bed. You make the sandwich, and I'll put that heavy crockery away for you." He picked up the stack of plates she had put down.

"No!" She spoke with unusual sharpness, surprising him. Then she smiled. "I mean, there's no need. It can wait until morning." She moved swiftly in front of him, blocking the storeroom door. "Go back to Axel. He's your guest and you're leaving him on his own."

"He'll be all right. It's you I'm worried about." He reached her with the plates. "Step aside now."

"Tom!" It was a desperate cry of appeal. "Please do as I say."

"My dear girl. What is it? What's the matter?"

While standing in front of the storeroom door, she had inadvertently touched it with her heel. Not completely closed, it began to swing open until stopped by Gunnar. He was hiding behind the door gun in hand. At that moment Steffen began to regain consciousness, emitting a groan. Tom, with apprehension, put down the plates and shoved Johanna aside, to stare, appalled, at the wounded man on the makeshift bed.

"Who is he?" In panic Tom seized Johanna by the shoulders and shook her. "Who have you brought into my house?"

"You must let him stay! I love him, Tom. He was wounded this evening, and there was nowhere else for him to go."

He shook a fist at her. "You might as well ask me to cut my own throat! I'm denouncing him!"

She swung herself in front of him as he made for the hall. "I'll swear you were in it as much as I! I'll tell the Nazis that this house is a resistance hideout and your hospitality to the Wehrmacht is a cover-up. I'll say that my lover isn't the first secret agent we've sheltered together. And some of the lies I'll tell them will stick. There is even a chance that you'll end up in a concentration camp with me!"

At that moment Axel stepped into the kitchen. "What's going on here? I came to tell you that soldiers are searching your grounds now, Major Ryen. I'm going outside to hear if there's any fresh news. Perhaps you would like to come with me." He went past the open storeroom without a glance and reached the back door. "Well?" he asked with impatience. "What is the matter with you? You look as if you've just faced the end of the world."

Tom opened his mouth and closed it again. Out of the corner of his eye he saw Johanna move swiftly over to the storeroom door and shut it with a click. "I'll join you," he said woodenly to Axel, following after him.

Gunnar raised both hands expressively when Johanna reentered the storeroom. "Well done! You were fantastic."

"I worked that threat out long ago, in case Tom caught me taking information from the files. Luckily he doesn't suspect that you're here too." She knelt down beside Steffen, lovingly taking the hand he held out.

"You really are here, then." His voice was blurred with weakness. "I thought I'd been dreaming."

"I'm here and it's no dream. Drink some water for me now and then sleep. We want you to get your strength back." He did what she asked.

"I feel as if I'm surrounded by live grenades that might go off at any minute," she confessed to Gunnar. "We can't trust Tom. Karen hasn't returned. Upstairs there are two sleeping Nazis, with a third prowling around outside the house like a leopard."

Gunnar chuckled. "At least we're not lacking excitement."

His cheerful attitude helped to raise her spirits. In the kitchen she prepared a sandwich for Axel and carried it through to the rose-ceilinged room to await his return. Tom brought him back into the house by the front door, giving her a murderous look as they came into the room.

"Have the soldiers gone?" she asked Axel.

"Yes. There should be no more disturbances tonight." He flung himself down into a chair and took the sandwich from the tray put beside him. Seeing she was about to leave, he indicated with a wagging finger that she should sit down. "There's something I want to ask you."

Her fear increased again. Was Axel about to play some trick? She sat on the edge of the chair, hands linked tightly together.

"It was the colder temperature outside that reminded me. I need some advice about furs and I know you worked in the fur trade. Some silver-fox skins came into my possession a few weeks ago. They look good to me, and I thought how much my wife would like a new fur coat for the winter ahead."

"What did you want to know?" Her question was abrupt.

"If there are enough skins for a coat and whether they're of good enough quality to be made up."

"I'm not an expert, but I could tell you that."

"Then I'll bring them along next time I'm here." He stretched his neck to glance across at Tom. "Would you arrange that? I wouldn't want to find Johanna had gone home that weekend."

"Johanna will be here." His gaze switched to meet hers, his murderous look unabated. "We can arrange that, can't we?"

"Easily." She felt almost sorry for him.

The next morning Axel was up by seven o'clock and away from the house half an hour later. By midafternoon the other houseguests had departed. Johanna went into the rose-ceilinged room, where she knew Tom would be awaiting her. He sat with his head in his hands, elbows on his knees. His wrath of the previous night had gone, but anxiety had taken its toll. At the sound of her step he spoke without looking up. "You said something last night about being in love with the fellow in the storeroom."

"I do love him. We want to spend the rest of our lives together."

"What of the risk to me by your taking him in?"

"I thought only of him."

"Are you involved in his work?" He dreaded her answer.

"I know nothing about his life away from me."

"Does Karen know he's hidden there and will she keep silent?"

"I let her go to her sister's last night. She hasn't returned."

"Then she'll have been taken away with the rest."

"I'm hoping she somehow avoided that. Tom, would you let me remain here until the weekend with my friend? He's very weak and in a lot of pain, and shouldn't be moved yet."

"He would have to be gone by Friday."

"He will."

"Could we get him to a bed, do you think? It can't help for him to be lying in his present quarters. The sooner he recovers the better. I want him on his way as much as you do."

She made up a bed for Steffen on the divan in the small sitting room, and when Tom came to move him, Gunnar remained in concealment. Tom departed later in his car without the least idea that a second agent was sheltered in his house.

All that week Gunnar, except when doing his share of nursing duties, kept tactfully away from Johanna and Steffen, who had eyes only for each other. At dawn on Friday, Gunnar and Steffen prepared to leave. They were taking one of the rowing boats. Steffen, who was still unable to walk without support, shared a long farewell kiss with Johanna, while Gunnar ostentatiously busied himself with the boat. Then she stood on the bank and watched the boat with their two silhouettes disappear into the mist that lay like a veil over the water.

FOR A WHILE IN THE OFFICE Johanna was even more cautious than before. Then gradually she saw that Tom did not suspect her of engaging in subversive work, and had accepted her denial of involvement with Steffen's activities.

Tom flatly refused to find out where Karen had been taken. "It's an army matter. Nothing to do with me. It's not healthy to show interest in those incarcerated in punishment camps."

Later, by chance, he did discover Karen's fate. A baby-farm had been started not far from Oslo. Golden-haired, blue-eyed girls were being mated there with young soldiers of Aryan looks in the furtherance of Hitler's aim towards a master race. Tom thought Karen fortunate to have escaped the concentration camps; nevertheless, he chose not to tell Johanna. He did not think she would view the girl's fate in the same light as he did. Meanwhile, he had hired a new housekeeper—a woman of dedicated Nazi principles. She did not like Johanna, and Johanna did not like her.

On the first weekend at Tom's house after the snows came Johanna learned of an Allied bombing raid on the hydro plant in Telemark. The air raid indicated to her that the Allies had become concerned again with the plant's heavy-water production. There was talk about the raid among those present until Axel Werner arrived, bringing the box of furs. Then everyone gathered round to watch Johanna open it.

Taking the skins out in turn, she held each one by the head and smoothed it down to the tail before blowing on it lightly to divide the fur, checking for colour and quality. These pieces would never have made Leif Moen's salon in the days of luxuriance, but they would pass muster now for her purpose.

"You have enough skins," she said. "They're not top quality, but they'll make a nice coat. What about measurements?"

"I'll send for them."

"And the design?"

"I'd like to leave that to you. Could it be made locally?"

"Not as far as I know. I should like to take them to my former employer in Oslo. He's a genius with furs."

"No difficulty," Axel assured her. "I'll ask Major Ryen to let you have a couple of days off to do this for me."

She was quick to seize her chance. "It would take more than one trip."

He gestured nonchalantly. "There's no problem. I'll give you an open travel permit valid for three months."

Someone in the group spoke up. "Is there any chance that this man will have any skins tucked away somewhere? My fiancée would go crazy over a fur coat."

"So would mine," said somebody else.

Johanna sank her chin into the soft fur she had drawn across her neck, her thoughts busy. Her original aim had been to establish three or four legitimate trips to Oslo in order to act as courier for the Resistance, as Steffen had wished. Now she saw that these trips might be stretched out indefinitely. It would depend on whether she could persuade Leif Moen to part with the precious furs he had in his vault.

"I can't make any promises. All I can say is that if it's possible to locate any furs for you when I get to Oslo, I shall do so."

AT JOHANNA'S NEXT MEETING with Gunnar in Astrid's cellar, he gave her some rare praise for the trips to Oslo that she had arranged. "Let me know when you've fixed the first journey," he said, "and I'll set up a contact for you." He thought there was something else she wanted to say. "Yes?"

"Nothing. That's all." There was no point in saying that she hated more and more her enforced association with the enemy. It had come to a point when her flesh crawled at the duplicity of the smiles she had to return. But her contribution to the saving of human life, no matter how indirectly, kept her going. She merely shook her head and said nothing more.

When Johanna arrived in Oslo early in the new year of 1944, war weariness lay like a cloud over the city, dragging at the faces of the people. At the railway station a military car arranged for by Axel was there to take her and the box of furs to the fur shop. When she alighted she saw the windows were bare. Leif was waiting for her, for she had telephoned him in advance. He was wearing his overcoat as a protection against the bitter chill. Owing to the electricity restrictions, the premises were unheated.

"It's good to see you, Johanna." He was thinner and greyer than when she had last seen him. When the driver had put down the box of furs and departed, Leif bolted the door and took her into his office. "How have you been?"

She made an unhappy grimace. "Everyone thinks that I'm a Nazi collaborator."

His face was full of sympathy as he pulled up a chair to sit opposite her. "One day the truth will come out."

"Not before we're free, I hope," she joked uneasily. "I hardly go home any more. For my parents' sake, it's really better if I stay away." She switched the subject. "I've brought you some work. You won't like making a coat for the enemy, but it's enabling me to travel to Oslo in the cause we both support, and I'm hoping you will help me to make further trips in time to come."

"How may I do that?"

"By releasing some of the lovely furs that you have in storage. On the pretext of getting them designed and made, I'll be able to extend my courier work indefinitely."

His expression of regret told her at once that her hopes would come to nothing. "You should have had them if they had still been here. Black marketeers broke into the vault and stole every garment."

"I'm so sorry."

"My chief regret now is that they're not here to be of use to you. Let me see the skins you've brought to be made up. I promise to make as many visits as possible for you out of them."

There proved to be more than he would need for one coat if a simple design was decided upon. He thought he could get two short capes from the remainder.

"Knowing Axel, I should think he would be prepared to sell the extra skins," Johanna said. Together they settled on the style. He promised to deliver a pen sketch of the coat and one of each proposed cape to her hotel before she left Oslo in the morning.

After leaving the fur shop Johanna went to her hotel. It was a well-established one. In peacetime it had been popular with tourists. Now the guests were mostly German officers. She had not been in her room long when there was a knock on the door and a chambermaid entered.

"Is there anything you require, frøken?" the woman asked.

Johanna sensed that this was the contact she was expecting. "I would like to know about buying a flower to wear this evening."

"You would like a bloom that never fades?" The password.

"I would indeed."

"You'll want a red carnation." Symbol of the royal house.

"I think we understand each other." Johanna went to her coat in the wardrobe. From a secret pocket, she took out a paper and handed it over. Her courier assignment for this trip had been fulfilled.

AXEL WERNER WAS NOT a frequent visitor to Tom's office, but he did call in occasionally. "I see you're hard at work," he greeted Johanna. "I'll not disturb you, because it's Major Ryen I've come to see. However,

I received your message about the surplus silver-fox skins and I'm prepared to sell them at market value. Major von Clausen and Ober-leutnant Hendrich are both interested. Perhaps you would discuss the matter of design with them."

"I will." Johanna smiled to herself. It was extremely satisfying that Axel's greed should aid her resistance work.

While he was in with Tom and after she had served them coffee, she returned to the task in hand, which was copying a letter that had reached Tom from Oslo that day. It was from one of the most treacherous ministers in the Quisling government, and gave instructions for a special registration for labour service by all males between the ages of eighteeen and twenty-five. Tom was to be in charge of it in his area. She was puzzled as to why only those of a prime age group should be required to register, and decided to pass on the information to Gunnar without delay. It suddenly occurred to her that perhaps this was what Axel had come to talk over with Tom. He had had a leather folder under his arm, but then he usually did when he came. Many a time she had wished she could get access to it.

The copy finished, Johanna folded it and slipped it into a secret pocket under the waistband of her skirt. That evening she left the copy of the letter under a loose slab of stone in Astrid's cellar floor, after letting Gunnar know by secret message that something important would be waiting for him there.

Gunnar's arrival late at night coincided with Steffen's return to Ålesund from his thoroughly successful recent mission—an act of sabotage that had sent the final shipment of heavy water from the Telemark plant to the bottom of the fjord.

"There's new work for us here," Gunnar said, banishing Steffen's hopes of a day or two alone in Johanna's company. "Before I go into details, I'll see what has been left for me." He took the paper from under the stone and gave a low whistle of satisfaction. "Here's something. It couldn't have come at a better time. Intelligence was notified as to what was in the wind some weeks ago. Now Johanna has given us a detailed report on the local moves that will be taken in a compulsory registration."

"What registration is this?" Steffen asked.

"Officially it's for labour service. In reality it's Quisling's camouflage for conscription. He has offered the Third Reich seventy-five thousand young Norwegians in an allotted age group as cannon fodder for the Russian front.

"We must get to work at once. Warnings must not be delayed. The men concerned must disappear into the mountains and the forests, get into Sweden or across to England. It's the only way. For us there'll be the sabotage of offices where registration is to take place. We must foil this scheme from every angle."

The next half hour was taken up in drafting plans; then Gunnar left to start putting the operations in motion. Alone, Steffen went up into the quiet house that had been his home from boyhood. Silently he climbed the stairs and opened the door to Johanna's room. She had pulled back the blackout curtains before getting into bed, and the white moonlight shone through the canopy of icicles outside the window. He could see her form moulded by the quilt and looked down on her sleeping face. He spoke her name softly, sitting down on the bed to smooth a strand of hair back from her brow. "My love. I'm here."

She opened her eyes lazily and smiled without the least surprise, as though he were a natural extension of her dream. She reached out her arms to him in passionate tenderness.

Chapter Thirteen

On the morning of June 6, Johanna was entering Tom's office when she overheard a conversation between two German officers going down the stairs. "It happened early this morning. An Allied invasion of Normandy."

"Normandy! That's crazy. They'll never gain a foothold there. They'll be back in the sea by now." Their voices faded as they left the building.

Johanna went into her own office and sat down at her desk in a daze. After more than four years of brutal occupation, of fear and persecution, a sense of isolation had been dispelled. At last there was light at the end of the tunnel. Her heart went out to those courageous men fighting on the beaches. She knew she would never forget them, or this moment, or this day. Something splashed down on her hands folded in her lap and she saw it was a tear.

It had been a busy time for Johanna. She had completed several courier missions to Oslo before the excuse for her journeys came to an end. One message she had carried concerned the punishment of those evading registration for service at the Russian front. Thanks to the Resistance, thousands of young men had escaped that fate. They were camping out in isolated mountain hiding places, often in great hardship, surviving on such food as could be got through to them and whatever wildlife could be trapped. The few who had registered, either not heeding the warning or receiving it too late, had been shipped out immediately. Nobody knew how they had fared before the Russian advance.

One piece of good news had arrived in a letter delivered to Ryen Farm during one of Johanna's infrequent visits there. Her brother Rolf had married the English girl he loved, Wendy Townsend. Upon reading the news, Gina had clasped a hand to her brow. "Great world! An English daughter-in-law. I won't be able to talk to her."

Johanna and Edvard exchanged a smiling glance. He patted his wife on the shoulder. "When the day comes, just say *'Velkommen'* to her, as you do to anyone else you welcome to our home. It has the same sound in every language."

It was not long after Normandy that Tom's weekend parties all but faded out. Rations could no longer be subsidized for him from army quarters, and the only drinks available were beer and a raw German wine. His duties had also been extended. Hitler had been caught off guard in Normandy, but he retained his determination not to be similarly surprised in Norway.

The iron fist had never been tighter on the Norwegians than it was in the summer of 1944. The firing squad took its position almost daily in the small courtyard of Akershus Castle in Oslo. Often the condemned patriots, broken physically and mentally by the Gestapo, could not walk unaided or stand for their last moments.

When his time came Erik Ryen did manage to shuffle ahead of his guards, although his whole body was a mass of pain. He no longer thought about it. Before coming out into the sun for the last time he had Karen to dwell on, childhood memories of the farm and his parents, the good times he had had in his life and throughout his years at sea. In his mind he was at peace. He had given nothing away. In spite of all that they had done to him, he had told them nothing of value.

He came to a standstill. The sounds of the harbour reached him in the clear early-morning air. His last sight was of a seagull wheeling against the Oslo sky.

DAILY THE GERMANS received news of the Allied advance on the Continent and that of the Russians to the east. But those who visited Tom's office were as arrogant and confident as ever about their own position in Norway. They had made the country into a stronghold fit to withstand any onslaught. Among themselves, they were highly critical of German forces that had fallen back before the Allies. "It won't happen here," was their confident opinion, voiced many times over.

Johanna had not seen Steffen since the night she had awakened to find him in her room. All Gunnar would say was that the Englishman had important work in hand. She could guess what it was. A new and intensive wave of sabotage actions had hit the occupation forces. Ships in Oslo harbour had been blown up, as had fuel and ammunition dumps, railways and bridges and selected factories.

Late in July came the news that a group of German generals had attempted to assassinate Hitler. Axel Werner took an almost fiendish pleasure in this foiled attempt on the life of the Führer, taking it as proof of the unreliability of the army in comparison with the unquestioned loyalty of his own SS security force. "If I had been there, I'd have hanged the lot on the spot," he declared one Friday morning when he strutted through Johanna's office, already in conversation with Tom, whom he had met on the stairs.

Judging the moment to be right to make coffee, Johanna put the cups on a tray and, when it was ready, took it into Tom's office. Axel had his leather folder open on the desk and was referring to a paper on top. They stopped talking when she entered. Johanna left the door ajar when she returned to her own office, but their remarks held no substance and she gave up straining her ears from her desk.

Her curiosity persisted. She decided to fetch the tray. The door, still as she had left it, pushed open silently. Axel and Tom were by the window, looking out at some military activity in the street below. On the desk was Axel's folder, half zipped up again, but with the top paper projecting from it. Her action was almost a reflex. She simply took a corner of the paper and whipped it out, at the same time stepping back out of the office. Outside the door she held her breath, expecting a shout. They had not noticed anything. She snatched a glance at the paper. It looked interesting. She slipped it behind a picture on the wall.

Now she returned again to the doorway of Tom's office, as if she had just entered. "May I remove the tray?"

They both turned. Tom answered her. "Yes, of course."

Johanna collected everything and carried it out. Axel came after her. "I'm going to Major Ryen's this weekend. Shall you be there this time?"

"Yes. I'm driving out with him this evening after work." It was not something she was looking forward to, but Tom had asked her particularly. A Quisling Nazi party leader was to be a weekend guest, and Tom wanted the man to have the best of service and attention.

"Good." Axel smiled and turned back into Tom's office. She was still taut with suspense. As he emerged with the folder under his arm he saluted her cheerily. The paper had not been missed. With luck he would not discover where it had been "mislaid".

Johanna had the document folded into her secret pocket when she went from the building at the end of the working day. Unable to wait for Gunnar, she left the paper under the cellar stone and was ready at the gate when Tom arrived to pick her up.

The weekend was as dreary as Johanna had expected it to be. The Quisling party leader was pompous and objectionable, and it made her despair to see how obsequious Tom was to him. It was Sunday evening when the housekeeper informed Johanna that Frøken Larsen wished to speak to her on the telephone. Johanna was filled with misgivings. Astrid never telephoned her at Tom's house. She took the receiver. "Hello, Astrid."

"You must ask for tomorrow off from work. I'm not well."

"What's the matter? Have you had the doctor?"

"Yes. It's a chill. He's coming again tomorrow. I must stay in bed."

Johanna replaced the receiver and went back to Tom and his guests. She told him about the call. Tom was annoyed. Monday was always busy, but reluctantly he granted her the time off.

When he dropped her at the gate that night, she ran up the path and into the house. She was surprised to see Astrid looking over the banister and not seeming in the least ill.

"There's nothing wrong with me," she announced at once. "Steffen was here. He says you must meet him in the cellar at four o'clock tomorrow morning. Wear your office clothes and sensible shoes in case you have to run. Don't ask me what it's about, because I don't know."

Johanna set her alarm clock but woke before it rang, excitement priming her. At five minutes before four she went down to the cellar. Steffen was waiting for her. They wrapped their arms about each other, relishing the pleasure of being together.

"Hey," he said, drawing back, "how are you?"

"Better for seeing you. Why am I here at this unearthly hour?"

He frowned. "In brief, that paper you took for us revealed the latest Quisling move to get Norwegians into service at the Russian front. There's no time to tell you everything now. Gunnar is waiting for us with a farm truck." His hand took hers. "I have to ask you if you're willing to play a risky part in today's events."

"You don't have to. Let's go."

He took her out by the long, winding tunnel entrance of the cellar. When they emerged into the rosy daylight, they were deep in the forest. He led her to a lane where the farm truck was waiting, Gunnar at the wheel. Steffen helped her into the back, where she was concealed behind boxes of vegetables. He could talk to her by holding back the dividing canvas behind the driver's seat as they drove along.

"As you know, everyone in the country has to register again for new ration cards. That German document told us that only those who apply personally will receive a card, which automatically cuts out those in hiding. Without the use of their ration cards it will be impossible to get enough food to them. The Germans are hoping to force them out of hiding by starvation. We're out today to help ourselves to ration cards being delivered from the printers. No resister will starve after this venture, I promise you."

She raised her eyebrows. "Where do I come in?"

"During the morning the boxes of cards we're after will be dropped off at a small depot. You'll be in the office to sign for them. We shall have removed the girl who is normally there, and she'll be tied up somewhere until we're safely away. The same applies to the caretaker, who would normally help unload the boxes. You'll see Gunnar and me taking over that task. Then Gunnar will leave with the goods reloaded in this truck, and you and I will depart in a van that will be waiting for us."

"What if other people come to the office in the meantime?"

"You'll bluff your way through somehow. We'll have plenty of time for you to get a grasp of what goes on there." He lowered his voice. "We're approaching the ferry now. Sorry, but you have to make the fjord crossing out of sight."

The canvas screen dropped back into place. She heard the German guard ask for papers, and there was a noisy clatter as the truck went up the ramp onto the ferry. The crossing took twenty-five minutes. Then they went rattling off the ferry onto a country road.

Their destination was a depot in a woodland area on the outskirts of a small town. Gunnar drew up in line with several farm trucks, a dairy next to the depot providing perfect cover for the vehicle. The van in which Johanna and Steffen would leave was parked nearby. They alighted. Due to the early hour there were few people about. They reached the rear of the depot, a sturdy wooden structure in need of a coat of paint, and Steffen opened the door with a key from a ring of master keys.

Johanna waited in silence as Steffen and Gunnar surprised the caretaker. There was a scuffling sound before he was bound and gagged and put behind a locked door. Then Steffen took her through to the office at the front of the building, to look around. It was not long before she felt she could have taken over the simple work there in full capacity. Steffen locked up the office again when it was time for her to go into hiding, and she waited in the caretaker's vacated quarters while the two men kept watch.

The office girl arrived on time at eight thirty. She sang to herself as she hung up her jacket and tidied herself before a mirror. Her eyes went wide as Gunnar clapped a hand over her mouth and carried her out of the office. Johanna went to take the girl's place behind the counter desk. Then there was nothing to do except wait.

The expected truck arrived at midmorning. Knowing she would have to sign the receipt forms, Johanna left the office to go through the building to the unloading area. An armed soldier was leaning against the doorjamb, watching idly as Gunnar trundled the first batch of ration cards through on a trolley. Outside, the driver, a thickset fellow with a ruddy face, was in the back of the truck swinging the packages down to

Steffen, who was stacking a second trolley. As the last package changed hands the driver leaped down from the truck and refastened the back. Then he came strolling into the building, mopping his sweaty brow with a dark blue handkerchief, in time to see Johanna padlock the door where the packages had been placed.

"Say! Where's Christina? And who are you?"

"She's having some time off," Johanna said. She experienced a qualm. Neither Steffen nor Gunnar had expected the driver to know the office girl. Looking bored, Johanna took the clipboard from him with the papers she had to sign, using a signature she had invented for herself at the bottom of each sheet. "There you are," she said, handing the clipboard back to him. "I'll tell Christina you asked about her."

The man hesitated. "Yes, do that. Bjorn is the name. She'll know me all right." Then he went back to clamber up into the truck with the soldier. As he drove away he glanced in his side mirror. "That was odd," he remarked, drawing out onto the main road for the return journey north.

"What was?"

"Christina not being in the office. I spoke to her on the phone last week. She said nothing about having today off."

"Your girlfriend, is she?"

"No. She's my sister-in-law." There was a lapse of time while he watched the road ahead, the heat shimmering up from the dusty surface. Then he gave the wheel a thump with his fist. "I tell you there was something fishy going on at the depot. Those fellows who unloaded were strangers to me. And why wasn't the caretaker giving a hand? I've been to that place three times this year and the caretaker was always there."

The soldier had begun to listen sharply. "What could be wrong, do you think?"

"I don't know, but I'm going to turn back and find out." He began to strain his neck, looking for a place to turn.

The soldier sat forward. "Keep going. There's an army pillbox a little way ahead. I'll make a report there."

At the depot, Johanna helped load the cards into the farm truck, which had been brought to the door, the crates of vegetables now removed. It was swift and desperate work, for all three had been left with the impression that the driver was far from satisfied with the explanation for the office girl's absence. Johanna's back was feeling the strain of the heavy lifting, every muscle aching.

"That's it!" Steffen proclaimed. "We've enough ration cards now, so in with the vegetable crates to hide this load."

When that was done, Gunnar took the wheel of the farm truck again and turned onto the road. Then Steffen and Johanna ran for the van, she taking the passenger seat. As he backed out he saw an army truck approaching in the distance. Gunnar's truck had met and passed it, which was a good sign. Steffen turned the van in the opposite direction to speed back conspicuously through the town and take the road beyond that would lead him to the ferry. A last look as he turned the corner showed him the army truck drawing up outside the depot.

"It looks as if they're on to us," he said. "At least Gunnar has slipped through, thank God. That's what matters. That and your safety. I'm going to make sure of that now."

He drove on. The gravel road was rough and pitted, and Johanna, bouncing on the old leather seat, held on tightly. She had no illusions about the danger they were in. When the Germans discovered two people tied up and the packages missing, it would not take them long to learn that a speeding van had been seen in the vicinity. She and Steffen had become far more of a quarry than Gunnar ambling along at a farmer's pace.

The road took them to the brow of a hill, with the wide fjord lying below. A ferry was drawing close in to shore. "We must catch that ferry before it leaves again!" Steffen exclaimed. He gave her instructions as the van charged down the winding road. "I'll slow down before we get to the jetty. Then you'll get out and run to board it. You can't risk remaining in the van with me. I'll time the driving to get on the ferry just behind you, but you must not speak to me or acknowledge me in any way. Once you're on the other side of the fjord, catch the bus into town and go back to Astrid."

"Why don't you dump the van and run with me?"

"I don't want to leave it on this side of the fjord. The longer I can make the Germans think I have the packages in the back of this van, the better chance Gunnar has of getting away." Below them, military and civilian vehicles had begun to roll off the ferry. Steffen drew into a side track and put an arm around her, gathering her to him. "It's time for you to go now."

She clung to him, returning his kiss with her whole being. Then he leaned across to open the van door for her and she jumped out. As she ran towards the road she saw an open staff car passing at full speed, Axel and another SS officer sitting in the back. She could not be sure whether Axel had glimpsed her. At least the car had been driving away from the ferry. She began to race down the last slope to the fjord. Her hair streamed out, her legs flew. The ferry was on the point of departure. She waved frantically in a plea to wait and saw the ferry hand let the half-lifted ramp fall back for her. A guard stepped forward. "Papers! Papers!"

She had her identify card ready and he OK'd it at a glance. Leaping on board, she swung round as Steffen began to drive at full speed for the ferry, ignoring the guard who was shouting at him. It was only then that she saw that Axel's car, somehow alerted, had turned round and was coming after him. The junior officer beside the driver was standing, one hand gripping the top of the windscreen, the other hand raised in an imperious command to delay the ferry. Johanna stood numbed by a sense of disaster as the ferry hand obediently kept the ramp in position after Steffen had shot on board and braked to a halt. The German car was close enough now for her to see Axel's iron face clamp into full recognition as he stared directly at her.

The front wheels of the staff car rolled onto the ramp. Johanna stared in disbelief, seeing that although the ramp had been kept in position, the ferry hand had not signalled the skipper at the wheel. The ferry was moving. As she watched, the whole sequence was seemingly almost in slow motion, and yet it took place in a matter of seconds. The back of the large car began to dip. She saw Axel's expression change. Then, like a child's toy, the car was completely upended as the gap between the jetty and the ferry widened swiftly. Amid the Germans' terrified shouts the whole vehicle plunged down under the swirling water. Johanna covered her eyes with her hands.

When she looked again, the ferry was several metres out into the fjord on its unhalted way. People on shore had rushed to the scene. The junior officer was being hauled out of the water, but of Axel and the two other occupants there was no sign. Johanna could guess at the depth of the water there. Trapped under the upended car against the rocks, they would have had no chance. Slowly she turned her head and looked towards the ferry hand. Their eyes met, and deliberately he looked away from her towards Steffen. He had saved them. He had seen the pursuit and he had saved them.

Shakily she went to the saloon and sat down on one of the seats. Nobody else was there. Steffen seized the opportunity to come in search of her. He slid onto the neighbouring seat and put an arm round her. "Listen to me," he said urgently. "All hell will be let loose after this. I expect a full military reception for me on the other side. But you should be safe. There's no reason for anyone to suspect you were with me."

"True. That was Axel Werner in the car. But he disappeared just after he recognized me."

"When the ferry arrives, as I said before, simply walk off with the other passengers and take the bus into town."

"But what will you do?"

He gave her a smile. "I'm going to swim for it. Now. When everybody's attention is elsewhere."

He would not let her watch him go, for it would have involved her in an unnecessary risk. On deck, he slipped off his shoes, stuck them into his belt, clambered up onto the rail and dived into the sun-shot water. He struck out strongly, his aim being to put as great a distance as possible between himself and the ferry landing.

When Johanna came out on deck again, she glanced around at the water and could not see him. On the approaching shore army vehicles formed a blockade, and there were soldiers with rifles on the quay. The moment the ramp was lowered they rushed on board to surround the van and search the ferry. Passengers and crew were herded into the saloon for questioning.

When it became obvious that the driver of the van was not among them, the soldiers made a second search. A child's remark that he had seen a man go for a swim solved the mystery for the officer in charge. In exasperation he permitted the passengers to leave.

Johanna took her place in the bus, her thoughts with Steffen. He had promised to contact her and let her know he was safe. She would go home to Astrid's house and hope for news that evening.

Steffen had chosen to come ashore where boulders from an ancient avalanche made for easy access. When he threw himself down, gasping for breath, on the soft grass and fir cones beneath the trees, red squirrels bounded away at his intrusion.

He was almost rested when there came a crackling of twigs underfoot that made him freeze through to the marrow of his spine. Scrambling up, he stood poised for flight. On the sun-patched slope between the trees were a dozen soldiers with rifles pointing directly at him. He took a step backwards in the direction of the water.

"*Achtung!* Hands up!"

Every rifle had slipped its safety catch with an ominous click. There was no chance. Inwardly a surge of wrath overcame fear. He saw everything sliding away from him: his liberty to help his country, his future with the woman he loved. Her name was a silent shout, a last link with hope and sanity. Johanna!

NO WORD CAME that evening. When Johanna went to work next morning, she was surprised as time went by and Tom did not appear. She went down to the reception area and asked the soldier on duty if Major Ryen had left any message for her.

"No, fräulein. I have heard he is under arrest."

"On what charge?" she demanded incredulously.

"SS Obersturmbannführer Werner discovered an important paper was missing from his files yesterday morning. The folder had been in a safe, where he had placed it after leaving Major Ryen's office. Ryen was the only one who could have taken it. Did you hear that Werner died in an accident later in the day? A sad business."

To be accused by the Nazis was always tantamount to being found guilty. There was nothing Johanna could do for Tom.

Two nights later Gunnar came to the cellar. It was after midnight. Sliding back the panel, he entered the house. A fan of light shone from the kitchen, and he saw Johanna in a striped robe standing at the kitchen table. He spoke her name and she gave a start. Then, seeing him, a tremor of fear went through her. "How did it go?"

"The sortie was a complete success. The ration cards are already in the right hands. But that's not why I'm here. The Gestapo have Steffen."

She sank down onto a chair, as if the power to stand had deserted her. Gunnar went to stand beside her. She was shuddering violently.

"Don't," he muttered, putting his hand momentarily on her shoulder. "Steffen is a fighter. They won't break his spirit."

After a brief silence she whispered, "Thank you for coming to tell me."

"I don't know when I'll see you again. Our rules require that we go to ground when a close contact is captured. As for you, don't go to the cellar any more. As a precaution, I've made the place appear long abandoned."

She nodded that she understood. He gripped her shoulder again in sympathy and encouragement before leaving her. How long she sat there, she did not know. When she finally went upstairs, she slept in exhaustion and awoke in the morning to find the nightmare still with her. Astrid, courageous as always, strengthened her by example.

Johanna went to work as usual. The rule of the Resistance was to carry on a normal routine. It was often the best protection. At midmorning two SS security guards marched into her office.

"SS Oberführer Richter wants to see you at headquarters. If you have a coat here, bring it."

It was Axel's successor who had summoned her, a man new to the district, whom she had yet to meet. The instruction to take a coat was not a good sign. It was always the first announcement that one's fate was sealed. She went with the guards downstairs and outside to a waiting vehicle.

At the headquarters, where she had first attended a Wehrmacht party with Tom, she was taken to Richter's office. He was a sharp-faced man with closely cropped grey hair and gold-rimmed spectacles. He did not rise when she entered, merely indicating that she should take the chair set before his desk.

"*Guten Morgen*, Fräulein Ryen. I'm informed that your German is fluent, so I shall address you in my own language. You will answer my questions truthfully and without deviousness. You were well acquainted with the late Axel Werner, I believe."

"We knew each other as children."

"Were you lovers?"

The suggestion was ludicrous. "No!" burst from her.

"Major Tom Ryen has suggested to me that you were."

She stared incredulously. "You must have misunderstood him. He knows there was never anything between Werner and me."

Richter cleared his throat. "You and Werner were often together at Ryen's weekend parties. Do you remember the night a neighbouring village was the scene of a hunt for two resistance men?"

"I do." She was deeply alarmed at the way the interview was going. Tom's treachery was beginning to get through to her.

"One of the wanted men was killed attempting to escape. The second was wounded but never found. We now know that he came to Major Ryen's house. You let him in and nursed him until he was fit to leave."

She bluffed fiercely. "No fugitive in his right mind would have come to a house full of Wehrmacht officers."

"Let us have no more pretence, fräulein. You took that man in. Major Ryen discovered you and reported the facts to Werner, whose infatuation with you stopped him from making an arrest." His accusing finger shot out at her across the desk. "You were Werner's downfall! He threatened Major Ryen with imprisonment on a trumped-up charge if he gave you away. His last act was to make Major Ryen a scapegoat for his own carelessness in mislaying an important document." He thrust his face towards her, his spectacles glinting. "Now, I'll have from you the name of the wounded man you took into the house that night!"

The time had come for the stock answer that she had been instructed to use if she ever found herself in such a situation. "I know nothing."

She was to repeat those words as long as she had the strength to say them. Fainting gave her some respite from the pain imposed on her. "I know nothing" became her litany. They extracted nothing from her.

Chapter Fourteen

In Grini concentration camp, thirty-five miles north of Oslo, a grapevine kept the several thousand prisoners informed of outside events. Johanna had been in the camp for over seven months by April 1945, when she heard of the death of President Roosevelt. It saddened her. He had been a good friend to Norway. When the crown princess and the royal children had taken refuge in Sweden at the start of the occupation, Roosevelt had sent a warship to transport them to the safety of American soil. Later he had held up Norway as an example to the world of what human courage could do in the face of adversity. She wished he could have lived to see the end of the war.

Although almost every other occupied country had been liberated in the Allied advance towards Berlin, Norway was still as isolated as ever within the Nazi grip. It was the boast of the Germans in Norway that they were equipped to fight on indefinitely, no matter how many other annexed territories were lost.

These days Johanna was always hungry. Her stomach had curved inwards between her hipbones. The food was abysmal, often the smell of it so revolting that in spite of hunger she would exchange her small bowl of victuals for a needle and a length of thread. Sewing helped to pass the time. Any small scrap of material could be utilized. Occasionally she bartered a finished article for a stub of pencil or a sheet of paper on which to write her continuous love letter to Steffen. Through it she felt in constant touch with him, even though she did not know where he was— mail was not allowed to be sent or received. She simply knew in her heart that he was alive, somewhere, and she set down her loving thoughts to him.

Every morning Johanna and the other women in her work group took mops, scrubbing brushes and buckets to carry out their allotted chores. And whenever it was possible in the course of her days, Johanna stood by the high encompassing barbed-wire fence to gaze out at the wooded countryside. Beyond that lay Oslo, where life was normal despite the occupation, normal in comparison with the wretched existence of those imprisoned within Grini's confines.

The women were divided off from the men and, although contact was strictly forbidden, at times they could see them through the fencing, black-jacketed, striped-trousered figures. Some had special marks on their jackets so that they could be picked out by the guards for harsher treatment. The saddest task for Johanna was when she was assigned to clean out the hut in which those condemned to death spent their last hours. The walls were covered with last messages, sometimes in pencil, more often scratched with the point of a sharp rock or the edge of a tin food bowl. *Please tell my wife . . . Let my parents know . . . My loving thoughts are with . . . Last greetings to . . .*

From the first she decided to do what she could to help fulfil those last requests. Each time she went there she noted messages and names; there were always means by which they could be smuggled out of the camp. One such route was concealment in the corner of a fish crate during the delivery of fish to the kitchens.

By the time Johanna heard of President Roosevelt's death, everything in the camp had begun to change. The guards were restless, some even making overtures of friendship to the inmates. On the first of May word flew round the camp that Hitler was dead. When the news was confirmed, several guards committed suicide. But the camp commandant was a cruel and brutal man; even now his vicious hold did not lessen. If anything, punishments became more frequent. Unspoken dread was in everyone as to how he would deal with them when total German defeat was secured by the Allies.

Johanna was sent again to the condemned cell, where the previous night a man had been held before being taken at dawn to his place of execution. Upon entering, she set down her mop and bucket to look for his signature. Each wall was like a familiar map to her and she could usually spot a new message straightaway. It was the same with this one, except that it sent waves of shock washing over her, his name going straight to her heart. She went stumbling towards it, with hands outstretched, reading what was there. *To Johanna of Ryendal, my love into eternity. Steffen Larsen. May 5, 1945.*

She uttered a sharp cry of grief and threw herself against the wall, pressing her cheek against the writing while terrible sobs tore out of her body in utter desolation. He had been in Grini, and she had not known. He had been in this hut and breathed this air and walked this floor, and she had not known. Everything he must have suffered over the past months had not saved him. In the end the Nazis had murdered him.

Shock made it impossible for Johanna to sleep that night. She lay awake, staring upwards in the darkness, and she went round in a daze the next day, to face another terrible night. She collapsed on the morning of May 7 while labouring at a laundry tub. Other women carried her to her bunk, where she finally slept.

Not yet recovered from her exhaustion, she was the last to wake during the night when there was a disturbance in the camp. She sat up in her bunk to see all the women huddled together in terror. As the guards unlocked the door of the hut and ordered everyone outside, she shared the same thought with the rest of the women: when the last day came, the Germans would shoot their prisoners down.

"Out! All of you! Move!" The guards were in a savage mood.

Some of the women began to cry. Johanna put her arm round one who had an injured leg and helped her down the steps. All the camp lights were on as the women gathered together in the compound. Searchlights added to the blaze. They drew nearer to one another for support when, from the direction of the barracks, there was the dreaded sound of military footsteps approaching at a sharp pace.

"They're coming!" one woman exclaimed tremulously. Johanna closed her eyes briefly to summon up courage.

A man in a uniform they did not immediately recognize came striding into the compound, followed by several others. Quickly he mounted some steps in front of a building and turned to address them. "Ladies! We are the Swedish Red Cross and we have come to take care of you. The

504

war is over. Germany has surrendered to the Allies. You are free!"

There was a long silence, and then a spontaneous outburst of joy. The women began to dance and laugh and hug each other, every one of them crying with happiness. Johanna stood motionless, thinking of Steffen. If only he could have been allowed another forty-eight hours. He would have been rejoicing in the men's compound, where a great shout had gone up that must have been heard far across the neighbouring hills.

Returning to their huts, the women dressed and began gathering together their few possessions. The Red Cross had bus transportation to the Oslo region waiting at the gates. Johanna collected her small treasures: a rag doll she had sewn, a patchwork scarf and a plaited belt. Last of all she took her letter to Steffen.

"Are you ready?" A Red Cross woman was at her side. "Good. Where is your home?"

"On the west coast, but I'd like to be taken to a house in Grefsen. That was my second home for a long time."

Johanna joined the rest of the women. Once outside the open gates she stopped to breathe free air deep into her lungs. In the distance was the sweet sound of a church bell chiming in freedom. It was a deeply moving moment.

In Oslo, the Norwegian flag had appeared everywhere, as if there had been a sudden blossoming of red, white and blue in the dawn light. All government buildings and former military headquarters were being guarded by members of the Resistance in white armbands. Their aim was to prevent vengeance against the enemy. Johanna guessed the situation was still extremely delicate. The Germans in Norway, unlike their comrades elsewhere, had yet to lay down their weapons. Johanna knew she had her own personal battle waiting for her in the Alsteens' house. It had been confiscated as Jewish property, and a high-ranking Wehrmacht officer had been living there.

She was dropped at the gate. As the bus drove away she went up the path, memories flooding in on her. As soon as she entered, she realized that the Nazi occupant had departed recently, in haste. In the kitchen the coffeepot was still warm.

After getting her bearings, she lifted the telephone receiver in the hall and rang home. Her father, up for the milking, answered.

"It's Johanna. I'm free," she said huskily. It was the most emotional call she had ever made, speaking to her father and mother in turn, all three of them overwhelmed. Afterwards came the saddest call. She rang Astrid, and they spoke quietly together for several minutes. Astrid was brave and did not give way. "Come and see me as soon as you can, my dear."

"I will."

Filled with sorrow, Johanna went upstairs to run a hot bath. The Nazi officer had left soap and shampoo. It was therapeutic to immerse herself in the steaming water after months of only occasional cold showers. Now she washed her hair into a luxurious lather, and when she stepped out of the bath, there were soft towels to wrap round her. Nothing seemed quite real.

Still in a towel, she wondered if there was anything in the house she could wear until she had laundered her camp clothes. Suddenly she remembered leaving a box of clothes in the cellar. Was it possible they were still where she had hidden them?

In her bare feet she hurried down. At first glance she thought there was no hope. All of Anna's lovely things were gone. The old cupboard was still bolted to the wall, the doors removed, probably for firewood. Kneeling down, she stretched her hand underneath, felt the corner of the box and pulled it forward. When she lifted the lid, it was like discovering a treasure trove. On top of some evening clothes were some items of satin lingerie, a couple of dresses, skirts, jackets and a pair of evening sandals.

While dressing in her old room, she thought she heard a vehicle draw up in the lane and depart again, but paid no attention. She had just finished fastening her dress when she heard the front door open. Had the Alsteens returned home already? Uncertainly she went out onto the landing.

A tall man stood in the hall, a raincoat over black prison garb, a package under his arm. At the sound of her approach he looked up, his face lighting in welcome and joy. He was far too thin and pale, his cheeks hollow, his bones sharp. She could only gasp his name rapturously. "Steffen!"

"Jo, darling!"

She flew down to meet him as he flung aside the package to hold out his arms to her. They melded together in a passionate embrace, unable to speak or even to think beyond the mind-dazzling moment of reunion.

"Tell me I'm not dreaming," she implored frantically, her fingertips running over his face as he still held her in his arms.

"As you once said to me, this is no dream. We're together, Jo. No more partings."

Her voice was choked. "I saw your last message to me in Grini. We must ring Astrid. She thinks—"

"I've already done that. It's how I knew you were here. She had just spoken to you when I called."

"How did you escape being shot?"

"Hundreds of special prisoners, against whom the Nazis had a particular grudge, were hurriedly transferred to Mysen, a camp near the

506

Swedish border that had been laid with explosives. At the moment of liberation we were to be blown up in our huts. Fortunately, the commandant got cold feet at the last minute. Local resistance fighters freed us, issued each of us a package of new clothes and brought us to Oslo by bus. My only thought was to find you."

She was filled with wonderment that so much happiness could come at once. After Steffen had bathed, put on his new clothes and burned his prison uniform, they went to join the celebrations in the city. Oslo was alive with flags carried by the crowds and unfurling on flagpoles. A placard in a shop window summed up the atmosphere of the day: CLOSED BECAUSE OF JOY!

Policemen who had refused to collaborate, or had worked secretly within the Quisling ranks as resistance contacts, had donned their dark blue uniforms again and were hailed enthusiastically as they directed traffic and controlled the rejoicing crowds with grins and laughter. Bands played, people sang and danced, and young children were wide-eyed at the festivities, having no memory of anything but fear on the streets. The celebrations went on all through the night, but Steffen and Johanna returned home to the peace and comfort of the house.

Behind the festivities in the city and elsewhere, much was going on. The Gestapo had fled from their headquarters in Victoria Terrasse. Quisling had been arrested. Reichskommissar Terboven had committed suicide. The prisons were filling up with collaborators, black-market racketeers, former secret police and Nazi informers. Throughout the country the traitors known as quislings had had their windows smashed and their possessions taken out of their houses and burned. Yet few, if any, suffered personal attacks. In the hour of liberation the people were remarkably tolerant. It was a national characteristic to forgive but never to forget. Each quisling was destined to live with the stigma of traitor to the end of his or her days.

The telephone awoke Johanna in the morning. It was her mother, calling to say a cable from Rolf in England had arrived.

"It says, 'Safe and well. Coming home soon. Wendy and your new grandson will follow shortly. Fond greetings to all, Rolf.' "

"That's wonderful news! There's nothing from Erik yet?"

"Nothing."

Johanna and Steffen decided to have a week on their own together before going home. They needed the time to adjust to life away from camp routine. They saw the exuberant return of Crown Prince Olav, and watched British-trained Free Norwegian troops march with other Allied soldiers down Karl Johans Gate. Garlanded with flowers, the men were cheered until they were deafened by the joyous noise. Overhead, Norwegian flight squadrons came home. Rolf was among them, flying his

Spitfire into Gardermoen Airport near Oslo. When he jumped from it onto Norwegian soil, he felt himself take root again.

On her last day in Grefsen Johanna was sitting in the flower garden when a taxi pulled up. She hurried over to see who had come. It was Anna Alsteen herself. When she saw Johanna, she exclaimed with delighted surprise, and they rushed to hug each other joyfully.

"Let me look at you." Anna held her back to study her face. "You're too thin. I must cook you some good meals." Then she saw the question in Johanna's eyes and smiled sadly. "My dear Viktor died over four years ago, on the way into Sweden. He never knew that we reached safety."

"I'm so sorry. That dear man."

Anna looked nostalgically towards the house, her voice softening. "It's good to be home again. I've always loved this house. All this time I've longed to be back here."

"There's somebody indoors you'll be glad to see. He's putting new doors on a cupboard in the cellar."

"Is it Steffen?"

"That's right. The man I'm going to marry."

Anna's face bloomed anew at this announcement and she embraced Johanna again. "That's marvellous! I always wanted you to meet each other."

Johanna laughed. "Let's go inside. I'll tell you all about it."

IN THE MORNING Johanna and Steffen departed for the west coast. Rolf was home when they arrived. Johanna was met with smiles again. Neighbours came running to their gates to wave to her and, when the chance presented itself, apologized for not having guessed she had been engaged in secret work. The pleasure of being home was shadowed by sorrow when Rolf broke the news of Erik's death. When Johanna was able to accept what had happened, she was thankful that her parents would have a grandchild to bring them some comfort in the years ahead. Nobody would ever take Erik's place, but the newest member of the family, when Wendy arrived with him, would give them a new and healing interest.

At Astrid's home, Johanna and Steffen found his aunt in full possession of her whole house again. "I did what I always said I would do when liberation came," she told them. "After scrubbing the place from cellar to attic, I invited the neighbours in to drink up the wine in the cellars. We had a wonderful liberation party!"

They stayed several days with her. During that time they heard that Tom Ryen had been arrested and could expect a long prison sentence when brought to trial. And Johanna received a courageous letter from Karen, who had phoned Gina and learned of Erik's death. At the baby-farm Karen had had a son, who had been taken from her and sent to Germany; there was no way of tracing him. Then she had given birth to a daughter before the liberation. She intended to keep this baby and bring her up on her own. Her brother-in-law and her sister had come through safely. They wanted her to live with them, but she needed to be independent. Did Johanna know of any accommodation?

"I do!" Johanna exclaimed aloud. She knew that Anna Alsteen dreaded the loneliness of her house without Viktor. It would mean everything to Anna if she had a baby to love and care for. And Karen could find herself a job in Oslo and have no worries about the baby during the day. Knowing both women—Anna with her generous heart and Karen with her sweet nature—Johanna foresaw this as a most satisfactory arrangement for them.

Johanna and Steffen were married in the local church by the fjord. In the congregation Wendy, Johanna's sister-in-law, newly arrived from England, saw the national costumes, worn on special occasions, for the first time. She was as intrigued by the embroidery and gold ornaments as she was by the richly decorated interior of the ancient church, painted by valley craftsmen more than two hundred years ago. Johanna wore a white gown previously worn by Astrid's grandmother—a high-necked, long-sleeved garment of lace and silk that had simple lines and suited her slender figure. When the bride and groom emerged into the sunshine there was no chiming of the church bell, for it had been rung with such enthusiasm on liberation day that it had cracked.

The wedding feast was set out on long tables in the shade of the trees by the farmhouse. Throughout the meal there were songs dedicated to the bridal couple, and there were also plenty of speeches. Gunnar, who was best man, spoke of knowing the bride and groom during the Resistance, but he did not refer to any specific venture. That had become the unspoken, accepted rule among them all, thus drawing a veil over individual achievements.

Johanna and Steffen returned to Oslo to see the king come home. It was June 7, exactly five years to the day since he had sailed into exile. The city burst into rejoicing on a scale that surpassed even that of liberation day. In an open car the king, in naval uniform, rode up banner-hung Karl Johans Gate to the palace. On the balcony he took the salute as those of the Resistance marched past him by the thousand, wearing the weatherproof jackets and rucksacks that had been their everyday gear throughout five years of hiding in the mountains and of secret work. Steffen and Johanna were among their number. It was the greatest procession the city had ever seen and a day to remember all one's life. The exhilarating cheering for freedom was to echo down the years in hearts throughout the land.

Epilogue

In 1984 Johanna was in London shortly before Christmas. Steffen, who had substantial interests in a Norwegian oil company, had had a business meeting with his British counterpart. She had accompanied him from their home in Oslo, seizing the opportunity to do her seasonal shopping in her favourite London stores. Both their sons were married, with three children each, and she had a long list. At the end of a busy day she was on her way back to the hotel in a taxi when she noticed they were passing Trafalgar Square. Suddenly she leaned forward and tapped urgently on the glass, calling to the driver, "Stop here, please."

"Your hotel isn't around here."

"I know. I've changed my mind for the moment."

She got out and paid, then turned to look across at the Norwegian Christmas tree by the fountains in the lee of Nelson's column. Her gaze travelled slowly up its great height of forty feet to the crowning star. Its thick branches sparkled with white lights and swayed in the chill breeze, an aura of brilliance hanging about it. The glow fell full on her upturned face, whose beauty had defied the passage of time.

Every year a Norwegian tree was sent to London at Christmastime, as it had been during the war to remind an exiled king of his homeland and of his people who awaited him. It came nowadays as a link between the friendship of the past and the friendship of the future. Memories stirred within her as a boys' choir filed into place by the tree. There was some shifting of feet, a fluttering of song sheets, and then the choirmaster raised his arms. They opened with "Silent Night". Johanna lost track of time as she listened to their clear, high voices.

Somewhere a clock struck, reminding her that Steffen would be back at the hotel and looking for her. They were still like lovers. There had never been anyone else for either of them. Leaving the Christmas tree, she hailed another taxi and it drew up at the kerb. She paused for a moment before getting into it, looking back over her shoulder. The tree was a beautiful sight, the lights as white as the snows of Norway.

ROSALIND LAKER

During World War II Rosalind Laker was an art student in West Sussex, painting by day and on fire watch through night air raids. It was then that she met her husband, Inge, who—like Rolf in *This Shining Land*—had escaped from occupied Norway to join the Royal Norwegian Air Force. "Inge escaped twice," Miss Laker says. "The first time he and his friends made the harrowing thirty-six hour crossing to the Shetland Islands, a strong wind blew their small fishing boat back across the North Sea. They made it on the second try." Many of the incidents in *This Shining Land* are based on the true experiences of Inge and his family. For instance, like Mrs. Ryen, Inge's mother instinctively knew he was leaving for England and her parting words were, "Don't let the Germans get you"; and his father became very ill just when the Nazis came to take him hostage.

Rosalind Laker has an infectious enthusiasm for the past. Historical detail blended with fiction is her particular métier, and two of her novels have been popular Condensed Books selections: *Banners of Silk* and *Gilded Splendour*. "Thorough research is the key," advises Miss Laker. "Once you have gathered all the facts about a person and a period, you can then start to ask what may have influenced their actions. Then doors start to open."

Miss Laker now writes about one book a year and has just completed her latest novel, based on the life of the eighteenth-century silversmith, Hester Bateman. "Hester had no formal training as a silversmith, but learned her craft from her husband John, who was a maker of gold watch-chains," says Miss Laker. "I recently went to St. Paul's Cathedral to see a wand made by her. It is quite exquisite: such artistry from a woman who could not even write her own name!"

Rosalind and Inge live on the Sussex coast, but they often spend the summer at their restored four-hundred-year-old Norwegian farmhouse, where the lyrical mountain setting provides a restful air for new ideas to take shape.